Golden Age

II

The Great Explosion

By Michael Robert von Blucher-Altona

31-March-2025

Library of Congress Control Number: 2024920286

ISBN: Hardback 978-1-7637277-4-8
Paperback 978-1-7637277-3-1
Kindle 978-1-7637277-2-4

First published 2025

Books by Michael Robert von Blucher-Altona

ForkBraid
Book 1: ForkBraid – The Price of Peace
Book 2: ForkBraid II – The Cost of War
Book 3: ForkBraid III – Just Rewards

Golden Age
Book 1: Golden Age – The Unexpected Conflict
Book 2: Golden Age II – The Great Explosion
Book 3: Golden Age III – The Outer Satellite Insurrection

My first three novels were one story laid down in three instalments,
completing my first trilogy.

I deliberately left enough loose ends in the first trilogy,
so as to allow for the writing of future novels or trilogies,
with the intent of fleshing out the universe of the first trilogy.

My fourth novel,
the first of my prequel trilogy,
was different,
as it was one complete story in its own right,
all with a history of its own.

I am planning to write the third novel of this trilogy,
as one complete story in its own right was well
and of course that novel will soon follow this novel.

That of course creates the ever so small problem,
of how to get from the first novel to the third novel,
which of course is the purpose of this second novel.

So this novel is the bridge between the first and third novels of this trilogy.

Unlike the other novels,
this novel is a collection of interrelated short stories,
each complete in their own right,
that bridge the gap between the events of the first and third novels in the trilogy.

Any one of these short stories,
could itself be spun off into an entire novel
and if given sufficient time to do so,
I will write them.

Enjoy

A soul is an infinitesimally small,
yet infinitely powerful
pinpoint of radiant and luminous energy.

All souls were wrought by the creator
in the image of the creator.

All souls reflect every other soul and
all souls are reflected, within the creator.

The creator, created the universe without
from within and of itself.

You are all souls,
you pilot your physical body
as a pilot pilots his plane.

Be consciously aware of who and what you are.
Living conscious souls,
created in the image of your creator!

Folcrom Tafazah. Winter Solstice 2028

Table of Contents

1. History Class.

Miss Bream set the date on her desk calendar to Monday, the Eighth of April, Thirty Four Ninety Five. The very first day of term two on the Earth's universal calendar, which was used all across the colonised worlds of the Earth's Interstellar Alliance. In this case, Xi Bootis A Secundus, the Thol homeworld, Homwol, also called Vale, depending on which native species you ask.

Miss Bream spoke to her class in fluent Carlinish, "It is good to see you all here once more. I do hope you all had a wonderful term break."

Miss Bream looked around the classroom. Some students definitely understood what she had said. There were, however, more than a few Humans in the classroom who looked utterly confused and even somewhat perplexed.

"I see", Miss Bream noted to herself, then asked, "How many of you actually understood what I just said? Come on now, raise your hands."

All of the Thols, both Mimasian and Indigenous, raised their right hand, as did all of the Carlins. The only Martian Human in the classroom, Saffiera, who was a non-verbal telepath, also raised her right hand. Of the Earth Humans, who were all verbal non-telepaths, less than a third raised their hand.

Miss Bream looked around the classroom, "Take note, students. This is important. Not all Humans have the linguistic skills to learn Carlinish."

"Why is that important, Miss Bream?", a young girl Mimasian Thol named Yeannah enquired, her hair was white blond hair, her skin tone alabaster white and her great leathery wings a creamy white.

Yeannah's purple eyes showed a high level of intellect and analytical ability, a Mimasian Thol trait.

"Over the term break, some Indigenous Thol parents wanted to know why our school's classes were taught in English", Miss Bream replied, adding, "They felt that Carlinish would be more appropriate. We did explain the reasons for this, however, that did not satisfy them."

"Oh! They wouldn't have been my people. We've lived amongst Humans for many centuries. We do know about Human linguistic limitations", Yeannah replied with quivering wing tips.

"Yes, Yeannah. Your people are descendants of Thols from Mimas in the Sol system", Miss Bream explained, adding, "The parents in question were Indigenous Thols. They have known us Humans for only a quarter of a century. They don't fully understand us Earth Humans just yet."

"Miss Bream", another Thol, an Indigenous Tholish boy named Yookey, asked, "I don't understand it either. Why can't Humans just learn Carlinish?"

Miss Bream tried to explain, "Well, obviously, Humans of Martian descent are non-verbal telepaths, so they can't speak Carlinish. They simply don't need to. Humans of Earth descent, however, have varying levels of multi linguistic ability. Some Humans are quite adept at picking up languages, many, however, simply don't have that skill set. Yookey, I took several months, lots of tutoring and practice to become proficient in Carlinish. Not all Humans can do that."

"It still doesn't make sense. We've been taught that Humans on Earth speak well over two hundred languages and over a thousand or more different dialects. How can this be so, Miss Bream?", Yookey asked, he was quite confused and his purple eyes showed it.

"Yes, that is true, Yookey. Of all of those languages, there are twelve main languages and of those, six are most commonly spoken internationally. Yet off world, you will find that ninety nine percent of Humans speak English, as either their first or a second language", Miss Bream replied.

"Beyond the Earth, Humans learn English out of necessity, usually at a very early age", Miss Bream explained to her class.

Yookey frowned, his broad, creamy white wings fluttered slightly and the spade-like tip on the end of his tail slapped the floor in annoyance. Yookey's purple eyes took on an almost defiant look. Other Indigenous Thols in the classroom were beginning to nod their heads in agreement with Yookey's body language. They didn't understand. Humans flew across the void between stars, how can they be stupid!

Miss Bream picked up on this silent exchange, it was quite typical of Indigenous Thols to use their body language in class as a form of silent communication, *"This is not going well"*, she thought to herself, *"I'm doing more harm than good."*

The young Martian girl named Saffiera picked up on Miss Bream's thought, which was quite loud to a Martian telepath, the only one in Miss Bream's class, *"Miss Bream. Perform a comparative. Show them why Humans of Earth descent are different."*

Miss Bream looked up at the smiling young Martian girl with her golden-hued skin, almost perfectly yellow blond hair and bright emerald eyes, *"Thank you, Saffiera"*, she thought back, knowing Saffiera would pick it up.

Miss Bream thought for a moment, then asked, “Name some major, possibly sapient species on this world that are not represented in this classroom.”

A pretty Human girl named Aria put up her hand immediately and spoke one word, ”Chittens.”

“Yes. Very good, Aria. Does anyone here perchance speak Chitten?”, Miss Bream asked.

Kethera, a Carlin girl, a hairless humanoid species with a great many feline features replied, her whiskers twitching with excitement, “No one speaks Chitten, Miss Bream. Anyone who gets close enough to a Chitten, to study their language, does not survive long enough to tell their tale. They get eaten alive”, she purred, as her long hairless tail swished back and forth.

“We Thols can fly away real fast and hide in the tree tops, but we're not stupid enough to even go near Chitten territory”, Yookey added.

“Yes, Yookey, but you forget, we Carlins are very fast afoot and can easily outrun a Chitten”, Kethera replied with a broad catlike Cheshire grin.

“We can't”, Aria remarked, “We'd be eaten in a heartbeat. I'm not going anywhere near a Chitten.”

Aria's twin Sister, Ariel, commented, “Chittens are like giant Ants, Miss Bream. They probably communicate using pheromones.”

“Yes, the Chittens are very dangerous indeed. Yet our insectoid neighbours in their territory to the far west do speak a language and may even be sapient, yet we know so very little about them”, Miss Bream replied, “and none other than the Chitten themselves speak Chitten.”

“Okay, what's another one?”, Miss Bream asked, continuing on with another example.

Aria's twin sister, Ariel, spoke up again, “The Harricks, Miss Bream.”

“Anyone here perchance speak Harrick?”, Miss Bream asked.

Yookey replied, “Harricks are the equivalent of the Earth's monkeys. They don't speak”, he laughed.

To which Ariel replied, “Monkeys have tails. Harricks do not. If anything, they'd be the equivalent of a Gibbon or a Siamang, except they're largely arboreal.”

Miss Bream pressed on, “We Humans have studied the Harricks using trail cams. Hiding as they might amongst the forest undergrowth, we have filmed them and we have recorded them. They appear to be small humanoids, no more than a foot and a half tall at the very most. They also appear to have a language of their own. Yet no one but the Harricks speaks that language."

Miss Bream continued, "Any others?"
Saffiera broadcast telepathically, *"The Tarlaks, Miss Bream."*

Miss Bream clapped her hands together loudly, "Yes, Saffiera. The Tarlaks. Saffiera, tell us what you know of the Tarlaks."

Saffiera stiffened slightly and almost shivered, then began, *"The Tarlaks of Mimas in the Sol system were brutal Slavers and cannibals. They are all extinct now, which is a good thing. They were a truly malevolent species. The only Tarlaks still in existence are here, south of the Southern Mountain Range, in Tarlakand, south of the Shar Wastelands. A vast desert. A brutal place, for a brutal species. They appear to be the descendants of the lowest Tarlak caste. As much as Thols look almost angelic, the Tarlaks look like devilish gargoyles crossed with gorillas. The lowest cast of Tarlak's are the Grunts."*

"The Grunts? They have language, yes?", Miss Bream enquired.

"Yes, Miss Bream. They spoke in a strong guttural voice amongst themselves, their language included indecipherable cackles, barks and grunts. They speak almost like hyenas", Saffiera explained.

"Do the contemporary Tarlaks speak the same language?", Miss Bream asked.

"That's very doubtful, Miss Bream. There are six million years of time and genetic drift separating the Mimasian Tarlaks and those on this world. Their language will have changed significantly, Miss", Saffiera replied.

"That is true. Very true, my dear. Does anyone here know of anyone, anyone at all, who speaks Tarlak?", asked Miss Bream.

Yookey replied, "No one but the Tarlaks speak Tarlak, Miss Bream. We Thols and Carlin don't go anywhere near them. They are extremely dangerous and we are very glad that they are trapped in their lands beyond the Southern Mountain range."

Yeannah, of Mimasian Thol heritage, stepped in, "My people take no pleasure in the fact that genetically speaking, the Tarlaks are the closest living relatives to we Thols."

Yookey, of Indigenous Thol heritage countered, "My people would dispute those facts. Tarlaks are nothing like we Thols! They are monstrous evil creatures!"

Kethera remarked, "It's a very good thing that the tunnels under the Southern Mountain Range are all blocked off. If the Tarlaks could access the Masula Valley, the violence would never end."

Yookey added, "There are tunnels under both the Northern and Southern Mountain ranges. We know the entrances to the Tunnels of Dread in the south and why they were purposely blocked. The tunnels in the north have been so long forgotten that we don't even know where their entrances are."

Kethera replied, "That is true, Yookey. There are even tunnels under the Western Mountains, however, they are in Chitten territory. So, no one goes anywhere near there."

Saffiera remarked, *"Since the arrival of Humans and Thols from the Sol System, we have no need of tunnels. If we need to travel beyond the Masula valley, we can simply fly there using our aircraft."*

Yookey replied simply, "We Thols have no need to leave this valley."

Miss Bream nodded in agreement with the Tarlaks being a dangerous species, then pointed to Yookey and Kethera, "Please Stand."

Yookey and Kethera stood up, "Okay. Why do Carlins and Thols not speak Chitten, Harrick or Tarlak?", Miss Bream asked.

Kethera quickly answered, "We have no need to, Miss. The Chitten have their own territory and we keep clear of it. The Harricks hide in the undergrowth and they keep clear of us."

Yookey stepped in, "And we are not stupid enough to go anywhere near the Tarlak lands."

"My point is simple", Miss Bream replied, "and Kethera hit the answer in one. You have no need to learn the languages of the Chittens, the Harricks or the Tarlaks. So, why do we know each other's languages?"

Kethera again quickly replied, "Because we need to Miss Bream. Our two species interact regularly and intermingle quite a lot. We need to understand the Thols and they need to understand us."

"It's far more than that, Kethera. Your two species have lived side by side for at least six million years and probably even millions of years before that", Miss Bream explained.

"Okay", Miss Bream clapped her hands together once more, "Kethera. You understand Tholish?"

"Yes, Miss Bream, I do. Both kinds, modern and ancient", Kethera replied.

"Can you speak Tholish?", Miss Bream enquired.

"No, Miss. No, Carlin can. We don't have the vocal capacity of the Thols", Kethera responded.

"Thank you, Kethera. You may sit down. Now Yookey, why can Carlins understand Thols but not speak Tholish?", Miss Bream enquired.

Yookey replied, "As Kethera noted, Carlins do not have the vocal capacity to speak our language. We can intone sounds, that are far beyond any Carlin's ability to speak. As for understanding us, it's all in the ears", Yookey pointed to Kethera's long, feline shaped ears.

"Correct, Yookey. Carlins have evolved the ability to hear the full extent of Tholish speech, which is precisely why they can understand it", Miss Bream confirmed.

Yookey nodded in agreement.

"We Humans, however, do not have the auditory capacity to hear the higher, or even the lower frequencies of spoken Tholish. We simply cannot hear nearly a third of the Tholish speech. Please take your seat, Yookey", Miss Bream explained.

"Yookey spoke up, "But why can't all Humans just learn Carlin?", he then turned to Saffiera and clarified, "Earth descended Humans that is?"

"I'm just getting to that Yookey", Miss Bream replied, explaining, "Carlins and Thols have lived together, side by side, for millions of years. You've adapted to each other. Your respective species have developed some quite wonderful linguistic abilities."

"And the Earth's Humans?", Yookey queried.

"Humans from the Earth, that is to say, my species, have not existed for more than a few hundred thousand years, Yookey", Miss Bream informed him, "On the Earth, Humans mostly live in their own diverse language, cultural and even ethnic groups. As long as a Human stays within his or her group, they have no need or requirement to ever learn another language."

"What about the boundaries of those groups or those Humans who travel beyond their group?", Yookey enquired.

"Well, those who live on the boundaries of two or more language groups, have the opportunity to become multilingual", Miss Bream replied, adding, "Those who travel outside of their particular language region, either learn the language of the region they're travelling to, or they rely on other Humans in that region to translate for them. On the Earth, translator is actually a profession."

Kethera stepped in, her whiskers twitching once again, "So the Humans on the Earth, are a relatively young species and have not yet developed wide spread, extensive multi linguistic skills, or for that matter, a universal language?"

"That is largely the case Kethera", Miss Bream confirmed, then qualifying, "Although once Humans leave the Earth, they quickly find that the Earth language English, is predominantly used. As noted before, many Humans who come from the Earth do still speak their native languages, but they generally learn English as a second language out of necessity."

"So, away from the Earth, English has become the 'default' language?", Saffiera questioned.

"Effectively, Saffiera, off-world, English has become the lingua-franca ", Miss Bream confirmed.

Miss Bream then asked of the twins, "Aria, Ariel, you both picked up Carlinish quite quickly. Where on the Earth did you parents come from?"

Ariel flicked her brunette hair and replied, her blue eyes almost sparkling, "Miss. Our parents immigrated here from Switzerland."

"Now that is interesting. It's also a very good example. Switzerland is in the interior of a continent, bordered by nations that speak different languages", Miss Bream replied, then asked, "What languages do your parents speak?"

Ariel replied, "I believe my parents can speak Swiss, French, German, Italian and English."

Aria stepped in, "And Carlinish."

"You see, class. On the Earth, if you live in a nation that is bordered by other nations that speak different languages, then you have the opportunity to learn those languages and develop multilingual skills", Miss Bream informed the class.

Miss Bream looked around the class once more and pointed to one of the other Human students of Earth descent, who had not raised his hand at the beginning of the class, "Richard", she called out, then asked, "Where do your parents come from?"

"From the Earth Miss, from Australia, the land down under", Richard, a tall sandy-blond haired boy with hazel eyes replied.

"And what languages do your parents speak?", Miss Bream asked.

Richard smiled broadly and almost laughed as he answered, "English, Miss, English, bad English and worse English."

All of the other students in the classroom burst into laughter.

Miss Bream raised her right hand, "Now, that is quite enough, students", and the room fell silent once more, she continued, "Australia is a large English-speaking nation surrounded by oceans and seas. The opportunity to learn and speak other languages in Australia is quite limited. Do your parents speak Carlinish Richard?"

"They try. They really do", Richard admitted, then he added, "but Carlinish is not so easy to learn. I can't make sense of it either", he replied honestly.

"Thank you, Richard, you have just made my point", Miss Bream replied.

Kethera's tail was swishing, her ears focused on Richard, here whiskers raised, *"Hmm, Richard's terrible with Carlinish, but he seems so nice. So good looking!"*, she thought to herself.

Saffiera raised her right hand and stepped in telepathically, *"When my people first went to the Earth, depending on where they went, which language region they were in, they had to learn a different language. We could get by for a while with just English, but we quickly found it necessary to learn the local languages as well. This was far easier for us, as we are telepaths, which makes learning languages somewhat easier."*

Miss Bream replied, "I expect that would be the case, Saffiera. For a short stay in a non-English speaking region, English would be okay, but for a much longer stay, you would need to learn at least enough of the local language to get by."

"Another language that my people found very useful was a sign language called USLAN", Saffiera noted, adding, *"Universal Sign Language. It is an amalgam of American Sign Language and Australian Sign Language."*

"I'd forgotten about that one. Thank you, Saffiera, for reminding me. Yes, Universal Sign Language, it's mainly used by Humans who are deaf or mute", Miss Bream replied.

"My people found that knowing English and USLAN worked well in many situations", Saffiera replied, explaining, *"Many Earth Humans learn Sign Languages so that they can communicate with the deaf and mute people, along with sub-sapient apes."*

"How does that work?", Yookey asked.

Saffiera, who was close friends with the twins, said to them, *"How are my two friends today?"*

Aria and Ariel, who had both learnt sign language from Saffiera long before, both replied in sign language, *"We're okay, everything is good with us."*

Aria replied in sign language, *"When's our morning break. I'm starving."*

Yookey watched in fascination before asking, "What did you say?"

"Just small talk", Saffiera replied both telepathically and in sign language, before adding, *"I taught sign language to Aria, Ariel, Kethera and Yeannah last year."*

Yookey spoke a handful of trills, soft barks and a couple of clicks of faltering ancient Tholish to Yeannah, *"This is awesome! Can you teach me, Yeannah?"*

Yeannah replied in kind, with a perfect string of trills, clicks and soft barks in modern Tholish, *"Sure, Yookey. Why not? You don't live too far away. Your ancient Tholish does need some work as well. I can help you with that at the same time."*

"Was that anything I need to know about?", asked Miss Bream.

Kethera, who could understand both ancient and modern Tholish, replied, "Not much, Miss Bream. Yookey wants to learn universal sign language. Oh, and Yookey's ancient Tholish is pretty terrible."

Yookey's face turned bright red with embarrassment, something impossible to hide with a Thol's alabaster white complexion.

"Okay then, Class. You now understand, that while some Humans can learn Carlinish, there are many more, who simply do not have those multilingual skills", Miss Bream told the class, adding, "Please let you parent's know that this is the case and that is why our school uses English as a common language."

"Yes, Miss", the whole class replied in English, almost in unison.

2. Paleo-history.

"Miss Bream. When are we going to learn about how Thols got to the Sol system?", asked Yookey.
Miss Bream quickly checked through the syllabus, "That topic won't be covered until the second term in year twelve Yookey. "

"Really, Miss! It's only the second term of year ten. Do we really have to wait that long?", Yookey questioned.

"Well, it's not a class that I actually teach, Yookey. The whole of year twelve history covers paleo-history and that is taught by Miss Evans", Miss Bream explained.

Yookey's face took on a sad pouting demeanour, to which Miss Bream responded, "Now Yookey, pouting does not suit you. I'll see what we can knock together."

Miss Bream looked around the room and her eyes settled on Yeannah and Saffiera, "Ah. There we go. Yookey, the answer to your question is just to your left."

Yookey looked to his left at Yeannah and Saffiera.

"Last term, we touched on part of this question", Miss Bream remarked, then asked, "Yookey, what do you remember about the Martian terraforming incidents and the Mimasian War?"

Yookey's face showed a small smile, "Well, Miss, there were the incidents involving sabotage and the attacks by the Mimasian Tarlaks on Mars. Then there was the Mimasian conflict fifteen years later, in which the generation ship Mimas attacked the Human colonies in the Saturnian orbital zone and the Human colonies closer to the Earth. The Mimasian Tarlaks were defeated and they became extinct as a result of the conflict."

"Yes, Yookey. That is correct", Miss Bream confirmed, then requested, "Saffiera, are you able to shed more light on this period of Human history?"

Saffiera stood up and spoke telepathically, "*Well, Miss, Martians were Slaves back in those days. After the sabotage and the attacks on the terraforming equipment, there was a period of time in which the terraforming process proceeded without issues. The Martian scientists had convinced their Tarlak slave masters that the terraforming project was actually beneficial to the planet and that it should be allowed to continue. They succeeded in that respect. It wasn't until fifteen years later, when the new Martian atmosphere was beginning to settle down, that things descended into conflict.*"

"Yes, Saffiera. First, the Earth's colonial forces liberated your ancestors on

Mars. Then your ancestors provided the colonial forces, the very technology they needed to defeat the Mimasian Tarlaks. The battle in space, outside of Mimas, was very fierce and the battle inside the interior of Mimas was even more so. However, in the end, it was the colonial forces that won the day. What happened next, Saffiera? Please, reveal as much as you remember", Miss Bream requested, expecting Saffiera to recount the previous terms group project.

Saffiera was quiet for a long moment, collecting her thoughts, as if reading her own memories, then continued, *"We need to step back quite a bit and cover something much more important, Miss Bream."*

"Yes, Saffiera, please do", Miss Bream agreed.

Saffiera continued, *"There were a pair of Earth terraformers. They had been captured by the Tarlaks on Mars while they were inspecting the terraforming and seeding process up close. While they were in captivity, my ancestors made some psychic changes to them. They developed telepathy at first, which was what my ancestors were aiming for. After my ancestors on Mars were liberated by the colonial forces, the two Earth terraformer's psi abilities developed rapidly in ways that were not anticipated nor intended. They became very powerful."*

"Saffiera, these are passed down memories you're revealing, aren't they?", Miss Bream enquired.

"Yes, Miss Bream. These are passed down memories", Saffiera confirmed.

"That explains why I haven't heard this part of the story. I knew that Martians could pass down memories telepathically, down the generations, but this is the first time I've actually come across it", Miss Bream noted, "Saffiera, please continue."

"The Earth Humans, two terraformers, a man and a woman, they joined with a female Martian and began to aid in the effort to defeat the evil Emperor Ahriman", Saffiera revealed, she smiled and almost giggled, *"They were a throuple."*

"A man with two wives?", Miss Bream questioned, her hand resting thoughtfully on her chin.

"Yes, Miss, although not officially, just under their own personal commitment", Saffiera confirmed, before continuing with the reveal, *"After the colonial forces had defeated the Tarlaks inside the generation ship Mimas, Ahriman had plans to use the General in charge of the colonial forces as his new host. He was going to go to the Earth and repeat there what he had done here many millions of years before. He wanted to possess the Earth Humans, as many as he could and then use them to take control of the Earth. Moving from one powerful host to the next. That was what he had done here, more than six*

million years before, only with the Thols."

"Saffiera. What happened to the Mimasian Tarlak's?", Yookey quickly asked.

"Ahriman's evil had a powerful effect on everyone inside the Mimasian interior", Saffiera replied, continuing, *"He pushed both sides into a fight to the death. He took great glee from the bloodshed. When the fighting had stopped, many millions were dead on both sides and all of the Tarlaks had been slain. The Mimasian Tarlaks in the Sol system became extinct."*

Shocked murmurs filled the classroom with that revelation.

Miss Bream raised her right hand for silence and then asked, "Saffiera, has any of this been written down? I don't think I've come across anything about this."

"No, Miss. This information is private to those who were there. I only know of these things because the memories were passed down to me by one who was involved in the events", Saffiera replied.

"Do you know their names, Saffiera?", Miss Bream enquired.

"There was the lead terraformer scientist, Doctor Gideon Reas, his lead engineer and wife, Sandra Danker and Winchilly, their Martian wife", Saffiera divulged, adding, *"Winchilly was a direct ancestor of mine. Winchilly is the source of these memories."*

"Well, history does confirm Doctor Gideon Reas and Sandra Danker. Winchilly is only mentioned as a fleeting footnote", Miss Bream replied, "You really need to write all of this down, Saffiera, my dear, perhaps dictate it into a recording device and have it transcribed."

"Yes, Miss, perhaps at a later date", Saffiera replied, continuing, *"Gideon and Sandra teleported to Mimas, into Ahriman's throne room and there, they defeated Ahriman. They rent him asunder."*

At the words teleporting and rent asunder, murmurs in the classroom began once more and Miss Bream once again raised her hand for silence, "I can see why this isn't written down anywhere, it almost seems like magic. Please continue Saffiera."

"After the defeat and elimination of Ahriman, Gideon and Sandra purged Mimas clean of all of Ahriman's filth and evil", Saffiera informed the class, *"Then they located Mimas's environmental control systems and adjusted them to enhance the interior environment of Mimas. While scanning Mimas, as part of the process, they discovered Yeannah's ancestors in cryogenic suspension pods, deep within the rock behind the throne room. At first, they only located two. The Patriarch and Matriarch."*

A slightly upset Yeannah asked, "If you knew all of this already, why did you not tell me?"

"I didn't know, Yeannah. It's only now that I can see these memories. Something Miss Bream said to me triggered their revelation", Saffiera replied, then, turning back to Miss Bream, she continued, *"Gideon and Sandra flew Mimas from Earth to Mars and they offered Mimas to my ancestors as a new home. My ancestors, after evaluating Mimas, accepted and nearly every Martian, two and half million of them, made the exodus from Mars to Mimas."*

Saffiera paused, looked around the classroom and then continued, *"It was during the evaluation of Mimas as a suitable habitat that the remaining cryogenic suspension pods were located. There were forty two cryo pods in all. My ancestors revived the Thols and Sandra Danker found a way to communicate with them. Sandra was multilingual and she psychically installed language abstraction layers into their minds. That made it possible for telepaths to read their spoken thoughts and for the Thols to hear telepathic replies. After settling into Mimas, my ancestors flew Mimas back to Saturn and placed the generation ship back into its original orbit."*

"I still find it quite remarkable, Saffiera, that hardly any of this is known", Miss Bream remarked.

"Some of this is known, Miss Bream, just not all of it. Gideon and Sandra had spent literally months inside Mimas before it was replaced back in Saturnian orbit. They also spent years living with the Martians and the Thols in the Mimasian interior", Saffiera replied, explaining, *"Imagine spending your days in high Martian orbit, in the Aries colony monitoring the Martian terraforming project. Then jaunting back to the Mimasian interior to spend your nights with the Martians and Thols."*

"Jaunting?", Miss Bream queried.

"Jaunting, blinking, these are just what they called teleporting", Saffiera explained.

"That's one hell of a long distance commute", Yookey remarked.

"Not really, Yookey. They crossed the distance from the Aries colony to Mimas in a split second", Saffiera replied, before turning back to Miss Bream, *"Miss. The Thols were found hidden within the rock behind Ahriman's throne, in his very throne room. At the other end of Mimas, the Northern end, there was a disabled emergency evacuation ship. It also had a throne room and another throne. Behind that throne, my ancestors discovered a vault buried deep inside of the rock. It contained all of the information from before Mimas departed from this solar system."*

"Is that significant, Saffiera?", enquired Miss Bream.

"Well, yes, Miss. After several centuries hidden inside of Mimas, my ancestors and the

Thols were eventually revealed to the rest of Human civilisation. A group of powerful Earth's psychics had decided it was the right time for us to reveal ourselves", Saffiera replied, then revealed, *"All of your information on this world's paleo-history comes from that hidden vault behind the throne, in the disabled emergency evacuation ship inside of Mimas."*

"That does make sense, Saffiera. When the Martians and the Thols were revealed, they released their entire history to the public at large", Miss Bream confirmed.

Yookey then asked an odd question, "So what's our world's original name? Is it Homwol or is it Vale?"

Miss Bream blinked, thinking to herself, *"That ridiculous old argument."*

The Indigenous Thols called their world Homwol, meaning trees, specifically the tall Jula Jula trees. The Carlins called their world, Vale, quite literally, the Valley. The Thols had named the world after the trees in which they lived and the Carlin after the Masula Valley in which they lived. A broad rift valley with the mighty Masula River running down its centre and the broad Masula Lake at its Eastern end.

This valley was slowly growing in width over time as the rift gradually spread wider and wider each year. There was no common name for their planet and each species used their own name for it. At least the two names for their world didn't translate as dirt.

Saffiera smiled and almost laughed, replying, *"Yookey, it's a Tholish history, written by Thols, it only refers to this world as Homwol."*

Another student who had been listening intently, a Carlin boy named Lviv, asked, "Saffiera, how do you pass down memories?"

Saffiera frowned for a moment, she didn't actually know, so she decided to look deeper into her newly awoken memories, she answered slowly, *"It appears to be tied to telepathic sharing. Two telepaths bring their foreheads together and the one who wants to share selects the memories that they want to share and telepathically transmits them directly to the other person. Gideon, Sandra and Winchilly shared their memories quite regularly."*

"I have heard about that", Miss Bream remarked, "but I have never seen it happen."

*"You wouldn't have Miss. It's usually a private matte*r", Saffiera replied.

"So how does that tie in with passing down memories?", Lviv asked.

Tears began to well up in Saffiera's eyes, *"Shortly after Winchilly gave birth to her children, she shared her memories with them. Her Daughters then did the same and then their Daughters did so as well and so on and so on. My Mother shared her memories with me shortly after I was born. All of these memories are cumulative. They remain dormant until something triggers them to awaken."*

"So that means, if the chain of sharing is unbroken, then you have all of their accumulated memories going back a long way?", Lviv queried.

"Effectively, yes. For Martians, when our loved ones pass on, they are never really gone. They are always within us", Saffiera confirmed.

"Why doesn't your head explode? I know mine would!", Lviv asked half-jokingly, as his tail swished back and forth.

Saffiera laughed telepathically and answered, *"I have no idea?"*

Yeannah stepped in and noted, "When I was a young child, my parents used to read me the history of our ancestors. Kind of like bedtime stories, only it was our history instead. They used to say it was really important so that our people would never forget who we were and where we came from. Thols from the Sol system all do this."

Yookey's ears picked up on this, "So you can tell us how your people, Thols from this system, got to the Sol system. I mean, we know it was in a generation ship, but why?"

Saffiera sat back down. She had seen in her passed down memories, her Mother's smiling face, as she pressed her forehead to her own, shortly after her birth and began to share. It had been an extremely emotional experience for her.

Miss Bream noticed Saffiera's teary eyes and that she had sat back down and requested Yeannah to take over, "Yeannah, if you can, please stand up and tell us what your parents told you."

"Well, Miss Bream, this is all based on the histories from inside of the vault on Mimas", Yeannah noted, "and it goes back more than six million years. It was a time when our world had an advanced civilisation. We Thols and Carlins, were at that time, a highly capably space-fairing species."

"Well, Yeannah, don't keep us in suspense", Miss Bream replied.

Yeannah began, "Over six million years ago, an evil entity came to our world. Ahriman. He had no body of his own and he was powerful, very powerful. Able to possess many people at a time and even able to use some of them as his hosts. Ahriman possessed Thol and Carlin alike, turning them into his minions, in that regard, he was not fussy. For whatever reason, he chose a Thol to be his first host and from that moment on, he chose only Thols as his hosts."

"Why Thols?", inquired Kethera, her whiskers twitching.

"We don't really know, Kethera. Nobody does. It could be that he just liked having wings", Yeannah replied before continuing, "Ahriman moved from one host to another, always choosing Thols of higher and higher rank. Our people knew something was happening, but because of the mass possessions and high ranking figures turning against the government, it appeared to be some kind of rebellion."

Yeannah paused to look around the room. All of the students were listening intently.

Yeannah continued, "Not knowing what the true nature of the threat was, the government decided to protect the High Matriarch and her family. They placed the High Matriarch, her Husband, her Son and the forty most prominent members of their court into cryo stasis and then hid them away. This was done for their own protection."

"Well, that must have worked", Kethera noted, her long tail swishing from side to side with excitement, "If it hadn't, you wouldn't be here today."

"Not quite Kethera", Yeannah replied, before continuing, "They were betrayed and their hiding place was discovered. Ahriman inspected the cryo suspension pods and chose the Matriarch's Son for his next host. Then he left the remaining pods to be destroyed by his possessed minions."

"Wait!", Richard interrupted., "That can't be right. You are here!"

Yeannah smiled, "Yes, Richard. Ahriman's minions were slaughtered and the remaining forty two cryo suspension pods were saved. Then they were hidden once again. Ahriman thought that they had been destroyed and so he never questioned their fate."

Once again, Yeannah paused to look around the room. All of the students were listening intently.

Now, even Miss Bream was intrigued, " Yeannah, my dear, don't stop. Please continue."

Yeannah smiled once more and then continued, "Once Ahriman had complete control of the planet, he could do whatever he liked. He set up a selective breeding program in the south lands beyond the Southern Mountain Range. That's where he selectively bred the various castes of Tarlaks. The Princely caste from which he chose his hosts, the Commander caste, the

Technician caste and finally the Grunts. Ahriman bred his precious Tarlaks for their height and their intelligence. The taller, the smarter. The shorter, the duller. The Grunts were his foot soldiers, so to speak, with I.Qs well left of the bell curve."

"I bet Ahriman was the tallest, so that everyone would have to look up at him", Yookey commented.

Yeannah confirmed this, "Yes, Yookey. He did exactly that", before continuing, "Ahriman ruled our world for tens of thousands of years. Exploiting every aspect of it. Eventually, he came to the conclusion that he'd gone way too far with his exploitation and that our world was dying."

"Whoa! He almost killed off our planet!", Yookey exclaimed.

"No. Not quite Yookey. I'll get to that part soon enough", Yeannah replied.

Yeannah paused to look around the room once more and noticed Miss Bream motioning her to continue. Yeannah smiled, she actually liked telling stories.

"Ahriman instructed our people, both Thols and Carlins, to build him a generation ship. A small moon of one of the outer planets of Homwol's solar system was chosen for the task. It took several thousand years of hard work to create the generation ship and the result was the ice moon we now know as Mimas", Yeannah informed everyone.

Yeannah continued, "Everyone thought our world was dying, so the Thols retrieved the forty two cryo suspension pods and secreted them away in the one place Ahriman was unlikely to find them. Deep in the rock wall, directly behind his throne!"

"That must have taken quite some audacity", Miss Bream remarked.

"It did, Miss and it worked, otherwise, I wouldn't be here", Yeannah replied, before continuing, "The Thols had also built a huge emergency evacuation ship inside of Mimas as well, just in case the generation ship failed at some point. It also had a throne room and hidden within the rock wall, directly behind the throne, they built a chamber and secreted away the history of our world within it."

"And that's how and why Thols got to the Sol system?", Yookey queried.

"Yes, Yookey. Although there is a bit more to it", Yeannah confirmed.

Lviv commented, "Yeannah, if your people are all descendants of those forty two Thols in cryosleep, then you people are all descendants of nobility, some are even descendants of royalty."

"Yes, Lviv, but my people don't tend to dwell on such matters", Yeannah confirmed.

"Ahriman betrayed both Carlin and Thol alike", Yeannah continued, explaining, "All of the Carlins were returned to our world, along with most of the Thols. Ahriman then shipped in his precious Tarlaks from our world to Mimas, as many as he could take. He then ordered the remaining Thol engineers to teach his Tarlak technicians how to manage and repair Mimas. Once that final task was done, the remaining Thols were discarded, cast into space to die. After that, the generation ship Mimas left our solar system forever."

Shocked murmurs filled the classroom once more and Miss Bream had to raise her hand for silence.

Yeannah continued, "Ahriman could not take all of his Tarlaks with him. He left a large number of his Grunts behind in the south lands, beyond the Southern Mountain Range. That is the only reason why Tarlaks still exist. Had Ahriman not done that, they'd all be extinct. After Ahriman left, without his massive exploitation of our planet, our world slowly began to heal. I can only assume it took many tens of thousands of years, as the history stops with Mimas's departure from our solar system. We have no idea how long it took for Mimas to reach the Sol system either, nor which route Mimas took. The Tarlaks did not record any flight paths or flight plans."

Yeannah bowed slightly, curtseyed and then, with a smile on her face, sat back down.

"Thank you, Yeannah. Nicely done", Miss Bream commended, then turning to Yookey, "There you have it, Yookey. That is how Thols ended up in the Sol System. If you need any further information on the subject, you can either wait until paleo-history class in year twelve or perhaps visit the school library and do some actual reading for a change."

"Or I could just ask Yeannah", Yookey replied with a smile.

Kethera's ears flicked in Yookey's direction, her whiskers twitched and her vertical pupils blinked, she commented, "Yookey's in love! Yookey's in love!"

Aria, Ariel and Yeannah all began to giggle and laugh, then the rest of the class joined in. Yookey went bright red and lowered his face into his hands.

Miss Bream raised her hand for silence, "Class. That will be enough, thank you!" and the room quickly quietened down once more.

After the class had settled down, Miss Bream announced, "Class. Please check your term assignment online. It is a group assignment, just like last term. You will all be using the same groups as last term as well. Same deal as last term, have it finished two weeks before the end of term. Class, you are now dismissed."

3. Tree Houses.

It was now the school's lunch period and Yeannah, Kethera, Saffiera, Aria and Ariel had all collected under the shade of a large, broad tree to eat.

Yookey approached the group of teenagers and asked, "Yeannah, when do you want to come over to my house to teach me sign language?"

"Maybe sometime on the weekend, Yookey. We need to get our heads around our term project first", Yeannah replied.

Yookey looked disappointed, "Oh, okay."

Aria and Ariel began clapping their hands together and singing a rhyme, "Yeannah and Yookey sitting in a tree, K-I-S-S-I-N-G! First comes love, then comes marriage, then comes baby, in a baby carriage!", then they repeated, "Yeannah and Yookey sitting in a tree, K-I-S-S-I-N-G! First comes love, then comes marriage, then comes baby, in a baby carriage!"

Yookey went bright red in the face with embarrassment and quickly walked away.

Yeannah snapped at Aria and Ariel, "Aria! Ariel! Will you not!"

"Why Yeannah? ", Aria queried, adding, "Yookey deserves it. He distracted Miss Fish Face with his silly questions and she didn't have time to explain the term project to us."

"Miss Fish Face?", questioned Kethera.

"Bream is a species of Earth fish. So Miss Bream is Miss Fish Face", Aria explained.

Kethera's eyes blinked as she shook her head and rolled her eyes, her whiskers twitching, "Humans!", she thought to herself.

Saffiera telepathically remarked, *"Yookey has very strong feelings for Yeannah. A crush!"*

"His feelings need to be discouraged", Yeannah replied, "but gently. Please don't make fun of him."

"You don't like Yookey?", Kethera enquired.

"No, Kethera. Not in the way that he wants. Yookey is just a friend. Nothing more", Yeannah replied, explaining, "I can tutor him in sign language. Maybe even help him with his ancient Tholish and Carlinish, but nothing more. His own parents will discourage him from anything further anyway."

"Why would they do that?", Kethera asked, "You're both Thols. Don't they like you?"

"For the very same reason that you don't see any Carlin Thol relationships either, Kethera. We are both Thols, yes, but we are different species of Thols", Yeannah informed her friends.

Ariel questioned, "Yeannah, how is that even possible? Indigenous Thols look almost identical to your people. You are the same!"

"No. Not the same! Think about it, Ariel. My ancestors spent over six million years asleep in cryo suspension pods. Our dna is identical to the Thols from over six million years ago", Yeannah explained, then added, "The dna of the Indigenous Thols has changed significantly over that time. Mimasian Thols and Indigenous Thols may look the same, but they are very, very different. We are two different species and not genetically compatible at all."

"So Yookey's parents know this and they haven't told Yookey yet?", Ariel asked.

"Probably not. It's something that Thols tell their children at around our age", Yeannah replied, "It's likely they haven't told Yookey yet. So I expect he doesn't know. He'll find out soon enough."

Kethera queried, "So the same inter-species relationship prohibitions exist between Yookey's people and your people, just like it does between Thols and Carlins?"

Yeannah answered honestly, "Yes, Kethera. It's considered inappropriate at best, bestiality at worst."

Kethera replied with equal candour, "We Carlins are not beasts and neither are your people."

Yeannah sighed, "Even my people consider relationships with Humans inappropriate. Yookey's people are just extremely strict on the matter."

"Shouldn't it be about consenting adults?", Saffiera asked telepathically.

"It's actually all about the genetic incompatibility. We Thols produce so few children, so producing children is considered to be extremely important. It's pretty much mandatory, you know, like a duty! Genetically incompatible relationships don't produce children, so they are discouraged. Pretty much forbidden", Yeannah tried to explain, finishing off with, "It's a Tholish thing."

Aria's and Ariel's tune changed drastically and they exclaimed in unison, "Poor Yookey!"

Kethera's whiskers twitched and her long tail swished from side to side excitedly, "The other day, I saw a Human boy and a Carlin girl kissing behind the shelter sheds."

"Who?", the twins, Aria and Ariel, enquired in unison, both wanting to get in on the gossip.

"I don't know. They were older students. The Carlin girl's tail was swishing excitedly from side to side, so she was definitely enjoying herself", Kethera replied, admitting, "I was so embarrassed, really embarrassed! So I turned around and went back the way I'd come."

"That is so disappointing, Kethera", Aria commented, the disappointment showing on her face, then she asked, "Are you sure you didn't recognise them?"

"No. I didn't get a good look at their faces", Kethera admitted.

"So, Kethera. Human boys! Who would you snog if you had the chance?", Ariel queried, prompting her, "Richard maybe?"

"Ariel!", Kethera exclaimed, her nostrils flaring, "I have no interest in snogging Richard!"

Aria then teased, "Richard probably doesn't like cat whiskers anyway."

"Aria! I am not a cat!", Kethera replied in a definite upset tone.

Aria teased further, "Are you sure, Kethera? Are you sure? You have cat's ears, cat's eyes, cat's whiskers and even a long cat's tail."

Kethera snapped back angrily, "Having features similar to an Earth cat does not make me a cat! And for your information, we Carlins swish our tails when we're happy. Earth cats swish their tails when they're angry and annoyed."

Ariel added in, "I don't know, Kethera, you also have ankles like a cat. You know Cankles!"

Aria piled on, "and you do walk on the pads of your feet like a cat."

Carlin's legs were very similar to Human legs, except for the thighs and calves being somewhat shorter, while their metatarsals were much longer, shifting their entire ankle joints off of the ground. This allowed Carlins to walk silently on the pads of the feet, their movements were fluid and precise, enhancing their agility and giving them the distinctive, graceful gait of a creature with a distinct digitigrade stance.

Kethera replied sharply, taking a different tact, "Your fury, four-legged Earth cats, just happen to look like Carlins! I am not a cat! I don't even have fur!"

"Egyptian sphynx cats don't have any fur either", Aria noted.

"I'm a two-legged Carlin, not a bald, four-legged Earth feline! We are nothing like those wrinkled little creatures and we are not house pets!", Kethera spat back.

The twins both giggled, then quickly reached out and hugged Kethera tightly, "We're just teasing, Kethera", Aria replied, adding, "You're our best friend."

Ariel added, "We love your feline features, Kethera. Especially your blue stripes. It's one of the things that makes you Carlins so endearing", finishing off with, "Kethera, your people are the perfect sapient species."

Aria corrected, "Adorable, Ariel. Carlins are adorable!"

Kethera's eyes blinked rapidly, as emotional tears welled up in the corner of her catlike eyes, "Maybe that's what the Human boy, behind the shelter-sheds, thought about his Carlin girlfriend", she replied with a giggle and a twitch of her whiskers, there was a distinct purr in her voice. Her tail was even swishing from side to side.

Yeannah remarked cheekily with a wry smile, "It's a shame you didn't see their faces, Kethera. You could have asked that Carlin girl what a Human boy's tongue tastes like."

Kethera replied in disgust, "Ugh! Yuck!"

"Yeah, Yeannah. That even grossed me out", Aria replied.

"So. Whose house are we studying at tonight?", queried Ariel.

Aria answered quickly, "I vote for Yeannah's house."

Yeannah responded with a question, "Aria, you do know that Thols live at the tops of giant trees?"

Aria answered, "Of course, Yeannah. We should have a sleepover!"

Aria's twin Sister, Ariel, agreed, "A sleepover in a Thol tree house. That sounds way cool!"

Kethera threw in with the twins, "Yeah, a sleepover. I've never seen a Thol tree house before!"

"That's because they're four hundred feet up in the tree tops!", Yeannah replied, then turned to Saffiera for some sanity.

Saffiera agreed with the twins, replying telepathically, *'I've never seen a Thol tree house either."*

"Okay, okay. I'll call my Mum and organise a sleepover over", Yeannah finally gave in and agreed.

Kethera, Saffiera and the twins contacted their parents to let them know that they were going to a study session and sleep over at Yeannah's house. Their Mothers turned up at the school before school was over and dropped off their overnight bags, with everything they'd need for their sleepover. Then, finally, at the end of the day, they all caught a school hover bus to the Thol villages further to the north, where Yeannah's family lived. As their school was at the edges of the forest in the Human colony, in between the Carlin villages in the broad Masula Valley and the Thol villages in the forest, the hover bus ride did not take very long at all.

They all stepped off of the hover bus, along with all of the other students, who, of course, were all Thols. The other Thol students, most of whom were Indigenous Thols, stared at the Humans and their Carlin friend with curiosity. All except Yookey, who seemed to only have eyes for Yeannah. It was so unusual for Humans and Carlins to enter their environment. Neither Humans nor Carlins could fly and climbing the giant Jula Jula trees was no easy feat.

"Where are the houses?", Ariel enquired.

Yeannah pointed to the tall Jula Jula trees that were growing everywhere all around them, their trunks were massive, easily much, much wider than their hover bus had been long.

"Wow!", Ariel remarked and then Yeannah pointed up to the tree tops way above them.

"I don't see anything", Ariel commented.

"The houses are all near the upper canopy. You can't see them from here, there are too many branches and foliage in the way", Yeannah replied.

As the small group watched, the other Thol students from the hover bus began leaping into the air. With powerful strokes of their wings, they soared upwards towards the high canopy far above them.

"Yeannah. How are we getting up there?", Saffiera asked telepathically.

"Well, in the old days, before Humans and my people came to this world, you had to climb. There was no other way", Yeannah replied, then she informed them, "My people found that bothersome. Most Humans don't like heights and they do make for poor climbers, so we installed elevators. That makes things much safer, don't you think?"

Kethera replied, “Okay. Elevators are cool. We Carlins don't mind climbing, but that”, she looked up at the canopy far above them, “that is just plain ridiculous.”

Aria was looking around the forest floor and the undergrowth, “Are there Harricks around here?”
Kethera replied, “There are Harricks everywhere, you might not see them, but they're there.”

Yeannah pointed to an odd small piece of what looked like a clump of soil and Aria reached down to pick it up, “That's Harrick poo!”, she announced.

“Eww!”, Aria exclaimed, as she dropped the Harrick turd, “That's gross!”, then she reached into her backpack for a bottle of water to wash her hands.

“I didn't say to pick it up”, Yeannah replied.

Aria finished washing her hands and asked, “So, where's your house?”

Yeannah pointed to an incredibly tall tree, farther off in the distance, a tree with a trunk so broad it defied the imagination, “Up near the top of that Jula Jula tree”, she informed them all.

The five school friends then started walking in the direction of the tall Jula Jula tree with the exceptionally broad base.

“Always keep to the paths. Do not deviate. It's for your own safety”, Yeannah advised the others.
“What happens if we don't?”, Aria queried.

Yeannah pointed into the distance at a rather large roundish object, then she pointed to another and yet another, they were everywhere, “Those really big round things are seeds. You don't want one landing on your head. My people have cleared the trees above the paths of all seeds for safety reasons.”

“Don't the Harricks get squashed?”, Ariel asked.

“Oh, heavens no. They're too smart for that. The Harricks look for places that have already been crushed by a falling seed”, Yeannah informed her, explaining, “That way, they know the tree above that spot has no seeds. All of my Dad's Human colleagues reckon Harricks are Sapient.”

Eventually, they came to Yeannah's home tree and they walked up to a door set into its trunk.

“A door?”, Aria questioned.

"Yeah. Why is there a door in this tree?", Ariel asked.

"To keep the Harricks out, of course", Yeannah answered, commenting, "If there was no door there, the Harricks would move in and make a huge mess."

Ariel shook her head, "No. That's not what I meant, Yeannah. Trees don't have doors. I mean, they're trees. So why's there a door?"

"Jula Jula saplings have solid trunks, but when they get to a certain height, they develop a hollow in their centre", Yeannah explained, elaborating further, "As they continue to grow, that hollow also grows and becomes quite large. They're very useful spaces, so we carve openings into the hollowed trunks for access. We need the doors to keep the Harricks out, otherwise, they create all kinds of havoc."

Yeannah opened the door leading into the tree trunk and gestured to her friends to enter. Yeannah then followed behind her friends as they walked down the tunnel that was carved out of the tree trunk. Eventually, they came to the hollow centre of the giant Jula Jula tree. Automatic lighting switched on and lit up the entire hollow space.

The hollow was quite large and an elevator had been built into the middle of it. They all looked up. The tree hollow looked like it continued all the way to the very top of the tree, almost five hundred feet above their heads. The walls around the inside of the hollow were lined with secure storage. These storage vaults had also been carved out of the tree's trunk. They were quite large and there were quite a few of them.

Yeannah noted, "Each family is assigned a storage vault or two. They come in quite handy. Although, the Indigenous Thols don't generally care to uses these hollows, just my people."

"You're not flying up, Yeannah?", Kethera asked.

"Normally I would, but without me, you would never find my house", Yeannah replied.

"Are all of the other Jula Jula trees like this one?", Kethera enquired.

"All the mature trees have hollows just like this one", Yeannah confirmed, adding, "Normally, they're just used for storage. If my people live in the tree, then it will have an elevator just like this one. Indigenous Thols have no use for elevators."

"Why is that?", Ariel asked.

"My people, the Mimasian Thols, worked and lived alongside Martians for many centuries inside of Mimas. After coming out of hiding inside Mimas, my people lived and worked alongside the Earth Humans for centuries as well", Yeannah explained, then noted, "Indigenous Thols are happy to work with Carlins, as they have for thousands of years. They are even happy to work alongside Humans. They are, however, extremely unlikely to invite you to their nests. They don't even invite us."

Your people and the Indigenous Thols are so different, Yeannah, yet your species look almost the same. So similar!", Ariel noted.

"Looking the same is not being the same. We are two very different species, Ariel", Yeannah explained once more.

As they all climbed into the elevator, Yeannah began explaining the structure of the tree above them.

"There are four landings. The lowest landing is about three hundred feet up and it is private. Only Thols may go there. That level is where most of the Indigenous Thols live, where they have their nests. The middle landing is about three hundred and fifty feet up. That level has a mixture of housing, both Mimasian Thol and Indigenous Thol. The upper landing is the level where the majority of my people live. It's about four hundred feet up. That is where my house is", Yeannah informed them all.

"You said four landings, Yeannah", Saffiera noted telepathically.

"The uppermost landing is not used for housing. It's at the very top of the tree, four hundred and fifty feet up. It's a communal gathering place used by all Thols, at the very top of the canopy", Yeannah explained, "Up there, the view is spectacular and at night, the stars are so brilliant."

They all arrived at the upper housing landing and stepped out of the elevator. Yeannah led them around the landing to a tunnel carved into the tree's trunk on the northern side. They followed the tunnel and soon found themselves standing on a broad balcony that surrounded the tree trunk. The students noted that it had a strong safety railing. Stairs wound upward around the tree trunk in a clockwise direction and as they looked up, they could see at least two other balconies above them on the same level.

Yeannah smiled, "My people are very big on safety. We often invite our friends over and we want to ensure that they are safe."

"Do the Indigenous Thols do the same?", Aria enquired.

"Not so much, Aria. They are very unlikely to invite non-Thols to their nests. My people do still ensure the balconies are safe, though. Safety is a necessity", Yeannah replied.

Saffiera looked out over the balcony, to the two levels below them, *"What are those?"*, she asked.

"Those are nests, Saffiera. Indigenous nests. Olden style! They have not changed in many thousands of years", Yeannah replied.

The nests were large, circular, almost a shallow cup shape. They were constructed with tightly woven branches, all tied together with strong vines. Each nest was fastened tightly to a broad tree branch. Each of the nests looked to be large enough to house four Thols comfortably. Above each nest was an even larger canopy that overhung the entire nest below it. These canopies were constructed in the same fashion as the nests, except that they had a waterproof layer of broad leaves covering them. Between the canopy and the walls of the nest were open spaces for easy ingress and egress.

None of the traditional nests could be reached except by flying or by carefully climbing along the tree branches. This perhaps explained why Indigenous Thols rarely invited non-Thol friends to visit their homes. It was simply far too dangerous. There were a great many Indigenous Thol nests, too many to easily count.

Yeannah smiled and then pointed to other, more elaborate structures, "Now that's a proper nest! My people build tree houses. Some of the Indigenous Thols do as well, but very, very few of them. Most are happy with their traditional nests and they don't want to change. Come along, follow me!"

Yeannah led her friends up the winding stairs to the next balcony. There, Yeannah led them to a strong suspension bridge that led out from the balcony towards one of the larger tree houses.

"That's my house over there", Yeannah informed her friends with a great deal of pride, "Isn't it beautiful?" and it was.

Yeannah's home was at least three levels tall, that they could see and built in modular sections. Each section had a basic design, that was based around the traditional Thol nests. However, there were as many as ten or perhaps more circular nests, spread across three or more levels. Each and every module was fastened tightly to multiple broad tree branches. Each nest was also built of tightly woven branches and tied together with strong vines, however, instead of a canopy to keep out the rain, they had true roofs and even had enclosed walls, with windows and doors.

Each of the modular nests connected to the other nest modules, sometimes directly and sometimes through covered walkways. Covered stairways linked the nests across the structure's multiple levels. The suspension bridge extended from the broad balcony to a porch at Yeannah's tree house, which was built into the structure at its mid-level.

The base modules rested securely on a large branch, itself branching out into many others, with the tree house fastened securely to these points for stability. The mid and upper levels were anchored to branches higher up, secured with treated vines that, according to Yeannah, were as strong as steel cables, if not stronger. There were a few of these tree houses scattered here and there, but not nearly as many as the Indigenous nests.

Yeannah led her friends onto the suspension bridge, informing them, "Normally, we access our house from the balcony and walk across this bridge. So you could say that the balcony back there is like an airport for us. We fly in and fly out from there."

Yeannah let out some loud trills, a couple of soft barks and a handful of clicks. Before the students had crossed the suspension bridge, her Mother and Father were on the porch at the other end to greet them. Her younger brother was behind them but completely disinterested. Yeannah stepped onto the porch and moved to one side.

"You must be the twins, Aria and Ariel", Yeannah's Mother remarked, her voice laced with trills, clicks and soft barks, commenting, "Thol families never have same-faced younglings.".

Then she gave them both a huge hug and squeezed their cheeks, "And you must be Kethera", who also received a huge hug.

When Saffiera stepped onto the porch, Yeannah's Mother's wings fluttered slightly and an excited look came across her face, she reached out and took Saffiera's hands in her own.

"You must be Saffiera! I am so happy to meet you. Martians are so few and far between on this world", then she gave Saffiera a huge hug that lasted far longer than with the others.

"Is your Mum always like this?", Saffiera telepathically asked Yeannah.

Yeannah thought back to Saffiera, knowing that her friend would pick it up, *"Yes. Mum loves having guests over and she especially loves Martians. Mum had a lot of Martian friends back inside Mimas."*

"Come now, children. You must all come inside and make yourselves at home", Yeannah's Mother trilled and clicked, inviting them all in.

The girls entered Yeannah's tree house and the main things they all noticed about Yeannah's home was that the rooms were all circular in shape and quite spacious. Far more spacious than you would have thought, looking at the tree house from the outside.

Yeannah informed her friends, "This level is our living space. The level below is for our utilities, you know, like the bathroom, toilet and laundry. That sort of thing. Our bedrooms are all in the upper level", and then she led them all up the stairs.

Yeannah's bedroom was more than spacious enough for them to all sleep over. The room looked comfortable enough. A single large bed was to one side, there were cupboards for clothing, a dressing table and plenty of shelving with lots of books.

Apart from that, its decor had an austere simplicity to it. This appeared to be a characteristic of Thols in general, both Mimasian and Indigenous. They enjoyed simplicity and their lifestyles generally showed it.

"Just drop your backpacks anywhere convenient", Yeannah told her friends, "then follow me back downstairs to the dining room. My Mum has prepared a small feast. Tonight, we eat well!"

4. Disambiguation.

The girls all sat at the dinner table in Yeannah's dining room. Yeannah's Mother, Father and younger brother sat with them. Arranged on the table before them, as described by Yeannah earlier, was the small feast. Mimasian Thols were all vegetarians and the food on the table reflected that. There was a variety of lightly sauteed mushrooms and other fungi in one large serving bowl.

Another large bowl contained a stir fry with various local vegetables. There was a separate bowl that contained delicately cooked noodles made with a local grain and another large bowl that contained *'fluffy'* rice. A grain that Humans from Earth had introduced to both Martians and Mimasian Thols. There were also plates of sliced bread and sliced fruits.

Saffiera, also being a vegetarian, remarked telepathically, *"Wow! This all looks amazing!"*

Aria noted, "I keep forgetting that Thols don't eat meat."

"No dear", Yeannah's Mother, Yealah, replied, trilling, "We Thols do not eat meat. I do suspect our vegetarian fare will surprise you, though. Please do try it."

Aria placed small portions of each dish on her plate and tried some, after which she remarked, "This is actually very good. The mushrooms are especially nice!"

"You see. My wife knows how to cook", Yeannah's Father, Yannick, replied with a smile and trill.

Yealah reached over and touched his hand affectionately.

Everyone sitting at the table ate their fill of the food provided and then Yealah asked, "So, how was it? Good?"

Yeannah's friends all replied in the affirmative, agreeing that they have enjoyed the meal.

Yealah then enquired, with trills and clicks, "So, what are you all studying?"

Yeannah replied to her Mother, "We aren't really sure. It's our term assignment but..."

Aria stepped in with, "Yookey distracted Miss Bream with useless questions, so she didn't have time to discuss it with us. We have to look it up on the network."

Kethera chimed in, "Not entirely useless, Aria. We now understand why our classes are in English and not Carlinish."

Saffiera added telepathically, *"We also learnt how Thols ended up in the Sol system and, more importantly, why."*

Yealah replied, trilling and clicking, "Yeannah could have told you that, Saffiera. We Mimasian Thols learn the history of our people at a very early age."

Saffiera replied, *"It was actually Yeannah who provided the information."*

"Oh really. Well done, Yeannah", Yealah commended.

Yannick spoke up about the school's choice of languages, "That language issue came up during the term break at a school community meeting."

"Yes", Yealah confirmed, explaining, "Some of the parents among the Indigenous Thols had trouble understanding how Humans can build interstellar spacecraft and yet not be able to master Carlinish. They find that quite perplexing."

"Miss Bream explained that quite well", Saffiera replied, adding, *"She even gave us some good examples as to why some Humans are good with languages, whilst others are not."*

"Richard was funny, so funny", Kethera commented, with a broad smile on her face that accentuated her cat like features, then she explained, "His parents apparently speak English, bad English and even worse English", then she frowned a catlike frown, with her whiskers down, "Not so much Carlinish."

Yealah blinked and gave Kethera an astonished look but said nothing about her comment. Carlins could be both flippant and whimsical at the same time but never meant any disrespect by it. Thols understood this very well, even the more recently arrived Thols from the Sol system.

"Well, let's hope your classmates pass that information onto their parents", Yannick replied.

Aria inquired with a wry smile, "About Richard's parent's language skills?"

Yannick blinked twice then replied, "Ah, no, Aria. More about Human linguistic skills in general."

Yeannah informed her parents, "Yookey has asked me to tutor him in universal sign language."

"Oh, okay. Do we know Yookey?", enquired Yealah.

"No. You haven't met him", Yeannah replied honestly, explaining, "His family live in the tree next to ours. Quite close, actually, our tree branches overlap. I could actually walk there if their nest was on the same level as ours."

Kethera added, "His ancient Tholish needs a lot of work as well."

"Oh, so Yookey is Indigenous?", Yealah realised and sought confirmation.

"Yes, Mum. Yookey is Indigenous", Yeannah confirmed.

"Will you be tutoring him at his nest?", Yealah asked.

"Probably", Yeannah replied.

"Then you'll need to remember this. To enter their nest, land on the main supporting branch and climb into the nest", Yealah advised, adding, "Don't do what they do!"

"What do they do?", Yeannah asked.

"They approach their nests from underneath, then they fly up between the canopy and the side wall of the nest", Yealah began explaining, finishing off with, "They fold in their wings at the very last second. If they get the timing wrong, they risk breaking their wings."

Yannick added, "Our Indigenous cousins can be quite reckless at times."

"Okay, Mother, that does sound dangerous", Yeannah agreed.

"It is. I've come across quite a few broken wings at the clinic", Yealah commented, "and broken wings never really heal right. Sometimes, they don't even heal at all. Always remember, Thols have hollow bones."

"Point noted. Land on the main supporting branch and climb into the nest", Yeannah confirmed, then she added, "Yookey's parents may be Indigenous, but they're not entirely traditional. Yookey once told me that his family's nest was actually five traditional nests all clustered together."

Aria opened her big mouth and let out, "Yookey has a huge crush on Yeannah."

"Oh dear!", Yealah exclaimed, commenting, "That is not a good thing! You might be better off tutoring him here, Yeannah."

"Yes, I agree", Yannick replied, explaining, "Once his parents learn about his crush, they'll banish you completely. You won't even be allowed to be friends."

Yealah shook her head, "Why do they always wait until an issue arises before telling their children that they and we are completely different species? I will never understand!"

Yeannah's face took on a perplexed expression.

Yannick explained, "It's not the first time, Yeannah. We told you, what, three or four years ago. For some unfathomable reason, the Indigenous Thols always wait until the very last minute."

Yealah remarked, "That poor young boy will be heartbroken."

Saffiera noted, *"When the Thols were awakened inside of Mimas, there were only forty two of them. With so few individuals, those first few generations would have been extremely difficult, especially with the limited genetic foundation. The loss of any single individual Thol would have weighed heavily on the entire population. That might have caused Mimasian Thols to develop a more cautious mindset in general, perhaps even a far more forward-looking mindset. The Indigenous Thols did not have that particularly limited population pressure."*

"Astonishing", Yannick replied, then he asked, "You thought of that all by yourself, Saffiera?"

"In a way, yes and yet, no. My passed down memories have awoken and I can see so many things far more clearly now. It's like I now have a lens with a far sharper focus", Saffiera admitted.

Yannick speculated, "We Mimasian Thols may have inadvertently selectively bred ourselves to be the way we are. Saffiera, your perspective is very valid and quite interesting. Thank you."

Yealah reached across the table and touched Saffiera's hand, tapping it gently several times. Mimasian Thols and Martians had always been close and Yealah was more touchy-feely than most.

Yealah remarked, "I would very much like to meet your parents, Saffiera."

Saffiera simply smiled in return.

Aria speculated, "Perhaps the Indigenous Thols are normal and the Thols from Mimas are the more unusual ones?"

Yealah replied, "Aria, honey, we Thols are two different species. What's normal for them is not normal for us and vice versa. It's kind of like comparing Martian Humans with Earth Humans, you have a lot of differences, although in the Human example, you are at least the same species."

"Okay, Mum. So I'll invite Yookey over here to tutor him and I'll tell him myself. Hey, Yookey, we're a different species. Did you know that?", Yeannah replied, adding, "Problem solved."

Yeannah's school friends began to giggle.

"Yes, well, if you do, Yeannah. Make sure he knows not to tell his parents that you've told him", Yannick replied, informing his Daughter, "They will consider that interference."

Yealah then turned to Yeannah's little brother, "Yarris. You're on dish washing duty", then to the girls, "If you're all finished eating, wash up and head upstairs to study."

The girls all went upstairs to Yeannah's bedroom. Once they were inside, they quickly made themselves comfortable, spreading their sleeping bags out on the floor. The floor was covered in floorboards, which hid the tangle of tightly woven branches and vines beneath them. Lying over the top of the floorboards were several thick, shaggy rugs. As the girls looked around, they noticed two maps on the wall, side by side.

"What are those?", Kethera asked.

"Oh, those. Maps of Homwol of course", Yeannah replied, informing Kethera, "The map on the left is Homwol, as the original forty two Mimasian Thols reawakened inside Mimas remembered it. Six million years in cryosleep was a very long time. The map on the right, you'll probably recognise as Homwol as it is today."

"Yeah, both maps of Vale, but why are they different?", Kethera queried.

"Six million years is lot of time Kethera", Yeannah replied, explaining, "Our world has only the one continent, Masula. The Masula valley has a huge rift valley running through the middle of it. It was much narrower six million years ago and grows wider, little by little every year."

Aria commented, "You know, you guys could call your world Masula."

Ariel agreed, "That actually does sound like a good idea. It kind of makes sense."

Kethera looked at the twins, her whiskers twitching once more, then she replied, "Nah. That would be silly. We Carlins would never agree to that", her tail was straight and unmoving.

"The Indigenous Thols would never agree to that either", Yeannah noted.

"Such a strange notion. The land is moving beneath our feet, spreading apart", Kethera considered.

Saffiera stepped in, adding telepathically, *"The rift is responsible for the*

Northern and Southern Mountain ranges. As the rift spreads Masula apart, the oceanic crust to the north and south is pushed down underneath the continent. These are called subduction zones and they generate volcanic activity and the rise of mountain ranges."

Kethera was impressed and replied, "I keep forgetting how smart you Martians are, Saffiera", then she asked, "How will this spreading end?"

Saffiera thought for a moment while staring at the maps, *"The Masula River runs eastwards down the centre of the rift valley, eventually flowing into the Masula Lake and then, from there, flowing out to Eastern Sea. If the rift continues to spread as it is, the Masula River will become a vast inland sea. The Isle of Sorrows will eventually collide with Tarlakand and a new mountain range will form. The continental drift is actually quite uneven. The west of the continent is not actually spreading, so we will effectively end up with two continents, connected in the far west, by the high Western Mountains."*

Kethera's whiskers twitched and she nickered, "You sound like a prophet, Saffiera, making some kind of weird prophecy."

Saffiera frowned before replying, *"Before my parents emigrated from Mimas, they studied Homwol in great detail. My parents explained plate tectonics to me and how it will affect Homwol."*

Yeannah stepped in, "Saffiera is right. My parents explained plate tectonics to me as well."

"Is everyone from the Sol system taught this stuff? Are you all really smart?", Kethera enquired.

Aria responded, "Don't ask me, Kethera. I don't know squat."

Ariel replied as she looked out of the window, where she could see the main branch upon which the tree house sat, reaching all the way out to the next tree, "I think plate tectonics is a part of next year's geology class. Do the trees actually touch each other?"

"They do, Ariel. All of the trees have intermingling branches. When I was younger, I used to run along the branches and leap across to the tree next door. It was quite a lot of fun", Yeannah confirmed.

Kethera's cat-like eyes blinked, "You won't find me leaping from tree to tree."

"Don't worry, Kethera. If you fall, you'll land on your feet", Aria commented.

Kethera threw her pillow at Aria, "Aria! I am not a cat!"

Aria tossed it back, "I'm just teasing."

Saffiera placed her sleeping bag on the right-hand side of Yeannah's bed, *"Is this okay?"*, she asked telepathically, then when Yeannah nodded in the affirmative, she sat herself down upon the bed.

Curiously, Ariel asked, "Why's that island called the Isle of Sorrows?"
"I don't know why. It just always has been", Kethera replied, she was also curious.

Yeannah answered Ariel's question, "That name goes back a long way. Six million years ago when the evil Lord Ahriman ruled the planet. Carlins were spread out over the whole of Masula at the time, beyond the Northern and Southern Mountains. When Ahriman bred his Tarlaks, he wanted to test their effectiveness, so he set them loose on the Carlins. First in the north and then later in the south. His Tarlaks were brutal, they slaughtered every Carlin they came across and as a reward, Ahriman gifted them the whole southern region, naming a large part of it Tarlakand."

"What about the Isle of Sorrows?", Ariel asked.

"I'm just getting to that, Ariel", Yeannah replied, before continuing, "Ahriman tested his Tarlaks a third time on the Isle of Sorrows and they slaughtered every Carlin there as well. Later, he set up the whole Island as a training ground for his Tarlaks. Over the centuries, tens of thousands of Carlin's were shipped there to be hunted. The Tarlaks would hunt them downs, kill them and eat them."

Kethera's face took on a shocked look, her ears pressed back, her whiskers were down, "That explains why no one goes there. It is said to be haunted by many ghosts", she told the others.

Yeannah then switched on the vid screen that was mounted to the wall and accessed their worlds data and communications network. Each of the students took out their data tablets and connected to the communications network as well. They quickly accessed their inboxes and located the relevant communique concerning their term project. Yeannah's tablet was cast to the wall-mounted vid screen. Up came the title, The Great Explosion! The five friends all looked at each other, then back at the screen with perplexed looks on their faces. That was all the information provided, just that single sentence. The Great Explosion!

"No way!", Aria exclaimed. "Is that it? What's old Fish face up to?"
No one had noticed that Yeannah's Mother, Yealah, was standing in the

doorway with a tray of sandwiches and five cups of Chillic juice, "Old Fish face?", she questioned.

"Um. Bream is a kind of Earth fish", an embarrassed Aria slowly replied, "Miss Bream. Miss Fish."

"That is terribly disrespectful, Aria. You do understand that, don't you?", Yealah replied as she placed the serving tray down on a dressing table, then as she left Yeannah's bedroom, she spoke something in a few short trills, clicks and soft barks of ancient Tholish.

Aria didn't reply but did display a contrite look on her face.

After Yealah had left, Aria asked quietly, "Yeannah, what did your Mum say?"

Yeannah didn't answer, instead, Kethera translated, "Something about you needing to learn to respect your elders and develop a better attitude. Oh, and that you should know better", then she added, "It actually sounds much better in Tholish."

Yeannah replied in confirmation, "That's pretty much it", adding, "Aria, you are officially in my Mother's bad books."

"Yeah, Aria, way to go with the oops of the day award", her twin, Ariel, chided.

"Sorry", Aria replied meekly.

Yeannah looked at the screen and noted, "Miss Bream likes us to think for ourselves", as she entered a question into her data tablet's AI search prompt, "What is the Great Explosion?"

The AI search engine responded with, *"Disambiguation. The Great Explosion", this was followed on the screen by four topics, "Disambiguation 1. The Great Explosion – The Galactic Core. Sagittarius A. Disambiguation 2. The Great Explosion – The Betelgeuse Supernova. Disambiguation 3. The Great Explosion – The Outward Interstellar Expansion. Disambiguation 4. The Great Explosion – The Outward Interplanetary Expansion."*

Aria sighed and tossed her data tablet aside, exclaiming, "No way! Do we have to do all of that?"

Saffiera replied, *"I don't think so. The assignment is 'the Great Explosion' singular, not 'the Great Explosions' plural. I think we have to choose one."*

Ariel then asked, "Yes, Saffiera, but which one?"

Yeannah popped up the first disambiguation in a separate window on the screen, the title came up as, *"The Great Explosion – The Galactic Core – Sagittarius A"*

Yeannah quickly scanned the information displayed on the main vid screen, "This one is to do with the black hole in our galaxy's core, Sagittarius A. It's a supermassive black hole with a mass of over four million solar masses. Apparently, a couple of centuries back, gravitational waves were detected. Those indicated that the Sagittarius A black hole, had swallowed another supermassive black hole with the mass of a quarter of a million solar masses."

Saffiera shook her head and replied, *"I'm pretty sure we can rule that one out."*

Kethera twitched her whiskers and agreed, "Yeah. I don't think black holes are in the curriculum."

Yeannah looked at the twins, "Your opinions?"

Aria replied as she put on her pyjamas, "I have no opinions on black holes. What even is a black hole anyway?"

Ariel, Aria's twin, replied as she put on her pyjamas, "It looks like we can rule out that one."

As Yeannah closed down the window with disambiguation one, the other girls changed into their pyjamas. Yeannah popped up a window with the second disambiguation onto the screen and the title came up as, *"The Great Explosion – The Betelgeuse Supernova."*

Aria jokingly commented as she watched Kethera change into her pyjamas, "Kethera, I'm jealous. You have six and I only have two!", then she glanced down at her own chest with mock disappointment.

Kethera smiled back, her whiskers twitched upward and she replied, "Carlins are born in litters, so we need six. You Humans only need two."

Aria replied with a cheeky smile, smirking, "Just like a cat?"

Kethera rolled her eyes and blinked, she twisted her hip, swished her tail and gave Aria a gentle slap on the arm with its tip, "Carlins are not cats, Aria."

Ariel chimed in with a wry grin, "I don't know, Kethera. Richard might like six."

"Not you too, Ariel", Kethera replied, swishing her tail once more, giving Ariel a gentle slap on the shoulder, "Maybe Richard just likes my legs? Hmm, what would he think of my blue stripes?"

Ariel leaned forward curiously and asked, "Has Richard even seen your blue stripes, Kethera?"

Aria quickly tossed in, "Which blue stripes, Kethera? The ones that swirl around your boobs or the ones running down your legs?"

Kethera chuckled ever so softly, a brief flicker of self-consciousness in her eyes, "Not on my legs, he hasn't! And most certainly not on my breasts, Aria!"

Aria's grin turned mischievous, "Maybe you should show Richard your legs, Kethera. He might even like that!"

Kethera arched an eyebrow and flicked her tail, gently brushing Aria's left cheek, "Maybe you should show Richard your legs, Aria! And while you're at it, show him those two as well!", gesturing playfully toward Aria's chest.

Aria feigned a shocked look before bursting into laughter, "Maybe you just want to see what's dangling between Richard's legs!", she shot back, then all three of the girls laughed and giggled.

Their laughter turned into playful wrestling before settling themselves down on their sleeping bags, which were spread out next to each other, on the rugs on Yeannah's bedroom floor.

Saffiera, observing their interaction, rolled her eyes and sent a telepathic message to Yeannah, there was a slight sense of jealousy to it, *"Why do Earth Humans get on so well with Carlins?"*

Yeannah thought back to Saffiera, knowing that Saffiera would pick it up, *"I think it's because Carlins do look remarkably like Earth cats and Earth Humans do adore cats."*

"You're probably right, they do tend to anthropomorphise everything", Saffiera replied.

"Saffiera, you are Human, yourself, remember?", Yeannah reminded her with another thought.

"True", Saffiera admitted, *"but we Martian Humans are still somewhat different."*

Yeannah pondered for a moment, then thought back, *"You know, it's really ironic."*

"What is?", Saffiera asked telepathically.

"My people and the Indigenous Thols look identical at a glance, you can barely see the differences, yet we are genetically incompatible. You Martians and the Earth Humans are so easy to tell apart, yet you're able to interbreed. I have trouble wrapping my head around that", Yeannah replied, with a perplexed look on her face.

Saffiera considered her response carefully before replying telepathically, *"My people genetically altered the Earth's Humans to be compatible with us. We've had less than a hundred thousand years of accumulated genetic drift separating our peoples.*

Your people have six million years of genetic drift separating you from the Indigenous Thols. It's all about time."

"That makes sense, Saffiera. I'm starting to see why my parents like Martians so much", Yeannah nodded, thinking back, *"Your people and mine are like kindred spirits intellectually. Earth Humans, though, they're so unpredictable and inconsistent. Fascinating but so enigmatic. Humans, yes, but so much different from Martian Humans."*

"That's probably the reason why my people find them so intriguing", Saffiera replied.

"Are there many Martian Earth Human relationships?", Yeannah enquired.

"Oh yes. Not so much here, because here we are so few, but back in the Sol System, it is not uncommon. There are even quite a few hybrids", Saffiera noted, adding, *"None on Homwol that I'm aware of, though."*

Yeannah smiled as she formulated her next thought, *"I think Kethera likes Richard far more than she lets on. She's just too scared to admit it, even to herself."*

Saffiera smiled, being a non-verbal telepath she understood, then she revealed, *"Yes she does and Richard likes her just as much."*

Yeannah continued scanning the information on the screen, "This one is all about the Betelgeuse super nova. That was over five centuries ago. I don't think we need to worry about this one either."

"Yeah", Saffiera agreed, commenting, *"These first two are something you'd expect in a university astronomy class, not at secondary school level."*

Kethera added, "So we can cut out the first two."

The twins, Aria and Ariel, both replied in unison, "Done!"

"Okay then, disambiguation three", Yeannah remarked as she dropped one window and brought up the next, the title came up as, "*The Great Explosion – The outward Interstellar Expansion.* "

Yeannah quickly read through the first paragraph, "I think my parents told me about this one. At least some of it. It was in the stories they told me when I was a little one. It's about the rapid colonisation of the stellar systems that were close to the Sol system."

Kethera replied as she lay on the floor, "Well, Yeannah, give us the low down."

"It's the period when Humans spread out of the Sol system and into the nearby star fields", Yeannah began, then continued, "When Humans first flew their interstellar spacecraft to the Alpha Centauri system. They were surprised to find that Humans had already colonised the four habitable planets they *'discovered'*, some two centuries earlier. Alpha Centauri A, the planets Gaia and Aries. Alpha Centauri B, the planet Odhinn and Proxima Centauri, the planet Twilight, a tidally locked world."

"That can't be right! How is that even possible?", Aria asked.

Yeannah replied simply, "The Human colonists that they found there were all Earth psychics."

Saffiera's passed down memories surfaced once more, her eyes looked down to her left as she accessed her memories, she smiled and replied, *"The first actual star ship was commissioned by a powerful Earth Psychic named Folcrom Forkbraid. It was constructed by a Master Engineer named Varakhan Utana and its control systems were created by a Positronic Matrix Engineer named Peter Swann. They were all exceptional people!"*

Saffiera paused a moment before continuing, the other girls were all watching her intently, *"Forkbraid and his crew of twelve flew out to several nearby star systems, including the Alpha Centauri system. There, Forkbraid set up small temples with psychic teleportation portals. Once back in the Sol system, Forkbraid then taught the other psychics, those who were powerful enough, how to access those portals. Those psychics were then able to jaunt, teleport physically to those worlds and take other less powerful psychics along with them."*

Kethera waited for a moment to make sure that Saffiera was finished before replying, "There is a legend among we Carlins and the Indigenous Thols as well, that Humans came to Vale, long before the first starships arrived. They were called star walkers by the Carlin and star striders by the Thols."

Yeannah responded with, "We Mimasian Thols have heard of those stories. They were always considered nonsense. The wingless star striders of myth and legend!"

"Perhaps myths and legends have a kernel of truth behind them", Kethera replied.

Yeannah replied, "Perhaps Kethera. Anyway, it was during this particular Great Explosion that the Humans discovered Homwol, when their starships arrived at Xi Bootis A."

Kethera smiled, her tail swishing excitedly from side to side, as she interrupted, "Vale", she noted.

"Vale?", Yeannah questioned rhetorically, then she replied, "Vale. Homwol. Whatever. It is certainly better than the designation, Xi Bootis A Secundus, that the Humans use."

"My Dad says the Tarlaks call this world Tarlakand", Ariel noted.

"Great, let's just add that one to the list, shall we, Homwol, Val, Tarlakand, Secundus", Yeannah commented, joking, "Shall we ask the Harricks and the Chittens what they call this world?"

Saffiera informed everyone, *"The official designation for our world is still Xi Bootis A Secundus. The Earth's Interstellar Alliance won't officially give it a proper name until the Indigenous species, that is to say, Carlins and Thols, choose which one to use."*

"Oh shit! That's never going to happen!", Aria commented.
Ariel added, "That's for sure", then asked, "So we can skip this one too, yeah?"
"It is weird, though. Carlins and Thols agree on the names of their Suns, Cathol and Cythol, and even their Moon, Luns, but not the name of their world", Saffiera remarked.
"Yes, I agree, it is weird, Saffiera", Yeannah replied, then agreeing with Ariel, "I think so too. These events, that is, this particular Great Explosion, took place long after the Horridian War in the twenty three sixties and that was centuries after the Mimasian conflict, which of course, we studied last term."
"Did we?", Aria questioned and everyone just rolled their eyes and shook their heads, including Aria's twin, Ariel.

Kethera remarked, "It's weird, you Humans have colonised worlds for dozens of light years in all directions around the Earth. You've even taken we Carlins and Mimasian Thols out to some of those colonies. Yet, only the Earth and Vale were found to have sentient life. Why is that?", she questioned.
Saffiera replied, *"No one really knows, Kethera. The worlds of the Alpha Centauri system had complex life but no sapient life. Likely, sapience hadn't evolved there yet. Of course, my ancestral homeworld, Mars, also developed sapient life, my people. That was long before the Earth did and even then, my people had a large hand in that. Perhaps sapient life is really rare. The Earth, Mars and Vale might just have been lucky."*

Kethera noted as her tail swished back and forth, "We have three species of sapient life on Vale, five if you include the Harricks and the Chittens."

Saffiera responded, *"On the Earth, the only sapient native species are the Humans, however, there are probably at least six other pre-sapient species. Perhaps even more. Yet, only the Humans achieved true sapience. I think true sapient life is very rare."*

Yeannah noted, "That could be the case. Most of the colony worlds I've read about, had lesser forms of life, hardly anything like the diversity we have here on Homwol or back on the Earth."

"And many of the colony worlds were barely habitable, so they had to be terraformed. They had only very simple lifeforms when Humans arrived", Aria added, while absently staring out the window.

Everyone stared at Aria in disbelief, thinking to themselves, *"How did Aria know that?"*

Aria turned around and looked at her friends, she shrugged and answered their surprised looks, "I saw it somewhere on the network. The Discovery

Network, I think."

Everyone rolled their eyes once more, Aria was a paradox, she was clever, almost brilliant in fact and then she had her moments, where she appeared almost scatterbrained or absent-minded.

Kethera quickly changed the subject in an attempt to get their study session back on track, "The last one on the list must be Miss Bream's Great Explosion. Open it up, Yeannah."

Yeannah closed the window on the screen and opened up disambiguation four. The title that appeared in the window that popped up was, *"The Great Explosion – The Outward Interplanetary Expansion."*

Ariel read out the first paragraph, after the title, aloud, *"The Outward Interplanetary Expansion was the rapid colonisation of Interplanetary space, including the inner and outer regions of the Sol system. This rapid colonial expansion took place between the years twenty sixty and twenty one eighty two. During this period was the Mimasian War and the Great Conceal. The Outer Satellite Insurrection, otherwise known as the first Horridian War, brought this period to an end."*

"Bingo!", Aria shouted, then questioned, "Why didn't you start with this one first?"

"What and miss out on all of the fun going through the other three first?", Saffiera replied.

"That was fun?", Aria questioned rhetorically, adding, "Wow, Saffiera, you need to get out more."

Kethera's whiskers twitched once more, "Well, now at least, we know what we're doing."

"We should have known. We studied the Mimasian War last term", Ariel remarked.

Yeannah confirmed, "The Great Explosion, the Outward Interplanetary Expansion."

Everyone was in agreement and they began to eat their sandwiches and drink their Chillic juice while reading through the notes on the vid screen. They began popping up windows on their individual data tablets, each with different historical aspects of the period known as the Great Explosion.

The group of five school friends were just beginning their term two group project.

5. Cis-Lunar Expansion.

James Carter, the President of the Earth's Cis-Lunar colonies, looked out of his office window. The vast expanse of Colonial Central Command's southern end cap spread out before him. Across the end cap, he could see across to the bulkhead mountains, more than two kilometres away in the distance.
Colonial Central Command was huge, it was the first of the mega colonies. An enormous O'Neil-style cylindrical colony, its main cylinder was twenty kilometres long and four kilometres wide.

Within this enormous space, there was no need for artificial weather, internal weather patterns developed naturally of their own accord. At each end of the main cylinder were hemispherical end caps with a radius of two kilometres. The whole colony construct orbited in a halo orbit in the Moon Earth Lagrangian point five. Automatic attitude control thrusters kept the colony precisely aligned, with its northern end cap always pointed towards the Sun.

Three enormous long mirrors extended out from the rear of the main cylinder at a precise angle so as to catch the Sun's rays and reflect them inwards towards immense strip windows running the length of the main cylinder. Each end cap had a circular window running around it, where they joined the main cylinder. Mirrors reflected sunlight through these windows as well. The whole structure rotated at point six-seven revolutions per minute to produce centrifugal force, creating an artificial gravity of one Earth g for its interior. Well over ten million people lived within this one cylinder.

It had taken two decades to build Colonial Central Command, simply called Central by its inhabitants and the colony was not that old either, having been completed for the turn of the century celebrations in the year twenty one hundred. It was a colony built to last the test of time. No other colony ever created across the entirety of the solar system could compare to Central.

Yet, that would not last. The blueprints and designs for the immense mega colony had been placed in the public domains and shared with the Trojans, the Jovians and the Saturnians. In the due course of time, they, too, would build their own versions. As would others, as colonists pushed outward to Uranus, Neptune and beyond.

President Carter's Mother had named him after an ancestor of theirs, who had been a president of a great nation in the twentieth century. His Mother had always told him that he was destined to greatness and pressed that belief on him all through his upbringing. James Carter felt anything but great. His colonies had suffered a disaster, twenty-five of them had almost been massively damaged, two others were heavily damaged and they had all been evacuated. A major calamity had befallen the entire solar system. James Carter had only been elected President six weeks prior to the catastrophe.

Two figures stood to one side of the President's office, their psychic obscuration fields keeping them completely hidden. They wore long, hooded cloaks of shimmering black, like the colour of a raven's feathers. President Carter and his secretary knew not of their presence nor even of their existence.

"Carmen", the President called out softly to his secretary, "The universe is a dangerous place. Had we been on the Earth, that micro meteor shower would have been nothing more than a light show in the skies above the Earth. Here in space, it caused enormous damage."

"It could have been much worse, Sir", Carmen replied, explaining, "Those meteor showers were very patchy, Sir. They only hit certain places. If they had been more widely spread, they could have destroyed everything."

"True enough, Carmen. The Venusians were spared. The Saturnian colonies were devastated, though. Not much is left out their way or so the reports tell me", President Carter replied, considering, "I guess we were lucky in comparison. Only twenty seven colonies here and Eros out at Earth Sun L-Five. As you said, Carmen, it could have been worse."

"Yes, Sir. It could have been much, much worse", Carmen agreed.

"My big concern is that those micro meteor swarms were undetectable", President Carter noted, "Their particles were too small to detect and they travelled at the speed of bullets."

"Yes, Sir, however, my understanding is that they're likely to be very rare", Carmen replied.

President Carter thought for a moment, then replied, "Rare or not, Carmen. We need to be prepared. Write up a communique and send it to our boffins. I want them to figure out a way to detect these micro-meteor swarms. No matter how rare those meteor swarms are or how small those meteors might be, we need to be able to detect them."

"Yes, Sir. I'll be on it straight away, Sir", Carmen replied as she took down notes.

Unseen, Folcrom Orpheus telepathically spoke to his protege, *"Freyja, it looks like the memory alterations are holding."*

Equally unseen, Freyja agreed, "*Yes, Orpheus. They've completely associated the Mimasian War with an interstellar micro-meteor swarm disaster. We might just get away with this cover-up.*"

"*Well, that is the general idea, Freyja*", Folcrom Orpheus replied, "*The public at large are not ready to know about aliens, especially in our own solar system.*"

"*Cousin Tina certainly did good work on their memories*", Freyja commended.

"*Yes, Freyja. Cousin Tina did very well indeed. Her work is so subtle. She wove and blended our cover story with their memories almost perfectly*", Orpheus agreed.

"*Their own trauma helps with that. The mind naturally wants to bury this sort of thing*", Freyja replied, then asked, "*So, Orpheus, when will we let them know about the Martians and the Thols?*"

"*Perhaps three to five centuries into the future*", Orpheus speculated, admitting, "*We won't be alive to see it. It will be our descendant's decision.*"

"*Understood. Let's hope we successfully can guide our people into the future and avoid any future pitfalls*", Freyja replied.

"*That is our purpose, Freyja, that is our purpose*", Orpheus confirmed.

"*They will be wasting their time trying to detect those non-existent interstellar micro meteor swarms, Orpheus*", Freyja commented.

"*That's perfectly okay, Freyja*", Orpheus replied, "*They might develop some new technologies out of all of their efforts*", and Freyja gave Orpheus a psychic nod in reply.

President Carter noted, "You know, Carmen, they made a mistake when they built this colony."

"Really? In what way, Sir?", Carmen enquired.

"Well, every other O'Neil-style cylindrical colony we've built has the governance, commerce and business all in their northern end caps. All of the engineering and control is down in the southern end cap", the President noted, adding, "When they built Colonial Central Command, they reversed all of that. I'm mean, look where we are. We're in the southern end cap."

"Does that matter, Sir?", Secretary Carmen enquired.

"Well yes", the President replied, explaining, "When people come here from the other colonies, it does cause a great degree of confusion until they get used to the fact that everything is flipped."

"I expect that we can't change that now, Sir. It would be frightfully expensive", Carmen replied.

"Yes. Yes, of course it would be", President Carter replied as he walked back to his desk, remarking along the way, "Remind me later Carmen, after we get this mess sorted out, to recommend that future mega colonies, conform to the old north south standards."

"Yes, Sir. I'm just noting that down now, Sir", Carmen replied.

President Carter sat down at his desk and looked across to his secretary as she sat at her desk, putting together the communique to their research and development division.

"Carmen. I need to send a communique to Eros", the President informed her.

"Yes, Sir", Carmen looked up and replied.

"Write me up an email to the Security Council of Sol", President Carter requested.

"Yes, Sir, I'll start right away", Carmen replied.

"Request from the Security Council, a full copy of their damage reports. Detailed copies", the President noted.

"Yes, Sir. I'm taking notes as we speak", Carmen commented.

"Request that they highlight and annotate any issues that they need us to help with", the President continued, adding, "and let them know that there will be no limitations on the aid we provide."

"They will appreciate that, Sir. I'm certain of it", Carmen remarked.

"I'm sure they will, Carmen", President Carter agreed, then instructed, "Put that email together, then send it to me. I'll have a look at it, make any changes that I need and then I'll send it off."

"Yes, Sir. I'll get started on it straight away, Sir", Carmen replied.

A short while later, President Carter was reviewing his communique to Eros. He read through it carefully, made a few minor adjustments and then clicked send.

"Carmen, thank you for that. I've just sent it off", the President thanked her, then asked, "Can you send me the damage report for those twenty seven damaged colonies. I'm interested in those summary pages in particular. I need to refresh my memory on the level of damage."

"Yes, Sir", then a couple of minutes later, "It's on it way now Sir."

"Now what to do with those twenty seven damaged colonies", James Carter thought to himself, before he read through the overall damage report summary, thinking, *"Hmm, it will take a bit of work. Still, we could repair them."*

Still observing silently and unseen, Orpheus remarked, *"Freyja, this is why we're still here."*

"Okay", Freyja replied.

"Carmen. I'm just looking at the level of damage and the repair cost estimates", the President noted, "It does look like we can repair those colonies. Your thoughts?"

"Well, Sir, not that my opinion on the matter is relevant, but I'd be more concerned about the evacuees myself", Carmen suggested.

"Of course. Of course, Carmen", the President replied, continuing, "My understanding is that half of those two hundred thousand evacuees have been placed in housing up here with other colonies and that the other half are down on the Earth."

"Yes, Sir, that is my understanding as well", Carmen replied, adding, "It is also my understanding that they have their belongings as well. Except for the larger items that are being held in storage."

"So we have a choice then, Carmen. We can repair those colonies or we can scrap them and replace them with new ones", President Carter replied.

"Repairing them would be quicker and more cost effective, Sir", Carmen suggested.

"And that is what we cannot allow", Orpheus informed Freyja, *"We can't have engineers pawing all over those colonies and repairing obvious weapons damage."*

"Too right, Orpheus", Freyja agreed, *"Micro meteor strikes don't really match up with particle beam and laser beam damage."*

"You work on the secretary and I'll work on the President", Orpheus instructed, adding, *"Let's just give them a subtle nudge in the right direction."*

President Carter sat frozen at his desk for just a moment, as did Carmen at hers. It wasn't long, just a few long seconds, then the moment passed.

"This could be an opportunity, Sir", Carmen commented, then asked, "Those colonies were quite old. Mostly over eighty years old, a few are close to ninety. Could replacing them be better?"

Freyja looked at Orpheus and smiled.

"While I do agree they are old, Carmen. Replacing them would be far more expensive", President Carter replied, adding, "It will also take longer, much longer."

"Slipping Orpheus", Freyja cheekily transmitted telepathically.

Orpheus gave Freyja a dirty look and then entered the President's mind once more.

The President's secretary, Carmen, replied, "Just thinking, Sir. Replacing those colonies would boost our economy. After this disaster, wouldn't that be a good thing, Sir?"

Freyja looked at Orpheus and smiled once more.

"Yes, Carmen. I have to agree with you on that point", the President replied, adding, "It will take much longer, but the result will be much better. A huge boost to the economy and twenty seven brand spanking new colonies. The latest designs, greatly improved colonies, perhaps even larger."

Orpheus looked back at Freyja, this time, he smiled a broad smile.

Freyja smiled back and replied simply, "*Touche.*"

"I'm sure the extra costs involved will be worth it, Sir", Carmen replied.

President Carter agreed, "Yes, yes, Carmen. The costs will be worth it. I'll need to run it by my cabinet, however, I'm sure they'll all agree. Please send out a meeting invite to all of the cabinet members for tomorrow afternoon at two pm."

"Yes, Sir, I'll organise that straight away", Carmen replied.

"And Carmen. Assuming they all agree, which I'm sure they will, be ready with some dates for a press conference, later in the week", the President instructed.

"It looks like our job is done, Orpheus", Freyja suggested.

"Not quite Freyja. When is our job ever done", Orpheus replied.

"Now. What to do with those old broken colonies?", the President thought out aloud.
Carmen responded as if it was a question directed at her and replied, "Well, Sir. Won't they just all get scrapped and recycled?"

Orpheus looked at Freyja and raised his index finger before pointing to the President.

President Carter looked at his secretary, "We could do that, although I'm getting a better idea."

"Getting a better idea, Sir?", Carmen queried.

"Yeah, Carmen. It's just popped into my head right out of nowhere", the President replied.

Orpheus turned to Freyja with a huge Cheshire grin on his face.

President Carter continued as the thought solidified, "We can push those twenty seven broken colonies out to the Belters. Separate the twinned colony cylinders, fold in their long strip mirrors and have them hauled out to the Belter colonies."

"They are all twinned colony cylinders, Sir", Carmen noted, adding, "We'll need at least fifty four space tugs."

"Yes we will, Carmen, but you know what", President Carter replied, explaining, "Belters love something for nothing and that's what they'll be getting. They can scrap them, repair them, do whatever they want with them."

"That is actually a very good idea, Sir", Carmen agreed, "I've been taking notes, Sir. I'll put together a standard offer agreement and have it ready for you to discuss at your cabinet meeting tomorrow."

"Excellent, Carmen. Offering those colonies to the Belters should demonstrate good will to our neighbours", President Carter replied, "I am certain cabinet will agree with me."

"Sir, I won't put in anything about transport costs", Carmen suggested, "That way, the Belters might offer to haul the colony cylinders out to their colonies themselves. They are free, after all."

"Yes. Yes. Very good, Carmen. Excellent idea", President Carter replied.

"That is how it's done, Freyja", Orpheus commented.

Freyja replied, questioning, *"Won't the Belters notice the weapons damage?"*

"Perhaps, Freyja, but Belter engineers aren't the same as Cis-Lunar engineers. They won't care! They've got something for nothing and that will be first and foremost on their minds", Orpheus replied.

"So that's it then. L-Five gets twenty seven brand new colonies and the Belters get the old ones. Everybody is happy", Freyja commented.

"And that is the general idea. Colonial Central Command shows the Belters good will. The Belters are grateful to receive the old colonies, broken though they may be. Everybody is

happy", Orpheus agreed, informing Freyja, *"and now, dear cousin, our job is done. We can leave."*

There was an ever so slight shimmering in the air in the President's office and the pair was gone.

President Carter remarked, "Carmen, please check the thermostat. It seems a bit chilly in here."

"Yes, Sir, I'll do that straight away", Carmen replied.

The following day, the cabinet meeting went just as President Carter had expected. The good will gesture, gifting the twenty seven damaged colonies to the Belters, was agreed to. Notes were added to the standard offer agreement and it was then altered accordingly. The damaged colonies were described as being "gifted to the *'Belter colonies'*, as is, with complete ownership, full rights and authority over them, clear of any encumbrances or impediments. To do with as seen fit, be it scrapping, repairing, refurbishment or on selling etc.".

It did not matter that they were damaged, even as scrap, their value was immense and the Belter colonies would be more than happy to have them. The damaged colonies had all been built within the same time period between seventy five and ninety years ago. They were all O'Neil-style twin cylinder colonies of the same model, each capable of housing ten thousand people each. At the time of the disaster, they housed eighty percent of capacity, around two hundred thousand colonists.

There were thirteen Belter colonies in the Asteroid Belt: Ceres, Vesta, Pallas, Hygiea, Interamnia, Davida, Europa, Sylvia, Euphrosyne, Eunomia, Juno, Bamberga and Psyche. Each Belter colony was allocated two of the damaged colonies and the names of those colonies were listed in their individual offer agreements. That left one colony unallocated, the youngest, which had been named Malibu. The fate of the final colony, Malibu and its twin cylinders, was yet to be decided.

The thirteen individual offer agreements had a transport stipulation, "Haulage of the damaged colony cylinders from Cis-Lunar L-Five to the *'Belter Colonies'* will be the responsibility of the 'Belter Colonies', including all arrangements for haulage, including all of the costs incurred, etc." This would be no impediment to the Belters, as the scrap value of the damage colonies alone far exceeded the cost of haulage by orders of magnitude.

Each colony had two main cylinders. Once they were separated and prepared for transport, each would require a powerful space tug to haul it to its destination. Gifting two damaged colonies per Belter colony, meant four main cylinder sections and four space tugs. The space haulage industry was about to get a major boost as well and one company, Cis-Lunar Haulage, was well positioned.

The fate of the Malibu colony was decided at the same meeting, which ran from two p.m. in the afternoon to well into the night, close to nine pm. It was decided that that the Malibu colony would have its main cylinders separated and prepared for a much longer journey. President Carter had decided that it would be gifted to the Saturnian colonies, which had suffered greatly during the disaster, which resulted in many thousands of deaths. Scores of thousands, in fact. All four of their O'Neil-style colonies had been destroyed.

The offer agreement for Saturn was almost the same as for the Belters, except that President Carter insisted that Cis-Lunar L-Five pick up the cost of haulage to Titan Saturn L-Five. It was the very least that they could do, considering the extreme distances involved and would extend their good will to the people of the Saturnian colonies.

The President's cabinet had decided to tender out the contracts for the construction of the new colonies. They had decided that the new colonies should be of the latest designs, very much larger designs. The colony replacement program had grown from simply replacing twenty seven damaged colonies to a more ambitious colonial expansion plan.

Each of the twenty seven new colonies would be capable of housing five times the number of colonists. The total housing capacity would be one point two five million people. The new plan was ambitious, very ambitious. It would not only house the refugees, it was also going to require a campaign to attract new colonists from the Earth to L-Five.

The following Monday, after checking through the standard offer agreements, Carmen asked, "Mr President, Sir. These all appear to be in order. Would you like me to transmit them?"

President Carter replied, "What's the date?"

"Monday, December Fourteenth, Sir". Carmen responded.

While the Earth had multiple times around the planet, the colonies of Cis-Lunar L-Five all used the one time zone, Greenwich meantime.

"Hold off on the Belter agreements, Carmen", the President decided, explaining, "I'd like those to be sent next Monday, the Twenty First. That will be a nice Christmas present for them. A nice surprise!"

"Yes, Sir and the offer agreement for the Saturnian colonies?", Carmen enquired.

"Find out who the current Administrator is", the President requested, adding, "I'll send him a personal message and let him know our plans."

"Yes, Sir", Carmen replied, as she quickly tracked down who the current colonial Administrator of the Saturnian system was, a few minutes later, "His name is Administrator Mark Spencer, Sir. I've sent you his contact details"

"Thank you, Carmen", the President replied as he put together a communique and sent it off.

The turnaround time for communications to Saturn takes hours due to the distances involved. It was not until the next day that President Carter received the reply.

"Administrator Spenser is a happy chappy, Carmen", President Carter informed her.

"Is he, Sir?", Carmen enquired.

"He certainly is, Carmen", the President replied, "The Administrator is thanking us for the Malibu colony and is informing us that his engineers should be able to repair and refurbish it. He is looking forward to its arrival. He is also asking for any further assistance that we can provide or arrange from the other colonies in the inner system."

"Well then, Sir. I'll send off that offer agreement for his perusal straight away", Carmen replied.

"After you've sent it off, pass Administrator Spenser's contact details to our colonial construction department. They'll take over and organise the preparation and shipping", the President replied.

"Yes, Sir, consider it done", Carmen replied.

On the Monday of the following week, the other offer agreements were been sent off to the Belter colonies. By Wednesday, the replies were coming back.

"We have received replies from the Belter colonies, Sir", Carmen informed the President.

"All good, I hope, Carmen?", the President enquired.

"They are all thanking us for the gift and wishing us a Merry Christmas, but they all want to know what the catch is", Carmen replied.

President Carter laughed, "Belters! Give them something for nothing and they want to know what the catch is. In your reply, let them know there is no catch. A gift is a gift", then he enquired, "Is there anything else?"

"Ah, yes, Sir. The Ceresian Administrator wants to know if we can help out with the transport costs", Carmen informed him.

"That would be right. Those gifted colonies are worth magnitudes more than the cost of their cartage and he still wants us to cover the costs", the President commented, then asked, "Who's their Administrator?"

"Harcourt Moon, Sir?", Carmen replied.

"What do we know about Administrator Moon?", the President enquired.

"Hmm", Carmen murmured, as she started looking up information on her computer, "Sir, it appears every Ceresian Administrator since colonisation has the surname Moon. Harcourt Moon appears to be a businessman. I'd say he's trying us on, trying to save his colony a few credits."

"Okay. Okay", the President replied, then instructed, "Carmen, inform Administrator Moon that we can't help with his cartage expenses, however, we can pass his contact details on to our finance division. They may be able to provide Ceres with a line of credit, at a relatively low interest, of course."

"Yes, Sir", Carmen replied, "I'll do that now, Sir."

"Excellent, Carmen. After you've done that, notify our construction department to start preparing the damaged colonies for shipping", President Carter replied.

"Sir, I'll monitor the progress and if the Belters are tardy with their haulage arrangements, I'll keep reminding them", his Secretary replied.

"Thank you, Carmen. Thank you", the President replied.

"Talking about our construction department, Sir, I've just sent you some documents that require your signature. Your authority is required, Sir", Carmen informed President Carter.

The President opened his mail and read through the first document, "It seems we'll be needing four new ore processing and smelting facilities in Cis-Lunar L-Four", he remarked.

"That does make sense, Sir. Twenty seven new colonies are going to need a lot more processed materials", his Secretary, Carmen, agreed.

President Carter digitally signed the document, attached the Presidential seal and then sent the document back to his Secretary for her to send it off, "That one's done", he noted.

The President opened up the next document and read through it, "It seems our construction department is recommending a second catch-all in Cis-Lunar L-Four as well."

"Catch-all, Sir?", Carmen queried.

"They're those big lunar ore receiving stations that they use to catch ore packets that are catapulted into space from the lunar surface", the President explained, "It seems they'll need a new one. That makes sense, too. We are going to need to scale up everything in the pipeline to get those new colonies up and running."

The President digitally signed the document, attached the Presidential seal and then returned the document to his Secretary, "There's another one for you to send off Carmen", he noted.

"Document number three", President Carter commented as he opened it up, "Yep, just as I thought, here's the trifecta. An extra Catch-all and new ore processing facilities are going to require more ore Carryalls for ore transportation."

"Yes, Sir. More ore, more facilities, equates to increased transport requirements.", Carmen agreed.

"Yep, we'll be increasing the ore Carryall fleet by fifty percent", the President noted, then signed the document, sealed it and sent it back to Carmen to be sent off, "Is that the last one, Carmen?", he asked.

"No, Sir, there is one more", Carmen replied.

President Carter opened up the forth document, "Of course Carmen. We need more ore. We can't built new colonies without the raw materials", he noted as he read through the document, adding, "I'll authorise the Lunar Mining Consortium to scale up their ore production to meet the new requirements."

President Carter signed the document, sealed it and then sent it back to Carmen.

Cis-Lunar L-Five had found itself with a major colony construction boom on its hands, while at the same time the old damaged colony cylinders being pushed out to the Belter colonies, caused a small construction boom in the Asteroid Belt as well. This construction boom would extend and continue for almost forty years.

6. Lunar Mining Liaison.

Kasim Khan was new to the sprawling lunar mining colony, he'd only been working there for four months. The whole operation was run by a private company, simply called the Lunar Mining Consortium. It had taken Kasim the best part of two weeks just to get use to the Moon's lower gravity, being that it was so low at one sixth of the Earth's.

Kasim was the company's liaison officer and it was his job to deal with official communications with Colonial Central Command. Generally, things went quite smoothly, with little more than requests to adjust the lunar ore extraction to suit the capacities and requirements of the ore processing facilities in the Moon's L-Four Lagrangian point. Often, they would request ores that were richer in one resource element over another, which then required adjusting the outputs of the various lunar ore fields. Generally speaking, it was fairly routine work.

Kasim read through the latest colonial Cis-Lunar construction schedule, he was rather surprised by what he saw, *"This is ridiculous. It must be a mistake",* he thought to himself.

What Kasim was reading was so ridiculous, in fact, that he contacted the Colonial Central Command, the colony construction department. After a short discussion, it was confirmed that the latest construction schedule was not a mistake. Kasim transferred the document to his tablet and quickly walked off to the Administrator's office.

As Kasim entered the Administrator Baxter's secretary's office, he greeted the Administrator's Secretary, Sharon Charters, "Is the Administrator available, Sharon?"

"I'll just check", Sharon replied, picking up the phone, "Sir. I have Kasim Khan here to see you."

Sharon put down the phone, "Please go straight in, Mr Khan."

As Kasim entered the Administrator's office, he asked, "Administrator Sir, have you seen the latest construction schedules?"

"No. Not yet, Kasim", Administrator Baxter replied.

"Sir. We have our current schedule. We, are over the next decade, are producing enough ore and raw materials for fifteen new colonies", Kasim reminded the Administrator, then he began tapping on his tablet, "I'll transfer the latest schedules to you Sir. This is straight from Colonial Central

Command."

Administrator quickly read through the document, after a minute he replied, "This can't be right Kasim. Surely this can't be right."

"Sir. I have contacted Central Command. The colony constructions department assures me that this new schedule is correct", Kasim replied, informing him further, "These changes are straight from the President's cabinet."

Administrator Baxter looked back down at the document, then back up to Kasim, "Twenty seven extra new colonies, big ones with twin cylinders. All in the same time frame as the schedule for fifteen. That's forty all up. That's a lot of ore. Is that even possible?"

"Ah, no, Sir", Kasim replied, informing Administrator Baxter, "It's almost tripling our ore production. We'd be hard pressed to double our production, let alone triple it."

"We'll need to open up more mining operations", Administrator Baxter noted.

"We'll need to break ground on at least six new mines, Sir, at a guess", Kasim replied

"Where did they even get this crazy idea from?", the Administrator enquired.

"I did ask. They're not going to repair the damaged colonies", Kasim informed him.

"They're not. So they want to build brand new, bigger ones instead?", the Administrator queried.

"Apparently, Sir", Kasim confirmed, adding, "With five times the capacity of the old ones."

"And the twenty seven old colonies? Are they just scrap?", Administrator Baxter enquired.

"No, Sir. They're gifting them to the Belters, to do with as they see fit", Kasim replied.

"It seems that Central Command has given us quite a headache", the Administrator noted, then instructed, "Kasim. Scale up production at our existing mines as much as you can. Then check with our Lunar Geology Exploration Lab. Find out what promising new ore fields they've discovered."

“Yes, Sir, that's next on my to-do list”, Kasim replied.

Kasim left the Administrator's office and the Administrator leaned back in his chair, he sighed and then shook his head in disbelief.

Brian Henderson was staring into his screen, inspecting the results of the latest shallow ore samples taken from a large strip of land in the Sea of Tranquillity. He had a broad smile on his face. Kasim Khan entered the Geology lab and, seeing that Brian was busy, settled down in a chair to wait. Brian's wispy grey hair was short and unkempt, giving the geologist the dishevelled appearance of a man who had never owned a comb. Of course, he did own a comb, he just rarely ever used it.

Brian looked up from his screen, “Seventy three parts per billion”, he commented to himself, finishing off with, “Outstanding!”

“Seventy three parts per billion?”, Kasim enquired.

Surprised, Brian spun around on his swivel chair, “Mr Khan! Are you trying to give an old man a heart attack?”

“Sorry, Brian. Did you just say seventy-three parts per billion? ”, Kasim apologised and queried once more.

“Helium three, lad, helium three”, Brian replied excitedly, explaining, ”Most regolith mining fields on this rock are lucky to reach ten parts per billion. Helium three mining doesn't even get economic until you get into double figures and seventy three parts per billion is just outstanding! It is phenomenal! If we're going to colonise the entire solar system, we're going to need a lot more helium three for ship fuel. The new fusion drives are hungry little beasts.”

“Good to know”, Kasim replied, “but I'm not here about the helium three.”

Kasim looked around the geology lab, “Aren't there supposed to be a dozen geologists running around down here?”, he enquired.

Brian replied, “Ah, yeah, they've gone for an early lunch break. Today's one of the Girl's birthdays”, then he added, “Although Thomas Levi is off Lunar, on sick leave. He's got a bad case of the HOS.”

“The HOS?”, Kasim queried.

“Hypo-gravitational Osteopenia Syndrome? Have you forgotten your induction so soon, lad?” Brian replied, then he asked, “You haven't been down here that long, Kasim. Have you been taking your stimulants and your supplements? You don't want your bones turning brittle! Not at your young age."

"Yes, yes and I've been doing all the mandatory strength exercises as well", Kasim assured him.

"Good, good. Make sure you keep that up. Thomas let things slide and ended up with green-stick fractures in both legs and now he's back up at L-Five", Brian replied, adding, "It's unlikely he'll be back down here anytime soon. We've lost more than a few good people to the HOS, so keeping to the Company's guidelines is essential, no matter how strict they are."

"How'd Thomas break his legs?", Kasim queried.
"He was changing a light bulb in his quarters", Brian replied matter-of-factly.

"Changing a light bulb?", Kasim queried incredulously.

"Yeah. He was standing on a chair, he had just changed the bulb and jumped down", Brian replied, adding, "When he hit the floor, both of his legs gave way."

"Just like that?", Kasim asked.

"Just like that. Of course, Thomas missed his shift without any word. So, a couple of us went over to his quarters to check on him and found him lying on the floor in agony. Apparently he'd been like that all day", Brian explained.

Kasim considered that for a few moments, the Moon's sixteen percent gravity could cause all kinds of health issues if one didn't follow the Lunar Mining Consortium's strict guidelines. The stimulants, the vitamin and mineral supplements and with the special exercise regimen were all exceedingly important.

The HOS wasn't the only health condition that the lower lunar gravity could cause, there was also Hypo-gravitational Muscular Atrophy, Hypo-gravitational Pulmonary Insufficiency and a whole raft of other Hypo-gravitational syndromes. It was imported to adhere to the Consortium's guidelines as strictly as possible.

"So no partying for you then, Brian?", Kasim asked.

"Well, you know how it is, Kasim. Some intriguing preliminary test results came in. I saw those and I just had to complete the full battery of tests to see what we had", Brian replied, "and the results are spectacular. These are the highest concentrations of helium three we have ever recorded on the moon!

The only place where we might find better results would be on Mercury."

"Mercury?", Kasim queried.

"Mercury is much closer to the Sun", Brian replied, then explained, "That close, the solar wind is far more intense and its helium three deposition rate would be much higher. If Mercury's magnetic field was much stronger in the past, there could be rich helium three deposits all around Mercury's poles."

Kasim nodded, he understood the importance of discovering helium three deposits and their use as a fuel in the latest spaceship fusion drives, but that wasn't the reason for his visit to the geology lab.

"Brian, how many lunar ore fields do we have that could be opened up for extraction?", he asked.

"Ore fields?", Brian asked, more of himself than of Kasim, then he replied, "We have a dozen or so ore fields ready for mining operations, Kasim. How many do you need to open up?"

"We need to open up six new ore fields, Brian. At least six", Kasim informed him.

"Six?", Brian queried rhetorically, "That's a lot of groundbreaking lad. Why do we need six new mines?", he asked.

"Central Command is pushing through a construction boom and they estimate we'll need a lot more ore", Kasim replied, adding, "At least six more mines worth."

"Six mines worth. That's a hell of a lot", Brian noted, then remarked, "You know lad, we are already in the middle of a large construction boom. L-Five's being building fifteen colonies per decade since the turn of the century."

Kasim passed his tablet to Brian, it was open to the appropriate page, "Well, Brian, our construction boom just got bigger, much bigger."

Brian read the open file on Kasim's tablet, "Sweet Mother! Another twenty seven colonies. All double cylinders and they're big bastards as well. In what time frame? Shit! Ten years!", he passed the tablet back to Kasim, "Are you sure six new mines will be enough?"

"At least six, Brian. At least six", Kasim replied.

"Well, Kasim, we have plenty of ore allotments to break ground on", Brian replied, then noted, "You'll need to check with our machinery department. We're going to need a lot more bulldozers, diggers and hoppers."

"Hoppers? I'm not familiar with those?", Kasim admitted.

"You're relatively new, Kasim, you wouldn't know everything yet", Brian replied, explaining, "The bulldozers scrape the regolith into ore piles. The diggers load the ore into hoppers. When the hoppers are full, they lift of and fly the load to the mag-lev mass driver. Then they fly back for the next load."

"Got it, Brian. Then the ore is pressed and packaged, loaded into the magnetic levitation mass driver's buckets, to be launched towards L-Four", Kasim replied, showing that he understood the process to at least some degree.

"Yep. That's it, lad. You may even need a second mag-lev mass drive as well", Brian replied.

"Jesus, Brian, this stuff never ends", Kasim remarked, questioning, "Where the hell are we going to get a second mass driver from? I'm assuming that these things don't just pop out of the ground like bloody mushrooms."

Brian laughed out loud, it was a quite a raucous laugh, "We've got another one already, Sunny Jim", he remarked.

"What are you talking about, Brian?", Kasim asked, commenting, "I'm only aware of the one mag-lev mass driver on this entire bloody rock."

"Remember that huge mega monstrosity, the one we all call Colonial Central Command", Brian replied, once he had his laughter back under control.

"Yeah, sure. That's where we're getting these damnable new schedules from", Kasim replied.

"Okay. To build Colonial Central Command, they needed more ore than you can imagine and an extra mass driver. So they built a second mass driver over in the next valley across from the first", Brian informed him.

"So we already have a second mag-lev mass driver?", Kasim asked for clarification.

"Yes, lad, we do. When Colonial Central Command was completed, it was shutdown, dismantled and mothballed. It is still there, unused, exactly where it was left", Brian informed him further.

"Well, I guess that will help", Kasim commented.

"Don't get too happy just yet, lad", Brian replied, noting while chuckling, "You'll need to check with our maintenance department. Those poor bastards are the ones that are going to have to put that bloody thing back together again."

Kasim replied with a wry smile on his face, "That does not sound like fun, Brian. Not one bit."

"It won't be. It's been shutdown, dismantled and mothballed for forty plus years", Brian agreed, noting, "They won't like being to told to put it all back together again and make it work."

"Oh shit! That's my job", Kasim realised, "I'm not looking forward to that. Not one bit!"

Brian quickly compiled a file and sent it to Kasim's data tablet, "That's a list of a dozen mining allotments. I've ordered the list by their assessed level of ore quality. Break ground on the first six and if you need more ore, then work your way down the list. They're all good ore fields and not that far from our main operations."

Kasim opened up the list and glanced over it, "Okay, so we have ore fields we can crack open. That's a good starting point."

"As I said before, check with our machinery department for the heavy equipment. You'll need to requisition all of that from them. Then you'll need to go upstairs to personnel. Each mine is going to need eight to ten people, at least, to operate it", Brian informed him.

"And then I head off to the maintenance department, to give them the bad news about rebuilding that other mag-lev mass driver", Kasim followed on.

"There you go, lad, your days all planned out", Brian replied as his colleagues began returning from their long lunch break.

"Okay then, I'd better get started", Kasim replied, as he acknowledged the other geologists with a quick nod, "I'll check you later, Brian and thanks again."

Kasim headed off downstairs to the Mining Consortium's machinery department. When the elevator reached the lowest level, he stepped out and had a look around. The foyer was bright, neat, very tidy and very clean. There was a series of offices and storage rooms down the corridor, off to the right and a receptionist's counter and desk across from the elevator. It could have been an office space anywhere. The corridor continued further down to the right into the distance. To Kasim's left was a bulkhead and an embedded airlock door.

Kasim approached the secretary, "Hi", he greeted, looking at the secretary's name badge, "Tanya. I need to speak to someone about requisitioning mining machinery."

"And you would be?", Tanya enquired.

"Kasim Khan", he replied, informing her, "I work for Administrator Baxter. I'm his Operations and Administrative Liaison Officer."

Tanya pressed a button and then spoke into her intercom, "Hank. I have Operations and Administrative Liaison Officer Khan here to see you."

"Thanks, Tanya, I'll be straight out", came the reply from the other end of the intercom.

Hank Sharky left his office and came walking down the corridor towards Kasim and greeted, "I'm Hank Sharky, the Head of the Machinery

Department. What can I do for you, Mr Khan?"

Kasim blinked, Hank Sharky was a tall bloke, easily six and half feet tall, with a head full of carrot orange hair and an orange goatee, "Ah yes, Mr Sharky. We'll be breaking ground on six new mining allotments. I need to organise some machinery", he held out his data tablet.

Hank Sharky held out his own data tablet and once they were in close proximity, the document Kasim had selected was transferred across.

Hank quickly scanned the document, "Six new ore fields. You'll need two bulldozers, two diggers and four hoppers for each of those fields. That's not an easy order to full fill, My Khan."

"You do have the machinery, Mr Sharky?", Kasim enquired.

"Follow me, Mr Khan", Hank requested, then he started walking over to the airlock door.

Kasim followed Hank through the airlock door, there was a second airlock door beyond that and the space in between was actually an emergency airlock. Beyond the second airlock door, Kasim found himself inside a huge cavernous space. It had been a rather large lunar lava tube. The walls and ceiling had been reinforced with steel beams, mesh and a specially formulated shotcrete, a form of concrete made from lunar regolith.

The cavern was enormous and lined up along one wall was the mining machinery and equipment. Off to one side in the distance to his right was a pair of large, thick doors. Off in the distance to his left was another pair of large, thick doors. Both pairs of doors were easily large enough to drive the mining machinery through. Kasim had not been in this level of the Mining Consortium's lunar base and everything he was seeing was being seen for the very first time.

Hank noted, while pointing to the heavy machinery, "Six bulldozers, six diggers and ten hoppers. We are going to be somewhat short, I'm afraid."

"So we only have enough for three new mines?", Kasim enquired.

"In terms of bulldozers and diggers, sure we have enough for three new mines, but we are still short by two hoppers as well", Hank admitted.

"Well, that is going to be a problem, Mr Sharky. We need to open up at least six new mines", Kasim replied, noting, "Perhaps even more."

"Well, Mr Khan, that could be problem", Hank replied, then pointed over to his right, to a pair of huge doors off in the distance, "The maintenance department over yonder, has two more hoppers under maintenance. So when they're all fixed up, you'll have enough hoppers for three mines."

"At least we'll have that", Kasim replied, then asked, "What about the rest?"

"Well, Mr Khan, I'll have to push that back upstairs, back to you", Hank admitted.

Kasim nodded, he understood, “I'll contact Central Command later and request they send us the heavy machinery we'll be needing. Six, Six and twelve yeah?”

“Double that, Mr Khan”, Hank replied, then explained, “If you need to open up more than six new mines, you'll need extra. In case of break downs. We are already stretched thin.”

“Go that. Order double what we need”, Kasim acknowledged, then asked, “How do you get stuff in and out of this place?”

Hank pointed to the huge doors, far off to the left, “We open those huge inner airlock doors, drive the equipment into the airlock. Close the inner doors, evacuate the air, open the outer doors and just drive all the equipment straight out into the staging ground.”

Kasim nodded in understanding, asking, “And delivery to the new mining allotments?”

“We have eight carryalls stationed out there. Delivery will not be a problem. We already have the coordinates”, Hank replied, holding up his tablet.

Kasim nodded once again, “Okay then, it seems I'll need to talk to our maintenance people about those other two hoppers. What's the quickest way to our maintenance department?”

“That would be back the way we came”, Hank informed him and then led him back through the airlocks and into his department's offices.

Once they were inside, standing in front of Tanya's desk, Hank pointed down the corridor, “Mr Khan, the maintenance department is down that corridor, right at the very end.”

“Thank you, Mr Sharky”, Kasim replied and started walking down the corridor.

Hank transferred Kasim's document to his secretary's data tablet, “Tanya, we're breaking ground on six new ore fields. We've got enough equipment for the first three on the list, please put together a schedule to have the machinery delivered to the ore sites.”

“And the other three new ore fields Mr Sharky?”, Tanya enquired.

“Young Mr Khan will be ordering new machinery from Central Command, including extras for possible further expansion”, Hank informed her, adding, “No doubt they'll be advising us of their delivery schedules.”

“And when the new equipment arrives, you'd like me to schedule delivery to the remaining three new ore sites, yes?”, Tanya enquired.

“That's the plan, Tanya, that's the plan”, Hank confirmed.

“Why do they need six new mines, Sir?”, Tanya enquired.

Hank looked further into the document, "Ha! They want to build twenty seven new colonies. O'Neil-style twin cylinders, big ones. That's a huge uptick in construction. Tanya, they'll be needing more than six new mines. Trust me on that!"

Kasim walked further down the corridor. The corridor was just as bright and clean as the foyer. Kasim passed by several offices and storage rooms, after which he found the lighting was scaled back and the corridor became somewhat dimmer. Kasim stopped and looked into the distance, the corridor was quite long, although he could see the end of it. Kasim started walking again and picked up his pace. The corridor was eerily quiet and the dim lighting made it feel rather creepy. After a short while, Kasim came to the end of the corridor and entered the Consortium's maintenance department.

The foyer was not bright, neat or tidy, neither was it very clean. It was filthy! There were what looked like grease or oil stains on the floor. Hell, there were what looked like grease stains on the walls. Off to Kasim's right were a series of offices and storage rooms. Off to Kasim's left was a bulkhead and an airlock door. Directly across from the corridor was a secretary's counter and desk. It, too, did not look the cleanest, it was also unmanned. Behind the counter and desk was a large door. Spare parts was written on the sign above the door.

Kasim walked up to the counter, there was a bell on it and Kasim tapped it three times. Bing! Bing! Bing! Nothing happened, nothing stirred. Kasim sighed and tapped the bell five more times. Bing! Bing! Bing! Bin1 Bing!

Roxy Wallabeye was the maintenance department head, a hands-on sort of a woman who didn't mind getting her hands dirty. Her face was smudged with grease and her dark hair looked as though she'd run her greasy fingers through it several times. Roxy was the epitome of the term, grease monkey.

Kasim heard the distinct words, "Hold on. Hold on. I'll be with you in a minute for fucks sake!", come from behind the spare parts room door.

Several minutes later, when no one had appeared, Kasim tapped the bell three more times. Bing! Bing! Bing!

Roxy shoved the spare parts room door open abruptly, "Really!", she exclaimed, "I said, I'd be with you in a minute", she scolded, before looking up at Kasim, "Oh! What can I do for you handsome?", she ran her greasy fingers through her hair.

Kasim replied, "It was a very long minute", then he introduced himself, "I'm Kasim Khan, I work for Administrator Baxter. I'm his Operations and Administrative Liaison Officer."

"So you're Baxter's new gopher", Roxy quipped.

Kasim looked at the name badge on Roxy's coveralls, “Ah, no, Ms Wallabeye, I'm his Operations and Administrative Liaison Officer.”

“That's the same thing, handsome”, Roxy replied.

“No. I liaise with Central Command up at L-Five and I ensure the smooth flow of the Consortium's operations here on Lunar”, Kasim informed her.

“Yep. You're Baxter's new gopher, alright”, Roxy quipped once more.

Not seeing the point of continuing this particular discussion, Kasim changed the subject.

“So, Ms Wallabeye, where is everyone?”, Kasim enquired.

“The same place I was. Working on shit out the back. That's what the maintenance department does”, Roxy replied, “And my name is Roxy, by the way”, then ran her greasy fingers through her hair.

Kasim nodded, “That makes sense.”

Roxy looked at Kasim, “Now, handsome, what brought you all the way down to my grease pit?”

Kasim replied, “Well, Roxy, a couple of things, three to be exact.”

“Okay, spill it”, Roxy requested.

“You guys have two hoppers over here for maintenance”, Kasim noted, adding, “We'll be needing those back in service, operational, sooner rather than later”, he held out his data tablet.

Roxy picked up her data tablet from the secretary's desk and held it out, the selected document transferred across straight away. Kasim noticed that Roxy's data tablet was also grease-stained. Roxy opened the document and scanned through it very quickly, running her left index finger through each page. It took very little time for her to read it in full.

“Ah ha. Ah ha”, Roxy spoke to herself, then looked up at Kasim's astonished face, “I speed read”, she explained, then remarked, “Twenty seven extra colonies, bloody big ones! Six new ore mines. That's quite the construction boom.”

“Yes, it is, Roxy. Which brings me to the hard part”, Kasim replied.

“The hard part”, Roxy's face had a wry smile on it, “I take it you mean hard work and not what I was thinking.”

“Yes, hard work, unfortunately”, Kasim confirmed, then informed her, “Out there on the surface, there's a second mag-lev mass driver. It's been dismantled and mothballed. The Consortium needs that to be put back together and operational. Sadly, as soon as possible.”

“Sweet Mother! When you said hard work, you meant fucking hard work”, Roxy replied, commenting, “That thing has been sitting out there in pieces, in the open for forty fucking years. Even if we can get it back together again, I cannot guarantee that it will work."

"Well, that's why I'm here, Roxy. Send out a maintenance crew or two, to look into what's required to put that mag-lev back together. Then send me a report of what you need. It's my job to source everything you require", Kasim informed her, he smiled and added light-heartedly, "I'll go for this and I'll go for that. It seems I'm your gopher as well."

Roxy smiled back and agreed, "My people don't particularly like working on the surface, but I do have more than a few people rated for that kind of work. I'll organise a couple of crews straight away."

"Excellent", Kasim replied, then looking at the empty secretary's desk, asked, "What happened to your secretary?"

Roxy looked at the empty desk and chair, her face taking on a sad look, "Holly passed away three weeks ago. We haven't found a replacement yet. The poor girl was only twenty eight."

Kasim looked at the chair where Roxy was staring, "Passed away. Only twenty eight?", he queried.

"Yeah. The HPI got her", Roxy lamented, "She had a massive coronary. Passed away really quick. Some of us just aren't suited for working in low gravity environments, not in the long term anyway."

Kasim nodded, he understood. Hypo-gravitational Pulmonary Insufficiency was one of the many low gravity syndromes that could affect human health and physiology, one that could be deadly if not caught in time.

Roxy continued talking, her face taking on a very sad appearance, "I was talking to Holly at the time. She was sitting right there in that chair. One second we were talking, the next an odd look came over her face. She reached for her left arm and began to stand up. I could see her trying to say something, but nothing came out. Then she collapsed onto the floor. When I checked her pulse, she was already gone. The emergency response team said that Holly was dead before she even hit the floor. I can still see the terrified look on her face", tears were welling in Roxy's eyes.

Kasim commented, "The geology lab recently lost one of their geologists to the HOS. He fractured both of his legs changing a light globe, of all things and he's now back up at Central Command."

Roxy nodded, "Yeah, this low gravity is a bitch. It just shows how short life can be. We should all enjoy it while we can."

"That is true, Roxy, that is so true", Kasim agreed.

Roxy reach down to a shelf under the counter and picked up a card, it had her contract details on it. Then she grabbed a pencil and added some more information, before passing the card to Kasim.

Kasim looked at the card. Roxy had added her personal contact number and the address of her quarters to it. Kasim looked at Roxy with a puzzled look.

"Handsome, you're taking me out to dinner tonight. Pick me up at seven pm", Roxy informed him.

"Roxy, I don't remember asking you out", he protested.

"You didn't. I figured you're the shy type, so I'm making the first move", Roxy smiled back, "Life's too short. Let's enjoy it while we can."

Kasim still looked puzzled, "Don't worry, Kasim. I scrub up real nice. You'll see", Roxy assured him, "Now remember, pick me up a seven p.m. sharp."

This was not expected, Kasim smiled back, agreeing, "Okay, seven p.m. sharp it is."

"Good then, handsome, I'll have your hoppers ready in a couple of days. That report on the mag-lev, hopefully by the end of the week", Roxy replied, then reminded him, "Seven p.m. tonight. Don't forget."

Kasim nodded, confirming, "I'll see you at seven then", then turned around and started walking back down the corridor towards the machinery department and the elevator.

Roxy smiled a broad smile to herself and then did a little happy, happy joy dance, before walking back into the spare parts storage to get back to her work.

Kasim nodded to Tanya, the machinery department's secretary before stepping back into the elevator and heading upstairs to the personnel department. The Consortium's personnel department was on the same level of his own office and Kasim was quite familiar with its location. It didn't take long for Kasim to reach the personnel department.

Upon entry he was greeted straight away by the department's secretary, Cassie, "Mr Khan. How nice to see you again. What can we do for you?"

"Nice to see you again, Cassie. Is Julie in? I need to discus some new personnel requirements", Kasim informed her.

Cassie pushed a button and spoke into her intercom, "Julie, I have Mr Khan here to see you. Shall I send him down?"

"Yes, Cassie, send him straight down", the voice on the other end of the intercom replied.

"Thanks, Cassie, I know the way", Kasim replied and then walked off down the corridor.

Julie Danton's office door was open and Julie was waiting for Kasim when he arrived. Kasim had met Julie before when he first started work at the Lunar Mining Consortium's complex. She was a tall, stout woman with short cropped hair and a plan looking appearance.

"Kasim, nice to see you again. Please come in", Julie greeted, then asked, "How have you been settling in? Everything going well, I hope?"

"Everything is going very well, Julie", Kasim replied.

"Good to hear. Now what brings you to my department, Kasim?", Julie asked.

"We need to organise personnel for six new mines", Kasim informed her.

"Okay then, so what do we need?", Julie requested.

"Each mine will have two bulldozers, two diggers and four hoppers. So we'll need operators for each of those", Kasim noted.

Julie was already taking notes, then she informed Kasim, "You're also going to need four maintenance engineers, a communications officer, a geologist and a supervisor. Not to mention a portable office and a housing complex on site."

"I had not thought of that, Julie", Kasim replied honestly.

"You wouldn't have. You've not setup a lunar ore mine before", Julie commented in reply.

"So, what's that. Fifteen personnel per mine?", Kasim queried, then asked, "Who do I talk to, to organise the portable office and housing?"

"Yes, fifteen people per mine. So we need ninety all up", Julie confirmed, then added, " The portable office and housing are my problem. We take care of that here in my department."

Kasim held out his data tablet and Julie picked up hers and held it out. Kasim's document transferred across and Julie quickly scanned her way through it.

"You did say six new mines, didn't you?", Julie enquired.

"Yes. That's Central Command's request", Kasim confirmed.

"Kasim. I'm not seeing six. If Central Command wants to build these twenty seven new O'Neil-style colonies with twin cylinders, in any reasonable amount of time, I'm seeing eight new mines", Julie chuckled, almost laughed.

"Are you sure?", Kasim questioned.

"I've been doing this a long time, Kasim. Trust me, you'll be breaking ground on two more. Upstairs at Central Command, they just haven't figured it out yet", Julie informed him.

"Okay. So what's the plan?", Kasim enquired.

"We'll plan for six mines and we'll factor in two more", Julie replied, adding, "I'll be organising up to a hundred and twenty personnel. I also recommend that you notify Central Command, that they may need eight new mines not six."

"I'll do that when I get back to my office", Kasim agreed.

"Kasim, it will be difficult to get all of these workers", Julie remarked, informing him, "At the moment we have five percent of our people up at Central Command, in hospital with Hypo-gravitational syndromes."

"That many? I know we've had issues with low-gravity syndromes, but that many?", Kasim queried.

"Yeah, it has been getting worse of late, I'm afraid. We've even had several deaths", Julie admitted.

"Why, though? We do have the stimulants and the supplements. Aren't they meant to protect us from low-gravity syndromes?", Kasim replied.

"We do, Kasim and they've worked well in the past, but now, something has changed", Julie replied.

"Changed? What could have changed?", Kasim enquired.

"That I do not know. The boffins up at Central Command are working on it", Julie informed him, adding, "Administrator Baxter has approved mandatory fortnightly health checks for all personnel. That email is going out this afternoon, along with the requisite schedules."

"Well, if Central Command wants us to supply them with the extra ore, then they're going to have to sort this out. We need those workers, Julie", Kasim replied

"And I will get them for you, Kasim, leave that to me", Julie confirmed.

Kasim left Julie's office and headed back to his own department. Soon, he was sitting in his own chair in his office putting together a communique to Central Command. Kasim requested that they double-check their requirements for the six new ore mines, noting that his colleague had suggested that eight would be required.

Julie's revelations about the situation with low-gravity syndromes and their effect on the mining Consortium's personnel were unsettling. He'd known they could be a problem, but weren't the stimulants and supplements meant to fix that? Something had changed, Julie had said.

True to Julie's word, the email about the new mandatory health checks arrived in his in box. Kasim read through the email, it noted the new mandatory fortnightly health checks and had a link to his calendar. Upon checking that, he found a schedule for his health checks were in place for the next six months. No doubt all of the other Consortium personnel had received the same.

Kasim had been quite busy all day, organising the opening up of the six new lunar ore mines. When he finally returned to his quarters, he quickly washed and prepared for is seven p.m. date with Roxy Wallabeye, the maintenance department head. That didn't take him too long and Kasim soon found himself navigating the lunar complex's tunnel system to the lower level's quarters where Roxy lived.

There were just as many quarters in this section of the complex as there were in his, fortunately, they were all set up and labelled using the same methodology. Kasim quickly located Roxy's quarters and pressed the intercom. It was seven p.m. on the dot.

Roxy opened the door and looked Kasim up and down, "Well, handsome, you scrub up well. Real nice, in fact."

Kasim looked Roxy up and down as well, she was gorgeous, her wavy dark hair accentuating her facial feature beautifully. Roxy's dark eyes shone brightly, she had high cheeks and full lips. Kasim definitely noticed her ample breasts and slender waist, it was hard to believe this was the same woman he'd met earlier in the day wearing grease stained coveralls. Roxy was no longer the grease monkey.

"Wow!", Kasim exclaimed, adding, "You look so different without all of the grease and coveralls."

"I did say that I scrub up real nice, handsome", Roxy commented, then she gave a slight frown, "I have some bad news and I have some good news."

"Well, what's the bad news?", Kasim asked.

"I'm not feeling very hungry right now. I think I've lost my appetite", Roxy replied, frowning.

"Oh okay, I was actually looking forward to dinner though. What's the good news then, Roxy?", Kasim enquired.

Roxy smiled a wry smile, "I've developed a completely different kind of appetite", then she reached out, took Kasim by the hand and dragged him into her quarters.

Kasim did not resist, he could not resist and the door quickly closed behind him.

The next day, Kasim notified the Administrator's secretary, Sharon, that he'd be late into the office. Roxy also notified her maintenance department manager, that she would be late in as well. They both used the same excuse, something had popped up. Apparently, that something had popped up several times during the night and the next morning, they were tired and exhausted, having had very little sleep.

Life was simply too short.

7. The Gravity of the Situation.

The President's Secretary, Carmen, had just finished preparing the conference room table for the President's cabinet meeting. The table itself was shaped like a horseshoe, with the President's seat at its centre and on his right was his Vice President's seat. Colonial Central Command's Department Secretaries had their seats positioned around the table. On the President's left was his Secretary of State.

The name tags on the table in front of each seat contained the department name and the name of its relevant secretary. There were sixteen departments besides the State Department. On the President's right, beyond the Vice President, were the departments of Agriculture: Miles Freemen, Commerce: Maxwell Thompson, Construction: Charles Gardner, Corrections: Clyde Kola, Defence: Samuel Shostakovitch, Education: Miriam Dervish, Foreign Affairs: Marcella Baxter and Science and Technology: Leto Trevaine. On the President's left, beyond the Secretary of State, were the departments of Telecommunications: Harold Haroldson, Health: Alyssa Galen, Labour: John Thrall, Public Safety: Leanne Fish, Natural Resources: Carmela Black, Security: Liam Murphy, Revenue: Tyler Green, and Transportation: Andrew Jackson.

The seating had all been arranged, folios with the latest information placed in front of each seat and glasses provided. Carafes of cold water with ice cubes in them were strategically placed around the table. Carmen gave the table a quick once-over just as the Cabinet members arrived. They were earlier than expected and Carmen moved out of the way, leaving the conference room and taking up a seat at the desk outside. The Cabinet members all filed into the conference room, greeting each other before taking their seats.

President Carter requester, "Please give the folios a quick perusal before we begin. My Secretary Carmen has been quite thorough in summarising the current situation with the replacement of the twenty seven damaged colonies."

All of the cabinet member opened up their folios and began quickly reading through them.

The Secretary of Natural Resources, Carmela Black, noted as she cross-checked the folio with her data tablet and her own documents, "Well, the Lunar Mining Consortium has plenty of mining allotments to break ground on. They have even chosen the allotments closest to the mag-lev mass driver for optimal efficiency."

"Yes, Carmela", Charles Gardner, Secretary of Constructions, agreed, "However, Mr Khan, the Consortium's Operations and Liaison Officer, would like us to double check our ore needs. Mr Khan's people believe we'll need eight new lunar ore mines, not just the six we have requested."

"That is very concerning, Charles", Carmela admitted, "Have your people rework their numbers, then have them contact my people and between our two departments, we'll work out what the correct requirements are."

Both Carmela and Charles started adding notes to their respective copies of the folios on the conference room desk.

Charles Gardner looked up from his note taking, "The Lunar Mining Consortium only has enough machinery to break ground on three mines at present. Mr Khan is telling us that each mine requires two bulldozers, two diggers and four hoppers."

The Vice President, Bartholomew Mason, noted, "So they need six bulldozers, six diggers and twelve hoppers."

"Yes, Bart, six, six and twelve", Charles confirmed, "I'll have my people start work on the machinery construction straight away."

"And if your people find we do need eight new mines instead of six?", Vice President Mason asked.

"Six, six and twelve to start, with the option to manufacture another four, four and eight", Charles replied, noting, "That should cover it."

President Ford stepped in, "Charles, you may as well just organise enough machinery to cover the five new mines. The Lunar Mining Consortium has enough machinery for three, so just build enough to cover five more. Even if it does turn out we only need six new mines in all, it won't hurt for the Consortium to have the extra machinery on site."

"Good point, Mr President", Charles replied as he noted down more notes on his copy of the folios.

The Transport Secretary, Andrew Jackson, then stepped in, "Charles, when your people have the machinery ready, let my people know. They'll arrange pickup and delivery", then he added some notes to his own folio copy.

"So noted, Andrew", Charles replied, adding more notes to his copy as well.

Charles noted, "It's not in the folio, but I have a communique from Mr Khan on my data tablet. The Consortium is assessing the old mag-lev mass driver, the one that was used during the construction of Central Command. They're going to need it to ship the extra ore packets up to L-Four."

Charles placed his data tablet on the table and tapped the document in question three times, transferring it to the data tablets of the other department secretaries.

Vice President Mason enquired, "Will this be a problem, Charles?"

Charles replied, "The old mass driver was decommissioned. Dismantled and left on the lunar surface. That was forty years ago, so some of its components may need replacing."

State Department Secretary, Robert Martins, remarked, "Forty years on the lunar surface! A lot of components will need replacing."

"Yes, Bob. We'll know what needs replacing when Mr Khan sends me the assessment reports", Charles informed him.

Vice President Mason commented, "You'll be adding any required components for the mag-lev to your list, no doubt, Charles."

"As soon as I get the reports", Charles confirmed, adding, "We may need to drag out the old mag-lev specifications and blueprints, but yeah, my people have got this."

President Carter then questioned his Revenue Department Secretary, Tyler Green, "Tyler, these twenty seven new colonies are going to be rather expensive. How are we covering the costs?"

"I'm glad you asked, Mr President", Tyler replied, then informed him, "This is a massive uptick in colony construction, so our Colonial Construction Fund won't be able to cover it."

President Carter frowned, "Well, Tyler, the twenty seven new colonies are still going ahead, so I hope you have a plan in place."

Tyler smiled, "Always, Mr President. We'll be using some of the interest being earned by L-Five's Sovereign Wealth Fund."

"Some of the interest?", President Carter enquired.

"Ah, yes, Mr President", Tyler confirmed, "We'll be transferring a portion of the interest across to the Colonial Constructions Fund to cover the costs, but only for the duration of the project."

President Carter nodded in agreement, then stated for the record, "Agreed!"

"Now if you guys have finished talking about making your new toys and playing Monopoly", Joanne Thrall, Secretary of Labour, began, "I've noticed that the Consortium is hiring one hundred and twenty new mining staff."

"Well, of course they are. They are opening six new ore mines after all", Carmela Black replied.

"My information from Mr Khan is that each mine requires fifteen personnel", Joanne remarked, then added, "The Consortium should only need ninety new staff, not one hundred and twenty."

Carmela replied, questioning, "Perhaps the Consortium is expecting us to agree that six new mines won't be enough and they're preparing for eight new mines instead?"

"That was what I was thinking", Joanne agreed, then added, "The Consortium should be waiting for our go-ahead first."

Charles stepped in, “The Consortium does have some damned good people. It's quite likely that they're correct and we've underestimated the requirements. They're probably just expecting us to confirm that they're right. We'll have a better understanding once we've reassessed just how new many mines we actually require.”

Alyssa Galen, the Secretary of Health, stepped in, “You know, they may be hiring more people than they need for other reasons.”

“Other reasons?”, Joanne Thrall, Secretary of the Labour questioned.

“They are short on workers at the moment”, Alyssa Galen informed everyone.

Leanne Fisher, Secretary of Public Safety, nodded in agreement, “Yes, that thing!”

The Secretary of Commerce, Maxwell Thompson, inquired, “What thing was that exactly?”

Alyssa Galen replied, “Only a handful of you actually know this”, then she looked at President Carter, who nodded before continuing, “Almost five percent of the Lunar Mining Consortium's personnel are actually up here in L-Five, in either hospitals or in rehabilitation facilities.”

“Five percent! The Consortium has almost ten thousand personnel. You are talking about five hundred people!”, Joanne Thrall noted.

“That is correct, Joanne”, Alyssa Galen admitted.

Leanne Fisher stepped in, “They all have Hypo-gravitational disorders, syndromes if you will.”

Alyssa Galen quickly added, “We've been keeping it on the down low, a need-to-know basis only.”

President Carter stepped in, “That was my decision and my decision alone.”

Those handful of department secretaries in the know all understood, the others, the majority, were all shocked and their faces showed it. The conference room fell silent for many long moments.

Samuel Shostakovitch, Secretary of Defence, broke the silence, asking, “I thought the problems with Hypo-gravitational disorders had all been resolved, so what's going on?”

“Yes, I'd like to know that as well”, Maxwell Thompson remarked, then commenting, “I do recall the evacuation of all of the lunar colonists. That was quite an expensive exercise. There are whole cities down there, all locked up and decommissioned. The only reason the Lunar Mining Consortium is still operating is because the problem was resolved.”

Alyssa Galen replied, “Well, Max, the problem was never completely resolved. If it was, all of those lunar colonies would still be occupied with happy, smiling colonists."

"Yes, I know, Alyssa, the stimulants, the supplements and the strict exercise regimen", Maxwell replied, letting her know that he understood the situation, adding, "We can't expect colonists to adhere to those requirements, but for the Mining Consortium, they are mandatory. That is the law!"

Samuel stepped in, asking, "Are the Consortium workers not sticking to the requirements?"

"No. No. They're doing everything they should be doing", Alyssa replied, explaining, "Something has changed and our people are struggling to get their heads around it."

"Perhaps Alyssa, you should start at the beginning", President Carter suggested.

Alyssa flagged a series of documents in a folder on her data tablet, then she tapped the folder three times and the folder with its document transferred to the data tablets belonging to the other Cabinet Secretaries.

Alyssa Galen then took a deep breath and began to explain the situation, "We've had nearly five hundred Consortium workers come through our health system of late. Most of those workers are now in rehabilitation, recovering from their various Hypo-gravitational syndromes. Around fifty or so are still in hospital. There have been six deaths. Further deaths are expected!"

"Did you say deaths?", Leto Trevaine, Secretary of Science and Technology, asked.

"Yes, Leto. Six deaths so far and the likelihood of more to follow", Alyssa Galen confirmed.

The conference room took on a sombre atmosphere as Alyssa Galen continued, "The most recent death was one, Holly Wheeler, a Secretary with the Consortium's Maintenance Department. My understanding is that she just dropped dead in front of her coworkers. The initial Consortium autopsy put it down to a Hypo-gravitational syndrome. Our own autopsy found that the cause of death was Hypo-gravitational Pulmonary Insufficiency. Most of those who have died or are in the process of dying have either Hypo-gravitational induced Pulmonary Insufficiency or Cardiomyopathy. These are not medical conditions that we can easily treat. Patient survivability is low."

"Short of a heart transplant, I suspect", Leto Trevaine tossed in.

"Sadly, Leto, that is correct", Alyssa Galen confirmed.

Alyssa Galen looked around the room and then continued, "Ms Wheeler had only been working at the Consortium for just under five years. Now, there are people working down there who have been there very much longer. We requested that the Consortium's longest serving employees be given a thorough examination, using our own testing protocols and that they send the results back to us. The longest serving employee at the Consortium's complex is their Head Geologist, Brian Henderson. Professor Henderson has worked at the complex for more than twenty years and he shows absolutely no signs of any Hypo-gravitational syndromes at all."

"Wait! So short-term employees are dying and longer term employees aren't even affected", Leto Trevaine remarked, adding, "Your researchers must be going nuts trying to work that one out."

Alyssa smiled, it was a sad bitter smile, "Our researchers do have a theory."

"Well, Alyssa, if you need to borrow some of my scientists to help you out, I'd be happy to lend them to you", Leto offered.

"Thank you, Leto, I may yet take you up on that", Alyssa replied.

"Now, Alyssa, you mentioned your people had a theory?", Leto enquired.

"Yes, but it's not a simple one", Alyssa replied, before continuing, "As we all know, the supplements are supposed to be taken up by the body and used to repair any damage caused by the low-gravity lunar environment. The exercise regimen is meant to help trigger the body to repair and heal itself. The most important component are the stimulants."

The Secretary of Education, Miriam Dervish, noted, "Yes, Alyssa, we do understand all of that. The stimulants are meant to stimulate the body's uptake of the supplements and aid the exercise regimen."

"Yes, that is correct, Miriam", Alyssa confirmed, then informed everyone in the room, "The stimulants are failing."

"Failing?", Miriam questioned.

"It seems that some of the workers, not all of them, mind you, are developing a tolerance to the stimulants, which severely reduces their effectiveness", Alyssa explained, adding, "My people believe that this variation in who it affects and who it does not is genetically related."

Leto stepped in, "So, for some of the workers, there is no issue at all, but for those workers with the genetic predisposition, the stimulants will become far less effective."

"Yes, Leto, that is the problem", Alyssa confirmed.

"Then we're going to need a test to determine who is and is not genetically susceptible", Leto noted.

"Bingo!", Alyssa exclaimed, "and that is precisely what my people are working on."

Leanne Fisher stepped in with, "From what I've been told, the genetics involved are quite complex and it may take years to develop a test for susceptibility, so we have developed a plan that we can implement in the meanwhile."

"Yes. Thank you, Leanne", Alyssa replied, then explained, "First, any

Consortium employees who have been down there for ten years or longer and have shown no symptoms are free to stay at the complex as long as they wish to work there. For all of the other Consortium employees, they can work there for six month or twelve month stints. Six months on the Moon, then two years back up here in the colonies, twelve months on the Moon, then five years back up here in the colonies."

"That's all very good, Alyssa, but what will they be doing up here when they're not down there at the lunar mining complex?", Maxwell Thompson asked.

Joanne Thrall quickly replied, "Dual skill sets, Max. They'll be trained to have duel, complimenting skill sets. That way, they will be valuable employees whether working down there at the mining complex or back up here in the L-Five colonies. We can even arrange refresher courses for them, when they swap from one to the other. No problem. We've got this."

Maxwell smiled back at Joanne and nodded in understanding.

Alyssa continued, "We do have one very strong recommendation. A new law. I call it the Gravity Law", she paused and looked around the table before continuing, "For all colonies, that derive their gravity via artificial methods, i.e, centrifugal force, that artificial gravity shall not deviate from one Earth g, by more than plus or minus ten percent as applied to the colony's main living surface."

"Except for military training facilities, of course", Samuel Shostakovitch commented.

"Of course, Sam. We can make an exception for military training facilities", Alyssa agreed.

All of the Cabinet Department Secretaries had been annotating their folio copies with numerous notes throughout the meeting.

President Carter remarked, "If everyone is in favour of this new Gravity Law, I can have my secretary, Carmen, run up a draft law this afternoon. We can knock it around over the next few days and when we've all agreed to its precise wording, I'll sign it into law."

Everyone around the conference table nodded in agreement.

Leto Trevaine then queried, "What's the scope of this new Gravity Law? I mean, I know it will apply to Cis-Lunar space and our trojan colonies, but what about beyond the Earth's orbital zone?"

Vice President, Bartholomew Mason, who hadn't said much throughout the meeting, noted, "These new Gravity Laws should apply to all of the Earth's colonies, irrespective of where they might be."

State Department Secretary, Robert Martins, who had also been quiet, added, "Central Command does not have any jurisdiction beyond Cis-Lunar space and the trojan colonies, however, Eros does. If we send a recommendation to Eros at the Earth's Lagrangian point five, along with all of the supporting documentation, they will make a binding Gravity Law for the whole solar system."

Leto replied, smiling, "Excellent. There are a lot of colonies out there and they'll be starting to have the same problems we're coming across soon enough."

Robert Martins enquired, "What action is the Mining Consortium taking with regards these issues?"

Alyssa informed him, "All of the Mining Consortium's personnel are undergoing mandatory fortnightly medical checks."

Robert Martins nodded, "That is something, at least. We need to prevent deaths at all cost."

"What about the outer satellites, the Moons of Jupiter and Saturn?", Carmela Black inquired.

Leto responded, "Well, the Moons of Jupiter are well within Jupiter's powerful radiation belts, so I don't expect there will be any surface colonies on them. At least not yet."

"And Saturn's Moon, Titan. There's a huge colony on Titan", Carmela commented with concern.

Leto was slower to respond, "There is no technology to alter the gravity of an entire moon."

President Carter interjected, "I believe Administrator Mark Spencer is still in charge on Titan. We can send him copies of our research, findings and recommendations. That should help them, at least."

Alyssa Galen noted, "It is highly likely that they're struggling with the exact same issues. They're just so far out that we haven't heard about it yet."

Vice President Bartholomew Mason wrote down some notes on his copy of the folios and replied, "I'll take that one on board, Mr President and have my people send Administrator Spencer everything he needs. The Saturnian colonies took the brunt of those interstellar micro meteor swarms, so anything we can do to help them, we will do."

"Thank you, Bart. Thank you", the President replied.

Alyssa leaned back in her chair with a thoughtful look on her face, then she leaned forward, "This one is straight out of left field. It's very, very odd."

"Alyssa?", Leanne queried.

"Oh, it's nothing to do with low-gravity health issues", Alyssa replied and then tried to explain, "We've had many people come through our psychiatric departments", she stopped for a moment, gathering her thoughts, then continued, "They all have very similar psychopathology symptoms."

"Psychopathology symptoms?", Leto Trevaine queried.

"We've had well over a hundred so far", Alyssa noted, "They all show signs of post-traumatic stress and they insist that there's something out there trying to steal their memories."

"Trying to steal their memories?", President Carter queried.

"Well, yes, only they can't tell us who or what, let alone how", Alyssa replied, noting, "Many of them wear tinfoil hats as a defensive measure. They said it protects their memories from theft."

"Extraordinary!", the President exclaimed.

"Here's the thing. We bring them in for evaluation and treatment, as we do and apart from their psychosis, we can't find anything else wrong with them. It is baffling!", Alyssa reported.

"So we have patients in our psyche wards with psychoses that have no physiological or neurological basis?", Leto questioned.

"Yes, Leto and it gets even stranger. We keep them under observation, sometimes for days or weeks and then their psychosis just disappears. One day, they were obviously mentally ill, then the next, it's as if they never were. It is all very baffling!"

The conversation continued along those lines until the meeting ended fifteen minutes later. Standing in one corner of the conference room, two pairs of eyes watched completely unseen. Hidden by their psychic obscuration field, the pair stood unseen, wearing long hooded cloaks of shimmering black, like the colour of raven's feathers. They watched unseen, gathering information and making sure things were unfolding as they required.

"Orpheus, some of our younger cousins could do with a bit more training", Freyja remarked telepathically to her mentor and older cousin.

"To true, Freyja. We have had to fix over a hundred failed memory alterations in Colonial Central Command alone", Orpheus replied, but then explained, *"The Mimasian War was devastating and covering all of that up, altering so many memories was never going to be perfect."*

"So for just how long are we going to be fixing these things?", Freyja enquired.

"It's hard to say, perhaps the better part of a decade", Orpheus considered.

"Hmm, I suppose we can't leave loose ends lying around", Freyja noted.

"No, Freyja, we can't leave any loose ends lying around", Orpheus agreed.

"They actually thought that wearing tin foil hats would stop us", Freyja almost laughed.

"Yes, Freyja, I thought that was amusing as well", Orpheus agreed, noting, *"Our work appears to be done here, shall we leave?"*

"Yes, time to go", Freyja replied.

There was an ever so slight shimmering in the air in the conference room and the pair was gone.

Aria and Ariel lay on their sleeping bags, on their stomachs, with their heads propped up their hands on either side of Kethera. The young Carlin girl could not lay on her stomach due to the peculiarities of Carlin physiology, namely having six breasts. It was terribly uncomfortable for Carlins to be lying in a prone position. Instead, Kethera was lying in a more supine position, with her head positioned for a good view of Yeannah's bedroom screen. They had all been reading through the data feed on the screen. The data feed contained voluminous amounts of information, far more than they expected.

Aria looked across to her twin sister, Ariel, "Seriously, Sis, there's way too much info! My brain might explode out of my ears! "

"You and me both, Aria. Do we have to read through all of this?", Ariel queried.

Kethera replied, "Sure, if we want to get good grades on our term project."

Aria looked at Kethera, noticing how she was lying, she asked with a broad Cheshire grin on her face, "Would kitty like a belly rub?"

Kethera turned around to face Aria, a very annoyed look on her face, "I'm not a cat, Aria. Please stop!"

Aria frowned, "I'm just teasing", then she gave Kethera a huge hug.

"Do you two need a room?", Ariel asked.

Both Aria and Kethera turned around to look at Ariel, at first, they looked angry, but then they both burst out laughing and Ariel joined in.

Saffiera and Yeannah were both lying on their stomachs on Yeannah's bed, their heads propped in their hands. Yeannah's great leathery wings were spread out and gently flapping in small circular movements. Something that Saffiera had noted and commented on.

"Yeannah, do you always do that, you know, flapping your wings like that?", Saffiera enquired.

The telepathic message was directed at Yeannah, so she replied with a thought that she knew Saffiera would pick up on, *"Yes, quite often, we Thols find it relaxing. It also makes a nice breeze, don't you think?"*

Saffiera agreed, *"It kind of does."*

Yeannah then commented, "I've always wondered where the gravity laws came from, not that it applies us, living down here on Homwol."

Saffiera replied telepathically in a way that all of the girls could pick up, *"The gravity laws only apply to rotating colonies in space. What I'm surprised about is the level of interference by the psi-corps. They went out of their way to cover up the entire Mimasian War."*

"Yeah, that's crazy", Ariel agreed, "What gave them the right to do that?"

"My parents once told me that it was done to prevent a solar system-wide panic amongst humanity", Yeannah replied, informing her friends, "It was the psi corp that convinced we Thols and Martians to emerge from Mimas. They'd said that the time was right and that it was now time to open up all of the records. They'd kept everything, every single record going back for centuries, along with the proof of it all in immaculate detail and then just surreptitiously released it into the wild."

"Still, my people could never have done that. We Martians don't believe in that kind of interference", Saffiera told them, explaining, *"It would be just so unpalatable to us!"*

Aria simply noted, "We humans do what the Martians cannot."

"Does it make it right?", Saffiera questioned.

"Saffiera, I don't know. It's just recorded history", Ariel replied.

"Hidden and then unhidden. Just because they're so powerful, they think that they can do anything", Saffiera vented with her mind so *'loudly'*, that everyone in Yeannah's bedroom blinked several times.

"Which brings me back to my question. Do we have to read through all of this?", Aria reiterated.

"I thought I'd already answered that", Kethera replied.

"You did Kethera, but I didn't like your answer", Aria commented.

Saffiera sighed, neither of the twins were known to like studying, *"I've been lying down here taking notes, Ariel. I'll give you all copies when I'm finished."*

"What kind of notes?", Aria's twin Sister, Ariel, enquired.

"A whole document, with section headings, numbered points, bullet points and hyperlinks", Saffiera explained, adding, *"I am very thorough!"*

"Okay, it's just, there seems to be a lot of information to sift through", Ariel replied.

Saffiera sighed once more, *"Which is why I'm building this document. Once I'm finished, we can divide it into sections and each work on a portion of the project."*

Aria looked at Saffiera, who noticed her gaze, *"Yes, Aria?"*

"Are all Martians as smart as you, or are you just a one-off?", Aria questioned.

"We Martians are all very focused, Aria. It comes with being a telepath", came Saffiera's reply.

Kethera had been answering her emails on her data tablet, "Forget the first three, it's the fourth one you want. The Great Explosion, the Outward Interplanetary Expansion", she replied to Richard's email.

Richard and his friends at another house in the Human colony on Homwol had accessed the same information online and they had been wondering which was the correct data feed to use, "Are you sure?", he double-checked.

"Yes, silly. It's the interplanetary expansion you need to be studying. The one that occurred between twenty sixty and the Outer Satellite Insurrection in twenty one eighty two. It included the Mimasian War", Kethera confirmed.

"Ah, of course", Richard replied in understanding, "We studied the Mimasian War last term."

"Precisely, so it all makes logical sense, Richard", Kethera replied, visualising Richard in her mind with his sandy blond flowing locks.

Aria looked over Kethera's shoulder, then reached over and subtly poked her twin Sister, Ariel. Then Ariel also looked over Kethera's shoulder as well, specifically at her data tablet and the email exchange. Then it began!

Aria and Ariel sat up and began clapping their hands together above Kethera, "Kethera and Richard sitting in a tree, K-I-S-S-I-N-G! First comes love, then comes marriage, then comes baby, in a baby carriage!", then they repeated again and again, " Kethera and Richard sitting in a tree, K-I-S-S-I-N-G! First comes love, then comes marriage, then comes baby, in a baby carriage!"

Kethera sighed, her whiskers drooped downwards and her tail fell flat, then she pulled her pillow up around her ears and closed her eyes. It was going to be a very long night.

Saffiera touched Yeannah on the shoulder as she began to sit up. Yeannah folded back her wings so that they were out of Saffiera's way.

"Seriously! Will you two grow up!", Saffiera telepathically admonished the twins, *"How do you think Kethera feels with all of this constant teasing?"*

The twins both stopped and looked down at Kethera, noticing her offended and embarrassed countenance. The twins looked back up at Saffiera and then looked across to each other, they silently stared into each other's eyes, both showing clear feelings of remorse.

Aria lay back down beside Kethera and Ariel did the same on Kethera's other side. They both put their arms around Kethera and held her tightly.

"Sorry, Kethera", Aria apologised.

Ariel also apologised, "Sorry, Kethera", explaining, "Sometimes we just get carried away."

Aria commented with teary eyes, "We both love you to bits."

A tear ran down Kethera's cheek and Aria gently wiped it away with her index finger. Then the twins noticed Kethera's tail begin to swish back and forth and her whiskers begin to twitch once more, so they both hugged her even more tightly. Kethera began to gently purr, she really liked the twins.

Saffiera laid back down on Yeannah's bed and Yeannah began gently flapping her wings once more in the way that she did to relax. It wasn't long before the twins and Kethera had fallen asleep still in their mutual embrace. Saffiera and Yeannah continued to read through the data feed and take notes on The Great Explosion, the Outward Interplanetary Expansion. Their study night continued.

8. The Earth's Libration Points.

Within the Earth's orbital region are a number of Lagrangian points, zones in space where the gravity of the Earth and the Moon, and the Earth and Sun cancel out. The Moon Earth Lagrangian points were heavily utilised.

Cis-Lunar L-Four was sixty degrees ahead of the Moon, leading in its orbit around the Earth. This was where the catchalls were, giant stations that were designed purely for the purpose of catching Lunar ore thrown into space by the mag-lev mass drivers on the Lunar surface.

Cis-Lunar L-Four was also where all of the dirty and heavy industries were situated. Where all of their ore processing and heavy manufacturing stations were. Of course, Cis-Lunar L-Four was also where the spaceship and colony construction yards were, both civilian and military. Military training cylinders were also located within the Cis-Lunar L-Four zone, both low and high gravity training cylinders, plus the military bases themselves.

Then there was Cis-Lunar L-Five, which was sixty degrees behind the Moon, trailing, in its orbit around the Earth. This was where all of the civilian population lived and there were hundreds upon hundreds of colonies, including the older Bernal Sphere and Stamford Torus style colonies. By far the most common style of colony were the O'Neil-style twin cylindrical colonies and there were hundreds of them, ranging in sizes from those capable of housing ten thousand colonists to those able to house populations in the low hundred thousands.

The largest colonies were the massive single cylinder O'Neil-style colonies, capable of populations from hundreds of thousands to millions of people. Colonial Central Command was the largest of them all, its main cylinder being twenty kilometres long and four kilometres wide. At each end were hemispherical caps, two kilometres in radius. This one colony was capable of housing far in excess of ten million people, but being only around forty years old, was currently housing around five million.

All of the colonies used solar power as their main source of energy. The O'Neil-style cylinders having three long strip mirrors that reflected sunlight through three equally long slit windows, to the land regions on the opposite sides. Each hemispherical end cap had windows all around to reflect the sunlight at centralised hemispherical redirection mirrors. The Bernal Spheres and Stamford Toruses used similar techniques. The largest of the colonies and the more power-hungry smaller ones augmented their energy requirement with multiple fission reactor piles. As did the ore processing and manufacturing stations. Fusion reactors were still quite rare in the civilian sector, almost unheard of.

Beyond those two Lagrangian points, there were also Cis-Lunar L-One and Cis-Lunar L-Two. The first of these two Lagrangian points was between the Earth and the Moon, but far closer to the Moon at a distance of only around fifty eight thousand kilometres from the lunar surface. This was where the lunar orbital way stations and hotels were. They were much smaller colonies, usually of the Bernal Sphere and Stamford Torus style. The way stations were used for the transit of people and equipment to and from the lunar surface, in particular the Lunar Mining Consortium and its Lunar surface mining complex.

The hotels were privately owned resorts with perfect views of the near side of the Moon. Some of these were older, refurbished O'Neil-style twin cylindrical colonies. They also organised multiple kinds of tours, with tours to the surface of both the near and far side of the Moon, where they often had shared common surface facilities. Tours of the Lunar Mining Complex could also be arranged along with regular Lunar flyovers. These hotels were particularly popular with honeymooners.

The second of these Lagrangian points, L-Two, was on the far side of the Moon just as far from the lunar surface as L-One. This region was very similar to L-One, in that it also private orbital lunar hotels, only these had perfect views of the far side of the Moon. They also provided all of the same tour functions and facilities as with L-One.

There was one major difference, however, regulations were far stricter in L-Two, as light and other electromagnetic pollution was to be kept minimal, almost non-existent. Orbital lunar satellites provided tight beam laser communications only. This was because the other component of Cis-Lunar L-Two included a copious number of research stations, space telescopes, telecommunications arrays and military surveillance facilities. In Cis-Lunar L-Two, they were the priority.

Of course, beyond Cis-Lunar space, the Earth had its own Lagrangian points with the Sun. The Earth's Lagrangian point L-One, one point five million kilometres from the Earth in the direction of the Sun, was filled with a great many solar arrays, all collecting solar energy to be beamed down to the Earth. A series of satellites in geostationary orbit above the Earth captured the energy beams and then re-transmitted them to surface collectors on the Earth below. On the opposite side of the Earth, at the same distance away, was the Earth's Lagrangian point L-Two. Just like Cis-Lunar L-Two, this zone was used for research stations, space telescopes, telecommunications arrays and military surveillance facilities. No other usage was allowed in that zone at all.

Farther afield from the Earth itself and Cis-Lunar space, there were two major Earth Lagrangian points, L-Four and L-Five, Earth's leading and trailing trojan points. These are very stable Libration points, sixty degrees ahead and sixty degrees behind the Earth in its orbit around the Sun. Around the same time that the construction of the mega O'Neil-style cylindrical colony of Colonial Central Command began, a plan had been put in place to protect the Earth and its Cis-Lunar colonies from asteroidal collisions.

The Earth's government had prepared the plans and then put those plans out to tender. The project planned to identify fifty asteroids that had Earth-crossing orbits and were potentially able to collide with the Earth itself. Those fifty asteroids were to have their orbits adjusted so as to make them far safer and reduce any likelihood of future collisions with the Earth or any of its Cis-Lunar colonies.

Various companies replied to those tenders with detailed tender submissions. One company in particular presented its bid and that bid undercut the competitors by more than a third. That company was simply called Cis-Lunar Haulage Pty Ltd, its CEO was one, Stuart Dumas.

Stuart Dumas had hated high school, the other students had teased him mercilessly, calling him Dumas the Dumb-arse and Stupid Dumb-arse, among many other derogatory names. He hated the constant ribbing, especially as he was actually quite smart. Not smart in intellectual pursuits, but smart in other areas, the areas of business and commerce.

As soon as his parents allowed him, he dropped out of high school. He was only seventeen. At first, his parents were disappointed. They were simple farmers and they had wanted their son Stuart to make something of himself, however, Stuart did not disappoint them for very long at all.

Stuart worked several minor jobs while he obtained his pilot's accreditations, both space and atmo-rated. As soon as he'd saved enough money, he used it as collateral to take out a loan and then purchased a moderately sized Cis-Lunar space tug. It was a smart move! Stuart Dumas then registered his first business, Cis-Lunar Haulage Pty Ltd. By the end of his first year, profits had been so good that he'd purchased four more space tugs to expand his company's fleet.

It was the fifth year that Stuart had been in the space haulage business and he now had twenty space tugs in his fleet, including some of the most powerful space tugs available. His business had been highly profitable and his company's loans were all paid off. Stuart's company had hauled everything imaginable in Cis-Lunar space and even hauled a few of the older O'Neil-style colonies farther afield. That was when the Earth government put out their plans for asteroid risk mitigation to tender.

Stuart Dumas has replied with an official bid for the business, a bid that at a glance appeared to be ridiculously low. So low, in fact, undercutting the competition by so much, that the Earth government department manager responsible for the project called him down to the Earth for a meeting. Stuart Dumas also had a plan, a complementary plan and he turned up at the meeting with a suitcase and many copies of his own plan. During the meeting, he passed copies of his plan to the project management team while they discussed his exceedingly low bid.

Stuart informed the project management team that his bid was so low because he was only interested in recovering his costs and that the real money was to be made in his own project. This supplemental plan was contained in the documents that he had passed around the conference room table. The project management team read through their copies as quickly as they could.

The original project was to mitigate the threat of asteroidal collision by hauling the most dangerous asteroids into far safer orbits around the Sun. Stuart Dumas's plan was to move those same asteroids into the Earth's L-Four and L-Five Lagrangian points and to accumulate them there, all together into an aggregated or conglomerated asteroidal mass. Twenty five asteroids at each Lagrangian point to start with and more asteroids to be added as the mining operations processed the conglomerated mass.

Stuart explained that the real money to be made was in the mining of the accumulated masses of the asteroids and that he wanted exclusive rights to the expanded project. Imagine all of the Nickel, Iron, Cobalt, Platinum, Gold, Manganese, Copper and Zinc, he had told them, not to mention the industrial slag from the smelting processes, that could be fashioned into astcrete radiation shielding. Then, of course, there were the rare earth metals. The project management team was intrigued by Stuart's plan.

It took the project management team more than two weeks to look into Stuart Dumas's proposals, but in the end, Stuart's bid was accepted and his expanded proposal was given the green light. They also gave him exclusive mining rights to any conglomerate asteroidal masses he accumulated. Thus, the Earth Trojan Mining Corporation Ltd was registered and Stuart Dumas became its CEO.

So much for Stuart Dumas being a Dumb-arse, he went on to found a third company, Astro Economics Ltd, for trading with future Belter Colonies farther out in the Asteroid Belt, which had not even been colonised yet. Stuart planned for things that were yet to even happen.

Later in his career, he made a separate deal with the Venusians, forming a new company, Venusian Trojan Mining Ltd. The same methodology, making use of Venus crossing asteroids to build up conglomerated asteroidal masses in both of the Venusian Trojan Lagrangian points to mine.

Stuart's undertakings were not cheap at all and he had to borrow vast sums of money to finance his endeavours, however, when his financiers saw his plans and that he already had the approvals, they literally threw money at him. They all had Golden Credits in their eyes and could already see the profits rolling in. All of Stuart's companies were highly successful and with those four companies, Stuart Dumas became one of the richest humans to ever live.

Stuart considered success to be the best revenge of all and amongst some of his many thousands of employees, were even those who had teased him mercilessly in high school. Stuart had forgiven them long ago, as they had provided him with the very drive to be where he was. Had his fellow school students not done that, he might have become just another simple farmer, taking over his parent's farm. They were all treated fairly and even sent Christmas and Birthday cards, along with small gifts.

During the Outward Interplanetary Expansion, by the time of the Mimasian War, both the L-Four and L-Five Lagrangian zones had grown and developed considerably. The original conglomerated mass of twenty five asteroids had grown to over a hundred asteroids at each zone, although much of the original asteroidal materials had already been mined and processed by that time. In this way, the Earth government's asteroid mitigation risk became an ongoing project, a mere side effect of Stuart Dumas's mining operations.

The conglomerated asteroidal masses did not rotate and sat in the very centre of the L-Four and L-Five Lagrangian regions, perpetually orbiting the Sun in those zone's gravitational sweet spots. The orbital regions around those accumulated masses included colonial structures in concentric rings. There were mobile mining stations. These were designed to work in micro-gravitational environments. They could land on the accumulated asteroids, mine them, fill their ore hoppers and then lift back off again to deliver their ore to the orbiting processing stations.

The ore processing stationed themselves pulverised the raw ore and then smelted it into various huge billets of Nickel, Iron, Cobalt, Platinum, Gold, Manganese, Copper and Zinc, not to mention the copious quantities of rare earth metals. Most, but not all of these were exported to Cis-Lunar L-Four, for use in the orbital manufacturing stations there. Nearly all of the slag left over from the smelting process was turned into astcrete and exported to both Cis-Lunar L-Four and the Belter colonies further out.

Beyond those, there were in higher orbits manufacturing stations, which could turn processed materials into various products. Jewellery made from precious metals was in the highest demand. The Dumas family had always believed in value adding, as well as exporting the processed materials themselves. Stuart Dumas had always said, "Diversify your interests", that was his lifelong motto.

In the higher orbital regions beyond the manufacturing facilities were the colonies themselves, where the workforce and the other colonists lived. There were not that many of them, only a dozen O'Neil-style twin cylinders at L-Four and L-Five, but they were at the time of the Outward Interplanetary Expansion, vibrant communities, developing their own cultures. They had managed to survive the Mimasian War virtually unscathed.

Looking back, one of the biggest changes in the Earth's Trojan points occurred in the L-Five zone, the Earth's trailing Trojan point. This also occurred around the time of the construction of the mega O'Neil-style colony cylinder, Colonial Central Command. That mega colony was designed and constructed to take over control and governance of all of the Cis-Lunar space colonies. Cis-Lunar space was to be governed along the lines of federal democracy, with alterations that the colonists of L-Five would ultimately decide, that is to say, their own constitution.

However, the colonies had expanded beyond Cis-Lunar space. Colonies were now starting in the Venusian orbital zone and even colonies in the Asteroid Belt. Colonists were even pushing out to Jupiter's Trojan Asteroids and the outer Moons of Jupiter. Then, of course, there was a push ship full of colonists on its way to Saturn. Now, with the development of mining operations in the Earth's Trojan points, the Earth's government had to take further action. Things were exploding outward rapidly!

Colonial expansion had to be managed and it could not be managed from the Earth or Cis-Lunar L-Five. The new plan set forth by the Earth's parliament and government involved Earth's Trailing Trojan point and a rather large asteroid named Eros. As the Earth's Trojan points were being managed by the Earth Trojan Mining Corporation, Stuart Dumas was contacted.

At first, Stuart Dumas was annoyed, he himself had wanted Eros to be moved into one of the Earth's Trojan points and then added to one of the conglomerated masses for mining purposes. The Earth's government, however, was having none of that, they had their own purposes in mind. Stuart Dumas was surprised when he found out their plans, strangely enough, he approved of it.

Cis-Lunar Haulage Pty Ltd was contracted to haul Eros out of its current orbit around the Sun and to move Eros to the Earth's Trailing Trojan point.

There, Eros was to be placed into a high halo orbit around the Earth's L-Five Lagrangian point's sweet spot, effectively with the conglomerated asteroidal mass in the sweet spot itself. The company's largest available space tugs were all put to the task and Eros was gently moved, or more correctly nudged into place.

What happened next was the part that Stuart Dumas was happy about. The Earth Trojan Mining Corporation was given the mining rights to Eros, however, it had to be performed in the fashion spelled out by the Earth's Government. Eros was to be reshaped. Currently shaped like an elongated peanut or potato, twenty one miles long and seven miles wide, Eros's surface was to be mined and reworked into a cylindrical shape and its ends flattened out. Once that was completed, the surface of Eros was to be melted, fused and hardened into a rock-like shell. Stuart was more happy about the mining part.

Beyond that, Eros was then to be carved out and hollowed to form a huge internal cylinder. That cylinder was to be eighteen miles long, with a diameter of four point seven five miles. That was a huge space and would require a lot of digging. Mining, to be more specific. Stuart was happy about that as well. Once Eros was hollowed out, its entire structure from the inside out was to be heated and fused into solid vitrified rock.

The engineers were then to take over and turn the interior of Eros into a colony, almost as big as Colonial Central Command. That process would take just as long and the two colonies were scheduled to come online within months of each other, with Central Command coming online first. As Colonial Central Command was being built to govern Cis-Lunar space, Eros was being reworked to govern and control the solar system's colonisation. Stuart Dumas felt proud to be a part of the process.

While Stuart Dumas was exceedingly happy with all that he had achieved, he did have some setbacks. Another clever entrepreneur copied Stuart's methodology and managed to be awarded the mining rights to the Martian Trojan Lagrangian points. That entrepreneur, named Victor Himmelstaff, set up a very similar method, using Mars-crossing asteroids to build up his own conglomerated asteroidal masses to mine.

Victor Himmelstaff's Mars Trojan Mining Ltd was a direct competitor to Stuart's companies and Mars was far closer to the Belter Colonies in the Asteroid Belt. Stuart was peeved by this development, as he too had plans for the two Martian Trojan points. Luck was on Stuart's side, however, and the future unfolded in surprising ways.

Victor Himmelstaff had two children by his wife Carolina, Victor Junior and Hypolita. Victor's Son, Victor Junior, was very hands-on, always believing that if he wanted something done right, he had to do it himself. That was his downfall, as when doing something himself, in setting up a mobile mining station, there was an accident in which he lost his life. Victor Himmelstaff Junior was crushed to death literally and both of his parents, Victor and Carolina, along with their Daughter Hypolita, were crushed emotionally as a result.

Stuart Dumas himself also had children, several in fact and his eldest son was Baron. At a function back at Cis-Lunar L-Five, Baron just happened to meet up with Hypolita Himmelstaff and they hit it off immediately. It was love at first sight and led to a long two-year courtship, after which they were both married. This took place years before the death of Victor Himmelstaff Junior.

Several years later, Victor's wife Carolina passed away and with that passing, Hypolita became the sole heir to the Himmelstaff corporations. With the later passing of Victor Himmelstaff himself, the entire Mars Trojan Mining company, amongst others, came under the full control of the Dumasian Corporate umbrella. There was, of course, much more to this particular story.

Yeannah turned to Saffiera and whispered, "That name, Dumas is very familiar", then she popped up a new window on the screen and performed a quick search.

Right at the very top of the search came up an entry in bold, with more detail information, Dumas Incorporated Industries Ltd. Yeannah clicked on the link and the Dumas Incorporated Industries network site came up. It was a fancy site with lots of information, one of the options was simply Consolidated Industries. Yeannah clicked on the option and a new page opened up, it was a list of companies under the Dumas Incorporated Industries umbrella. Yeannah scrolled down the list.

"Oh my god!", Yeannah quietly exclaimed, "This list is endless. There are thousands of companies under their corporate umbrella!"

Saffiera watched the list scroll down the screen and telepathically, *"And to think, that all started with a farmer's son!"*

"One man started that ball rolling", Yeannah whispered in confirmation, then she stopped scrolling on one of the corporate links on the screen, Dumas Planetary Transformations Ltd.

Yeannah whispered excitedly, "I knew I recognised that name. They terraform whole planets and moons!"

"Amongst a lot of other things. Dumas Incorporated Industries is a commercial and business empire! They are huge!", Saffiera replied telepathically.

Yeannah nodded and then quietly replied as she cancelled the new window, "It's also way beyond the scope of our term project as well. We already have way too much information to wade through."

"That's true. I'm summarising and linking as much as can", Saffiera replied, adding, *"The twins are both going to have to step up and focus as well. They distract Kethera far too much."*

"How are our girls doing, Saffiera?", Yeannah whispered.

Saffiera moved to the edge of the bed and looked down at Kethera and the twins. Kethera was lying on her back, her arms completely outstretched. Aria was snuggled up to Kethera on her left side, while Ariel was snuggled up to Kethera on her right side. Both twins had their heads resting gently on Kethera's upper arms and chest, their free arms wrapped around Kethera's lower abdomen, hugging her in a warm embrace. All three girls were fast asleep and Kethera was purring contently.

Saffiera noticed that Kethera's pyjama top was dishevelled and her lower pair of breasts were clearly visible. Saffiera reached down, carefully and gently adjusting Kethera's pyjama top to cover her lower breasts from view. Saffiera understood that Kethera would not like her breasts on display for everyone to see. Most Carlin girls and women had an innate shyness to them, although they could become quite promiscuous at times. Saffiera then activated the camera on her data tablet and held it out above the three sleeping girls, she quickly took a photograph, a stolen photo and then she smiled to herself.

Saffiera passed her tablet to Yeannah, commenting, *"They look so cute, don't they?"*

Yeannah looked at the stolen photo thoughtfully, then thought back, *"True. They do look cute, but when the twins are awake, they can be like a pair of little vipers!"*

Saffiera began to giggle telepathically before asking Yeannah, *"Why do Carlins have blue stripes?"*

Yeannah stopped the slow, rhythmic flapping of her great leathery wings and thought for a moment before answering with carefully composed thoughts, *"Camouflage I think"*, she replied, explaining, *"It's an adaption that allowed them to move unseen, within the blue Savannah grasslands that line both banks of the Masula River."*

"That does make sense", Saffiera replied.

"Why do you ask?", Yeannah asked, moving from thoughts to whispered vocalisation.

Saffiera replied telepathically, *"I was just wondering, why they evolved their stripes"*, then she noted with a little embarrassment, *"They even have blue areolas."*

Yeannah blinked at the remark but said nothing in reply, thinking to herself, *"I had not noticed."*

Yeannah enquired is a soft, quiet voice, "What's it like? You know, when you read minds?"

"It doesn't work the way you might think it does", Saffiera replied honestly, *"We don't actually read minds and we don't push thoughts into minds either, not in the way that you're thinking, anyway."*

"Then how does it work?", Yeannah thought, enquiring, *"How do you pick up these thoughts?"*

"It's a perception, Yeannah", Saffiera replied, adding, *"We perceive other minds"*, wondering whether that would make any sense.

"That doesn't make any sense at all, Saffiera", Yeannah thought back, asking, *"How are you picking up my thoughts?"*

Saffiera was silent for a long moment before replying, *"If I turn the light off and on, you perceive the light turning off and on, yes? You perceive the light, yes?"*

"Yes, but what has that got to do with it? A light is just light!", Yeannah in a whisper once more.

"Bear with me for a moment, it's not so easy to explain", Saffiera replied, then after a moment, she attempted to explain, *"In this bedroom, I can perceive five minds, including my own. If I reach my mind out, I can perceive your parents and your brother's minds. If I reach out further, I can perceive the minds of the families next door and even further afield, the further I reach out, the more I perceive."*

Yeannah was quiet in thought for a moment, then replied with a thought, *"I thought I had it for a moment there, then I guess I lost it."*

Saffiera plucked three of her golden blond hairs from her head and then scrunched them all together into a tangled hairball in her hand, *"This is how we perceive another mind, although there would be a lot more hairs, anywhere from fifty to a hundred or more, and the hairball would appear as a golden ball of threaded thoughts, all tightly interwoven. Each thread rippling with vibrant emotions and thoughts, with many, many interconnections. It's the surface of these thought balls that is the easiest to see"*, she held the hairball out to Yeannah.

Yeannah took the hairball and looked at it closely, *"So our minds look like a tangled ball of golden thoughts, like a web of thoughts"*, she thought back.

"Yes and a telepathic mind is like a field in which the other nearby minds are all embedded, with their own thoughts all interacting like a tapestry", Saffiera replied, then she added a qualification, *"Actually, all minds are fields in their own right, it's just that telepaths are able to use and expand those fields and communicate across them."*

"So you literally see thoughts, Saffiera?", Yeannah queried in a whispered voice.

"You could say that, Yeannah", Saffiera replied.

Yeannah decided to test that theory, "So Saffiera, who's thinking about me?", she whispered.

Saffiera frowned, then allowed her mind to drift outward, "*Your family are all asleep*", then her mind spread even further like the ripples in a pond, after a few minutes, *"Yookey is still awake. He's in his nest in the tree next to this one, on a lower level. He's thinking about you, Yeannah."*

Yeannah knew where Yookey lived and Saffiera appeared to know as well, but she wasn't convinced, "Okay", she replied, then she asked, "Is Kethera dreaming?", she whispered.

Saffiera glanced to her right, *"Yes, Kethera is dreaming."*

Yeannah thought to Saffiera, not wanting to be heard, *"What is Kethera dreaming about?"*

"Yeannah. We should not peek. We should not pry. It is not considered polite", Saffiera protested, this was something that was ingrained into Martians since birth.

Do not pry. Do no harm. Respect fellow minds. These were principles etched into every Martian child's mind, unspoken laws that minds were sacrosanct.

"We won't tell anyone, Saffiera. Who is going to know?", Yeannah thought back.

Saffiera frowned, guilt was rising in her chest. Yeannah's unrelenting curiosity tugged at her thoughts, leaving Saffiera with little choice.

She turned reluctantly to her right and focused on her Carlin friend once more, *"Kethera is dreaming about Richard"*, she informed Yeannah with obvious embarrassment.

"Oh, so Kethera does like Richard. What kind of dream is it?", Yeannah thought back.

Saffiera's golden complexion took on a reddish tint, the colour of rose gold came across her cheeks, *"It is a very personal, romantic dream. I should say no more, Yeannah."*

"Oh, okay. So Kethera is having a wet dream about Richard?", Yeannah replied in a hushed, whispered voice.

Saffiera looked a little annoyed and upset at having pried into Kethera's dreams and replied, *"Yes, but do not ask me again and you must promise never to tell Kethera or Richard. Is that understood?"*, it was a rebuke.

Yeannah's wings shifted uneasily, her gaze dropping to her hands, "I am so sorry, Saffiera. That was very wrong of me. I promise that I shall not tell anyone of this."

Saffiera began to giggle telepathically and Yeannah asked her with a whispered voice, "What's so funny, Saffiera?"

"The girls. They're asleep and even in their sleep, they're distracting us", Saffiera replied.

"I think that's more on us than them, Saffiera", Yeannah thought back, explaining, *"Our girls are asleep after all."*

"Our girls?", Saffiera queried.

"Yeah, I reckon so, Saffiera. They are our girls", Yeannah confirmed in a whispered voice.

"And we love them to bits, as Aria would say", Saffiera agreed.

Yeannah smiled and replied, "We'd better get back to studying. This project won't write itself."

9. Eros Controls it All.

The Government of Earth and their expert engineers had underestimated how fast the Earth Trojan Mining Corporation worked. Instead of shaping the exterior of Eros first and hollowing out the interior next, Stuart Dumas instructed his people to work on both simultaneously. Stuart Dumas was eager to get his hands on the mineral wealth inside of the asteroid Eros.

Silicates like Olivine and Pyroxene, Nickel, Iron and even Nickel-Iron alloys, Platinum, Palladium and Rhodium, even Water and of course regolith for making radiation shielding panels. Most of all, however, Stuart Dumas was eager for the Rare Earth Elements, such as Neodymium and Yttrium, etc. Mining Eros was extremely lucrative, paying off all of his company's many debts and filling his company's coffers with trillions in golden credits. The riches were beyond belief and propelled Stuart Dumas and his companies into the stratosphere of human influence and politics.

The name Dumas became a household word and everyone knew his name. Even so, his own employees and others who knew him would often describe Stuart Dumas as a humble man who always looked out for those less fortunate than himself. Eros was shaped into a cylinder and hollowed out inside, two years ahead of schedule and then the engineers from Earth quickly got to work.

It was in the year twenty ninety eight AD that Eros came online and was opened up for habitation. Both the Colonisation Committee of Sol and the Security Council of Sol moved from their medium-sized toroidal colony at Cis-Lunar L-Five, which had been their home for half a century, into their new home within weeks of Eros's opening. That single event began the largest drive of humanity into the farthest reaches of the solar system in terms of both exploration and colonisation. The Golden Age of Humanity had begun!

By the time of the Mimasian War, Eros had been turned into a beautiful world on the inner surface of a cylinder eighteen miles long and four point seven five miles in diameter. In the very centre of that cylinder was a two-mile-wide sea that ran around the entire circumference of the cylinder. If laid out flat, it would be close to fifteen miles long.

Two more seas extended from this central sea, running along the length of the cylinder in both directions. Both of these seas were a mile wide and six miles long, connecting up with the central sea at the centre of the cylinder. At the junction of these seas was an island shaped like an eight-pointed star. Eros

Central, the capital of Eros, was covered in many buildings, the tallest of which was nearly five hundred meters in height.

One hundred and twenty degrees around the cylinder on either side of Long Sea, there were four other seas. These were five miles long and one mile wide and each was separated from the central sea by a mile of land. Twin broad canals connected each of these seas to the central sea itself.

In between the seas from their coasts, plains swept inland. Near the central regions, these grew into small mountains about fifteen hundred meters tall. A light scattering of snow accumulated on their peaks in winter, snow that was destined to melt in the summer months. Both summer and winter were controlled, but beyond that, the weather was largely its own.

On the plains, crops grew in large patches and at the base of the mountains, small towns and villages had been built. Along the coasts themselves, built around small bays, small towns had also been constructed. A network of roads crisscrossed the lands in every direction. Orchards and vineyards were plentiful across the landscape. Small lakes, rivers and streams also existed, flowing from the mountains to the seas.

Most of the industry on Eros was built into the ends of the asteroid and built deep into the crust. The entire region between the spaceports and the interior was taken up by power generation stations and air and water recycling systems. They were all constructed on an enormous scale.

The crust in the cylindrical section of Eros had housing and light industry to a depth of two hundred meters. The light industry was towards both ends of Eros and the housing being towards the central sea. All of the towns and villages of Eros were of a set size. They could not grow and expand as towns and villages on a planet could. Even though Eros was huge compared to most colonies, it was nonetheless a colony itself and limited in land area. Much of Eros's living areas, shops, offices and entertainment complexes were all underground. This underground structure surfaced in the villages, towns, and Eros Central. It was all serviced by highly efficient rapid transit systems.

The asteroid Eros housed a population of over five million people and those people came close to losing it all during the Mimasian War. The Mimasian Tarlak attacks had caused significant damage to the Eros colony, the city within the rock that was Eros and that damage had to be repaired.

Of course, in the aftermath of the Mimasian War, a hidden branch of the Earth's psi-corps had been busy covering up the War. Using the natural trauma that all Wars generate and their skills at memory alteration and manipulation, the Council of Shadows covered up the existence of aliens and the War, relegating it to a natural yet exceedingly deadly event.

The peoples of the Earth and their colonies believed that the disaster was caused by the solar system passing through a region of interstellar space that contained dangerous micrometeor swarms and other potential hazards. Mimasian Tarlaks, Thols, and Martians were reduced to little more than myth and were carefully excised from Human memory.

The Council of Shadows, occult and hidden, even from the psi corp itself, had as its core purpose the maintenance of stability within all Human civilisation. They moved unseen in the background, doing what they believed to be necessary. While the psi-corps could be controlling, the Shadow Council controlled from within the hidden shadows of the psi-corps itself.

Even though it was not his responsibility, Stuart Dumas had told both the Security Council of Sol and the Colonisation Committee of Sol that he would donate funds from his personal accounts towards the reconstruction of Eros. When he was asked how much, Stuart Dumas replied simply, *"Whatever it takes."*

To his credit, Stuart Dumas was true to his word, providing immense funding towards Eros's reconstruction efforts, always waiving off any need of repayment, stating, "*You are not indebted to me, you owe me nothing. It is I who owe humanity everything.*"

His name and his philanthropy were reaching legendary status, although some pushed odd conspiracy theories about the Dumas family, its origins and his companies. The conspiracy theorists saw Stuart Dumas as just another tall poppy to be cut down.

Tables had been set up for the various delegates. One table at the centre of the conference room, running along one wall, a large permanent desk facing out over the entire conference room, was set up for the Colonisation Committer of Sol. That committee currently had three members, the Central Speaker, Professor Daniel Forbes, the Speaker in his right, Professor Dorian Voss and on his left, Professor Althea Morgan.

There was room on this desk for up to thirteen speakers, however, the Colonisation Committee only required three. On other occasions, the Security Council of Sol held proceedings in the same conference room and they indeed had thirteen members. The Colonisation Committee of Sol and the Security Council of Sol, together, controlled humanity's outward expansion and the colonisation of the solar system from Eros. Essentially, Eros controlled it all!

In front of their slightly raised desk, other tables had been set up. One table in the centre of the room had been set up for representatives of the local Eros government. The local Eros government consisted of a local Eros Council, which was chosen democratically under the concept of universal suffrage. One person, one vote across all of Eros's citizenry who were of the age of suffrage, being the age twenty one and higher.

The members of the local Council of Eros were all independents, with no political parties, choosing to affiliate as they saw fit, a system designed to ensure that personal agendas could not overshadow the greater good of the colony. As a part of their task, they would elect the Major of Eros Central, who would be the head of the local Eros Central's Council, who in addition, would become the Governor of Eros itself. The selected Governor would then propose Secretaries to oversee the various *"higher"* government departments for the whole Eros and the Eros Central Council would either approve or reject those appointments. That was how Eros, the city within the rock, was governed.

Six seats had been set at this table and the name plaques placed on the table in front of each seat read, front left to right. Mr Dmitry Ivanov, Councillor, Miss Svetlana Kuznetsov, Councillor, Mr Darius Shahriari, Major and Governor, Miss Nyabol Nyaluak, Governor's Secretary, Mr Louis Rousseau, Councillor and finally Ms Sakura Takahashi, Councillor.

A smaller table with two seats had been set up to the right of the centre table, it was slightly forward and allowed the occupants a good view of the councillors on their left and the committee members on their right. The name plaques in front of the seats read, Mr Tory Marshal, Security Council Liaison and Miss Oriya Patel, Secretary.

Another smaller table had been set up to the left of the centre table, also with two seats, it too was slightly forward and its occupants had a good view of the councillors on their right and the committee members on their left. The name plaques, Mr Stuart Dumas, CEO of the Earth Trojan Mining Corporation Ltd and Miss Ritu Dharma, Secretary. In all, there were ten representatives and interested parties at the meeting and they had all taken their seats. They all waited patiently for the Colonisation Committee members to arrive.

While the delegates and committee members went about their business, none noticed the three entities at the back of the room, concealed by their psychic obscuration fields. These figures sat in the shadows, their presence completely undetectable to the human eyes in the room. These observers wore black robes, shimmering like raven's feathers and they'd taken seats at the back of the room.

To the others in the room, they were completely unseen. Even the seats they sat upon were invisible to the others, who only saw the stacks of unused chairs lined up along the back wall of the room. Everyone was already seated in their allocated seats, except for the Committee members themselves.

Unseen by the others, the three Folcrom, Orpheus, Freyja, and Tina, sat at the back of the room, concealed by their psychic obscuration fields, an ability that made them invisible even to the most discerning eyes. The psychic obscuration fields were powerful, making the three Folcrom not only invisible to the human eye but also undetectable by even the most advanced surveillance systems.

The three Colonisation Committee members entered the conference room from a door behind the central seat of the main desk. The central speaker, Professor Daniel Forbes, sat down in the central seat. His colleagues sat in their seats, Professor Althea Morgan in the seat to the left and Professor Dorian Voss in the seat to the right. This was a less formal meeting than the usual Colonisation Committee meetings and Professor Forbes introduced himself and his colleagues. In most other meetings, they were simply unnamed speakers.

"Greetings Ladies and Gentlemen, welcome and thank you for attending this meeting", Professor Forbes greeted everyone in the room, then he gestured to his left, "This is my esteemed colleague, Professor Althea Morgan", and then he gestured to his right, "and my esteemed colleague, Professor Dorian Voss".

Professor Forbes was an older man, his hair silver grey from age. He looked around the room before his eyes settled on Tory Marshal, the Security Council Liaison, "First thing on the agenda, I'd like to know how it is that we are all still alive. Mr Marshal, the Security Council is responsible for the docking hubs and all of Eros's external systems. Please explain."

Tory Marshal looked back at the Professor and replied, "Professor, the Security Council has people working on that very question."

"Surely you have an answer by now?", Professor Althea Morgan chimed in, "That swarm of micrometeors took out both of our docking hubs and all of the facilities on them, including the attitude control systems. By rights, we should all be dead. I still remember how our gravity spiralled out of control on that day."

Tory Marshal accessed his data tablet and checked the latest information they had on the subject, he nodded in agreement, "While that is true, we have found that the attitude control thrusters kicked in and slowed Eros's rotational rate. While our artificial gravity did peak at three point seven five gs, the thrusters managed to slow down our rotation, bringing our artificial gravity back down to normal."

Professor Althea Morgan gave the Security Council Liaison an incredulous look, questioning, "And all without the attitude control systems? You might need to explain that one a little better, Mr Marshal."

"We have found that our attitude control thrusters were", Tory Marshal paused, "How do I put this. The attitude control thrusters were hacked and controlled externally."

Now, Professor Dorian Voss was giving him an incredulous look, questioning, "How? How is that even possible, Mr Marshal?"

"To be quite frank, it isn't", Tory Marshal replied honestly, "The systems are supposed to be unhackable. As Professor Morgan stated, by rights, we should all be dead."

Darius Shahriari, the Major of Eros Central and Governor of all of Eros interjected, "I must say, Mr Marshal, you are not installing us with any degree of confidence."

Mr Marshal replied, "I can only tell you what we know", then he tagged a document and tapped it three times, the document was then transferred across to the data tablets of those present for the meeting.

Data tablets in the room all beeped for attention at once and their owners opened the document, giving it a quick perusal.

Mr Marshal explained, "This document is a summary of our investigation. If you scroll down the second last page", he paused for a moment as they scrolled through the document, "We found that message embedded in our computer control logs."

The message read, *"Attitude control thrusters adjusted. Eros's rotational axis and rotational rate stabilised. You're welcome. Doctor Gideon Reas and Sandra Danker."*

Unseen at the back of the room, Orpheus performed a perfect facepalm.

"It appears our attitude control thrusters were accessed and controlled by Doctor Reas and Miss Danker from high Martian orbit, from the Aries Colony", Tory Marshal informed them, adding, "Hell, they continue to tap in on a regular basis, just to make that sure we're okay.

Althea Morgan looked at the Security Council liaison, "Have you contacted them? Ask them how?"

"Yes, we have. They admit that they have accessed our thrusters. They are not telling us how", Tory Marshall replied, informing them, "They've told us to get the thrusters back under our control as soon as possible. That they can't keep monitoring them and tweaking them indefinitely."

"How? How did they even know we were in trouble?", Professor Althea Morgan asked.

"We. We have no idea, Professor Morgan", Tory Marshal replied honestly.

Professor Forbes noted, "So our attitude control thrusters are being controlled from high Martian orbit and we don't even know how. I suggest your Security Council get on top of this situation and get those thrusters back under our control. It seems we owe Doctor Reas and Miss Danker our gratitude."

Security Council Liaison Tory Marshal agreed, "Yes, Professor, our people are working tirelessly on the issue as we speak. I should note, Miss Danker is a Master Engineer, a highly capable one."

"They didn't know, Orpheus", Freyja's voice echoed in his mind, calm but insistent, *"This was before their induction, before they even knew of the Council of Shadow's existence."*

"Don't we need to adjust this?", Tina enquired, her tone questioning yet neutral.

Orpheus paused, his thoughts weighing the situation for a moment before answering, *"No. No, let them have this mystery."*

"Let them have this mystery! That's not very much like you at all, Orpheus", Freyja replied, a note of surprise in her voice, *"No loose ends, you always say."*

"This is a minor issue, Freyja and life does need some small mysteries after all", Orpheus explained, his tone carrying a rare hint of amusement.

Professor Forbes moved on to the next topic of discussion, "Very good, then. We've had some news from Cis-Lunar L-Five. Those twenty seven damaged colonies, they have all been written off. They are going to be replacing them. The new colonies will have five times the capacity of the older ones that they're replacing."

One of the Eros Central Council Members, Dmitry Ivanov, remarked, "That is a huge uptick in construction. Do they have access to all the materials they need?"

"They are breaking ground on six or more new mines on the Moon", Professor Forbes replied.

"They are going to need a lot of rare earth elements for those new colonies. More than they will find on the Moon in a dozen mines, I'd wager", Stuart Dumas chimed in.

"Perhaps, Mr Dumas", another Council Member, Ms Sakura Takahashi, replied, adding, "Your asteroid mining operations may be able to help them in that area."

"I can do far better than that, Ms Takahashi", Stuart Dumas replied, he requested his secretary Ritu Dharma to take detailed notes before addressing

Professor Forbes, “I have voluminous stores of rare earth elements at both Trojan points and also in my warehouses in Cis-Lunar L-Four. Please, Professor Forbes, offer those stores to Colonial Central Command for their construction efforts.”

“And your terms for their use Mr Dumas?”, Professor Forbes asked, “Will you be offering these materials to them at a discounted price?”

Mr Dumas smiled, the lines and creases on his face accentuating his advanced age, “Professor. You misunderstand. I offer these rare earth elements to Colonial Central Command's use for free! Call it a gift. I will have a contract written up accordingly.”

Professor Althea Morgan's interest was piqued, “Why, Mr Dumas? Rare earth elements are highly valuable. Your offer makes little sense.”

Mr Dumas smiled once again, “My warehouses are currently full of rare earth elements. My mining operations have extracted far more than we can currently use. Now, we have a use for them, so I'll empty my warehouses for other, newer stocks. This is to my advantage, otherwise, I will have to construct more warehouses and that is a cost burden. Besides, I've driven the price of rare earth elements down significantly, so it's far easier for me to give away my excess stocks. As I said, let these be my gift towards their colony construction.”

“Well, this is most unusual, Mr Dumas, however, if you are willing to provide the appropriate contract to that effect, we are certainly more than happy to make the offer on your behalf”, Professor Morgan replied.

“My secretary, Ritu, will have the contract ready by tomorrow afternoon”, Mr Dumas replied.

“What is Central Command doing with the twenty seven damaged colonies that they have written off?”, Councillor Svetlana Kuznetsov enquired.

Professor Forbes answered her, “They have gifted them to the Belters. Two colonies each to the thirteen Belter colonies. The last remaining colony is being gifted to the Saturnians. These are all twin cylinder colonies, by the way.”

“Very generous of them", Miss Kuznetsov noted, "They are still extremely valuable, even as scrap."

“Yes, but they may not get scrapped. Central Command is replacing them more due to their age, not so much because they are damaged. Don't get me wrong, they are quite heavily damaged, however, Central Command's focus is on the future, not the past", Professor Dorian Voss informed her.

"So, they may even be repaired and refurbished. The Belters are very good at these things. They will profit either way", Miss Kuznetsov concluded, "I am sure that the Belters and the Saturnians will be very happy with these gifts."

"Quite Miss Kuznetsov, quite", Professor Forbes agreed.

Professor Forbes moved on, "Colonial Central Command has offered all and any assistance that we might need in our reconstruction efforts here at Eros", he turned to the Security Council Liaison, "Mr Marshal. Can you put together a detailed list of what you require and highlight where Central Command can help out?"

"It is funny that you should mention that, Professor. Our people are putting together just such a list", Tory Marshal replied.

"Very good, Mr Marshal. Make sure your list is clear, concise and correct. Anything where Central Command can help out, make sure it's highlighted", Professor Forbes commented.

Professor Dorian Voss added, "Before you send that list to Central Command, please do us the courtesy of sending us a copy first. We would be interested in running our eyes over it."

"Yes, of course", Tory Marshal agreed, then he turned to his secretary, Oriya Patel, "Have you got all of that, Oriya?"

"Yes, Sir", Oriya replied, "All neatly noted down."

"Right, now for our next topic of discussion", Professor Forbes started, turning to the Security Council Liaison, "Mr Marshal. Our docking hubs? Please enlighten us."

Tory Marshal stood up and buttoned his suit, he stepped around his table and began to explain, "As you all know, Eros has two docking hubs, one at our North end and one at our South end. These are basically identical. Large squat cylinders, one kilometre in diameter and one kilometre deep. Now Eros rotates at almost point five revolutions per minute. That generates roughly one standard gravity via centrifugal force. Our docking hubs are embedded into the ends of Eros, in equally large, special receptacles and they are fitted rather precisely. Those docking hubs are supposed to remain stationary while Eros continues to rotate around them."

"Yes, we know all of that, Mr Marshal", another Councillor, Louis Rousseau, remarked, "Could you please get down to the damage?"

"I was getting to that, Mr Rousseau", Tory Marshal replied, then continued, "Apart from peppering the exterior of Eros with somewhat minor damage, the micrometeor swarms have destroyed all six of the external local docking ports on both hubs. They also destroyed most of the external facilities, including our attitude control relay stations, our communications arrays and the six main doors to our internal interplanetary docks. The internal docks themselves have also been devastated. To make things worse, both docking hubs have welded themselves into their receptacles and are now rotating along with the rest of Eros."

"Wait!", Darius Shahriari, the Major and Governor exclaimed, "Are you telling us that we have no method of ingress or egress from Eros?"

"Almost none", Tory Marshal admitted, "We have cobbled together one operational port out of the devastation, however, we can only dock one small ship at a time."

"Sweet Mother of god! We have five million people living inside of this rock! If we need to evacuate Eros, we're all screwed", he turned to his secretary, Nyabol Nyaluak, a very tall, dark skin girl with South Sudanese features, "Nyabol, make sure you're getting all of this down", he looked back to Mr Marshal, "And the Security Council's plans? Please tell me you at least have a plan?"

"We do have plans, Governor Sir and we will definitely need Central Command's assistance", Tory Marshal replied.

Darius Shahriari stretched out his arm with his palm up, gesturing to the Mr Marshal, "Speak!", is the one word he uttered.

"Well now. The process is not an easy one", Tory Marshal began, he looked at the faces of the people in the conference room and then continued, "We first need to release the docking hubs from Eros. They are currently heat-welded to their receptacles. Once we have done that, we need to pull the docking hubs out into space. We then need to repair the docking receptacles, after which we then repair the docking hubs. Once we're done, we have to carefully pop the docking hubs back into their receptacles."

Everyone in the room looked shocked, Professor Forbes spoke up, "Mr Marshal, you have just told us that those docking hubs are one kilometre in diameter and one kilometre deep. Exactly how are we going to do this?"

"Once we've released the hubs from their receptacles, it's just a matter of pulling them out with several space tugs", Tory Marshal explained, "Trust me, Professor, we've got this."

Darius Shahriari asked, "Just how long is that all going to take?"

"Well, Governor, it does depend on the precise level of damage, however, we believe it will take three to five years to complete the process", Tory Marshal replied, quickly adding, "For each hub."

"Three to five years for each hub!", Governor Shahriari shouted.

"I'm sorry, Governor, but they each have to be pulled out and worked on separately", he replied.

Everyone in the room, except for the Security Council Liaison, had defeated looks on their faces.

Stuart Dumas stood up and reached for his walking frame, which was beside his table. He slowly walked around his table, he was slow and everyone followed him with their eyes. Stuart Dumas was old, very old and yet, he still had this odd charisma about him.

"Sit down, Mr Marshal, you're giving an old man a heart attack", Stuart commented, before addressing the room, "This entire process sounds like it will be a frightfully expensive business, even with all of the help from Central Command. I'm going to open up my personal accounts to help fund this entire process."

Professor Althea Morgan responded, "Mr Dumas, that is incredibly generous of you, but this is not your responsibility."

"Nonsense, I came through that cobbled-together space dock. I've seen the devastation inside that docking hub. I most definitely have a responsibility to help out wherever I can", Stuart replied.

"But opening up your personal accounts?", Professor Morgan questioned.

"Woman, look at me. I'm old, very old. Those accounts of mine have enough credits in them to last a hundred lifetimes", Stuart explained, adding, "I can't take it with me, you know!"

Professor Voss asked, "Are you proposing a loan of some kind, perhaps a low-interest loan?"

"Hell no, Professor", Stuart replied, "I'm proposing to donate as much money as it takes."

Professor Althea Morgan replied shaking her head, "It is still not your responsibility, Sir."

"Isn't it, Althea?, Stuart replied rhetorically, using her first name, "I've had a good life. I've been given one opportunity after another and sure, I took advantage of those opportunities, but those opportunities were given to me. I most definitely have a responsibility to help out with this and I fully intend to do so. It's time for me to pay back that debt to society that I owe."

Professor Morgan replied, "If you insist, Mr Dumas, but I do recommend that this goes through Eros's legal department to make sure it's all kosher."

"My secretary, Ritu, will make the arrangements", as he slowly walked back to his seat, he asked, "Have you got all that noted down, Ritu?"

"I sure have, Mr Dumas", Ritu replied.

"Excellent, Ritu. You know, I might even live to see the repairs completed", Stuart Dumas noted, "This sort of thing kind of gives an old man a reason to keep on living."

Orpheus had been quietly scanning the surface of Stuart Dumas's mind, he noted silently to Freyja and Tina, *"Old man, Dumas there is a true philanthropist, all of his motivations are altruistic."*

"Seriously?", Tina questioned rhetorically, *"That would be so unusual. I'm used to seeing ulterior motives everywhere I look."*

"That's not always the case, Tina", Freyja replied, remarking, *"The two most powerful psychics I've ever met turned out to be incredibly selfless. It kind of makes a lie of that old saying, power corrupts and absolute power corrupts absolutely."*

"More powerful than Orpheus?", Tina questioned.

"More powerful than great grandpops, Folcrom Tafazah himself", Freyja replied.

Tina gave Orpheus a look that requested his opinion.

Orpheus replied honestly, *"It is possible, perhaps. I'd never seen such raw power and they weren't even naturally born psychics either. Gideon Reas and Sandra Danker are anomalies."*

The trio fell silent amongst themselves once more as Professor Morgan began to speak.

Professor Morgan addressed her peers and Stuart Dumas, "This next issue is a new law being implemented by Central Command. They call it the *'gravity law',* and it applies to all colonies in Earth's orbital zone that rely on centrifugal force for their artificial gravity. It does not apply to planets or the moons thereof."

This piqued the interest of Darius Shahriari, the Governor, "The gravity law?", he enquired.

"Yes, Governor. The Gravity Law", then Professor Morgan stated the law, "For all colonies, that derive their gravity via artificial methods, i.e, centrifugal force etc., that artificial gravity shall not deviate from one Earth g, by more than plus or minus ten percent as applied to the colony's main living surface. With the exception of official military training facilities."

The Governor quickly answered, "Eros has one point zero seven gs of gravity, so we are already in compliance with this new Gravity Law."

"Yes, Eros is within the ten percent tolerance this new law stipulates", the Professor replied, then turning to Stuart Dumas, "Mr Dumas, the only other colonies in Earth's Trojans are your corporate colonies, your cylinders. Are they in compliance with this new law?"

Stuart Dumas replied, "Professor, we have a corporate regulation to the same effect as this new law", then he turned to his secretary, Ritu Dharma, "Ritu, please take note, to have our corporate gravity regulations reworked to match the wording of the new Gravity Law."

The Governor questioned, "Why now? Why are they making official Gravity Laws now?"

Professor Morgan then noted, "Along with this new law, we have been provided with a whole lot of documentation and research. It seems that longtime exposure to extreme low gravity environments causes detrimental physiological changes, even life-threatening ones."

The Governor then queried, "We are aware of these issues already, Professor. Aren't the stimulants and the supplements meant to mitigate those issues?"

"Some of us apparently develop a tolerance to the stimulants that appear to render them ineffective. That, in turn, affects the uptake of the supplements. It appears that there are genetic factors involved, which are currently not understood. At the Lunar Mining Complex, workers have died as a result. This is why the new law was implemented", Professor Morgan informed the room, then noted, "They've even created new regulations for the Lunar Mining Consortium. Six months on the Moon, then two years back up in the colonies, twelve months on the Moon, then five years back up in the colonies."

"That kind of employee rotation is going to be a scheduling nightmare, although, I have no doubt that they'll make it work", Stuart Dumas replied.

"Well, as we are all currently in compliance, we should not have those issues", the Governor replied.

Professor Morgan nodded in agreement with the Governor, then noted, "Central Command is requesting that we recommend this new Gravity Law to the other colonies beyond Earth's orbit."

Stuart Dumas remarked, "The other colonies are under no obligation to follow laws from Central Command."

"We will be recommending this new Gravity Law nonetheless", Professor Morgan replied, noting, "It is up to the individual colonies beyond our jurisdiction as to whether they adhere to it."

Stuart Dumas responded, "I have mining ventures in both Venusian Trojan points and my eldest son, Baron and his Wife, Hypolita, have mining ventures in both Martian Trojan points. They all follow the same corporate regulations as my Trojan Mining Corporation here."

"So, Mr Dumas, you'd be recommending this new law as well?", Professor Voss questioned.

"Absolutely. My son and I will be lobbying the relevant governments to take up this new Gravity Law, although, there's isn't much I can do beyond Martian orbit", Stuart Dumas replied.

"We are more than happy to have you recommending this new law alongside us, Mr Dumas. The fact that your operations also have the same regulations, does add weight to the matter", Professor Morgan replied, "Thank you."

Svetlana Kuznetsov brought up an issue that had been sitting on her desk back in her office, "There is another problem that needs to be addressed."

"What problem might that be, Miss Kuznetsov?", Professor Forbes enquired.

"We cannot get out so easily, so we are effectively sealed in, like a world in a bottle", Miss Kuznetsov replied, noting, "We need to consider the mental health of our population."

"Have there been issues?", an interested Professor Morgan enquired.

"Yes. We have come across this thing. Ah, what is the word?", Svetlana paused in thought, English was her second language, not her first, she turned to Dmitry Ivanov and asked, "Как в английском языке называется тот, кто слепо следует, даже вопреки здравому смыслу?", in Russian.

Dmitry answered in English, "Those who blindly follow, even against all common sense? The word you are looking for is cult. They are cult members."

Svetlana replied, "Thank you, Dmitry, yes, that is the word. Cult!"

"Cult?", Professor Forbes inquired.

"Yes, Cult. They have no name for their cult, yet they all have similar things about them", Miss Kuznetsov replied, noting, "They wear hats made of tin foil when not in public. When in public, they always wear hats that they have lined with tin foil on the insides."

Orpheus, sitting at the back of the room unseen, could see where this was going and he facepalmed.

"Why, Miss Kuznetsov?", Professor Voss asked.

"They believe that there are aliens who are going to probe them all over and steal their minds. They meet in quiet, hidden places and they seem to be actively recruiting new members", Svetlana replied, hoping that she was understood and not coming across like an idiot or worse, a crazy woman.

Orpheus looked at Tina and asked telepathically, *"Cousin. I thought you had this under control?"*

"I thought that they were hilarious, Orpheus", Tina replied silently, *"So I left them alone."*

Orpheus facepalmed again, *"Tina, this is not funny!"*

Freyja agreed, *"Tina, this is far too big a loose end to leave to chance!"*

Professor Forbes asked, "Have they caused any problems?"

Svetlana replied, "Not really, but their numbers are growing. Their cult is expanding. It could become a dangerous conspiracy in our confined space."

Professor Forbes noted, "This could become a public health and safety issue. We need to keep on top of this, cult."

The Governor, Darius Shahriari, commented, "This is something in my area. I'll have our public health department and our public law compliance departments keep an eye on it."

Svetlana Kuznetsov replied, "I will send you what information I have on this matter."

"Tina, this is an unacceptable situation and you need to get it under control", Orpheus chastised.

Freyja, who had been silent for several minutes with her eyes rolled back, then came out of her trance noted, *"That won't be so easy, Orpheus. I'm detecting thousands of cult members. Literally thousands!"*, then she added, *"Those tin foil hats really don't work at all!"*

"What a mess!", Orpheus exclaimed, *"I might have to jaunt to Aries colony and rope in Gideon and Sandra to help with this one."*

"I thought that they were living inside of Mimas", Tina commented.

Freyja explained, *"They do. They live inside of Mimas with Winchilly and then they jaunt to Aries in Martian high orbit each day to manage the terraforming project."*

"Tina, there is nothing funny about loose ends, especially one like this, where the mere mention of aliens is involved", Orpheus explained.

Freyja spelled it out, *"Our people are barbaric, Tina. Have you forgotten how our fellow Humans behaved during the Mimasian War? The Tarlaks are now extinct! We must protect the Martians and the Thols, which is why we covered up the entire Mimasian War in the first place. That was a monumental task and we cannot have it all unravelling on us!"*

Orpheus looked at Freyja, then back to Tina, *"After we finish up here, we'll jaunt to Aries and explain the situation to Gideon and Sandra. It will take all five of us to clean up this loose end."*

Professor Forbes stood up, "Well, if no one has any more points of discussion to raise, we can close this meeting."

Everyone looked around, there were no more points of discussion. Professors Morgan and Voss were satisfied that there was nothing more to discuss.

At the back of the room, three unseen watchers shimmered slightly and then they were gone. No one had noticed them leave and no one had known that they were there, although there was an ever so slight chill in the air after they'd left.

Professor Forbes was still standing when he noticed three empty chairs at the back of the room, *"Were those chairs there the whole time? Funny, how I never noticed them"*, he thought to himself.

The repairs to Eros's docking hubs proceeded as planned. The first docking hub, the northern hub, was replaced into its receptacle and opened to the public in the year twenty one forty six, four years after the repair process began. Stuart Dumas, now of very advanced age, was present for the ceremony. Unable to use his walker, he sat in a wheelchair pushed by his nurse.

The docking hub's opening ceremony took place in the vast main entrance hall of the interplanetary spaceport. Elevators lined two walls, whisking travellers down to Eros's main living surface miles below. Information kiosks dotted the floor, providing easy access for visitors. A massive polymerised glass window spanned one wall, offering a breathtaking view of Eros's cavernous interior. Opposite it, entrances to the main port and interplanetary customs bustled with activity. There were many thousands of people present for the opening ceremony.

As Stuart's gaze lifted, he froze, stunned by what he saw above the enormous window, a rather large portrait of himself. The image, vibrant and larger than life, depicted a much younger Stuart Dumas, captured at the height of his achievements. It was positioned to greet every visitor to Eros's northern entry portal.

Baron Dumas gently rested a hand on his Father's shoulder. "Dad, I insisted on that," he said quietly.

Stuart's voice wavered with emotion as tears welled in his eyes. "You didn't need to, son. Now I feel like an old fool."

The southern docking hub was pulled from its receptacle shortly after the northern docking hub was reinserted, ensuring uninterrupted operations. Four years later, in twenty one fifty, the southern hub was fully repaired and reinstalled. It opened to the public soon after.

The opening ceremony unfolded in the expansive main entrance hall of the interplanetary spaceport. Identical in layout to the northern hub, this vast cavern echoed with the voices of thousands of attendees. It was a momentous occasion, with dignitaries and citizens alike gathered to celebrate.

Despite his doctor's strong objections, Stuart Dumas insisted on attending.

"I'm going to this ceremony if it's the last thing I do", he had declared with characteristic resolve. Seated in his wheelchair, a drip now attached to his arm, he was pushed to his designated position for the ceremony by his nurse.

Stuart took in the familiar grandeur of the hall, noting its striking similarity to its northern counterpart. Yet, something different caught his eye, a large object draped in vibrant sheets of fabric. As the speaker's words resonated faintly in the background, Stuart's attention remained fixed on the concealed structure. Slowly, the fabric was drawn away and the crowd erupted into applause and cheers. All eyes turned to look at Stuart. The people had genuine affection in their eyes.

Before Stuart could fully process what he was seeing, he found himself face to face with a towering bronze statue of himself, cast in his younger years. The statue stood proud, its polished surface gleaming under the bright lights of the hall, a testament to his enduring legacy.

Baron Dumas placed a reassuring hand on his Father's shoulder, just as he had four years prior.

"Dad," he said gently, his voice barely audible over the clamour, "They all insisted on this," he gestured to the applauding crowd.

Stuart's eyes welled with tears as he struggled to find the words. He looked at the statue, then at the cheering faces around him.

"Fools," he murmured, his voice thick with emotion, "That money could have been better spent."

Later that night, Stuart Dumas lay in his bed. The drip still fed its precious, life-sustaining fluid into his frail body, a silent lifeline tethering him to the world. Another bottle of fluid hung beside the bed, its contents slowly dwindling as the seconds ticked by.

Stuart stared into the darkness, "God," he called out, his voice barely above a whisper.

"I've had a good life. I've done all I could do, seen all I could see," he paused, his breath shallow but steady, "It's time for you to take me home."

With trembling fingers, Stuart reached for the cannula in his arm. His movements were deliberate, filled with purpose. As he pulled it free, the fluid spilled out onto the floor, forming a small, glistening pool beside his bed.

"It's time for me to come home," he murmured once more, his voice soft and resolute.

Unseen by Stuart, three silent watchers stood in the room, Orpheus, Freyja, and Tina. They had come to pay their final respects, sensing his end was near. When Stuart pulled out the cannula, Tina instinctively moved forward, her heart aching to intervene, but Freyja caught her by the arm, shaking her head gently from side to side.

"No, Tina. It is his time", she transmitted, her voice steady but tinged with sadness.

"Is there nothing we can do?", Tina asked, her eyes brimming with tears.

"It is his time, Tina", Orpheus replied quietly, *"This is a part of life. We cannot interfere."*

They stood in solemn silence as Stuart closed his eyes and drifted into sleep. Moments later, his breathing stilled, and he was gone. The trio watched as a faint light emerged from his body, rising slowly. It coalesced into the shape of Stuart's very essence, his soul.

Stuart's soul turned to them, his gaze warm and filled with peace. It was as if he, now being free from the mortal coil, understood who and what they were, previously hidden knowledge now at his disposal. He raised an approving hand, pointing to them with a gentle smile and a nod, before dissolving into the ether. His presence lingered in the room for a short while, a quiet farewell.

It was the year twenty one fifty, and Stuart Dumas was one hundred and two years old.

"Has he gone forever?", Tina asked.

"No, dear cousin. Death is just the beginning", Orpheus replied, adding, *"It is a doorway, one that we must all pass through.*

"He showed no fear", Tina noted.

"He lived a good life, Tina. Why should he be afraid?", Freyja replied.

"And had his life been the opposite of good?", Tina enquired.

"You are not yet ready for that lesson, youngling", Orpheus pronounced.

The trio wiped their tears away and then there was a shimmering in the air, as the trio jaunted and disappeared, leaving the room quiet once more.

Yeannah's wings stopped their gentle flapping as she looked up from the screen, Yeannah rolled her head around on her neck, which had become a little stiff.

"That business executive, Stuart Dumas, he was only one hundred and two when he died", Yeannah remarked to Saffiera in a whispered voice.

"That was well over thirteen hundred years ago, Yeannah", Saffiera replied, noting, *"They didn't have anti-agathic compounds back then. People were lucky to live to even*

eighty."

"So, he was actually, really old?", Yeannah quietly questioned, her voice incredulous.

"He was for his time, yes, Yeannah. Lives were much shorter back then", Saffiera explained.

"Are our three beauties still sleeping?", Yeannah asked in a whisper.

Saffiera looked over the edge of the bed and smiled, replying telepathically, *"Yeah, exactly as they were when I last looked"*, she giggled, *"Just like the picture we took earlier."*

"You've got all the notes down, yeah?", Yeannah softly asked.

"Yep. Everything is documented with hyperlinks", Saffiera replied.

Yeannah yawned, "It's getting late. What say you, we get some sleep and start on the next section tomorrow", she whispered so as to not wake the twins or Kethera.

"It is a good idea", Saffiera also yawned, *"I am getting tired and we can start on the Venusian section tomorrow. It looks like it's just as big as the section for the Earth."*

"Good, agreed then. Whose house tomorrow night?", Yeannah asked.

"I kind of like it here, to be honest. Your parents are way cool", Saffiera commented.

"Yeah, no. Aria has kind of poisoned the waters with her old Miss Fish Face comment earlier", Yeannah noted, adding, "I'm not sure that my Mother will want to see her back so soon."

"Kethera's house then", Saffiera suggested.

Yeannah looked at Saffiera and smiled, whispering, "Yeah, Kethera's house. That's a great idea."

They both agreed and then adjusted their pillows to the end of the bed and were soon fast asleep.

The next day after school, the girls all jumped onto another school hover bus, the one that Kethera usually caught. Instead of heading north into the tall Jula Jula forests and the tree houses of the Thols, this bus headed south, towards the villages of the Carlins, nestled along the broad plains of the Masula Valley. The school was positioned in the centre of the large Human colony, which itself was positioned halfway between the villages of the Thols and the villages of the Carlins. Small stands of forest were occasionally seen off into the distance, to either side of the well-travelled pathway.

The hover bus stopped and all of the Carlin students alighted, along with Kethera and her friends. The Carlins didn't stare at the Humans, as it was a common sight to see Humans in the Carlin villages. The two species got along together extraordinarily well. Martian Humans, on the other hand, were extremely rare on Vale and the Carlins did take notice of Saffiera, her golden-hued skin tones shining in the afternoon sunlight. They also took notice of Yeannah, even Thols would often visit the Carlin villages, but Yeannah was a Mimasian Thol and they were almost as rare as Martians.

Carlinish villages had roadways made of cobbled blue stone and on either side of the broad roads were dry-stone walls. One could almost mistake their surroundings as being in Yorkshire, in the north of England, back on the Earth. Of course, this was the Carlinish world of Vale and they were in the broad Masula Valley plains. Within the dry-stone walls were quite reasonably large plots of land, within which Carlin families would grow food produce and raise farm animals, like large hobby farms back on the Earth.

The houses within the plots of land were always in the centre of the plot. They were made of blue stone and timber. The walls were double thick stone and self-supporting. Kethera explained that timber was used for floor joists, the flooring itself and also for the roofing.

Most of the houses also had a stone basement and many houses had an upper level, where the bedrooms were all situated, although some houses simply sprawled. The roofs of the houses were covered in a thick layer of sod, upon which rich blue grass grew. Many goat-like creatures were standing on the roofs, grazing, using them like elevated pastures.

There were a few broad trees scattered here and there about the plots, mostly around the houses. The goat-like creatures could be seen to jump from soil-sodden roofs to branches in the trees and back again. They were agile like mountain goats and it was easy to see how they got onto the rooftops. The one thing that every plot of land and house had in common was groups of Carlin children, kits, playing outside of their homes. Some were even climbing the broad trees along with the weird goat thingies.

"This is so very different from how Thols live", Ariel noted.

"Yes. Very different", Yeannah replied, "This is all new to me as well. It kind of reminds me of Yorkshire back on Earth. My parents once stayed there for a couple of years before emigrating here. I think the locals thought we were weird and strange. Thols were so very rare in the north of England."

Aria glanced at the house roofs, "Those goat thingies look weird, kind of like they've been shaved", she muttered under her breath.

Kethera sighed but said nothing. Aria could be such a pain at times.

Kethera led the group along the winding cobblestone paths, her steps confident as they turned at various junctions and meandered through the heart of her village. The twisting streets and closely packed houses soon left the group disoriented, realising they would undoubtedly need Kethera's help to locate the school bus stop in the morning.

All except Yeannah, of course. With great leathery wings of creamy white that shimmered faintly in the soft evening light, she could easily soar above the village and find her way from the air. But for the others, the labyrinth of narrow paths and identical dry-stone walls felt endless, never-ending.

At last, Kethera stopped before an ordinary-looking, well-kept wooden gate set neatly into the dry-stone wall. She glanced back at the group with a satisfied smile.

"This must be Kethera's house", they all thought to themselves, as they exchanged knowing glances, relief washing over their faces.

"Micasa su casa", Kethera nodded, gesturing to the plot of land behind the wall.

True to form, Kethera's house was made of blue stone, two stories high and had those odd goat-like animals grazing on blue grass on the roof.

Kethera opened the gate and they entered her parent's property. Aria was staring at the goat-like creatures. There were eight of them on the roof in all, more were in the nearby trees. They superficially looked like goats, but they were definitely not goats. They were about the right size but had no hair and no fur at all. Their skin was a dullish grey colour and they had odd blue stripes. Aria almost giggled at that. They had long tails, almost as long as Kethera's, which they held up straight.

The pupils of their eyes were vertical slits and their irises were of a lavender colour. They had four eyes! They also had horns, but those were not overly long and they were quite straight. They even had a goatee, just like an Earth goat does, only they appeared to be flesh tendrils, they each had a great many flesh tendrils on their chins!

"Kethera, what are those goat thingy creatures?", Aria enquired.

Kethera replied flippantly, "They're just Gudongs and no, they don't look like goats, Aria. Your Earth goats just look like Gudongs!"

The eight Gudongs bleated at them as they approached.

"Kethera, they bleat just like goats", Aria noted.

"Argh, your Earth goats bleat like Gudongs, Aria!", Kethera replied.

In contrast to Yeannah's parents, no one greeted them at the front door of the house. In contrast to Yeannah's home, with its neat and tidy appearance, Kethera's home was chaotic and looked, well, lived in. It was easy to see why, when Kethera's nine siblings surged past in a lively stampede, their laughter echoing through the hall. Moving in age-defined clusters, the older triplets led the way, followed by three sets of twins of varying ages. Their nimble, padded feet barely made a sound as they disappeared out the front door.

One of the siblings, a younger boy, had turned around and smiled mischievously, then he turned back around to run and catch up with the others. They moved so fast and silently on the pads of their Carlinish feet. The girls continued further into the well-lit house and found Kethera's Mother, Kayala, in the kitchen. She was making a stew, the smell of which wafted throughout the house.

"Gudong stew?", Kethera asked with a smile on her face.

"Yes, but not for you. The stew is for our kits. For you, I made some pies", Kayala replied as the oven timer went off, "Kethera. Please take the pies out of the oven and place them on the table."

Kethera did as her Mother asked, placing the pies on the small kitchen table, as her Mother noted, "Your Father is in the garden", she smiled, "That Earth corn is ready for harvest."

The pies glistened with the faintest blue sheen under the kitchen lights, their crusts golden and slightly puffed. The aroma of the pies drew everyone's attention and the girls all breathed in deeply.

It was then that Kethera noticed a stack of steaming corn cobs sitting on a large plate on the kitchen bench, "Earth corn! It will be nice to try it. Do we have any butter?"

Kayala noted, "Yes, of course, Kethera. I milked the Gudongs myself this morning", she wiped the sweat from her brow with a small towel, "The butter is as fresh as can be."

Another pot was also on the stove, it appeared to contain something that looked like rice, but it had a distinct blue colouration to it.

Kethera noticed her friends looking at the pot, "That's our staple grain, masuli. We eat masuli with nearly every meal. It tastes kind of like Earth rice but it's sweeter and of course, it's blue. I'm sure you'll love it. That's also why the pies look a little bluish, the pastry is made with masuli grain."

Aria looked into the large pot of Gudong stew, "It smells delicious!", she exclaimed, then noted, "Hey, those look like carrots and potatoes", she added in surprise.

Kayala smiled, "Yes, little one, they are. We Carlins have been planting and trying lots of Earth foods. We are finding them quite delicious and easy to grow."

Kethera looked a little embarrassed, "Mum, this is Aria, Ariel, Saffiera and Yeannah."

"It's always nice to meet Kethera's friends", Kayala remarked, then looked at Saffiera with her golden-hued skin, "You're a Martian, Saffiera?", she asked rhetorically, "Very few Martians on Vale."

Saffiera replied telepathically, agreeing, *"Yes, there are only a few Martian families on Vale."*

Kayala replied, "Oh! Your thoughts went straight into my mind. How strange that felt."

"I'm sorry, I didn't mean to startle you", Saffiera apologised.

"No need to apologise, little one", Kayala replied, then looked curiously at Yeannah, "Hmm, Yeannah, you're one of the new ones from the Sol system, aren't you?"

"Yes, my people are from Mimas in the Sol system", Yeannah confirmed.

"So, Mum, what kind of pies did you make?", Kethera asked, noting, "Saffiera and Yeannah are both vegetarians."

"Yes, I am aware of that, little one", Kayala replied, pointing to the pies, "Those six pies with the X on them are many mushroom pies. All of the others are Gudong pies."

Yeannah curiously asked, "Many mushroom pies?"

"A selection of our finest mushrooms, little one. All different. All subtly flavoursome", Kayala replied, noting, "Kethera's Father grows them in a shed at the back of our plot."

Kethera held Yeannah's arm gently, "My Mother made them, especially for you guys."

Aria looked a little sad, "Will there be enough for me to try one?"

Yeannah smiled, looking at Aria, "I'll share one of mine with you, Aria. You won't miss out."

Kayala looked approvingly at Yeannah, understanding that Indigenous Thols were not so generous and that Mimasian Thols appeared to be somewhat different. Yeannah was, of course, the first Mimasian Thol she had ever met.

Kethera's siblings charged back through the house, their energy charging the air. They flowed into the dining room, taking their seats with practised ease, their excited chatter muffled only by the rapid movement of their Carlinish feet. The chaos seemed to settle into a strange harmony as they waited, their anticipation palpable. There was only one seat left and ordinarily, it would have been Kethera's.

Kethera's Father, Krylor, walked into the kitchen, "I thought I'd better chase our kits back in. I could smell your wonderful cooking clear across the plot."

Kayala introduced the girls, "Krylor, these are Kethera's school friends, Aria, Ariel, Saffiera and Yeannah", she got Aria and Ariel wrong way around, but they were identical twins and didn't mind.

"Pleasure to meet you girls", Krylor greeted, then noted, "I've seen lots of Humans around of late, not so much Martians and Mimasian Thols though."

Saffiera replied telepathically, *"My people and Yeannah's people are very few and far between on Vale, Sir. Not very many of us here at all."*

"Whoa! Isn't that the strangest?", Krylor replied, almost in disbelief, "Your words went straight into my head. What they say about Martians appears to be true."

"Yes, Sir, we Martians are all non-verbal telepaths", Saffiera confirmed.

Krylor took in Saffiera's reply and then looked to Yeannah, "Oh my, Mimasian Thols look so much like our native version, don't they? It is remarkable."

Yeannah smiled, she had been compared to the Indigenous Thols more times than she could remember, "Yes, Sir. We do look very much alike, however, we are very different species."

"So I have heard", Krylor noted.

Kayala sniffed Krylor, "Argh. Of you go and wash, husband. You smell like the fields", she sniffed him again, "and something else", then she turned to Kethera, "My, little one, please give me a hand to feed our kits."

"Please wait here", Kethera requested of her friends.

Together, Kayala and Kethera took some large bowls of masuli and corn into the dining room and placed them on the table for Kethera's siblings to eat.

"Uh uh uh. Not yet", Kayala told them, "You wait until we're finished or you won't get any stew."

The Kethera helped her Mother place large bowls of Gudong Stew on the table.

Once they were finished Kayala told them, "Okay, little ones. Dig in and try not to make a mess!"

Krylor returned from his washing up and addressed the girls, "Normally we Carlins feed our kits in the one big room. We ourselves tend to eat here in the kitchen. So that does not leave us a lot of room", he explained.

"Kethera, little one. Please put the food on some trays and take it upstairs to the attic room. You may all eat your supper up there. We have set up some ground mats for you all to sleep on and you have access to the big screen and the network", Kayala instructed.

Kethera thanked her Mother before placing their food on trays and showing her friends upstairs to the attic room, "Trust me", she told them,

"Eating with my siblings would have been pure chaos."

The attic room was an enormous space at the top of the house, above the second story. Its roof was angled, yet still tall enough for them to stand comfortably. The girls looked around, noticing it had been cleaned up very recently. Five large, thick ground mats had been placed on the floor and a large screen was mounted onto the wall at the far end of the room. At the other end of the attic room was a large window that let in copious amounts of light. There was a tree beyond the window which blocked any further views. Kethera sat her sleeping bag down on a ground mat and the twins took up positions on either side of her.

Yeannah thought loudly enough that Saffiera would surely pick it up, *"Thick as thieves those three."*

Saffiera tried not to laugh and repeated, *"Yes, thick as thieves",* in reply.

They all began eating their supper. Kethera's Mum had been very thoughtful, eating pies while sitting on ground mats made things much easier.

"Gudong tastes just like a goat!", Aria commented, her face scrunched in surprise.

The flavour was sharp yet earthy, reminding her of the tanginess she'd tasted in goat meat, which had a similar gamey bite and the pies gravy accentuated the flavours perfectly.

Kethera sighed, she was determined to flip Aria's thinking, "No, Aria. Goats taste just like Gudong", she replied with a soft determination.

Saffiera and Yeannah, both noted how incredible the *"many"* mushroom pies tasted and both Aria and Ariel agreed when they tried some for themselves. The pies literally had many different kinds of mushrooms in them, each with its own unique flavour profile.

The girls all enjoyed the steamed masuli, which was sweeter than steamed rice from the Earth, it had a soft texture to it that made eating it so much more enjoyable. The light blue colour did not faze them at all. Kethera found the sweet taste of the buttered corn delightful as well, the taste of the Earth staple being entirely new to her.

Ariel remarked, "I would have loved to try that Gudong stew."

Kethera noted in reply, "Stew is too messy to be carrying up two flights of stairs, Ariel."

While they all finished off their supper, Yeannah switched on the attic's big screen and accessed the household network. The girls all took out their data tablets and linked up to the household's network hub. The Great Explosion, the Outward Interplanetary Expansion, came up on the screen and Yeannah quickly scrolled down to the section on Venus. Then they began their studies for the night.

10. The Venusians.

The Earth-Moon system has five Lagrangian points, four of which are stable enough to be considered useful. Similarly, the Earth-Sun system also has five Lagrangian points, with four of them being stable and useful. The same pattern applies to other planetary systems, including Venus and the Sun, which also have five Lagrangian points. Of these, four, L-One, L-Two, L-Four and L-Five, are stable enough to be considered useful.

The Earth with its volcanic eruptions, earthquakes, tsunamis and plate tectonics, along with its cyclones, hurricanes, tornadoes and lightning storms could be thought of as a death world. Even more so when you add in the predatory animals on land and at sea, as well as all of the bacteria and viruses that kill just as easily. Yet, Humanity survives regardless. The resilience of our species is remarkable.

If the Earth is a death world, then Venus, in comparison, is a hell world. The Venusian atmosphere is dense and thick, having a pressure ninety two times that of the Earth's. Its clouds are composed of sulphuric acid and its winds whip around the planet at a phenomenal three hundred and sixty kilometres per hour in the upper atmosphere.

Due to the dense Venusian atmosphere, the surface winds are sluggish, one to three kilometres per hour. Venus's surface temperature is so hot that it can melt lead at four hundred and sixty-five degrees Celsius.

Venus has numerous large volcanic structures, some of which are very similar to those on Earth. These include shield volcanoes, which are broad, gently sloping volcanoes built up by the eruption of low-viscosity lava, and lava plains that cover large areas of the planet. Some volcanic features are over one hundred kilometres in diameter. Venus has no plate tectonics as such, instead, it has smaller crustal converting cells, like mini-plates that drive its intense volcanism.

Nothing lives on Venus, at least nothing known to Humanity and Humans cannot colonise the planet as a result. Venus is our literal conception of hell! A world upon which we may never live.

The first Venusians looked upon Venus with trepidation. There was no way to colonise hell! Yet they found a way nonetheless. They first looked at their options and there weren't that many, but they had to start somewhere and that somewhere was the Venusian Lagrangian points. The first point that they looked at was Venusian Lagrangian point one, a mere one million kilometres from Venus in the direction of the Sun.

Once the decision had been made, the colonists sought financial backing and when their financiers saw their plans, they gave them a line of credit, knowing that they would make good profits in return. This was not just to see if colonising Venus could be done, but more importantly, the colonists had plans to capture and mine Venus crossing asteroids in the Venusian L-One orbital zone.

Old twin O'Neil-style colonies in Cis-Lunar L-Five were purchased and then refurbished. Venus, being far closer to the Sun, the cylindrical colonies needed many modifications. The colony cylinders required thinner strip windows, as the Sunlight was far stronger at Venusian L-One, likewise, the land surface areas could be widened accordingly. This gave the Venusians a greater land surface area for their crops and orchards.

The external strip mirrors that redirected sunlight through the strip windows could be significantly reduced in width as well. The mirrors for the northern and southern end caps needed to be reduced in size as well. There was little if any need for supplemental fission reactors, instead, there was a much greater need for heat radiators. Being far closer to the Sun, at point seven two AU, the radiation shielding was doubled. Twice the moncrete and astcrete were required for the colony shielding.

Then, when the first O'Neil-style colony was ready, with its twin cylinders, the Venusian colonists contracted Stuart Dumas's company, Cis-Lunar Haulage, to haul the two massive cylinders into broad halo orbits of Venusian L-One. A halo orbit enables the colony to circle around the gravitational sweet spot of Venusian L-One, maintaining a stable position with minimal energy expenditure. There, the two cylinders were linked together with guy wires and transport tubes, completing the first Venusian colony, with a capacity above twenty thousand colonists.

This was soon followed by another colony and then another and before long, there were half a dozen O'Neil-style colonies in the Venusian L-One region. These six colonies combined could house well over one hundred and twenty thousand colonists, the new Venusians.

Once this was completed, the colonists hired Stuart Dumas's Cis-Lunar Haulage once more to transport mining stations, ore processing stations, and manufacturing hubs into the Venusian L-One region. These were placed in halo orbits close to the colony cylinders, but in tighter paths nearer the gravitational sweet spot.

Stuart Dumas quickly grasped the colonist's ambitions and helped them acquire specialised space tugs designed to lock onto asteroids and carefully tow them to Venusian L-One. Here, the asteroids could be mined for their wealth of rare and valuable metals, trapped volatile gases, and the all-important water essential for sustaining life and industry.

When the Venusian mining began at the heart of the Venusian L-One gravitational zone, the Venusian colonies were finally becoming profitable. Their company, Venusian Mining Incorporated, was off the ground and running fast. Their financiers were ecstatic, not only were the associated loans being repaid, but they had heavily invested in what become known as the Asteroidal Commodities Market. Better yet, they had also negotiated a small but significant percentage of the profits from the Venusian Mining operations.

This, of course, coincided with another startup, who actually got his idea from the Venusians.

Stuart Dumas had seen what the Venusians had planned and he thought to himself, "I can do better than that", which of course he did.

The Venusians had developed one Mining operation at the Venusian L-One Lagrangian point. Stuart Dumas had set his mind to and concentrated his efforts on the Earth's L-Four and L-Five Lagrangian points. This doubled the size of the Venusian mining operations but in the Earth's orbital zone, within the Earth's jurisdiction.

Stuart Dumas made significant improvements to the Venusian methods. Stuart Dumas's Earth Trojan Mining Corporation, instead of working on one asteroid at a time, focused initially on building up asteroidal conglomerated masses by hauling and accumulating multiple asteroids at each of the Earth's Trojan points. Once a conglomerate mass had reached the target of twenty-five asteroids, mining operations would commence, extracting valuable metals and resources

This was also in the interests of both the Earth government and the Cis-Lunar government, in that they wanted the most dangerous Earth-crossing asteroids dealt with. Stuart provided a method of both achieving their aims and his at the same time.

This did have an initial detrimental effect on the Asteroidal Commodities Market, the stocks of which began to plummet. With no fewer than three asteroid mining operations coming online almost one after the other, there was suddenly a glut, an oversupply of valuable and rare earth metals in the marketplace. This caused their values to plummet almost overnight as a result.

To combat this crash in the value of stocks, the Earth's government stepped up the production of spacecraft and space exploration in general. Metals such as iron, platinum, tungsten, copper, aluminium, chromium, lithium, titanium and rare earth elements were crucial to spacecraft production.

The Cis-Lunar government, on the other hand, stepped up the production of colonies in the Moon's L-Five Lagrangian zone. The very same elements used in spacecraft production were also crucial in colony production and far larger quantities were required. Both of these ideas had been lobbied by Stuart Dumas, who was instrumental in a great many initiatives of the day.

This led to the re-balancing of the supply and demand equation and the value of asteroidal metals and rare earth elements began to rise once more. The Asteroidal Commodities Market quickly regained its losses and the value of Asteroidal Commodities stocks rose to new heights as a result. Everybody had profited in the end, after the market turmoil had subsided.

Still, Stuart Dumas had seen the results of an oversupply in the Asteroidal Commodities Market and the devastation caused by it. Stuart decided it was better to moderate the supply of many of these asteroidal metals and rare earth elements. His answer was to build massive warehouses in space, where the excess asteroidal metals and rare earth elements could be stored long-term.

Stuart Dumas had theses massive space warehouses built initial in Earth's L-Four and L-Five zones and also in the Moon's L-four zone in Cis-Lunar space. Stuart's company, Astro Economics, was placed in charge of these warehouses.

That way, the oversupply could be controlled and managed, stabilising the markets and their stocks. This was extremely expensive for his business, as his companies had to bear the cost of warehousing and storage, yet this was far better than flooding the market and causing everything to crash and burn. It was far better for everyone to win than for everything to burn down.

With the Asteroidal Commodities Market stable and a constant stream of credits flowing into everyone's coffers, be it the Venusian Mining Corporation or Stuart Dumas's Earth Trojan Mining Corporation, the Venusians embarked on another venture, albeit a much smaller one. They looked at the Venusian L-Two Lagrangian point, which was one million kilometres from Venus, on the side away from the Sun.

That stable gravitational point was quite literally in the shadow of Venus itself. In this zone, the Venusians set up research stations, massive space telescopes and a surveillance network. They even set up a single-cylinder O'Neil-style colony, as a University, albeit one powered by no fewer than five fission reactors. It was, of course, dark in the shadow of Venus after all.

The Venusians could never hope to colonise the hell world that was Venus itself, but its stable orbital zones offered them the heavens of an opportunity.

"These mats are really comfortable, Kethera. I've never seen anything quite like these before", Ariel remarked, lounging comfortably while gazing at a glowing screen.

"Carlins don't use beds, Ariel. We all sleep on ground mats", Kethera replied with a casual shrug.

"No beds?", Aria's voice carried a tone of disbelief.

Kethera paused thoughtfully, her ears tilting slightly forward, "We Carlins only need three bedrooms", she explained, "One for our parents and one each for the boy kits and the girl kits. Most of the floor is covered in ground mats and we all just snuggle together with our blankets."

"So, just like one big bed on the floor?", Aria persisted, intrigued.

Kethera's whiskers twitched upward in amusement, "Yes, just like one big bed on the floor", she laughed, the sound light and infectious.

Meanwhile, Saffiera found herself drawn to the attic window. The twilight hues painted the village beyond and shadows danced between the trees. She squinted, spotting a flicker of movement, a small figure leaping from one branch to another. For a moment, she thought it was a Gudong but quickly realised it was far too small.

"Are there other animals out there in the trees, Kethera?", Saffiera's question came through telepathically, her tone laced with curiosity.

"Yes. Why?", Kethera's reply was sharp with interest.

"I saw something small jump through the branches of that tree", Saffiera explained, her gaze fixed on the canopy.

"Small? Jumped? Ah, that was a Boobook", Kethera said, her tone shifting to a matter-of-fact calm. "There are a quite few living in the trees."

"A Boobook?", Aria echoed, leaning closer to the window with wide eyes.

"They kind of resemble a hairless Earth Monkey with a long tail", Kethera explained, her whiskers twitching contemplatively, "or more correctly, your Earth Monkeys resemble our Boobooks."

While the group crowded around the window, peering into the thickening dusk for a glimpse of these curious creatures, Kethera assured them, "Boobooks are completely harmless. At this time of year, they're very quiet. You should hear them during mating season. Their mating sounds are enough to make anyone blush!"

As they watched, something else darted across their view. It moved with startling speed, its leathery wings slicing through the air with ease. They all gasped in unison.

Kethera remarked nonchalantly, "That was a Thrixan. They start to stir around dusk. There are a lot of Thrixan in the village. They roost in our trees. We catch them in nets and they are quite tasty."

Vale's primary star, Cathol, a yellow G-type dwarf star slightly smaller than the Sun, had already set, while Vale's secondary Sun, Cythol, an orange K-type dwarf star, remained well above the horizon. It appeared small but was nonetheless clearly visible. Cythol's feeble light cast an eerie orange hue over the garden scene beyond the attic window. Vale's large Moon, Luns, cast a silvery light, giving the scene an otherworldly quality. Though they were accustomed to the night sky on Vale, it seemed far more alien when seen through Kethera's attic window, with the exotic trees and alien creatures.

Yeannah's wings rustled softly as she added, "You can find them in the Jula Jula forests as well. We Thols call them Zrrakil. The Indigenous Thols like to eat them as well."

"Wait, Yeannah. I thought Thols were vegetarians?", Ariel asked, her brows furrowing in confusion.

"Mimasian Thols are", Yeannah clarified, "but Indigenous Thols aren't. They eat what we eat, as well as insects, bugs and small animals like Zrrakil. They are more far more primal."

"Wow! I had no idea. Your two species really are different", Ariel commented as she leaned back.

A curious Aria asked, "What does a Thrixan taste like?", as she reached for another Gudong pie.

"I have heard that your Earth Chickens taste just like Thrixan", Kethera replied with a broad smile.

"Shouldn't that be the other way around? You know, Thrixan tastes like Chicken", Aria remarked.

"No. I believe I had it right the first time", Kethera smiled back, her ears focused on Aria and her tail swishing from side to side in playful satisfaction.

Aria then remarked with a broad Cheshire grin, "It kind of looked like a bald flying fox."

Kethera flipped Aria's observation, "Your flying foxes look like hairy Thrixan", she stated smugly.

Ariel rolled her eyes as she enquired, "Are there any Harricks in the village?"

"There are Harricks everywhere, so there are probably some in the village", Kethera replied, noting, "We just never see them. Harricks prefer to remain hidden."

"Then how do you know that they're there?", Ariel asked.

"Poo", Aria replied loudly, remembering her experience in the Jula Jula forest, accidentally picking one up, then explained, "Harrick poo. The Carlins would see their droppings."

Kethera confirmed, "Yes. We do see what they leave behind."

The attic grew quieter as the group reflected, their thoughts filled with the strange and vibrant life that surrounded them in Kethera's world.

Kayala entered the room with a tray, upon which were five glasses and a large jug of Gudong milk, infused with a flavour extracted from masuli grain. A drink that was both sweet, milky and refreshing. The closest analog from the Earth might have been goat's milk mixed with a touch of maple syrup. Kayala placed the tray down on a small, squat table.

"I am so sorry, little ones. I forgot to bring up something for you to drink. You must be terribly thirsty", Kethera's Mother apologised, her whiskers twitching accordingly, her ears held back emphasising her apologetic tone.

"That's fine, Mother. I could have come down to collect the drinks myself", Kethera replied.

"Saffiera, Yeannah, are you both able to drink Gudong milk?", Kayala asked.

Yeannah nodded, "Yes, milk, cheese, yoghurt, even ice cream, especially ice cream. All dairy products are fine."

Saffiera agreed telepathically, *"Yes, the same for me. I can eat dairy products as well."*

Aria poured herself a glass, noticing a slight blue tinge to its colour, an effect from the masuli grain used in the infusion and tried it, "Oh my, it's sweet and milky! Not like any milk I've ever tasted before!", there was no comparison to Earth goats and that made Kethera smile.

Kethera picked up her data tablet and opened up the picture that Saffiera had taken of her and the twins, sleeping at Yeannah's tree house the previous night. During the day at school, Saffiera had shared the picture with Kethera and the twins so that they all had copies. Kethera passed the data tablet to her Mother so that she could see the picture.

Kayala looked closely at the picture, which showed Kethera asleep in the middle, with the twins Aria and Ariel sleeping on either side of her, cuddling her tightly. The twins looked at each other with concern and trepidation.

Kayala's ears stood up, her whiskers twitched with excitement and her tail swished quickly from side to side, a broad smile appeared on her face and she looked directly at the twins, "You all slept like Carlin kits last night!", she exclaimed, true joy on her face.

A look of relief came over the twin's faces.

Saffiera looked around at Yeannah, silently transmitting, *"What is it with Carlins and Humans?"*, with a truly baffled look on her face.

Yeannah looked back and simply shrugged, thinking back, *"Beats me, I have no idea."*

"I should adopt you two kits as my own and then you can sleep over every night!", Kayala pronounced as she smiled at the twins, her ears focused forward and her whiskers twitching.

Kayala handed the data tablet back to Kethera and whispered with excitement, "Send me a copy, Kethera. I can't wait to show your Father. He will be so excited!", then she left the attic and rushed downstairs.

Saffiera looked at the twins, pondering why Carlins and Earth Humans got on so well, then she turned back to Yeannah, *"My Mother did try to explain it to me once. You know, why Earth Humans get the reactions they do. She said, there are so few Martians here and that when I'm older, I'll probably see Earth boys differently. Then I'll understand."*

Yeannah thought for a moment then realised what Saffiera's Mother had meant, she leaned in closer to Saffiera and whispered in her ear, "Few Martians, many Earthlings. You might end up marrying an Earthling and having hybrid children."

"Yes. My Mother says hybrid children are delightful. They do take after their Mother and they are always telepathic, but they are just so different", Saffiera replied, with an unconvincing smile.

"You never know, Saffiera. You might actually find a nice Earth boy that you really like", Yeannah whispered, trying to reassure her.

Saffiera smiled back, but did not feel reassured, here on Homwol, there were still so few Martians and so many more Earth Humans and Saffiera could not see what the future had in store for her.

Saffiera looked at Kethera curiously, a Carlin who had an Earth-Human boy on her mind.

The girls all poured themselves glasses of Gudong milk and after trying it, they all agreed it was unique. Not even Kethera could tell them of an analog, Earthen or Vale, although she did mention that Gudong milk was lactose-free.

At that comment, Aria had noted, "Well, that makes for a fart-free night!", which elicited giggles and laughter from her friends.

"Kethera, what did your Mum mean when she said, we all slept like Carlin kits last night?", Ariel enquired with true curiosity.

Kethera thought for a moment before replying, "Hmm, my Mother meant that we all slept like Sisters, the way Carlin Sisters sleep. All in the same room and cuddled together on the one big mat."

Yeannah interrupted abruptly, wanting to steer them all back to their studies, "So which of you has been taking down notes?"

Saffiera replied, *"Who do you think?"*, it was usually Saffiera that took down all the notes.

"Why would we bother? This Venus stuff is like, all economics, not even history", Aria complained.

Yeannah rolled her eyes and replied, "Aria. History does include economics. We need to cover that as well", then she noted, "At least Saffiera is taking notes."

Saffiera mock saluted the others and telepathically replied, *"Saffiera, Notetaker. That's me!"*

Their Gudong and Mushroom pies eaten, their masuli-infused Gudong milk drunk, the girls busied themselves with the task of studying once more.

11. The Venusian Libration Points.

Beyond the planet Venus and two colonised Lagrangian points L-One and L-Two, there were two more useful Lagrangian points, L-Four and L-Five. The Venusian leading and trailing Trojan points, sixty degrees ahead and sixty degrees behind Venus in its orbit around the Sun, are the two most stable of the Venusian Lagrangian points. Two perfect orbital locations in which to accumulate asteroidal masses for mining purposes.

No sooner than Stuart Dumas had his latest company, Earth Trojan Mining Corporation, up and running in the Earth's Trojan Points, he eyed the Venusian Trojan points, thinking to himself, *"I can repeat the process in the Venusian Trojan points."*

The Venusian colonies were relatively new and were run by a Governor and their Venusian Colonial Council. They would, at some point in time, develop their own constitution and democratic government, but that was far off in the future. The Venusians did have representatives in Cis-Lunar L-Five and that is where Stuart Dumas went first.

Stuart was disappointed, the Venusian officials in Cis-Lunar L-Five had no real authority, they were only there to pass on information and decisions made by the Venusian Governor and Council. Those officials recommended that Stuart travel to the colony cylinder of Venus Central Command, from which the Venusian colonies were run. Venus Central was in the midst of the Venusian L-One Lagrangian point, which posed a major logistical challenge for Stuart Dumas.

Stuart had stressed the urgency of getting a decision on the matter, however, the Venusian officials had told him, "It was well beyond the scope of their job positions and that they were not authorised to make decisions of such magnitude."

Stuart had replied to them, "Then why are you even here?", a rhetorical question.

The Venusian officials didn't give Stuart a good answer, apparently, their job was simply to issue passports and visas and authorise shipping manifests, things of that nature. They repeated their stance and showed a complete indifference without addressing any of Stuart's concerns. They remained impassive, only repeating their scripted responses from which they did not deviate. With mounting irritation, Stuart walked off, determined to cut through this bureaucratic red tape on his own terms.

There was a cycler transport system in which interplanetary transports and liners continuously travelled between Cis-Lunar L-Five and Venusian L-One in what was known as a cycler orbit. This allowed flybys of both Earth and Venus without continuous propulsion. It was a highly efficient system. This *"Venus Cycler"* was run by a private corporation called the Venus Orbital Transfer Line Ltd.

Stuart Dumas sighed deeply and frowned, the cycler had a twelve-week travel time and that was for either leg of the journey. Six months for a return trip! The Venus Cycler was slow, but it was also highly energy efficient and far cheaper for the average citizen, at least in economy class. The system did have a business class and a first class, which was more akin to luxury travel. However, for Stuart Dumas's purposes, it was far too slow. Stuart Dumas did not like to waste time.

Stuart Dumas contacted another of his companies, Cis-Lunar Haulage. It would be expensive to take one of his space tugs out of company operations, especially just to use it as a taxi to fly to the Venusian L-One colony of Venus Central Command, but it would be quick. A flight to Venusian L-One space would take around six weeks. It would not be a comfortable trip, however, Stuart was used to space tugs as he used to pilot them. There was also one added bonus if he was successful, then Stuart would already have one of his space tugs in Venusian orbit to start work immediately. Of course, he would need to call in at least another nine space tugs to get the process up and running.

"Tegan. I need a visa to travel to the Venusian colonies. Please organise that for me", Stuart Dumas instructed his personal assistant as he walked into the foyer of his office.

"Yes, Sir. I'll get on it straight away", his personal assistant replied.

"Excellent, Tegan. Contact Cis-Lunar Haulage. I'm going to use one of their space tugs as my ride", Stuart advised, noting, "Let them know I'm taking the big one, Chugga. Let them also know that if all goes well, in six to eight weeks, I'll be needing another nine more. The biggest we have."

"Okay, Sir. I am noting that down. Is there anything else you require?", Tegan asked as she noted down Stuart's instructions in short-hand.

"Chugga's head pilot. Find out from him the flight time from Cis-Lunar L-Five to Venusian L-One, Venus Central colony. Then make arrangements for me to meet with the Venusian Governor three days later", Stuart Dumas instructed, then he touched his chin thoughtfully, noting, "Take into account any lead time for an expedited Venusian visa."

"Yes, Mr Dumas. That is a good idea, it wouldn't do to travel without the correct stamp in your passport", Tegan replied.

"Quite", Stuart agreed in reply, then he noted, "You'll be dealing with those feckless retches in the Venusian Consulate. Unpleasant bureaucrats, all of them. Remember to smile a lot and lay on the charm."

"Yes, Mr Dumas. I will certainly do so", his personal assistant replied, then commented, "Mr Dumas, Sir. I took the liberty of organising some modelling performed on the current Venusian colonial setup. Some interesting issues have cropped up. I'll provide you with the details when I have your passport stamped and ready, Sir. I am certain you will find it useful."

"Yes, thank you, Tegan. Every little bit helps", Stuart replied, then he opened the door of his office and walked in, thinking to himself that it had been a long time since he'd flown Chugga, the largest space tug in his fleet. Perhaps Chugga's lead pilot would allow him some flight time along the way. He could always ask.

Seven weeks later, Stuart Dumas was at the Venus Central Command colony in the Venusian L-One Lagrangian point. Venus Central was unlike the other O'Neil-style colonies in the L-One orbital zone, which were all twin-cylinder colonies. Instead, Venus Central was a single-cylinder colony of immense size. It was quite underpopulated at present but did have the capacity to house two hundred and fifty thousand colonists. Little did Stuart Dumas realise that Venus Central would just be the first of many colonies to bear that name. Several centuries later, its namesake colony would be one of the mega colonies, with up to fifty times its capacity.

Stuart had enjoyed his time flying from Cis-Lunar space to Venus Central. His space tug, Chugga, was captained by one, Jabari Mwangi, a tall, dark man of Kenyan birth. Jabari was also Chugga's highly qualified head pilot. When Stuart requested some flight time during their trip to Venus Central, Jabari checked Stuart's current pilot status and was pleased to see all of Stuart's accreditations. Next thing Stuart Dumas knew, he had been scheduled as a regular a pilot on the space tug, Chugga. When Jabari passed the schedule to Stuart, he read it with surprise, then nodded in agreement.

"Thank you, Jabari. Chugga is a working vessel and I'm more than happy to pull my weight", Stuart told him with a grateful smile on his face, thinking to himself, *"I do need to clock up the flight time."*

"No. Thank you, Sir", Jabari replied, explaining, "It is always good to have an extra, qualified pilot on board. It makes for less stressful pilot flight schedules."

"Yes, very true, but thank you again anyway, Jabari", Stuart Dumas replied.

Stuart Dumas's personal assistant, Tegan, had performed her job well and his meeting with the Venusian Governor was just two days away. That time flew quickly by and Stuart was soon sitting in the Governor's conference room. The conference table was big and square. Only five chairs had been set up, three at one end, one at Stuart's end in which he sat waiting patiently and a single chair off to Stuart's right. All the remaining chairs appeared to have been stacked along one wall.

On the table, in front of the single chair to the right, there was a keyboard. Along the top of the keyboard was a screen that was little more than a strip, three inches wide. The name plaque in front of the seat read Gaylene Arkroyal, Stenographer. At the other end of the table, the name plaques read from left to right, Councillor Jewel Barton, Governor George Cartwright and Councillor Ethan Buckminster. Stuart picked up his name plaque, it read, "Stuart Dumas, CEO Earth Trojan Mining.

Stuart smiled, thinking to himself, *"Professional with a personal touch."*

Stuart stood up as the others entered the conference room from a door behind their seats. They greeted Stuart and quickly took their seats. Gaylene, the stenographer, began typing the second the discussions began.

"Now, Mr Dumas. You requested this meeting and that fact that you've come all the way from Cis-Lunar L-Five, in your own ship no less, does indicate to us that you consider this both important and urgent", Councillor Barton commented.

"From a business perspective, yes, Councillor Barton", Stuart replied, as he placed his suitcase on the table and extracted two folios, he stood up, walked around the table and passed them to the Councillor before returning to his seat.

Upon sitting down, Stuart explained, "The first, red folio contains economic predictions based on the current Venusian economy, governmental policy direction and the colony's financial situation. The second, green folio is my detailed proposal for opening up the Venusian Trojan Points for mining operations, whilst at the same time mitigating any possible danger from Venus crossing asteroids with untoward orbital parameters."

Councillor Barton looked at Governor Cartwright and Councillor Buckminster. They returned her look and then they all looked back at Stuart.

Governor Cartwright remarked, "That is quite a lot to take in, Mr Dumas."

"I expected it would be Governor", Stuart Dumas agreed, then he cut to the chase, "As my people have explained it to me, your colony has over-leveraged your mining operations. You have multi-trillion credit loans all predicated on the Venusian L-One mining operations and that is highly problematic."

"How so, Mr Dumas?", Councillor Buckminster enquired.

"Well, Councillor, this zone we are in, Venus Lagrangian point one, just happens to be your primary colonisation zone", Stuart noted in reply, explaining, "Sure you have Venus L-Two, however, that's really only a special purpose zone in Venus's shadow. Here, right here, in Venus L-One, is where you are building all of your colonies. Basically, your housing infrastructure!"

Councillor Buckminster looked confused, "Yes, Mr Dumas, but I'm still not seeing the problem."

Stuart replied as he took a small holographic projector out of his suitcase and placed it on the table in front of him, "Our projections are that you will run out of ore from that asteroid you have in Venus L-One's gravitational sweet spot in just under ten years."

Councillor Barton quickly replied, "We are aware of that, Mr Dumas and we have plans to drag another asteroid into that sweet spot before the ore runs out."

Stuart turned on the holographic projector and it displayed a simulation of the Venusian L-One orbital zone. There was a small asteroid in the zone's gravitational sweet spot. That was surrounded by ore processing stations and further out there were manufacturing stations. Even further out, there were two dozen O'Neil-style colonies with twin cylinders and one rather large single-cylinder colony, Venus Central Command. The colonies all orbited in clearly defined and stable halo orbits around Venus L-One's sweet spot.

Governor Cartwright remarked, "Venus L-One. I do recognise our colonies, Mr Dumas."

"Yes, Governor", Stuart agreed, "Now watch the simulation as we move in a new asteroid."

The simulation showed an asteroid being moved into the zone, slowly approaching the sweet spot. As the asteroid approached, the halo orbits of the colonies began to change. The closer the asteroid came, the more chaotic the colony orbits became, eventually two of the Venusian colonies twin cylinder collided. The councillors all watched in horror, even the stenographer, Gaylene, had stopped typing. All eyes turned to Stuart Dumas.

"This can't be right!", Governor Cartwright shouted in abject disbelief, thinking to himself, *"No, this is simply not possible. Not possible!"*

Stuart rubbed his chin then replied, "Governor. My people have run thousands of simulations. Some are worse than others, but they all end in chaos and disaster. The problem is that this gravitational zone is both your primary colonisation zone and your operational mining zone. The result was predictable."

Councillor Barton stated the obvious with serious concern evident on her face, "If this is true, then when the ore runs out, we won't be able to harness a new asteroid. All of our loans! The banks will foreclose! The colony will go bankrupt!"

"It is true, Councillor Barton, hence the second folio. Feel free to have your experts review the first folio. I'll even leave you the simulations", Stuart Dumas calmly advised, then added with confidence, "Every problem has a solution and I am confident that we can resolve this one."

An equally concerned Gaylene Arkroyal typed away at her keyboard, her face just as shocked as the councillors. Gaylene Arkroyal had never typed minutes for a meeting this tense or critical.

"And this second folio? It contains your solution?", Governor Cartwright questioned.

"Yes, Governor, indeed it does", Stuart Dumas replied with confidence.

Stuart Dumas stood up and began to explain his plan, first stating the cause of the current problem, "Governor, Councillors, Miss Arkroyal. This problem started at the very beginning. Your engineers moved a single asteroid into Venus L-One's sweet spot, intending to move in another when the original asteroid was depleted and so on. Now, that was not a bad plan if this gravitational zone was simply a mining zone, however, it has become your primary colonisation zone as well."

Governor Cartwright was nodding in agreement, "I can see that now", he admitted.

"And your solution, Mr Dumas?", Councillor Buckminster enquired.

"We move all of the mining operations to the two Venus Trojan points, L-Four and L-Five. They are far more stable than L-One as well.", Stuart Dumas stated boldly.

Councillor Barton was shaking her head, "No. No. No, Mr Dumas. We are already severely over-leveraged. The banks would never loan us the money and once word gets out about our current predicament. Well things do not bode well. The banks will almost certainly foreclose."

"Yes", Councillor Buckminster agreed, "We can all expect to be spilt out at the next election. The electorate will be baying for blood!"

Councillor Barton scoffed, "Really! That's your concern, Ethan! Personally, I'm thinking of immediate bank foreclosures. Imagine our colonies being taken over by banking bean counters!"

Governor Cartwright stepped in, "Calm down Jewel, Ethan, I have a feeling that Mr Dumas has covered those bases."

"Indeed I have, Governor. Venus Central can't take on any more debt, but I can. I'm going to, or more correctly, my companies are going to finance the whole shebang", Stuart informed them.

"Very generous of you, Mr Dumas. Obviously, you will make enormous profits. How do the Venusian colonies factor in with your plans?"

All through the discussion, Gaylene continued to type as the drama unfolded.

"Governor, I will set up a new company, Venusian Trojan Mining Ltd. It will be run along the same lines as the Earth Trojan Mining Corporation. The company will have the mining rights to both the leading and trailing Venusian

Trojan points and the Venusian colonies will get twenty percent off of the top. I will, of course, finance the entire operation. It is a good deal", Stuart Dumas explained.

Governor Cartwright leant back in his chair, "How will you avoid falling into the same trap that we have here in Venus L-One?"

"Well, that is actually quite easy, Governor. I'll do the same thing that we did with the Earth's Trojan points", Stuart replied.

"And that was exactly?", Governor Cartwright asked, wanting more details.

"Well, Governor. We'll target fifty Venus-crossing asteroids, ones with dangerous orbits", Stuart began, pausing ever so slightly before continuing, "The two largest are hauled into the Venusian Trojan Point's gravitational sweet spots. Then we haul in the remaining asteroids and build up a conglomerated asteroidal mass for mining purposes at both points. So, twenty five asteroids at each sweet spot."

Councillor Barton shook her head, "Why the hell didn't we do that?", she asked rhetorically, "If we'd done that, we would not be in this predicament."

The Governor remarked as a side note, "You've just answered my next question, Mr Dumas. How this mitigates asteroid threats."

Stuart Dumas nodded, "Yes, Governor. The mitigation of asteroid threats is inherent in the process."

Councillor Buckminster enquired, "Won't we eventually run out of ore to mine? It will take longer, but we will run out?"

Stuart smiled, "Yes, Councillor, however, as the Venusian Trojan points will be designated mining zones, there won't be many colonies there. Only around six O'Neil-style twin cylinder colonies, for the mining personnel and their families."

Councillor Barton noted, "So, you'll be able to haul more asteroids into your conglomerated asteroidal masses, whereas we can't."

"Further mitigating the problem with dangerous asteroids", Governor Cartwright interjected.

"Yes", Stuart confirmed, informing them, "We've had mining operations up and running in the Earth's Trojan points almost as long as you've been operating in Venus L-One."

Councillor Buckminster questioned, "Where the fucking hell were you when we were setting up? We could have used someone like you with your foresight!"

Gaylene Arkroyal giggled under her breath as she took down more notes, the drama was exciting and almost intoxicating.

Governor Cartwright instructed her, "Gaylene, please delete Councillor Buckminster's profanity. It would not do to leave that on the record."

The stenographer did as she was asked but thought to herself, *"I will still remember it."*

"Well, Councillor Buckminster, I was kind of busy developing the Earth Trojan Mining Corporation's operations at the time", Stuart Dumas replied as he thought to himself, *"It was the Venusians who'd actually give me the idea for the Earth Trojan Mining Corporation and the Earth's Trojan Points in the first place."*

The meeting ended shortly thereafter.

Stuart Dumas stayed at the Venus Central colony for the next two weeks waiting for a decision from the Governor's office. The full Venusian Council of twenty five council members had held several combined meetings with the Governor's cabinet and their staff. The results of these meetings were never to be released to the general public. Only the Councillors, the Governor and his Cabinet, their staff and the meeting stenographer, Gaylene Arkroyal, would know the unvarnished truth.

Anything censored in the meeting minutes would eventually be fully covered in Gaylene Arkroyal's published memoirs, *"Venusians! The Arkroyal Files. What your Government tried to hide from you! By Gaylene Arkroyal"*, which became a best seller in Venusian space.

The Venusian's first combined meeting had been to discuss the findings of their experts concerning Stuart Dumas's report in his first red folio. The Venusian experts were all in agreement with the findings of Stuart Dumas's own people. Their simulations matched those that Stuart provided with little, if any, deviation. New asteroids could not be hauled into the Venusian L-One gravitational sweet spot.

What the council wanted to know was how they had not been aware of this situation and more importantly, who was responsible for such an egregious oversight. That meeting resulted in an official investigation. The Venusian Council and the Governor's office were all looking for someone to blame.

The Venusian's second combined meeting was about the financial ramifications of the situation that they found themselves in. If the Venusian Council and Governor's office ignored the situation, then the human effluent would definitely hit the spinning turbine. It would become an economic disaster, with the banks calling in their loans, the citizenry revolting against the current political leadership and finally, bankruptcy, resulting in a takeover by financial Insolvency Practitioners and Trustees.

Governance by Bean Counters as Councillor Barton had derogatorily called it. Doing nothing and ignoring the problem was not an option. Nothing was achieved in that meeting, with perhaps the exception of people pulling at their hair and banging on the conference room table. Gaylene Arkroyal was having great difficulty with her note-taking. Many of the Councillors and

Cabinet members had been quite animated and their language colourful. Several times, she marked expletives to be deleted. Gaylene would, of course, remember everything!

The Venusian's third combined meeting was the most productive. In this meeting, they discussed Stuart Dumas's second green folio and his proposal. There was a lot of talk about why Mr Dumas was able to foresee the problem and yet not a single person in the Venusian L-One zone had had the slightest clue. The Councillor's repetitive arguments revealed their frustration with the current predicament.

They all agreed that they were in financial dire straits and that Stuart Dumas's proposal was not only fair but the perfect solution. That Stuart Dumas was willing to finance the solution himself and still allow the Venusians a twenty percent cut of the profit pie was overly generous, considering their precarious financial position. A more ruthless businessman might have taken advantage of them.

Councillor Barton had even remarked, "I've gone through this proposal and the associated contract with a fine-toothed comb. I'm telling you, I can't find any loopholes that Mr Dumas could take advantage of. There's no fine print either. Based on what I've seen, the man is being incredibly honest and generous."

The Venusian's L-One mining operations would eventually come to a halt and the Trojan mining operations would simply take over and provide the raw materials required for future Venusian colonial expansion.

When the vote finally came after many hours, all of the Councillors raised their hands and they all replied with, *"Aye."*

Stuart Dumas was waiting patiently in his hotel room when the email came through. His proposal had been accepted and the contract he had provided with it, in the green folio, had been signed by all the councillor members and ratified by Governor Cartwright's own signature. Stuart Dumas smiled to himself, the deal was done and so he sent off a communique to his office in Cis-Lunar L-Five to begin the process of setting up mining operations in the Venusian Trojan Points. It had been a time-consuming process and yet, it had been worth it.

The news came over the video screen in a special new bulletin, *"Breaking news from the Venusian News Network, Camilla Ocarina reporting. Governor Cartwright has just announced a highly profitable deal with Asteroid mining magnate Stuart Dumas to open up mining operations in the Venusian Trojan Points. Mr Dumas's new company, Venusian Trojan Mining Ltd, will have exclusive mining rights within those two orbital zones. The rich rewards of this new mining venture are to be shared with the Venusian people and utilised for our future developments. For further news on this announcement, see our main news broadcast at six pm."*

Stuart Dumas watched the breaking news. He had low-balled the incompetent Venusian Government with just a twenty percent share of the overall profits, knowing they wouldn't notice the disparity. However, to ensure the Venusian people would actually see the benefits, Stuart quietly funnelled an additional ten percent through his non-profit organisation, Dumas Philanthropic.

There was no contractual obligation for this, but Stuart Dumas understood that the Venusian Government could not be trusted to act in the best interests of the Venusian people. His own organisation, however, could be trusted to put the money where it was needed most, into the hands of the Venusian people through humanitarian and socioeconomic projects.

The five schoolgirls all paused in their studies for a short while.

"How are the notes going, Saffiera?", Yeannah asked.

"Going quite well actually, Yeannah", Saffiera replied in her usual silent way.

"Argh! It's all economics! I hate economics!", Aria almost screamed.

"Aria, I did say before that history does include economics", Yeannah reminded her, as she looked at Ariel to impart some sanity into her twin.

Ariel acknowledged Yeannah's look with a nod, telling her twin, "Aria, when you read that section, did you even notice that the Venusian colonies almost went bankrupt?"

"Companies go bankrupt all the time, Ariel", Aria replied.

"Companies, yes, but not whole colonies. If the Venusian colonies had gone into bankruptcy, the whole colony could have failed", Aria tried to explain.

Saffiera chimed in tried as well, *"Imagine twenty five colonies being stripped of their assets by the receivers and then sold off as scrap."*

"What would happen to all of the colonists?", Aria asked.

"Eviction. They'd lose everything and somehow have to return to Cis-Lunar L-Five space or the Earth, with nothing", Ariel replied with a highly unlikely worse case scenario.

Aria said in reply, "I get it, Ariel, colonies are big but still, eviction? Surely something that big can't be allowed to just fail!"

"Imagine all those colonists losing their homes! Tens of thousands of them! That Venus Cycler of theirs would have been busy repatriating colonists for years. Wow! Bankruptcy's a bitch", Saffiera remarked uncharacteristically.

"No! The page mentioned something about governance by Insolvency Practitioners and Trustees", Aria protested.

"Seriously, Aria? That's literally their job! They wind up failed businesses", Ariel replied dryly.

"Yeah, maybe, but surely not failed colonies", Aria replied in disbelief.

Yeannah stepped in with, "It appears you were actually reading, or were you just skimming for the fun parts, Aria?"

"Fun parts! Yeannah! That was all doom and gloom with numbers!", Aria replied.

"The Venusians were actually very lucky", Yeannah remarked.

"How so?", Aria asked, eager to move away from the uncomfortable notion of economic collapse.

"If that mining magnate hadn't turned up, the Venusians might have tried to move another asteroid into their L-One gravitational mining sweet spot", Yeannah explained, her tone serious.

Kethera's ears picked up and her whiskers twitched, "Colonies in collision! Ooh, that's bad, very, very bad!", she exclaimed, her voice rising with alarm.

"Yeah, Kethera. Colonies in collision", Yeannah agreed, nodding grimly.

Aria suddenly realised what she had missed, had the mining magnate not turned up, his simulations would have come to pass and tens of thousands of people could have died, "Holy crap, that would have been disastrous. He saved them all with a business deal!"

Saffiera chimed in with, *"Fortunately, they were saved by a white knight, Aria!"*

Aria thought for a moment, Saffiera was right, the mining magnate, Stuart Dumas was the Venusian's white knight!

Saffiera asked something of Kethera, which she wasn't sure she should ask, so she directed her thoughts to Kethera in such a way that she would know it was more personal, *"Kethera. Carlin litters. How do they work? I mean, you were born as a litter of one, weren't you? If you don't mind, of course."*

Kethera concentrated and thought back as best she could, not being telepathic and all, *"I don't mind, Saffiera"*, then she remarked aloud, with a smile on her face with her whiskers twitching, "Saffiera just asked me about Carlin litters."

Yeannah took note, "I've always wondered about that myself, Kethera."

The twins, Aria and Ariel, both nodded in agreement, with Ariel asking, "Yeah, how's that work?"

Kethera explained, "The first litter has only one kit, the next few are twins, that's followed by triplets, then later quads and so on. The usual result is twenty or more kits in all."

"Your parents only have ten kits?", a very curious Aria questioned.

"Yes, Aria. I was talking about how things were before your people, Humans, came here. Carlin families were much bigger back then", Kethera replied, explaining as best she could.

Kethera frowned, her ears pressed back, her whiskers lowered and her tail stopped swishing, "Before Humans came here, nigh on sixty percent of Carlin kits died before even reaching adolescence and after having so many kits, Carlin Mothers often died quite young. The strain of so many births I believe", her voice was truly sorrowful.

"Oh, that's truly awful, Kethera. I had no idea", Aria replied.

"How did we Humans change things?", Aria's twin Ariel asked curiously.

"Your people provided us with better healthcare. We now have new medications, antibiotics and vaccines. Those help us greatly. The things that once killed the foundling kits no longer killed", Kethera replied, her tail was swishing once more as the mood of the conversion changed.

"And the Carlin Mothers?", Ariel enquired, more curious than ever.

Kethera smiled, it was a coy smile and she whispered loudly, "Contraception, of course!"

Ariel smiled and replied loudly, "Okay. So you have fewer litters and fewer kits."

Kethera frowned, her whisker twitched down once more, "The Humans say that even with ten kits per family, we'll quickly overpopulate Vale. They recommend we have less than four kits."

Saffiera commented in reply, *"That does make sense, Kethera. If your people continue to have ten kits per family, they'll need to do what the Earth Humans do and colonise the stars."*

Kethera was still frowning, "It is a topic of much discussion among Carlin kind."

Yeannah replied thoughtfully, "We Thols have the opposite problem. Both my people and the Indigenous. Too few children. The Earth Humans help us with that as well, they provide us with fertility medications."

Ariel was again curious, "Do they help, Yeannah?"

"Yes, they do", Yeannah replied, although her face was now quite pink, instead of its usual alabaster white, showing her embarrassment with the discussion.

Saffiera sent a thought directly to Yeannah, she had a revelation, *"This is why Carlins like Earth people so much. They feel indebted to them as a species and yet, the Earth Humans have never expected anything in return!"*

Yeannah blinked twice and her wings twitched slightly, Saffiera was right, the Human colonists never asked for anything in return for the aid they provided. They just helped out wherever possible!

"Hmm, I was thinking it might be pheromonal on the Human side, remember, Martians also find Earth Humans fascinating. Still, you could be onto something", Yeannah thought back to Saffiera.

Ariel inquired curiously, “Yeannah. When your people first came here, how did they discover that your two peoples are different species?”

“The Humans figured that one out. They'd been helping us Mimasian Thols for centuries”, Yeannah replied, then began to explain more fully, “When their fertility drugs failed to work on the Indigenous Thols, they wanted to know why. After all, what worked on one group of Thols should work on another. At least that is what they had thought.”

Aria quickly said, “So they investigated and discovered your people had entirely different genetics?”

Yeannah was surprised by Aria's interest, “Yes, Aria”, she confirmed, adding, “Your people discovered the genetic differences and designed new fertility drugs specifically for the Indigenous Thols.”

Ariel remarked, “That must have caused quite a stir!”

“It did. No one had expected my people and the Indigenous Thols to actually be completely different species. It took a while for all of Thol kind to wrap our heads around it”, Yeannah replied.

Yeannah, her cheeks flushed pink with embarrassment at the discussion of contraception and infertility, quickly redirected the conversation, “We really need to get back to our studies”, she said, her voice tinged with a mix of awkwardness and determination.

12. The Rise of the Sky Cities.

Councillor Jewel Barton found herself in Governor Cartwright's office, attempting to dust off a project that had been on the back burner for so long it had been almost completely forgotten.

"Seriously George, with the new Trojan mining zones coming online, we have more credits flowing in that we know what to do with. We're even making huge dents in our loans", the Councillor stated as she tossed the file onto the Governor's desk, it was labelled, *"The Venusian Sky Cities."*

"This damnable scheme again", the Governor replied as he picked up the file, asking, "Do you really think these Sky Cities are safe?"

"Our engineers certainly think so and besides, it will take some pressure off building new colonies in the Venusian L-One Lagrangian zone. They are twenty times more expensive", Jewel Barton replied.

The Governor flicked through the file, he had read it several times before in the past and quickly scanned it for anything new.

There wasn't, *"Same old, same old"*, he thought to himself, then something caught his eye, that he'd complained about previously, "Thermally Induced Thermodynamic Suspension, T.I.T.S", he blurted out in annoyance.

"Say what, George?", Jewel Barton enquired with a puzzled look on her face.

"It's an acronym, Jewel. Thermally Induced Thermodynamic Suspension, T.I.T.S. One of our engineers worked way too hard to make that acronym work", George Cartwright explained.

"What's a Thermally Induced Thermodynamic Suspension?", Jewel asked.

"They are the Gas Buoyancy Envelopes, GBEs. Those are the huge bags of gas that keep airships aloft", George informed her, adding, "Some idiot engineer got creative and renamed them to Thermally Induced Thermodynamic Suspension, T.I.T.S. Very funny! Ha-ha!", he said sarcastically, "How that short, fat little fucker got that report past the committee, I'll never know."

Councillor Barton looked at that page where the Gas Buoyancy Envelopes were depicted, she turned her head to the side, replying, "That's entirely beside the point George. Our engineers say it's safe and we have the credits, so we should at least make an attempt to build one Sky City as a prototype", Councillor Barton insisted, then noted, "Those Gas Buoyancy Envelopes do look kind of pendulous don't they?"

The Governor sighed at that remark and then offered, "I tell you what, Jewel, you have this document modified to remove any mention of that term, Thermally Induced Thermodynamic Suspension, T.I.T.S. and I'll free up the funding. The last thing we all need is having the very thing keeping Sky Cities aloft, called Tits! We'd all become a laughing stock!"

"Done!", Councillor Barton readily agreed, then she picked up the file to have it modified.

"And the plans and blueprints. Don't you forget those plans and blueprints? I don't want to see that acronym anywhere ever again", George Cartwright shouted as Councillor Jewel Barton left his office.

Much to Governor Cartwright's chagrin, not only did the acronym T.I.T.S. endure for centuries to come, but future generations of engineers would find increasingly creative ways to work it into official reports, monuments and documents. The engineers became exceedingly creative with its usage.

The original engineer who had coined the acronym went on to build his own space yacht, he christened it, *"The Titty McTitface",* and he gleefully registered it with the Venusian Department of Space Transport.

The bureaucrat who processed his registration form laughed as he read the name and remarked, *"That is seriously too funny. I can't possibly deny this one!"*

The Venusian Space Yacht, Titty McTitface, quickly gained notoriety and its name was emblazoned across the news networks and news feeds, as a shining example of bureaucratic oversight and unchecked engineering humour.

There was even a romantic ballad written about the Venusian Sky Cities called, "Hanging on TITS" that topped the charts several years before becoming a cult classic.

The sheer audacity of one short, chubby but clever engineer was written into history for all time.

The first Venusian Sky City, Venusville, was, oddly enough, built in space. Building within the Venusian atmosphere was not yet something that humanity had mastered. Venusville started off as a huge bulkhead base disk of specially formulated plasteel, five hundred metres in diameter. The base disk had been printed by massive three-D printing robots in high Venusian orbit. The special plasteel formulation itself was impervious to the Venusian sulphuric acid clouds.

Once the base disk had been built, a massive bulkhead side wall, forty metres tall was printed around the entire circumference of the base disk. It too was printed using the same machinery as the base disk and of the same formulation of plasteel. When the bulkhead wall was finally completed, the entire wall was topped with a hemisphere of clear, crystalline aluminium, which was also impervious to the Venusian sulphuric acid clouds.

Access points were strategically cut into the bulkhead wall, allowing access to and from the interior. Both the interior and exterior were finished to perfection. The entire structure was strong, resilient and most importantly, it could be hermetically sealed.

The underside of the base disk of Venusville was crisscrossed with eight massive arch reinforcement structures. The peaks of these arches met the base disk in the centre, with their bases extending down well below the outer edges of the base disk. Connecting the arches to the sides of the base disk were huge upright buttresses. These buttresses ran from the base of the arches up to the base disk and further up along the outer circumference wall.

The eight buttresses extended far beyond the height of the circumference wall by at least three hundred metres and at their tops were massive anchor points for the attachment of cables to connect Venusville's Gas Buoyancy Envelopes. The buttresses themselves were hollow and contained special compressed gas tanks, the valves of which were at the top, close to the anchor points. The base of the buttresses contained both main thrusters and attitude control thrusters and all the equipment thereof.

Around the base disk, between the buttresses, were eight landing platforms, several levels tall. These matched up precisely with the strategically placed access points. The tops of these platforms had specially marked landing points for shuttles and transports. Grapples would reach up and lock onto the spacecraft, holding them tightly in place and then an umbilicus would rise up and form hermetically sealed passages for accessing Venusville. The lower levels contained plentiful emergency escape pods, just in case the Sky City concept turned out to be a failure.

Everything was manufactured using the same three-D printing techniques, using the same extremely strong and resilient plasteel formulation. Except for the dome, which was constructed of specially formulated clear, crystal aluminium.

The interior of Venusville had five concentric rings of housing, business and commercial structures. Their heights were staggered, reducing the closer they came to the centre of Venusville. The outermost ring, which was against the circumference bulkhead wall, was ten levels tall. The next ring within that was eight levels tall, the one within that was six levels tall and then within that one, four levels tall. Finally, the innermost ring was only two levels tall.

The lower two levels of the concentric rings contained office business space, commercial spaces, shops of various kinds and recreational facilities, etc. The rooftops of the concentric ring structures were public garden spaces, open to all of the citizens of Venusville. The uppermost two levels of the four inner rings were apartments, which had direct access to natural light and the rooftop gardens. The levels beneath those held more apartments, but those relied on artificial lighting.

At the very centre of the main disk of Venusville was a cylindrical tower of plasteel and clear aluminium. The tower stood majestically at a height of twelve levels. It was Venusville's Government Centre. This central tower contained Venusville's government, bureaucrats, scientists, engineers and maintenance personnel, in that order from the top down.

Between the Government Tower and the Concentric Rings lay a verdant open garden space, a commons designed for the delight and relaxation of Venusville's inhabitants. Lush gardens, tree-lined paths, vibrant flower beds, and even a sparkling lake invited citizens to gather and unwind. This central space also hosted sporting facilities and a state-of-the-art aquatic centre.

Beneath this idyllic haven, Venusville's lifeblood thrummed quietly in the form of atomic fission reactors. These reactors, powered by uranium fuel imported from Earth, were securely housed beneath the main base disk, nestled between the massive underside arches. Encased in layers of radiation-shielded plasteel, they provided the energy needed to sustain the sky city's operations and inhabitants.

Venusville was designed to be a comfortable, low-density living space for a population of around ten thousand people. A milestone in humanity's achievements, Venus itself could now be colonised. Venusville marked the dawn of a new era, proving that even the most inhospitable of hell worlds could be tamed through ingenuity, technology and perseverance.

It took nearly five years for the Venusians to construct Venusville. When they'd completed it, they spent another year testing every aspect of her. Once they were satisfied with their accomplishment, they attached eight massive, pendulous Gas Buoyancy Envelopes, the G.B.E.s. The engineers burst out laughing, they could not control themselves. Each of the G.B.E.s had been labelled in big bold letters, T.I.T.S. one through eight. A certain short, chubby, very clever engineer had struck once again!

While the engineers couldn't help but laugh at their inside joke, there was no mistaking the sheer precision and complexity of the task ahead. With the Gas Buoyancy Envelopes securely in place, Venusville was gently lowered into the dense clouds of the Venusian atmosphere.

As Venusville descended into the murk of the Venusian atmosphere, the compressed gasses stored in her buttress's gas tanks were piped up into the Gas Buoyancy Envelopes. The Tits as they were affectionately known, slowly yet surely expanded as more and more gas was piped in. As the Tits slowly filled to their enormous pendulous size, the thrusters were wound back and after several tense hours, they were finally shut off.

Venusville was now floating in the Venusian upper atmosphere. Floating high above the seething cauldron that was the surface of Venus, amidst the swirling, yellow, golden clouds and tempestuous winds, Venusville became the first of the Venusian Sky Cities. Delicately perched and floating fifty kilometres above the surface, the ethereal habitat with its glorious dome offered a breathtaking vista of the endless expanse of the Venusian skies above.

Venusville underwent extensive testing for over six months. Every aspect of the city was examined for stability, functionality and safety before the first colonists could move in. After the testing period was completed, the first colonists were allowed to step aboard Venusville. They found their new home a true marvel of modern engineering, with spacious apartments, multiple levels of gardens, and a serene atmosphere that contrasted sharply with the violent chaos many kilometres below.

The Hanging Gardens of Venusville would soon become the symbol of humanity's ability to thrive in the most hostile of environments. It was their slice of heaven floating high above the Venusian version of Hell, a sanctuary amid the swirling tempests and broiling heat below. The settlers looked down at the chaos beneath, knowing they had created something truly extraordinary, an oasis amongst the Venusian clouds.

The one true constant in the universe, is that all things change. So too with the colonisation of the Venusian sky scape. The Venusian Sky Cities were significantly cheaper to build than the O'Neil-style twin cylinders in the Venusian L-One Lagrangian gravitational zone, especially the bigger ones. So with the incredible success of Venusville, the Venusian Government put out tenders to build another dozen more sky cities.

The successful bidder, who had in fact built Venusville itself, was the company, Sky City Constructions Ltd. They had the know-how, they knew exactly what they were doing and they had promised, that with new efficiencies and their latest equipment, they could complete the massive undertaking in a decade.

One by one, new Sky Cities came online and by the time the tenth Sky City was opened for colonists, Venusville had reached its breaking point. The population of the first Sky City had breached fifteen thousand and the citizens were complaining that their lifestyles were deteriorating. It was decided by the government at Venus Central Command that the eleventh Sky City would be used for the expansion of Venusville. When this new sky city was lowered into the Venusian upper atmosphere, its attitude control thrusters were used to manoeuvre it alongside Venusville. Special new adaptors, purposely constructed for the task, forever linked the two sky cities together, the new with the old. Venusville was a decade old when it was upgraded to Venusville Two.

The upgrades didn't end either. By the time the thirtieth Sky City came online, the original Sky City, Venusville, had been upgraded with two more additional Sky City expansion modules. Venusville Three was capable of housing up to forty thousand people with comfort and room to spare.

Throughout the years more and more Sky Cities came online and Venusville was upgraded once more, with Venusville Four completed and coming online. Venusville Four had its original Sky City as its central hub but now had six more Sky Cities attached to it, creating a Sky City Cluster. The Sky City Cluster could house seventy thousand people.

At this point, it was decided that Venusville could not take on any further modules. Instead, a process of gradual Cluster consolidation took place. First, the atomic fission reactors were replaced with newer, more powerful and efficient fusion reactors. Next, massive air conduits were positioned, taking air from Venusville's outer rim towards its centre for atmospheric processing and thrust.

The massive air conduits had equally massive air-multiplying turbines installed. Venusian air was sucked in from the outer rim of Venusville and directed through special filters to mine elements from the atmosphere, carbon, oxygen and hydrogen. Carbon was to be used for making nanofibers and oxygen and hydrogen were to be used for making water. The downward thrust from the air multipliers was actually capable of aiding in holding Venusville aloft.

Then, the structural integrity of Venusville was increased with extra bracing and stanchions. A part of the process was the linking together of all seven base disks, creating one single huge base disk, fifteen hundred metres across. Around the rim of this new *"super"* disc were installed newer, far more massive Gas Buoyancy Envelopes, seventy two of them in all. They were enormous and literally looked like enormous pendulous upside-down tits. They were all labelled as T.IT.S, one through to seventy two.

That had set the stage for the next two instalments. Around this super disk was built a single huge, bulkhead wall, fifty metres tall. Then, the finale was one huge, clear crystal aluminium dome covering the entire Sky City Cluster. Every aspect of these upgrades was performed in situ, within the Venusian skies with its sulphuric acid-laden clouds. The final task in the upgrade process was the removal of the seven smaller, interior bulkhead walls and crystal aluminium domes, which had now become completely superfluous. The whole Cluster of colonies that was Venusville Four was now a super Sky City capable of sustaining a population of well over one hundred thousand people.

Venusville Five was now online! It could expand no more and would be a constant reminder of humanity's ingenuity and technical prowess for centuries to come. No other Sky Cities became a Super Sky City like Venusville, each of the others stopping at the seven-cluster configuration, leaving Venusville as the singular shining light and crowning glory.

Aria stretched, rolled her neck and yawned, then she remarked, "That was far more interesting."

"Really, Sis, anyone would think you were bored, yawning and all", Ariel replied.

"No, my darling, Sister. I'm just tired", Aria replied honestly, as she was feeling very tired.

Kethera piped up, "One day, I'm going to the Sol system. I want to see the Venusian Sky Cities for myself. They sound so romantic, floating around a hell world, with heavenly hanging gardens."

The twins both blinked several times.

Yeannah swung her head around from the screen to look at Kethera and Saffiera just thought to herself, *"Oh dear, she doesn't know."*

Saffiera called up a search on her data tablet, *"The fall of Venusville and its aftermath"*, then she passed her data tablet to Aria, who then passed it on to Kethera.

Kethera began reading the information on Saffiera's data tablet screen, "The fall of Venusville in the year twenty three sixty two was caused by fundamentalist terrorists, *'The People of the Prophet'*. The terrorists surreptitiously placed explosive charges on the anchor points of the Sky Cities seventy two Gas Buoyancy Envelopes. The charges in themselves were not sufficient to break the anchor points, however, they did weaken them so that they would break gradually under the strain. Ostensibly, this was done to allow the inhabitants of Venusville to evacuate", she looked from one twin to the other, "So Venusville was destroyed?", her eyes were beginning to show horror within them.

Aria looked at Kethera with sorrowful eyes, "Keep reading, Kethera, there is more."

Kethera continued, "The panic that ensued as the Gas Buoyancy Envelopes broke away one by one caused a mass stampede for the emergency evacuation pods. The air multipliers went into overdrive, attempting to stabilise the stricken Sky City. In the end, they maxed out and failed one by one. There were only enough emergency evacuation pods for a third of Venusville's population. With the chaotic evacuation underway, emergency evacuation pods, which could hold up to twenty people, were being launched with as little as one or two people on board", she stopped and looked up, "Only one or two people on board?", she queried

Saffiera chimed in, in her silent, telepathic way, *"It was pure chaos. People dove into the emergency evacuation pods and launched without waiting for others. I cannot imagine the fear."*

Kethera turned back to the data tablet and continued reading, "In the end, just over twenty thousand people survived, with well over eighty thousand fatalities."

Kethera's ears flattened, her whiskers drooped as her eyes brimmed with tears as she repeated in a whisper, "Well over eighty thousand fatalities?"

Ariel chimed in, explaining, "Yeah, that happened in the middle of the second Horridian War. It was what brought the Venusians into it, on the side of the Earth and Cis-Lunar L-Five."

"How did all of those people die?", Kethera asked, her voice little more than a squeak.

"Well, at that time, the Venusian atmosphere was over ninety times normal atmospheric pressure and the planet had temperatures hot enough to melt lead", Ariel informed her.

"Not to mention the sulphuric acid clouds", Aria reminded her twin Sister.

Kethera's tail lay flat on the ground mat as she questioned, "So, Venusville cracked open like an egg, the people choked on sulphuric acid and then they burnt to death like they were in a furnace?"

Aria bit her bottom lip, "Yes, Kethera, try not to think about it", she reached out and held Kethera's forearm, trying to comfort her.

Kethera, continued reading into the aftermath section, there were tears in her eyes and streaming freely down her cheeks and her voice quivered as she read, "As a result of the Fall of Venusville and the subsequent loss of life, all confidence in the Venusian Sky Cities vanished overnight and the people demanded to be evacuated. There were over a thousand Sky Cities, with a population of over one hundred million people demanding to be evacuated. The task of evacuation and resettlement took over two decades and cost the Venusian Government trillions in credits. A thousand new colonies were required to resettle the evacuees and those were built all across the inner solar system."

Saffiera looked to Kethera and remarked, *"The sad tale of Venusville is known to every citizen of Sol. We are taught about it in primary school as a cautionary tale of what can happen when extremist views take hold."*

That did not console Kethera one bit, who asked, "What became of the Sky Cities?"

"Well, if you read further, you will find out", Yeannah informed her, then instead, she decided to explain it, "Each Sky City's thrusters and Gas Buoyancy Envelopes lifted it into low Venusian orbit, before space tugs hauled them into high orbital scrap yards for recycling. Everything was reused and recycled. Sky Cities were abandoned forever. I can't recall anything like them since."

A teary Kethera questioned, "Except for Venusville?"

Ariel gave Kethera a hug and carefully explained the cold, stark, harsh truth, "Kethera, Venusville was a melted ruin on the Venusian surface. Its inhabitants rendered to less than burnt ash spreading on the slow Venusian winds."

"I don't want to study anymore", Kethera cried.

"I don't feel like studying anymore either", Aria agreed.

"Neither do I", Ariel sighed, agreeing softly.

Saffiera had tears in her eyes now, her empathy had kicked in almost as soon as Kethera had begun crying, *"Enough study for tonight, yeah?"*, she questioned telepathically.

Yeannah turned off the big screen, "Agreed, let's get some sleep. We'll all feel better tomorrow."

As Kethera laid down on her right side on her floor mat, she remarked, "So, Venus, the hell world won in the end."

Aria laid down beside and looked into Kethera's eyes, "Venus, the hell world lost in the end. It pushed the Venusians into terraforming Venus. Venus, the once hell world is now a blue paradise", she put a comforting arm around her.

Ariel laid down on Kethera's other side and embraced Kethera, noting, "The remains of Venusville are now under six thousand feet of water", as the three girls slowly fell asleep.

Saffiera wiped her eyes, unshed tears welling up and silently remarked to Yeannah, *"I keep forgetting how sensitive Carlin girls are. They wear the hearts on their sleeves."*

Yeannah wasn't a telepath but focused her thoughts on Saffiera, *"Yeah, Carlins don't do trauma very well"*, then she did the math in her head, that was her sort of thing, *"Even when it's eleven hundred and thirty three years in the past."*

"I think that has something to with their recent past and how they used to lose sixty percent of their kits to natural causes", Saffiera speculated.

Yeannah yawned and thought back, *"Possibly"*, before they both gradually fell asleep.

A little while later, once Kethera's parents had noticed the quiet from the attic, they both snuck upstairs to see how the girls were settling in for the night. Through the dim light, they both stared at the five sleeping angels on the floor mats. The twins and Kethera were a tangle of arms and legs. Even Saffiera was embracing Aria and Yeannah herself was on her side and, in turn, embracing Saffiera. Yeannah's great wings were lying sprawled lazily behind her back.

"You see, Krylor. I told you they sleep just like Carlin Kit Sisters", a smiling Kayala noted.

"Well, Kayala, I didn't believe that photo, but I can't deny my own eyes now", he smiled back.

"There must have been a time in their distant past when Humans also had too many kits and not enough space for them all to sleep", Kayala replied, her thoughts wandering about ancient human families, all huddled together in ways now long forgotten.

Krylor tried to imagine Humans living like Carlins, but he could not, so he simply nodded to Kayala and then they both went back downstairs to their own bedroom and went to bed for the night.

The following day after their morning classes, the girls headed off to their favourite place to eat their lunch. The school's eastern quadrangle was a reasonably-sized square open space that was not regularly used by other students during their lunch break. They all sat down at their regular table, a rectangular table with bench seats running down two sides.

"Why don't we see native animals in the colony?", Ariel asked.

Kethera, who was feeling much better after the previous night's emotional study session, replied, "Look around, Ariel. Do you see any native trees?"

Ariel looked around. There was only one tree in the quadrangle, a tall maple tree, native to the Earth. It provided shade for the quadrangle but only towards its centre. Beyond that, there were thick, low shrubs around the edges of the quadrangle. Ariel did not know what kind, but one thing was clear, they were also from the Earth. To all but Kethera, their surroundings were familiar and comfortable. For Kethera, not so much. Comfortable, yes, but alien in many ways. It saddened her that the Humans did not plant more native species of flora.

When Ariel's eyes fell upon Kethera's once more, she explained, "You see, Ariel. There are no native trees in the colony. Gudongs, Boobooks and Thrixan all prefer native trees, all native species do. Native trees are their source of food."

"I guess that makes sense", Ariel agreed.

Saffiera asked curiously, *"We know the Gudongs eat grass and leaves, but what about the Boobooks and Thrixan? What do they eat?"*, as she asked, Aria got up and walked over to the shrubbery.

Kethera thought for a moment and then replied, "Well, you already know that Gudongs are herbivores. Boobooks are largely insectivores, they largely eat bugs, insects, spiders and grubs. Though they do eat fresh leaf shoots as well."

"And the Thrixan?", an even more curious Saffiera enquired.

"Thrixan, Zrrakil, are frugivores", Yeannah chimed in, using both the Carlinish and Tholish names for the winged creatures, she added, "They eat Chillic and Bell Nut fruits, among many other fruits."

"Which is why they taste so nice. Sweet fruits make sweet meats", a smiling Kethera commented.

"I know what Chillics are, but what's a Bell Nut Fruit?", Saffiera enquired.

Kethera explained, "The trees in our village are mostly Bell Nut Fruit trees. The Bell Nut Fruit is about the size of a Chillic, only it's bell-shaped. Before it ripens, it grows a nut under the fruit. The fruit resembles a bell with a clanger hanging underneath it. We call the nuts Clanger Nuts."

Saffiera was even more curious, *"Do the Thrixan eat the nuts?"*

"Oh, no, Saffiera, they just eat the fruit and let the nuts fall to the ground. They do have a hard shell", Kethera replied, then she added, "Clanger Nuts are delicious. We collect them and they have a really sweet, creamy taste", then she noted, "The Bell fruit itself tastes like a lemony Chillic."

Yeannah chimed in once more, "Chillics are basically peaches. So lemony peaches."

Saffiera's curiosity seemed never-ending, *"What pollinates the Bell Nut tree?"*

Kethera smiled, she loved informing her friends about Vale and its ecology, "A bug, of course. It's kind of Vale's equivalent of an Earth bee, but much bigger. The Boobooks love eating them, but they do hate their stingers."

Ariel turned to look at her twin Sister, "What are you doing, Aria?"

"Harricks are everywhere, right?" Aria asked as she walked along the edge of the quadrangle past the shrubbery. Harricks are a diminutive humanoid native species that may even be sentient.

Kethera confirmed, "Yes, Harricks are everywhere, Aria."

Aria smiled, "That's what I thought. There are three Harrick turds at the edge of this shrubbery."

Ariel threw her hands up into the air with disgust, "Aria! Are you serious? We are eating! Couldn't you wait until after lunch to point out turds?"

Kethera frowned, her whiskers were slightly downcast, not because of what Aria had said but for another reason, she remarked, "In our village, we have to be very quick to collect the Clanger Nuts. If we are too slow, the Harricks get to them first. There are too many Harricks in our village. They are omnivores and highly opportunistic. They eat what we eat. That's why they're here. They eat your leavings, your rubbish."

"Just like humanoid rats!", Aria exclaimed.

"Kind of ,Aria but rats that could be sapient", Kethera replied but not really agreeing with her.

Ariel thought for a moment, about tailless, two-legged, upright-walking rodents and then she shook her head gently to clear the thoughts.

As the group of friends sat at their usual spot, enjoying their lunch in the quiet corner of the quadrangle, two classmates unexpectedly entered the space. This was unusual. Not many students ventured into this particular area, which is exactly why the girls chose to eat there whenever the weather allowed. The quadrangle, surrounded by tall buildings with a single tall maple tree in its centre and surrounded by thick, verdant shrubbery, felt peaceful and secluded, far from the hustle and bustle of other lunch spots.

The newcomers were two Human boys, Richard and Thomas. Richard, a tall, sandy-haired lad with hazel eyes, walked with a slight hesitation, as though unsure if he should intrude on the girl's usual territory. His friend, Thomas, a tall ginger boy with bright green eyes, walked a bit more confidently beside him, looking around with casual interest.

Richard's gaze shifted toward Kethera almost immediately. She could feel his eyes upon her, though he tried to act casual. Richard had a secret crush on Kethera, a fact she suspected but never acknowledged openly. Despite the obvious differences between their species, Richard found himself drawn to her, though he often kept his feelings to himself.

Kethera, for her part, shared the sentiment, though she was much better at hiding it, but not from her friends who saw straight through her subterfuge. Kethera's tail twitched subtly and her whiskers were forward, as if standing to attention, betraying her emotions for just a moment. Thomas started walking over to the girls while Richard held back, as if embarrassed.

"Kethera. Get up, go and talk to Richard", Aria prodded, with a mild nudge.

Aria's twin Sister, Ariel stood up and took Kethera by the arm, lifting her gently to her feet, "Come on then, Kethera, we know you like him. Don't be shy", she said as she walked her over to Richard.

When they were both standing in front of Richard, Ariel declared, "My job is done", and rushed back to the table and her friends.

Kethera's blue stripes began to broaden with embarrassment, displaying a slight iridescence and she wanted to run back to her friends. Richard, however, had plucked up some courage and gently took her by the hand, "Let's talk", he told her in a soft and uncomfortable voice.

Meanwhile, Thomas had reached the girl's table and sat himself down right next to Yeannah, he winked at her, "Hello there, Angel eyes" , he told her in a suave voice.

The alabaster white skin of Yeannah's face went bright pink with embarrassment and she looked to her friends, whose focus was purely on Richard and Kethera. Yeannah said nothing in reply. A Thol does not enter into relationships with other species, ever and she felt utterly confused. That simply was not her. This Human boy made her feel different!

Richard and Kethera were talking softly, she looked so bashful and kept turning away from Richard, looking back to her friends and then returning her gaze back to Richard once more.

Saffiera remarked, *"Kethera looks so coy, but my mind can sense her purring from here."*

Aria tried not to laugh as she replied, questioning, "Like a kitten?"

Ariel smirked, "Maybe they're talking about the Thrixan and the Bugs."

Saffiera smirked and gave a little telepathic nod at the Birds and Bees reference.

As they watched, Richard placed his hand gently on Kethera's chin and then he leaned in and kissed her ever so gently on the lips. Kethera did not resist and soon they were in a passionate embrace, kissing for many long moments.

The girl's eyes were all wide open with shock, their jaws all dropped, "No way!", Aria exclaimed.

Thomas looked at Yeannah and smiled, he took her hand and brought it up to his lips, kissing it gently, "I prefer my woman to be more Angelic, Yeannah. I will see you around my, alabaster beauty", he stated in his suave voice, he then gently touching the tip of her chin and smiled.

Yeannah's face went bright red with embarrassment and she felt a hot flush coming on.

Aria looked at Thomas in utter shock and disbelief, "No effing way!", she exclaimed.

Thomas blew Yeannah a kiss as he got up from the table and walked over to Richard, "Time to go, lover boy. We still have our study session, remember?"

Richard gently broke away from Kethera, "Maybe we can catch up later, Kethera?"

Kethera did not answer, she herself was in shock and simply bit her lower lip and nodded as the two boys walked off in the direction of the school's senior study hall.

Kethera stood perfectly still for several long moments, her tail was oddly not moving at all, just standing out straight. She did not hear her friends calling to her, which was odd for a Carlin with their exceptionally focused hearing. A brief thought crossed her mind. *Did she feel wet?* She certainly felt hot, far too hot!

Then she heard Saffiera's soft whispered thoughts in her mind and she turned around to her friends, a look of pure bewilderment on her face. That look did not last long.

A huge beaming Cheshire grin came over Kethera's face, her whiskers rose up and her ears redirected toward her friends, her tail began to swish swiftly from side to side. The shock of the experience had worn off and Kethera was excited.

Kethera's hands came up to her face and cheeks. She felt hot, ever so hot and she did a little, happy, happy joy dance, before excitedly running back to her friends, her pupil slits wider than they'd ever been. Her friends hadn't realised how fast Kethera could run, she covered the distance ever so quickly.

When Kethera reached her friends, she asked, almost screaming, "What just happened?", as if it was some weird surreal dream that had happened to someone else, before biting down on her lower lip.

Aria blurted out, "You just snogged Richard, silly!", then the girls all burst into giggles and laughter.

The laughter died down somewhat but then picked up again into even louder bursts when an irreverent Aria asked, "So what does Richard's tongue taste like?"

Kethera's eyes looked downwards, then slowly she looked back up at her friends, "It was nice, really nice", she replied in the coyest of voices.

Then the girls all burst into laughter and that laughter became uncontrollable.

After their laughter died down, Saffiera silently asked Yeannah, if she was okay, laughter aside, Yeannah was showing signs of deep internal turmoil, *"Yeannah? You seem out of sorts."*

"Thomas!", Yeannah focused her thoughts back to Saffiera, *"Why did he do that to me? Why did he have to say that?"*

"For all of his bravado, he actually does like you. A lot in fact. Thomas covers his heart with a mask. It's how he copes with the world around him", Saffiera replied, being a telepath, she'd know.

"You know, this inter-species restriction, for the Indigenous Thols, it's a fucking cultural taboo. For us Mimasian Thols it's more of a practicality issue", Yeannah replied back vocally, explaining, "I mean, all Thol women want to have children and that simply cannot happen with a Human."

Kethera and the twin's ears picked up at that, normally private internal dialogue between Saffiera and Yeannah, didn't become *'loud'* and Yeannah rarely ever swore, Aria commented, "You can always play the field you know. Before you marry one of your own people and have kids, Yeannah."

"No. I can't, Aria. It does not work that way. I would be considered dirty and wrong", Yeannah responded, tears welling in her eyes.

Aria replied, suggesting, "There's always artificial insemination and in vitro fertilisation."

Ariel calmly told her twin, "Not helping, Sister!"

"Why would he do that to me?", Yeannah asked, she was now sobbing freely.

Ariel replied, "Thomas didn't know. He doesn't understand. How could he?"

Aria added quite bluntly, "He is also an idiot. I mean, what an effing jerk!"

With that one remark, Yeannah wiped away her tears, pulled herself back together and began to smile once more.

Yeannah was back to her stoic self once more, the real Yeannah, "Let's get to the study hall. We do have a lot of ground to cover."

With that the girls made their way to the school's senior study hall, in order to continue working on their term project, the Great Explosion, the Outward Interplanetary Expansion. When they arrived and found a table to sit around, Kethera kept an eye on Richard with his mates on the other side of the hall.

Yeannah did her best not to look anywhere near Thomas. He affected her in ways that did not make sense. It frightened her and she did not understand why. The girls connected their data tablets to the school's network and got down to business.

13. The Martian Libration Points.

Stuart Dumas sat behind his desk in his home office at his luxurious house in his Cis-Lunar L-Five Corporate Colony Cylinder, Dumas Incorporated Industries Ltd. The paperwork seemed endless. His desk was strewn with reports and files and his data tablet was networked to his company's computer processing systems. It displayed daily tasks, notifications, touch-points that needed his attention and stock market valuations.

Underneath of all of that "*crap and crud*" was even a large inlaid computer touchscreen, not that you could even see it. His entire desk was itself a large, powerful data tablet. The monotonous drudgery of the paperwork seemed never-ending, it was just everywhere.

Stuart was now in his early forties and he thought to himself, *"Is this what my life is now, just continuous paperwork? I need to go back to my roots"*, he brushed the thought aside for the moment.

Stuart remembered the fun days and how he started his Cis-Lunar haulage company with a single space tug. That same company now had hundreds of space tugs, he wasn't even sure how many, perhaps even a thousand or more. Two walls bore his family photos, a testament to the moments he cherished outside of his work. Interspersed were images of ribbon-cutting ceremonies, milestones in his empire's journey.

Bookshelves lined another wall and the final wall was lined with filing cabinets, atop which were his two favourite space tugs. The first one he'd ever owned, named Charity and his favourite one of all, Chugga! Stuart was described as a space-hauling magnate by some and due to his massive mining operations in the Earth's and Venus's Trojan points, a mining magnate by others.

Stuart's huge space warehouses in those Trojan points, as well as in Cis-Lunar L-Four, were responsible for maintaining the Asteroidal Commodities Market, balancing the equations of supply and demand so precisely, ensuring that everyone profited and that the market didn't collapse. Stuart, his wife Maria, hell his whole family, were virtually household names.

Stuart was awoken from his reverie by a knock at his office door. It was his son Baron, a tall strapping lad with his Father's dark hair, only far longer and tied back in a ponytail, he had his Mother's good looks. Baron had a brilliant mind and academic record to match, but he also had a penchant for partying, which his Father and Mother both hoped he'd grow out of.

“What can I do for you, Baron?”, Stuart asked.

“Just letting you know I'm heading off to a party”, Baron replied.

“Another party. You seem to have a party to go to every weekend”, Stuart noted in reply.

“Well, yes, but this party's really important”, Baron explained.

“More so than the others?”, his Father questioned.

“Yeah. I met a girl a couple of months back at another party. I'm meeting up with her again tonight. We're kind of an item and have been for a while now”, Baron replied.

“Oh, I see. Make sure you keep your Mother in the loop, yeah”, Stuart replied.

The Stuart had a thought and he followed it, “Baron. Can I ask you a question, a business question to be more precise?”

“A business question?”, Baron was perplexed, “Dad, you're the businessman. Why would you even consider asking me?”

“Ah, Baron, my Son, let me be the judge of that”, Stuart replied with a broad smile.

“Okay then, Dad, shoot”, Baron responded.

“Now I don't want you to think about the question, Baron. Just give me the first thought that comes to mind. The very first thought. Do you think you can do that?”, Stuart asked his Son.

“I think so, Dad. What's your question?”, Baron enquired.

“Okay then, Baron. What is the next big business venture I should undertake?”, Stuart asked.

Baron froze, startled by the enormity of the question. He began to mull it over in his mind.

Even before Baron could answer, his Father interrupted his thoughts, “Stop! Baron, I don't want you to think about it. Just, without thinking, spit out the very first thought that pops into your mind, completely unbidden. Okay. Can you do that?”

“I think so”, Baron replied.

“Okay then. What is the next big business venture I should undertake?”,

Stuart repeated.

Baron spat out without even thinking, "The trifecta."

That caught Stuart by surprise, "The Trifecta?", he questioned.

Baron sang a short line from an old song, "Venus and Mars are alright tonight!"

Stuart gave his Son a questioning look.

Baron caught the look and explained, "You have the Earth's Trojans, right? You also have the Venusian Trojans. The Trifecta would be to sow up the Martian Trojans as well."

Stuart looked at his Son with both pride and admiration and then he remarked, "Another grand undertaking, another five year plan", he looked daunted by the thought of it all.

Setting up mining operations at the Martian Trojan points would be a huge undertaking. Even though he'd done it before elsewhere, was he too old for this? Should he pass the baton?

"Dad! You've done this before. It's your bread and butter. You know big plans, big deals", Baron reassured him, adding, "You always said, *'go big or go home',* and you are not the type to go home."

"You are right, Son. I've got this, only this time, I'll be showing you the ropes", Stuart replied.

"Me?", Baron asked, thinking to himself, *"What have I gotten myself into?"*

"Of course, you. It's time you learned the family business", Stuart explained to his Son, then he added, "You start on Monday, make sure you're at my corporate office at nine a.m. sharp. Wear a suit."

Baron gulped softly, "Are you sure, Dad?"

"Absolutely. You've finished your University courses and it's time you started working", Stuart told his Son, "I'll even make sure you have an office on the top floor, relatively close to mine."

Baron wasn't sure. He thought about complaining to his Father and saying he wasn't ready, but then he looked at his Father's desk, covered with all that paperwork. This was his Father's home office and he was drowning in paperwork, even at home.

"I have to take some of the burdens", he thought to himself, then replied,

"Dad. It's a deal", heck, did he just sound like his Father?

"Good then, Baron. Now off you go to your party and you know the rules. Come home before one a.m. Make sure you're not drunk", he told his Son and then he added, "And always use protection."

Dad! Really!", Baron replied as he headed off to meet his girlfriend and the party.

After Baron had headed off to his Saturday night party, his wife Maria poked her head inside his home office door., "Honey, it's Saturday night and I think you've done enough paperwork for the day."

Stuart looked up from his ridiculously messy desk, ridiculous yes, but to Stuart's mind it was controlled chaos, "You're right, Maria", he gestured to his desk, "This '*shit*' will be the death of me."

"Good then. It's agreed, you're taking me out to dinner", Maria informed him.

"I am?", Stuart considered, "Yes, I suppose I am. Our nanny can look after the kids."

"I'm ready to go, so get yourself cleaned up and we'll head off", Maria told him.

As Stuart stood up from behind his desk, he noted, "You know, that Son of ours is quite the genius."

"Of course, he is, Stuart, he is my Son after all", Maria agreed.

Stuart smiled, "Yes, Maria, but that isn't what I meant. I asked Baron a simple question, wanting an instinctive reply. He answered with two words, *'The Trifecta'*."

"And that was genius?", Maria inquired, with a slightly puzzled look.

"Indeed it was, Maria. We have mining operations in the Earth's and the Venusian Trojan points, but not Mars", Stuart informed her, adding, "Setting up a Martian Trojan mining operation completes the trifecta. It's kind of like the full set. It completes a Grand design."

"It seems I taught our Son very well indeed", Maria smiled.

Stuart smiled back thinking, *"If it pleased her to think so"*, then he replied, "You did indeed."

Maria then instructed Stuart, "Now get cleaned up and get dressed. I've already made the booking with our favourite restaurant", then she put on an alluring smile, "When we get back, I have some new lingerie to show you. After which, I might need your help to take it back off ."

Stuart smiled back with an artful smile, "I will be ready in twenty minutes", he replied as he quickly rushed out the door.

Maria jokingly reminded him, "Just remember to put your clothes on, Stuart. They won't let us in the restaurant if you're not appropriately dressed."

"Hell, Maria", Stuart shouted back as a joke laughing, "I'd just bribe the waiter to let us in any way."

Maria laughed to herself internally, *"Oh, Stuart, you crazy nut bag"*, a wry smile came over her and she stated aloud, "Your nuts are mine tonight, Stuart."

The following Monday, Stuart was in his office, on the top floor of his corporation's headquarters. His Son, Baron, was there well before nine a.m. and had waited patiently in a conference room for his Father to arrive. He was all suited up with a fine business suit and sporting a new professional office hairstyle. Baron Dumas looked the part and seemed ready for his new role.

Stuart's secretary showed Baron into Stuart's office, "Wow, Dad. Nice digs!", Baron noted.

The office was set up in a highly consistent way with his home office, complete with controlled chaos on his desk. There were files and papers cluttered everywhere and his desktop touchscreen/data tablet was buried beneath them all. The only real difference was the view from the ten-story office window. The whole northern end cap of the colony sprawled into view.

"I'm glad you like it, Son", Stuart replied, then he turned to his personal assistant, "Tegan. My Son will require his own office. Could you arrange that for him, please?"

"Noting that now, Sir. Your Son will have an office before midday ", Tegan informed him.

"Excellent. My Son will also need an assistant. Someone who can show him the ropes and ease him into the business", Stuart remarked.

"So noted, Mr Dumas. I will organise that for him as well", Tegan replied with her usual level of efficiency.

Baron looked at his Father's desk, “If I may be so bold. Looking at my Father's desk and having seen his desk at home, my Father is drowning in paperwork. Does my Father have a sufficient number of assistants?”, he enquired.

Stuart cocked an eyebrow, “Baron, it is only your first day. Don't you think it's a little early to make *'bold'* inquiries?”

“Not at all, Dad. Neither Mum nor I want to lose you to a coronary before you're fifty. You are heavily overworked and you know it” Baron replied, then he asked, “You know I'm right?”

Stuart was silent taking in his Son's bold statements, until Tegan stepped in, “Sir, if I may be equally bold, your Son is one hundred percent correct. You are buried in work, Mr Dumas”, she turned to Baron, “In answer to your question, young Sir, I am your Father's only assistant.”

“You too, Tegan?”, Mr Dumas questioned.

“Yes, Sir. Me too”, Tegan replied, explaining, “How could I not agree, Sir?”

Baron folded his arms, “Dad. This simply has to change!”

“I will make the arrangements, young Sir”, Tegan replied, fully agreeing with Baron, she added, “Two assistants should be sufficient. Your Father has been working like three men for a long time.”

“Tegan, I haven't approved that”, a slightly concerned Mr Dumas replied.

“Mr Dumas. Your health is of primary concern here. You are woefully overworked and haven't taken a proper break in forever. Your Son, Baron, is entirely correct, Sir”, Tegan explained.

Stuart raised his hands in mock defeat, “Okay, okay. I will approve two assistants and no more. And Tegan, they will need to be fully vetted and qualified.”

“Yes, of course, Sir. I will organise everything myself”, Tegan informed him.

Stuart turned to his Son, who replied to his look, “If you didn't want me to help out, I wouldn't be here, would I?”, the question was entirely rhetorical.

Stuart slowly replied, “Son, while that may be true, I didn't think you would start so quickly.”

Baron smiled at his Father, “Dad, I'm pretty sure Mum would agree with me. And besides, I am putting on a new hat after all.”

Stuart thought to himself, *"Like Father, like Son. Baron is one of my apples."*

"Okay. I'm glad that's out of the way. Now, Tegan, the order of business for the day. Who controls the Martian Trojan points, both leading and trailing? I need to know which bureaucracy I'm dealing with", Mr Dumas requested.

"Sir, which bureaucracy and for what purpose? If I may enquire?", Tegan asked.

"Ah, yes, of course, Tegan. I want the mining rights to both Martian Lagrangian points. We are going to develop them. New Trojan mining operations", Stuart informed her.

Tegan's eyes lit up, it had been a while since her boss had a fire in his belly, "Yes, Sir. This sounds very exciting."

"Good then. Baron. Shadow Tegan for the day, she will show how we do things around here", Stuart advised his Son, "At least until your assistant is arranged."

Tegan spoke to Baron, "Come along, young Sir. I have quite a lot to show you."

Businessman Victor Himmelstaff was at Eros, the City within the Rock in the Earth's trailing Trojan point. He had business with the Colonisation Committee of Sol, a small three-person committee that oversaw the colonisation of the solar system. Of course, behind that small committee was a vast bureaucracy. Unbeknownst to Stuart Dumas, Victor Himmelstaff's purpose was exactly the same, to develop the Martian Trojan Points as mining operations.

Just as Stuart had copied the mining operations at the Venusian L-One Lagrangian point, albeit with major improvements, in order to develop his mining operations at the Earth's two Trojan points, now Victor Himmelstaff was doing the same, but with a twist. Victor had acquired the mining rights to the Martian Trojan Points and now, any development thereof must run across Victor's desk. It was a predatory move on his behalf.

It was later in the day when Tegan found out about the Colonisation Committee of Sol having control over the development rights to the Martian Trojan points. When Tegan delved deeper, she came across the bad news. The mining rights to the Martian Trojan Points had already been allocated to a rival businessman, Victor Himmelstaff, just a mere five days earlier. Baron Dumas was shadowing her at the time. Tegan's jaw dropped when she came across the information.

"This is bad, very bad", Tegan mumbled, then she looked up at Baron, "Young Sir, we need to see your Father straight away."

"Is it anything I can help with?", Baron enquired.

"Very doubtful, young Sir, very doubtful. Your Father will know what to do", Tegan responded while thinking to herself, *"He always does."*

A short while later, Tegan and Baron were back in Stuart's office.

Tegan began explaining the situation, "Sir. The mining rights to the Martian Trojan Points have already been allocated."

"Are you sure, Tegan?", Stuart enquired, he wasn't angry or upset, it was just another problem to be worked on and problems always had solutions.

Tegan responded with the requisite information, "The mining rights were assigned five days ago to one Victor Himmelstaff."

Stuart stroked his chin, "I'm not familiar with him. He must be one of the smaller players. This was bound to happen. I copied Venus L-One. Now, someone has copied me and five days before I'd even decided to make my own move. Hell, I only decided last night."

Baron pipped up, "What was that surname again, Tegan?"

Tegan replied, "Himmelstaff. Why, young Sir?"

"Give me just a second, please", Baron took his flip communicator out of his pocket and called a number, when the call was answered he spoke, "Honey. What was your surname again?", he asked, after a moment, "Your Father. He wouldn't happen to be one, Victor Himmelstaff, would he?", then after he got the reply, "Thanks Hon, I'll explain it to you later. Love you, by", then he hung up.

"Dad. Victor Himmelstaff is my girlfriend's Father. I'm currently dating his Daughter, Hypolita Himmelstaff", Baron informed them both.

"Two coincidences?", Stuart asked himself, musing, *"Or is the universe talking to me? Trying to tell me something important?"*

Baron noted, "We had no plans to open up mining operations in the Martian Trojan Points until last night and Victor Himmelstaff acquired the mining rights five days ago."

Tegan chimed in, "Young Sir. If I may interject. The rights were signed at the Eros colony in the Earth's trailing Trojan point. It takes six weeks by interplanetary cycler to get to Eros. This would have been planned perhaps two months or more ago."

"That would have been before I even met Hypolita and I met her purely by chance at a random party. One that I decided to attend at the very last minute", Baron explained.

"That would truly make this a coincidence and your dating Hypolita makes this extremely fortuitous for us", Stuart surmised, his mind already working out strategies.

Stuart decided upon another approach, "Think fast, Son. Options?"

Baron was in thought for a moment, "We could always throw money at the problem and buy out Victor's mining rights?"

"That was my first thought too, but Victor is a businessman with good leverage. He won't go for it, I know that because I wouldn't either. His leverage is far too strong", Stuart replied.

Tegan chimed in, "He is a smaller player, Sir. Largely unknown. You can leverage that, Sir."

Baron stepped in, "Victor will need finance. He has to go to a bank. That gives us leverage."

"If he's smart, he will have already done so", Stuart mused, then he enquired "Tegan. We deal with just about every bank there is. Do you have time to send some feelers?"

"Yes, of course, Sir", Tegan replied, already knowing what Mr Dumas was going to say.

"Okay then. Victor Himmelstaff wants to play with the big leagues. Question the banks and venture capitalists. Have they loaned Victor the funds for his venture? If they have, request that they cancel the loan. If they haven't, request that they reject his loan applications. Any bank that does not comply will never do business with Dumas Incorporated Industries or any of its subsidiaries ever again. That should force Victor to come to us for finance", Stuart instructed.

"Dad, do we own the banks and the financiers?", Baron asked, thinking it was impossible.

"Son, our companies are bigger than most banks and many of the financiers and we have enormous leverage", Stuart explained, adding, "They do not want to lose our business. Trust me on that."

"So how does this work? How does it play out?", Baron eagerly enquired.

"We make Mr Himmelstaff an offer that he simply cannot refuse", Stuart informed his Son.

Tegan smiled, she understood, "You are going to be magnanimous aren't you, Sir."

"Yes, Tegan, I am", Stuart replied and then instructed, "Write up an offer contract. We provide the expertise and the equipment and we cover all these costs. I will generously offer him fifty one percent of the pie. That gives him power over *'his'* company, but he will be forever beholding to ours."

"Isn't fifty one percent a lot?", Baron questioned, it certainly did seem so.

"I'm generous, Son. First, I let Victor find out that he can't get the money he needs anywhere. Then I make him the only offer he can take. If he procrastinates, he loses percentage, one percent per day for his lack of diligence", Stuart explained.

Tegan smiled a gentle smile and then added, "Young, Sir, it puts the onus on Mr Himmelstaff to act swiftly, or else his financial position deteriorates."

"I don't know, Dad, that doesn't seem fair?", Baron questioned with genuine concern, he was of course dating Hypolita Himmelstaff, Victor's Daughter.

"I'm being exceedingly generous, Son. Most businessmen would lowball him, with offers of twenty percent or less", Stuart explained, adding, "My offer lifts Mr Himmelstaff straight into the big leagues with all of the big fish. He will have more credits and opportunities than he knows what to do with for the remainder of his life."

"Your Father's approach is the best one, young Sir", Tegan advised, noting, "The next approach, would be to flood the Asteroidal Commodities Market with our surplus stocks, which would lower the commodities prices to such low value as to make those Martian Trojans worthless. It would completely destroy Victor's leverage. I do not recommend that approach."

"And that, Son, would send our entire solar system's economy into a decade long depression, which is why we won't be doing that", Stuart completed.

Three days later, a frustrated Victor Himmelstaff asked his personal assistant, Susan Carter, “Susan. Why won't these blasted banks lend me any money?”

“I don't really know, Sir. They appear to be rejecting your loan applications on the grounds that you don't have sufficient collateral or enough experience to carry forward with your mining operation plans”, Susan informed him.

“My mining operation plans are basically a copy of the Earth Trojan Mining Corporation's plans. How can that even fail? It is fucking ridiculous!”, Victor spat back, he was quite angry with the entire situation, then he enquired, “How many applications have been rejected so far?”

“Every single loan application has been rejected, Sir”, Susan replied and she was quite unhappy with Victor's language, considering it quite inappropriate.

It was then that a communique came in and Susan eyed it over, “Sir, this will be of interest to you”, she hoped it would drag Victor back into a reasonable frame of mind and she sent it across to him.

Victor read through the document, put his hand to his bald head and began to summarise sections aloud, “The Dumas Corporation will provide all financing, expertise and equipment to develop the mining operations for both of the Martian Trojan points. Mr Victor Himmelstaff Esquire will retain full control of the new business entity, Mars Trojan Mining Ltd, via a fifty one percent share in the corporation. Fifty one percent, geez, that is actually quite generous. They aren't even trying to lowball me. What gives with that?”

Susan stepped in, she had been reading the original copy of the offer document, “Sir, if I may. The Dumas Corporation will still control the purse strings. You will control Mars Trojan Mining, however, with them in charge of the purse strings, they do have a heft of leverage over you.”

“You are right, Susan, but still, they are not lowballing me. They could just as easily offered me twenty percent or worse ten or fifteen percent”, a much more reasonable Mr Himmelstaff noted.

“Sir, who retains control of the mining rights?”, Susan enquired.

“According to this offer document, I do”, Victor replied, he was more than happy with that.

Then Susan read the fine print, “Oh, that's not good! Sir, you need to sign and return this document back to Dumas Corporation by midnight tonight."

"What?", he quickly read through the fine print, "Oh shit! Clever but shit! They will penalise me a one percent share for every day that I delay signing this document. Damn. This is bloody controlling, yet fair, but it's also forcing my hand", Victor noted.

"Sir, it is very clear. If you don't sign and return it by midnight tonight, you will lose the controlling share. If you wait another day, Dumas Corporation will have the controlling share", Susan explained, adding, "Sir, you have a difficult choice to make."

"And if I sign this today?", Victor enquired.

"Then the terms as stipulated will be binding", Susan answered, noting, "Based on the earnings of the other Dumas mining ventures, you will become exceedingly rich. You'll have access to people, you would never have met otherwise. However, Dumas will control the purse strings!"

Victor gripped his bald head tightly, he was sweating profusely, "Susan, please read through this entire document. Then, print out a copy with any pitfalls highlighted. If it is as it says on the surface, then I'll have to sign it. I don't seem to have a lot of choice in the matter."

As requested, Susan went through the offer document with a fine-toothed comb looking for any hidden bombshells. It was as it seemed, no more and no less, generous to a *'t'*, yet controlling nonetheless. Susan frowned, she'd almost hoped to find something fishy, fishy enough for it to be rejected, but the only fine print was the one percent per day procrastination stipulation. At eleven p.m. that evening, Susan Carter handed the document to Victor Himmelstaff for signing. Victor scanned through it, there was nothing highlighted that they didn't already know.

After much umming and ahhing, Victor made a decision. Victor's bald pate still sweating, he put pen to paper, then he passed the document back to Susan, who promptly scanned it and sent it through to the Dumas Corporation. Victor wiped the sweat from his head, it was done. Victor Himmelstaff would become a rich man, very rich indeed, but at what cost.

A document arrived at the Dumas Corporation's servers, it was parsed and then passed onto Stuart Dumas, it's timestamp, twenty three fifty five p.m. Victor has secured his controlling share in the new corporation, Mars Trojan Mining Ltd.

In the due course of time, the Himmelstaff and Dumas families become much closer, when two years later, Hypolita Himmelstaff married Baron Dumas, their union was of love and not a partnership. During those first two years, Victor Himmelstaff kept a sharp eye out for that *'hidden'* cost that having financial overseers at the Dumas Corporation would bring. All he found were business opportunities and a constant inflow of credits that sometimes sent him dizzy about how quickly his wealth accumulated. Instead of *'hidden'* costs, he found silver lining after silver lining.

In his many meetings with Stuart Dumas, Victor was introduced to more and more powerful players in the business world. Each player he met was more powerful than the previous one.

Victor had thought to himself, *"Dumas is bringing me into the big leagues one step at a time!"*, it was perplexing until one day Dumas himself explained it.

Dumas had said, "I may be hard, Victor, but when I uplift a man into my world, it uplifts all of those people that, that man employs."

"Was that what Dumas was doing, uplifting him, into Dumas's world?", Victor had thought.

By the time of his Daughter, Hypolita's, marriage to Baron Dumas, Victor now owned two more companies. Stuart Dumas had advised registering a third company, Himmelstaff Consolidated Industries Ltd, explaining that by doing so, he could manage all three of his businesses from that one umbrella corporation. Susan Carter, his administrative assistant, readily agreed and helped him with the entire process.

Stuart Dumas was at least ten years younger than Victor Himmelstaff and yet, he became Victor's mentor and gave him free advice at every opportunity. Every Christmas from the union of their children onwards, Victor's entire family were invited to Christmas lunch at the Dumas mansion. Stuart was not just Victor's mentor, but also became his confidant and somehow, Stuart Dumas was even his friend.

Victor looked back to that vexing offer document that had him rubbing his sweating bald pate and wondered just how that one document had changed his life in so many ways. In the news, he sometimes saw his own name and himself described as a rising business mogul.

Where was the *'hidden'* catch?

Where was the trap?

Victor could not find one. All he found was opportunity after opportunity and his star rising.

Victor Himmelstaff was soaring high above the clouds and all he could see before him was blue skies and silver linings in his future and that was how his dreams were of late.

Aria lowered her head onto the table and placed her hands over her head, she just groaned.

"What's wrong, Aria?", her twin Sister, Ariel, enquired.

Aria lifted her head, "It's all economics and business!", she moaned, then she turned to Saffiera who was note-taking as usual, "Do not assign any of that economics crap to me, Saffiera!"

"Aria, the work has to be done. It is just a part of the history, an important part", Saffiera told her.

Ariel focused her thoughts carefully, hoping Saffiera would pick them up as she often did, thanks to her telepathic gifts, *"Saffiera, I know my Sister. If we assign stuff to Aria that she doesn't like, she won't do it, or worse, she will mess it up."*

Saffiera was quite concerned, *"The work has to be done and I have to be fair when I assign it."*

Ariel replied aloud, "Saffiera, just assign the stuff that Aria hates to me. I'll deal with it."

"My, Sister to the rescue!", Aria exclaimed, then she hugged Ariel and stated, "I love you to bits!"

Ariel shrugged her Sister off, "Aria! I hate economics just as much as you do!", she exclaimed.

Saffiera looked at Kethera, whose eyes seemed focused on Richard most of the time, then she turned to Yeannah, who was doing her best not to look at Thomas, even though every few minutes, she would sneak a quick peek. Saffiera shook her head, her two friends were quite distracted. Something that was very unusual for Yeannah, not so much for Kethera.

Kethera targeted her thoughts to the twins, *"Is there some way you guys can get Kethera and Yeannah to refocus on our work?"*

Aria and Ariel repositioned themselves on either side of Kethera and began clapping their hands together, softly they sang into Kethera's ears, "Kethera and Richard sitting in a tree, K.I.S.S.I.N.G. First comes love, then comes marriage, followed by a baby in a baby carriage."

"By the Gods", Saffiera thought to herself, *"That is not what I meant."*

The twins repeated, "Kethera and Richard sitting in a tree, K.I.S.S.I.N.G. First comes love, then comes marriage, followed by a baby in a baby carriage."

It seemed to work, however, as Kethera reached out to grab the twins clapping hands, she then looked from Aria to Ariel with a hint of anger.

Aria looked at Kethera, "Then stop staring at Richard and focus on the assignment!"

"I wasn't staring", Kethera replied, then realising she actually was, she asked with a quiet, embarrassed voice, "Was I? Did anyone notice?"

Aria replied honestly, "Yes, Kethera, you were staring and yes, people noticed. Everyone noticed!"

Kethera looked across to Richard once again and saw Richard waving back, her blue stripes broadened with embarrassment, displaying a slight iridescence. She turned back around and put her hands to her now hot flushed face, he whiskers were downcast and she bit down on her lower lip.

Why couldn't she stop looking at Richard?

It was as if her eyes had a will of their own, betraying her every single time.

"What's wrong with me?", Kethera asked.

Saffiera's silent voice softly entered Kethera's mind filled with gentle amusement, *"You're in love, Kethera. It's as simple and as complicated as that."*

Yeannah was equally distracted and noticed none of the interactions.

Aria asked her quite bluntly, "What's your excuse, Yeannah? Why are you continuously sneaking peeks at Thomas?"

Yeannah snapped out of her reverie and answered, "What? No! I wasn't!"

"You kind of were, Yeannah, my alabaster beauty!", Aria replied, using the very last compliment that Thomas had given her.

Now Yeannah was the one biting down on her lower lip, her face felt hot and was bright red with embarrassment. Had she really been sneaking peeks at Thomas? Then she realised she had!

"No one noticed, did they?", Yeannah quickly asked, then she added, "No one saw me? Did they?", then she thought to herself, *"Gods, let no one have noticed."*

Ariel took Yeannah's hand in hers and placed her other hand over the top, "Yeannah. I don't think anyone else noticed. Just us", she tapped the back of her hand gently.

"He can't know Ariel. He must never know!", Yeannah replied, her irises open wide, "Thomas is not a Thol, not of any kind of Thol, let alone a Mimasian Thol. He must never know!", she snuck another look and Thomas waved back at her, "Oh, Shit!", she exclaimed.

Saffiera calmly and gently entered Yeannah's mind with her soft thought, *"Yeannah, you are attracted to him nonetheless"*, it was a thought open to Kethera and the twins as well.

Yeannah looked at Saffiera, her eyes wide, with an almost horrified look, "That cannot be, Saffiera. That must not be, Saffiera. A Thol must not love someone who is not of their own kind!"

"Why?", Aria asked, noting, "Yeannah. This is the thirty fifth century, for Christ's sake. In this day and age, you can love whoever you like."

"It does not work that way with my people, Aria", Yeannah replied, she had tears welling in her eyes and the twins got up and sat on either side of her, "It is the duty of all Thol women to bear young and that cannot happen with one who is outside of our species."

Ariel put her arm around Yeannah, gently caressing her great leathery wings, she passed her a tissue, "You can like Thomas without being involved with him you know."

Aria put her arm around Yeannah from the other side, caressing her wings as well, agreeing with Ariel, but in her more usual blunt fashion, "Ariel is right. You can love someone without bonking them. Just be his friend and chill, hang out", then with unusual wisdom, "Let's just focus on the assignment for the moment and put Thomas out of your mind."

Kethera chimed in, beaming with a smile, "Was that wisdom from Aria?"

Aria replied nonchalantly, "Meh, I don't know, Ariel got me all soppy. Thomas is just a jerk anyway. We have better things to do", then she turned to Yeannah, kissing her gently on the cheek, "We love you to bits, my alabaster beauty!"

Yeannah began to smile and with their emotional turmoil subsiding, they all focused back on their second term assignment.

14. Phobos and Deimos.

In the two years after signing the contract with the Dumas Corporation, a lot of things were in motion. For one, the mining operations in the Martian Trojan points were almost ready to begin. Conglomerated Asteroidal Masses had been built up in the sweet spots of both Trojan points. These, of course, were built up using fifty Mars-crossing asteroids, the ones with the most dangerous orbits. That helped to mitigate issues of possible asteroidal collisions. The mining stations had already been put in place in orbit around the conglomerate masses. Mining was soon to begin!

There was still much more to do, however, with the need to haul in and, of course, place into safe halo orbits the ore processing stations, the manufacturing stations and of course, the big ones, the six twin-cylinder O'Neil-style colonies. The financial costs were substantial, hell, they were enormous and true to his word, Stuart Dumas's Dumas Corporation was underwriting all of the expenses.

Victor had agreed to the five year plan put forward by Dumas Corporation's experts and in another three years, his Mars Trojan Mining company would be in full operation. Victor Himmelstaff smiled at the prospects, not that he needed the credits, he had two other companies and his umbrella company to manage them. They were all profitable and the credits just kept rolling in.

Victor could not understand how all of this remained on schedule. The financing, the resourcing, all of the expertise, even the actual work itself. There were no delays, every aspect of the process was smooth and progress never wavered, not by one iota. Stuart Dumas had once explained to Victor that it's all about respect.

If you pay your people very well but also make them understand that you expect hard work out of them in return, then that is what you will get. Good conscientious workers who go the extra mile. Do the opposite and all you get is griping and groaning, continuous bellyaching. The Dumas Corporations paid top credits for their workers and their workers appreciated it.

There was a meeting at the Dumas Corporate Tower in the Dumas Corporate Colony, a large single cylinder O'Neil-style colony in the Cis-Lunar L-Five gravitational region, in which Stuart Dumas lived and worked. The entire colony was Dumas Incorporated Industries and that was its registered name. Victor Himmelstaff and his staff had been requested to attend, requested meaning, he had to be there.

Victor left his office at the Mars Trojan Mining corporate offices in the colony where he lived, with his personal assistant, Susan Carter. Susan was the only staff Victor required, she knew everything Victor knew and then some. Victor trusted her completely.

As the pair travelled by inter-colony taxi from Victor's home colony to Dumas Incorporated Industries, he asked himself, *"Is this where I find out what the catch is?"*, his mind held fear and trepidation, he still held deep doubts.

The inter-colony taxi had left the docking ring at Victor's colony and he was expecting much the same at his destination. They would alight at the docking ring and catch a pod or a runabout to the corporate tower. Instead, however, the taxi was directed into the docking ring, then through several airlocks, before flying across the northern end cap directly to the Dumas corporate tower itself, landing on its roof. The process was so efficient!

The sheer size of this corporate colony did not go unnoticed as Victor and Susan had approached, *"These were the big boys. I am so out of my league!"*, he had thought to himself with clear unease.

"Mr Himmelstaff, Sir. If I might say so, you are looking a little flustered. I recommend you take a moment to compose yourself, Sir", Susan told him, bringing him back from his anxious thoughts to reality.

"Yes, yes, you are so right, Susan. I don't know what's the matter with me today. I have been here before many times after all", Victor replied, as he began to compose himself for the meeting, he added quietly, "Every time I come here, it just seems so daunting!"

Tegan Smith was waiting for them on the rooftop, there was an ever so slight artificial wind and it played with Tegan's curly auburn locks, "Mr Himmelstaff, Susan. Welcome", she greeted as they alighted the taxi, "Please follow me."

Tegan led them directly to Stuart Dumas's office. There were several comfortable chairs all arranged in a circle in the office's central open space. Five chairs in all. A chair for Mr Dumas, his Son, Baron, Tegan, Susan and himself. A platter of sandwiches had been placed on a low coffee table in the centre, along with several folios containing documents. There was a bar set up at the edge of the circle.

Stuart walked straight over to Victor and greeted him warmly, taking his hand in his with a firm handshake. Stuart had that odd habit of being firm and turning his hand over the top the other person's. Victor subconsciously gulped nearly every time he did so.

Noticing Victor's mild discomfort, Stuart placed his other hand around Victor's, "It is so good to see you again, Victor. Please, everyone, take a seat."

Stuart noticed the sweat on Victor's hand and as they sat down, he said to him, "Victor. You're always so apprehensive when you come here. We are family now, my Boy is your Son-in-law", then he turned to Baron, "Lad, get your Father-in-law a drink. Brandy I think", then he reconsidered, "No wait. Make that Cognac, VSOP, on the rocks. It is a nice drop!"

"And yourself, Dad?", Baron enquired.

"The same, of course, Baron. This is a time for celebration", Stuart replied.

Baron placed the glasses of cognac in front of his Father and Father-in-law, then asked, "Ladies. What would you like?"

"Perhaps a nice glass of red wine, young Sir", Tegan requested, then Susan agreed with her stating, "Yes, that would be nice."

Baron placed a bottle of expensive Shiraz on the table along with two glasses and generously filled them both before passing them to Susan and Tegan, in that order

"Victor, please, take a drink, it will calm those nerves", Stuart implored.

Victor felt slightly embarrassed, he asked, "Is it really that obvious?"

"Honestly, Victor, yes, it is. You need to let that apprehension go. You are family, after all. I'll be entirely honest with you, Victor. I still get nervous as well", Stuart replied, then he added, "And besides, today is a good day. We have opportunities galore!"

"You mentioned opportunities, Stuart?", Victor asked, using his first name, as he downed his cognac in two swigs, placing the now empty glass on the table.

Before placing the bottle of cognac on the table, Baron asked his Father-in-law, "Father, would you like a top-up?", distinguishing between his biological Father as Dad and his Father-in-law as Father.

Victor replied, "Yes, thank you, Baron."

"Yes, well, Victor. You may not know this, but the Dumas Corporation has purchased thirty six percent of the Lunar Mining Consortium's stock", Stuart informed him.

"Interesting. I did not know that", Victor admitted, then asked, "How does this opportunity work?"

Baron passed Victor a folio, the front cover was labelled Lunar Mining Consortium Proposal.

"Ah, yes. Well, Victor. I was thinking that if Himmelstaff Consolidated invested in a fifteen percent share of the Lunar Mining Consortium's stock, together we would have fifty one percent of the company shares and effectively control the whole lunar mining consortium."

Victor thumbed carefully through the document, he noted the finance options, "Okay, Stuart. So I can finance this myself through Himmelstaff

Consolidated, or I can finance it through Dumas Incorporated. Both appear to be good options", he passed the folio to his assistant, "Susan will perform the due diligence, of course, and if it stacks up, Himmelstaff Consolidated will make the purchase. At a glance, it does look quite lucrative", he made the decision surprisingly quickly.

Susan placed the folio into her briefcase and remarked, "Mr Himmelstaff, Sir. I will look into this proposal once we're back in the office", Victor nodded in reply.

Baron noted, "My Dad could have purchased that stock himself, but he wanted to allow you the opportunity to expand your business holdings."

"Yes, Baron. That was very generous of your Father", Victor agreed as he downed his second glass of cognac, he noted, "This is a very fine cognac, by the way. Very smooth, in fact."

"Father, I would recommend eating a couple of sandwiches to soak up the booze", Baron noted.

Victor nodded and picked a ham and cheese sandwich.

"Now for the really big opportunities, Victor!", Stuart remarked.

"I thought that was the big opportunity", Victor replied, then he smiled, "Of course, Stuart. The playing field you're on is so much higher up."

"To be entirely honest, Victor, it is, but you know what? You will be playing on those same levels very soon. Mark my words. You have places to go, people to meet and deals to make", Stuart replied.

Baron passed Victor another folio, its front cover was labelled Cis-Lunar Constructions Acquisition.

Victor thumbed carefully through the document, he was a little confused, "Wait a minute! I know this company. It was in the news a while back. Isn't it on its last legs, almost about to fold?"

"Absolutely, Victor. You'll get to acquire it for a rock-bottom price. Once you've done that, you can White-Knight it back into prosperity", Stuart agreed, with just a hint of the plan.

Baron chimed in with, "Think about it Father, you will save tens of thousands of jobs."

Victor was not yet convinced, "She sounds like a dark horse, Stuart, a very dark horse."

"It is indeed, Victor, but did you notice the number one on the folio's front cover, it's a water mark", Stuart replied, with a wry smile upon his face.

Victor immediately took notice of the watermark on the folio's front cover, a clear one, that he had not noticed before.

Baron passed his Father-in-law another folio, "Father, this one is number two of three", the front cover read Port Phobos Construction Initiative, it had the distinctive watermark, two.

"Port Phobos Construction?", Victor read out the title questioningly.

Stuart smiled, "Once you buy out Cis-Lunar Constructions, you rename it to Himmelstaff Interplanetary Constructions Ltd."

"Himmelstaff Interplanetary Constructions", Victor repeated, it rolled off the tongue nicely, he liked the sound of it, "How does this save the company?"

"Oh, Victor. I know the right people. I drop your name here and there. I'll mention Himmelstaff Interplanetary Constructions in a glowing light."

Then Baron chimed in, too eager to hold back, "Father, you'll get the contract to build Port Phobos!"

As Victor carefully thumbed through the document, he realised the enormity of the project, the Martian Moon Phobos was to be excavated and built into a major port in Martian orbit. It was a huge undertaking, a huge opportunity, a major construction project, a very lucrative one at that!

Victor looked at Baron and then the implications dawned on him, he looked back to Stuart, "With your backing, I'll have contracts thrown at me, hand over fist", he was beginning to realise what playing in the big leagues truly meant.

Baron noted, "We will need to nudge Phobos into a safer, more stable orbit, but Cis-Lunar Haulage is good at that sort of thing."

Victor smiled and nodded, the Martian Moon Phobos was going to become a major space port and he was going to build it!

It was as if it was never going to end, Baron passed another folio to Victor, "Father, it gets even better, much better, this is folio three of three", the front cover read, Deimos Military Base and Re-fulling Station Initiative, it also had a distinctive watermark, three.

Victor looked at the document and then began to thumb through it carefully, "Oh my God! This is huge. A massive military base and refuelling station carved into the Martian Moon Deimos!"

"And Victor, your company, Himmelstaff Interplanetary Constructions, will be the one to build it", Stuart informed him.

This was way too much excitement, Victor topped up his glass with cognac and downed it in one, "Are you sure I can handle all of this?", he asked Stuart, feeling somewhat inadequate.

His personal assistant, Susan, had a cross look on her face, "Mr Himmelstaff, Sir. You are more than capable of handling these opportunities. Do not underestimate yourself."

Tegan piped up, glass of red wine in hand, "Here, here!"

Stuart smiled, "There's your answer, Victor."

Baron then remarked, "Father, when I ran these files past Hypolita, she thought it was a wonderful opportunity. Your family prospers, your companies prosper and even your employees will prosper."

"Oh. Wait a minute. You informed Hypolita before you informed me?", Victor questioned.

"Father! I tell my wife, Hypolita, everything, she is my better half after all", Baron replied, then noted, "Hypolita wanted to keep it all a secret, a pleasant surprise for you. And it is your birthday after all!"

Victor laughed, "Huh, huh! I'd forgotten all about that!"

"Baron telling his wife aside, these deal can not become common knowledge just yet", Stuart noted, explaining, "We have to do the leg work first. Buying shares in the Lunar Mining Consortium is the easy part. Very simple. Those other three folios are more difficult, they have to be actioned in the order presented with very precise timing. One step after the other."

Victor replied after eating another couple of sandwiches, "So, how do we proceed?", he asked.

"Highly methodically. Tegan knows what to do, she will liaise with Susan and the process should be completed before the month is out", Stuart informed him.

Tegan noted, "Mr Himmelstaff, Sir. Our people have even mapped out a five-year plan for both projects. I will help Susan with all of it, show her the ropes, so to speak."

Susan looked to Tegan, "Thank you, Susan. I will appreciate your assistance."

Stuart also noted, "Victor, just like the Martian Trojan mining operation, you will have our full and complete backing. Whatever you might need, resources, technical assistance, financial, anything you need. Anything!"

"You're always so generous, Stuart", Victor noted.

"Think about it, Victor. How many people have you employed since we started working together?", Stuart asked.

Victor looked at Stuart, admitting, "I don't really know, thousands upon thousands, I guess."

Susan put a number on it, "Sir. Over thirty six thousand employees in the last two years alone."

"That many! I knew it was a large number, but that many? Wow!", Victor replied.

"And all of them have good jobs, good pay and good lives. All of them uplifted. At the end of the day, that's what this is all about", Stuart replied, then he smiled, “And it is, of course, your birthday.”

“Great timing, I think”, Baron added.

“Stuart. That very first contract, the one offering to finance the Martian Trojan Mining operation. I'm just wondering. Why was their time limit with growing penalties?”, Victor enquired, he added, admitting, “I've always wanted to know. I guess I've never had the courage to ask.”

“Oh! Yes, that one percent per day penalty”, Stuart remembered, then explained, “Back then, I didn't know who you were, Victor. You had purchased the Martian Trojan mining rights just five days before I was going to purchase them. So, I already had the Earth's and Venus's Trojans all locked in and all of a sudden, I was blocked from completing the trifecta.”

“The trifecta?”, Victor enquired.

Baron answered, “The trifecta would have been locking in all three Trojan orbital zones, Father. You managed to get in before we did.”

“And because I didn't know anything about you when I made our offer, I decided to include a Sword of Damocles clause”, Stuart admitted, to which he then apologised, “I can only imagine how stressful that day became, for which I do sincerely apologise.”

“A Sword of Damocles clause?”, Victor enquired.

“Yes. I needed to test your mettle, Victor. I needed to know how your mind works. I gave you the option of fifty one percent in the company, a controlling percentage in the Mars Trojan Mining Corporation. No lowballing. That's not something I do when dealing with individuals or competent parties. Yet, at the same time, Dumas Incorporated Industries held all of the purse strings”, Stuart explained.

“Stuart, that implies that you do occasionally lowball?”, Victor noted.

“Yes, when it involves corrupt or incompetent governments spending and wasting other people's money”, Stuart admitted, remarking, “So I limit their supply of funds and inject my own funds where necessary using my own trustworthy people. I offered you fifty one percent, I offered the Venusian Government only twenty. They almost sleepwalked into a disaster of their own making. The Dumas Corporation compensates the Venusian people by donating significant funds for Venusian Schools and Hospitals”, the discussion was getting off track.

Tegan stepped in, clarifying, “Not just Schools and Hospitals, Mr Himmelstaff, Sir. Parks, Gardens, Open spaces, Social injustice and a lot more. All to the tune of about a thirty percent difference.”

Baron chimed in, “My Dad absolutely hates seeing people go hungry, especially children. That inequity just isn't right”, then he returned the discussion back on course, "So Father, you would control your company, but Dumas Incorporate controlled the financial oversight."

"Yes, thank you, Son", Stuart replied, then he continued, "You would obviously realise that and that alone would give you a severe case of fear, uncertainty and doubt. So then, I added urgency to the equation, with a Sword of Damocles clause. For each day, you procrastinated, you'd lose a one percent share of the business, starting at midnight. I needed to see if you'd bite the bullet and take the deal."

"And just before midnight on the first day, I signed the paperwork and Susan sent it off", Victor stated, remembering the moment, "I must admit, it worked. I definitely bit the bullet."

"And that, Victor, was what I needed to see", Stuart admitted, finishing off with, "Would you sign the document under pressure, knowing that another corporation had leverage over you and not knowing whether there were any hidden catches? Would you step past your fears, your uncertainties and your doubts?"

"I took a leap of faith, Stuart, and look at where I am today. I'd say that the stress of that one day, that one decision was actually worth it", Victor replied, closing with, "I'd make that same decision all over again if I had to", then he noted, "Thirty percent of your Venusian profits go to charitable works! Wow! I really need to step up."

"How you spend your credits is up to you, Victor. Personally, I recommend philanthropic practices", Stuart commented.

Within two weeks, Susan and Tegan had navigated the bureaucracy of acquiring the Cis-Lunar Constructions company and re-branding it as Himmelstaff Interplanetary Constructions. Then one week after that, Himmelstaff Interplanetary Constructions was awarded the contract for building Port Phobos on the Martin Moon, Phobos in Martian orbit. This was followed one week later with the awarding of the contract for building the new Military base and Refuelling facilities on the Martian Moon, Deimos. The plans, as discussed with Stuart Dumas, were all coming together.

Himmelstaff Interplanetary Constructions broke ground on both Phobos and Deimos one month after that, officially kicking off the five year plans to construct the two projects. Once that had happened Victor asked Susan to look into setting up a *'philanthropic'* system to donate funds to worthy, charitable causes.

To do this, Susan, looked into how the Dumas Corporation handled their philanthropy, it turned out they had created a special division to handle these things, The Dumas Philanthropic Foundation. So Susan discussed this with Tegan and together they set up a new division, The Himmelstaff Philanthropic Foundation. Victor's instructions were clear, but they were also ambitious.

Victor wanted ten percent of his Mars Trojan Mining profits channelled into worthy charitable causes by the Himmelstaff Philanthropic Foundation by the end of the financial year. That was no easy task, as there was not a lot out in the Martian orbital zone at that time. Worthy charitable causes had to be located on the Earth and within Cis-Lunar L-Five. By the end of that financial year, however, Susan had achieved her boss's requests.

With the creation of The Himmelstaff Philanthropic Foundation and its ongoing philanthropic efforts, Victor Himmelstaff himself was becoming a household name.

Stuart Dumas was quite surprised when he saw the news, so much so that he had to check it twice.

Stuart had thought to himself, *"Go hard or go home. Victor is going hard! I should have expected this, my personal assistant, Tegan, is of course showing Susan the ropes."*

The girls had finished reading through the pages about the Martian Moons Phobos and Deimos, Ariel turned to her twin, Aria, who had a huge frown on her face.

"Do not say a word, Aria! I do not want to hear it! So don't you dare!", Ariel snapped at her Sister, vividly remembering that the last time Aria opened her big mouth, she'd volunteered to do Aria's work.

The kind of work she knew she would end up doing because Aria always found ways to avoid it.

Aria, instead of saying what was on her mind, mouthed the words without making a sound, *"I hate this economics bullshit!"*, it was silent but irritating, except of course, Saffiera's telepathic mind heard her quite clearly.

Ariel turned to Saffiera, projecting her thoughts as loudly as possible so that Saffiera would hear them, *"Can you do anything to tweak my Sister. You know, make her more reasonable?"*

Saffiera replied, *"Sadly, no, Ariel. As much as I might like to, that would be against Martian law."*

Ariel thought back quickly, *"I didn't hear a no, so you could do it, just not legally."*

"Yes, Ariel. Tweaking Humans is illegal. Only the Martian Elders may do it and even then, the decision has to be unanimous", Saffiera explained.

"So they've done it in the past?", a very curious Ariel asked silently with another thought.

"Yes, however, the first time they did so was during the Mimasian War many centuries ago. The Elders somehow created the two most powerful Earth psychics to ever exist and

they didn't even understand how", Saffiera explained, adding, *"Now, they are very reticent to tweak Humans at all. It is just far too dangerous."*

"So, your Elders made a huge mistake back in the Mimasian War?", Ariel asked curiously.

"Yes and no. It was a mistake that turned out serendipitous. Those two Earth psychics ended up defeating the Mimasian Emperor", Saffiera remarked, then noted, *"That was no mean feat!"*

The silence between Ariel and Saffiera was palpable and Aria spat out, "Will you two stop thinking about me! I am right here, you know!"

"Aria, did you not read those pages? They explained how the Martian Trojan mining operations were developed and the construction of Port Phobos and the military bases on Deimos", Ariel scolded.

Kethera had turned around, having been distracted yet again by Richard, "And who was instrumental in making those events happen. You mustn't forget that. Very important it is!"

Aria replied with a shrug, "Meh. It was all boring. Too much economics!", she whined.

Saffiera rolled her eyes, *"Let me try something. It is legal, I just would prefer not to do it."*

"It's fine by me, Saffiera. Anything that helps us get the work done", Ariel suggested.

Saffiera moved closer to Aria and remarked, "Aria, this will help you handle the assignment better."

"Is it painful? My brain won't bleed out of my ears, will it?", Aria asked, feeling quite reluctant.

"It is completely harmless, Aria", Saffiera assured her.

Saffiera leaned forward and gently touched Aria's forehead with her own, then she focused on her memories, the ones from studying the historical document pages on the network. Slowly Saffiera built her memories into a coherent stream and because they were intended to be delivered to Aria, she built up visualised imagery as accurately as possible to match the history that she had just read about.

At first, Aria baulked when the first memories began streaming into her mind and she resisted, but Saffiera held onto Aria's arms firmly to ensure that her memories were delivered without interruption. All of the *'economic'* bullshit that Aria had derided, began to stream into her mind with coherence and clarity, only this time with the historical contexts highlighted, along with telepathic notation and tied to Saffiera's relatively accurate visualisations.

After several long minutes, the flow of memories and information slowed and then finally stopped. Saffiera gradually backed away from Aria, she had a trickle of blood in her right nostril, which she quickly dabbed with her handkerchief.

Aria declared, "That was amazing. I didn't realise I'd missed so much!"

Ariel asked Saffiera, "Are you okay?"

"Yes. It's the first time I've attempted this with an Earth Human, especially with something so complex. I'll be okay in a few minutes", Saffiera replied, adding, *"Thank you for asking."*

Aria was excited, but for all the wrong reasons, "We no longer need to study! Saffiera can just read it all and push everything straight into our brains, complete with visuals", she declared.

"And that is why I don't like doing this", Saffiera transmitted silently to Ariel, *"It is not a shortcut!"*

Ariel's eyes rolled, then she looked at her Sister, "Are you fucking serious, Aria!", she scolded, gesturing to Saffiera who was still recovering.

Aria looked at Saffiera, she looked pale and drained, and she was still dabbing at the trickle of blood coming out of her nostrils, "I am so sorry, Saffiera!", she told her with true remorse, as she placed her arms around her and hugged her tightly, "I had no idea it would have this effect on you!"

Saffiera replied silently to her friends, *"While sharing memories works well amongst Martians, it is so much harder with other species. Especially those with chaotic minds, like Earth Humans."*

"Are our minds so different?", Aria asked with curiosity.

"Martians have orderly structured minds and we are used to sharing. It is something we have done for countless millennia", Saffiera informed them.

"Other non-Martian minds tend to have a distinct lack of structure and a degree of chaos that makes it somewhat more difficult. It can be quite a strain for us", Saffiera explained.

"Let's not do that again then, Saffiera", Aria decided, remarking, "I'll try not to be such a bitch in the future. I love you to bits", then she gently kissed Saffiera on the cheek, rocking her gently, feeling fully remorseful for her earlier behaviour.

While the girls had been talking and completely distracted, Richard and Thomas had sauntered across from their table on the other side of the study hall. Richard pulled up a chair and sat down in front of Kethera. He reached out his hands and took Kethera's hands in his. The pair just stared at each other in silence, taking in each other's gaze. Thomas, on the other hand, had walked over to Yeannah and he too pulled up a chair, however, before he could sit down, Aria reacted to his presence defensively.

"Don't you dare sit down! Not after what you've done! Turn around and go back the way you came", she told Thomas in no uncertain terms.

"After what I've done?", Thomas questioned, he was quite confused and asked, "What am I suppose to have done?", he didn't even know which twin he was talking to, "Which twin are you anyway? You are both identical."

Aria smirked, "It's very simple", she gestured to Ariel, "That is Ariel, she's the good twin", then she gestured to herself, "I'm Aria and I'm the bad twin. Would you like to see just how bad I can be?"

Thomas almost laughed, he was tall and lanky, standing a full foot taller than Aria, "What? I should be afraid of a little girl."

Ariel rolled her eyes as Aria began to wind up, she held up her hand and pointed at Thomas, "Do not go there, trust me. My Sister, Aria, will rip you a new one", she told Thomas in no uncertain terms.

Thomas put up both hands in mock defeat, "Okay. Okay. Could someone please tell me what I did wrong? I'm kind of confused over here."

"You hurt our friend, Yeannah!", Aria snarled at him.

"I did not. The last time we spoke, I complimented her in fact", Thomas replied in bewilderment.

"Perhaps you should learn more about Thols and their culture", Aria snarled back.

"Culture?", Thomas questioned rhetorically as it dawned on him, he may have inadvertently said something untoward, he sat down in front of Yeannah, who averted her eyes, "Yeannah, if I said something that offended you, I do apologise. It was most certainly not my intent."

Saffiera silently entered Thomas's mind with her thoughts, *"You need to learn a few things about Thols and their cultural prohibitions and taboos"*, she snapped sharply.

That took Thomas aback, he almost trembled, he had heard Saffiera communicate many times before, but never with such potent force.

"Prohibitions? Taboos?", he thought to himself, obviously he'd missed something, he faced Yeannah and ever so gently lifted up her chin, so that he could look in to her eyes, "Yeannah. I am so sorry! I did not mean to hurt you", then he complimented her again, in the one way he shouldn't have, "I think you're the most beautiful girl in the whole school. Truly!"

Aria palm faced, "You just did it again, you stupid twat! Just get the fuck out of here! Go!", she shouted out at him.

Thomas was obviously triggering Aria's anger and aggression, he wasn't even sure why and would definitely have to do some research on Thol kind, "Okay. Okay. I can see that I'm just causing more issues here, I'll go", then he got up and walked back to his table on the other side of the hall.

Richard took that as his queue to follow Thomas back to their table, he leaned in and kissed Kethera, their lips met and lingered together for many long moments.

"I'll see you later, my love", Richard told Kethera as he stood up and followed Thomas.

"My love?", Ariel repeated, "I think you two are officially an item now, Kethera."

Kethera's whiskers twitched and her tails swished excitedly from side to side, the blue stripes on her face broadened and glowed with slight iridescence, in a coy voice, she excitedly told Ariel, "His tongue tastes like Chillics!"

In a dull, almost monotone voice, Yeannah replied, "Too much information, Kethera", then she added dryly, "They were eating Chillics with their lunch earlier."

Saffiera asked her, gently pushing her thoughts into Yeannah's mind, *"Are you okay?"*

Yeannah was clearly upset, but understood that it was not Thomas's fault, how could it be, he could not possibly know about Tholish taboos, "I'm alright Saffiera. It wasn't Thomas's fault. Our people have prohibitions, we have taboos and we just don't talk about them. How would he know that Thols can't have relationships with other species, not ever."

"Then, when he finds out, two will have been hurt. Thomas dropped his mask and I saw his motivations. He has deep feelings for you, Yeannah", Saffiera informed her, then she turned to Aria, *"He is neither the jerk nor the twat you think he is, Aria, under that mask of his, he is quite insecure."*

"No, I am not going to apologise to him", Aria replied.

"I didn't ask you to", Saffiera clarified.

"He will be hurt, he will be upset", Yeannah commented with sadness and true empathy, "These stupid taboos will now hurt two boys, both Yookey and Thomas."

"Thomas still has to be told", Saffiera replied.

"I'll explain it to Richard next time I meet him, then he can explain it to Thomas. Then he will understand his missteps", Kethera volunteered.

A single tear ran down Yeannah's cheek and Aria leaned in, gently wiping away the tear and cradling Yeannah in her gentle embrace, Aria then stated calmly, "We need a distraction. Let's put this crap behind us and get back to work."

Yeannah's mind was still in turmoil, taboos aside, understanding genetic incompatibilities aside, she actually had feelings for Thomas, though she denied them, even it to herself.

Ariel looked at Aria in mock shock, "More wisdom from my evil twin Sister", she joked and then the group got back to studying for their second-term assignment.

15. The New Tortugans.

The octocopter flew around Hebes Chasma in the upper central reaches of the Valles Marineris chasm complex. Powered by a single micro-fission generator, the artificially intelligent drone was tasked with scanning the upper walls of the chasms in the Valles Marineris complex, searching specifically for cave and cavern systems that may have the potential for developing into underground colonies. The octocopter was the size of a large truck, not a huge lorry, but the kind of truck people living in rural or remote areas might own. Something that had grunt and the ability to tow and carry large loads.

There was a badge on the side of the octocopter that simply had the letters E.A.S.A, the East African Space Alliance. This alliance comprised seven countries, Ethiopia, Kenya, Somaliland, Somalia, South Sudan, Tanzania and Uganda. Their project was ambitious, send an orbiter and a drone to Mars, to investigate the Valles Marineris region for suitable colony sites. No one thought that they could do it and yet, there it was, the E.A.S.A Droni la Uchunguzi octocopter flew through the chasms of Mars successfully for more than two Martian Sols.

The Hebes Chasma was the last chasm in the complex to be investigated. This was the octocopter's second sweep of the Hebes Chasma and now the central mesa, Hebes Mesa, was being scanned. Many cave and cavern systems had been discovered and logged, all around the Valles Marineris chasm complex. These discoveries were transmitted to the orbiter flying high above at regular intervals and then transmitted all the way back to the Earth.

Just in this one chasm alone, the Hebes Chasma, many promising cave systems had been discovered on the southern side of the chasm. More promising cave systems had also been discovered on the Hebes Mesa, however, the most promising of all was the enormous cavern complex discovered on the mesa's southern flank. It was huge, a cavern that opened up into three immense, deep branches.

The branches on her left and the right were large enough to be extraordinarily useful, however, the central cavern was the largest of them all. The central branch was broad and led deep into the mesa, miles deep and at the very back, it connected with a cave system that extended for many more miles. This one cavern alone was so huge, it had the highest potential for turning into a colony.

Many international space mission and engineering specialists had been hired by the E.A.S.A for their ambitious projects. When reviewing the data from the E.A.S.A Droni la Uchunguzi octocopter, a Spanish mission specialist hired by the E.A.S.A, had noted that from the inside of the cavern looking towards its entrance, the left and right branches were like flippers on either side of a turtle's body. That led to the almost immediate naming of the cavern *'New Tortuga'* cavern. The name stuck and it became official.

After the survey of the Valles Marineris chasm complex was completed, the Droni la Uchunguzi octocopter was re-tasked with surveying the nearby Perrotin region in between the Hebes Chasma and Ophir Chasma for possible skylight caves and lava tubes.

The E.A.S.A. had definite plans to colonise the New Tortuga cavern system, only there was one small problem. Like nearly all major scientific discoveries of the day, their findings were all published and made public. So the world at large knew of the successes of the E.A.S.A's mission and that meant the world also knew about the New Tortuga cavern system. A far more powerful space-faring nation, the Russian Federation, was the first to launch with its own colonisation mission. Their target was Novaya Tortuga.

As much as the E.A.S.A Nations were incensed by the Russian's move, there was nothing they could do about it. So the E.A.S.A put together a backup plan. They would instead take advantage of the cave systems on the south side of Hebes Chasma and those they'd discovered in the Perrotin region. The newer Perrotin discoveries had not been released to the public. So it came to pass that the Russians were the first to land on the Hebes Mesa, to make the Novaya Tortuga cavern system their own.

The Russians landed their space transports on the southern side of the Hebes Mesa, well above the Novaya Tortuga cavern system. As the Russian spacecraft approached during their landing, they immediately noticed that a low mountain range ran east to west along the centre of the Hebes Mesa, effectively dividing the mesa in half.

The first action the Russians performed upon accessing the cavern system, was a full and complete survey. They located the region at the very rear of the central cavern, where there was access to a vast cave system. They did not survey the cave system, their main priority was the Novaya Tortuga cavern.

They brought in their high-powered laser rock-melting equipment into the cavern and used these machines to rework the walls of the cavern system's Eastern and Western branches. Having reshaped the walls, they then used the machines to level the floor of each cavern branch. The Western branch was much larger by far and was designated as a port for mid-sized space transports. The Eastern branch was designated as a port for smaller spacecraft. All left over detritus was simply dumped into the depths of the Hebes Chasma. Once finished, they then expanded and squared off the cavern's main outer entrance and then reinforced it with heavy bulkheads.

The leader of the Russian colonial expedition sent one of the laser rock-melting machines to the low mountain range to the north. Their surveyors had located useful trails that led to the mountain range in the south and further trails leading away from the mountain range on the other side. There were no natural passes through the mountains, so the Russians bored one straight through the highest mountain in the range with their laser rock-melting machines. The tunnel was several hundred metres long and now accessing the northern lands on the Hebes Mesa would be a reasonably simple hike.

Once the outer cavern structure had been modified as per their plans, the Russians began work on the central cavern itself. First, they built in heavy bulkheads and an airlock system at the very rear of the cavern, separating the main central cavern itself from the larger, almost unexplored cave system it connected to. The central cavern itself was a huge space, but the cave system was only partly explored and seemed to go on and on for mile upon mile. It appeared to be never-ending.

Where the main central cavern connected to the smaller Eastern and Western caverns, they also put in place massive, heavy bulkheads. Built into these bulkheads, they built a series of airlocks so that cosmonauts could travel from the exterior of Novaya Tortuga to its main interior colony space. Having created a sealed space within the central cavern, they then pumped in the thin Martian air.

They weren't concerned about the constituents of the atmosphere they were creating in the central cavern, they were simply testing for leaks. After all, if the colony couldn't hold an atmosphere, they needed to know about it. They slowly built the central cavern's pressure up for two Earth weeks, from point six millibars Martian standard to one thousand millibars Earth standard. Then they monitored the air pressure for a further two weeks to see if it dropped. The pressure remained stable, they were in luck, the rock walls of the cavern seemed impervious to air. There were no leaks.

The Russians released the air from the central cavern and continued their work. On the eastern and western walls of the central cavern, they used their laser rock-melting machines to sculpt terraces into the cavern's rock walls. Above the cavern floor, they built six terraces on both sides reaching up high into the heights of the cavern. Into these cavern walls, at floor level and the six terraces, they used smaller laser tunnelling machines to carve out a great many *"standardised"* colonial apartments. They were creating housing for thousands of Russian colonists.

As they carved out the *"standard"* apartments, their engineers got busy, a colony of this size still required air and water purification systems, along with power supply transmission systems amongst other infrastructure. Other engineers installed lighting along the full length of the central cavern, while still more engineers toiled on the surface of the Mesa installing six small, yet efficient micro-fission generators. They all worked hard, they all worked long hours and the Russians worked like robots.

At the very rear of the central cavern, they built hydroponic systems that reached from the cavern floor to its ceiling. Artificial lighting was spread throughout the structure. Behind the hydroponics, at the very rear wall of the cavern, they built a high single broad terrace. Into the rock wall at the back of the terrace, they bored out more *"standard"* apartments for the hydroponic farmers who would soon be arriving. The central-most apartment had a direct connection to the cavern's rear airlock and the mysterious cave system beyond it.

All of the tunnelling using laser rock-melting machines was creating a major problem with molten *"slag"* runoff. Waste not, want not, the Russians had a plan for that too. Unlike previously, where they had dumped the detritus into the Hebes Chasma. This time, they pulverised the slag and remelted it, forming it into slag stone blocks, a building material.

At the front of the central cavern, on the inside of the main bulkhead, with its airlocks, they marked out a township in concentric circles. In the very centre of it would be a town plaza, Novaya Tortuga Plaza, the town being simply Novaya Tortuga. The slag stone blocks were used to build the town and they had an ample supply of them.

The final step in the process was, of course, a breathable atmosphere and water supply. For a water supply, they bored a deep hole under the floor of the cavern. Once it was deep enough, they expanded it out to be large enough to hold the town's water and then some. They specially fused the walls of their *"well"*, so that they were like glass and impervious to water. Beyond that, the water in Novaya Tortuga was to be fully, one hundred percent recycled.

For the air, they had a problem. An atmosphere needed a *"filler"* gas to give it volume. On the Earth, that filler gas was nitrogen. On Mars, for nitrogen, they needed to catalyse ammonia, a gas that might be found near volcanic vents. They sent scouts over to the shield volcanoes on the Tharsis Bulge with ammonia detectors and they found several volcanic vents where they could obtain the gas.

The task was difficult, but they managed to capture ammonia in large quantities, compressing it into spent fuel tanks and then moved it to the top of the Hebes Mesa. From there, it was catalysed, the nitrogen being pumped into the Novaya Tortuga colony and the hydrogen being compressed into another spent fuel tank.

As part of the process, they also catalysed atmospheric carbon dioxide. The oxygen was pumped into the Novaya Tortuga colony, with the carbon being compressed into carbon blocks for future use. The hydrogen they'd captured from catalysing ammonia was combusted with some of the oxygen, forming water. This was pumped into the water containment hole, their *"well"*.

It took nearly a month of Earth days to complete the process of pressurising the colony, but in the end, they'd created an atmosphere inside the Novaya Tortuga colony of one thousand millibars, with twenty one percent oxygen and the rest mostly nitrogen with traces of argon, carbon dioxide and water vapour. Two more weeks later and the pressure was declared stable. There were no leaks!

Everything was going well and the last thing on the list was the hydroponics planting. With nearly everything else completed, the hydroponics planting was performed at a more leisurely pace. The seeds germinated, the plants began to grow and soon they were looking forward to their first harvest. Literally the fruits of their hard labours.

Then the bad news hit and it hit like a rock slapped to their faces. The Russian economy had collapsed due to rampant corruption and mismanagement, for the second time in this century. It resonated harshly with the cosmonaut's minds. All funding for Russian space exploration had dried up. The new Government in Moscow was calling for their Martian cosmonauts to come home! A major problem, as the colonists had used a lot of their resources to build the Novaya Tortuga colony. They did not have the resources to return everybody home.

A good fifteen percent of their number had volunteered or were volunteered to remain behind in Novaya Tortuga. All of them were older men amongst their number. They alone remained as *"caretakers"* until the time that their comrades would return for them. They waited and they waited and still their comrades did not come. As time went by, they no longer even received contact from Russia, from Moscow. In the end, they resigned themselves to their fate as *"caretakers"*, accepting the fact that they would never be going home.

These Russian *"caretakers"* were dutiful till the end. They maintained Novaya Tortuga's systems and looked after their hydroponics, all while knowing full well that they were never returning home nor that their comrades were returning to re-colonise Mars. They were all older men and one by one, they succumbed to elderly health issues.

One by one, they died off and the surviving *"caretakers"* did their duty. The bodies of the deceased were cremated and their ashes were mixed with a slag concrete slurry. This was hardened into a large block, which was inscribed with the cosmonaut's name, his birth and death dates and a single sentence summing up his life. Then the block was added into a *"wall of remembrance"*. One block after another, as their numbers dwindled, the wall of remembrance grew.

If their comrades on the Earth ever returned in the future, at least they would be remembered, but their comrades never came back. When the last Martian cosmonaut died, he passed away alone at his work station, dutiful to the very end. There was no one left to bury him and so he, too, was lost. The colony, once brimming with hope, was abandoned and all but forgotten.

The Mars Horizon Homesteading Group, M.H.H.G, was an ad-hoc collective of over a thousand individuals, all of whom wanted to colonise and homestead Mars. Many of its members were wealthy and were actually willing to fund the organisation, which had only a handful of paid employees. One of these was Moira Priestly, their researcher, whose job it was to locate a suitable colony site on Mars.

Moira was looking through some old records that she'd found in an archive in Juba, South Sudan. They were written in three languages, Dinka, Nuer and Kiswahili. The Kiswahili was the easiest to translate. Moira was looking for information on the former East African Space Alliance, E.A.S.A, Mars colonisation plans and what happened to their Martian colonists.

The East African Space Alliance had fallen apart due to economic turmoil less than a year after the economic collapse of the Russian Federation. There was a global economic downturn at that time, precipitated by Russia's collapse and it spread to many parts of the globe. However, what caught Moira's eyes was the fact that these were surveillance records taken by the East African colonists of the Russian colonisation of Novaya Tortuga.

When the translation came back, she was stunned. While the East African Space Alliance was colonising the southern cliffs of the Hebes Chasm, they were also watching ever so closely the Russian operations on the Hebes Mesa and Novaya Tortuga. Moira eagerly read through the translations. It was incredible, she had to read it a second and even a third time.

Moira Priestly jumped on her communicator to her boss, a transport magnate and member of the Mars Horizon Homesteading Group, Magnus Larson.

"Magnus! I've found it. The perfect place to colonise!", Moira exclaimed, she was excited, "It's brilliant, absolutely brilliant. I couldn't believe it when I came across it."

"Slow down, Moira. Slow down. What have you found?", Magnus asked.

"New Tortuga, Magnus. New Tortuga!", Moira almost shouted into her communicator.

"Wait! Moira. Isn't that the failed Russian attempt, Novaya Tortuga?", Magnus queried.

"That's the thing, Magnus. They didn't fail. According to East African Space Alliance records, the Russians actually succeeded. They just abandoned the colony when their economy collapsed. It was one hundred percent completed", Moira informed him with so much excitement in her voice that she was almost shouting.

Magnus Larson thought about the implications, "Oh my. The Russians are still suffering from internal conflict, they are not going back any time soon", he muttered into his communicator, adding, "This is salvage. Straight-up salvage. They've abandoned their colony, they've lost all claims to it."

Moira was quick to make a correction, "Magnus, they did leave caretakers."

"Then it's not so abandoned after all?", he asked.

"Well, here's the thing. We know who came back. We know who they left behind. Their caretakers were all in their sixties, Magnus. That was twenty years back, they are likely all dead by now", Moira explained.

Magnus considered the implications further, the caretakers were likely all dead and the Russians were not going back any time soon, he replied, "Moira. We need to act fast on this one. Fast, but quietly. Very quietly, Moira. I need you to rein in that excitement."

Magnus Larson was a very rich and successful transport magnate. He had ships, plenty of them and he had friends, rich friends, quite a few were, in fact, Mars Horizon Homesteading Group members. Based on the East African Space Alliance records, they could ascertain how large the entrance to New Tortuga was and what ships they should send.

That was no problem for Magnus, he allocated four ships for the task, long-range, mid-sized, that could easily dock at New Tortuga. Each ship could hold a crew complement of twenty five. Moira and Magnus were amongst them. Magnus had the ships ready and crewed before the month was out. On the last day of the month, they launched into the void from Cis-Lunar L-Five, with the destination simply noted as, exploratory.

The four ships in Magnus Larson's little fleet, each had six highly advanced and efficient micro-fission reactors, they reached Mars in just over three months. Once they had achieved orbital insertion, their lead ship sent a military-grade reconnaissance drone down to Hebes Chasma. The drone had the latest A.I. Technology and it carefully scanned Hebes Mesa, most especially the region around the New Tortuga caver structure. Their information was accurate and the entrance was of sufficient size to accommodate their ships.

The drone was then ordered to scan the Hebes Chasms south cliff face. The East African Space Alliance records had made no mention of the colonies in that area nor in the Perrotin region. The drone found no signs of the African colonists, if they still existed, it was a mystery. Magnus sent the drone into the New Tortuga cavern.

Magnus was very pleased to find the Western branch would accommodate his ships with ease. The drone settled down on the Western cavern's floor and Magnus ordered the Captains of his four ships to make haste for the New Tortuga colony. Within two hours, all four ships had entered New Tortuga using their control thrusters and settled down gently in the Western Port Cavern.

Space suits on, the ten-man excursion party, including Moira and Magnus, left their command ship and sauntered over to the central cavern's thick, heavy bulkheads and its airlock system. Interestingly, the airlocks were not locked and the excursion team was easily able to enter the colony. Once inside, they all quickly realised that New Tortuga had an atmosphere, a breathable one at that. After performing some standard tests, they removed their helmets and switched off the oxygen valves in their space suits. The air was not only breathable, it was also clean, crisp, almost sweet. That last one was most surprising.

They looked at the completed yet abandoned town before them, they noted the terraces along the cavern walls, six stories high. It was amazing, absolutely amazing, it was also effing huge! Magnus's team released small A.I. Drones into the cavern and they immediately began scanning and mapping the huge expanse of New Tortuga. While the drones performed their task unattended, the excursion team looked for a base of operations.

They quickly noticed an operations centre tucked into the Western wall of the cavern, up against the main bulkhead. It was a large building and was probably constructed for managing the twin port facilities, however, it was also a larger building than would ordinarily be required for that purpose.

Magnus pointed to the structure and simply said, "That way!" and they all marched towards the building while the drones continued to gather their information.

After entering the building, one of their drones, which had already performed a sweep, led them to the main operations room. It was a big room with multiple workstations, a great many of them. It had an odd, musky smell to it. All of the equipment was still functional, it was all set to run on automatic.

Everything from air purification, water reclamation and power distribution was still running. At the master control station, they found a loan Russian slumped over his workstation. He was dead and, by the looks of him, had been for quite a while. The last of the caretakers? They speculated. It certainly explained the odd musky odour, the lingering scent of death.

The dead man had a name on his coveralls, *"Yuri Belyakov"*. On the workstation's flickering screen, an open file glowed faintly. The text was in Russian, dense and meticulous, very detailed, a digital record of Yuri's final days.

Moira spoke to the drone, "Access this log and translate. Provide side-by-side translation of Russian to English", then the drone began its work, it didn't take long, just a few minutes.

Moira looked at the log, it was now translated as requested, "Shit!", she exclaimed, "Yuri here, has been dead for under a year! It seems he kept everything running right up to the end."

Magnus asked, "Does it say what happened to the other caretakers?"

Moira replied, "According to Yuri's log. The other caretakers had been cremated and transformed into cement blocks, forming a wall of remembrance. Yuri was the last. Severe chest pains signalled his end was near, yet his final act was to ensure that the airlocks remained unlocked for any of his comrades who might return."

"Dedicated to his work until the last!", Magnus exclaimed, adding, "We will honour him and follow his instructions and place his remains with his friends. That's the very least we can do for the guy."

One of the other team members remarked, "I cannot imagine how lonely he must have been."

Moira looked further into Yuri's log, "There are details in here about all of his fellow caretakers. Poor Yuri was on his own for nearly three years", she replied

Moira sighed heavily, "His mind appears to have been deteriorating, yet he still soldiered on with his work. He wrote about the silence, the endless hours maintaining systems and how he longed to hear the sound of another Human voice."

Moira quoted from Yuri's log, "The silence grows heavier each day. I dream of voices and laughter, but all I awake to is the endless hum of machines."

Another team member noted, "Like a Russian robot. They work until they drop."

"Yuri Belyakov wasn't just a machine," Moira said sharply. "He kept this place alive for years when no one else could. Show some bloody respect!"

The team member, Benson, lowered his gaze and nodded.

Magnus fixed Benson with a stern look, "You've just volunteered for undertaker duties. Read Yuri's notes and honour him properly. We'll join you when you're ready", his tone softened. "It's important. Yuri deserves this.'"

Benson didn't argue. He glanced at the log, his expression a mix of regret and determination.

Honouring Yuri Belyakov's last wishes felt like the least he could do.

Benson processed Yuri Belyakov's body as prescribed in his notes. First, his body was cremated in the colony's crematorium. After this, any remaining bone fragments were ground down into dust. The ashes and dust were then mixed with a special concrete mix made with Martian rock slag. This was then poured and hardened in a mold form that was specifically used for the task. It took some time for the block to harden.

Once the block had hardened, Benson christened it "Yuri". He then placed it in a milling machine. To Benson's surprise, Yuri had set up his own epitaph before his death. Only his date of death was missing. Moira Priestly checked Yuri's log and advised Benson of the correct date. Yuri's full name, date of birth, date of death and a small statement were milled into the block in an elegant Russian Cyrillic font. Yuri's last words were, Последний выживший человек. Moira gave the translation as *"The last man standing"*. He literally was.

Moira was present for the entire process as Benson performed the task, not because she didn't trust Benson, it was more about having another person present to watch the process out of respect. Moira probably shouldn't have, she cried silently throughout much of the process and the morbid process gave her nightmares for years to follow. Not everyone was meant to be an undertaker.

The wall of remembrance stood on a platform that was thirty two feet long, three feet wide and a foot high. Running straight down the middle of the platform were perfectly formed and milled blocks. Thirty long and stacked five high, one hundred and forty nine in all. There was a single space on the end that was empty. Yuri's space. Benson very carefully cemented Yuri into position, then checked that he'd done a perfect job before stepping away and wiping tears from his eyes. The wall of remembrance was complete, there were now one hundred and fifty blocks in all.

"Why am I crying?", Benson asked, "I never even knew the man!"

"Not in life perhaps, but you know him now", Magnus replied, placing his hand on his shoulder.

Moira asked, "Benson, can you make more of those blocks?"

Benson replied, after wiping more tears from his eyes, "Yes, of course, but why?"

"I think we should surround the wall with blocks and form an earth bed", Moira commented, then informed the others, "We should plant flowers around the wall. Typical Russian flowers."

Benson nodded, "Consider it done, but I'm not sure where I'll find the flower seeds."

"That's my problem", Moira informed him.

The excursion team expanded from ten to eighty, leaving only five men on each of their four ships. The engineers were busily going through the data feeds from all of the A.I. drones and studying every aspect of the colony. After all, they were now becoming the new colony managers and needed to know every aspect of the colony and its systems. The colony was a complex system and it did need management, even though many of its processes appeared to be automated.

It was a pleasant surprise to find out about the floor to ceiling vertical gardens of hydroponics at the far rear end of the cavern. They were so far back in the distance, that they could not be seen from the township, the central cavern was immense and several miles in length. The hydroponics were heavily overgrown, almost wild looking and in need of a few farmers. They, of course, had none with them and would have to improvise.

Magnus Larson sent word back to the Mars Horizon Homesteading Group to activate their colonisation plans. This was the moment that the group had been waiting for, for many years. Within weeks, the plans were implemented and four ships per month were launched towards Mars, destination New Tortuga. Although officially, their destination was listed simply as exploration. Magnus still harboured concerns about the Russians finding out and how they would react. Four ships per fleet, one hundred personnel, by the end of twelve months there were thirteen hundred colonists in New Tortuga, with fifty two ships lined up neatly in New Tortuga's Western Port.

Along with people, other supplies were also delivered and along with those supplies, there were Russian flower seeds. There were Snowdrops, Chamomile, Forget-me-nots, Violets and Primrose.

Moira made it her task to plant them neatly around the Wall of Remembrance.

The colony was working well, it was stable and secure, so Magnus made a decision an important decision. He could not leave their ships lying idle in the port and at the same time, he wanted to bring across more colonists. So Magnus cycled the ships in New Tortuga's Western Port back to Cis-Lunar L-Five, to bring more colonists across.

This was a risky move, as there would be insufficient ships for any future evacuations. His engineers told him that the colony was sound and that any evacuation would be highly unlikely, so he bit the bullet and set the ships to work. After their second year, the New Tortuga colony had grown, becoming a vibrant community of over twenty five hundred people.

The years rolled on by, many decades worth in fact and the terraforming of Mars had begun. All known colonies were notified and informed that due to the nature of the terraforming process, evacuation was mandatory. The process was simply far too dangerous to leave colonists on the Martian surface.

Most of the officially known colonies were evacuated, but a few colonists stayed behind, refusing to leave. Of course, there were also many unofficial colonies, New Tortuga was one of them and they did not even receive any notification at all. There were other colonies south of New Tortuga and they too were completely unknown.

When the terraforming began in the year twenty one twenty five, the greatest light show in Martian history began. Two Centaur bodies, Chariklo and Chiron, had been manoeuvred into Mars Sun L-One and there they were being carefully dismantled and fragmented. Those fragments were seeded with fusion detonators and then hurled toward Mars with absolute precision. Upon arrival in the Martian atmosphere, they were detonated, exploding high in the Martian skies and releasing all of their volatile gases and water vapour.

One by one the bolides exploded high in the Martian skies and as they did so, those unknown colonists below described them as the falling skies. With each explosion, the Martian atmosphere grew thicker and thicker. The Martian skies slowly began to turn from salmon pink to azure blue. Then the new Martian atmosphere began to develop and billowing clouds of water vapour formed.

These new Martian clouds continued to grow and before long, they had grown to impossible proportions, almost covering the entire planet. Then, one eventful day, they burst forth with torrents of rain, far heavier than any torrent of rain on the Earth. These Martian torrents were impossible, not only in size and volume but also in duration. The long rains is what they would be remembered as, by the colonists huddled in their colonies in the surface below.

The Martian regolith, now soaked by torrents of water falling from the skies, reacted and what remained of Mars's ancient atmosphere, long regolith locked, began to release. There were eruptions of atmospheric outgassing from the Martian regolith, further building up the new Martian atmosphere. The rapid, widespread outgassing had not been predicted by the terraformer's modelling, it was completely unexpected. The terraformers had believed that the regolith-locked ancient remnant atmosphere of Mars would outgas slowly and gradually over many decades. They had not factored in such rapidity!

It was difficult to know what was more frightening, the exploding icy bolides, the massive torrents of never-ending falling rain or the huge region-wide eruptions of ancient atmospheric outgassing. They'd set up video cameras at the top of the Hebes Mesa, four in all, surveilling in all four cardinal directions. The video feeds were accessible within New Tortuga. They couldn't hear the bolides exploding nor feel the vibration of the shock waves, their colony was deep below the Mesa's surface, far above them. The colonists watched the events with a combination of horror and fascination, the exploding bolides, the torrential rains, they watched it all.

As the long rains continued with their unabated torrents, the basins of Mars began to fill with water and the Hebes Chasma was no different. It would soon be known as the Hebes Sea and the Hebes Mesa would become Hebes Island. All across Mars, other basins were slowly filling, including the entire Valles Marineris system. It would soon become a large sea, large enough to rival the Mediterranean Sea back on the Earth, only with a fast current from west to east.

All was not well though, the new Martian atmosphere was full of toxic chemicals, toxic and exotic gases and far too much water vapour. As the atmospheric pressure rose, pressure suits were no longer required, but the sheer toxicity of the new Martian air required the use of rebreathers and fine filters.

Then there was the smell, a smell that would make people wretch, the smell of vile farts intermixed with the stench of death. There was no other way to describe it! It was expected that these toxicity issues would be washed out of the atmosphere in time, but that time was to be measured in long decades, perhaps even in centuries.

The New Tortugans watched as the process unfolded. During this terraforming process, no one could leave the surface colonies by ship and even venturing beyond their airlocks was dangerous. As the New Tortugans watched, other unknown colonies to the south with their own colonists also watched.

For generations to come, the descendants of those Martian colonists would say, *"The skies fell, then the long rains came and Mars itself convulsed, with the release of its ancient breath."*

The girls finished studying the section on New Tortuga. Although there was some economics involved in New Tortuga's story, there was so much more.

Ariel remarked, "Those poor caretakers. Dying off one by one until there was only one man left. I can't imagine that man's loneliness."

Aria replied, "Yep. Yuri must have been one lonely man, that's for sure, but it seems he covered that by burying himself in his work."

Kethera looked up, she had just sent a message via her data tablet to Richard before answering Aria, "To work until the end like that showed both sacrifice and dedication. It was wrong for those caretakers to be abandoned like that", the sheer horror at the thought of their casual abandonment.

Yeannah commented, "The Africans, they discovered that place and the Russians, they just stole it from under them. Sometimes being transparent is not in one's best interests."

"Yeah, that was a dog act, Yeannah, there's no other way to describe it. Then abandoning the place and leaving people behind, that's just double dog!", Aria replied.

Saffiera remarked telepathically, *"It was actually very sad. They were just left there, all alone!"*

"If the Russians hadn't dogged on the Africans in the first place, they wouldn't have double dogged on their own people. That's just one despicable act after another", Aria noted.

"What happened to the Africans? They did have a backup plan?", Ariel asked.

Saffiera answered in her usual silent way, transmitting, *"That looks like it's in the next section."*

Richard had walked over and took a seat in front of Kethera, "You wanted to discuss something my love?", he enquired.

"I meant later, Richard, not now!", Kethera replied, but then she reached out and took his hand in hers anyway.

Aria commented, "It's about your friend, Thomas, he's such a dick."

"What, because he told Yeannah that she's the most beautiful girl in the school?", Richard asked.

Kethera gave Richard a slightly disappointed look, Richard took note and quickly added, "That is just his opinion. Personally, of course, I believe Kethera is the most beautiful girl in the school."

Kethera squeezed Richard's hand, smiled and batted her eyelids at him in approval.

Aria was quickly getting sick of all the soppiness and told him straight up, "No. I'm talking about why he's upsetting our, Yeannah."

Kethera bit her lower lip, "Yes. Richard, about that. Thols have some cultural things that Thomas is probably not aware of."

"Cultural things?", Richard curiously enquired.

Aria was about to jump in, but Ariel cut her off, "No, Aria! It's better if

Kethera explains it."

Kethera did her best to explain, "We Carlin have lived side by side with the Thols for millennia. We understand their foibles. You Humans do not. Thols are forbidden to enter into a relationship with any other species, ever!", she explained.

"Forbidden?", Richard enquired curiously once more.

"For the Indigenous Thols, it is one of their greatest Taboos. For the Mimasian Thols, it's more of a practical genetic compatibility issue. They are more neural on the subject. Nonetheless, for Thols, interspecies relationships are simply not allowed. They are taboo!", Kethera answered as best she could and then looked to Yeannah for approval.

Yeannah nodded back and smiled in appreciation.

Richard considered that for a moment, "So, no Thol can ever have a relationship with a non-Thol?", requested clarification.

Kethera replied with more information, "It's far more complex than that, Richard. The Indigenous Thols and Mimasian Thols are different species as well. So this taboo applies to relationships between their two species as well."

Richard ran his hand threw his sandy blond hair, "Okay. Okay. Now I get it. I'll have to explain all of this to Thomas. Fuck! He's going to be so upset! Still, he has to be told."

Aria burst in with, "I don't care if he's upset, that ginger-haired bastard is messing with my girl's head and he needs to stop it!"

Richard looked Aria directly in the eyes and gave her a cold stare, "I will tell him, Aria. Thomas will do the right thing", then he turned to Kethera and kissed her on the lips, before walking back to his friend Thomas.

Kethera got up and quickly sprinted around the table, sitting down in front of Yeannah, "Please tell me I said all the right things?", she was so unsure if what she'd said, was actually said right.

Yeannah wrapped both of her arms around Kethera, who wrapped her arms around her in return. Kethera's arms were between Yeannah's shoulders and her great leathery wings. Slowly, Yeannah wrapped her great wings around Kethera, completely enveloping her in a double embrace.

Yeannah whispered into Kethera's ear, "You did very well, Kethera. I really do appreciate it."

Kethera didn't reply, she just thought to herself, *"A Tholish double hug"*, it was such a rare privilege, usually reserved for Thols and Thols alone.

Richard sat down with his friend Thomas, "Dude, you really need to leave Yeannah alone."

"Why? What's the problem?", Thomas enquired, he was completely clueless.

"Thols have cultural taboos, Thomas and you have been trampling all over them", Richard told him.

"Cultural taboos?", a still clueless Thomas enquired.

"Thols are forbidden from having relationships with non-Thols", Richard spat out, adding, "Thomas, you are messing with Yeannah's head and it is upsetting her. You need to stop it!"

Thomas was beginning to understand, however, he wasn't happy, "But, I love her!", he exclaimed.

Richard shook his head, "Dude, that doesn't matter, it's entirely irrelevant. It's a forbidden love. You are going to have to let it go. Let Yeannah go!"

Thomas replied, his voice becoming choked with sadness, "I don't know that I can, Richard."

"Dude, you're hurting her. Is that what you want?", Richard asked.

"No. No. You know I don't want that", Thomas replied, he was literally shaking.

Richard placed his hand on Thomas's shoulder, he was firm but gentle, "Thomas, if you truly love her, you will let her go!"

Thomas nodded. He quickly typed in an email on his data tablet.

The girls were watching from across the study hall, they saw Richard place a consoling hand on Thomas shoulder and knew that he was receiving the bad news. Less than a minute later an email notification came up on Yeannah's data tablet.

Yeannah opened the email, it was from Thomas, "I am so sorry, Yeannah. I had no idea that I was hurting you. Please forgive me!" and that was when Thomas's heart broke, ripped asunder, sadly Yeannah felt almost the same.

"I didn't ask for any of this", Yeannah declared to her friends, thinking to herself, *"There's something about Thomas's ginger hair and his confidence. I still love him"*, thoughts were never hidden when there was a telepath around.

Saffiera's soothing mind gently sent wave upon wave of gentle love to Yeannah, to help her cope with her emotional turmoil.

Aria, ever the wordsmith, smirked and remarked, "Well, when you're the most beautiful girl in the school, weirdos are bound to show up. Rangas always cause problems."

"Seriously, Aria! Do you really think that's going to help? For fucks sake!", Ariel scolded.

Aria replied matter of factly, "Probably not, Sis. Sorry, Yeannah. You know me and my big mouth."

Yeannah smiled and replied without any hint of being upset by her comment, "It's okay, Aria. I know that you mean well."

Aria replied, somewhat more thoughtfully, "I think the best thing to do is to dive back into the project. You know, get on with our studies and get Thomas out of our minds."

Kethera smiled as she returned to her original seat, "More wisdom from Aria. Who'd have thought?", then out of left field, "Shall we study at my house again tonight? My Mum loved having you guys over."

"Are you sure, Kethera? Aria can be quite a lot to put up with, you know", Ariel asked.

"Hey. I'm an acquired taste", Aria retorted and the girls all started laughing.

16. New Africa.

The fourteen colony ships of the East African Space Alliance had achieved orbital insertion. They were now all orbiting Mars in low Martian orbit. No sooner than the fleet of colony ships had entered orbit, they released a series of drones that all descended to the planet's surface far below.

The drones all converged on the southern Hebes Chasma region and the lands even further to the south, known as Perrotin. Their objective was simple, to locate all of the cave and cavern systems that were known to be in those regions. The ones that had been discovered by the E.A.S.A Droni la Uchunguzi octocopter mission and to take far more detailed scans.

These drones were not only capable of entering the caves and caverns, but they were also carriers of far smaller drones. These much smaller drones were capable of navigating tighter spaces that the carrier drones could not. Having surveyed a cave, they would then return to the carrier drone ready for their next deployment. Their data having uploaded to the E.A.S.A's colonisation fleet in low Martian orbit.

Each ship held two hundred and fifty colonists, carefully chosen for the project. All up there were three thousand five hundred colonists from the seven East African member countries. There were two ships from each country, Ethiopia, Kenya, Somalia, Somaliland, South Sudan, Tanzania and Uganda.

That division of the ships along national lines was probably their biggest mistake. Worse, the crews of each ship were also divided along tribal lines. Of the two South Sudanese ships, one was Dinka and the other Nuer. For Ethiopia, one was Oromo and the other Amhara, for Kenya one was Kikuyu and the other Luhya, for Somalia one was Darod and the other Hawiye, for Somaliland one was Isaaq and the other Dhulbahante, for Tanzania one was Sukuma and the other Chagga and finally for Uganda there was Baganda and Banyankole. National and tribal divisions would lead to rivalry and a lack of consensus. Something that should have been foreseen, considered and mitigated.

They were not integrated crews either, as they were divided along tribal lines. It was quite a mess and to make matters worse, the Somali and the Somalilanders did not even like to deal with each other. This was due to historical issues harking back to the division of Somalia into two countries in the late twentieth century. Their unity was little more than a thin veneer, a facade and they were, as a whole, highly fragmented, even the names of their ships reflected their tribes.

Language was also a problem. While they had all agreed that their language of common use would be Kiswahili, on their own ships, they all spoke their native tongues. This would spill over into inter-ship communications, where it would take precious minutes for the crews to realign their communications to the Kiswahili tongue, their lingua franca. The Captain of the fleet's flagship, the Kikuyu, Captain Njoroge Mugendi, had always argued that they should have chosen English, the colonial tongue, as their common language. His advice had fallen on deaf ears and the corrupt politicians made their own choices instead. Such was the nature of politicians.

Fleet Captain Njoroge Mugendi addressed the assembled Captains, their faces flickering in thirteen separate windows on his ship's bridge main screen. He straightened his posture, projecting calm authority despite the turmoil simmering beneath the surface.

"As you all know", Mugendi began, his voice steady, "There was supposed to be a dedicated follow-up mission after the Droni la Uchunguzi octocopter exploratory mission. A mission to conduct detailed surveys of every cave and cavern system, every single thing that we had discovered."

Captain Gatluak Thok of the Nuer leaned forward, scowling, "And we all know why that did not happen, do we not?"

Captain Deng Kuol of the Dinka slammed his palm on his console, his face dark with anger, "Those damnable Russians stole New Tortuga right out from under us! And our precious E.A.S.A. sat back and let it happen. They said nothing! They did nothing!"

Njoroge Mugendi raised a hand for silence, his tone clipped, "Yes, Captain Kuol. We are all painfully aware of this. That loss forced the E.A.S.A. to roll the follow-up mission into this one. It is why we are here now, balancing colonisation and exploration in a single effort."

Captain Kato Sseggwanga of the Baganda smirked, leaning back in his chair, "Spare us the history lesson, Captain. What did our scans find?"

Njoroge Mugendi hesitated, exhaling slowly, "The results are somewhat disappointing. The other cave systems are significantly smaller than New Tortuga. They may not support long-term habitation without significant expansion. It will be a big undertaking!"

A murmur of discontent rippled through the screens, and Captain Kuol shook his head. "So, we have come all this way to scrape by in glorified wormholes, living like maggots in the ground!"

An angry Captain Thok spat out, "We should take New Tortuga back!"

"Yes!", an equally angry Captain Kuol agreed, "We should land there, on the Hebes Mesa and take back New Tortuga from the Russians."

Captain Njoroge Mugendi exhaled deeply, letting the murmur of discontent settle before speaking, "I understand your frustrations, Captains. We are all aware of the importance of New Tortuga and the cost of its loss. Let us not waste our energy on futile anger."

Captain Gatluak Thok leaned forward, his glare sharp, "Futile? That was our future, Captain Mugendi. We would not be scraping for survival if the E.A.S.A. had taken action!"

"And what would you have them do?", Mugendi retorted, "Declare war on the Russians? We came here to build a future, not to fight battles we cannot win."

Captain Deng Kuol slammed his palm against his console, "We have fought with less, Captain. I brought my Father's spear with me on this journey. The Russians have taken what was rightfully ours and we can take it back!"

Njoroge Mugendi's gaze hardened, "Your Father's spear, Captain Kuol, is a proud legacy, but it cannot stand against Russian guns. This is not a battlefield, it is a colonisation mission. We must act as leaders, not warriors."

Before Kuol could respond, Captain Ibrahim Mahmud interjected, his voice calm but firm, "Enough! Violence will not solve this problem! Our ships carry generations of hope, men and women relying on us to find a way forward. Let us focus on what we can do."

"Thank you, Captain Mahmud", Njoroge Mugendi nodded at the screen, "We need to work on this problem together. I am transmitting you all full copies of the scans. Assign your best people to work on them. We all need collaboration, not conflict, to survive this. "

The colonist's experts spent a gruelling week analysing the survey data, their debates growing increasingly heated. The Nuer and Dinka fiercely defended their chosen cave systems, barely eight miles apart along the southern Hebes Chasma rimlands, with one along the actual rim itself. Here, they could bore deeply into the existing cave systems and expand them all along a length of tall escarpment.

"Proximity gives us an advantage, Captain Mugendi", Captain Deng Kuol argued, "We can pool our resources when needed. We Dinka and Nuer can work together on this!"

Captain Gatluak Thok had noted, "There will be underground aquifers below those escarpments."

The Ugandans, the Baganda and Banyankole, meanwhile, championed two other cave systems further east, insisting their chosen sites offered even better access to potential underground aquifers as well. It was a very similar pair of cave systems to the ones found by the South Sudanese, only on the eastern side of the very same escarpment. They too had proposed resource sharing as an advantage.

Captain Tumusiime Rwomushana of the Banyankole had remarked consistently, "These are the best caves my people have seen so far. They are perfect!"

In other windows on the screen, the Somali and Somalilanders muttered in tense agreement, if agreement it could be called at all.

"Separate habitats", Captain Mohamed Hassan of the Hawiye repeated firmly, "That is not negotiable. We will work with these people, but we will not live with them!"

The Kenyans, Tanzanians, and Ethiopians stood apart, presenting a united front for their ambitious plan further south in the Perrotin region.

"We believe the interconnected cave systems in this region of Perrotin, far to the east of the crater itself, are the key", said Captain Haile Tadesse of the Amhara, "Our geologist, Doctor Ayele Bekele, swears by them, but time and resources are required. It could take five, perhaps six years to fully develop."

Doctor Ayele Bekele was even on the bridge of the Amhara to add voracity to his beliefs, "There will be a vast, deep aquifer directly under those cave systems. We will have water on tap!"

Captain Omar Ali of the Dhulbahante had remarked, "We do not agree with Doctor Bekele's assessments. There are other cave systems further west, in the eastern outer rim of the Perrotin Crater itself. They look far more promising. I, for one, have no intention of leaving my people in orbit for five or six years. That is simply preposterous!"

"I have seen those cave systems, Captain Ali. I am not convinced. I suspect the terrain will be unstable", Doctor Ayele Bekele replied with concern.

An angry Captain Mohamed Hassan remarked, "We found those caves first, Captain Ali. Your people have no rights to them!"

Captain Ibrahim Mahmud stepped in belligerently, "I suspect there are caves in the depths of Hebes Chasma that would suit you better!"

Captain Mohamed Hassan retorted, harking back to the Somali, Somaliland split, "I would expect no less from secessionist scum!"

His counterpart, Captain Abdirahman Warsame of the Darod, added, "We will never live even close to Somaliland filth!"

"Enough of this madness. We must work together or not at all!", Captain Mugendi shouted at them, thinking to himself, *"We should never have come here!"*

That was the crux of the problem. The Perrotin caves could only house a thousand colonists in the first phase. The rest would have to remain in orbit, potentially for half a decade or longer. That was not something anyone liked. As the discussions dragged on, frustration simmered.

How could they build a future when the present itself seemed impossible?

Two windows on the main screen, on the Kikuyu's bridge dropped out, it was the Nuer and the Dinka. The South Sudanese had discussed this in advance privately and they were implementing their own plans. This was quickly followed by two more windows dropping out, it was the Baganda and the Banyankole, the Ugandans, they also had their own plans to implement.

"Get them back online!", Captain Njoroge Mugendi commanded his Communications Officer.

"They are ignoring our hails, Sir", the Communications Officer replied.

"Sir!", the Kikuyu's Officer of the Watch called out, "The Nuer, the Dinka, the Baganda and the Banyankole are all breaking orbit!"

"Breaking orbit! Where the hell are they going?", Captain Njoroge Mugendi urgently requested.

"It is too early for me to tell, Sir", the Officer of the Watch replied.

The other nine Captains were all still online.

Captain Haile Tadesse of the Amhara remarked, "Captain Mugendi, they have already told us where they are going. They have already picked their own cave systems. They will be going alone!"

Captain Mugendi shook his head, "This is madness", he stated far more loudly than he'd wanted.

Then things got worse, two more screens dropped out, it was the Isaaq and the Dhulbahante. The Somalilanders went offline.

"Get them back online now!", Captain Njoroge Mugendi pointed to his Communications Officer.

"Sir. They have gone dark. They are ignoring our hails and they have shut off their transponders", the Communications officer replied.

"They are breaking orbit as well, Sir", the Kikuyu's Officer of the Watch noted.

"Perrotin's rim! Fuck it!", Captain Mugendi muttered, he knew exactly where they were going, then he quickly reached out to the Somalis, "Do not follow them!", he implored.

"Why shouldn't we?", Captain Mohamed Hassan asked.

"You cannot build a colony and fight each other at the same time", Captain Mugendi told them, "Mars is a harsh place. You follow them, both you and they will die!"

Captain Mohamed Hassan was silent, considering Mugendi's words and then Captain Abdirahman Warsame interjected, "Captain Mugendi is right, Mohamed. We chase after them and we all die!"

Captain Hassan nodded his head, he knew it was true.

"Captain Hassan. Captain Warsame. It is important that what remains of us, work together", Captain Njoroge Mugendi stated, trying to get back some modicum of control.

The Somali windows both dropped out, "Shit!", Captain Mugendi exclaimed, "Get them back online now!"

"They are ignoring our hails, Sir", the Communications Officer replied.

After several minutes of silence, the Officer of the Watch noted, "They are still there, Captain."

Then the windows popped back up. Captain Abdirahman Warsame and Captain Mohamed Hassan were back online.

Captain Njoroge Mugendi leaned forward towards the main screen, "Thank God you are back!"

"Captain Mugendi. We have decided to go to the surface. We will make our own way", Captain Warsame informed him.

"No! No! Why? We need to work together on this!", Captain Mugendi was beside himself.

Captain Hassan replied, "Captain. The Alliance is broken, we will make our own way."

Captain Warsame stepped in, "We will look for a suitable cave system. When we have found one, we will go down to the surface."

"Captains, this is madness. We stand a much better chance of survival if we all stick together", Captain Mugendi implored.

"Perhaps, Captain, but you must remember. Each of our ships is a complete colony in its own right. We will survive", Captain Hassan replied.

Captain Warsame added, "The decision is made, it is final, Captain."

Then the two windows dropped out and they went offline.

Captain Mugendi commanded, "I want eyes on every ship heading down to the surface. If they switch off their transponders, then track them the old way. They may be going their own way, but they are still my responsibility!"

The Kikuyu's Officer of the Watch responded, "Yes, Captain!"

Captain Mugendi added, "Log their landing coordinates, nearby cave systems and any notable local resources, everything. I want to keep track of our people. It is probably all we can do now."

The colonisation team of the East African Space Alliance was now broken beyond repair.

The eight break-away colony ships each landed on the Martian surface and immediately began seismic testing for underground aquifers. Once satisfied that water was available, they then began excavating their selected cave systems, boring deeper and deeper into the rock using their high-powered laser rock-melting machines. Each colony ship was a complete colony in its own right, so the colonists lived aboard their ships while they burrowed out the cave systems to build their new colonies.

The relatively broad escarpment that ran south of the Hebes Chasma would become home to four colonies. The South Sudanese, Nuer and the Dinka were on the western flanks, with the Nuer being closer to Hebes Chasma. The Ugandans, Baganda and the Banyankole were on the eastern flanks, with the Baganda being closer to Hebes Chasma.

Further to the west was the Perrotin Crater, which was roughly eighty eight kilometres across. The Somalilanders, Isaaq and Dhulbahante had chosen cave systems on the outer Eastern rim of the crater itself, positioned north and south of each other.

For all of their talk of not wanting to be anywhere near the Somalilanders, the Somalis, Darod and Hawiye, chose cave systems on the outer Western rim of the same Perrotin crater, also north and south of each other. Both the Somalilanders and the Somalis began to excavate their chosen cave systems.

The remaining three countries, Kenya, Tanzania and Ethiopia, followed through with their chosen plans, the same plans rejected by the others. Now down to only fifteen hundred colonists, they could see a way through to building their colonies in a way that suited their population. After a week of adjusting their plans, they, too, broke orbit for the Martian surface.

In the centre of the Perrotin region, well east of Perrotin Crater itself, they landed in an area with multiple cave systems. Each tribe had been allocated a suitable cave and they began their work, excavating and boring into them. The Kenyans, Kikuyu and Luhya, the Tanzanians, Sukuma and Chagga, the Ethiopians, Oromo and Amhara. Six colonies in a clustered region in the centre and over the whole of the Perrotin region, south of Hebes Chasma, fourteen new Martian colonies in all.

The Martian colonies of the East African Space Alliance, although now splintered into tribal factions, were quickly developed. They were hard at work tunnelling and boring out their respective cave systems and although now fiercely independent, they still collaborated and worked together when necessary. Cooperation was a matter of survival. It took much time and effort, but they worked hard, tirelessly and before the year was out, most of the colonies were ready for habitation.

These colonies were all very similar. They were not so deep below the surface like New Tortuga. They were shallower and being these were African folk, they wanted natural lighting. Be the natural feature an escarpment, a cliff or a crater rim, they carved and shaped the outer surfaces, then vitrified them, making them like glass. Into these surfaces, they carved many windows, behind which would be the rooms of their underground houses.

The windows were lined with sealed metal frames that contained outer shutters, just in case, this was Mars after all. Each window was quadruple-glazed. The outer pane was thick, clear crystal aluminium, with a thin coating of gold to aid in blocking solar radiation. The middle two panes were of the same material but had polarising filters. The innermost pane was of the same material but just as thick. The colonists would be able to see out clearly, yet they were nonetheless protected from the harsh radiation in the Martian environment.

The interiors of the colonies were multi-level and bored deeper into the rock. Some reaching from the base of their natural features, almost to the top. All of the walls, floors and ceilings were vitrified and like smooth glass. At the very back of the colonies, they build large caverns for hydroponic vegetable gardens and even caverns for aquaponics. Deep bores were dug to reach the deep Martian aquifers and the water was filtered and purified before being stored in deep cavernous chambers. Air and water recycling systems were put in place and then finally, the colonies, one by one, came online.

When the Nuer folk brought their colony online, theirs was the first, Captain Gatluak Thok had told his people, "We shall all live here, like peas in a pod."

One of his fellow colonists had called out, "Then we shall call our new home, Pod Village!"

All of the Nuer colonists cheered at the suggested name and it stuck, Podville, a name that would be shortened in later years to simply, Podvil. Many of the Nuer couples changed their surname to Pod in deference to their new Martian home.

The colony ship Nuer had been repositioned closer to the escarpment and the colony within it. An umbilicus was extended from the ship's main hatch, connecting to the colony's main entrance. An airtight seal was achieved and the two hundred and fifty Nuer folk moved effortlessly into their new colony home. The colony ship would, of course, be kept intact, a backup plan was always needed and this was, of course, Mars after all, with its deadly environments. One by one, all of the other fragmented colonies of the East African Space Alliance came online.

The Somaliland and Somali peoples had fortuitously positioned themselves on either side of the Perrotin Crater's outer rim. As such they found themselves frequently working with each other on their colony's projects. Over time, they let go of their historical animosities and merged their four tribes into one people, the Samar. In the many decades to come they would be known as the Samar people of the Perrotin's Rim or simply, the Rim Folk.

The six tribes of the Kenyans, the Tanzanians and the Ethiopians never did manage to link all of their colonies via underground tunnels. Once they'd provided for their numbers and room enough for future expansion, interlinking of their colonies was first placed on the back burner and then later forgotten. In future centuries the whole region would become known as New Africa or Little Africa and the people would be called the Africans or more commonly, they were known as the Bush Folk.

Mars changes all things and along with it, it changes all peoples.

The years rolled on by, many decades passed and then the terraforming of Mars had begun. In the years in between the East African Space Alliance's colonisation of Mars and the beginning of the terraforming process, the East African Space Alliance back on Earth had also fragmented. The cause of the collapse was massive governmental corruption and economic mismanagement, as always.

As their economies crumbled, their funding dried up and their Space Alliance dissolved. Then, there were internal conflicts in the former countries of the East African Space Alliance and their records were largely lost.

Over the decades, the East African Space Alliance's colonists became as forgotten as the Russian caretakers left behind at Novaya Tortuga. No one knew that the Bush Folk were there, they had been long forgotten, not that they would have evacuated if they had been notified of the dangers of the terraforming process.

Eighty percent of the icy fragments from the dismantling of Chariklo and Chiron at the Martian Sun Lagrangian point one had been directed to detonate and explode in the skies high above the Northern and Southern Martian Ice Caps. The remaining twenty percent were detonated as bolide randomly throughout the temperate and equatorial regions of Mars.

Nyabol Pod sat in her small bedroom in the heart of Podville, the dim light of her desk lamp casting shadows over the homework scattered across her stone desk. Though her assignments demanded attention, her gaze was fixed outside the window. There, above the red Martian sky, the bolides streaked by in their fiery arcs. It was her favourite pastime, one that grounded her in the endless horizon beyond, where the past and present collided in the briefest flashes of brilliant, explosive light.

Most of the bolides exploded and flashed briefly in the distance, too far away to hear or even feel their shock waves. Nyabol had counted six! Six bolides in three hours, that was extraordinary! A few days earlier one, particular bolide had exploded high above Podville. That one shook the colony with its shock wave, not enough to cause damage, but enough to know that they were real. Then the boom came over the colony, muffled by the four thick layers of clear crystal aluminium in their windows. That one had been exciting. Her parents had not thought so. Yet Nyabol watched, wrapped in the fabric of excitement as the sky outside of her bedroom window continued to fall. Day and night, it fell. The Martian skies were falling and the excitement in watching it was palpable.

Long before the last bolides had fallen, the skies had thickened, Nyabol had watched as the Martian sky gradually changed from salmon pink to azure blue. She watched the huge billowing clouds develop and cover the skies, then the clouds burst forth and the long rains began. It rained and it rained, never-ending torrents of water streaming down from out of the now azure blue Martian skies.

The other colonists were all excited by the fact that the Hebes Chasma was now filling with water, becoming a new sea, the Hebes Sea. Nyabol, however, was more interested in the bolides exploding across the Martian skies. The bolides were still falling, still exploding, only now the sound and shock waves travelled much further and were much louder, in the far new thicker Martian air.

Nyabol had watched with her wrapped attention and everything she saw, she noted down in her diary, along with copious photographs taken through her bedroom window. Her window was literally the window of change. In decades to come the *"Diary of Nyabol Pod"* would be published and remain in print for countless centuries and even longer. Scientists and historians would study the observations and the thousands of photographs that Nyabol had taken. All meticulously written down as witnessed, history in the making.

Later in her life, Nyabol Pod would become the Mayoress of Podville and centuries in the future, her descendants would reshape the solar system and the motto of her family would be, *"Mars changes everything and everyone."*

For generations to come, the descendants of those East African Space Alliance colonists would also say, as many other Martians who were descended from those who lived through the terraforming process, *"The skies fell, then the long rains came and Mars itself convulsed, with the release of its ancient breath."*

Kethera mouthed the words, "Mars changes everything and everyone."

Aria looked at Kethera, shrugged and replied, "I've never been there, so I wouldn't know."

Ariel commented, "Mum and Dad have, that's where they met. That's why we exist!"

"Yeah, but we've never been there. We were born in Colonial Central Command in the Cis-Luns L-Five Trojan point", Aria reminded her twin Sister.

"Well, Aria, don't you think that their meeting on Mars, maybe, just maybe, Mars had something to do with that", Ariel told her twin.

"Meh. We weren't there, so we can't know", Aria shrugged again and Ariel just rolled her eyes.

Saffiera broke in with her observation, transmitting to the others, *"Those colonies had lots of windows. Many of them were likely bedroom windows. Lots of those colonists would have watched the terraforming process unfold."*

Yeannah chimed in, "Yet only that little girl, Nyabol Pod, had the wherewithal to write her observations down and take photographs of the whole process. We owe a lot to her foresight!"

Saffiera noted, *"The New Tortugans videoed the terraforming process, but it looks like were just live feeds and not actually even recorded. I couldn't find any links to their videos at all."*

Kethera queried, "So the only real record that we have of that entire event, from the surface, was recorded by a little girl? In her diary?"

Yeannah confirmed, "That dear, Kethera, appears to be one hundred percent correct!"

Kethera frowned, her whiskers were downcast, "Those African colonists were forgotten! Just like the ones at New Tortuga. Is that a common theme in Human history?"

Saffiera replied, *"Kethera, you have to understand. That was back in the twenty-first century. It was a tumultuous period. There were multiple wars, pogroms, terrorist atrocities, corruption and economic collapses. During that century a lot of records were lost or destroyed."*

Ariel added, "Saffiera is right. It wasn't until the later part of the twenty-first century that we Humans got our act together."

Kethera remarked, "I cannot imagine what life for Humans would have been like back then."

"None of us can, Kethera", Aria even agreed.

"That surname *'Pod'*, it rings a bell", Yeannah remarked, as her fingers glided across her data tablet's virtual keyboard, then a window opened up.

A picture of a bronze statue appeared in a small town square, the plaque at its base read, Zuawalo and Zeealas Pod, twenty three sixty five. The statues depicted two tall, beautiful women with distinct South Sudanese features, one about six foot three, the other six foot two, they were Sisters. They stood side by side, arms folded. The taller of the two was holding what looked like an oversized ferret about the size of a small coyote. The ferret's name was Zigg, he was Zuawalo's pet.

"The statue was made only a few years after the Horridian War ended, people must have really admired them", Kethera remarked.

"These are descendants of Nyabol Pod. They helped defeat the Horridians during the Horridian War", Yeannah informed them all, as she ran her fingers over her virtual keyboard once more.

Another window popped up, it contained a photograph of a spaceship crew all dressed in crisp, stylish navy blue uniforms.

"The crew of the Mars Defence Force Ship Solstice", Yeannah noted, as she magnified the image to the full size of her data tablet's screen.

Kethera read out their names, "Captain Folcrom Forkbraid. Officers: First Officer and Tactical: James Murphy. Engineering: Varakhan Utana. Helm and Navigation: Marcus Greyhelm. Communications: Charlene Fewkes. Science: Peter Swann. Security: Zuawalo Pod and Zeealas Pod. Engineering Assistant: Nyaliep Pod. Special Consultant: Leroy McGuvan."

"There are those two Pod women again", Yeannah noted and then added, "That crew and their spaceship, the Solstice, literally saved millions of lives."

"More importantly, the Horridian Dynasty lost the War. Had they won, we'd be living in the Horridian Imperium. If they hadn't stopped the Horridians, we'd all be living under their rule. No freedom! No future! They were true psychopaths!", Saffiera informed them all.

"Well, that would have sucked! Big time!", Aria noted.

"It would have been very bad, indeed. They were also Slavers. The Horridian Dynasty controlled the Jovian Realms and they wanted to expand across the entire solar system as their new Horridian Imperium. In the Jovian realms, all non-Christians were Slaves. They would have done exactly the same thing with non-Humans as well. They also hated all psychics with an irrational fury.", Saffiera told everyone.

"Aria's right, that would have really sucked big time!", Ariel agreed.

"So they're the ones that reshaped your solar system!", Kethera suddenly realised and then remarked, "It's hard to believe that people like them even existed. They literally saved everything."

Yeannah nodded, "Yep. They sure did."

Saffiera noted, *"The Captain of the Solstice was Lord Folcrom Forkbraid! He and his wife, Lady Folcrom Selene, were two of the most powerful psychics in recorded history. They rediscovered psychic teleportation, which is called jaunting or blinking and they started the Human psychic colonisation of the worlds of the Alpha Centauri system! Up until then, jaunting was thought to be a myth, that is, until Lord Forkbraid and Lady Selene proved it was real."*

"Wow! That's incredible", Aria exclaimed.

"No, Aria, they were incredible. The Folcrom are all powerful psychics. They are the pivotal points, around which our entire reality is wrought", Saffiera explained, that one statement temporarily stunned Aria into silence.

"They were no ordinary crew either, Saffiera, look at those notes", Ariel pointed out, then reading them, "Marcus Greyhelm and Charlene Fewkes were a married couple. As were Varakhan Utana and Nyaliep Pod. Nyaliep was also the Pod women's Aunt. And look here, Zuawalo Pod, Zeealas Pod and James Murphy were a married throuple! Looks like the Solstice's crew wasn't just a team, they were a family as well."

The word throuple had Aria giggling, she looked at Ariel and she joined in.

Saffiera then noted, *"And now we are getting off track. We need to focus on our term assignment."*

Yeannah nodded in agreement, "Yes, of course, Saffiera."

"Do we have to do that now? We can do that at Kethera's house, it is almost bell time", Aria noted.

"Aria does have a point. The school day is almost over and we are way behind", Ariel agreed.

Kethera checked her messages, "My Mum has agreed to another sleepover and your Mums have been to my house to drop off your things for you, so we're all good to go."

At that, the girls packed up and headed off to the school buses to catch one to Kethera's village.

17. Protect the Gudongs.

As the girls casually walked up to Kethera's home plot once more, they all noticed something different. A large hovercar was parked on the bluegrass in front of Kethera's house.

"Hmm. That is my Mum's hovercar", Saffiera noted

Saffiera reached out gently with her mind, her Mother was there as expected and so was Yeannah's Mother, Yealah, *"Your Mum is here too, Yeannah."*

Yeannah replied, "My Mum did say she wanted to meet your Mum, Saffiera."

The girls entered Kethera's house, with Kethera leading them straight to the kitchen, where they found Kethera's Mum, Kayala, sitting at the kitchen table between Saffiera's Mum, Sarlia and Yeannah's Mum, Yealah. The remains of three many mushroom pies were sitting on the table, as were empty glasses of masuli-infused Gudong milk. There were also some pieces of Gudong parchment, on which Kethera's Mother had written down the recipe for her many mushroom pies.

"Hi girls", Kayala greeted them, then asked, "How are your studies going?"

Kethera replied to her Mum, "We are a bit behind at the moment, Mum."

Ariel added in, "Yeah, we got a little sidetracked by some related history a couple of centuries later."

"Yes", Saffiera agreed, "There were links between our study material and the second Horridian War of twenty three sixty two."

Yealah replied, her natural trills and clicks still present, even when speaking perfect English, agreed, "Ah yes, Saffiera. That would have been some very compelling reading. It was a pivotal moment in Human history. Had the Horridians won that War, we Thols and Martians would not be free today!"

Kayala smiled and noted, "I have made many mushroom pies for your supper and", she paused for just a moment, "Some deep-fried Thrixan pieces. Your Father, Krylor, netted over a dozen of them this morning and put them in the coop."

Kethera clapped her hands together excitedly, "That means we'll be getting Thrixan eggs! They are so yummy!"

Aria queried, "Thrixan are born from eggs?"

"Of course they are, Aria", Kethera replied in surprise, "Thrixan make nests and so they lay eggs."

Aria looked surprised by that and asked, "Thols also build nests, but Thols are not egg-born."

"Too true, young Aria", Yealah agreed, seeming to be able to tell the two identical twins apart at a glance, "Yet, even though our species are live-born, there are some significant differences", she trilled.

"Perhaps I'd better explain", Saffiera's Mum, Sarlia, remarked, then launched into the explanation, *"You understand how Humans develop in the womb, yes? One umbilicus and one placenta per fetus."*

Sarlia's telepathic *'voice'* came through loud and clear, Aria replied, "Yes."

"Okay. Very good. Carlins are very similar, although they have one large placenta with multiple umbilici, one for each fetus. Multiple births are common and tend to be fraternal", Sarlia continued.

Kayala chimed in, "When our kits are born, they are much smaller than either Human or Thol kits. However, they do develop very quickly and catch up in size, walking by the time they reach six months old. And we do occasionally give birth to same-faced kits, Sarlia. Just not as much as we'd like."

Kethera chimed in, "A Carlin kit is usually up and running well before they're one year old."

"And the Thols?", Aria's twin Sister, Ariel, who was now equally curious, asked.

Yealah took over, "Human babies and Carlin kits come out head first, then their shoulders, then their arms and then finally their feet. Of course, Carlins also have a tail, but that does not affect the process. Thol babies, on the other hand, have arms, legs, a tail and, of course, a set of wings", she stressed that last word with a single trill.

"So the wings can cause complications?", Aria enquired, noting, "That does kind of make sense."

"They could, except we evolved a method to mitigate that", Yealah replied, explaining, "Thols have a womb, just as Humans and Carlins do, however, our placental development is different. The placenta connects to the womb, yes, but then it encapsulates the developing fetus, like a leathery protective sac. The umbilicus is within this sac."

Ariel thought she understood, "So baby Thols pass through the birth canal, protected in an *'egg'* like membrane. I can see how that would make the process somewhat easier."

Aria threw in, "Yeah, no arms, legs and wings poking out all over the place."

Yealah smiled a broad Tholish smile, "Yes, Girls, that is correct. The new youngling is curled up inside its protective placental membrane, which, upon contact with the outside air, begins to break down. Then we just pull the baby out of the sac and voila, a new youngling Thol!", she trilled.

Yeannah told her friends, "It is also one of the reasons we Thols have so few babies. We can only ever have one baby at a time, never more and the process takes time, twelve to thirteen months, not nine as with Humans or seven as with Carlins."

Yealah admitted, "It is a slow process and in the later months, a pregnant Thol cannot fly."

The twins were silent as all the information sunk in, not so much Saffiera, Kethera, or Yeannah, who all had some previous understanding of the processes involved.

Kayala broke the silence, commenting, "Kethera told me about the *'double hug'*, that was such a privilege."

"Yes", Yealah agreed, noting, "It is very rare for our people to give outsiders a *'double hug'*. It is usually a highly emotional moment, rarely seen by outsiders", she looked at her Daughter and asked softly, "Yeannah, which was it, elation or sadness?"

Yeannah bit her lower lip, her face began to grow pink with embarrassment and she did not answer, so Aria blurted out, "It was definitely sadness."

"Sadness!", Yealah nodded, then took a guess, "Boy problems perhaps?"

Yeannah didn't answer, so Yealah continued, her English interspersed with a few clicks, trills and soft barks, "That Indigenous boy, Yookey, who lives in the tree across from ours? Your Father and I have already spoken to Yookey's parents. By now they will have explained to him...", she paused momentarily, "What he needs to know as a Thol. He will get over his crush, given enough time."

That was not the problem, but the girls did not want to upset Yeannah any further, so they said nothing and kept quiet.

Sarlia, of course, was a telepath and had a fair inkling that the girls were not being forthright, *"The truth would come out soon enough"*, she thought to herself, *"It always does in the end."*

"So girls", Kayala was addressing the twins, "Your Mother dropped off your bags, but then she had to go to work. She did seem very busy", then she enquired of them, "What do your parents do exactly?", she was genuinely curious.

Aria replied, "Dad works up in high orbit. He's a space traffic controller, he works two weeks on and two weeks off. Mum works the afternoon shift at the spaceport, she's their head security officer."

"Interesting jobs", Yealah noted, then asked, "How'd they manage to get those?"

Aria replied, with a degree of pride, "Mum and Dad were Special Forces

Operatives in the Colonial Defence Force. They were trained in a lot of different skills. When they came out here, their skill sets put them in high demand."

"Special forces Operatives?", Kayala queried, "That must have made things hard for you growing up."

Aria shrugged, "Meh. It had other benefits. Ariel and I have been trained in mixed martial arts since the moment we could walk."

"Mixed martial arts?", Saffiera's Mum, Sarlia, asked.

"Watch", Aria replied swiftly, "Ariel, square off! Demonstration time!", as she rolled her head on her shoulders to loosen up.

"Are you sure, Aria?", Ariel questioned as she turned sideways to Aria, taking up a solid stance.

"Yeah, sure", Aria replied.

Ariel stepped precisely one step back and raised her left hand, "Say my left hand is my head and my palm is the right side of my face", and then she nodded to Aria.

Aria's right leg swung out to the right, then quickly swung back to the left, crossing above her left foot and then rotating in an arc. The right side of her right foot connected with Ariel's left palm with a resounding slap. The whole motion took a split second, probably less.

Ariel shook her left hand, then grabbed her wrist, "Damn it, Aria, did you have to hit it so hard?"

Aria shrugged again, "You know me, Sis. I don't know any other way."

Saffiera, Kethera and Yeannah were looking from one to the other, none of them knew that the twins had been trained since toddlers in martial arts. Sarlia, Kayala and Yealah looked at the twins in shock.

After a few long moments of stunned silence, Sarlia remarked, transmitting, *"That was fast. Quicker than a blur. You moved like lightning. I did not even detect the thought that triggered the motion!"*

Kethera remarked, "I had no idea you could do that!"

Kayala also noted, "I could not follow the movement! It was too quick!"

Aria shrugged once more, "Ariel is faster", she told them.

Ariel, still holding her wrist, smiled wryly, "Yes, but you hit harder. You never pull back, do you?"

Aria smiled, a touch of mischief in her eyes, "Never saw the point of holding back."

Yeannah's Mother, Yealah, queried, "Muscle memory?"

Ariel smiled, "Mum would say, muscle memory combined with distributed reflex memory. Not that I fully understand what she means. Mum once explained it to us, but I guess it didn't sink in."

Sarlia cautiously looked into the twin's minds, *"They are so protective of their friends"*, she thought to herself.

Loud enough though for Saffiera to pick up, *"Yes. They love us to bits and will always protect us, Mother"*, she thought back to her.

Sarlia thought back to her Daughter, "*Saffiera, why do I find that both frightening and reassuring?"*

"They have martial arts skills, which goes against everything we Martians hold sacred. Combat is not our way and yet, they protect their own with such fierce loyalty. They are fiercely protective of their friends, one of whom just happens to be your Daughter", Saffiera replied, smiling.

Kethera suddenly giggled, her tail swished from side to side, her whiskers were twitching and she noted, "You weren't bluffing, Ariel. When you told Thomas that Aria would rip him a new one, you actually meant it."

Ariel looked at Kethera, thinking to herself, *"Why did you have to mention Thomas?"*, but replied anyway, "Yes, Kethera. I was giving Thomas a fair warning."

Sarlia asked, her curious telepathic mind reaching out, *"Why did you need to warn Thomas?"*

Ariel replied, "He was pushing all of Aria's buttons and I had to let him know what a bad idea that was", she held up her left palm, it was still bright red where Aria had struck it with her foot.

Kayala looked at Sarlia, then she turned back to Ariel, she asked, "Why was this Thomas, pushing Aria's buttons?"

Aria did not like people talking about her while she was right in front of them and she blurted out, "Thomas was upsetting my girl, Yeannah", she gestured in Yeannah's direction.

Yealah looked at her Daughter, "Yeannah? How did this Thomas upset you?"

Yeannah's face turned bright red, and she quickly covered her cheeks with trembling hands. She tried to hold back the tears, but they welled up in her eyes and in an instant, they spilled over. She couldn't contain herself any longer and burst into sobs, her shoulders were shaking.

Yealah stood up, quickly rounding the kitchen table. As her leathery wings unfurled, there was a distinct audible cracking sound and then she held her Daughter, Yeannah, in her tight embrace. Her mighty wings wrapped around Yeannah and held her protectively. The warmth of her mother's wings wrapped around her like a protective cocoon. Another Tholish double hug. Yealah slowly rocked her Daughter, Yeannah, from side to side, trilling melodically into her ear.

Sarlia was surprised by the emotional display, Thols, especially Mimasian

Thols, were normally such stoic people and yet here were Tholish emotions, raw like an open wound for all to see.

Sarlia and Kayala both looked to Aria for more information.

Aria replied to their looks, telling them, "Thomas is in love with Yeannah."

"Is Thomas a Thol?", Kayala enquired, noting, "It does not sound like a Tholish name."

Ariel gently kicked her Sister in the shin and replied, "Thomas is Human."

Yealah turned to face the twins, incredulity in her melodic voice, "A Human boy? This Thomas?"

"Yes", Ariel confirmed, adding, "and he's been showing his affections to Yeannah and it has been upsetting her. Quite a lot, actually."

Yealah replied, "I imagine it would. First, Yookey and now this Human boy, Thomas. No wonder my Yeannah is so upset", then she asked, "Does this Thomas not know of Tholish customs?"

Kethera chimed in, "He didn't, but he does know now", then added quickly, perhaps too quickly, "I explained it to Richard and then Richard explained it to Thomas. Richard is Thomas's friend. That's why Yeannah gave me the double hug."

Yealah responded, "That is good to know, Kethera. Thank you. Under Tholish customs, this love Thomas has for Yeannah is considered forbidden."

Yeannah clenched her fists, she wanted to scream, her chest felt so tight, *"I love Thomas"*, the thought echoed in her mind and then she thought to herself, *"Why do we have to have these stupid damned rules!"*

Sarlia heard Yeannah's tormented thoughts and looked cautiously into Yeannah's mind, then carefully sent her thoughts to Yealah, *"Your gentle Yeannah is conflicted, she loves this Human boy, Thomas. You will need to give her gentle guidance."*

Yealah was a Mimasian Thol and had been raised around Martians, she was not upset with Sarlia's prying, it was the Martian way of helping, they actually made great therapists.

Yealah carefully thought back to Sarlia, "*Thank you for the observation, Sarlia. I will guide her as best I can. For us, Mimasian Thols, this taboo is not absolute, although it is still problematic, nonetheless. Unfortunately, the Indigenous Thols push their taboos on all Thols, even though we are a different species. Their rules are strict and quite, harsh, my people not so much.*"

"Why is that, Yealah? The Mimasian Thols are a separate distinct species", Sarlia enquired.

"Yes, Sarlia but there are millions of Indigenous Thols. They live all along the

Northern and Southern Mountain Ranges. We Mimasian Thols live in a few dozen villages just north of the Human colony", Yealah thought back trying to explain the situation.

"But still, it does not seem right", Sarlia commented.

"Mimasian Thols make up around point zero one percent of the Thol population on Homwol. The majority never allows separate rules for a minority", Yealah thought back in reply.

Sarlia looked at Yealah with ancient Martian understanding, *"Yes, that is always true."*

"When the Humans first found Homwol, our lost ancestral homeworld, we Mimasian Thols were ecstatic. Up till then, we had never left the Sol system. We lived inside Mimas, on Mars, on the Earth and even on Venus. Some of us even lived in off-world colonies. Then the home-world of the Thols was found and a great many of us came here with the Humans. We had not understood how different the Indigenous Thols would be to us returnees", Yealah's thoughts lamented, she added, *"Very similar in many ways, but so different in many others. Many Mimasian Thols now live off-world in the colonies of Cis-Luns L-Five, precisely because the Indigenous Thols with their ancient taboos don't."*

Kayala suddenly realised something she'd barely noticed before when the girls had first walked into the Kitchen. She had smelled all the usual scents. The girls all carried each other's scents, which was quite normal, but there was another scent she'd noticed and could not put a name to. Now, Kayala had a name to put to that scent, Richard.

"Kethera, little one, who is this Richard?", Kayala curiously asked of her Daughter.

Kethera's whiskers drooped, her ears went flat, her blue stripes broadened and a slight iridescent glow of embarrassment came over her face, "He's a Human boy, Mother", she said quickly, then she bit her lower lip, not want to say anything else.

Ariel looked at Kethera, who nodded, then she turned to Kayala, "Richard is in love with Kethera."

Yealah released her embrace and stepped slightly back from Yeannah, wiping her Daughter's tears away, "Humans!", she exclaimed as she looked at the other two Mothers and rolled her eyes.

Sarlia chimed in, *"Yes indeed, Humans. Their males will fall in love with any female and it does not matter the species. They can love anything."*

Aria thought she was lightening the conversation and blurted out, "Yep, better hide the Gudongs."

Kayala looked confused for a moment and asked, "Why do we need to hide our Gudongs, Dear?"

Ariel pinched the bridge of her nose and replied, "Aria was making a joke, a very bad joke", then she turned to Aria and whispered, "A really stupid joke. Not funny at all, Aria!"

Kayala thought for a moment, then she blinked a few times and her whiskers twitched, "Oh! Oh! Hide the Gudongs!", the thought of Human men chasing Gudongs across their plot crossed her mind and she shook her head to chase the thought away, "I'm certainly glad you were joking, Aria."

Sarlia picked up Kayala's thought telepathically and likewise shook her head.

Aria smiled, ruffling her hair, "Yeah, sorry about that. I don't have much of a filter."

After the heavy moments of comforting Yeannah, a small distraction arrived at the perfect time.

One of Kethera's siblings, oblivious to the tension, chose that precise moment to walk past the kitchen, "Why do we need to hide our Gudongs?", he asked.

"My Sister, Aria has a really big mouth", Ariel replied glaring at her Sister, then she covered up quickly by adding, "and she'll eat all of the Gudongs. Gobble them all up, she will", then she quickly gnashed her teeth.

Aria turned to the little Carlin kit and gnashed her teeth as well.

Kethera caught on and told her little Brother, "Quick, quick, go outside and protect the Gudongs."

The little kit darted outside with his hands waving in the air, his tail held perfectly straight, "Protect the Gudongs. Protect the Gudongs. Aria wants to gobble them all up, shell eat them all!", he cried, making wild arm gestures, his high-pitched voice echoing across the yard.

Another older kit quickly joined in and shouted, "I am Kriltak, the Protector of Gudongs. I will defeat the ravenous monster, Aria!"

Kayala smiled, almost laughed, her whiskers raised in amusement, "Well, that game, Protect the Gudongs, is going to keep them busy for at least a couple of days. That will keep them out from under my whiskers for a while."

Kayala looked back to her Daughter with a gentle smile on her face, "Under Tholish customs, inter-species relationships are considered forbidden. Under Carlinish customs, they are not. Kethera, if you love this boy, that is okay. Just remember, if you experiment with him, use protection."

Kethera was wishing she could just vanish, she felt so embarrassed, he Carlinish face was iridescent, glowing with embarrassment, "Mum! I'm still far too young for that! I'm still years away from being able to bond."

Aria made matters worse by asking, "Protection? Carlins and Humans aren't genetically compatible. Our species evolved on completely different worlds."

Yealah was now sitting on the edge of the table, "Oh, that old assumption", then she looked at Aria and noted, with her melodic trills and clicks, "Thols and Carlins are incompatible, yes. Thols and Humans are incompatible, yes. Even Mimasian Thols and Indigenous Thols are incompatible, yes. So, naturally, you would think that Carlins and Humans are incompatible as well. It does appear to be a fair assumption, doesn't it?"

Kayala then dropped the clanger, "The assumption is a false one, little one. Carlins and Humans are compatible sexually, even compatible genetically."

The girls all blushed, each in the way of their respective species.

"That isn't possible. Our species evolved on worlds twenty two light years apart", Aria replied, not thinking it was even possible.

"A one-in-a-trillion chance, perhaps and yet it is true", Kayala replied.

Yealah noted, trilling and clicking, "I have seen Carlin Human hybrids born in the clinic. A perfect blend of Carlin and Human. They have the most delightful shocks of Human hair. The Mothers are always Carlin, although I'm not sure why that is. That is currently a mystery to us."

Ariel thoughtfully added, "Perhaps the attraction is from male Humans for Carlin females and not the other way around. Attraction is entirely subjective after all."

Kayala looked at Kethera, "Little one, do you remember your Aunt Kearill?"

"I think so. Doesn't Aunt Kearill work in a Primary School, somewhere in the Human Colony?", Kethera asked.

"Yes, kind of. It's a Primary School in a small village to the west of the Human Colony", Kayala informed her, explaining further, "That village has mixed families, Carlin Mothers, Human Fathers and hybrid kits. Lots of hybrid kits. Your Aunt Kearill has a Human husband and four hybrid kits."

"No way", Kethera replied, then asked, "Why didn't anyone tell me?"

"Your Aunt Kearill didn't want to confuse you. Maybe one day soon, we'll go there for a visit", Kayala told her.

Aria was confused and blurted out, "Why do they have their own village?"

Kethera frowned and her whiskers became downcast, "Not every Carlin is as accepting of mixed relationships. The Human men feel uncomfortable here in the village. Carlin folk always stare at them. It can be quite disconcerting. Very uncomfortable, in fact. Some can be downright disrespectful."

"Okay, but surely they can live in the Human Colony?", Aria questioned, that made sense to her.

Sarlia chimed in, in her usual telepathic way, *"Aria. Do you think Humans are any different from Carlin folk?"*

Yealah chimed in and explained, "Human folk can be quite cruel and judgemental at times. Not many of them mind you but enough to cause problems. Xenophobia and speciecism does occur."

Ariel became curious, remarking, "Racism no longer exists. That's all in the distant past, why do we have the xenophobic issues? It makes no sense!"

Sarlia frowned, her Martian mind looking for an adequate response, she settled on, *"I have no answer for you, Ariel. I can only say, that there are always outliers with negative mindsets and this occurs in all societies, no matter how civilised."*

Kethera's whiskers drooped, "So they are ostracised and forced to live in their own village?"

Kayala smiled at her Daughter, "Little one. Have you noticed that we Carlins live in our villages? That the Thols live in theirs and that the Humans live in their colony. They are happier living in their own village. There is no xenophobia there."

Yealah chimed in, with her melodic voice, "Only the most progressive of each species live together in one community and that usually means living in off-world colonies", she frowned, "Sadly, that does not include Indigenous Thols. They hold onto their old ways and their ancient taboos. There are many outliers, as Sarlia described them, amongst the Indigenous Thols and very few amongst those of Mimasian descent."

As always, Aria had to know more and asked, "How do Carlin Human hybrids compare to Martian Earthling hybrids?", a subject that Saffiera, being there were so few Martians on the planet, was completely uncomfortable with.

Saffiera's Mother, Sarlia replied, *"Humans, whether of Earthling or Martian descent, are closely related subspecies of Homo Sapiens. So we do have a very high genetic compatibility."*

"So for us Humans, hybridisation is simple, even normal, whereas Human Carlin hybrids are a cosmic fluke?", Aria questioned.

"A one-in-a-trillion chance of species compatibility would indicate so", Sarlia replied, her Martian mind going into an analytical mode, then she added, *"There are of course some intriguing observations."*

Saffiera frowned as Aria continued with her questions, "Intriguing observations?"

Wanting to end this particular discussion quickly, Saffiera responded, *"All Martian-Earthling matings involve Martian women and Earth men. All the hybrids born take after their Mother and are non-verbal telepaths. The Martian genetics are favoured"*, rattling off some quick facts.

"Yes. Yes, Saffiera but it gets more intriguing. Overtime and if no more Earthling genetics are added, the descendants of the hybrids revert back to pure Martian over time", Sarlia responded, then added, *"Except for of course, throwbacks."*

"What's a throwback?", Aria enquired.

"The random occurrence of a Martian Earthling hybrid, even when hybridisation was

not known in one's ancestral lineage", Sarlia explained, then she added, *"It can be quite the shock when it happens and usually leads to genealogical research on the part of the family involved. We Martians love a mystery, especially solving them."*

Aria's twin Ariel chimed in and asked, "What is the source of attraction between Martian women and Earth men? Is it pheromonal?"

Sarlia smiled, she liked the way the twins took a keen interest in other species, *"We thought it was pheromonal at first, Ariel, but it turns out that Earth men just find Martian women attractive and Martian women find Earth men attractive as well. There's apparently more passion involved in these relationships."*

Both twins nodded in unison.

Sarlia had finished answering the twin's questions and Yealah stepped in with what she knew of Carlin Human hybrids, "From my work at the clinic, I can tell you a few things about Carlin Human hybrids. Unlike Martian Earthling hybrids, they don't favour one species over the other. They are a perfect blend of both."

"How is that even possible?", Aria asked, "I mean, given the completely separate evolution?"

"Well, Aria, that is the big cosmic mystery, perhaps convergent evolution?", Yealah replied, her trills appearing to highlight the mystery part.

Ariel was more interested in another aspect of these Carlin Human hybrids, "Why isn't this common knowledge? I mean, even Kethera didn't know about it."

Kayala frowned, her whiskers drooped and her ears flattened, "That is partially the fault of we Carlin folk. As a people, we just don't talk about it and as the hybrids and their parents live in a separate village, it's kind of out of sight, out of mind, I suppose."

"These hybrids are born in the colony, at a Human clinic?", Ariel questioned.

"Yes, they are Ariel", Yealah confirmed, then admitted, "It is the colony's policy not to publicise the existence of the hybrids, so as not to cause alarm amongst the Human colonists."

"What!", Aria exclaimed, "Why does that excuse ring hollow?", she blurted out.

Sarlia stepped in, explaining, *"Aria, the Human colony has only been on this world for two and a half decades. We Martians, Earthlings and even Mimasian Thols are all new here and no one wants to rock the boat."*

Yealah added, "These Carlin Human hybrids are very new. Not a single one is older than eight and as far as we can tell, they represent a new species, half Carlin and half Human."

Ariel asked, "Why always Human men and Carlin women?"

Yealah smiled and almost gave a Tholish, melodic chuckle, "We don't really know. That is still being studied, but my best guess would be a personal sense of attraction, as your Sister, Ariel, suggested earlier. Carlin men and Human women don't seem to have that same attraction."

Ariel's twin Aria found that answer perplexing "The universe is far weirder than I'd ever thought", Aria blurted out.

"What?", Kethera asked, "Don't you think I'm attractive?"

Aria gave Kethera a hug, "Of course I do. We both do. We love you to bits, Kethera."

Ariel smiled in agreement, "To true. To true. I love you to bits, Kethera", she responded.

Sarlia transmitted a private observation to Yealah, *"It seems that both human males and females are attracted to Carlin females."*

Yealah looked at Sarlia and simply nodded in agreement.

Sarlia provided more information than perhaps even Yealah was ready to hear, transmitting, *"There even seems to be an attraction between Humans and Mimasian Thols and it appears to cut both ways. The possibly of producing offspring appears to be an irrelevance, perhaps even an afterthought."*

Yealah nodded in agreement once more but thought back, *"This disturbs me. The breaking of young hearts is not something we Mimasian Thols can stomach. The Indigenous can do so in a heartbeat, for us, it is so much harder."*

Saffiera took charge of the discourse, she had had enough of all this talk about hybridisation. As one of the few Martians on Vale, it was a path she would likely be forced into, assuming she was to have children of her own. Saffiera was conflicted by the issue but then again, she was still quite young and it was possible she would find a suitable mate amongst the Humans of Earth descent, given time.

Saffiera pushed the thought out of her mind, telepathically she transmitted, *"This is a lot to take in, but we are really behind on our studies and we really need to get back on track."*

Sarlia remarked telepathically, *"The mind of a Martian at work, always returning to the subject and one's purpose. Do not be so dismissive of Earth boys, my child, you are a descendent of Winchilly and Gideon Reas, so there are hybrids in our ancestry. More than you might think"*, she nodded at her Daughter with respect.

Yealah asked her Daughter, "Yeannah, are you still okay to study? You don't want to go home?", she gently trilled and clicked.

Kethera added, "We will understand if you're not feeling up to it, Yeannah", then she implored, "Please stay, we all love you to bits!"

Yeannah's eyes were still red from crying, but her determination was fierce, "We are way behind on our assignment and we really do need to catch up. There is work to be done! I will stay."

"Well then girls, go upstairs and study, you already know the way. I'll bring up your supper as soon as I've heated it up", Kayala told them.

As the girls all made their way upstairs, Kayala commented, "These girls are just like my own kits and I will always treat them as such", she smiled and both Sarlia and Yealah appreciated the sentiment.

The girls all went up to the attic room and straight away they noticed their duffle bags and sleeping bags neatly lined up against one wall. Yeannah switched on the main screen at the other end of the attic and connected her data tablet to the network. The other girls connected their data tablets to the network as well. The sounds of playing kits wafted into the attic and Aria walked over to the big attic window, which was next to the stairs.

Aria looked outside at the big Bell Nut Fruit trees, she could not see any Thrixan or Boobooks, it was likely far to light outside for them to show themselves. There were certainly no Harricks visible, day or night, they were rarely ever seen. The Gudongs, however, were highly conspicuous, they all appeared to be in the closet Bell Nut Fruit tree.

Seven of Kethera's siblings were running around the Bell Nut Fruits, chaotically waving their arms in the air and shouting out, *"Protect the Gudongs. Aria will eat them all."*

One of Kethera's siblings, an older boy kit, had strapped a bin lid to his left arm and in his right hand, he held a long stick.

"I am Kriltak, the Protector of Gudongs", he shouted, as he was swashbuckling his way around the base of the tree, lunging his stick at invisible ravenous Arias. Apparently, they were everywhere, gnashing their savage teeth.

No wonder the Gudongs had all taken to the tree to escape the chaos below. Kethera's siblings had corralled them there for their own protection.

"Guys. You have to see this. It is hilarious", Aria called to her friends.

The girls all walked to the window and looked outside, they all began to laugh. Kethera noticed one of her nine siblings was missing.

"Where's Ketran?", Kethera enquired, Ketran was Kriltak's fraternal twin Sister.

"I'm over here, silly", a shy young girl answered from the top of the stairs.

"I thought you'd be playing with the other kits", Kethera commented.

"I just wanted to check", Ketran replied shyly, then she asked, "Aria's not really going to eat all of the Gudongs, is she? She doesn't look like a monster."

The twins giggled as Kethera explained, "No, Ketran, Aria is not going to eat all of the Gudongs."

"Okay. I just wanted to check", Ketran replied in her soft, shy voice.

Aria decided to have some more fun and she said with a wry smile on her face, "It's the three fingers you really need to worry about, Ketran."

Ariel almost cracked up laughing but held it back, "Yes, it's definitely the three fingers", she confirmed.

"What's a three fingers?", Ketran asked, feeling a little sceptical.

Aria was quick with an absurd answer, she got down to Ketran's eye level and with a completely straight face, whispered loudly, "They look just like us Humans, except they have only three fingers."

"I've never seen a Human with three fingers", Ketran replied, even more sceptically.

However, Ariel covered her twin Sister, "No, that's not what Aria meant at all. They have five fingers just like us, but when they use them, it's as if they only have three."

Ketran looked up at Ariel and Aria in disbelief until Aria and Ariel held out their hands and splayed their fingers. They had a thumb, then two fingers joined together, index and middle fingers and then another two fingers joined together, ring and little fingers. That made it look as though they both had only three fingers on each hand.

Ketran put her hands to her face in shock and both Aria and Ariel gnashed their teeth with loud audible clicks. Ketran's pupil slits opened wide, her whiskers shot up and her ears pressed down. Then she jumped up and ran down the stairs on the balls of her feet.

"Aria and Ariel are three fingers!", she shouted as she quickly joined her siblings outside by the Bell Nut Fruit tree, "Aria and Ariel are three fingers! They're going to eat all of our Gudongs."

Kriltak yelled out, "Where are the three fingers? I will defeat them. I will protect the Gudongs."

The twins were snickering to themselves, it was a twin thing. Kethera joined in laughing as well.

Yeannah shook her head in mock disgust, "You three are incorrigible", she told them while holding back her laughter.

Saffiera just gave a little smirk, *"Earthlings!"*, she transmitted telepathically before laughing.

Kayala came up the stairs with the girl's supper, freshly heated, many mushroom pies and deep-fried Thrixan pieces. There was even a large bowl of steamed masuli, a staple grain similar to rice but sweeter with a slightly bluish tinge to it. Sarlia followed close behind her, with five glasses and a jug of masuli-infused Gudong milk. Something that she found quite refreshing.

"We nearly got bowled over by Ketran on the stairs", Kayala remarked, questioning, "She was shouting something about Aria and Ariel being three fingers?"

The twins both raised their hands, splaying their fingers in their three-fingered formats, "That would be us", Aria and Ariel replied in unison.

Kayala looked at their splayed fingers and laughed, "Are you sure you two aren't really Carlin kits in disguise? You both have Carlinish mischievousness."

Sarlia gave off a little telepathic giggle, *"It's an Earth Human twin thing, Kayala. They have their own internal language and natural mischievousness. We Martian Humans rarely have twins, but when we do, they exhibit exactly the same behaviour."*

Kayala and Sarlia passed the food to the girls before retreating back downstairs.

As they walked back downstairs, Sarlia noted, *"Only a pair of twins could turn their fingers into something that scary."*

"Are you sure that they're not Carlin kits in disguise?", Kayala jokingly asked.

Sarlia smiled and replied with a telepathic laugh, *"Oh no, they're definitely Human. Although, there does appear to be a lot of similarity between Carlin kits and Human twins."*

While eating a piece of deep-fried Thrixan, Aria noted, "This Thrixan tastes just like sweet chicken."

"That's the Bell Nut Fruit they eat. It sweetens their meat and their eggs as well", Kethera replied, adding, "Their eggs have a delightfully creamy texture and sweet flavour."

"Maybe next time we'll get to try some", Aria replied as she took another bite of deep-fried Thrixan.

"And by the way, your Earth Chickens taste like flavourless Thrixan", Kethera chortled.

That had the twins snorting with laughter.

Ariel remarked to her twin, "Aria, you really do need to think before you spit out one of your jokes."

"Why, Ariel?", Aria asked, adding, "I might not have much of a filter, but tonight went fairly well."

"Don't you even remember the look on Kethera's Mum's face when she realised what you meant by *'hide the Gudongs'* ?", Ariel reminded her.

"Kind of, why?", Aria asked.

Saffiera chimed in, *"Telepath here, both my Mum and I",* she announced, *"Kethera's Mum had an image of Gudongs running around the yard being chased by randy Human men. It took her a good few seconds to shake those images out of her mind."*

"Thank you, Saffiera", Yeannah replied, "Now it will take me a few good seconds to do the same."

"Sorry, Yeannah. I was just trying to get Aria to understand exactly what her jokes

actually do to people", Saffiera apologised.

Kethera laughed, "Gudongs being chased around the yard by randy men. That is so funny!"

"You too, Kethera? My Mum saw that image as well, you know", Saffiera pronounced.

The twins burst out laughing as well.

"Oh, I give up", Saffiera replied, then changed the topic slightly, *"Are the Gudongs okay being herded around by the kits like that?"*

Kethera recomposed herself and replied, "The Gudongs don't mind. The kits are like chaos, they mean no harm and the Gudongs just get out of their way."

"So when the kit get too rowdy, the Gudongs just jump into the trees?", Saffiera enquired.

"The trees or the house roof, either one. They're not too fussed", Kethera replied, explaining, "Carlin kits and Gudongs grow up with each other, so they know when to move to higher ground."

"If a Gudong was to say, hurt a kit, you know, bite one. What would happen?", Ariel asked.

"The next day it would be Gudong stew or perhaps roasted Gudong", Kethera replied, very matter-of-factly, explaining, "We cannot tolerate a viscous Gudong", then she noticed her friend's concerned looks and added, "It is very, very rare for that to happen."

"I wonder what they'd do in the Human colony", Aria smiled with a wide, wry grin.

"No, Aria! You are not sneaking Gudongs into the school", Ariel chided.

"Oh, come on, Ariel. I was only thinking about it", Aria complained.

Yeannah rolled her beautiful purple eyes and told her friends, "Guys, we are way behind. We have to get back to studying", she was still having trouble keeping Thomas out of her mind and needed to bury herself in work.

Saffiera caught on real quick, telling the others, *"Yeah guys, we really need to study, so let's get on with it."*

Kethera agreed, "Yeah, guys, we really should."

The twins sighed in unison and quickly agreed.

While Yeannah linked up to the site with the historical data they required for their assignment, Aria and Ariel taught Kethera how to splay her fingers in a way that displayed a three-fingered format.

Aria then said to Kethera, "Now tomorrow, when you get home from school, splay your fingers just like we showed you. It will freak the kits out, they'll think you've become a three fingers!"

Ariel added, "It will be hilarious!"

Kethera giggled and grinned, "It will be so funny!", she exclaimed.

Saffiera and Yeannah just shook their heads and rolled their eyes as the data came up on the screen.

The Great Explosion, the Outward Interplanetary Expansion was back on the attic's main screen and the girls dove into the studies once more.

18. High Martian Orbit.

Doctor Gideon Reas stood behind his office desk. It was a large behemoth of a desk with his data tablet and docking station sitting in the middle. The docking station gave him access to keyboards, cursor control devices, amongst several other devices and three large screens. The central screen was in landscape mode and gave him a clear view of his computer's systems. The other two screens, to the left and right, were set to portrait mode. The one on his right was used for the Mars Terraforming Project and the one on his right was used for the Management of the Aries colony, along with all of the other colonies in the Martian Orbit.

There were exceptions to this rule: the Martian Moons, Phobos and Deimos. Phobos was managed by the Port Phobos Administrator, a Lieutenant, at Port Phobos. Deimos was managed by the Military Commandant at the Deimos Military and Refuelling Base on Deimos. Both of those appointments were made by the Colonial Armed Forces, based in Cis-Lunar L-Four and therefore, they were Military.

Doctor Gideon Reas, however, was appointed as the Mars Chief Terraforming Project Manager by the Colonisation Committee of Sol, which was inside Eros, the City within the Rock, a hollowed-out Asteroidal colony. Gideon's other hat was as the Martian Colonial Administrator, that position was appointed by the Security Council of Sol, which was also inside Eros. As such, Gideon was responsible for Mars and all colonies in Martian orbit, except for the two Moons, Phobos and Deimos. He was not to interfere in any way, shape or form with the management of the Martian Moons. They were not within his remit.

Gideon's desk was split along similar lines, left and right, in terms of his work.

Everything on the right was for the ongoing Martian Terraforming project. Gideon had a trio of trays on the right side of his desk. From left to right, his in-tray was red, his in-progress-tray was orange and his out-tray was green.

Everything on the left side of his desk was for Martian colonial management. Gideon had four trays on the left side of his desk. From right to left, his in-tray was red, his in-progress-tray was orange and his out-tray was green. The fourth tray on the far left was purple. That tray was for things that had absolutely nothing to do with Martian colonial management and yet, somehow, they ended up on his desk anyway.

At the far left side of Gideon's desk was another smaller desk that connected to his big desk and the back wall. Overall, it gave the appearance of an even larger, L-shaped desk. On that desk were two out-trays, one labelled

Deimos and the other labelled Phobos, they were both coloured grey. The purple tray was the in-tray for those two trays and they were a source of continuous annoyance for Gideon, as their contents had no business in his office whatsoever.

The Aries colony itself was one of the larger O'Neil-style twin-cylinder colonies but nowhere near the largest. It had not been built in high Martian orbit. Instead, it had been towed there by eight space tugs from Cis-Lunar Haulage, a company of Stuart Dumas, all the way from the Dumas Colonial Construction yards at Cis-Lunar L-Four. The colony had arrived with its great strip mirrors, three per cylinder, all neatly folded in at each cylinder's sides. That was, of course, a long time ago, forty five years back.

Gideon had two sectaries just outside of his office door. Behind the desk on the right sat Zelda, his Administrative Assistant for the Martian Terraforming Project. Behind the desk to the left sat Marsha, his Administrative Assistant for Martian Colonial Management. Of course, just as Gideon's desk was complicated with *"files"* that had no business in his office, outside of his office door was a third desk. That desk was to the left and further beyond Marsha's desk. Behind that desk sat Leila, his Administrative Liaison to the Martian Moons, Phobos and Deimos. Her job should be completely unnecessary, except for the constant flow of work that was not meant to be coming across his desk.

Gideon's desk had very little clutter, except for two desktop photos of his two wives, Sandra Danker and Winchilly. Apart from that, his desk was spotless. Gideon's workflow was highly organised. Zelda would feed work, terraforming reports and projections, etc., into his right-hand in-tray and remove completed work from his right-hand out-tray. Marsha did the same on the colonial administration side, feeding his other in-tray and removing completed work from his other out-tray.

Another important aspect of Marsha's job was to isolate anything pertaining to Phobos or Deimos, which was then passed onto Leila, who perused it carefully before placing the more iffy issues into the *"purple"* in-tray. A tray that ought to be empty and yet, it was far more often than not, quite full. That *"purple"* in-tray would have been stacked three feet high if not for Leila's constant efforts in dealing with ninety percent of the misdirected workload.

Sandra Danker waltzed in her Husband's office, she held up her hands, which held two brown takeaway bags, "I brought lunch", she told Gideon verbally.

That was something they both preferred to do, even though Gideon and Sandra were both extremely powerful psychics and could have conversed telepathically. Very few people actually knew this, so they had to constantly keep up the appearance of normality.

"Great, Sandra. What are we having today?", Gideon asked.

"Well, you've got soft-shell crab Ramen with octopus balls and I have Pad Thai", Sandra informed him, then she asked, "How's your day going?"

Gideon pointed to his work trays for the Martian Terraforming Project, "These are no real problem. There are some more serious concerns and I'm ordering more modelling done, but it's our bread and butter. We know what to do", he then gestured to the Colonial Administration work, "Also not a problem", then he pointed to the *"purple"* in-tray, "I have no words for that mess!"

"Damn it, Gideon, we should jaunt you back to Mimas, you need one of Winchilly's massages", Sandra replied, adding, "Why the hell are you getting that Military crap across your desk anyway?"

"Heaven only knows, Sandra, heaven only knows", Gideon replied.

Leila walked into the office, "I'm sorry to disturb you, Doctor Reas, but I have some more contentious documents meant for Phobos and Deimos. I'm not even allowed to read these ones, Sir!"

Leila placed the stack of documents on top of the *"purple"* in-tray. Gideon glanced at the top document, one for Deimos. It was clearly stamped "*Top Secret*".

Gideon's frustration boiled over, "For fucks sake!", then he apologised and asked, "Sorry, Leila. These documents. Are they all marked top secret?"

"The entire stack is Doctor Reas", Leila confirmed, then she remarked, "Honestly, Doctor Reas, I keep fielding these misdirects, but it is just getting worse. It's getting like I need a clone of myself!"

Sandra chimed in, "I thought it was bad enough with contractors sending you invoices for what were military contracts, but top secret military documents. That is really, really bad!"

"Yeah, Sandra. Something is severely broken with the system", Gideon replied, then he assured Leila, "After lunch, Sandra and I will fix this problem personally. Leila, your workload is about to lessen somewhat."

"You and Sandra, Sir?", Leila asked, she was quite confused as to how that would happen.

"Don't worry about that, Leila. Just let us deal with it", Gideon assured her.

Leila left the office and then Gideon and Sandra went straight back to eating their lunch.

After lunch, Gideon and Sandra uncharacteristically left their empty food containers sitting on Gideon's desk. Sandra and Gideon then went through the stack of documents, separating them out into the Phobos and Deimos out-trays.

Once the documents were all sorted, Gideon asked his wife, "Okay, Sandra. Are you ready to play a little game of bad cop, worse cop?"

"Hmm", Sandra put he finger to her lips, "Is that something we can play later with Winchilly?"

Gideon sighed, "Focus, Sandra, focus. Now show me your scariest face."

Sandra smiled and almost giggled, "Really, Gideon. We can make them see whatever we want."

"Good point", Gideon replied, "Let's do Phobos first."

Gideon and Sandra astral projected across from the Aries colony to Port Phobos. They quickly found the Administrator's office and they observed him carefully for a few minutes. His name was Lieutenant Mackay and he had no idea that they were there. The Lieutenant was a short, overweight, portly chap and Gideon detected a distinct Napoleon complex. He was, as Gideon might describe, an unpleasant personage.

The duo both returned to Gideon's office, where Gideon picked up every document in the Phobos out-tray. Then, without adieu, they both jaunted across to Lieutenant Mackay's office. They did so in the most showy of fashions, it was completely unnecessary and they did so purely for the psychological effect. Two bright columns of light appeared in Lieutenant Mackay's office. They so ridiculously were bright and Lieutenant Mackay simply could not ignore them.

"What the fuck!", the Lieutenant shouted out loud.

Then in an instant, Gideon and Sandra appeared in the Lieutenant's office, "What the fuck!" he said again, as he stood up from his chair, "Where the hell did you two come from?"

Gideon put on a severely commanding voice, "Shut the fuck up and sit down you petty, perfunctory prick!", the Lieutenant felt completely compelled to sit down and did so, it was not of his own choice.

Gideon slammed the Phobos files down on the Lieutenant's desk. There were a lot of them.

The Lieutenant was astonished to see so many top secret files all at once on his desk, "What's all this then?", he murmured, as if he had a lump the size of a potato stuck in his throat.

Gideon leaned on the Lieutenant's desk and stared into his eyes, "Those are the files, that have been crossing my fucking desk!", he told him, then added, "They are not meant for my eyes!"

The Lieutenant murmured, "Yes. Yes, I can see that."

"Good then, Lieutenant. Do you know who I am?", Gideon asked.

"Yes. I've seen your picture in the news feeds. You're Doctor Gideon Reas, the Martian Colonial Administrator", the Lieutenant replied in the meekest of voices.

"Then tell me, Lieutenant. Why are top secret Military Documents crossing my fucking desk?", Gideon released more frustration than he'd wanted.

"I, I, I don't know, Doctor Reas. It must have been a mistake", the Lieutenant replied.

Gideon gestured to his wife, Sandra, who took over and she was frightening to behold. Sandra's face morphed and all the Lieutenant could see was an angry, red-faced, female Gargoyle complete with long pointed horns and chin, staring coldly at him. She looked at him with pure disdain!

Sandra put on a commanding voice, "My Husband is stressed and these mistakes", she slammed her right fist onto the documents on the Lieutenant's desk, "They need to stop!"

It was like venom in his ears, his brain wanted to bleed out, the Lieutenant replied in the softest and meekest of voices, his heart racing and the fear of God in his eyes, "Yes! Yes! I'll, I'll make it stop!"

Sandra replied matter-of-factly, "Good! Then I have no need to burn you where you sit!"

Sandra and Gideon stepped back from the Lieutenant's desk, there were two flashes of light and they were both gone. The Lieutenant reached for his desk drawer, opened it and pulled out a bottle of Kentucky Bourbon, he took a deep drink, not bothering with a glass. Bottle of grog in one hand, rosary in the other Lieutenant Mackay preyed for the first time in decades.

Gideon and Sandra reappeared in Gideon's office, "Was that over the top?", Sandra asked.

"Did you not scan his mind, Sandra?", Gideon questioned back, noting, "He has been brushing off his own work for years and his exasperated underlings have been shunting it everywhere else."

"Yeah, Gideon. I might have missed that part, I was having too much fun", Sandra admitted, "It was kind of like, a Satan Claus moment."

"Okay, let's have a look at Deimos, shall we?", Gideon suggested.

"Most definitely", Sandra replied.

Gideon and Sandra astral projected across from the Aries colony to the Deimos Military Base. They quickly found the Commandant's office and they observed him carefully for a few minutes. His name was Colonel Strong and in contrast to his name, he looked the complete opposite. The Colonel was thin, wiry and also quite old, almost retirement age, old. The Colonel had two simply grey trays on his desk, an in-tray and an out-tray. Both were full, the in-tray, the more so and his desk was completely cluttered with work. This was in

Gideon's mind, a very hard-working and overworked man. Gideon and Sandra both returned to Gideon's office.

"Gideon, we cannot play bad cop, worse cop with this guy. It would not be right", Sandra noted.

"Agreed, Sandra. We'll play good cop, nicer cop instead", Gideon replied.

"Good cop, nicer cop? Is that even a thing, Gideon?", Sandra asked, as she picked up the stack of documents that were supposed to be at the Deimos Military Base, then she added playfully, "Would Winchilly even want to play such a game?", then she smiled a wry smile, "Come to think of it, she probably would."

Gideon smiled back and they both jaunted to Colonel Strong's office. There was less of a display this time, just a pair of small bright lights that gradually blinked into existence and formed into Gideon and Sandra. Colonel Strong was astonished yet showed no sense of fear. He understood that psi-corp had powerful psychics around the place, he'd just never met one before. Although, he'd been told that psi-corps operatives could not function off-world.

"And you two would be?", the Colonel asked in a mild-mannered, polite voice.

"I am Doctor Gideon Reas and this is Sandra Danker", Gideon introduced themselves.

"So, Doctor Reas, why are you two here?", the Colonel asked, "As you can clearly see, I am a very busy man."

Sandra replied as she put the stack of files into the Colonel's in-tray, "This stack of documents crossed my Husband's desk. They are all labelled top secret and should never have ended up in the Aries Colony. There are not for Gideon's eyes, Colonel."

"Well, that is an oversight. A major oversight. Still, it just makes my work so much harder", the Colonel replied.

"It is more than an oversight, Colonel. Those are top secret documents and that means there is a systemic problem that needs to be fixed", Gideon politely explained.

"And what do you suggest, Doctor Reas?", the Colonel enquired.

"If I may, Colonel, I wear two hats. I'm not only the Martian Terraforming Project Manager, I'm also the Martian Colonial Administrator", Gideon informed him.

"Oh, I see, Doctor Reas. One of those is my job on the civilian side of things", the Colonel replied.

"Yes, quite. My point is, the only way I can manage my workload is with two Administrative Assistants and an Administrative Liaison", Gideon informed the Colonel.

Sandra chimed in with a voice that was almost like a soft cooing in the Colonel's ears, yet it held great command and strength, "Colonel, I am not detecting anyone outside your office apart from a single secretary. Looking at your desk and your workload, you definitely need more assistants", it was convincing, the Colonel could not say no.

Those words sunk into the Colonel's mind with great weight and he replied thoughtfully, "Yes, you are probably right, Ms Danker. I will discuss this with my secretary and endeavour to ensure that these unfortunate oversights never happen again."

"That is all we can ask for, Colonel. Thank you", Gideon agreed, "Have a wonderful day", and then they both blinked out of existence, returning to Gideon's office in the Aries colony.

Sandra's seed had been planted and Colonel Strong buzzed his secretary, "Gloria. Do me a favour. Organise an Administrative Assistant and a Liaison Officer for me. I really need to cut my workload down a bit. We appear to have top secret files being misdirected to civilians."

"Yes, Sir. I will start on that straight away, Sir", Gloria confirmed, thinking to herself, *"Why now? I've been suggesting that to him for years!"*

The Colonel buzzed Gloria once again, "Gloria, please put together a communique to Colonial Defence, High Command. Flag it, top secret. Doctor Gideon Reas and Sandra Danker are both psi-corp operatives and they are operating off-world", he instructed her.

"Are you sure, Sir?", Gloria enquired.

"They appeared out of nowhere, like only psi-corp operatives could. No run-of-the-mill psychic would have that much raw power", the Colonel explained.

The Colonel had made that assumption, as all psychics on the Earth were supposed to be, by law, inducted into psi-corp at an early age. Except, neither Gideon nor Sandra had ever been to the Earth.

"Yes, Colonel. I will do that straight away, Sir", Gloria confirmed, thinking to herself, *"Psi-corp? Here? This far from the Earth?"*

Back at the Aries colony in Gideon's office, Gideon buzzed his Administrative Liaison, "Leila. Sandra has made a few calls. With a bit of luck, a lot of those misdirected files you've been receiving will disappear. Let me know how things go. If nothing changes, I'll set Sandra loose on them again."

"Thank you, Doctor Reas", Leila replied, with a slightly mystified tone to her voice, she was wondering, *"How? I've been trying to stem the flow for years?"*

Gideon sat down behind his desk and Sandra plonked herself down on the desk's edge. Gideon picked up a file and began quickly scanning through it, refreshing his memory.

"This file, Sandra, this file is more important than all of those military files put altogether", Gideon informed her as he held up the file.

Sandra took the file and gave it a quick read, "Oh! I remember this. When we were on the Martian surface before the Martians were liberated. The stench of the new Martian atmosphere was awful."

"I was wrong!", Gideon admitted, explaining, "I believed the new Martian atmosphere was mildly toxic. I underestimated those volatile gases and toxic compounds. There have been a lot of deaths!"

"Deaths! No!", Sandra protested, "We haven't even opened up Mars for colonisation yet. Mars is still officially closed to colonists!"

"Homesteaders are bypassing Aries and Port Phobos and just landing on the planet without any real understanding of how bad the new Martian air is", Gideon informed her.

"How? When we escaped from the Tarlaks, we were breathing that air", Sandra recalled.

"The first time we had re-breathers. The second time, after escaping the Tarlaks, we were only exposed to the Martian air for around an hour", Gideon explained, adding, "It's all about the exposure times. Read the document a bit further."

Sandra read through the document a bit further, "After one hour of exposure, the headaches gradually begin. After the second hour, the headaches start to become unbearable. The headaches become intolerable and disabling at around the third hour. By the fourth hour, the vomiting begins, which is followed by diarrhoea at around the fifth hour. Dehydration sets in in around six hours, with death following before the eighth hour is up. Jesus, Gideon, this is horrendous!"

"Do you know how we have that information, Sandra?", Gideon asked.

"I have no idea, Gideon. Perhaps if I read a bit further into it", Sandra suggested.

"I'll save you some time, Sandra. That is an excerpt from a medical log", Gideon informed her, adding, "From the latest homesteaders to fall afoul of the Martian atmosphere. A whole extended family, thirty eight deaths in all and that is just the latest homesteading incursion. The Doctor died as well, they all did, even their livestock."

“How many others?”, Sandra asked.

“So far, twenty incursions that we know of. There have been hundreds of deaths”, Gideon admitted, “We usually find them long after they're all dead, so there could be a lot more.”

“And you never thought to tell me about this?”, Sandra asked, still shocked by the information.

“I thought it better not to tell you, Sandra. Imagine how that conversation would have gone”, Gideon explained, “Hi Hon, we found another thirty eight corpses today. What's for dinner? That's not a conversation I ever wanted to have with you, Sandra.”

“I'm stronger than you think, Gideon. When are you going to get that through your thick skull?”, Sandra reacted, “You need to stop protecting me from this shit!”

Sandra got up and walked over to a comfortable couch that was against the wall to the left of Gideon's desk, Gideon stood up and followed her. He sat down beside her.

“Haven't we released information on the toxicity of the Martian air?”, Sandra asked.

“We have, Sandra, but people think they know better”, Gideon replied, explaining, “They plan for the toxic air, not understanding how to really mitigate the issue. The only way to survive is to remain in hermetically sealed environments, you know, treat Mars as if it's in a vacuum. That way, no toxins can ever get in, but they don't have the credits to set up something like that. So they cut corners and that's their downfall.”

“They're homesteaders”, Sandra mused, “Of course they don't have the resources. But what on Earth were they thinking?”

Gideon shook his head, “From our analysis, they used modular homestead units that could be bolted together in various configurations. The problem is, they weren’t hermetically sealed at all. Instead, they relied on basic filtration systems and cheap rebreathers, trying to filter out the toxins. It was like slapping a filter onto an air conditioning unit. And to top it off, they had no airlocks. None at all!”

“Christ!”, Sandra exclaimed, her engineering instincts kicking in, “That was never going to work. Their filtration systems would’ve clogged up with toxins and failed in a week, ten days at the most. Sure, their rebreathers might’ve bought them some more time, but those need constant maintenance as well. Filters have to be replaced regularly or, at the very least, cleaned. And no airlocks! Every time they left their modules and reentered them, the toxins would have just flowed straight in. They were doomed the moment they touched down! They were absolutely screwed!"

"Right royally!", Gideon agreed.

"So, we can't allow this to continue. That much is obvious", Sandra remarked, then asked, "How do we stop these idiots?"

"Well, I've already quadrupled our surface scanning. Finding these homesteaders before they're dead is an important consideration", Gideon stated the obvious, "If we can extract them before the dehydration becomes irreversible, then they have a fifty-fifty chance or so, I've been told."

"So, before the sixth hour of exposure, their odds are much better", Sandra mulled over in her head, "That is not much of an extraction window. Locate them, assess their situation, extract them. Hell, they'll be dead anyway", she ran her hands through her hair.

"We still have to try. Our main plan is to prevent them from landing in the first place", Gideon noted, explaining, "I have low orbital patrols keeping Mars under surveillance for any attempted landings. I also have patrols in ultra-high Martian orbit, watching for approaching homesteaders. If we can stop them from landing, they will live."

"Gideon, since when do we have the resources for that?", Sandra questioned.

"We don't, not enough anyway. That file was from my out-tray. Zelda will collect the out-tray files at the end of the day and action them tomorrow morning", Gideon informed Sandra, "Then a communique goes off to Eros and the Colonisation Committee requesting fifty new surveillance craft."

"I never realised how complicated terraforming Mars was going to be, Gideon", Sandra admitted.

"Neither did I, Sandra, neither did I", Gideon agreed, "So many odd issues have popped up."

"Okay, Gideon, what is the long-term prognosis? When is our new Martian atmosphere going to be safe to actually breathe?", Sandra enquired.

"I'm requesting some more remodelling done on that very issue", Gideon advised Sandra, "I wasn't happy with the previous results."

"So what was the timeline on that one?", Sandra asked.

"The exotic gases and toxic chemicals are washing out of the atmosphere, but it is a very, very slow process. The last modelling suggested between one hundred and fifty to two hundred years", Gideon replied, adding, "I want to get a better handle on the timeline. Lock it down a bit tighter."

"Two centuries is a long time to be quarantining the whole planet", Sandra noted.

"Which is why I have asked Eros for adequate resourcing", Gideon informed her.

"My advice, Gideon. Those deceased homesteaders. Make the whole sorry situation public" Sandra recommended, "That should discourage any others."

"Or it will make them more creative, you know, a challenge", Gideon suggested, explaining, "It is a moot point anyway. I've already recommended that. The Colonisation Committee agreed, however, the Security Council vetoed their agreement. They did not want to alarm the public, especially considering the enormous expense of the project."

"We've been down there, Gideon. There are whole meadows and pastures of grass. New forests are growing. The biomes are all growing and developing. Those images are public record, it's leading those homesteaders to Mars, like moths to a flame", Sandra remarked.

"Yes, Sandra. The toxins aren't affecting the flora, only the fauna", Gideon agreed, reiterating, "It is exactly as you said, *'like moths to a flame'*."

Gideon switched on a screen on the opposite wall of his office and brought up a real-time image of Mars, it was now a blue ball, although you would not know it, the whole Martian globe was white with massive swirling storms. Thick, heavy rain clouds, one swirling hurricane after another, all bunched up around the Northern Hemisphere. The Southern Hemisphere was little different, except they were cyclones, all swirling in the opposite direction, right up against one another. The Coriolis forces were clearly visible from high Martian orbit.

"Every Martian year, the old red planet, used to get covered in a global dust storm", Gideon informed Sandra, "Now, instead of those global dust storms on our new blue planet, we get global hurricanes and cyclones."

"I thought that the global torrential rains had stopped", Sandra commented.

"They've largely ended, yes, Sandra, but in their place, once every Martian year, we get global hurricanes and cyclones instead", Gideon replied.

"Are those expected to settle down?", Sandra asked.

"Yes, the modelling suggests in about a century to a century and a half", Gideon noted, "I have requested a tighter timeline on that as well."

"So the Terraformers are doing a lot of modelling of late", Sandra noted.

Gideon looked at Sandra, "Here is the really sick, ironic twist. If I could click my fingers today and remove all of those disgusting stanky toxins from the new Martian atmosphere, we still could not live there. We would still have to wait for a century or more."

"The storms, right, Gideon?", Sandra queried, thinking to herself it was more complex.

"Yes and no, Sandra. Those hurricanes and cyclones are a problem, yes, but that is not the only issue", Gideon replied, he then asked, "Do you remember back when we were on the surface?"

Sandra reached back with her mind remembering the smell and taste of the new Martian air, "It was disgusting, stanky, toxic. There was also way too much oxygen. It made me giddy and the water vapour, the humidity was horrendous!"

"And there you have it, oxygen toxicity! We have to remove some of that as well. At least get it down into the low twenties as a percentage of the atmosphere", Gideon divulged, "But there is more, that humidity you mentioned. Remove those toxins and Humans can live longer, right up until pneumonia sets in and we drown in our own fluids."

"That's hard to believe, Gideon. That can't be right", Sandra protested, "I mean, oxygen toxicity I can understand, but drowning in the air?"

"Yep. I have been assured by our medical people that with the humidity levels down there and the sheer levels of water vapour in the atmosphere, all it will take is a day or two for pneumonia to set in. Then, if not extracted from that environment, death sometime on the third day, certainly by the fourth", Gideon explained.

"Pneumonia though, Gideon?", Sandra asked for clarification.

"Yes, Sandra, the lungs will be overwhelmed. Our bodies are full of symbiotic bacteria that usually work in harmony with us. Those very same microorganisms in that humid, wet air down there, they will go way out of balance and pneumonia will be the end result", Gideon explained.

"Gideon? What's the timeline for that to settle down?", Sandra asked.

"For the humidity and water levels, a century to a century and a half. A blink of the eye for Mars, a lifetime for us", Gideon replied, noting, "For the oxygen levels! We don't even have a handle on that yet. I've got the Terraformers working on new projections, but even they are unsure as to how long it will take to balance it naturally. Someone even suggested using insects to *'eat'* the oxygen and then wiping them out to turn them into organic fertilisers. Everyone has their own ideas", he chuckled.

Sandra looked at Gideon and remarked, "I remember two decades ago, before we started this terraforming process, you were all. No problem, we just break up Chariklo and Chiron into fragments and hurl them at Mars. Just blow them up in the upper atmosphere. You said it was an engineering problem and a solvable one at that."

"Yes, we were all so naive back then, weren't we? So easy. So simple. Now look at where we are. This is my life's work and I won't be around to see it completed", Gideon lamented.

"That's the thing, though, isn't it. It's not just your life's work. It's my life's work as well. Not to mention all of the scientists and engineers that put their whole lives into this project", Sandra replied.

Gideon smiled, "One bit of good news though, Sandra."

"Really, Gideon, today, I thought you were being Mr Doom and gloom guy", Sandra replied.

"Remember those giant space tugs? The Calypso and the Olympus?", Gideon asked.

"Yeah, they're the ones we used to haul Chariklo and Chiron out of solar orbit and into Mars L-One", Sandra recalled from memory.

"Yep. An expensive business that. The final payment on the loan for that operation went through over night", Gideon informed her.

"Wow! Two decades just to pay off that one process", Sandra remarked.

"Big credits equal big repayment times. That's always the way of it", Gideon replied, adding, "It's not a lot, but it does free up some funding for other endeavours, like preventing homesteaders from landing on Mars."

Gideon and Sandra both detected a slight change in the air in Gideon's office. They both looked around the office, but there was nothing to see.

Gideon shouted out, "You can come out of the shadows, we know you're here."

"Damn it, Orpheus. How did they know?", Freyja questioned.

"I don't know, Freyja. These two are wild cards. They are far more powerful than any of us", Orpheus admitted.

Folcrom Orpheus, Folcrom Freyja and their cousin Folcrom Tina all dropped their psychic obscuration fields and suddenly appeared in Gideon's office.

"Orpheus, Freyja", Gideon nodded, "I don't know you, Miss?", he gestured to Folcrom Tina.

"I'm their Cousin, Folcrom Tina", she replied.

Sandra stepped in, "You guys only turn up when you need something. What is it this time?"

Tina ran her fingers through her hair and answered, "I made a mistake and need your help to fix it."

"Tina, it's better for me to handle this", Orpheus advised, he explained, "We have a situation on Eros. Tina missed an opportunity to resolve that issue and now it has snowballed."

"A missed opportunity?", Sandra enquired.

Tina replied quickly, "There's a cult on Eros. They believe that there are aliens who are going to physically probe them and steal their minds and their memories."

"Tina, I did say let me handle this", Orpheus reminded her.

"This is my fault, Orpheus. I didn't take them seriously and now we have a problem", Tina replied.

Gideon raised his hand and answered, "It doesn't matter whose fault it is. I'm assuming you need our help to fix it?"

Sandra shook her head, "You people!", she shouted, "You induct us into your little Council of Shadows, but did you ever consider that we actually have lives? My Husband has two very stressful jobs and he doesn't need more stupid stuff just dumped on his head."

Having been inducted into the Council of Shadows, technically, Gideon and Sandra also held the title *'Folcrom'*, although they never bothered using it.

Freyja hadn't said anything since arriving, she sat down on the edge of Gideon's desk, laid back over it and looked up at the office ceiling, "Gideon is pretty cool. I have ways, techniques for relieving stress, you know", she commented, then asked, "Does Gideon need a third wife?"

Orpheus face-palmed himself and Tina's face went bright red.

Sandra's jaw dropped and she shook her head, "What?"

Freyja sat back up and looked straight at Sandra, "Does your Husband need a third wife?", she reiterated.

"My Husband does not need a third wife!", Sandra snapped back.

"I am being serious, Sandra", Freyja replied, "Gideon is really nice, he's intelligent and he's a brilliant man. We could make some really excellent babies together."

Gideon's face was also turning a decent shade of red, "No, Freyja. I do not need a third wife and you would never get Sandra's or Winchilly's agreement on the matter."

"More's the pity. Your loss and another missed opportunity", Freyja replied, with a flirtatious, almost predatory look, then she added, "I was serious, Gideon and the offer still stands. Think about it."

Sandra shook her head once again.

Orpheus looked at Freyja, "We'll be having a discussion about inappropriate behavior and professionalism later, Freyja."

"Oh, Orpheus. Lighten up, life is too short", Freyja replied.

"Sandra has a very important point, Orpheus", Gideon replied, having difficulty keeping his eyes off of Freyja, he could see into her mind and she was indeed serious about her offer and babies, he added, "A lot of work crosses my desk, Orpheus and I don't have a lot of time to run around *'tweaking'* people's memories. You need to give us more lead time when you need our help, unless it's an emergency, of course."

"I actually do understand, Gideon. We", Orpheus gestured to Freyja and Tina, "do this full-time and we would not be asking for your help if we didn't need it."

"Okay. You need our help and so you shall get it", Gideon stated.

"No. No, Gideon. You have way too much work on your plate as it is", Sandra told him, then glaring over at Freyja, "I'll help them with their little *'conspiracy cult'* problem. When you're finished here for the day, jaunt back to Mimas for some Winchilly time and I'll join you both later."

"Are you sure?", Gideon asked.

"Absolutely, I need to keep an eye on this little viper anyway", Sandra confirmed while still glaring at Freyja.

"I may be a viper, Sandra, but I am a pretty one and my offer was genuine", Freyja replied unrepentantly.

Gideon reaffirmed his previous statement, "I do not need another wife, Freyja."

Freyja shrugged, "So you say, Gideon. We shall see. I always get my way in the end."

Tina sent a private telepathic message to Orpheus, *"Is Freyja always like this?"*

Orpheus replied in kind, with a telepathic smile, *"Generally, yes, but somehow, she is worse around Gideon. She has aspirations with Gideon. I cannot see her stopping until she gets what she wants."*

"Are you two thinking about me again?", Freyja enquired as a lighthearted jab.

"Not at all, Freyja", Orpheus fibbed, "Tina was just anxious to get this *'cult'* issue resolved."

Sandra linked her mind to the minds of Orpheus, Freyja and Tina, then they jaunted as a group to Eros, the precise destination point being decided by Orpheus. During their transit from the Aries colony to Eros, Sandra caught a quick glimpse of Freyja's feelings. Indeed, she did like Gideon, in a big way as well. Freyja's brashness was just a mask that covered up the depths of her feelings.

Sandra thought to herself, *"Have I misjudged, little Miss Viper?"*

Gideon continued with his work, reducing the volume of work in both of his in-trays as much as possible in the remaining time available. Towards the end of the day, Zelda, Marsha and Leila entered his office and collected the files from their respective out-trays on Gideon's desk and placed them on their own desks for processing on the next day. Then, the three ladies left for the day. Once they had left, Gideon jaunted to Mimas, where he lived with Winchilly and Sandra. Their apartment at the Aries colony was just there for show and rarely ever used.

Gideon arrived at his home inside of Mimas, deep underneath of Mimas's

Southern Mountain Peak and immediately, quite heavily sunk into his favourite chair. Winchilly was quickly by his side and looked at him with concern, her empathy showing in the features of her Martian face, she smiled.

"You seem stressed, my Husband", Winchilly's telepathic thoughts entered his mind and she immediately began to soothe his mind, *"Was work that bad today?"*

"No, not at all, Winchilly. It's just been a weird day is all", Gideon thought back.

"We'll see", Winchilly leaned in towards Gideon and placed her forehead against his and he shared the day's memories with her. Winchilly saw all of the events of the day as if she had been there.

"Okay. I see, Gideon. Solve a niggling problem, I see. Sandra enjoys her theatrics way too much. Then you brainstorm terraforming issues with Sandra. Ah, of course, our friends from the Council of Shadows turn up. Now, everything makes perfect sense", Winchilly summarises her understanding of Gideon's day.

Winchilly sat down on Gideon's lap and kissed him gently, *"You had an offer of marriage, I see. Sandra's little Miss Viper? Folcrom Freyja is far more than she seems, she puts up a mask. Bring her here one day and I will evaluate her for suitability as a Sister-Wife."*

"Are you serious, Winchilly? Sandra and I have already told her no", Gideon argued gently.

"No, is only no, until it is not", Winchilly replied as she got back up, *"Supper is almost ready, Husband. Our children are playing outside, please round them up"*, she smiled at Gideon, *"We can both play with Sandra later."*

Gideon went outside to round up his children, both those he had with Winchilly and those he had with Sandra. They ate their supper at their large dining table, all together, Gideon and Winchilly, surrounded by their children. It was later that night when Sandra blinked into existence in their Mimasian home. It had been a long day and she too, shared her day's memories with Winchilly.

"I may have misjudged, little Miss Viper", Sandra told Gideon, as Winchilly watched and smiled.

"You too? Winchilly wants to assess her", Gideon replied, reminding her, "I've already said no."

"Perhaps, she will grow on us", Sandra tossed back, "You can always change your mind."

"Winchilly, Sandra! Little Miss Viper wants babies, you know children", Gideon pointed out.

Sandra replied, explaining the obvious to Gideon, "That tends to happen in familial relationships, Gideon. Wives have children."

Winchilly simply stated, *"The more, the merrier."*

It was as if they'd already made up their minds, "Yes and build another bed. One made for four!", Gideon sighed as his two wives cracked up laughing, Winchilly being Martian, laughed telepathically.

Aria looked away from the big screen, "Wait! So Gideon Reas and Sandra Danker were psi-corps?"

"Is that true, Saffiera?", Ariel queried, adding, "Winchilly was an ancestor of yours."

Saffiera looked down to her left as she accessed her shared memories, the ones in her very distant past, after almost a minute she replied, *"Yes and no. It is somewhat more complicated."*

Aria wasn't satisfied with that answer, "Complicated? How?", she asked, then added, "More information, please?"

Saffiera tried to unravel the complication as best as she could, *"Winchilly, Gideon and Sandra all shared their memories regularly"*, she began, then continued, *"Gideon and Sandra had never been to the Earth and so they could not have been inducted into psi-corp. To psi-corp, they were unknown."*

"Saffiera, you did say yes and no", Aria noted, she wanted more information.

"They were both inducted into the hidden, 'occult', organisation within psi-corp, the Council of Shadows, by Folcrom Orpheus", Saffiera divulged, thinking it best not to mention too much about the organisation that worked in the shadows and was very likely still around.

"We Martians do not like to talk about the Council of Shadows. Their reach is vast and I will say no more about them", Saffiera looked around the attic, *"They could have operatives in this very room and we would never know that they were here."*

Ariel chimed in, "So they were and they weren't?"

"I did say it was complicated. They were members of the Council of Shadows, yes, but they were not actually members of psi-corp itself", Saffiera explained.

Kethera wore a frown on her face, her whiskers were distinctly downcast, she asked, "What happened with Folcrom Freyja? Did she become Gideon's third wife?"

Saffiera looked at Kethera with surprise, of all the questions she could have asked, she was interested in Folcrom Freyja, she looked down to her left and accessed her deep shared memories once again, this time focusing on Freyja.

Saffiera looked up smiling, *"Yes, Kethera, Freyja did become Gideon's third wife. They even had four children together."*

Kethera's whiskers flicked up, she clapped her hands together with glee and smiled broadly, "How romantic!"

Aria rolled her eyes, "Romantic! Kethera, the man, had three wives. I don't see anything romantic about that. It sounds more like he was a collector!"

"Still romantic. His wives chose him", Kethera insisted.
"Kethera is right, his wives did choose him", Saffiera confirmed.
"Whatever", Aria replied in almost a disinterested mumble.

Yeannah noted, "I found it interesting. The terraforming, that is. We studied the Mimasian War last semester, so we should have a good handle on that part of things, but the sheer scale of the project!"

"Yeah, it was huge", Ariel agreed, "They pulled the two largest centaur bodies out of orbit. Placed them both in a convenient location and broke them apart, only to throw those fragments at Mars and detonate them in the upper atmosphere."

"Yeah, but that's not what I'm thinking of", Yeannah replied, explaining, "They delivered all of that material to Mars, which gave the planet air and water, but the problems, the side effects that arose from that, took another two centuries to wash out."

Saffiera caught on, *"Not a single person involved in the terraforming project at its beginning was alive to see its completion. Not a single one. All of their work and dedication was for the future generations to see and enjoy."*

"And that is exactly what I was thinking", Yeannah agreed.

"All of that work and they never saw the end result", Kethera mused.

"Yeah, Mars wasn't opened up for colonisation until well into the twenty fourth century", Yeannah replied, musing, "That's probably what makes Humans so different. They can be so far thinking."

Saffiera smiled and replied, *"They got that from us remember. We Martians created the Earth Humans by tweaking their native hominid dna over the course of a million years and more."*

"Right up until the Tarlaks conquered your ancestors and enslaved them", Yeannah noted, then added, "Even then, your ancestors foresaw that their creations would one day free their descendants, although that was ninety thousand years later."

Aria chimed in with, "Two things I'm seeing here. One, Martian dna is dominant, which explains why Martian hybrids revert to pure Martians over a handful of generations and two, Saffiera has hybrids in her ancestry."

Ariel replied to her twin Sister's observations, "Aria, you picked up on that? Normally, you don't seem to care."

Aria went back to her usual self, "Meh, it seemed pretty obvious to me."

Saffiera confirmed those two things, *"Yes, Aria. Martian dna is dominant and yes, I have hybrid ancestry. By now, it is likely that most Martians do"*, she did not want to talk about Martian hybrids.

Kethera could see the discomfort on Saffiera's face and changed the subject, inquiring of Yeannah, "How are you feeling? You have had an emotional day."

Yeannah replied with a smile and almost forced smile, "I'm feeling somewhat tired and drained Kethera. Honestly, I think I just need to sleep."

"Then sleep we shall", Kethera replied, then to her other friends she announced, "Yeannah is feeling a bit drained. Perhaps we should sleep now and worry about our studies tomorrow."

Yes, Yeannah had had an emotionally draining day and her friends could see it in her eyes, they all agreed to get a good night's sleep. The big screen was switched off, their data tablets were disconnected from the network and shut down and then they all changed into their pyjamas and lay down to sleep.

As Saffiera slowly drifted off to sleep, she felt happy not to delve deeper into her hybrid ancestry. There were so few Martians in this world, Vale, Homwol, whatever the name of it was and hybridisation was on her mind way too much. Her own future may very well include an Earth Human mate, for the simple lack of suitable Martian men.

The girls were asleep and their Mothers slowly crept up the stairs from the kitchen. Yeannah's Mother, Yealah, wanted to check that her Daughter was okay after the day's upsetting emotional turmoil. At the top of the stairs, sneakily peering over the top into the attic, a kit was watching the girls sleep.

"Ketran, why aren't you in bed with your Sisters?", Kayala asked as she twitched her whiskers.

Ketran turned around, "I was watching the three-fingers, Mummy. I wanted to see if they'd caught any of our Gudongs and were eating them."

Kayala sighed, "Oh, little one. They had many mushroom pies and fried Thrixan for their supper, the same as you. Now run off to bed, Ketran."

Ketran did as she was told and ran off to bed with her kit Sisters.

The three Mothers stepped onto the landing in the attic above the stairs and surveyed the room and the sleeping girls. Saffiera was in the middle with Kethera asleep snuggled up on her left and Yeannah asleep cuddled up on her right. One of Yeannah's great leathery wings was furled up and her right wing was unfurled and spread across both Saffiera and Kethera. Her right arm was around Saffiera, while her great leathery wing embraced them both. Kethera was purring contently. Aria was snuggled up behind Yeannah and her twin Sister, Ariel, was snuggled up behind Kethera, which gave the impression that the twins were holding them in a protective embrace. The three Mothers smiled and sighed, tears welling in their eyes.

"They look so beautiful", Yealah commented to the others, with a teary smile of joy.

"They sleep just like my kits", Kayala noted in reply.

Sarlia asked in her usual telepathic fashion, *"Would you like me to check their emotional states?"*

Yealah replied, "Normally I'd say no, but after today, I think it would be best."

Sarlia carefully and very cautiously probed the girl's minds and when finished, noted, *"It is done."*

The Mothers then withdrew back down to the kitchen, but not before Kayala stole a photograph of the sleeping girls, capturing the moment for all time.

As they sat back down at the kitchen table, Yealah asked with concern, "How is my, Daughter? How is my, Yeannah?", her voice urgent.

Sarlia replied in a professional clinical manner, she was not only a telepath, but also a therapist, *"Yeannah is fine, although she does have feelings for this boy, Thomas. Yeannah dreams of Thomas as we speak. He is on her mind quite a lot."*

Yealah frowned, "We Mimasian Thols are much more accepting of such things, but the Indigenous Thols are not. They will never accept this. They can be very unforgiving. If this relationship persists, they will ostracise my Daughter. Yeannah will be forced to live off-world."

Sarlia sent a calming wave across to Yealah's mind and replied, *"Perhaps it will not come to that."*

Kayala inquired curiously, "Does this not happen back in the Sol system?"

"In the Sol system, Earth Humans, Martian Humans and we Mimasian Thols all attend separate schools", Yealah informed her, then added, "There is no *'mixed'* teenage angst and by the time our children are young adults, they all understand our cultural boundaries."

"So it is only here on Vale, where all species attend the same school?", Kayala queried.

"Yes, Kayala. Even on the off-world colonies, it is the same with separate schools for each species", Yealah confirmed.

Kayala enquired, "If this *'forbidden'* love persists, will they not be ostracised in the off-world colonies as well?"

Yealah's expression took on a sad look, "There are no Indigenous Thols off-world. Such a relationship would, of course, seem odd, but they would not be ostracised off-world."

Sarlia sent another calming wave across to Yealah's mind and replied, *"It may not come to that."*

Kayala asked in a sheepish tone, "Did you peek at my, Kethera?"

"I did check all of their emotional states, Kayala", Sarlia admitted.

"And my Kethera is okay?", Kayala enquired.

"Your kit, Kethera, is fine, Kayala. She does have some minor turmoil with the revelation that Carlins and Humans are compatible, but otherwise, she is fine", Sarlia replied honestly.

"Will Kethera be okay? She is my eldest kit. I need to know", Kayala implored.

"Kayala, I am not one to predict the future, however, I do see an eighty five percent chance of mixed Carlin Human kits in the future", Sarlia replied, noting, *"But that is only my opinion and the future does not care what we in the present think. I could easily be wrong."*

"As long as Kethera is happy and any kits are born healthy, that is all that matters", Kayala noted.

"Based upon the dreams I saw in Kethera's mind about this boy, Richard. I feel that you should provide gentle guidance to your eldest kit or else the future will come quicker than you are ready for", Sarlia recommended her tone still very clinical.

Kayala smiled at Sarlia and agreed, "That is good advice, Sarlia. Kethera is still far too young to start having kits. I will speak to her when we can find a quiet moment together."

"And how is your Daughter, Saffiera?", Yeannah asked.

"Yes, Sarlia. How is Saffiera?", Kayala was also curious.

"Saffiera has other concerns. As you are aware, there are so few Martians in this world. Mimasian Thols came here because it is the ancestral Thol homeworld. The few Martians that came here, well, what can I say, perhaps we have too much hybrid Earthling dna in our blood and have inherited their wanderlust for travel", Sarlia commented dryly, adding, *"Saffiera's concern is for her future and the limited options in finding a mate. Saffiera does not like to be cornered and she feels boxed in with no choice but to end up with an Earthman. My Daughter struggles with that."*

"I noticed that Yeannah double hugs Saffiera and Kethera even in her sleep", a smiling Kayala noted, understanding how rare a Tholish double hug truly was..

"Yes. Yeannah is feeling uneasy, the turmoil of the day. She reaches out to her friends, embracing them both for comfort", Sarlia explained in her clinical fashion, noting, *"My Saffiera has positioned herself purposely in the middle of them both to soothe both Kethera's and Yeannah's minds. A Martian can do this even when asleep."*

"And yet, your Daughter, Saffiera, supports our Daughters unconditionally? Despite her own struggles?", Yealah questioned, seeking understanding.

"You already know the answer to that, Yealah. It is the Martian way", Sarlia replied.

"And the twins?", Yealah curiously enquired.

"Oh, the twins, Aria and Ariel. They are highly resilient. Their parents have not only taught them mixed martial arts but also resilience and survival skills", Sarlia explained, adding, *"They sleep as they appear, protectively embracing their friends. There is something about the twins."*

"I am glad that they had this second sleepover", Yealah noted, her words melodic with true affection, stating, "If they hadn't, we would never have known of these issues our girls were having."

Kayala chimed in, her whiskers standing up, "We would never have met either and I'm certainly glad we did."

"Yes, indeed, Ladies, yes indeed. We shall have to make a habit of visiting each other regularly", Sarlia replied, to which they all agreed.

The night was late when Sarlia and Yealah left the Carlin household, with Sarlia providing Yealah a ride home in her hovercar. It had been an emotional, tumultuous day and evening and Sarlia had assured the other Mothers that the girls would feel much better in the morning. An added bonus of the evening, apart from understanding their Daughter's emotional states and making new friendships. Sarlia and Yealah both left with recipes for many mushroom pies, written down on Gudong parchment.

19. The Belters.

Harrison Moon was in a crisis, he had ambitions, big ambitions and they were being thwarted. His organisation, the Ceresian Colonisation Project, was running short of funds at a critical juncture. His organisation had contracted the construction of a twin-cylinder O'Neil-style colony in the Cis-Lunar L-Four colony construction zones. It wasn't a big colony by modern standards, but it was big enough for the colonisation of Ceres.

At one point, six kilometres long and four hundred metres wide, the four end caps combined would easily house twenty thousand colonists with plenty of room for growth. The long cylinder sections would provide the land areas required to produce all of the food they required. The long strip mirrors were designed to be slightly concave along their length. This was to capture and focus more sunlight from the distant Sun, through the long slit windows, at Ceres distance from the Sun.

Once completed and ready for transfer to Ceres, both cylinders would have their strip mirrors folded in for transport. Each cylinder would be accompanied by three mobile mining stations and three mobile ore processing stations. These would be connected to both of the cylinder's southern extensible boom sections for transport and then they would disconnect once the colony was in orbit around Ceres. Once in orbit around Ceres, both cylinders would be guy-wired together and then their inter-cylinder transit tubes would be installed. After this, the cylinders would be rotated, producing centrifugal force for artificial gravity.

It was an ambitious Project and now, the construction was in dire crisis. Funding was running low. The banks and the financiers were refusing to lend the Ceresian Colonisation Project any more credit unless Harrison Moon could somehow guarantee a return on their investments. Some were even calling for foreclosure. Harrison Moon was at the end of his tether. He had nowhere else to turn! Harrison Moon was desperate. Harrison had one thing in his favour, his surname was, Moon and Moons never give up!

Stuart Dumas was running through the latest reports about his mining ventures in the Earth's Trojan points. Stuart's company, the Earth Trojan Mining Corporation Ltd, was doing better than expected during its fourth year of operations. The credits were rolling into Stuart's coffers and his actuals were far exceeding his projections.

Stuart Dumas was pleased with his original company, Cis-Lunar Haulage Pty Ltd, which was in high demand and he was expanding that as well, adding more space tugs and space tow ships hand over fist. His other company, Astro Economics Ltd, was also performing exceedingly well. Astro Economics was created to manage and warehouse his vast mineral and metal stocks, selling those raw materials into the market as necessary to balance supply and demand. Stuart's aim was stability in the Asteroidal Commodities Market so that everyone profited.

Tegan Smith entered Stuart's office, she had no need to knock, it was Stuart's way, "Mr Dumas, Sir, I've come across this little snippet of information", she informed him.

"By all means, divulge your snippet, Tegan", Stuart replied.

"Sir, there is a project, it's called the Ceresian Colonisation Project", Tegan informed him, adding, "They are in severe financial difficulty and their financial backers could foreclose on them."

"So, Tegan, you think this is an opportunity?", Stuart asked, his hands and fingers steepled in front of him with a great deal of interest.

"Yes, Sir", Tegan confirmed, explaining, "The Dwarf Planet Ceres has a lot of resources, especially concerning volatiles. There are also several smaller asteroids fairly close to Ceres that could be formed into a conglomerated asteroidal mass."

"Ah, Tegan. Thank you. This looks very similar to something we've already done, just a tad different. Perhaps it is a recoverable situation", Stuart's mind was already putting together an action plan to save the Ceresian Colonisation Project.

"Yes, Mr Dumas. That is what I was thinking", Tegan agreed, adding, "You could White Knight their project, Sir."

"Let me have a think about their situation, Tegan. I'll discuss it with you later and we can put together a proposal", Stuart Dumas decided, "This one could be lucrative. Very lucrative."

Tegan smiled, "I entirely agree, Sir", she replied and then left his office.

Harrison Moon buzzed his secretary, "Gig, please let me know when the creditors arrive", he requested, then he noted sadly, "Let's hope things go well this morning. If not, we'll all be out of a job by lunchtime."

His secretary, Gig Anderson, replied as two people walked through the door, "Yes, Sir. I think they've just arrived, although I am not familiar with these people. They appear to be different representatives."

Tegan walked up to the secretary and passed her two cards, Gig read them, "Mr Moon, Sir. You have one Stuart Dumas and his Personal Assistant Tegan Smith to see you, Sir."

That name caught Harrison Moon by surprise, it had been in the news feeds on and off for a few years now, "Stuart Dumas, the transport mogul and mining magnate?", he queried.

Stuart Dumas smiled and nodded, "That would be me."

"Yes, Mr Moon. That Stuart Dumas", Gig confirmed.

"Well then, Gig. What are you waiting for? Show them in", Harrison

Moon replied.

Gig Anderson showed Stuart and Tegan into Harrison Moon's office.

Harrison Moon rose to his feet and greeted his visitors, "Good Morning, Mr Dumas, Ms Smith. I'm Harrison Moon. What can I do for you?", he asked.

Stuart held out his hand and Harrison reached out his and they both shook hands, Stuart turned his hand over on top while gently squeezing, "A pleasure to meet you, Harrison. Please call me Stuart. This is my personal assistant Tegan Smith. I'm your new Creditor", he greeted.

Harrison Moon was taken aback, "My new creditor?", he questioned, then asked, "How?"

"I had a meeting with your former creditors yesterday at my office", Stuart informed him, explaining, "I made them an offer for your debt portfolios and they accepted it. I must be honest, they did seem quite happy to sign everything over to me."

Harrison Moon was incredulous, "Is that legal?", he asked.

"Yes. They had little faith in breaking even on your loans and I offered them a small profit. They were more than happy to sign your loans over to me", Stuart explained.

Tegan opened her briefcase and passed Harrison their official deed of transfer, it was official.

Harrison Moon felt resigned to his fate, "I guess that makes you my boss."

"Not at all, Harrison. I'm here because Tegan, my assistant, assures me that there is a business opportunity here", Stuart informed him, "One that your myopic, former creditors could not see."

Harrison reached up and stroked his chin, his fingers brushing the faint stubble that had appeared after a restless night, *"Was he dreaming?"*

The idea that Stuart Dumas, a figure who loomed large in the news and financial circles, was now sitting in his office as his new creditor seemed surreal. It felt like a twist too dramatic even for the uncertain tides of his life.

"Let me get this straight, Mr Dumas", Harrison began, his voice hesitant as he sought clarity. "You bought out my loans, just like that?"

"My name is Stuart, Harrison", Mr Dumas told him, adding, "Tegan can help you understand our new proposal."

"Your proposal?", Harrison Moon questioned as Tegan retrieved a folio labelled from her briefcase, *"Ceresian Colonisation Project Resurrection Proposal"*, she placed the folio on the disk in front of him.

"If you could please read the proposal, Mr Moon", Tegan requested.

"Take your time, Harrison", Stuart advised, adding, "Take as long as you require, we can wait."

Harrison Moon carefully read through the folio, he turned back to certain pages and reread them, some several times, then after several long minutes he looked up, "You will finance the Ceresian Colonisation Project, Mr Dumas?", he cautiously asked.

Tegan replied, advising, "Please reread page five, Mr Moon", and then Stuart nodded at Tegan.

Harrison reread page five more carefully, "Two financing options. One, you loan the Ceresian Colonisation Project more credits and we pay back the previous loans and the new credit line over time. Two, you take over all of the financing and provide all the expertise required, but you take a twenty percent cut of the profits for all time."

"The choice of which option is yours, Mr Moon", Tegan advised.

Stuart chimed in, "Harrison, please read the fine print at the bottom of the page", he instructed.

Harrison read the fine print, "If the proposal is not accepted, signed and returned to Dumas Incorporated by midnight tonight, option one becomes unavailable and only option two will remain."

The sword of Damocles was hanging over Harrison Moon's head.

"Why the deadline?", Harrison Moon enquired, he was confused, Stuart Dumas could have just offered option two.

"I work with people who think fast, make quick decisions and have no regrets about their choices. My world can sometimes be brutal. I need to test your mettle, Harrison", Stuart was brutally honest.

Tegan chimed in, "Mr Moon. One option favours you and the second option favours Mr Dumas. Will you make the decision quickly, bite the bullet, so to speak or perhaps procrastinate?"

Harrison looked at Tegan, she had been very honest and then he looked back to Stuart, he was equally honest, brutally so.

"I suppose I should be angry, but option one is more than fair. You could have left it out and just offered me option two, which would be fairly standard", Harrison bit the bullet, "I will need to go through this document several more times to make sure, but if it is what it looks like, I'd be a fool not to sign up for option one."

"You have until midnight, Harrison, the whole afternoon to analyse the document", Stuart replied.

Harrison Moon nodded.

"My former creditors were about to foreclose on me. How is it that you see a profit in this venture and they didn't?", Harrison asked.

"Ah, yes, Harrison. That is a very good question", Stuart replied and then nodded to Tegan.

Tegan took out another folio from her suitcase, it was labelled, *"The Ceresian Heptaluna Asteroidal Moon Project (CHAMP)"*, and then she placed it in front of Harrison, stating, "They lacked vision, Mr Moon."

Harrison Moon picked up this new folio and started reading through it. The first section was a fairly straightforward proposal to haul the new O'Neil-style colony, once completed and prepared to Ceres and placed into orbit. The haulage rates appeared to be fairly standard and the work would be performed by Stuart Dumas's Cis-Lunar Haulage company. The haulage would be financed by a separate loan, which would be paid back over time. It was more than acceptable.

Harrison Moon turned the page and was confronted by the titled proposal and a list of smaller asteroid names, the list of asteroids contained.

- Three three nine seven – Leyla
- One three seven two – Haremari
- Nine one six – America
- Two three three – Asterope
- Three one zero – Margarita
- Five eight one – Tauntonia
- Six seven four – Rachele

Harrison noted, "So, you're proposing, that after hauling our colony, Ceres Central, to Ceres, your space tugs are going to pull these asteroids out of their current orbits and pack them all together as a single conglomerated mass", he paused, then questioned, "You're building Ceres a Moon?"

"Yes, of course, Harrison. We did a very similar thing at Earth's leading and trailing Trojan points", Stuart pointed out.

Tegan chimed in, "Mr Moon, by taking those asteroids and combining them into one, then placing the resultant mass into orbit around Ceres, we effectively create useful Ceresian Lagrangian points."

Harrison understood, he rattled off, "Ceres, L-One, L-Two, L-Four and L-Five."

"Precisely", Tegan replied, adding, "We'll then place Ceres Central into a halo orbit in Ceres L-Five and you will have an analogue of the Earth-Moon system."

Stuart smiled as he watched Harrison's face change with growing realisation, "That's right, Harrison. You can mine Ceres for its volatiles, but also the new Ceresian Moon for other unique materials."

"And that is what my former creditors couldn't see", Harrison relied.

"And that is what my personal assistant, Tegan, saw", Stuart credited, adding, "An opportunity."

"I suggest you name the new Ceresian Moon, Heptaluna", Tegan suggested.

"I will indeed", Harrison agreed, noting, "You appear to be making your credits purely with the haulage contracts?"

"Yes, Harrison, but you're missing another very subtle point", Stuart told him.

Tegan chimed in, "There are at least another five big asteroids, like Ceres, out there. So we will be getting a lot of business coming our way. We can create new Moons around each of them! Vesta is looking particularly intriguing!"

"Damn. You've created a whole series of completely new business opportunities", Harrison laughed in full realisation of what Stuart was doing.

"Yes, we have Harrison, yes we have", Stuart confirmed, knowing that his company, Cis-Lunar Haulage, was the only space transport company with the specialised equipment and most powerful space tugs required to move asteroids.

Harrison Moon signed all of the proposals and returned them before the end of the business day. He had read through them thoroughly and could not find any pitfalls. Stuart Dumas was exceedingly fair. The line of credit was approved with Dumas Incorporated and before the end of the following year, the colony of Ceres Central was completed, packed up, and hauled out to Ceres. That was the completion of stage one.

After being delivered to Ceres, the space tugs went into stage two, moving smaller nearby asteroids out of their normal orbits and accumulating them in orbit around Ceres as a single conglomerated asteroidal mass. The asteroids Leyla, Haremari, America, Asterope, Margarita, Tauntonia, and Rachele, now forming a single Ceresian Moon, were renamed *Heptaluna.* This, as predicted, created stable libration points around Ceres, L-One, L-Two, L-Four, and L-Five, with L-Three being on the opposite side of the Sun and not terribly useful.

The new twin O'Neill-style colony cylinders, Ceres Central, were connected together and placed into counter-rotation at *two point one one revolutions per minute*, providing a simulated gravity of *one standard g*. Ceres Central was then positioned in a halo orbit around Heptaluna L-Five. The six ore processing and smelting stations were strategically placed in halo orbits around Heptaluna L-Four. This positioning ensured efficient material transfer between the mining stations and the processing hubs.

The six mobile mining stations, marvels of engineering, were initially split into two groups. One set tasked with mining Ceres itself for its water ice, ammonia and carbon-rich materials and the other focused on Heptaluna, extracting metals and silicates. The stations worked in seamless coordination, their automated systems operating around the clock to maximise output. Stage two was completed and stage three, the mining operations, had officially begun.

As Harrison stood on the observation deck of one of the twin colony cylinders, gazing out at the newly formed Heptaluna, he felt a surge of pride. What had once seemed like the end of his dreams was now a vibrant reality, brimming with potential. The steady hum of the colony's systems was a constant reminder of the work being done, of the countless opportunities Stuart Dumas had envisioned and delivered.

Stuart's vision had not only saved Harrison Moon's company but had transformed it into a cornerstone of the interplanetary industry. Ceres was no longer just a Dwarf Planet on the outskirts of the solar system, it was becoming a thriving hub of human ingenuity and progress. Stuart Dumas created a new company, Asteroid Belt Imports Pty Ltd, for the importation of Ceresian refined minerals, metal and volatiles. Taking into account transport costs, he offered the Ceresians a fair price for their exports. Stage three was now completed.

Stuart Dumas, however, wasn't finished, he and his personal assistant, Tegan Smith, had put together stage four. Implementing stage four would require Harrison Moon's help. When Harrison returned back in Cis-Lunar L-Five, having travelled back from Ceres, he found himself in a small conference with Stuart and Tegan. Harrison Moon was stunned by the level of Stuart Dumas's ambition and the heights of Tegan Smith's vision. Harrison could do nothing more than help push Stuart's new proposition forward.

The advertisement hit the news and entertainment feeds right across the inner system networks.

Stuart Dumas and Harrison Moon walked into view, between them was a hologram of the newly colonised Ceresian Dwarf Planet system complete with a newly created moon, Heptaluna. The caption above the hologram read, *"The Belter Project."*

"For those of you who don't recognise me, I am Stuart Dumas, owner and CEO of the Dumas Incorporated Companies. With me, I have Harrison Moon, Administrator of the Ceresian Colony and mining operations", Stuart addressed the camera and Harrison nodded in acknowledgement of his introduction.

Harrison then gestured to the hologram, *"This is the Dwarf Planet Ceres, the largest object in the Asteroid Belt"*, then he used a small laser pointer and pointed it to the new Moon, *"This is Heptaluna, the new Moon of Ceres that was created by*

Stuart's Dumas's Cis-Lunar haulage company."

Stuart took over, *"Heptaluna was created by capturing and consolidating seven smaller asteroids into a single conglomerated object, which was placed into orbit around Ceres."*

A list of the seven smaller asteroids appeared on the screen under the hologram.

Leyla, Haremari, America, Asterope, Margarita, Tauntonia and Rachele.

Harrison stepped back in, *"The creation of Heptaluna and its orbital placement, created stable libration points around the Ceres system. Heptaluna, L-One, L-Two, L-Four and L-Five*", then he used his laser pointer to highlight, Ceres Central, *"We placed Ceres Central, our new colony, in a stable halo orbit in Heptaluna L-Five"*, then he moved the laser pointer to the L-Four zone, *"We placed our six ore processing and smelting stations into stable halo orbits in Heptaluna L-Four."*

Stuart chimed back in with, *"Many of you who live in Cis-Lunar L-Five would be familiar with this setup. It is analogous to the Cis-Lunar L-Four and L-Five setup. Which brings us to the reason for this broadcast."*

There was a slight pause as a list of major Asteroids in the Asteroid Belt appeared on the screen below the hologram. There were twelve in all.

- **Vesta:** Approximate Diameter: 525 km
- **Pallas:** Approximate Diameter: 512 km
- **Hygiea:** Approximate Diameter: 434 km
- **Interamnia:** Approximate Diameter: 330 km
- **Davida:** Approximate Diameter: 326 km
- **Europa:** Approximate Diameter: 300 km
- **Sylvia:** Approximate Diameter: 288 km
- **Euphrosyne:** Approximate Diameter: 260 km
- **Eunomia:** Approximate Diameter: 255 km
- **Juno:** Approximate Diameter: 248 km
- **Bamberga:** Approximate Diameter: 230 km
- **Psyche:** Approximate Diameter: 225 km

Harrison ran his laser pointer across the listed twelve asteroids and looked directly into the camera, *"What we have achieved at the Dwarf Planet Ceres, can be achieved at the Asteroid Belt's other twelve largest Asteroids"*, he told the audience.

Stuart then added, *"Dumas Incorporated has the funds, Cis-Lunar haulage has the space tugs and the expertise. My people can make this happen"*, then he looked directly into the camera and asked, *"Are you interested?"*

Harrison stepped back in, *"Are you interested in becoming an Asteroid miner or a*

Colonist?", then a network address appeared on the screen and he highlighted it with his laser pointer, *"Then register using this form at this network address and we will make it happen."*

Stuart Dumas stepped back in, *"Are you interested in becoming a part of an Asteroid Colony management team?"*, then another network address appeared on the screen and Stuart highlighted it with his own laser pointer, *"Then register using this form at this network address and we will make it happen!"*

The two network links remained on the screen for ten seconds, bold and highlighted in vivid blue, with a faint pulsing glow to draw attention. They were accompanied by an audio prompt giving viewers both a clear view and ample time to click on them.

This was the beginning of stage four.

The two network links received a lot of hits. People were entering their details in rapid succession. Obviously, not everyone would succeed in their aspirations. Tegan Smith had both lists parsed with their A.I. Processors, which filtered candidates based on key qualifications and suitability. Anyone who was unsuitable for whatever reason received a polite email reply, letting them know that there was a large volume of applicants and that their application had been unsuccessful.

They were still left with a good-sized pool of applicants for both lists. The list of potential colonists was well above ten thousand per Asteroid, which was in line with expectations for the new colonies. For the management teams, with their more stringent requirements, there were well over two hundred and fifty, which would eventually be reduced back to one hundred and twenty, ten per colony. Those who didn't make the cut would have the option of becoming administrative assistants.

Stuart Dumas had informed Harrison Moon that as he still required colonists for Ceres Central, he would have the first pick of the *"cream of the crop"* of colony applicants. Harrison Moon's picks were his own to make and decide upon, as he was, of course, the Administrator of Ceres.

Tegan received a communique from Eros at Earth's L-Five libration zone, from the Colonisation Committee of Sol. They had seen the advertisement for colonists and managers and had concerns.

Tegan entered Stuart Dumas's office, "Mr Dumas, Sir. The Colonisation Committee is querying your Asteroid Belt Colonisation Initiative. They would like to know why they had not been consulted."

Stuart looked up from his work, he steepled his hands and fingers, thinking carefully before responding, "Has Administrator Moon registered the Ceresian Colony with both the Colonisation Committee of Sol and the Security Council of Sol?"

"Yes, Sir. That was done as soon as stage two was completed", Tegan advised.

"So this is not about Ceres, it's all about the new Asteroid colonies, none of which actually exist yet?", Stuart asked, his mind thinking quickly.

"Yes, Sir. That does appear to be the case", Tegan confirmed, she was smiling, knowing what Stuart Dumas was thinking, almost predicting his precise words in advance.

"Okay, Tegan, here is my response", Stuart replied and dictated his response, "As the colonies in question do not actually exist and will not exist until they have been constructed, transported to their final destinations and assembled, they are not within the remit of either the Colonisation Committer of Sol or for that matter, the Security Council of Sol. We believe it is premature to address such concerns before the colonies are fully realised. Simply put, they currently do not exist. "

Tegan quickly noted down the reply on her data tablet in shorthand with her stylus.

Stuart continued with the next section, "As each new colony comes online and is established, their administrative teams will register with both the Colonisation Committee of Sol and the Security Council of Sol. At such point in time, they come under your overall jurisdiction. We must also remind you that beyond the orbit of Mars, under the current legislation, registration is considered optional. The new Asteroid colonies will be doing so as a courtesy, nothing more."

Stuart paused to give Tegan time to catch up, which she did quickly.

Stuart then continued, "I will, as a courtesy, also keep the Colonisation Committee of Sol in the loop with each Asteroid's colonisation milestones. Regular, voluntary reporting will start as of this reply."

"I have that all noted down, Sir," Tegan replied.

"Good then, Tegan. Write it up and then send it off with your usual flare and we'll see what they come back with", Stuart instructed, noting, "They are clearly overstepping their reach and need to be told so."

Tegan replied, "Shall I prepare a summary of their currently defined protocols, just in case they challenge this stance, Sir?"

"An excellent idea, Tegan. Prepare that summary, but ensure it highlights the current limitations of their jurisdiction", Stuart replied, noting, "It is highly likely that they'll request changes to legislation to increase their scope, however, that will take years and by then, the colonies will be completed and online. Legislative changes take time and are never guaranteed."

"I'll have the protocols summarised and your response finalised by the end of the day, Sir. ", Tegan replied and left the office to write up Stuart's reply.

As Tegan left the office, Stuart remarked with a wry smile, "Tegan, slip into the reply somewhere that by building these new moons, we are performing Asteroid collision mitigation. We are actually doing them a favour."

Tegan smiled back, "Yes, Sir. That is a great idea."

Stuart Dumas created two new companies under the Dumas incorporated umbrella. The first was Dumas Colonial Financial Ltd, specifically created as the financial vehicle to funnel the credit flow into the twelve Asteroid Belt colonisation project. The second company was Dumas Colonial Constructions Ltd, which was initially created to construct the twelve O'Neil-style twin-cylinder colonies. As always, these companies did not have a single purpose. Colonial Financial financed many other projects as well and Colonial Constructions manufactured a lot more than just the twelve required colonies.

At the urging of his personal assistant, Tegan Smith, Stuart Dumas even created a personnel management firm, Dumas Personnel Ltd, ostensibly to manage the workforce for the colonies, both managerial and blue-collar workers. The company did, of course, branch out further into the greater corporate world at large.

The Belter Project was an almost ninety percent in-house project under the Dumas Incorporated umbrella. All of the financing was via Dumas Colonial Financial. The rare materials were provided by the vast stocks warehoused by Dumas's Astro Economics. The construction of the twelve new colonies, their mobile mining stations and orbital smelting and processing stations was to be performed by Dumas Colonial Constructions. Finally, the transportation of the new colonies, etc., to their respective asteroids and the construction of the twelve new moons from smaller nearby asteroids in the Asteroid Belt was to be performed by Dumas's original Cis-Lunar Haulage company.

The Belter Project was single-handedly driving Human expansion beyond Martian orbit and yet Stuart Dumas would not own any of these new colonies. They were all destined to become self-governing *"Belter"* colonies. Dumas Incorporated was making its credits through financial loans, business deals and ventures for its subsidiaries companies, new external unrelated work and technological developments and spin-offs.

It took ten years for the *"Belter"* project to reach completion and another two years after that to bring in all of the colonists and settle down into what would become thriving colonies. Stuart's Asteroid Belt Imports company were awarded the import contracts and his Cis-Lunar haulage company were awarded the transport contracts.

Many other lucrative opportunities began to arrive on Dumas

Incorporated's doorstep. There were submissions by new colonisers who needed Stuart's assistance to colonise Jupiter's leading and trailing Trojan points. Especially the asteroid Hector in Jupiter's L-Four region and the twin asteroids Patroclus and Menoetius in Jupiter's L-Five region. The plans for those were extraordinarily ambitious. There were even proposals to colonise the moons of Jupiter itself. Stuart instructed his people to put together plans for their colonisation and these new collaborations began.

Long afterwards, when the terraformers of Mars needed to move two giant Centaur Objects, Chariklo and Chiron, out of their orbits for use in the Martian terraforming project. Stuart had the two biggest space tugs ever built, commissioned for the project. The Calypso and the Olympus, both under the banner of his original company, Cis-Lunar Haulage. That was to be one highly lucrative contract.

All wasn't entirely well, however. Another corporate competitor rose up in the background, it was small and brash and flirted with illegality in many of its operations. It was the Horridian Dynastic Group. Then, of course, there were the legislative changes requested by both the Colonisation Committee of Sol and the Security Council of Sol, at the Eros colony, in Earth's trailing Trojan point. The City within the Rock that Stuart's Mars Trojan Mining corporation had helped to create. The Earth's Government and Cis-Lunar L-Five's Colonial Central Command had debated the legislative changes for more than a decade before finalising them.

Tegan Smith entered Stuart's office, "Mr Dumas, Sir. I've read through those legislative changes", she informed him.

"Please, Tegan, by all means, provide me with a quick summary", Stuart requested.

Tegan began first by noting, "Sir, they weren't at all happy with you pointing out the limits of their jurisdiction", then she began reading out the highlights, *"The scope of reach, responsibility and jurisdiction, of the Colonisation Committee of Sol and the Security Council of Sol, both situated at Eros, The City within the Rock, shall henceforth be extended, from the Martian Orbital Zone to the far outer reaches of the Solar System, beyond the Kuiper Belt and the Oort Cloud."*

"Wow! Those petty Legislators and Bureaucrats think that they have the right to inflict their rule and decisions on the entire Solar System!", Stuart commented with amusement, "Just how do they think that they're going to enforce that?", he questioned rhetorically.

Tegan smiled and read another highlight from the new legislation, *"New colonies, upon coming online, will register with both the Colonisation Committee of Sol and the Security Council of Sol within twenty eight standard Earth days of their first official operations. This is compulsory. There will be no opting out. Failure to do so will result in fines of one million credits per standard day, for each day that registration to either organisation is delayed."*

"No carrots. Just a bloody big stick!", Stuart remarked harshly, then he questioned, "Just how are they going to back that up? What if a colony is recalcitrant and simply refuses?"

Tegan had the answer for that as well as she read another highlight from the legislation, *"Any colony that refuses registration and refuses the payment of levied fines, shall first be sanctioned and their exports banned. Further recalcitrance"*, she stopped and remarked, "Sir. They actually used your term."

Tegan looked back down at her data tablet, continuing, *"Further recalcitrance, shall be met with escalating sanctions, as decided upon by the Security Council of Sol, leading up to the forcible removal of said recalcitrant colony's Colonial Administration and being replaced under new Administration being assigned by the Security Council of Sol, with the enforcement of the Colonial Armed Forces."*

"Oh my God. These people are absolute idiots. Creating this new legislation, with the inclusion of what I can only describe as military intervention and confiscation of property is disgraceful", Stuart noted, his face red with anger, "They are literally asking for civil unrest and rebellion! The best-case scenario is that neither the Colonisation Committee of Sol nor the Security Council of Sol enforce any of this. Doing so would lead to disaster."

"There is more, Sir", Tegan advised.

Stuart gestured with his hands for her to continue, *"Failure to abide by the rulings and decisions of the Colonisation Committee of Sol or the Security Council of Sol, from first notification, will result in the same escalating penalties, as listed for the failure to register, starting on the twenty eight standard days of non-compliance."*

"Jesus, Tegan. That just gets worse and worse!", Stuart exclaimed.

There is one little silver lining, Sir, *"Colonies planned or under construction do not come under the jurisdiction of either the Colonisation Committee of Sol or the Security Council of Sol until such time as their construction is completed and they officially come online."*

Stuart smiled, "I wonder what happens if a colony doesn't officially come online?", it was rhetorical.

Tegan answered anyway, "They haven't actually stipulated what defines a colony as being *'officially'* online, Sir."

Stuart snickered, "So Tegan, hypothetically speaking, what if the official online opening ceremony is held off for, say, ten years?"

Tegan smiled and replied, "As long as they have a *'valid'* reason not to *'officially'* come online, then they could, in theory, hold off for even longer, Sir."

Stuart replied, "It took them more than ten years to come up with this flawed legislation. What's the bet there are even more flaws? Rip it apart, Tegan, see what you can find."

"I will, Mr Dumas. We have already found one loophole and there are bound to be others", Tegan noted, adding with a smile, "It will take them just as long to close them."

Tegan and Stuart worked out new contracts for the twelve new Asteroid Belt colony Administrators to sign. They could not help Harrison Moon and the Ceresian colony, as his colony had already been registered with the Colonisation Committee of Sol and the Security Council of Sol. The new colonies, however, were not.

Tegan's first communique explained the new legislation and the effects it could have on their respective colonies. Tegan's second communique spelled out a "*hypothetical*" definition of when a new colony officially comes online, tying that to the final loan payment each individual colony had with Dumas Colonial Finance Ltd.

The Asteroid Colony Administrators all pointed out in their replies, that those loans were in fact multi-decade loans and that their final payments were forty years into the future. Tegan had agreed with them completely, pointing out that having their colonies officially come online, at their loan's final repayments, kept them out of the Colonisation Committee and the Security Council jurisdiction for four decades.

That bought them plenty of time for everyone to lobby both the Earth Government and Colonial Central Command to water down and weaken the legislation. All twelve Asteroid Colony Administrators agreed to the definition and signed the new contracts and Stuart Dumas placed the weight of his entire business empire behind them. Much to the chagrin of the legislators, it worked!

20. The Moons of Ceres.

The legislators of the Earth Government and Cis-Lunar Colonial Central Command may have been slow, but their bureaucrats were not, they were, in fact, highly efficient. When the new contracts between Dumas Colonial Financial and the twelve new Asteroid Colonies were registered in their respective archives, one bureaucrat, a low-level clerk, decided to officially record the definition of a new Colony Officially coming online. Up till then, it had not been defined. So the clerk thought he was performing a great service.

It was recorded thus, a new Colony is Officially online when their final loan payment is made. After all, until then, the colony is still officially owned by the financiers.

The clerk instructed the archive's A.I. processor to preserve that meaning for all time and he flagged it as *"unerasable"*. The A.I. processor complied and the change was implemented for all time. Every time a legislator searched their archives for the official definition of when a colony was officially online, that is what they were presented with and they could not change it! It had more than a few of them face-palming!

As time went by, the Belter Colony Administrators came up with cleverer and cleverer tactics.

Hunter Moon, Harrison's eldest Son, checked over the legislation very carefully. The main loophole was simple. It revolved around that last loan payment, however, it was too late. His Father, Harrison, had registered the new Colony of Ceres Central with both the Colonisation Committee and the Security Council before the new legislation had been drafted.

Then Hunter Moon noticed something, the registration numbers on the Official Registration Documents both the Colonisation Committee and the Security Council used the same numbers. Each registration had the same two numbers. Hunter looked into those registration numbers, he had a hunch.

Hunter checked the construction plaque on the Northern end cap of the Western Cylinder where he lived. The construction plaque in beautiful bronze spelled out the name Ceres Central, Western Cylinder and there in bright bold letters and numbers, was one of the registration numbers.

Hunter then travelled to the Northern end cap on the Eastern Cylinder and just as he thought, the construction plaque in beautiful bronze affixed to the Cylinder had both the name of the Cylinder, Ceres Central East and the other one of the registration numbers. Hunter smiled to himself as he travelled back home to tell his Father of the news.

"Dad, I have some great news", Hunter told him excitedly.

"Well then, you'd better spill it before you burst", Harrison replied, seeing how excited his Son was.

Hunter passed his Father a copy of the Official Registration Documents, "It's those registration numbers. Those are the officially stamped registration numbers on Ceres Central's two cylinders."

Harrison sat up in his chair, "You don't say!", he exclaimed.

"You know what that means, don't you, Dad?", Hunter queried, he already knew.

"It means that the registration with the Colonisation Committee and the Security Council is tied to the actual physical colonies themselves and not to Ceres itself", Harrison realised and then he exclaimed, "Hunter, my Son. This is golden!"

The next day, Harrison and his Son, Hunter, together drafted a very simple email to Stuart Dumas, *"Hi Stuart. My Son Hunter and I have found some intriguing information. Colonial registration is tied to actual hardware, that is to say, the Colony Cylinders themselves. We propose, to build a new larger O'Neil-style twin-cylinder colony with double the capacity of the one we have. Ceres Central Two. This will, of course, require new financing through Dumas Colonial Financial. The new colony, of course, will not be under the jurisdiction of the Colonisation Committee or the Security Council until it is registered, after the final loan payment."*

Stuart Dumas smiled, then he burst out laughing, a very concerned Tegan Smith was quickly in the office wondering what was going on. Stuart was still laughing when he forwarded the email to Tegan.

Tegan read it and understood the implications straight away. Harrison and Hunter Moon were going to build a new bigger, better colony, which would not be under the Colonisation Committee's or the Security Council's jurisdiction. What they did with the old colony was then up to them, keep it, scrap it, it made no difference, they would not have jurisdiction over the new colony at all.

Tegan Smith burst out laughing, so much so that she barely got out the words, "Sir. This is brilliant. Those clever", she was going to say *'Bastards'*, but held it back, instead saying, "I'll start making the arrangements straight away, Sir."

"Tegan", Stuart called out as she was leaving his office, "Perhaps an email to the other Belter Administrators is in order."

A wry smile crossed Tegan's mouth, "Oh yes, Sir. I'd already planned to send one."

A little over a decade later, Harmony Moon, Hunter Moon's youngest daughter, came up with another, very clever concept. Harmony was only twelve at the time. By that time, the original Ceres Central colony had been rechristened, amusingly to, "*Eros can have it*". They had an actual christening ceremony and everything, including the unveiling of a new bronze plaque, with the new name and the original registration numbers. The actual name didn't really matter, the registration was based on the actual physical registration numbers. The newer, bigger colony, had also been rechristened to, complete with a new bronze plaque to, Ceres Central.

The new colony was far bigger than the first, at two kilometres in length and six hundred metres in diameter. The two cylinders with their four end caps could easily house well over ninety thousand people at medium-density housing, not including the main cylinder. Both cylinders had been set into counter rotation at one point seven three rotations per minute, to generate one g of artificial gravity.

Harmony Moon fully understood, even at her tender young age, that "*Eros can have it*" was under the jurisdiction of the Colonisation Committee and the Security Council, but the larger Ceres Central colony was not. It was relatively safe, but Harmony had another idea, a very clever idea. Why not restructure their loans with Dumas Colonial Financial? Not all of them, just that one final payment!

Hunter Moon, laughed when his young girl, Harmony, suggested it. Hunter took his daughter to his own Father, Harrison and asked Harmony to explain it to him. Harrison Moon listened intently, his hand over his chin, as his granddaughter explained her simple, yet very ingenious plan. Then he laughed along with his Son, Hunter.

"Harmony, my child. You are most definitely a Moon", Harrison told her, then he mock scolded his Son, "Hunter, why hasn't my granddaughter got a big bowl of ice cream in front of her. Whatever Harmony wants, Harmony gets", he then winked at Harmony.

"Yes, Dad. I'll make it so", Hunter replied, smiling at his clever daughter, he then commented, "I'll organise the restructuring of our final payment."

"Hunter, don't keep this to yourself. Let all of the other Belter Administrators know", Harrison told him with a wry smile across his face.

"Consider it done, Dad", Hunter replied.

One by one, loan restructure applications arrived at Dumas Colonial Financial. The clerk who received them was perplexed, there were thirteen of them in all and he wasn't sure he should action them without proper authorisation.

"No, no, no. This can't be right. It's insane! They're insane!", the clerk thought to

himself before sending them upstairs to Tegan Smith for perusal and evaluation.

Tegan walked into Stuart's office, "Mr Dumas, Sir. You are going to love these", she assured him, as she passed him the first of the loan restructure requests, "There are precisely thirteen of them, Sir."

There was that number again, thirteen, the number of Belter colonies out there in the Asteroid Belt.

Stuart read the request, even he was perplexed, "They want us to restructure the final repayment of their loan, to one credit per standard year?"

"Yes, Sir. One credit per standard year", Tegan reiterated, noting, "At that rate, they will never pay back that final repayment. The repayments won't cover the interest, Sir. The loans will remain active until the Sun swells into a red giant and swallows everything."

"Are these all the same?", Stuart enquired, still looking perplexed.

"Every single one, Sir", Tegan confirmed.

"They do understand that they will never pay off those loans? I mean, they will be paying one credit per year, forever?", Stuart asked.

"I have emailed them all and clarified the situation, Sir", Tegan replied, adding, "Their typical reply is and I quote, *'We can afford one credit per year forever, we cannot afford Erosion'*, Sir."

"Erosion?", Stuart questioned.

"I clarified that as well, Sir", Tegan replied, explaining, "Erosion is the Belter word for Erosian Oversight. That is their word for Eros and its control, Sir."

"Financial impact?", Stuart enquired.

"Minimal impact, Sir. Those final repayments are less than a drop in the ocean", Tegan noted, adding, "We won't even notice them financially."

Stuart smirked, clearly relishing the brilliance of the move, "If the Belters do this, the Colonisation Committee and the Security Council, will never receive those registrations and it will all be legal! God, I've gotta love that", he replied, then asked, "What genius came up with this?"

Tegan smiled, "Harrison Moon's granddaughter, Harmony Moon, she's only twelve, Sir!"

"Really, only twelve", Stuart was astonished, "Two things, Tegan. First, approve the restructuring of those final repayments. Adjust their interest rates so that their debts don't grow overly large. We just want these loans to keep ticking along. Two, keep an eye on Harmony Moon. Watch her academic progress. If she's this brilliant at twelve, we'll definitely want her on our team someday."

"Yes, Sir. I'll start processing these straight away", Tegan confirmed as she turned to walk out of his office, pausing momentarily in the doorway for what she knew would come.

Stuart shouted out, "And Tegan. If and when the Belters want more finance to build new colonies, offer them a clause for their final repayment. One credit per year, indefinitely."

"Yes, Mr Dumas", then she continued walking to her desk.

And so it began, a game of cat and mouse between the Belter Colonies and Eros's Colonisation Committee and Security Council, although the Belters called their game, *"Screw the Leeches."*

These loan restructures did not go unnoticed. All business contracts, including loan contracts, had to, by law, be submitted to the Earth's archives for proper filing.

When the Colonisation Committer and Security Council, both situated at Eros in the Earth's L-Five Trojan region, submitted requests for the timeline, for when the Belter Colonies come online and therefore could be registered with them, they had quite a shock. What had been a timeline in decades, had been pushed out into eternity. None of them were happy!

Tegan Smith buzzed her boss, Stuart Dumas, "Mr Dumas, Sir. I have two men from Eros here to see you, Sir. One, Marriott Waters, a Colonisation Committee Liaison and one, Lance Bolton, a Security Council Liaison."

"Well, Tegan. They've travelled all this way from Eros, please show them in", Stuart instructed, then added, "Bring yourself in as well, along with your files."

Stuart Dumas politely greeted the two men who entered his office. They were both tall men, easily over six feet and both wearing the same black suits. They were meant to look intimidating. Stuart thought they looked comical, so he offered them a pair of seats in front of his desk. Tegan pulled herself up a chair on the right-hand side of Stuart's desk, carefully placing a neat stack of files on the desk in front of her. The two men glanced at Tegan and her files, they had no idea of the horrors of true efficiency, Tegan Smith efficiency!

"So what's this about then?", Stuart asked in the most innocent of voices.

"Mr Dumas, you know full well what this is about", Lance Bolton told him, he was the bad cop.

"Ah, yes. Certain loan restructures", Stuart mused, adding, "All perfectly legitimate", then he stressed, "All perfectly legal!"

"Mr Dumas. This is not about legality. It is about the spirit of the matter", Marriott Walters said, apparently he was the good cop.

"Spirit of the matter!", Stuart spat back and caught them both off guard, "There is no spirit in this new legislation, only control and disingenuity", he replied while Tegan opened the top file.

Tegan passed a document to Stuart, "If a colony fails to register or for that matter, comply with edicts from Eros, within twenty eight days, they get fined one million credits per standard day, for each and every day that they are in breach. You both understand that none of the Belter colonies can afford such ridiculous fines."

The two liaison officers looked at each other uncomfortably, they were the ambushes and yet, they were being ambushed.

Stuart continued, "Both the Colonisation Committee and the Security Council know this. They both know that the Belters could not possibly pay, so what is this really all about?", it was rhetorical.

Before either of the liaisons could answer, Stuart answered himself, "It's all about control, isn't it? The Belters get fined, they don't pay the fines, then the Security Council sends in the colonial troops to occupy their colonies and the Colonisation Committee sends in their Administrators. Eros gets total control, lock, stock and barrel. There is no justice in that!", he slammed the document down in front of Lance Bolton, the bad cop, Tegan was smiling thoughtfully.

Both men looked from one to the other, then back to Stuart. They had not been prepared for this.

Marriott tried to counter, "Mr Dumas, the system needs control, we cannot have colonists just running around doing whatever they want."

Stuart countered, "Those Belter colonists chose to colonise the Asteroid Belt precisely to get away from your control. No one likes living in the Erosian nanny state."

Lance chimed in, "Mr Dumas, the solar system needs strong leadership and that means centralised control. Eros provides that."

"Really. You really believe that?", Stuart asked rhetorically, "Well then. What do the Belters get when they bend the knee to Eros and submit? What do the Colonisation Committer and the Security Council bring to the table?"

Marriott answered, "The Colonisation Committee provides clearly defined rules and regulations."

Stuart shot back, "Clearly defined rules and regulations! The Belters have their own constitutions and they have their own clearly defined rules and regulations. Yours are just an overlay of control."

Lance counted, "The Security Council provides security for the whole system, for everyone!"

Stuart gave Lance a wry smile, "Security from what exactly? There is no one else in the Asteroid Belt but the Belters and they have their own police forces, their own security forces."

Tegan opened another folder and pulled out a document, "It was the

Belter's common Constitution, thirteen copies. Each Belter colony has their own agreed upon, signed copies", she gently placed the documents in front of Marriott.

Stuart summed up, "Gentlemen, neither you nor the organisations you represent have anything the Belters need or want. Eros is all stick and no carrots. You bring nothing to the table. Nothing at all!"

Both men looked from one to the other once more. Was this meeting being shut down in front of them so easily?

Stuart took on a more conciliatory tone, "Eros offers the Belters governance from afar without any form of representation. Laws thrust upon a people without representation are tyranny. Surely the two of you can see that?"

Neither of them had an answer for that one, it was so very true.

"If you want to be Eros's bulldogs, fine, but don't expect me to play along", Stuart informed them, then explained, "If Eros does not change its ways, I can predict where this is all heading, long-term."

Marriott looked at Stuart, he understood who this man before him was, Dumas was a self-made multi-trillionaire, he had extreme foresight, "And what do you predict, Mr Dumas?"

"If Eros does not change, the animosity between the outer colonies and Eros will grow", Stuart began explaining, "Not just the Belters either, Jupiter's Trojan colonies, Jupiter's colonies and eventually the future colonies of Saturn, Uranus and Neptune."

"What the hell are you talking about?", Lance questioned, adding, "There are no such colonies!"

"Really, Mr Bolton? So the colonies Dumas Colonial Constructions is currently building in Cis-Lunar L-Four, for the consortiums colonising Jupiter's Moons and Trojan points don't exist?", Stuart asked another rhetorical question.

That was news for both of the liaisons, who simply said nothing, staring in disbelief.

Stuart continued, "These colonial consortiums all have one thing in common. They've had a gut-load of living under the auspices of Eros and the Earth's central control systems. They want freedom!"

Marriott then asked, "What is your prediction? I mean, if Eros and the Earth don't change?"

Stuart replied, cautiously, he didn't want to start any drums beating, "I don't like to think about it, but if this continues without change, there will be open rebellion and eventually War."

Lance had had enough, "Bullshit! A handful of Belters are not going to declare War!"

Stuart sighed, "Lance, you are thinking short-term. We aren't talking about a handful of Belters now. We are talking about colonies across the entire outer solar system in, perhaps, a century from now. Maybe sooner. You and the organisations you represent really need to think long-term. Really long-term!"

The two men looked at each other once more. Stuart Dumas was making predictions, scores of decades into the future.

Stuart frowned, this meeting was getting nowhere fast and he told the two liaisons, "If Eros does nothing, what I have predicted for our distant future will come to pass. If Eros rethinks its ways and makes reforms, the future will unfold very differently, far more smoothly. Gentlemen, Eros is looking at a business opportunity! They just have to realise that!"

Both men still looked unconvinced, although Marriott showed distinct signs of doubt in his position. Lance was caught up with his own past in the military and was having trouble seeing beyond that.

Stuart shook his head, "Gentlemen, I can see that this is going nowhere", he gestured to Tegan who selected another folder, checked its contents and passed it to Marriott, "That folder contains the contacts for our legal department, Dumas Legal Incorporated. All future dealings with either the Colonisation Committee or the Security Council will proceed through them. Good day, Gentlemen."

Marriott Walters placed the other documents Tegan had provided into the new folder.

As the two men stood up to leave, they adjusted their jackets and began to walk towards the door, they both paused momentarily as Stuart instructed Tegan, "Ms Smith. Offer the Belter colonies all and any legal assistance, gratis. I will personally cover all of their legal bills", it was like rubbing salt into a wound.

Once the two men had left the office, Tegan walked to the doorway, checking to make sure that they had truly left, she knew Stuart had at least one final word to say.

"Tegan, our company, Earth Trojan Mining, dug out, Eros, that rat hole the Colonisation Committee and Security Council reside in", Stuart stated, adding, "If I'd known what Eros would become, I would have broken it up and mined it completely."

"We could always create a division to work on the problem of past mistakes and their temporal mitigation, Sir", Tegan joked.

Stuart smiled and then laughed, as Tegan left the office to return to her own desk.

Lance Bolton and Marriott Walters were on their way back to their hotel in

Colonial Central Command, "Well, that did not go well!", Marriott noted.

"Dumas is a fool", Lance replied, commenting, "The Security Council will economically break the stupid bastard."

Marriott stared at Lance in disbelief, "Agent Bolton, you really don't know anything about Stuart Dumas, do you?"

"What's to know? He's just a man and he can be broken like any other", Lance replied.

Marriott shook his head, "Stuart Dumas is not just any man, Agent Bolton. His corporations pretty much run the entire solar system economy. You break the man, you break his corporations, you break the entire solar system economy!"

"Don't be ridiculous! No one man has that kind of power!", Lance replied in abject disbelief.

Marriott took out his data tablet and quickly performed a search on Stuart Dumas.

He picked an appropriate network page and then passed his data tablet to Lance, "Agent Bolton, do a little bit of research. Then tell me again, exactly what the Colonisation Committee and the Security Council are going to do."

Lance began reading through the information and he was very, very quiet.

When he looked back up away from the data tablet, Marriott told him, "Our organisations are going to do nothing. Absolutely nothing!"

Some years later, Hudson Moon, Harrison Moon's great-grandson, had Ceres Central's rotation rate gradually slowed down to one point two one revolutions per minute. Hudson figured that point five gs would be fine and would actually be beneficial for the older folk in the colony, who were frail and would find half a gravity easier to cope with. Hudson did the same with their older colony, "*Eros can have it*", as well and that became the standard in the Ceresian colonies. The other Belter Colonies did the same and their colonies followed suit, slowing down their rotation rates and generating point five gs of artificial gravity.

Hudson's eldest Son, Harcourt Moon, had similar sentiments, although he could not see why O'Neil-style colonies needed gravity any greater than that of Mars. After all, Mars was well into the process of being terraformed and its gravity was only point three eight gs. That could not be changed.

So Harcourt Moon had Ceres Central's rotation rate slowed to a meagre, one point zero two rotations per minute, setting the artificial gravity to point three five gs. The other Belter colony Administrators were all a bit dubious at first, but they too implemented the same changes and point three five gs became the standard across all Belter colonies. After all, Ceres own gravity was only point zero three gs, almost micro-gravity and the other twelve Belter asteroids were smaller and their gravity was even lower than Ceres.

Of course, in later years, Belter colonists did build colonies and homes on their primary asteroids, like Ceres, in near micro-gravity and this would, in the generations to follow, have deleterious effects on their Human physiology!

When Harcourt Moon received a communique from Eros, from the Colonisation Committee, with regard to a new law, *"The Gravity Law"*, he read it with disdain.

"The Gravity Law – For all colonies that derive their gravity via artificial methods, i.e., centrifugal force, that artificial gravity shall not deviate from one Earth g, by more than plus or minus ten percent as applied to the colony's main living surface. With the exception of Military Training facilities."

The communique contained a lot of supporting documentation, including case studies and medical tests, along with blood and genetic analyses. Even the detailed descriptions of several dozen low-gravity syndromes. Harcourt looked at the information with all the suspicion of a conspiracy theorist.

"This was just another way for Eros to reassert their control", Harcourt thought to himself.

After all, the Belters did have the supplements and stimulants, just like every other people living in low-gravity environments. The Belters needed nothing from Eros and Harcourt copied the communique straight into his digital shredder. All of the other Belter colony Administrators had done the same.

Along with the communique from Eros, about the new Gravity Law, came another communique directly from the office of President James Carter in Colonial Central Command. The President of the Earth's Cis-Lunar colonies. This communique was different, it was business and business always piqued Harcourt's interest.

"Julia!", Harcourt called out to his wife, who was also his personal assistant, "I'm sending you a communique with an attached offer document. It's President Carter of the Cis-Lunar colonies."

Julia read through the document and printed it out before walking over to her husband's desk.

"It's to do with that great disaster a couple of years back", Julia explained, adding, "They had twenty seven damaged colonies and they want to *'gift'* two of them to us. They are gifting two colonies to each of the Belter colonies."

"That is what I thought it said", Harcourt replied and then he asked, "What's your take on this?"

"Harcourt, if this offer is real, then this is platinum!", Julia exclaimed, adding, "They're all O'Neil-style twin cylinder colonies, one point six kilometres long and four hundred metres wide. That's the same size as our first colony, *'Eros can have it'*. Capacity, twenty thousand plus colonists."

Harcourt's smile toned down somewhat, "It does say that they are damaged, Julia."

Julia was more upbeat, "It does say that they are reparable, Harcourt. President Carter is giving them away because he wants to replace them with new ones. An economic boost for the colonial construction yards at L-Four."

"Julia, take note. Send an email to Stuart Dumas about this. He probably already knows, but send one anyway, just in case he doesn't. Dumas Colonial Constructions will get a huge boost", Harcourt instructed his wife.

"I'll also run it past Dumas Legal, to see if it's legit", Julia noted, explaining, "It says here we will have title to those two colonies, free and clear, to do with as we see fit."

"Is Stuart still picking up our legal tab?", he asked his wife.

"Yes, Harcourt, at least for the term of his life and his Son Baron, has promised to do the same should his father pass on", Julia confirmed.

Harcourt Moon nodded, there was a profit to be had, but only if all of the i's were dotted and the t's crossed, "Another note, Julia. Query the President about helping with transport costs."

"Harcourt, you are incorrigible, you've been offered a gift horse and you want to inspect its mouth", Julia laughed a surprisingly boisterous laugh.

The following day, they received a series of replies. The first of the replies came in from Dumas Legal, even Stuart Dumas had his personal legal beagles looking into it thoroughly. The two colonies were indeed repairable and were being gifted, free and clear, to do with as they pleased. Stuart noted that Dumas Legal had received thirteen queries about these *'gift'* colonies, which was to be expected as there were thirteen Belter colonies. Each Belter colony would receive two *'gifted'* twin cylinder O'Neil-style colonies, enabling the colonies to expand by forty to fifty thousand colonists once they were repaired.

There was one hitch, one drawback. Each of the *'gifted'* colonies was free and clear, yes, except they were also registered with both the Colonisation Committee and Security Council at Eros. That was unavoidable, however, these *'gifts'* were too valuable not to accept. The Belters could simply scrap them if they wanted, but their use for colonial expansion was tremendous.

The second reply was from President Carter. The President stated very clearly that they could not help with the cost of haulage and he did point out that the value of the colonies outweighed the haulage fees by several orders of magnitude, even as scrap. President Carter included a list of Financial Institutions that could help him with the costs.

Stuart Dumas's Colonial Financial was at the top of that list. Harcourt smiled to himself. Stuart would give him rock-bottom rates. Another thing that Harcourt noted was a list of space haulage firms. Dumas's Cis-Lunar Haulage was at the top of that list, again Harcourt could see rock-bottom rates.

The third reply was from Stuart Dumas himself, recommending accepting the *'gift'* offer, noting that even with Eros's filthy hand on them, they were far too valuable not to accept. Stuart pointed out that *'free and clear, to do with as we see fit'*, meant exactly that. Harcourt could on-sell them for a profit, scrap them for a profit or use them for colonial expansion. The decision was his to make and his alone.

Of course, Harcourt Moon and his wife, Julia, even found a workaround for the *'gifted'* colony's registration with the Colonisation Committee and the Security Council.

"Julia, these colonies. They were gifted, that means that they were *'written off'*", Harcourt noted.

"That is this case, Harcourt", Julia confirmed.

Harcourt smiled a broad smile that showed he had an idea, one that bordered on genius, "We need to contact Dumas Legal and Dumas Colonial Financial Ltd. I have a plan, Julia."

"A plan, Harcourt?", Julia asked and then she smiled and asked, "A plan or a scheme, Harcourt?"

"Yes, Julia, my love, a plan and we need to keep Stuart Dumas and the other Belter Administrators in on it", Harcourt replied and then began to divulge his plan.

Stuart Dumas's personal assistant Tegan stepped into his office, "Mr Dumas, Sir. You are going to love this one", she informed him, noting, "It's from Harcourt Moon!"

"Really, Tegan. What does Administrator Moon have to say?", Stuart enquired, smiling.

"Sir, those *'gifted'* colonies. Mr Moon has pointed out that they have been written off, so therefore, their registrations with the Colonisation Committee and the Security Council are null and void", Tegan informed her boss.

"Now isn't that interesting, Tegan", Stuart agreed.

Tegan continued, "Sir, Dumas Legal is in agreement with Mr Moon. He and the other twelve Belter Colony Administrators are requesting finance for the repairing those *'gifted'* colonies through Dumas Colonial Financial!", she paused, then finished, "Complete with a refinanced final repayment!"

"God, those clever bastards! Sorry, Tegan", Stuart replied, noting, "That means that all of those *'gifted'* colonies will need to be re-registered under new colony identification numbers!"

"Yes, Sir", Tegan replied, commenting, "They are adding a hyphen two, to the numbers on their construction plaques. Legal says they're good to go."

"Harcourt Moon!", Stuart exclaimed, remarking, "He's a clever bloody man. With their final repayments being repaid at one credit per year forever, they will never officially come online. Eros will never see those colonies back under their jurisdiction! They will never be re-registered!"

Harcourt Moon was a man moulded in the likeness of Stuart Dumas, a man of Stuart's mettle. He thought fast, made quick decisions and had no regrets about his choices. Harcourt Moon bit the bullet with the stroke of a pen and then asked his wife, Julia, to counter-sign the document and email the offer agreement back to President Carter at Colonial Central Command, as accepted. He was Moon and true to his name and his heritage, his decisions once made were never regretted and always profitable!

Harcourt Moon was one of the many Moons of Ceres!

21. The Bonds of Love.

Four of the girls were eating their lunch at the usual table in the school's eastern quadrangle. The majestic maple tree in the centre was perfectly positioned to provide the girls with mottled shade from Vale's primary, yellow Sun, Cathol. Vale's secondary, orange Sun, Cythol, cast no light on the quadrangle, its feeble orange glow obscured by the shadow of a nearby building.

A slight breeze, barely above a whisper, rustled the leaves of the shrubbery surrounding the edges of the quadrangle. The shrubbery, they had leaned, was a combination of English Box and Blueberry bushes. The Blueberry bushes bore fruit seasonally on Vale, just as they would have on the Earth.

Aria had taken to leaving *"offerings"* of food, as she called them at the end of each day, for the Harricks that lived somewhere nearby. Titbits of bread, berries and pieces of apple. The next morning, the small offerings were always gone. Proof positive, Aria would say that Harricks lived nearby. Aria's ulterior motive was to hopefully make friends with the elusive little humanoids.

"Where's Yeannah?", Ariel curiously asked.

Saffiera informed them, transmitting, *"She said she needed to stretch her wings. Her Mother keeps telling her she hasn't been exercising her wings enough lately."*

There was the slight sound of flapping wings and Ariel noted, "Thols aren't allowed to fly within the school's grounds. Too many dangerous obstacles with Human architecture or something like that."

"Yeah, no one wants to get skewered on a spire or crash into a gargoyle", Aria noted dryly.

They all looked up to see Yeannah flying majestically, high above the quadrangle. The flapping of her mighty wings was clearly audible. Yeannah circled the quadrangle four times before swooping in at speed behind the tall maple tree. She glided under the branches, angled upwards and then descended, using her large, leathery wings like a parachute. A rush of wind washed past the girls seated at their table as Yeannah nailed the landing perfectly.

Aria cried out, "Way cool! My girl Yeannah is rebelling, breaking all the rules!", as Yeannah furled her great wings and approached them.

They rarely had the privilege of seeing Yeannah fly and Aria exclaimed, "That was awesome. You nailed that landing just like a superhero."

Kethera's whiskers stood to attention and she smiled broadly, "That was so impressive."

Yeannah replied, "It was reckless of me. If my Mother was here, she'd be scolding me."

For all of the exertion of flying, there was no noticeable sweat visible on Yeannah.

Ariel noticed that, asking, "How is it possible for you to fly like that and not even work up a sweat?"

Aria became curious and asked, "How do you even breathe when you're flying?"

Yeannah smiled and let loose a little trill of laughter before replying, "Ariel, Thols don't sweat. We don't have sweat glands."

"Lucky for you, sometimes I wish I didn't have sweat glands", Ariel replied.

Yeannah replied, "Our lungs are different, Ariel. You Humans have two lungs and so do we, except we also have upper and lower air sacs. When we breathe in, our lower air sacs fill first and then when they're full, the air pushes into our lungs. As more air is breathed in, the air is pushed into the upper air sacs and as the breath continues, the upper air sacs are emptied when we exhale."

"Wait! That means that spent air and new air never intermix in your lungs as it does with us", Ariel remarked.

"Yes, Ariel. Tholish lungs are much more efficient", Yeannah confirmed.

"Sounds pretty weird to me", Aria commented.

"Yeannah trilled another laugh and continued, "It gets even weirder. Our bones are hollow and there are tubules connecting the larger bones to our air sacs. So if we can't breathe for any reason, we can self-tracheotomy, just by breaking an appropriate bone", then she frowned, "That does sound painful, I never want to have to do that."

Saffiera, who had been quiet during this whole exchange, noted, *"Thols breathe just like terrestrial birds do. If Humans had the same kind of lung system, imagine how much faster and for how much longer we could run."*

"True", Kethera added, commenting, "Carlin lungs work the same way, except our bones aren't hollow and connected to our air sacs. We can run very, very fast!", the grin on her face spread from ear to ear, her pupil slits opened wide.

"Our Mother said that was because you had legs like coiled springs", Aria noted in reply.

"Your Mother is right. That just makes us even faster", Kethera replied with pride.

Aria noted curiously, "I've seen you run, Kethera. You are so fast. It makes me wonder how fast you'd be if you were trained in martial arts like Ariel and I. Would you be faster than Ariel?"

Ariel agreed, "Probably. I've seen how fast Kethera is."

Kethera's whiskers drooped and her ears flattened, "I don't want to hit people."

Ariel replied, "No, you don't, Kethera. That's probably why us Humans love Carlins so much."

Kethera smiled back, her whiskers stood up and her ears focused, "My people love Humans too!"

Aria noted in a more practical tone, "Our Dad says that if Carlin folk were to learn martial arts, they'd be unstoppable. He has recommended your people for military recruitment several times."

Kethera frowned again, drooping her whiskers, "Aria, my people don't like to fight. We only kill for food, only for necessity, nothing more."

Aria looked at Kethera, "I'm sorry, Kethera. This talk is making you sad. Perhaps we should go to the study hall and go over this morning's history class?"

Ariel rolled her eyes, "Wow! More wisdom from my evil twin! What is the world coming to?"

"Aria is not evil, Ariel, she's just uncomplicated and has no filter", Kethera replied, smiling.

"Yes, Kethera, we all know about Aria's lack of a filter", Ariel agreed.

Yeannah steered them all back on course, "To the study hall!", she cried out and they all packed up and started walking towards it.

Aria took Yeannah by the arm and whispered into her ear, Thomas's last compliment, "Love you to bits, my Alabaster Beauty."

As they walked, Yeannah asked Aria sceptically, "Am I really that beautiful?"

Aria replied, completely unfiltered, "Absolutely, First Yookey, then Thomas. You'll be beating them back with a stick next!"

Yeannah frowned, "Aria, I don't want to beat anyone back with a stick."

"It's all good, Yeannah. You don't have to. Ariel and I will always protect you", Aria noted in reply.

Such a strange yet comforting sentiment.

The girls entered the school's senior study hall and made a beeline straight for the table that they normally sat at. They all noticed Richard and Thomas sitting with their usual friends as they passed by on the way to their table. Other than that, the study hall appeared to be quiet. All of the other tables were empty and it was quiet all the way across to the far side, where the study hall adjoined the senior school library. Then again, the library was always quiet, that was the nature of libraries.

Saffiera noticed as they walked passed Richard and Thomas, two things that her telepathic mind had picked up. The first, Richard was overly excited to see Kethera, he was in love with Kethera, but this, this was something different. Very different, something much deeper, Saffiera had entirely no understanding of what it was. Love beyond love! It was perplexing to her Martian Mind.

The other thing Saffiera picked up on was Thomas's demeanor. Gone was his usual bravado, his machismo, replaced by something else. Thomas was downhearted, heartbroken and feeling rejected. The boy was miserable. Thomas had lost his mask entirely and the real Thomas was openly on display. Thomas's mojo was completely gone and he was in such a bad way that he looked almost pathetic. Thomas's unrequited love for Yeannah was ripping him apart!

As the girls walked past, Richard placed a consoling hand on Thomas's shoulder. Thomas averted his eyes away from Yeannah, he was inconsolable. Yeannah had noticed as well and she wasn't happy at all with the situation. Sure, Yookey's heart was also broken, but he was an Indigenous Thol, so he now understood their Tholish taboos. Thomas, however, was a teenage Human boy and simply being told something about Tholish taboos did nothing to alleviate his underlying feelings.

"This is my fault", Yeannah thought to herself, *"I did this to Thomas!"*

Saffiera reached out to Yeannah and sent her calming thoughts, *"This is not your doing, Yeannah. This is the result of irrational and stupid ancient Tholish taboos! Indigenous taboos that have nothing to do with Mimasian Thols"*, she took Yeannah's hand in hers as a comfort.

Kethera on the other hand, was completely oblivious to Thomas's and Yeannah's turmoil, instead, all she could see was Richard and she was eagerly awaiting the gentle caress of his lips once more. Perhaps more so than even she realised.

Saffiera, being the Martian telepath that she was, even picked up on Kethera's emotional state, *"Kethera's love for Richard is taking on similar dimensions to Richard's. Love beyond Love!"*, she thought to herself, how perplexing it was!

The girls all sat down at the table and began the revision of the morning's history class and the first thing that Aria noted was, "That Stuart Dumas guy is everywhere!", she exclaimed.

Yeannah agreed, distracted as she was, "Stuart Dumas was the richest business tycoon of that time. He financed the Earth, the Venus and the Martian Trojan mining operations. He was even responsible for the construction of Eros. Something he appears to have regretted later."

"Yeah, but also he financed and constructed all of the Belter colonies and even constructed their Moons", Aria replied, the incredulity of it was palpable in her voice.

"I thought that was amazing", Kethera replied, noting, "He not only consolidated dangerous asteroids into conglomerated masses for mining in the inner system Trojan points. He also had the foresight to build asteroids into artificial moons for the Belter colonies. That was brilliant!"

Ariel was astonished by how quickly Kethera had picked up on that, "Whoa, Kethera. You were actually paying attention? I thought you spent the whole class dreaming of Richard!"

"Yeah, that's what I thought as well", Aria agreed with her twin Sister.

Kethera sighed and drooped her whiskers slightly, "I can multi-task, you know. I am a woman after all", she reminded them.

Saffiera glanced back in Richard's direction, *"Richard certainly thinks so, Saffiera"*, she informed.

Kethera slyly placed another chair conveniently close to hers. Richard would come over soon enough and she was eagerly awaiting him. Carlins had no prohibitions with inter-species relationships and Kethera was a teenage Carlin girl in love.

Saffiera remarked, *"I found it interesting that Stuart Dumas used his corporations and economic clout to protect the Belters. He didn't have to do that!"*, her thought came across a little too strongly.

"Are you okay, Saffiera?", Ariel asked, "That was a potent thought, you're not usually that loud."

"Sorry, Guys. I guess I've got a lot on my mind", Saffiera replied and she did, Saffiera had her friend's emotional states, especially Yeannah's and Kethera's, weighing heavily on her teenage mind.

"Saffiera has a very valid point, though. Stuart Dumas did not have any obligation to protect the Belters, yet he did so anyway?", Yeannah agreed completely.

"I guess he was just that kind of guy", Aria replied flippantly.

"No, Aria. He was thoughtful and visionary. He wasn't all business and money", Ariel chided, explaining, "The man was considerate and a long-term thinker. Stuart Dumas was the true force behind the solar system's colonisation at that time."

"I think he was probably hot! Not as hot as my Richard, but still hot", Kethera added with a smile.

Aria raised her hand for a high-five, "Way to go, Kethera, my goofy girl!" and Kethera high-fived back, with her whiskers raised and a broad Cheshire grin.

"I know we haven't got to the next section yet, but Stuart Dumas also funded the colonisation of Jupiter's Moons and Jupiter's Trojan points", Yeannah noted, "Not to mention his involvement in the colonisation of

Saturn's orbital zone."

"Yep, he was a mover and a shaker", Aria agreed, asking, "Why is this called the Great Explosion again? Shouldn't it be called, Stuart Dumas does everything?"

That had Ariel and Kethera laughing. It had Saffiera and Yeannah rolling their eyes.

It was Yeannah's turn to reply dryly, "No, Aria. Stuart Dumas instigated a lot of things, but he did not personally do everything himself. He was just the triggering agent."

Saffiera added to Yeannah's statement, *"And he always followed up and oversaw the processes as they unfolded."*

It was Yeannah's turn to offer a high-five and Saffiera quickly returned it.

"What about the Moons of Ceres?", Kethera asked, "Reading their history, they come across as almost artful, sometimes just skirting the legalities of the day."

"Artful dodgers", Ariel agreed, "That's likely what they were."

Yeannah called up a window on her data tablet about the Moon family and its relationship to Ceres, then with a double tap, the network page appeared on her friend's data tablets which were all linked.

"Wow!", Kethera exclaimed, noting, "Every single administrator of Ceres has been a Moon family member since its first colonisation. Right up till this day! That is a very long time!"

"It is even more than that, Kethera", Yeannah replied, explaining, "Many Moon family members emigrated to the other Belter colonies, even to Jupiter's Trojan colonies. Those emigrant Moons become prominent figures within those communities as well. Many became administrators."

"And they were supported from the very beginning by Stuart Dumas", Ariel added.

Oddly, Aria had something constructive to say for once, "I think that the biggest takeaway from this entire period is how crucial Stuart Dumas was for the solar system's colonisation. Without Stuart Dumas, that might never have happened."

"Thank you, Sister", Ariel replied, giving her a huge hug, "For once you've said something useful."

Then the flippancy came out, "Meh! I've gotta be useful at some point, right!"

Richard came sauntering over from his table and sat down on the chair that Kethera had prepared for him earlier.

Yeannah asked awkwardly, "How is Thomas?", she did not want to ask, but was feeling quite guilty.

Richard didn't want to answer either, but ended up blurting out, “Let's see. Hmm. He's had his heart torn out, ripped into two, thrown on the floor and stomped on. All by stupid, primitive taboos no less. All in all, Thomas is feeling quite peachy, I'd say”, he replied with sarcasm, immediately wishing he hadn't.

Aria was quick to Yeannah's defence, “You need to be very careful with what you say, Richard. If you upset our Girl, Yeannah. Your being friends with Kethera will only go so far.”

Kethera gripped Richard's arm really tightly, “Please don't upset Yeannah, Richard. You really do not want to see what the twins can do first-hand."

Richard looked at Kethera, she seemed more than a little concerned, “Okay. Okay, Yeannah, I apologise. Now, could someone please explain to me why these stupid, ancient taboos are causing so much trouble?”

Yeannah began to explain, but she was struggling for words and Saffiera held her hand, sending soothing sensations into her mind.

With Saffiera's help, Yeannah began, “The taboos belong to the Indigenous Thols and they are truly ancient, dating back millions of years. They are ingrained into every aspect of their society, culture, even their language and the way they think. Their greatest taboo is the one about inter-species relationships. Every Thol relationship must be productive, as in offspring. It is a duty to them and that can never happen with inter-species relationships.”

“But you are not an Indigenous Thol, Yeannah. You're a Mimasian Thol”, Richard noted in reply.

Yeannah shook her head, “Their taboos apply to us as much as docs to them. Even Mimasian Thol and Indigenous Thol relationships are forbidden. Do you really that think that they will allow any Thol relationships with Humans?”

“Yeannah, surely they can't push their stupidity onto your people?”, Richard questioned.

Yeannah actually laughed, her melodic trills were as dry as her wry smile, “Do you not comprehend, that for every Mimasian Thol, there are ten thousand Indigenous Thols?”

And that was the one thing that Richard had not considered, things were beginning to make sense. “The rules of the many overrule the rules of the few”, he nodded in understanding.

“Yes, Richard!”, Yeannah nodded in confirmation.

Richard curiously, yet cautiously asked, “What would happen if you and Thomas were to enter into a relationship?”, he heard Aria crack her knuckles and he noticed her clench her fists, “If you don't mind me asking, that is,

Yeannah", he quickly added.

"It is somewhat hard to say. At the very least, I would be completely ostracised, forced to live here in the colony amongst Humans", Yeannah speculated, adding a possible worst-case scenario, "It could get even worse. I might be driven from this world completely, along with my Parents and my Brother."

"That does not sound good at all", Richard agreed.

"It could even be worse", Yeannah informed him.

"How so?", Richard asked.

"Thols, by and large, are a peaceful people, especially mine. The Indigenous Thols are also generally a peaceful people", Yeannah began, but then she noted, "There are always outliers. Radicals amongst any population and the Indigenous Thols are no different."

"I don't understand?", Richard asked, not knowing where Yeannah was taking this.

"One rule is paramount. Thols do not kill Thols, no matter how heated the issue might be", Yeannah explained, then added the darkness, "Thomas is a Human. I cannot guarantee his safety!", a single tear ran down her cheek.

"Those radicals might murder him?", Thomas asked incredulously.

Yeannah nodded, "They have taboos against Thols killing Thols, but none at all against Thols killing outsiders", her tears were running freely.

Saffiera took out her handkerchief and began wiping away the tears from Yeannah's cheeks.

"Jesus, Yeannah, I had no idea", Richard admitted, then he apologised, "I am so sorry."

Saffiera noted, *"This is why Humans are so careful not to upset the Indigenous Thols. The Human authorities understand more than you know, Richard."*

Kethera and her people, the Carlins, had lived side by side with the Indigenous Thols for many millions of years. The Carlins in their valley and the Thols in their tall trees in the mountains.

Kethera remarked, "We know there are radicals amongst the Indigenous Thols, but we would never see them. They look just like anyone else, they just think differently."

Saffiera stated something not considered, *"They may look just like any other Thol, but they cannot hide their minds, not from a Martian anyway."*

To which Yeannah smiled and trilled back, "There are even fewer Martians than Mimasian Thols."

"I really need to tell Thomas this", Richard noted.

"Do you really think it will help?", Ariel asked.

"It won't make him feel any better, but at least he will understand", Richard replied, adding, "He most certainly doesn't want to be murdered in his sleep."

"No, no, no, Richard, do that later. I've hardly seen you since yesterday", Kethera replied, then she stood up from her chair and sat down on Richard's lap, straddling his legs.

Richard was both surprised and very pleased, especially when Kethera wrapped her arms around his and began passionately kissing him. Richard kissed her back and their passionate embrace continued for long minutes.

Aria was both surprised and amused and commented, "Geez, do you two need a room or what?"

Kethera moved in closer to Richard, almost grinding up against, what could only be described as his overly excited state. Ariel, Aria, Saffiera and Yeannah gasped in shock!

"Holy shit!", Aria exclaimed, "Holy shit!", she exclaimed again.

Saffiera's mind was racing, the thoughts, *"Love beyond love!"*, popped into her mind and she transmitted urgently to the others, *"Something is very wrong. Separate them. Separate them now!"*

Aria and Ariel reacted straight away and pulled Richard and Kethera apart, they were completely unresponsive. Their eyes appeared glazed and they were resisting, trying to get back together.

Aria, true to her nature, chortled when she saw Richard's groin, Ariel chided her, "Not now, Aria!"

Saffiera gently entered their minds and both Richard and Kethera became calmer. Richard's eyes became clearer, but Kethera's eyes remained glazed over.

Yeannah was quick to instruct her friends, "We need to get them to sickbay, right now!"

The girls packed up their gear into their bags and then grabbed Richard and Kethera, almost dragging them off to the school's sickbay.

As they passed Thomas, he looked up. Yeannah gave him a slight smile, his heart picked up and Yeannah chided herself, thinking, *"Why did I have to do that?"*

Saffiera picked up on her thought and Thomas's state of mind, *"Actually, you made him feel a little better, with just that one small smile"*, she thought to Yeannah.

When the girls reached the school sickbay, the two school nurses, Ms Katla, a Carlin and Ms Yoolah, a Mimasian Thol, were at first not seeing what the issue was. The girls were all surprised, as they had not seen many Carlins working in the Human colony and did not know one worked at the school. Mimasian Thols often worked in the Human colony and that was not unusual at all.

Nurse Katla caught a glance of Kethera's glazed eyes and the glistening of her wet nose, "Oh my", she stated as she scanned Kethera for her dna imprint.

Nurse Katla's scanner beeped and Kethera's school profile came up on her data tablet, "Please bring Kethera over to the bed."

The girls brought Kethera over to the bed and laid her down upon it.

Nurse Katla looked at Richard more closely, "Of course", she stated as she scanned him for his dna imprint, her scanner beeped once more and she checked her data tablet, "Please take Richard over that other bed", she asked.

The girls took Richard over to the other bed. His eyes were no longer glazed, however, he did seem a little disoriented, so they laid him down on the bed as well.

"Good then, girls, please wait in the other room", Nurse Katla requested and they all obeyed, except for three of them standing in the doorway with concerned looks on their faces.

Saffiera was a Martian of course, she could scan the entire room with her mind and so she sat herself down on the nearest chair.

"You've seen this before, I take it, Katla?", Nurse Yoolah asked.

"Oh, yes, Yoolah, a few times", Nurse Katla confirmed, "See these scans. Carlins run hot at the best of times, but Kethera here is one point five degrees above normal and Richard is one degree above Human normal as well. His temperature would have been even higher, earlier though."

"Yes, I see", Yoolah commented, "The dna readings look a bit odd as well."

"Well, yes. We're detecting multiple dna signatures. Aside from Kethera's and Richard's, we've detected, let's see", Nurse Katla touched her data tablet with its stylus, "Aria Swanson, Ariel Swanson, Saffiera and Yeannah, corresponding to the girls in the other room. Saffiera is a Martian. How very unusual."

"That would be expected, they all appear to be close friends", Nurse Yoolah replied, looking back at the three girls standing in the doorway, all still looking extremely concerned.

"Yes, Yoolah, but look at the Kethera's and Richard's scans. They are smothered in each other's dna", Nurse Katla remarked, "This is an uncommon pheromonal cascade response."

"I'm not seeing any other issues in your scans, Katla. No dangerous bacteria, no viruses or parasites", Nurse Yoolah noted, "Just that pheromonal cascade response you've noted."

Nurse Katla looked at Nurse Yoolah, she smiled cautiously and whispered, "They were both in heat. Well technically, Kethera still is."

Nurse Yoolah stepped in, "Humans don't go into heat."

"Not normally", Nurse Katla agreed, commenting, "Unless there is a Carlin involved."

Nurse Katla walked over to a cabinet and unlocked it. She took out two boxes of pills and some smelling salts. The Nurse walked over to Richard first and popped open the smelling salts under his nose, holding them there while Richard shook his head. Then the Nurse walked over to Kethera and did the same, popping open another vile of smelling salts.

Nurse Yoolah asked, "Is that it then?"

"Pretty much, Yoolah. We just need to give Kethera a bit more time to come around, though", Nurse Katla replied as she walked back over to Richard.

"What happened?", a still slightly groggy and confused Richard asked.

Nurse Katla had her data tablet and stylus out and ready, "Richard, exactly how long have you and Kethera been an item?"

"What? How did you know?", Richard asked.

"Richard, you are both smothered in each other's dna and pheromones", Nurse Katla replied, "Now please answer the question."

Richard was still taken aback, but answered her question, "Three days, maybe a little longer."

Nurse Katla noted that down, mumbling to herself, "Three days", thinking to herself, *"That is so fast, much faster than a Carlin couple bonding."*

Nurse Katla gave Richard a packet of pills, "Richard, put those in your pocket and don't lose them."

"What are they for?", Richard asked.

"They are pheromone blockers. You will need them, trust me. Take one per day in the morning with food. Do you think you can remember that?", Nurse Katla instructed.

"Yes, of course, but why?", Richard enquired.

"I'll explain that to both of you in a few minutes", the Nurse replied.

Nurse Katla walked back to Kethera, who was now beginning to stir, her eyes looking much more normal. Nurse Yoolah watched, taking notes on her own data tablet with its stylus. This was something new to her and she wanted to record it properly. It was also something the school would need to develop a policy on. That a Human boy could trigger an underage Carlin, one that had not yet reached their quickening, into heat was something that needed careful consideration.

Nurse Katla looked at Kethera, "Well then, little one, has your Mother", she looked at her data tablet for the right name, "Kayala had the talk with you yet?"

Kethera nodded, she looked truly scared, her ears were flattened and her whiskers drooped about as far as they could, she nodded and asked, "What happened?"

Nurse Katla gently scratched the skin at the back of Kethera's ear, "The heat, little one. You came into the heat."

"No, no, no", tears welled in Kethera's eyes, "I'm far too young for that", she sobbed.

"Ordinarily, yes, I would agree with you, but little one, you've bonded with Richard", Nurse Katla replied, still gently scratching the skin at the back of Kethera's ears.

"Bonded?", Kethera queried, "How? That shouldn't have happened. I'm too young."

Richard, at hearing the word *"bonded"*, climbed off of the bed and walked over to Kethera's side. Pulling up a chair, he sat down and held Kethera's hand.

Nurse Yoolah sighed, "Humans, up and about when they should be lying down."

Nurse Katla smiled slightly, "Richard, go over to that basin and take one of those pills now, please", she gestured to a basin against the wall, "We don't want your pheromones triggering another episode."

When Richard came back, having done as Nurse Katla had asked, he sat back down and picked up Kethera's hand once more, the Nurse continued, "Kethera, the pheromones of Carlin Men are much weaker than those of Carlin Women."

Kethera nodded in understanding, Nurse Katla added, "The pheromones of Human Men are ten times as strong as Carlin Women."

Kethera bit her lower lip, seeing where this was going, "So, us, Richard and I being so close, triggered something?", she asked in the softest of voices.

"Yes, little one", Nurse Katla confirmed, "Bonding between Carlin couples can take several weeks. A Carlin woman bonding to a Human man can take just days."

"I didn't know", Kethera replied softly.

"Not many do and to be honest, not enough people talk about it", Nurse Katla replied, as she now gently stroked Kethera's cheek, thinking to herself, *"Carlin parents are always happy to see grand-kits, but never think critically about how they came into being."*

"Now, Richard. Do you remember my instructions?", Nurse Katla asked.

"Yes, Nurse Katla. One tablet each morning with food", Richard replied almost robotically, a side effect of his recent *"heat"* experience.

"Good then, Richard, do not forget", Nurse Katla told him, then she passed the other packet of pills to Kethera, "Now, little one, these are contraceptive pills. Take them in the sequence as noted in the instructions. One tablet at night, wash it down with a nice glass of Gudong milk."

Richard and Kethera both looked at Nurse Katla with concern, she explained, "If Richard forgets his pills even once, just once, you run the risk of succumbing to the heat again. If that happens, Kethera, you'll be glad to be taking those pills."

"And if we both forget?", Richard asked.

Nurse Katla shook her head, "Don't even think about that, young man. Make sure you both take your pills, because if you don't, you will both have kits seven months later. You have no idea how fertile Carlin women are!"

Richard nodded in understanding, "Okay. Take the pills religiously. No forgetting."

"What if the pills run out?", Richard asked, as he ran his hand through his sandy blond hair.

"You are both under eighteen. So you will need to discuss this with your Mothers", Nurse Katla informed them both, explaining, "Then you can go to your Doctor and get a prescription for a twelve-month supply."

Richard's face dropped, "Tell my Mother! I don't think she'll understand. She is very traditional", he looked at Kethera, "I love you Kethera, but my Mother. I don't think she'll understand. She might disapprove. No, she will definitely disapprove. My Mother is not just overtly speciesist, she's also racist", he was running his hands through his hair again, a clear sign of stress.

Nurse Katla sighed, "Humans! Okay. Kethera, you talk to your Mother, okay?", Kethera nodded and the Nurse turned back to Richard, "You should really tell your Mother as well, but until you do, Nurse Yoolah and I will arrange a backup plan. Just make sure you come to us before those pills run out."

"That's a deal. We can't afford to run out of the pills, that's for sure", Richard replied.

"What about the bond?", Kethera asked, her voice still low and full of innocence.

Nurse Yoolah stepped closer and replied, "I've heard about Carlinish bonds, honey. They are for life, just the way Tholish bonds are."

Nurse Katla confirmed, "Yes, little one, Carlinish bonds are lifelong. You are bonded, but not yet mated, Kethera."

"Richard is a Human though. Doesn't that make a difference?", Kethera asked, she was still thinking that she was far too young.

Nurse Katla shook her head, "Richard, being Human, makes that bond even stronger."

"How can you possibly know that?", Kethera questioned, quite firmly considering her state of mind.

Nurse Katla looked at Nurse Yoolah, then back to Richard and Kethera, "Little one, I can tell you from personal experience. I live in the little village to the west of the Human colony, my Husband is Human and my five kits are a perfect mix of Carlin and Human traits."

That revelation shook not only both Richard and Kethera but Nurse Yoolah as well.

Kethera's friends in the other room suddenly became aware of why Nurse Katla, a Carlin, was working in the Human colony.

"What would happen if the bond breaks?", Richard asked, he was curious and needed to know.

Nurse Katla sighed, "When Carlin-Human relationships first started appearing, their respective families would try to separate them and that was a very bad idea. Couples in a Carlin-Human bond would rather die than be separated. It was cruel and traumatic for both. That practice was quickly discontinued."

Kethera asked, "Will my Mother scent our bond?"

"Yes, Kethera. Your Mother is a Carlin. How can she not?", Nurse Katla informed her.

Saffiera stuck her head through the doorway between her friends, *"If you want Kethera, I can email your Mother to pick you up."*

Neither Nurse Katla nor Nurse Yoolah had experience with Martian telepathy before, it was a gentle shock, Nurse Katla replied, "That would probably be a good idea, Saffiera, but don't tell her why. I should discuss this issue with her myself."

"Okay. I'll email her to come and meet you and Kethera here", Saffiera replied.

After sending off the email to Kethera's Mother, Saffiera sent another more private message to Nurse Yoolah, who was less involved with Richard's and Kethera's case, *"Can I speak with you?"*, she asked.

Nurse Yoolah walked into the other room where Saffiera was sitting, the girls in the doorway all made room for her, she thought carefully back to Saffiera, *"What can I help you with, Saffiera?"*

"Are there any other Martians my age in the colony?", Saffiera enquired.

Nurse Yoolah connected to the colony's main network and accessed the colony records, then she focused her thoughts as best she could, *"Honey, there aren't that many Martians in the colony down here. Most are older than you by almost ten years, all couples. The others are younger by just as much, they're all in primary school."*

"So, there are no boys even close to my age?", Saffiera asked.

"Ah. Now I see. You have concerns about finding a mate?", Nurse Yoolah asked rhetorically, she already understood the answer, *"I have to be honest with you,*

Saffiera. There are not a lot of options."

"What options do I have?", Saffiera asked.

"Well, I'd say there are three", Nurse Yoolah replied, explaining, *"Martians are not averse to poly-amorous relationships. You could catch the eye of an older Martian man who already has a wife."*

Saffiera frowned, it was not only visible on her face but also telepathic, *"Okay, I see"*, Nurse Yoolah replied, *"Perhaps off-world in the colonies of Cis-Luns L-Five. There are far more Martians off-world than down here, but I don't have access to those records. That is an option, probably the most viable one available to you."*

"And the third option?", Saffiera questioned.

"Hmm, Saffiera, I think you already know that one. Perhaps, you'll find a nice young Earthman whose your age", Nurse Yoolah replied.

"Yes, thank you, Nurse Yoolah", Saffiera replied, noting, *"It always comes back to that last option."*

"Saffiera, honey. Perhaps you should talk to your Mother about this issue?", Nurse Yoolah recommended, *"There may be more options that I haven't covered."*

"Yes, I will do that. Thank you", Saffiera replied.

Nurse Yoolah sat herself down at a chair and announced, "Since I'm sitting here, does anyone else need to talk about anything? Now, don't be shy. You are all teenagers and you must have something to talk about. Teenagers always do."

The twins didn't say a word, but Yeannah asked cautiously, "What would have happened if Kethera had been a Thol and not a Carlin?"

"A Thol? What an interesting question. If you mean an Indigenous Thol, honey. That would never happen. They have way too many inter-species hang-ups", Nurse Yoolah replied.

Then Aria stepped in, blurting out, "What if Kethera had been a Mimasian Thol?"

"Now that is even more interesting. I am no history expert, but I cannot think of there ever being a Human-Mimasian Thol relationship. Not a single one ever", Nurse Yoolah replied.

Aria then asked, "But what if there was one here in the colony?"

Yeannah was becoming increasingly uncomfortable, thinking to herself, *"No more questions, Aria!"*

Nurse Yoolah thought for a moment, "Honey, that does not even bear thinking about. The only safe place for a Human-Mimasian Thol relationship would be in the Cis-Luns L-Five colonies. There are no Indigenous Thols off-world. That's the safest place."

And that was the answer to that.

About forty-five minutes later, Kayala arrived at the school. Kayala did not have transport, so she called Saffiera's Mother, Sarlia, who was very quick to help her. Sarlia suggested picking up Yealah, Yeannah's Mother, as well. Sarlia's reasoning was simple. All three of their Daughters were so very close, that they'd find them all together at the school's sickbay. A typical Martian trait, always helpful.

Sarlia parked her hovercar in the school's car park. The colonial school was large, with a fair-sized kindergarten, primary and secondary schools and even a tertiary institution. The buildings were tall gleaming stone and glass spires, although more correctly, the stone was faux stone, made from specialised concrete. The architecture was Gothic, an ancient Earth style, complete with flying buttresses, steeples, spires and gargoyles.

"Do you guys know where the sickbay is?", Sarlia asked.

Kayala replied, "No", while Yealah looked out of the window, replying, "I will not be taking flight in this place, stone and wings don't mix. You can sense trees, almost feel them, in this place, no. There is too much stone!"

"Okay then, I will search for my Saffiera. I'm certain your girls will be nearby. Give me a few moments", Sarlia replied, as she reached out, her powerful telepathic mind, her eyes closed in thought.

Several minutes later, Sarlia informed Kayala and Yealah, her eyes still closed as her mind wandered through the sick bay, *"Excellent. I have our Daughter's location and they are all together, with the twins. The sick bay has six beds in three rooms, a treatment room and an office. There are two nurses"*, her eyes opened wide, *"and a Human boy called Richard!"*

Kayala's cat-like ears flattened and her whiskers drooped, "This is not a good sign. That Human boy, Richard. His name came up at the sleepover last night. This can only mean one thing!"

Yealah had an inkling as to what Kayala meant, but Sarlia did not and queried, *"What one thing is it that you see, at the mention of this boy's name?"*

"I see my Sister, Kearill, in the past, eight years ago", Kayala replied with sadness.

"Your Sister, Kearill?", Yealah trilled, asking, "The Sister who is married to a Human?"

"Yes, Yealah, that Sister", Kayala replied, explaining, "One day, my younger Sister went to the Human colony. Kearill had never been to the colony before and she was very excited. Kearill found herself in a park surrounded by flowers from Earth and their pollen and scent filled the air."

"And what happened?", Yealah asked melodiously.

"Kearill came into her quickening right there in the park", Kayala replied, going deeper into the story, "A Human man, Norton Fairchild, became attracted to Kearill's pheromones and he sought her out. When he found Kearill, she was about to faint and he caught her in his arms before she fell.

He carried Kearill to a nearby seat, their eyes met and they smiled at each other. That was all it took."

"All it took?", Sarlia questioned, her mind needing to know and understand more.

"Norton showed Kearill around the Human colony. They spent the entire day together, not knowing that they were actually mate-bonding", Kayala replied, commenting, "After that, Norton brought Kearill home in his hovercar. It was very late and getting dark, so we insisted that he stay the night."

"What happened during the night?", Yealah enquired melodically, seeing where this was going.

"During the night Kearill's quickening drove her up to the room where Norton was sleeping", Kayala explained, adding, "They both entered the heat and the mating frenzy. Seven months later, Kearill gave birth to her first hybrid kit. It only takes half a day for a Human to trigger the heat! Then another half a day to go through the mating frenzy. They were fully mate-bonded in a single day!"

"And that's what you think has happened here?", Sarlia asked.

"Yes", Kayala nodded, she was thinking the worst.

"No, Kayala. Kethera is only sixteen. She cannot come into the heat for another two years, surely", Yealah replied, Tholish, clicks and trills laced her voice, trying to assure her that it could not be so.

Sarlia noted, her analytical mind at work, *"Humans take nine months to gestate and are capable of reproducing as early as twelve years of age, although society does place age limits on that."*

Kayala replied, "We Carlins gestate more quickly, only seven months, but once born, we take eighteen years before the quickening and bonding can take place."

"Quickening? You mentioned that earlier, Kayala", Sarlia enquired.

"You would call it puberty or menses", Yealah softly barked, then reassuring Kayala, "Your Kethera is not old enough to bond. She is still far too young."

"Perhaps, but these Human men are different", Kayala noted.

"That is true", Sarlia agreed, noting, *"Many a Martian woman has fallen for an Earth man, most especially those with stubble or facial hair. Martian men don't have facial hair"*, she smiled and admitted, *"When I have my needs, I choose a handsome Earth man with a three-day growth"*, then added, *"We should make haste to the sickbay."*

As they climbed out of Sarlia's hovercar, Yealah trilled, "What of Saffiera's Father?"

Sarlia stopped for a moment, her eyes showing a deep sadness, *"We lost him back in the Sol System. It was a stupid accident that should never have happened"*, she paused, then added, *"I have no wish to talk about it."*

Yealah and Kayala nodded in acknowledgement and they continued toward the school's sickbay.

When the Mothers arrived at the sickbay, Kayala immediately went to her Daughter, Kethera's side. Sitting beside her, holding her hand, was the Human boy, Richard. They were both sitting on the sickbay bed. Sarlia and Yealah located their Daughters, Saffiera and Yeannah, in the sickbay's office. The twins, Aria and Ariel, were with them. The girls all had very concerned looks on their faces.

Nurse Katla quietly and calmly explained to Kayala that Kethera and Richard had bonded and that it had been driven by a cascading pheromonal response. It was something that they had not known was possible for an underage Carlin. Kayala had tears in her eyes as she wrapped her arms around Kethera.

"Please don't be angry, Mother. Please don't be angry", Kethera implored.

Kayala smiled at Kethera, in only a way that a Carlin Mother could, "I am not angry with you, little one, not even with this boy, Richard. I am simply concerned. Last night, when I told you to use protection, I was not aware that you could go into heat so young, nor was I aware that a Human's pheromones could trigger this. Certainly not at your age", she turned to Nurse Katla, "When will the kit be due?"

Nurse Katla smiled back, "There will be no kit, Kayala. This occurred in an inappropriate place and the twins were quick to separate them."

"So they are bonded, but there is no kit?", Kayala asked for confirmation.

"There will be no kits, Kayala. Not as long as Richard here, takes his pheromone blockers and Kethera takes her contraceptive pills", Nurse Katla explained.

Kayala nodded in understanding, "That is a good thing. Kethera is far too young for kits. Perhaps in two or three years, they can have kits. I understand contraception. I can help her with that."

Nurse Katla noted, "Richard has concerns that his Mother may not be accepting."

Kayala nodded again, "Yes. Human Mothers can be like that. The Fathers not so much, but Human Mothers often do not understand or accept.

"You have experience with this, Kayala?", Nurse Katla enquired.

"My Sister, Kearill has a Human husband and lives in the village to the west", Kayala replied

Nurse Katla smiled and looked at Kayala, her pupil slits widened, her ears focused and her whiskers raised, "I live in that same village, my husband is Human and we do have a neighbour named, Kearill!"

"That would be my Sister", Kayala noted, then she turned to Richard and

Kethera, "We will be visiting my Sister, sooner than later it seems", her whiskers twitched in anticipation, she had not seen her younger Sister in many years.

Sarlia looked into her daughter, Saffiera's eyes, *"You seem troubled my child"*, she transmitted.

Saffiera was becoming overwhelmed with emotions, her eyes welled with tears, *"I have so many emotions in my head and most of them are not even mine. I feel like my head going to explode!"*

Sarlia immediately placed her hands on either side of Saffiera's head and leaned in close, touching her forehead to Saffiera's, she reached into Saffiera's mind and let her Daughter unburden herself, all of her emotions. Then Sarlia implanted a small ball of radiant and comforting energy into Saffiera's mind to alleviate the emotional discomfort before slowly stepping back.

"I see, Saffiera", Sarlia responded, then she turned her Daughter around and asked the twins, *"Aria, Ariel, Saffiera needs a hug. If you don't mind of course."*

The twins stepped forward and took Saffiera into their embrace, it was comforting and Saffiera began to cry, releasing all of the pent-up emotions, most of which was not her own.

As the twins continued to embrace Saffiera, Sarlia reached over Saffiera's shoulders and placed her hands on the shoulders of the twins. She directed her thoughts to the twins directly, leaving her own Daughter out of the loop as she recovered from her emotional turmoil.

"Aria, Ariel. You love my Daughter dearly. I can see that", Sarlia began, then explained, *"Recently, Saffiera's shared, passed-down memories have awoken. That alone can be extremely stressful. Added to this are her empathic emotional ties to her friends, four of whom are in deep turmoil. Kethera and Richard, Yeannah and this other Human boy, Thomas. These emotions are not her own and they are causing her great emotional stress."*

The twins both thought back simultaneously as only twins could, *"How can we help?"*, Sarlia isolated their thoughts to allow Saffiera some peace.

"Just do as you always have. Just be her friend. That is all I can ask", Sarlia replied, then she commented, *"But first, I should note, your emotions are not burdening my Daughter, not in any way."*

Ariel thought back, *"How is that possible? Saffiera is a telepath and an empath."*

"Trust me, Ariel. Saffiera is so much more. Her mind will adapt and grow much stronger in a very short time, I assure you", Sarlia explained, then added, *"However, it is the pair of you that has caught my mind's eye. You too are also empaths and I need to investigate that. If you don't mind, of course."*

Aria thought back, *"Surely not. You must be mistaken."*

"Aria, a Martian Elder is a lot of things, but never mistaken", Sarlia replied.

Ariel wanted to understand more, *"Sarlia, please investigate us. Deep dive if you must"*, she bravely asked, to her Sister she implored, *"Aria, you must agree"* and she did.

Sarlia's eyes closed and she concentrated, diving gently, yet deeply into the twin's psyches, there was something odd about these girls and Sarlia needed to understand exactly what it was.

Sarlia searched their memories but could not see anything out of the ordinary, except for the rigorous mixed martial arts training, *"These girl's martial arts skills could make a grand-master weep"*, she thought to herself.

Sarlia continued to dive deeper and began to look into those memories that ordinary, mundane folk could not unlock. Deep genetic memories were woven deeply into the twin's very dna, their very essence. Then, Sarlia found the reason why the twins were so different. Sarlia was excited by what she had found but could not allow her excitement to distract her. She dove deeper into their genetic memories, the way only a Martian Elder could and then it became clear. Slowly, yet carefully, Sarlia withdrew her mind from the twin's minds and her eyes opened once more.

Yealah and her Daughter, Yeannah, stood in the doorway of the sickbay's office, watching the twins, Saffiera and Sarlia. Something momentous was happening, but they did not know what. The twin's eye had been glazed over and when Sarlia withdrew, they came back to normal.

Sarlia informed them, allowing the others to hear, *"Aria, Ariel, you were both born with great potential. Only there was no one there to train you, so that potential has atrophied"*, then she announced, *"You are both scions of Folcrom Forkbraid and Folcrom Selene, which also makes you scions of Folcrom Tafazah himself."*

"How can you be sure?", Ariel asked vocally.

"It is written in your genetic memories, Ariel", Sarlia replied as if it were the simplest of things, then she noted, *"The Earth's Interstellar Alliance maintains a massive database, it contains genealogical data going back thousands of years. Dare I say it, you could confirm this for yourselves with a few quick searches of your family tree."*

"What does it mean?", Aria asked, also now vocally.

Sarlia smiled a broad smile and replied, "*To you twins, Aria and Ariel, by the powers and rights vested in me as a Martian Elder"*, she reached back into the twin's minds, *"I share with you both, a piece of my mind, that it shall awaken your natural gifts and latent talents in accordance with your will"* and it was done, the twins were destined to greatness.

Ariel questioned Sarlia, "Did you just break the law?"

Aria piled on, "Yeah. I thought Martians had laws against tweaking us Earthlings?"

Saffiera was now almost back to her normal self, *"Mum? What have you done?"*

Sarlia sighed, *"No, girls. I have not broken any laws"*, then she explained, *"Those laws are there to prevent the tweaking of Earthlings who are not natural-born psychics."*

"Wait!", Aria exclaimed, "So my Sister and I are natural-born psychics?", she questioned.

"You were, as was one of your parents before you and one of your grandparents before that. Only, no one knew, so you were never trained, never developed. Your skills atrophied. Many natural-born psychics, when not discovered and trained, funnily enough, end up in the military. Fully atrophied and reduced to mundane existence, but they still end up there nonetheless. Their gifts completely lost", Sarlia explained, again with sadness in her thoughts, for such a fate had claimed too many before them.

Sarlia noted, *"As a duly appointed Martian Elder and the only one on this planet, it is within my remit that when I find such as yourself, that I reawaken your gifts."*

"So you could awaken our Parent's gifts as well?", Aria asked.

"No. They are too old now, Aria. Their gifts are lost", Sarlia replied with a slight expression of sadness on her face, explaining, *"I could only awaken your gifts because you are both still young enough to do so. If we had met three or four years from now, that would have been impossible for me."*

"So what happens now?", Ariel enquired.

"Look within you. Look for that little piece of me, it will appear as a golden spark and it will guide you both", Sarlia informed them.

Aria joked dryly, "It's kind of like following the yellow brick road, only it's a spark!"

Ariel just shook her head.

Sarlia smiled, in that only a telepath could, visually and telepathically, *"A wight of my will is within you both. It will guide you and will always be there when you need it. If you need to meet with me in person, that golden spark will guide you to me or, of course, my Saffiera can."*

Saffiera finally realised why she and her Mother were on this planet, her Mother was the only Martian Elder here. The only one! It was a placement, a duty and she would take over from her Mother in the due course of time.

"Yes, my Daughter. We are placed here. Every colonised world has at least one Martian Elder", Sarlia confirmed with a private thought, noting, *"One of our tasks is to locate and awaken the lost scions of Folcrom Tafazah. The Folcrom are thinly spread in our time and they are necessary, always!"*

Understand dawned in Saffiera's mind, she linked back to the studies, that she and her friends had been working on, "*Mother, it was Folcrom Forkbraid and Folcrom Selene who prevented the creation of the Horridian Imperium, wasn't it?*", she asked.

Sarlia turned to her Daughter and transmitted this one all-important thought, *"A fulcrum is the pivotal point, around which a lever works. The Folcrom are the pivotal points around which our entire reality is wrought! It is they and only they who can switch our universe from one happen track to another. Such is their importance!"*

That thought resonated in Saffiera's mind, never would she forget it!

Kethera appeared in the doorway, she was looking tired and drawn out. Her Mother, Kayala, looked at Sarlia, "It has been a big day for my little one, Kethera", she noted.

Kethera was rubbing her weary eyes, her emotions raw, so raw any psychic within a mile would sense them. Sarlia's own Daughter, Saffiera, was holding onto her arm as if it was the only thing holding her up. Saffiera needed rest. The raw emotions within her mind, most of which were not even her own, needed to coalesce and collate. Yeannah just looked tired, ever so tired.

Yeannah whispered to her Mother, Yealah, in a teary voice, "I still love Thomas."

Yealah wrapped her arms and then her wings around Yeannah, protectively double hugging her, "We will work something out, Yeannah. We will work something out", her voice laced with melodic trills.

The twins, ever resilient, looked as though they could take on an army. Nothing at all phased them, yet another sign that they were different. Trained by parents in mixed martial arts, parents who themselves could have been so much more. The twin's latent potentials had been awakened and they would quickly become who they were meant to be.

Nurse Katla and Nurse Yoolah were both frantically taking notes on their data tablets with their styluses. They had to put together a report for the school board, concerning Human boys and Carlin girls within a certain age range. An age range that included the possibility of not just inter-species teenage angst, but the possibility of pheromonal triggering of premature heat and life-long bonding. All whilst keeping the privacy of the affected students intact. New school policies would need to be developed, and parental advice documentation would need to be drafted.

There was a lot that needed to be considered, as the cascading pheromonal response could happen so quickly. Literally three days from the first kiss to full-on heat and bonding, the situation was extremely urgent. For all that they knew, it might not have even been the first kiss, it could have been the first touch! The colony's health research department would need to be informed of the situation as well. The implications were staggering!

Sarlia agreed, all of their Daughters needed urgent rest, *"It has been a big day for everyone in more ways than one"*, she looked at her own Daughter, Saffiera, still holding tightly onto her arm and at Kethera, then to Yeannah, *"The girls need some rest. Quite a bit, actually. Some quiet time will do them all good. We should take them home to rest their weary minds and let their emotions settle down."*

The Mothers all agreed. They thanked the Nurses for their kind work and understanding and then they left the sickbay to take their children home.

Richard left for his home in the colony, unsure how, or even if, he should approach his Mother, he was thinking to himself, *"No way. I can't tell Mum! She'll freak out!"*

The twins, with newfound realisation as to their distant roots in the past, headed back to their home as well. They were latchkey kids, letting themselves into their home and cooking their own dinners. Their parents were both working hard and with odd shifts and hours, but they didn't mind, as their parents had trained them well. Teaching them every skill they could ever need, from household duties to mixed martial arts and even survival skills. Hell, they even knew how to field strip a rifle in the dark.

Yealah stepped into Sarlia's hovercar and wrapped a protective wing around Yeannah. Saffiera climbed in and sat down beside Yealah on the other side, so Yealah wrapped her free wing around her as well and watched, smiling as Saffiera fell gently asleep.

Sarlia's keen mind took note, she turned around to see Yealah, sitting with her left-wing wrapped around Yeannah and her right-wing wrapped around Saffiera, both asleep, a heat felt, *"Thank you"*, she transmitted to her.

As Kayala and Kethera stepped into Sarlia's spacious hovercar's rearmost seats, she told her Daughter, "Now, my little one, you understand the bonds of love", then she hugged her Daughter with intensity while thinking to herself, *"That Richard is handsome. They will make beautiful kits together."*

22. Hector, Patroclus and Menoetius.

Most of the roads within the Human colony itself were paved and ninety five percent of the vehicles had wheels. Hover buses, of course, travelled beyond the colony into places where the roads were unpaved dirt, which every year or so were regraded. For Humans that lived beyond the colony or had business beyond the colony, hovercars were essential.

Sarlia, as a Martian Elder and the Martian Ambassador to Homwol/Vale, was often outside of the colony, as was her home and so she owned her own hovercar. It was a large hovercar with three sets of seats, capable of seating eight people in comfort, although ten could be seated in it. Her hovercar was almost essentially a minibus, what in the ancient days on Earth before space flight was common, would have been called a people mover. Ancient vehicles with four wheels and an internal combustion engine running on refined petroleum products.

On the way to drop off Yealah and her Daughter, Yeannah, at their home, a tree house in the forests of the tall Jula Jula trees to the north, Sarlia offered, *"Yealah, Kayala, the girls have slept over at both of your houses, perhaps tomorrow night it's my turn. They are welcome to sleep over if it's okay."*

"Are you sure?", Kayala asked, noting, "My little one, Kethera, has had such a difficult day."

Yealah chimed in, trilling, "Yeannah's had an awful day as well, are you sure, Sarlia?"

"What better place is there, than the tranquil home of a Martian Elder?", Sarlia asked, then further offered, *"If you are both still concerned, you are both welcome to a sleepover as well. My house has plenty of extra bedrooms."*

Kayala noted, "It would be nice to get away from all of the kits for one night and Krylor won't mind looking after them. Perhaps a lady's night is in order."

Yealah softly trilled and barked, "You have ten kits, Kayala. I only have two, so it certainly won't be a challenge for Yannick to look after Yarris for one night. I could use a lady's night as well."

"So be it", Sarlia agreed, adding, *"I do have an ulterior motive. As I have awoken the twin's latent gifts, I must monitor them as well. I don't want them to become overwhelmed."*

Yealah replied, trilling, "Yes. That sounds very important, Sarlia. Our girls can let the twins know about the sleepover at school tomorrow."

"Excellent!", Sarlia exclaimed, noting, *"I can pick everyone up tomorrow when school finishes for the day. It will be nice to have people over for a change."*

Sarlia dropped off Yealah and Yeannah at the Jula Jula forest close to their home. She was surprised to see them both walk up to one of the tall and mighty Jula Jula trees, only to open a door in its trunk and walk inside.

"Extraordinary!", Sarlia exclaimed, she did not know the trees were hollow on the inside.

Saffiera climbed into the passenger seat beside her Mother, *"That's a modern Mimasian Thol innovation, basically for storage and the elevator. The actual tree houses are four hundred feet up. I'll explain it all to you later, Mum"*, she said as she sat herself down and closed the door.

Kayala and Kethera moved up into the centre row of seats, "One day I will have to visit Yealah's home. I've never seen a Tholish tree house before", Kayala noted.

Kethera noted as she cuddled up to her Mother, "They are impressive. Very impressive."

Sarlia then drove her hovercar to the south past the Human colony, to take Kayala and Kethera home. As she had been there a couple of nights earlier, she was familiar with the way there.

After dropping off Kayala and her Daughter, Kethera, Sarlia drove the hovercar back to their own house, which was southwest of the colony. Sarlia turned on her hovercar's satellite auto navigation and instructed the hovercar to bypass the Human Colony and drive directly to their house which was northwest of their current location. The hovercar increased its altitude to thirty feet and flew across the bluegrass meadows of the Masula Valley.

Along the way, Saffiera asked her Mother about their previous conversation, *"The Earth, Venus, Mars and all of the main worlds of the Alpha Centauri system, all have Psychic Academies. So Psi-Corp and the Folcrom still exist. So why are the scions of Folcrom Tafazah so important?"*

"All psychics when inducted into psi-corp are graded by their raw potentials. The more powerful, the higher the grading level. Most of their psychics are level eight or less. The Folcrom are themselves exceedingly rare, mostly level nines, with a few that are somewhat higher", Sarlia began explaining.

"And the scions of Folcrom Tafazah?", Saffiera asked.

Sarlia smiled and looked at her Daughter, *"Saffiera, many of the scions are level tens and higher. Not all, but enough to be so important! Other psychics can be a level ten and higher, but the scions of Folcrom Tafazah are usually the most powerful. That is why, when we find them and if their abilities can be awakened, we make it so. On the psi-corp scale, we Martians rarely rate at level eight. Most Martians are only level fives. That is why the scions are necessary. We cannot do the things that they can, not even us Martian Elders!"*

"So, they are the ones around which our reality is wrought?", Saffiera asked for clarification.

"Indeed they are my child. Only they can change our reality from one happen track to

another", Sarlia confirmed, telling her, *"You still have so much to learn."*

Saffiera had one final question, however, she was not sure if she should ask it, *"What about the Council of Shadows? Does it still exist?"*

Sarlia looked at Saffiera once more, *"My Child, that is a question, we Martians cannot answer. We have asked that same question of the psi-corp Folcrom. They do not know either."*

"They are recorded in our histories. Surely someone should know?", Saffiera questioned.

Sarlia tried to explain, *"At the time of the Great Reveal, when we Martians and the Mimasian Thols were unveiled to the Earth Humans, they revealed themselves as well. All of the hidden history of Humanity, including the entire Mimasian War. Everything that was covered up and the actions of the Council of Shadows had all been revealed as well. Then they vanished once more. Now, they are little more than myths and legends!"*, her explanation seemed inadequate.

"Surely though, if we have historical records of them, they must still exist?", Saffiera pressed on.

"My Darling, the Council of Shadows hid an entire devastating War for centuries and the Earth Humans did not have a clue, not even the psi-corp. It is still called, the Great Conceal to this day", Sarlia informed her, noting, *"The Council of Shadow members, were all scions of Folcrom Tafazah, level ten and higher. If they still exist, we can never know of it, until they reveal themselves once more. Thankfully, they are or at least were, benevolent overseers."*

Saffiera nodded in understanding as their hovercar landed at its usual landing pad.

The following day Sarlia picked up Kayala and Yealah from their respective homes and then drove her hovercar back toward the school.

"This is a good day for a lady's night and a sleepover", Sarlia told them, noting, *"Tomorrow is the weekend and the girls can all sleep in. It will do them good to have a lazy morning for a change."*

Kayala replied, smiling with affection, "We can make them something nice for breakfast. A bit of a treat", she suggested.

"That does sound lovely", Yealah trilled in agreement.

Sarlia noted, *"My house is surrounded by a number of Maple trees and they are all tapped. Perhaps pancakes and maple syrup for breakfast."*

Kayala smiled broadly, "Perhaps with ice cream? We rarely ever get ice cream in our village."

"Ladies, that can be arranged", Sarlia agreed.

Sarlia and the Mothers picked up their Daughters and the twins from the school and soon they were driving to Saffiera's house.

As they approached the southwest boundary of the Human colony, Sarlia switched on the hovercar's satellite auto navigation and instructed the hovercar's autopilot to fly directly to their house. The colony's paved roads came to an end and the hovercar increased its altitude to thirty feet and began flying across the bluegrass meadows of the Masula Valley.

Ariel remarked, "Wait! Hovercars can't fly this high!"

Sarlia laughed in her telepathic way, *"Ariel, darling. Martian hovercars can."*

Thols could fly, they had seen the meadows and plains of the Masula Valley, especially in the north. Carlins lived in the Valley and knew it very well. The twins had never really seen it and now they stared in awe out of the windows of Sarlia's hovercar. There were meadows of bluegrass as far as the eye could see. The sight was breathtaking!

Scattered here and there were scattered stands of forest. Most were small stands of forest, some were big and a few were quite large. As they watched, one of these stands of forest began to grow larger as they approached it. The closer they got, the larger it grew until it loomed large, directly in front of them. This was a big forest and they were heading straight towards it.

The hovercar increased its altitude once more as they approached the forest and they were soon flying thirty feet above the tallest treetops. The trees below them were all native trees, there were many Chillic Fruit trees and Bell Nut Fruit trees amongst them. The forest appeared thick and foreboding. This forest stand was far bigger than any of the others in the nearby meadows, being many miles across. The hovercar flew on its autopilot to a large clearing in the very centre of the forest.

As they flew over the clearing, they could all see the large house in its centre. It was partly above the ground and partly covered by soil, grass and shrubbery. Next to the house were four greenhouses and these and the house itself, were surrounded by its own smaller forest of Maple trees. Beyond those, there was a broad meadow several hundred metres wide, covered in bluegrass and wildflowers. The outer perimeter was lined by a tall cyclone wire fence, separating the clearing from the thick and foreboding forest of native trees. The hovercar landed at its usual landing pad and they all alighted the vehicle and stretched their legs. Yealah and her Daughter, Yeannah, unfurled the mighty Tholish wings with a crack and took to an impromptu flight around Sarlia's home before landing beside the hovercar.

"It feels so good to stretch our wings", Yealah remarked, trilling with joy.

Sarlia replied, *"You're welcome to fly anywhere you wish around this cleaning"*, but noted a warning, *"Be very careful of the forest beyond the fence line. There are predators in that forest."*

Yealah replied with a clear understanding, "Yes, we are aware of that. Our world, Homwol has many predators, even here in the valley. Far more so in the tall mountain forests to the north and south where we Thols live", her voice was laced with soft barks and clicks.

"Predators?", Ariel queried.

Kayala replied with a cautious tone, "Most are not a threat to us, but some are bigger and more dangerous young, Ariel. In the forests of Vale, you must be very careful."

Her Daughter, Kethera, elaborated, "The most dangerous is the...", she paused trying to translate the word from Carlinish to English, "I think that, Fearlessfang, is the best translation for it. We call them, Kyrrax. They run on all fours and are very fast, much faster than even us Carlin."

Yeannah nodded agreeing, "We call them, Zarynx. You don't want one of them stalking you. Seriously, you don't! Unless you are very quick and you can fly!"

Saffiera changed the topic, *"Now that you've planted those horrible images in Aria's and Ariel's minds, they'll be having nightmares all night. Perhaps we should all go inside."*

"Saffiera does have a point. Let's go inside and make ourselves comfortable", Sarlia agreed.

"Saffiera, Ariel and I don't have nightmares. We never have", Aria informed her, noting, "We've always turned our bad dreams into entertainment."

Sarlia took note of that, these twins were scions of Folcrom Tafazah and understanding them was extremely important.

Once they were inside Sarlia's and Saffiera's home, Sarlia told the girls, *"Follow Saffiera to her room and make yourselves at home. Your Mothers and I will prepare your dinner and bring it to you when it's ready."*

Saffiera took the lead, "Follow me, my room is this way, down the end of the hall."

The girls followed Saffiera to her room, while Sarlia led Yealah and Kayala to the main kitchen.

"While the girls are studying, we can prepare them something nice", Sarlia commented, then she placed a bottle of Martian Sweet Cherry Red wine on the kitchen table and added, *"Then, we can have a relaxing lady's evening."*

Yealah picked up the bottle of wine and read the label, trilling, "Martian Sweet Cherry Red wine from the CCF orchids of Hebes Island. I've seen this brand in the shops back in England. It is frightfully expensive. I can't image how much it costs out here, twenty two light years from Sol."

"One of the perks of my placement. The Council of Elders back on Mars sends me two crates of that wine every year", Sarlia noted, adding generously, *"I only drink*

maybe two bottles a year, so I have hundreds of them. I'll give you both a bottle or two each tomorrow before I take you home."

"That is very generous of you, Sarlia. This wine has a reputation. Those orchards are well over a thousand years old.", Yealah trilled, still holding the bottle and studying its label.

"Yes it is, but you know what, I can't drink over two hundred bottles myself", Sarlia confirmed, adding with a wry smile, *"Let's just hope that this one is not corked."*

Kayala asked, "But why do they send you so much of it?"

Sarlia replied, her eyes showing a great sadness, almost teary, *"To assuage their guilt and because they think I need it, Kayala. It was their decision that put my husband where he was when the accident that took his life occurred. Young, Saffiera, was only three at the time"*, she paused, as her tears flowed, and then she added, *"I drank a lot of this wine after that. I was a Martian Elder drinking far too much back then."*

"So they sent you here?", Yealah asked with a soft bark.

Sarlia wiped away her tears, *"Yes, they did and I refused to go at first."*

"The other Martian Elders all told me that I could not refuse them", Sarlia recounted, then she noted, *"They sarcastically told me, that they would send me a crate of CCF Sweet Cherry Red wine every year if I agreed."*

"I told them sarcastically, to make it two and they agreed and then they put Saffiera and me on the very next flight to Xi Bootis A Secundus", Sarlia continued, noting, *"I had no idea where this world was at the time. Such was their desire to be rid on me"*, the tears welled and Yealah embraced her with both her arms and mighty wings.

While Yealah held Sarlia, Kayala dabbed at her tears with a tissue, "Well you are here now and you do have friends", she comforted.

"Yes, thank you", Sarlia thanked them, as she pulled herself back together, self-consciously commenting, "*I cannot let Saffiera see me like this"*, then she gave a little telepathic chuckle, *"The irony is, now, I hardly drink at all anymore."*

Kayala joked, "If this wine is as expensive as Yealah says, you should have told them ten crates, just to annoy the hell out of them."

Sarlia smiled and gave off a small telepathic chuckle.

Kayala and Yealah helped Sarlia compose herself and then they went back to making dinner for the evening. Their children and the twins did need to be fed after all. The girls meanwhile, had already connected to the network and were calling up the next section of their studies, The Great Explosion, the Outward Interplanetary Expansion, the section concerning the colonisation of Jupiter's Lagrangian points, the Trojan Asteroids. The week it turned out had been harrowing, not just for Saffiera, Kethera and Yeannah, but also, surprisingly for Sarlia.

Stuart Dumas was waiting for some guests to arrive at his office. They were from the Jovian Trojan Colonisation Consortium, a loose group of companies, each with an interest in colonising Jupiter's Trojan points. Specifically, they wanted to discuss proposals to colonise the largest Asteroids in Jupiter's Leading and Trailing points. The asteroid Hector at Jupiter L-Four and the twin asteroids Patroclus and Menoetius at Jupiter L-Five. Stuart and his personal assistant Tegan had already read through the proposals.

They were not as simple as the consortium had thought. These asteroids were massive behemoths and Hector alone was three hundred and seventy kilometres long and one hundred and ninety five kilometres wide. The twin asteroids were much smaller, yet they were still enormous in their own right.

The largest component of the pair, Patroclus, was one hundred and seventeen by one hundred and ten kilometres in size. The smaller component, Menoetius, was more spherical, with a rough diameter of one hundred and four kilometres. All three were huge and presented a massive engineering challenge.

The guests arrived and were greeted by Tegan who led into a nearby conference room. Tegan showed them to their seats and pointed out the refreshments on the conference table in front of them. Then Tegan assured them that Mr Dumas would be with them shortly, after which, she left the room to notify Stuart of their arrival.

The guests were very anxious to discuss their proposals with Stuart Dumas. They had seen what Stuart had achieved in the Trojan points of the Earth and Venus, and along with Victor Himmelstaff, the Trojan points of Mars as well. Most impressive of all, was Stuart's work with the colonisation of the thirteen Belter colonies and the independent status they had achieved.

The guests had communicated with Harrison Moon, the Ceresian Administrator and he had given Dumas Incorporated Industries a glowing review. Most importantly Harrison Moon had described Stuart Dumas as both a visionary and a man who could be trusted.

The door of the conference room opened and in walked five people, including Tegan Smith, whom they had already met.

Tegan introduced the team that followed her into the room, "This is Mr Victor Himmelstaff, his personal assistant, Ms Susan Carter, Mr Baron Dumas and of course, Mr Stuart Dumas."

The three representatives of the Jovian Trojan Colonisation Consortium all stood up and Tegan introduced them, "Gentlemen. Our guests are Mr Ulrick Carlson, Mr Collin Nightingale and Ms Sheila Sharky", and the two groups began shaking hands.

The three guests sat at one end of the table. Stuart, Baron and Victor sat across from them at the other end. Their personal assistants, took seats at the sides of the table, Tegan on Stuart's right and Susan on Victor's left. Both women had folios stacked in front of them. Oddly enough, Stuart's Son, Baron, was sitting in between both Victor and Stuart.

Baron opened the meeting, "Ladies, Gentlemen. We have read your proposals in detail and we do find them highly intriguing. So much so that we invited Victor here for this meeting."

Victor spoke next, "Together, the three of us have more knowledge and expertise in what you're proposing than anyone else in the solar system", then he corrected himself, "My apologies ladies. I should have said the five of us. Susan and Tegan are most invaluable."

Stuart then spoke, "We ran your proposals past our engineers. All trusted people", he assured them, "They did find some problems. Minor problems that will require careful consideration."

"Problems?", Ulrick Carlson queried.

Baron smiled and replied, "Mr Carlson, your consortium wants to core out three asteroids, Hector, Patroclus and Menoetius. Essentially creating massive versions of Eros", he noted, then pointed out, "There is nowhere in this proposal, where surface reshaping and exterior regolith vitrification is mentioned. Those are critical for structural stability."

"Surface reshaping and exterior regolith vitrification", a confused Sheila Sharky questioned.

Baron launched into an explanation, trying not to be too technical, "Yes. If you want these behemoths to be rotated to generate artificial gravity, then surface reshaping to a more cylindrical shape is necessary. More importantly, they will need enhanced structural stability and of course, they need to hold in air, so melting and compressing the exterior surface is also necessary."

Collin Nightingale chimed in, "We were not aware of those requirements."

"That is why you came to us, Mr Nightingale", Stuart took over, noting, "Rotating asteroids of this size means you must increase structural integrity. You also need to hold in any atmosphere that you create. The remedy is the same in both cases. We basically heat up the exterior and vitrify or glass it to a depth of at least two hundred and fifty metres."

Victor Himmelstaff chimed in, "At least. Note that. The proposed asteroids are as Baron noted, behemoths. They may need to be glassed to an even deeper depth. Stuart's engineers can do the math to decide exactly how deep. We do have the technology to do this."

Sheila Sharky was quite surprised by all of this and replied, "Thank you, gentlemen. It looks like we came to the right people."

Ulrick Carlson and Collin Nightingale agreed almost in unison, "Definitely!"

Ms Sharky enquired, “Were there any other issues?”

“Well, yes, Ms Sharky”, Baron replied, noting, “Once cored out, the interior should also be vitrified to depth as well. That will ensure a double layer of structural integrity and imperviousness.”

Stuart chimed in, “Then of course, your plans also include massive docking hubs, the same as were created for both ends of Eros. Those are completely unnecessary in these cases. You will save a lot of time and a great deal of credits by simply dropping that concept entirely.”

Collin Nightingale was perplexed, “Wait! You told us, that we need to glass both the exterior and the interior to depth to hold in the air, but we don't need docking hubs?”

Baron supplied him with the answer, “Mr Nightingale, Hector will be rotating at point one zero nine revolutions per minute at the interior surface. That's one gravity of centrifugal force. The central axis is seventy five kilometres from the interior surface. You can have the central axis open to space and not lose any appreciable amount of atmosphere. It's the same for the smallest of the three as well. Menoetius is wide enough to provide the same effect. For Hector, you could have free spaceport access via an opening as much as twenty kilometres in diameter.”

Ulrick Carlson replied questioningly, “That sounds absolutely crazy! Are you sure?”

Victor smiled and chuckled, “The Earth's atmosphere has been contained by gravity for millions of years. Anything that is lost to space is just replaced by outgassing.”

Stuart chimed in, “In these cases, the Sun's solar wind will have almost zero effect. So any atmospheric loss will be minimal and easily topped up as necessary.”

“How much are we going to save on that point?”, Collin Nightingale enquired of his colleagues.

Sheila Sharky replied, “We can't really calculate that at present, however, I suspect, it is a lot.”

Stuart noted, “You have to remember, the three proposed asteroids are behemoths compared to Eros and the same rules can't be applied. Our engineering department can rework your designs for both cost efficiency and practicality.”

Tegan stepped in, “If I may, Mr Dumas. I took the liberty of running the concept for Hector past our engineers. Here is what they came up with. It's just a quick concept and needs more work, but it is a starting point”, then she passed a sketch to their guests.

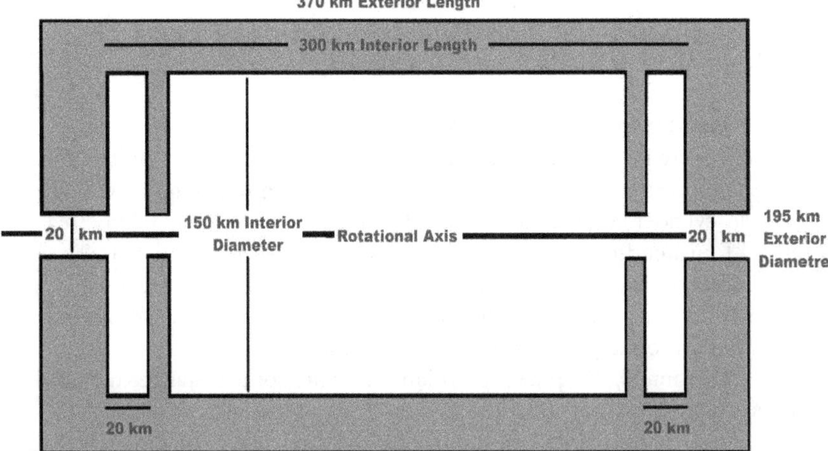

Ms Sharky enquired, "Why the two smaller chambers at both ends? Why not one huge cavity?"

Baron had seen the sketch and he explained, "It took two decades and longer to core out Eros. Hector is on a whole new scale altogether. You are talking about centuries, at the very least more than one. Our engineers used their experience with coring out Eros to come up with this quick sketch."

Tegan added, "This is a time scale issue, Ms Sharky. Those two cavities at either end are achievable within your lifespan. The main cavity is not. You won't see it completed, although your descendants will. So you can, using those two cavities at either end, colonise Hector, while the centuries-long work of coring out the big central cavity continues well into the future."

Ms Sharky cradled her chin in her hands, staring at the sketch for a very long minute, before replying, "Your people are very thorough, Ms Smith. Can they rework all of our designs?"

"If you wish, Ms Sharky, that will not be a problem. I assure you", Tegan replied.

Baron noted, "In the distant future, when the central cavity is completed, those two smaller cavities can become spacious spaceports with a huge docking capacity."

Stuart Dumas took over, "We can have our engineers put together a clear, concise path for terraforming Hector, Patroclus and Menoetius. If you want us to proceed with that, no problems, they are just engineering issues. Long-term engineering issues", he told them, however, we are in the here and now, "So here is what we can do for you right now."

Ulrick Carlson stepped in, "Mr Dumas, I can state right away that we are very interested in your company's engineering expertise."

Collin Nightingale and Sheila Sharky both agreed, with Sheila adding, "Let's hear what you can do for us, Mr Dumas."

Stuart nodded to Victor's personal assistant, Susan, who then began, "Well, if you are going to colonise the Trojan asteroid fields of Jupiter, you will need colonies to base yourselves in. We are recommending two O'Neil-style, twin-cylinder colonies. Each cylinder will be one point six kilometres long and four hundred metres wide, with two hemispherical end caps. The total combined capacity of all four end caps will be greater than twenty thousand colonists. That does not include the main cylinder surface areas."

"That does sound good", Ulrick Carlson noted.

Susan continued, "As Jupiter's Trojans are quite some distance from the Sun, the colony's main strip windows will be larger and given a concave surface along their entire length to increase the capture of Sunlight. The curvature will be calculated for maximum safe capture. We will also be installing the latest fission reactors. Five in all for each cylinder, installed into the cylinder's tail booms for safety reasons, of course."

Collin Nightingale started clapping as soon as Susan had finished and Ulrick and Sheila quickly joined in, "That sounds fantastic!", Sheila exclaimed.

Susan noted, "Wait. There is more. The two colonies will be constructed here in Cis-Lunar L-Four. You will have a choice of either Himmelstaff Interplanetary Constructions or Dumas Colonial Constructions. Both, if you wish. The end result will be the same, the same materials, the same quality and the same timeline. Our two corporations collaborate all the time."

Sheila, Collin and Ulrick all nodded in understanding.

Tegan Smith chimed in, "Of course, once those colony cylinders are built, you need to ship them to their respective Jovian Trojan destinations. For that, we have Cis-Lunar Haulage. We have space tugs more than capable of hauling those four new cylinders to Hector and the twin asteroids, Patroclus and Menoetius. Part of the service of hauling, includes, unfurling of the strip windows, aligning the cylinders with the Sun, guy wiring them together and installing the transport tubing."

Sheila asked incredulously, "You throw that all in as part of the service?"

"Of course we do, Ms Sharky. Our people will likely be the only ones out there with that expertise", Tegan informed her, noting, "We will even train your people how to run the fission reactors. If necessary, even seconding our own staff to your colonies until your own people are proficient."

"That is remarkable", Tegan replied, she had realised how support was being offered.

"We have to provide that level of service, Ms Sharky", Stuart replied, noting, "We cannot allow a single colony to fail. Not a single one, not ever!"

Susan chimed in, "Orbital stations, like mobile mining, ore processing and manufacturing stations can also be manufactured by either Himmelstaff Interplanetary Constructions or Dumas Colonial Constructions. Again, the choice is yours to make. They will be docked onto the colony cylinder's tail booms for transport with the cylinders themselves."

"So, pretty much everything we need to set up a colony, Dumas Incorporated can arrange", Collin Nightingale asked.

Victor replied, "That is correct, Mr Nightingale. By working under the Dumas Incorporated and Himmelstaff Consolidated Industries umbrellas, combined, we can achieve the economies of scale that enable us to provide complete colonisation solutions. Everything is included."

Sheila asked a question, that had been on her mind during the meeting, "Why Dumas Incorporated and Himmelstaff Consolidated Industries?"

Baron replied, noting, "We are family. I'm married to, Victor's Daughter, Hypolita. So when a proposal like this comes along, we both work together to ensure it gets done and done right."

Sheila nodded in understanding.

Tegan stepped back in, "We have designated the two colonies, Hector Central and Patroclus Central for the moment, you can change those later names if you wish. Once they're been completed, we move into the next phase. Our space tugs, two at each location, will haul together a number of smaller nearby asteroids into, what we call *'conglomerated asteroidal masses'*. These will be nudged into safe orbits around the relevant asteroids. One creates a new *'moon'* around Hector and the other creates a new *'moon'* orbiting the barycentre of the Patroclus-Menoetius twin asteroid system."

Ulrick Carlson commented, "Yes, Harrison Moon told us about that. We did wonder if you had something similar in stall for us."

Baron stepped in, "It creates stable libration points, L-One, L-Two, L-Four and L-Five, that are remarkably useful. You can place your colonies into halo orbits around the new L-Five points and your ore processing and manufacturing stations likewise in the new L-Four points. The other two points are a bonus. The mobile mining stations can then get down to the business of coring out those asteroids."

Ulrick Carlson nodded in understanding.

Then Sheila Sharky asked, "What about financing?"

Victor smiled, "That would be through Dumas Colonial Financial. Mr

Dumas might even offer the same deal that the Belter Administrators requested."

"I'm not sure I understand that one. Administrator Moon did explain it, but it sounded so esoteric", Sheila Sharky admitted.

Tegan explained, "The Belters didn't want to be under the jurisdiction of the Colonisation Committee or the Security Council, something about boots on throats. Anyway, we restructured their final loan repayments. One credit per standard year forever, with the interest rates reduced to not accrue an overly large debt."

Sheila put her hands to her chin wondering what Tegan meant.

Tegan elaborated, "Under the Earth Government's own definition, a colony is not officially online until the final loan repayment is completed. At one credit per year, the loan continues to remain open and the colony is never officially online, even though it is completed."

Sheila laughed, "Oh my God. That is brilliant! Who came up with that one?"

Tegan laughed, it was unprofessional, but Sheila's laugh was contagious, "Harrison Moon's twelve-year-old Grand Daughter, Harmony."

A shocked look came over Sheila's face, "Holy crap! A twelve-year-old!", she mumbled.

Ulrick chimed in, "We will definitely want that clause."

Collin agreed, "Absolutely!"

And so the colonisation of the Trojan colonies of Jupiter began.

The girls all began discussing the Trojan colonisation as their Mothers brought in their dinners. As Sarlia and Saffiera were Martians, the food was vegetarian fare, along with Sarlia's first attempt at making mushroom pies. Kayala helped out by showing Sarlia the finer points of pie-making, while Yealah helped prepare some Tholish vegetarian cuisine. The twins of course being Humans of Earth ancestry would have preferred meat, they did, however, find the food to be delicious.

Aria noted, "That Dumas guy had his hands in so many pies", as she bit into a mushroom pie.

Ariel replied, "Stuart Dumas, started off as a farmer's son, with only one space tug and one company, Cis-Lunar Haulage. From there he branched out into asteroid mining, massive scale warehousing, materials importation, construction, financial and even legal services."

"That's my point, Ariel. Stuart Dumas ended up providing end-to-end services to anyone who came to him with a viable plan to colonise the outer solar system", Aria explained, "He was quite brilliant."

"Wait!", Yeannah exclaimed, "Aria, I thought you hated economics?", she questioned.

"Well, yeah, Yeannah. I do, but that was before I could see where this was going", Aria replied.

"This is amazing", Kethera remarked, "I have never seen Aria being so constructive."

"Oh, Kethera. Do you really think that I'm the flippant arsehole that I pretend to be?", Aria replied not waiting for an answer, instead continuing, "Stuart Dumas came up with a winning formula for colonising the Asteroid Belt. He prototyped the method with Harrison Moon and Ceres and then carried it forward to twelve more asteroids in the Asteroid Belt. He then propagated the same methodology to Jupiter's Trojans asteroid fields. I can't wait to see what else he got up to!"

Ariel looked at her twin Sister with mock suspicion, "Who are you and what have you done with my Sister, Aria?", she laughed.

The Mothers all looked quite surprised and Sarlia sent Kayala and Yealah a private thought, *"Young Aria is evolving right before her eyes. Self-deprecating, self-aware, critically thinking. These are all remarkably positive developments."*

Aria looked up at Saffiera's Mother, Sarlia and commented, "I actually heard that thought."

Ariel noted as well, "Actually, so did I."

Sarlia looked surprised, *"Aria, Ariel. You both heard my thought?"*, she questioned, then noted, *"I transmitted it privately."*

Aria replied simply, "We both still heard it. You know, self-deprecating, self-aware, critically thinking. Positive evolution, that sort of thing."

Saffiera looked at her Mother, *"You did awaken their latent abilities and they are both scions. If I remember our history correctly. Martians can't hide their thoughts from the scions."*

"Yes", Sarlia agreed, *"You are quite correct. I did not expect the twins to awaken so*

quickly."

"So, Aria's new outlook is a part of her awakening?", Ariel asked.

"Yes, Ariel. You are both awakening", Sarlia confirmed and requested, *"Please allow my Saffiera to guide you. Her own experiences will be invaluable to you both."*

Saffiera replied, a big grin on her face, *"That's me, Saffiera, telepathic guide extraordinaire."*

The girls all cracked up laughing.

The Mothers all left Saffiera's bedroom and went back to the kitchen, they had a lovely bottle of Martian Sweet Cherry Red wine to drink. The girls then went back to recapping their studies.

Kethera commented, "Colonising Jupiter's Trojan asteroids was different to the Belter colonies. I mean, none of the Belters were hollowing out their asteroids."

"Kethera is right, that is a big difference", Yeannah agreed, then noted, "What they were doing was very similar to what was done to Mimas, where I was born. A hollowed-out moon of Saturn. Mimas was built as a generation ship long ago in the Xi Bootis system. My people built it, although it was the Tarlaks who took over it back then. After the Tarlak's defeat in the Mimasian War, it became my people's refuge."

Saffiera replied, noting telepathically, *"The intriguing thing is, it was all their idea. The colonists didn't even know that Mimas was hollow at that time."*

Ariel commented, "Mimas is a good analogy, but not quite. The asteroids that they were hollowing out, were planned to have cylindrical cavities so that rotating them would provide artificial gravity."

"That is true", Yeannah agreed, noting, "The interior of Mimas is spherical, so it uses a combination of rotation and gravity plating to provide artificial gravity. That does create some weird effects, especially in the tunnels inside its rock shell."

Aria commented, "Concealing your people's existence for so long was made so much easier because they all lived inside of an innocuous moon."

Yeannah smiled, "I guess it was, although, they did have Earth Humans living within Mimas. They dealt with all the outside communications at the time. Mimas was considered a private, sovereign colony during that period.

The Martians lived side by side with my Thol ancestors inside of Mimas, with a mere handful of Earth Humans protecting us for hundreds of years. Those few Earth Humans protected our peoples right up till the Great Reveal and they asked nothing in return."

Saffiera added to the story, *"It was a handful of Earth Humans that helped to conceal my people that remained on Mars as well. As you said, Yeannah, right up till the Great Reveal."*

Aria went back to her irreverent self, "I bet there were hybrids!"

Saffiera replied, smiling, *"Whenever you put Earth Humans and Martian Humans together, there will always be hybrids, Aria. That is a universal truth."*

Kethera had an important question, "The colonies in Jupiter's Trojans were set up in the same time frame as the Belter colonies, but the histories state clearly, that hollowing out those asteroids and terraforming would take centuries. It makes no mention of if and when they were completed?"

"Wow! Deep, Kethera, deep!", Aria replied, asking, "When were they completed?"

Yeannah replied, "Let's see", as she performed a few searches on her tablet and sent the results to the screen on Saffiera's bedroom wall.

Ariel read out the results, "The smaller of the twin asteroids, Menoetius, was completed in the later twenty forth century. The primary asteroid, Patroclus, was completed in the early twenty fifth century."

"So, that would be thirty to fifty years after the second Horridian War", Aria noted.

"Yes, Aria. That is the right time frame", Ariel agreed, continuing, "Hector was huge. Much, much bigger, that one was completed in the mid-twenty sixth century. They are all still inhabited to this day."

"Yes, I remember, Ariel", Saffiera remarked as she looked into her passed-down, shared memories, *"The Hector colony was completed about a decade after the Great Reveal."*

Aria noted dryly, "They started hollowing out those asteroids not long after the turn of the twenty second century. It literally took the builders centuries to complete!"

"That it did, Aria, that it did", Yeannah agreed.

The Mothers sat in the kitchen, they had already finished off the first bottle of Martian Sweet Cherry Red wine and were halfway through the second. Kayala had mentioned that she really shouldn't drink too much, something about Carlins getting drunk far too easily. Sarlia and Yeannah both agreed, yet somehow they finished the second bottle and started on a third.

They talked about their Daughters, comparing notes and parenting tips. Martians, Carlins and Mimasian Thols all had their own methods. None of them knew anything about Indigenous Thol parenting techniques, not even Yealah. They even discussed the twins and their latent abilities. At some point, Kayala even suggested bringing the twins Mother into their little group. They did not even know her name, something they decided to remedy. Then they opened the fourth bottle of Martian Sweet Cherry Red wine.

Kayala was more than a little tipsy when she mentioned that she would love to adopt all of the girls, unofficial of course, something about how they slept just like Carlin kits during their sleepovers. She did mention it more than once, Yealah and Sarlia found that endearing. They understood the strong maternal instincts that all Carlin Mothers had and the girls all sleeping together like Kit Sisters would definitely trigger those. Kayala more than once called them Sister Friends, declaring them to be kits.

After the fourth bottle of Martian Sweet Cherry Rad was empty, they decided to call it a night. They checked in on the girls, who were all sleeping together on the floor, as they had the previous sleepover at Kayala's house. Saffiera in the middle, Kethera on her left and Yeannah on her right. Ariel snuggled up beside Kethera and Aria snuggled up beside Yeannah. Kayala noted, that her Kethera was purring contently.

"You see! Just like Carlin Kit Sisters", Kayala had quietly remarked, reinforcing her beliefs.

Kayala was, of course, quite drunk.

Martian Sweet Cherry Red wine had a reputation for being both sweet, flavoursome and strong!

Then the Mothers went back to their rooms and changed into their night attire. Having done so, Sarlia and Yealah found Kayala standing in the doorway of her assigned bedroom, staring into it.

"Is something wrong, Kayala?", Sarlia telepathically asked.

"The room is too empty, too cold, too lonely. I cannot sleep in there", Kayala whispered in reply, her ears were folded down and her whiskers were drooping, there was no movement in her tail at all.

Sarlia was perplexed and turned to Yealah looking for an answer.

Yealah spoke softly, melodically to Kayala, trilling, "Hey, honey, it's only for one night."

Kayala shook her head, "It is too quiet. It is too unnatural."
"*Yealah, I don't understand*", Sarlia admitted.
"I thought that this might be a problem", Yealah noted, explaining, "Carlins never sleep alone!"
"Oh, really. I had no idea", Sarlia replied.
"Yes", Yealah confirmed, adding, "From the moment a Carlin is born, they never at any point sleep alone. As a newborn, they sleep with their Parents and later they sleep with their Brothers or Sisters. After they bond, they sleep with their Partner and then the cycle repeats. Kayala, being drunk certainly does not help", her voice laced with soft barks, trills and clicks.

Sarlia's solution was simple, she smiled warmly and told Kayala, *"It's okay. You don't have to sleep in that bedroom, Kayala. Tonight, we are all Friend Sisters, so we'll all sleep in my bedroom."*
"Are you sure?", Yealah barked softly.
"Absolutely", Sarlia confirmed.
Yealah took Kayala by the hand and told her, "It's okay, honey, let's all sleep in Sarlia's bed. Tonight, we are all Friend Sisters, just like kits", and Kayala began to smile.
The three Mothers then entered Sarlia's bedroom, climbed onto her bed and slept together for the night, just like Carlin kits with a tangled mess of limbs. They had all drunk quite a bit of the Martian Sweet Cherry Red wine and their pending hangovers were a tomorrow problem.
The Mother's Lady's night had come to a close.

23. The Jovian Dream.

Carlins live in households full of kits and in the mornings those kits awaken early and start to play. This in turn means the entire household awakens early. So naturally at Saffiera's house, Kethera was the first person to awaken. Kethera sat up and looked around, her friends were all still fast asleep, so she got up to find her Mother. After all, a Carlin Mother never had a chance to sleep in.

First Kethera walked down the long hallway to the kitchen, it was empty. As were the four bottles of Martian Sweet Cherry Red wine on the kitchen table. Kethera looked at the empty wine bottles. Carlins do not handle alcohol very well at all. Kethera picked up one of the bottles and carefully read the label. Kethera's Mother, Kayala, was likely still asleep, so back down the long hallway she went.

There were eight bedrooms off of the long hallway. Saffiera's bedroom was at the very end on the left and her Mother, Sarlia's bedroom was at the end on the right. All of the bedroom doors were closed, except for Saffiera's, which Kethera had just left and Sarlia's, which was slightly ajar. Kethera peeked inside the room. There before her were the three Mothers, all fast asleep on Sarlia's bed. Kayala was in the middle, with Sarlia on her left and Yealah on her right. Yealah was on the edge of the bed, with her left wing unfurled and lazily hanging down the side of the bed.

A bemused look came over Kethera's face and she silently giggled to herself, *"They look just like a bundle of Carlin kits, just bigger"*, she mused to herself.

It also made perfect sense, Carlins never slept alone. Sarlia and Yealah were both simply supporting Kayala. Kethera sniffed the air, it was stale and there was the distinct smell of wine to it, so she walked into the room and quietly opened the window on the far side to let in some fresh air. Vale's primary Sun, Cathol, was rising and as Cythol had already risen, the sky outside took on an eerie orange glow.

As long as one of Vale's two Suns was in the sky, it was never really dark on Vale and even when they weren't, Vale's large Moon, Luns, would cast its silvery reflected light as well. The sky would turn much brighter soon enough with Cathol rising. A slight breeze blew through the window, it was cool and crisp, smelling like the bluegrass meadows.

"Much better", Kethera thought to herself, *"This room needs some fresh air."*

Kethera made her way back down the hallway to the kitchen where she searched the cupboards, locating the glasses and a pitcher. Kethera went to the fridge and filled the pitcher using bottled cold water. The bottle was labelled *"Maple Water"*. After which, she placed three glasses and the pitcher on a serving tray, that she had also found in the kitchen. Then Kethera went back down the hallway, entered Sarlia's room once more and placed the tray on the dressing table. Kethera then sat down on the end of the bed and watched her Mother, waiting for her to awaken. Kayala purred with contentment, getting a very rare chance to sleep in.

Yealah awoke first and teetered on the edge of the bed, Kethera quickly reached out and grabbed her right wrist, steadying her, lest she fall off of the bed and onto the floor.

"Thank you, Kethera", Yealah whispered, trilling quietly so as not to wake the others.

"You're welcome", Kethera replied, then gesturing to the dressing table. "I brought in some cold water and glasses. It's Maple Water. I'm not sure what that is, but it smells slightly sweet."

Yealah got up and climbed off of the bed, then she walked over to the dressing table and poured herself a glass of water, "Thank you again, Kethera", after drinking some, she commented, "Kethera, honey. Last night we drank far too much Martian wine", her trilling sounded just a little rough.

A bemused smile came over Kethera and she replied, "I know. I found the empty bottles", then she noted, "Carlins are not noted for drinking strong drinks. That Martian Sweet Cherry Red wine had twelve percent alcohol in it, which is probably four times stronger than the Carlinish Chillic or Bell Nut Fruit wine that we make."

"Honey, when we were back on the Earth, we saw people drinking drinks that were much stronger", Yealah replied, remembering their time in Yorkshire in England, "Some Human drinks contain over fifty percent alcohol. No Thol nor Carlin could handle that. The Human tolerance for toxins is truly unbelievable. They can eat and drink things that would have us writhing with stomach pains. This Maple Water is sweet and refreshing by the way."

Yeannah and Saffiera in the meanwhile had woken up. They found their way into Sarlia's bedroom.

Upon seeing her Mother sitting on the edge of the bed, with both Kayala and Sarlia still cuddled up together and sound asleep, Yeannah commented, "Oh, that is so cute! We should take a picture!"

"Yeannah, honey, please don't. Mothers take stolen photos of their children, not the other way around", Yealah advised her Daughter in Ancient Tholish, their native tongue.

Saffiera's face took on a stern look, *"Did my Mother get you both drunk?"*, she transmitted.

"No, honey. No one forced us to drink the wine", Yealah trilled softly, "Although, I think Kethera's Mum will be wishing she hadn't when she wakes up."

Sarlia began to stir, she looked up with bleary, red eyes and found, Kethera sitting on the edge of the bed, with Yeannah and Saffiera standing on either side of her. Saffiera had her arms crossed in front of her. Yeannah passed her a cold glass of Maple Water.

"Thank you, Yeannah", Sarlia responded, then to Saffiera, *"Why are you looking so grumpy?"*

"Aren't you supposed to be a Martian Elder?", Saffiera replied accusingly

"Oh, my little darling. Even Martian Elders need to kick back and have some fun every now and then", Sarlia replied as she took slow sips of cold water.

Saffiera gave her Mother a little dig, *"At least you all still have your night clothes on!"*

Sarlia rolled her eyes, "*Trust me, Saffiera, we were all far too drunk last night to have a menage a trois"*, she repeated, *"Far too drunk"*, she looked down at Kayala with concern.

Sarlia checked Kayala telepathically, "*Your Mother is okay, Kethera. She is just recovering. I won't let her drink so much next time*", then she smiled, "*Carlins do like to party though.*"

Yealah asked quietly, trilling, "A menage a trois?"

Sarlia replied with a telepathic chuckle, *"Yealah, have you not looked in a mirror lately"*, then as Yealah turned to look at her image in the large mirror above the dressing table, *"I mean, Carlinish women are beautiful, but Tholish women are next level gorgeous. It's as if you were designed and created by the Gods themselves."*

Saffiera sighed, *"It's apparently a trait with us Martians. We are supposedly, incorrigibly promiscuous with either gender or any species"*, then she gestured to her Mother.

Sarlia sighed, *"To be entirely honest, Ladies, I cannot disagree with that statement."*

Yealah stared at herself in the mirror, trilling, "Back on the Earth, some people called us Angels."

"The more religious kind would", Sarlia noted, adding, *"In the Earth's deep past, Tarlaks visited and they were labelled as devils and demons. They ended up recorded as such and became myths and legends. To this day, the Earth Government does not even confirm the existence of Tarlaks on Homwol. They probably never will."*

Kethera commented "You guys go and make yourselves some breakfast. I'll stay here with my Mother until she wakes up", then she climbed onto the bed and wrapped her arms around Kayala.

The others all left the bedroom and walked down the hallway to the kitchen. The freshly awoken twins, having heard the commotion, quickly followed.

It had been around six thirty a.m. when Kethera had awoken, it was slightly after nine a.m. when Kethera and her Mother, Kayala, walked down the hallway. Kayala's ears were flat, her whiskers were drooping as far as they could and her eyes were bleary and red. Kayala's pupil slits were almost closed!

As Kethera helped her Mother to the kitchen, Yealah remarked, with a few soft barks, "Oh, honey, you do not look well at all", then she got up and helped her to the table, where she sat down.

"I'll feel better after I have something to eat", Kayala assured her, then she commented, "That Martian Sweet Red Cherry wine was so strong!"

"Ah ha", Sarlia replied, *"Kethera was saying, it's four times stronger than what you're used to."*

"That would do it", Kayala smiled.

Yealah smiled and replied, "Honey, next time, we'll not let you have more than two glasses. Okay!"

"That, sounds like a plan", Kayala agreed, then after looking around, "Where are the kits?"

Sarlia answered, *"They're in Saffiera's bedroom studying"*, then she apologised, *"I am so sorry, Kayala. I should have cut you off after two glasses."*

"That was on me. I should have stopped drinking much earlier", Kayala replied, with a slight smile.

Yealah, who was sitting beside Kayala, wrapped her right arm and wing around her in support.

"Are you going to be okay, Mum?", Kethera asked, then noted, "I really should join my friends."

"I am fine, little one. You run along and study", Kayala replied, managing to smile, her whiskers were beginning to lift once more.

Kethera skipped down the hallway towards Saffiera's bedroom.

Kayala remarked, still managing to smile, "It was quite a night", then she gave off a little giggle and her tail began to swish back and forth once more.

The Jovian Trojan Colonisation Consortium had chosen to split the construction of their two colonies between Dumas Colonial Constructions, to build Hector Central and Himmelstaff Interplanetary Constructions, to build Patroclus Central. Both colonies were being constructed in the company's respective construction zones within Cis-Lunar L-Four.

The designs were both identical and by choosing both construction companies, both of the colonies could be constructed simultaneously, saving considerably on time. The two companies would also construct the relevant mining, ore processing and manufacturing stations for each colony. There were three orbital stations of each station type, for each colony in the initial phase, with another three of each to follow later after the colonies were delivered to their respective final destinations.

It wasn't long before colony construction was well under, as the enormous frameworks for each cylinder began to show. Vast spans of thick metal girders were manoeuvred into place by even larger space cranes and space hauliers. The entire process had to be perfect.

In space, without the presence of an atmosphere and with clean un-oxidized, metal surfaces, the bonding is not simply a *"process used to connect them together"*, but a phenomenon, known as, *"cold-welding"*, where the metal atoms can fuse under certain conditions. The final result would be an enormous framework that appeared to be a single continuous construction.

They were huge skeletal structures, clearly forming into the shape of the four main cylinders and their end caps. Just like the building of the Belter Colonies before them, the inner solar system was abuzz with the news. News of the bold colonisation attempt of the Jovian Trojan points hit the news feeds. Those locations were so far from the Sun or the Earth. With the previous success of the Belter Colonies and now with this new *"Trojan"* development, more new clients turned up in Tegan's office reception area. They all had their own bold new plans.

The first of these new potential clients was an organisation calling itself, *"The Jovian Dream"*. It was a loose consortium of various small groups and companies. Other colonial financial institutions had called their plans insane. When news of Dumas Incorporated Industry's and Himmelstaff Consolidated Industry's, work with the Jovian Trojan Colonisation Consortium made headlines, they attempted to contact Stuart Dumas as soon as they could. They considered it urgent, as they wanted to be the first to colonise Jupiter itself and that meant being the first to get inside Stuart Dumas's office.

Tegan Smith answered her communicator, "Tegan Smith here. How may I help you?"

"It's security down in the lobby, Ms Smith", the security officer answered, "We have a couple of people down here who want to see Mr Dumas. They are saying it is urgent."

Tegan replied, "Mr Dumas does not have any meetings scheduled for the day. They will need to make an appointment", then she had a feeling in her gut, "Wait! Who are they exactly?"

"They say they are from a consortium called The Jovian Dream", the security officer replied as he read their business cards, then noted, "Their names Mr Adam Cain and Ms Evelyn Abel."

It all sounded normal the way the security officer read out their names, but Tegan noticed something and smiled in bemusement, that gut feeling of hers was getting stronger.

"Please ask them to wait, while I check my sources", Tegan instructed the security officer.

Tegan began making some quick searches on the network. One window was open searching on The Jovian Dream, another was searching on the name, Adam Cain, while a third searched on, Evelyn Abel. A lot of information came up on the screen and Tegan quickly started taking notes in shorthand with her data tablet and stylus. The financial information that came up was particularly interesting, as was the overall mission statement of The Jovian Dream consortium. The data tablet's translation matrix quickly converted Tegan's scribbles into legible documents that she could make use of later. After less than five short minutes, Tegan tapped the windows with her stylus to close them. Then she turned to her communicator once more and gave the security officer some instructions.

"Please perform your usual due diligence and then have one of your security team members escort them up to my office", Tegan instructed the security officer.

"Yes, Ma'am", the security officer replied.

Within fifteen minutes a security team member showed Adam Cain and Evelyn Abel into Ms Tegan Smith's office. At first impressions, these two appeared quite young. Adam could not have been much more than twenty five years old and Evelyn not much less than twenty five. They both carried briefcases. Tegan stood up from her desk and greeted them both warmly, before directing them to some seating arranged around a coffee table. As they sat down, Tegan dismissed the security team member and then took up a seat on the other side of the coffee table.

"So, Mr Cain, Ms Abel, what is so urgent that it could not wait for an appointment?", Tegan asked, then noted in warning, "If you want to speak to Mr Dumas, it will need to be a very good story."

Mr Cain and Ms Abel spent the next fifteen minutes explaining the consortium's plans, while Tegan took down more shorthand notes on her data tablet. Every now and again, Tegan would ask them some poignant questions and note their responses, even going so far as to instruct her data tablet's A.I. to gather further information. Her stylus was moving faster than either of her guests could follow.

When Adam and Evelyn had finally finished their pitch, Tegan commented, "You do have some interesting plans, however, I can see quite a few problems with them."

Evelyn sighed, "So you just think we're crazy just like everyone else."

"I did not say that, Ms Abel", Tegan replied reassuringly, "I said your plans have quite a few problems, however, problems always have solutions. We just have to look at them long enough. A lot of what Stuart Dumas does was considered crazy in the past. Now it's just run of the mill."

Tegan stood up and straightened her double-breasted blazer, "Please wait here. I will speak with Mr Dumas", then Tegan walked over to a door on the other side of her office, well behind her desk.

Tegan entered Stuart's office and asked, "Mr Dumas. Did you receive my message?"

"Yes, Tegan. I am looking at it now", Stuart replied, commenting, "Very quickly put together and yet, nonetheless thorough. So, The Jovian Dream? Are they worth our trouble? What are your impressions, Tegan?"

"Yes, Sir. This is an intriguing business opportunity", Tegan responded, but warned, "Their plans are very raw and have a lot of problems, Sir, but nothing our people can't fix."

Stuart nodded his head in understanding, "I can see that. No fewer than nine rejections for finance and I agree with you, their plans need considerable work."

"One of the banks they approached, the financial consultant called them insane, Sir", Tegan commented, then she smiled wryly, "It would be worth taking them on just put that smug consultant in his place. Success is always the best revenge, Sir. As you, yourself, have always said."

Stuart Dumas chuckled, "Oh, Tegan. Since when have you ever been vengeful?"

Tegan replied, just a little playfully, "Sir. It would be divine justice. Just look at their names."

Stuart smiled and chuckled, "Cain and Abel?", he queried.

"Adam Cain and Evelyn Abel, Sir", Tegan replied, explaining, "Adam and Eve. Cain and Abel. If that is not divine providence, then I don't know what it is. The universe is sending us a message and to be honest, my gut agrees."

"Okay then, Tegan. Bring them in and we'll discuss their plans", Stuart decided.

Tegan led Adam and Evelyn into Stuart's office and showed them to some chairs in front of his desk.

Stuart opened the discussion straight away, "I have read Tegan's preliminary report", he told them, "You have a fascinating, yet somewhat flawed concept."

Adam remarked, "Preliminary report? We were only talking for ten minutes or so. How?", he asked.

"My personal assistant, Tegan, is very, very good at her job", Stuart replied, noting, "Tegan is more of a personal adviser, to be honest. If we proceed with your plans, you will both get to know Tegan very well, she will become your personal mentor."

Adam and Evelyn both looked at each other at that last comment.

Adam opened his briefcase and passed Stuart a copy of The Jovian Dream Consortium's plans. Stuart accepted Adam's document and then looked at Evelyn, assuming that there might be more documents in her briefcase.

Evelyn smiled and commented, "Oh. My briefcase just contains copies. I don't know why I brought it really", she admitted.

Stuart looked up at Tegan, then he turned back to the document and began speed-reading through it.

After a few minutes, Stuart looked up from the document, "Tegan, please pull up a seat", he instructed as he passed the document to her, then commented, "I like what I see here, Adam, Evelyn. It's raw, it's incomplete, but it is a good start."

Evelyn smiled, "A good start!", she was a little excited, "That's better than being called insane."

Stuart smiled a warm and disarming smile, "Your Jovian Dream is a loose consortium of various small groups and companies, even individuals. According to your own documentation, over five hundred. Banks don't really like that kind of setup. That was your first hurdle", he turned to Tegan.

Tegan automatically kicked in, "Your second hurdle was your actual plan. Your consortium wants to colonise Jupiter's Galilean Moons. Given the strength of Jupiter's radiation belts, that is probably why one of those bank financing consultants called your plans insane."

Adam frowned, "So, you can't help us?", he queried prematurely.

Tegan put up her hand, "Slow down, Adam. That is not what I said nor what I meant. We just need to work the problem."

Stuart stepped back in, "What Tegan means, is that we'll run your plans past our science and engineering divisions. We'll see what our boffins can come up with."

"Mr Dumas, Sir, I'd like to bring in Himmelstaff Consolidated on this as well", Tegan advised, noting, "Their collaboration will be invaluable."

"Agreed, Tegan, give Victor a call. I'm sure this will make his day", Stuart decided.

Evelyn was smiling now, "So you'll help us?", she asked.

Stuart replied, "Me? No, not just me. You'll have the backing of both Dumas Incorporated and Himmelstaff Consolidated. We often collaborate on these big colonisation plans. We will organise another meeting in about two weeks. Rest assured, that during that period of time, we will not entertain any other Jupiter colonisation plans or proposals."

Their meeting ended and Tegan showed Adam and Evelyn out of the office, to the elevators. She watched with a smile as they high-fived each other as the elevator doors closed.

Later, Tegan commented to Stuart, "Mr Dumas, Sir. Think about it, we'll be helping Adam and Eve colonise Jupiter", and then she laughed.

Stuart Dumas joined in.

The next meeting was scheduled and occurred three weeks later. Stuart and his colleagues were waiting in the conference room. His Son, Baron, sat in the middle seat, with Victor Himmelstaff sitting on his left. Stuart sat on Baron's right. Their personal assistants, took seats at the sides of the table, Tegan on Stuart's right and Susan on Victor's left. Both women had folios stacked in front of them.

Tegan's communicator buzzed and she answered it, after a few moments she announced, "Our guests are on their way up. I'll just go and greet them", and then she got up and left the conference room.

A few minutes later, Adam Cain and Evelyn Abel entered the conference room with Tegan following closely behind.

Stuart stood up and introduced his colleagues, "Good morning Adam, Evelyn, this is my Son, Baron, my colleague, Victor Himmelstaff and his personal assistant Susan Carter", he then turned to his colleagues, "This is Adam Cain and Evelyn Abel from the Jovian Dream Consortium. Everyone, of course, knows my personal assistant, Tegan Smith."

They all shook hands before Adam and Evelyn sat down in the seats provided.

Evelyn noted, "I recognise everyone's faces from the news feeds", she was somewhat excited.

"Yes, we do appear to be in the news quite often", Stuart replied.

Baron then stepped in, "If I may", Stuart nodded and then Baron began the meeting, "The biggest problem your original plan had was that your target colony sites were the Galilean Moons. Colonising those particular Moons will not be possible."

Adam replied, probably too quickly, "But that was the whole plan. Colonise the biggest Moons for the maximum resources."

Baron nodded, he understood why the four Galilean Moons were originally targeted, "Yes, we are well aware of that, Mr Cain", he then nodded to Tegan.

Tegan took a data sheet out of one of the folios and passed it to Adam, "The problem with the Galilean Moons, Mr Cain, is that they are all within Jupiter's extremely powerful and highly deadly radiation belts. The problem is one of lethal doses of radiation."

Adam read the data sheet and then passed it onto Evelyn, she read out the summary at the bottom of the page, "Lethality of the Galilean Moons: Io, lethal within minutes. Europe, lethal within hours. Ganymede, lethal within days. Callisto, lethal within weeks. Is there any way to mitigate these radiation risks?", she enquired.

Baron gave her the bad news, "Not with our current radiation shielding technology. Io and Europa are completely out of the equation. Ganymede is a difficult prospect and likely out of the equation as well. Callisto is possible with our current technology, but we have been advised against it. Any failure and it would be lethal for all concerned."

Evelyn replied, a shocked look on her face, "Now, I'm seeing why our plans were described as insane", she turned to Adam, "This pretty much puts a stop to the entire project."

Adam nodded in agreement, "It does look that way, Evelyn. That is unless Mr Dumas's people have come up with a better plan."

Baron replied, explaining, "We do have our research department working on better shielding. What we have could work with Callisto, but ultimately, what we really want is shielding that can handle the radiation at Io's distance from Jupiter."

Stuart chimed in with, "Personally, I want to see our researchers take it even further. Amalthea is far closer than Io and it has extremely promising mineral scans. However, I have been told that radiation mitigation will probably require exceedingly thick astcrete combined with electromagnetic deflectors. That could take decades to develop and fine-tune. In the meanwhile, Victor can give you an idea of what we can do at the present moment."

Victor Himmelstaff chimed in, "Mr Cain, we do have a couple of options for your consortium to consider", he then nodded to his personal assistant, Susan Carter, who reached into her folios for a list of Jupiter's other Moons, she passed it to Evelyn.

"Jupiter has a very large number of Moons, Mr Cain, Ms Abel. Many of them are within Jupiter's radiation belts, however, some are not", Susan informed them both, "I've highlighted the *'safe'* Moons in green. There are eight Moons above twenty kilometres in diameter and fourteen smaller ones. Sadly, most of the best Moons are within the radiation belts."

"So we do have options, with more than twenty Moons?", Evelyn queried.

"Yes", Susan continued, adding, "There are others as well, but they are so small as to be useful as resource mining sites only."

"Okay, that is a start", Adam noted, looking over at the document, "I notice one of those eight you mentioned is significant in size, one is over one hundred and fifty kilometres."

"Now, that is the spirit, Mr Cain", Victor Himmelstaff remarked.

"Indeed", Stuart Dumas agreed, then added, "And there is more", he nodded back to Tegan.

Tegan took out another document and handed it to Adam, "We have modified your plans to do what can be done, what's possible. We recommend colonising three libration points. The first point is Jupiter's Moon, Himalia's trailing Trojan point. The second point is at Jupiter's Lagrangian point one and the third at Jupiter's Lagrangian point two."

Adam thought for a moment, "So three colonies? How does that work out?"

Stuart replied, explaining, "Well, Adam. We build your consortium three good-sized twin-cylinder O'Neil-style colonies and of course, all of the relevant mining, ore processing and manufacturing stations. Once completed, we haul them all out from Cis-Lunar L-Four to each of the selected libration points in Jupiter's orbit. Each colony will have the capacity for over twenty thousand colonists. Victor and I both have the manufacturing capacity to make this happen."

Adam questioned, "I can see how the colony in Himalia's trailing Trojan point will work. Jupiter has a plethora of Moons to mine but what about Jupiter's L-One and L-Two Lagrangian points?"

Victor smiled a broad smile, he turned to Stuart, "May I, Stuart?"

"By all means, Victor", Stuart replied.

"Adam, Evelyn. Stuart's Cis-Lunar Haulage company will haul your colonies to the chosen libration points. After that, Stuart's space tugs will take selected small asteroids from the Asteroid Belt and accumulate them as conglomerated asteroidal masses in the centres of Jupiter's L-One and L-Two Lagrangian zones. Roughly fifty four million kilometres in front of and behind Jupiter. Those conglomerate asteroidal masses will be your mining resources", Victor explained.

Susan added in, as Victor had not mentioned it, "Your colonies will be placed into halo orbits around those conglomerated masses. The process is relatively simple and has been used in the Earth's, Venus's and Mars's Trojan points. A similar process was used to build the new Moons for the thirteen Belter colonies that were set up and we'll be using a similar process again with Jupiter's Trojans."

"So you guys have done this, many times before. Well, that makes me feel better about the process", Evelyn replied.

"Yes, Evelyn. I have to agree with you there", Adam agreed.

"I have one question though", Evelyn noted, "Jupiter L-One is in front of Jupiter, so we know the colony there will be in daylight, but Jupiter L-Two will be in Jupiter's shadow. It will be in complete darkness?", she questioned.

Baron chimed in, "That's the beauty of libration points. If the halo orbit is inclined with a radius of five million kilometres or more, the colony will receive constant sunlight."

Adam looked at Evelyn, "Seriously, Evelyn, these guys think of everything."

Stuart took over once again, "Once the colonies are completed and hauled out to their respective target locations, my company, Cis-Lunar haulage will unfurl the strip mirrors, guy wire the cylinders together and connect them with transport tubes. We'll even train your people in fission reactor management. A full end-to-end service is provided."

"What happens, say, decades from now, when the conglomerated asteroidal masses are depleted?", Adam asked.

"That is a fair question, Adam. You simply notify Cis-Lunar Haulage and they'll provide you with a reasonable quotation to add more small asteroids to the conglomerate mass. The process can be repeated as long as the Asteroid Belt has asteroids", Stuart explained.

"Okay, now the big question, financing?", Evelyn asked.

Tegan replied, " Dumas Colonial Financial will provide all of the funding required for the project via a long-term lone and at very good rates."

Susan added, "If you wish to maintain autonomy and not come under the jurisdiction of Eros and the Colonisation Committee or the Security Council, we can work around that as well."

"I thought that would be unavoidable. That is what everyone else has said", Evelyn commented.

Baron provided the answer, "Registration is tied to each colony cylinder's identification number and you only have to register when the colony becomes officially online", he smiled broadly, "That is tied to your final loan repayment, which can be restructured to one credit per standard year at a bare minimum interest rate. That last repayment becomes manageable, never grows overly large and pretty much never finishes."

"So, the colonies will be fully operational and never officially online?", Adam questioned.

"Yes. It is a loophole in the law, that every Belter colony has used and the Trojans will be using", Baron confirmed, noting, "If you decide on that final loan payment restructure, Eros will never have jurisdiction over your colonies and it is all perfectly legal."

Adam and Evelyn looked at each other, "That is incredible", Adam commented.

Both Tegan and Susan each passed them a thick folio, "This is our detailed proposal. Two copies of the same. Please present it to your board of directors and let us know what they think."

Susan added, "It will be wonderful to take The Jovian Dream Consortium on as clients."

"Thank you", they both replied in near unison.

The meeting had concluded, but before leaving, Evelyn remarked, "When our board of directors heard that we'd managed to see Mr Dumas, they couldn't believe it. They were sure we wouldn't even get past the lobby's front desk."

"Yes and when we told them that we'd spoken to you and that you'd schedule a meeting, they could not believe it", Adam added, commenting, "Now they have a solid, well-thought-out proposal to read through. I think they will be extremely surprised, possibly even in shock."

Stuart replied, smiling, "Well, once they're given it their due diligence and they're ready, have them sign off on it and we'll get the ball rolling."

"Will do, Mr Dumas. I don't think we'll need to convince them, the proposal should do that by itself", Evelyn replied.

Then they both shook Stuart's hand before making their way back to the elevators.

"I have a good feeling about this one, Mr Dumas", Tegan noted, "A really good feeling."

"Practicalities, Tegan. We have two colonies already under construction, we will need to schedule three more", Stuart noted.

Victor chimed in, "Not a problem, Stuart. We'll just combine our resources as we usually do."

"Well, Victor, Baron and Ladies. In my office, I have a bottle of VSOP Cognac and a bottle of Red wine waiting. We can all toast to the success of The Jovian Dream", Stuart invited.

Ariel commented on the information they'd just been reviewing, "It seems to me that the Dumas Corporation came up with a successful formula for creating colonies."

"Well, yeah", Aria replied, explaining, "The original formula they used to create their mining operations in the Earth's Trojan points. All that they really did was copy that same formula for use with Venus and Mars. Then they tweaked it for the Belter colonies and Jupiter's Trojan colonies then tweaked it once again for Jupiter itself. What I find interesting, is that Dumas and Himmelstaff were willing to help anyone with a viable plan for expanding Human colonies."

"That formula did have its limitations though", Yeannah noted, pointing out, "They couldn't use it in the radiation-rich environment closer to Jupiter. Those radiation belts sound so deadly. I mean, Io, lethal within minutes, Europe, lethal within hours, Ganymede, lethal within days and Callisto, lethal within weeks. Not to mention that other Moon, what was it called? Amalthea? That one is even closer to Jupiter. That sounds like an impossible challenge!"

"I didn't understand the divine providence references. What was so special about those names? Adam and Evelyn, Cain and Abel? I didn't follow that all", Kethera complained, being a Carlin, she had no point of reference for Earth's religions.

Saffiera explained, transmitting, "*It's an obscure Earth religious thing, Kethera. Adam and Eve, their Sons, Cain and Abel, are all names referenced in one of the Earth's many religious books.*"

"Which is why you didn't catch the reference", Ariel added.

"We're not expected to know Earth's religions, are we?", Kethera asked.

"No, Kethera. I don't think that divine providence is something we need to worry about", Yeannah assured her, "Just the historical components. We can ignore any religious references or just note them down and move on."

"That's good. I don't want to get involved with the Earth's religions. We Carlins have our own beliefs", Kethera replied proudly, announcing, "The Carlinish Gods created Carlins in their image and the Tholish Gods did the same with their Thols. I just assumed that the Human Gods did the same with Humans, both Earth and Martian."

"*Not quite Kethera. We Martians created the Earth's Humans by gradually and carefully modifying the dna of the early Earth hominids for more than a million years*", Saffiera corrected.

Kethera smiled, "That may be so but then who created the Martians?"

Saffiera smiled back, "*A good question, Kethera, one that is open to speculation.*"

Kethera smiled again, her tail was swishing and her whiskers raised, "Humans are nice. I think that your Gods are probably nice as well."

Aria replied, explaining that she was not entirely correct, "Not all Humans are nice, Kethera. That's why we have the police and the colonial armed forces."

Kethera frowned at Aria's last remark then asked, "Those big moons of Jupiter, did they end up getting colonised in the end?"

Yeannah performed a few searches on her screen and checked the data on the screen, "That, Kethera, is what the next section is about."

Aria sighed, "Gods. No more study. Let's just go outside and enjoy the weekend."

Ariel for once agreed with her twin Sister, "Aria has a point. It's a nice day outside and we should really enjoy it."

Yeannah noted, "We are somewhat ahead of schedule, so yeah, why not?"

Saffiera let out a huge telepathic smile, *"Motion seconded!"*

Kethera smiled and stood up, her whiskers were twitching in excitement, "I vote for fun!"

Aria, Ariel and Yeannah all agreed and within minutes they'd abandoned Saffiera's bedroom and were rushing outside to enjoy themselves.

As they all ran past the kitchen on their way outside, Sarlia sent them a telepathic message, *"Play wherever you like in the glade but keep well away from the perimeter fence. It is electrified."*

And with that, the Girls all rushed outside.

24. The Glade.

Sarlia led the other Mothers out into the yard around her house. There was a nice shaded area near the rear entrance where several lounge chairs had been set up. The light from Vale's primary Sun, Cathol, filtered through the leaves of the nearby Maple trees. Vale's secondary Sun, Cythol, was approaching its zenith and its light, though still feeble, added an eerie orange hue to overall daylight.

The Mothers sat themselves down in the lounge chairs, placing their mocktails into their chair's drink holders. They had stripped down to clothing that was little more than bathing suits and took in the mottled sunlight with joy. Their Daughters were playing several hundred yards away in the glade, tag was the game that Sarlia had noted.

Angelique Swanson was flying her craft high above the clouds. It was only a short hop from the Human colony to the glade where, Sarlia, the Martian Elder and Diplomatic Ambassador to Secundus lived. Angelique, however, enjoyed taking her vessel high above Secundus and then gradually spirally back down to her destination. The view was spectacular from on high and Angelique loved those views.

Angelique used the Human designation for this world, Xi Bootis A Secundus or Secundus for short. It was not ideal but the native inhabitants had not agreed upon a name, the Carlins using Vale and the Thols using Homwol. Without a decision, officially, the Humans applied their own designation.

Angelique was the proud Mother of twins, Aria and Ariel and one of their best friends, Saffiera, was the Ambassador's Daughter. Angelique turned her craft into a slow spiral and began a slow descent once more below the cloud layer. Lower and lower the craft spiralled, then upon eyeballing her destination, she adjusted course into a tighter spiral to approach.

Angelique's destination was one of the many small stands of forest that were scattered across the Masula Valley where the Carlin folk lived. This stand of forest was larger than most, almost perfectly circular and over six kilometres across. The larger stands of forest contained thick tangles of native vegetation and many types of native fauna, including quite a few predators.

Angelique's destination was a fenced clearing in the centre of the forest stand, that was a kilometre in diameter. In the very centre was a partially soil-covered homestead surrounded by gardens, greenhouses and tall Maple trees, the residence of Sarlia, the Martian Elder and Ambassador.

Sarlia, Kayala and Yealah watched as a craft spiralled around the glade in a counterclockwise direction. It slowly descended and when it came low enough, they were able to see it more clearly. It was black in colour and shaped like an arrowhead, with a broad, short shaft at the rear. Weapon pods were clearly visible at strategic points along its hull, under the bow, at the tips of its wings and on its vertical stabilisers. Sarlia was able to make out the class of vessel that was slowly descending, she recognised what it was.

"That's a long-range Interplanetary Starfighter. A military ship!", Sarlia exclaimed, questioning, *"Why is a military ship coming here?"*

Yealah asked for clarification, with a soft trill, "A military ship?"

Kayala looked up at the ship. After the preceding night of wine drinking, the light was still a little too bright, so she lowered her gaze and covered her eyes.

Still recovering from the effects of last night's lady's night and still not thinking clearly, Kayala mumbled softly, "Please, let me know when the invasion is over."

"Yes, Yealah. A military ship. I've seen these before back home on Mars", Sarlia confirmed.

It was at that point that their Daughters and the twins came running over. Kethera, Yeannah and Saffiera were all pointing at the ship. The twin stood there with bemused looks on their faces.

"It's okay", Ariel told everyone, explaining, "That's Mum's ship."

"Your Mum's ship?", Sarlia queried, asking, *"Your Mum flies a military ship?"*

Aria confirmed, "Yep, that's Mum's ship. A Broad Head, Arrow Class Starfighter."

Angelique circled the glade in her ship three times before approaching the homestead, then she hovered her craft above a patch of blue grass close by. The ship's landing gear descended and slowly the ship lowered for a perfect touchdown. Its landing thrusters were whisper quiet.

A ladder descended underneath the ship and Angelique climbed down it. Once her feet were planted firmly on the ground, she opened up a device on her left forearm, it was a *'grip'*, a potable A.I. system. Angelique tapped its virtual holographic keyboard and the ship's ladder reascended into the ship.

The Mothers watched as Angelique approached. The woman was wearing blue flight pants and a utility belt. A pouch on her right hip contained some kind of instrument. She wore a sleeveless blue jacket which was open at the front, underneath which she wore a tight blue singlet. Her hips were wide, but not overly so, showing that she was a woman who had given birth to children, in this case, the twins, Aria and Ariel.

Her waist was thin, ridiculously so, the woman obviously had a vigorous exercise routine. Her chest was equally as wide as her hips and beneath her jacket an ample bosom was apparent. Her eyes were hazel in colour, just like the twins and her hair was long, wavy and brunette. The similarity between Mother and her Daughters was striking.

Angelique turned sideways and scanned her eyes around the glade. The three Mothers watching gasped, her arms were strong and rippled with muscles. The twin's Mother was beautiful, feminine and fierce, a warrior. The twins both ran up to their Mother and hugged her in a tight embrace.

Sarlia thought to herself, *"The Mother is a scion as well as the twins, not the Father."*

"Love you to bits, Mum", both twins told their Mother in near-perfect unison.

"I love you both to bits too", Angelique replied, instructing them, "Now off you go and play with your friends, so I can meet their Mothers."

The twins looked at each other and frowned but then did as their Mother had asked, running off with their friends to play tag.

Angelique approached the other three Mothers, "I'm Angelique Swanson, the twin's Mum", she greeted with a smile.

Sarlia smiled back and introduced the other Mothers, *"Nice to meet you, Angelique, this is Yealah and Kayala. I am Sarlia."*

"Yes, Ambassador Sarlia. Greetings, I am aware of who you are and your position", Angelique replied, then to the other Mothers, "Greetings ladies", she did not seem phased in the slightest, by Sarlia's telepathic communications.

"Please, Angelique. I am just Sarlia", Sarlia replied.

Angelique crouched down in front of Kayala, "My Daughter, Aria, did mention something about Martian Sweet Cherry Red wine in her email", she looked at Kayala and reached out to her chin, "Kayala, if I may."

When Kayala nodded, she gently touched her chin and raised her head slightly, assessing the level of Kayala's hangover recovery. Carlins were not known for their ability to drink heavily.

"I do recommend, that when you drink strong wine, moderation is the key and most importantly. Don't ever try to compete with Humans when it comes to drinking. You'll find yourself worse for wear every time", then Angelique reached into her jacket pocket, took out a pair of sunglasses and placed them on Kayala's face, "That should help with the bright sunlight just a little. I also recommend drinking lots of water, you really need to keep hydrated, especially after drinking heavily."

Kayala smiled back and mumbled softly, "Thank you."

Sarlia cautiously enquired, *"Angelique, how did you come across a Starfighter?"*

"Oh, that thing. That's my sweet ride", Angelique replied, explaining, "I work the late shift as Head of Security at the Space Port. That is a military position."

Yealah also enquired, trilling, "But a Starfighter?"

Angelique smiled, explaining, "My Husband, Bobby and I, have highly peculiar skill sets. Our day jobs seem normal enough. I'm Head of Security at the Space Port and Bobby's up at Cis-Luns L-Five working as a Space Traffic Controller. However, we are still military and on call twenty four seven, and as we both have Fighter Pilot skills, they like to keep our kit, our Starfighters, close by."

"So, you get to fly a warship whenever you want?", Sarlia asked incredulously.

"Ambassador Sarlia, Bobby and I are also special ops", Angelique replied, explaining, "If and when we get the call, they don't want us chasing around asking for our equipment. They call and we roll!"

"Angelique, just Sarlia please. I don't bother with the title", Sarlia reminded her.

"I will try to remember that, Sarlia", Angelique replied.

Kayala reached for her mocktail and took a sip, her head was slowly starting to clear, "Angelique, how did you even find us all the way out here? I couldn't even tell you where we are."

"Here, in the glade! I was the supervisor eleven years ago when we carved out this little piece of paradise for our Martian Ambassador here", Angelique replied, commenting, "I probably shouldn't tell you this, Sarlia, but back then, they kind of called you the Martian Diva."

"I know Angelique and that was my own fault. When I was sent here, it was not my choice and I made so many demands, hoping that someone would complain to the Council of Elders back on Mars and that I'd be recalled. However, that did not work. Those damnable Elders are even more stubborn than I am", Sarlia explained, along with a few telepathic chuckles.

Angelique's face turned slightly serious, "You have been monitoring those perimeter fences, yes?"

"The household A.I. monitors the fence line continuously. The only things that seem to get through are those little Harricks creatures and I have no idea how they do that", Sarlia replied, laughing.

"Harricks", Angelique rolled her eyes, "Yeah, those little buggers seem to get into just about everything. Those fences are fixed three feet into the ground, but you know what, I bet they've just tunnelled under them anyway."

At hearing that, Kayala almost had a giggle fit, her ears stood up, her whiskers raised and her tail swished, "You can't stop Harricks, not even the Chittens can stop them", she laughed.

"You're starting to feel a little better I see, Kayala", Angelique smiled.

Angelique mused, "This glade is actually one of the safest places to live on Secundus."

Yealah corrected her with a soft click, "Homwol."

Kayala laughed and corrected Yealah softly, "Vale."

Angelique shrugged, "Homwol, Vale, until your people make a decision, I'm calling it Secundus. Anyway, just outside of that fence, you have two and a half kilometres of thick, tangled forest, teaming with wildlife, including lots of predators. The only way in is by air."

Yealah agreed, clicking and trilling, "Even we Thols don't like to fly over these lowland forests. The trees are all too close together and the undergrowth is far too thick. Definitely not safe for Thols."

"Actually, that is why I chose this location. When I first came here with Saffiera, I had virtually no knowledge of this world. So I was kind of anxious and more than a little scared and demanded somewhere safe to live", Sarlia recalled, noting, *"I chose this place."*

Angelique laughed, "And the merry chaos you caused when you did so. My bosses just gave in and said to me, *'Just give that damned Martian Diva everything she wants'* and so we did."

Sarlia laughed, *"I really was that bad back then, I have to admit it"*, she recalled.

Angelique took out a device from the pouch on her utility belt, it turned out to be a small telescope with an odd sort of handle, that looked more like a mount. Angelique stepped further away from the house, took the lens caps off and began to scan the fence line. The scope's A.I. was not detecting anything of interest and so did not transmit any data to Angelique's neural implants.

Angelique then swept her gaze across to the children and watched them play, "Kids, they are such fun to watch", she noted as she gazed.

The girls were playing tag and Yeannah quickly unfurled her great leathery wings with a crack, that sounded like the cracking of a whip. She then leapt into the air with two quick flaps of her mighty wings and then hovered fifteen feet above her friends, her wings gently flapping.

"Yeannah, that is not fair", Aria complained.

"The rules for tag don't mention anything about wings or flight", Yeannah counted as she lowered herself gently to the ground with both poise and elegance, softly touching back down.

The telescope picked up the girl's banter and its A.I. processor automatically transmitted it to Angelique's neural implants.

Angelique took the telescope away from her eye and looked at Yealah, "Mimasian Thols look just like Angels", then she commented, "Yealah, your young girl is so beautiful. She must have the boys chasing her all over the schoolyard."

Yealah sighed, trilling, "We have had some issues lately with boys."

"Don't tell me! Indigenous Thol boys whose parents have neglected to tell them that Mimasian Thols are a completely different species, right?", Angelique enquired.

"Half right. One Indigenous Thol boy and a Human boy", Yealah clicked and trilled in reply.

"A Human boy? Well, that's a new one", Angelique replied, noting, "I can't remember ever hearing of that happening before. That's kind of unique!"

Sarlia commented, *"It's the colonial school. Off-world and back in the Sol System, each species has its own schools. Here in the colony, the school is a multi-species campus."*

"Ah, so the boys are having crushes on the girls, before even finding out about each species foibles", Angelique surmised.

Sarlia then added, *"You notice that Yealah, occasionally trills, clicks and barks when speaking English and Yeannah doesn't."*

Yealah explained, clicking and trilling mildly, "I was taught English in a Mimasian Thol school, in the equivalent of high school. Yeannah went to school here and learned English from a much earlier age. It actually does make a huge difference."

Angelique replied, "So there are some benefits, it's just that the curriculum needs to be adjusted. The school needs to teach the kids about species customs and differences much earlier."

Something in Angelique's mind twigged and she placed the telescope to her eye once more, gazing at the children while they played. Her neural implants dialogued with the telescope's A.I. processor.

"Subject, Saffiera, Martian. Physical parameters", her neural implants requested.

The telescope's A.I. processor transmitted the requested information back, *"Height, five foot eight inches tall. Skin tones, light golden hues. Hair colour, light golden-yellow. Eye colour, light emerald green."*

For a few short moments Angelique was in thought. Martians all had the same height, five foot ten inches. They all had golden-hued skin tones and golden-yellow hair. Their eyes were mostly either a bright, sparkling emerald green or occasionally vibrant purple. The differences were very subtle and most people would not even notice. For Martians, those parameters never changed. Saffiera was an outlier and that meant only one possible thing.

Angelique took the telescope away from her eye and turned to Sarlia, she was about to ask a question, but Sarlia caught the thought and got in first, *"Please don't say anything, Angelique. My Daughter, Saffiera, she does not know."*

Angelique had spent years on Mars with her Husband, she had lived side by side with the Martians, she concentrated her thoughts and replied back, *"How can she not know?"*

Sarlia explained with sadness in her thoughts, *"My Husband was an Earth Human diplomat. He was always off on diplomatic missions. When he passed away, Saffiera was only three. When we came here, she was only five years old and she does not remember her Father at all. As there are so few Martians in this world, she does not know that she's a hybrid. I really don't want to confuse her."*

Angelique nodded in reply and deflected, remarking, "It won't take long for our girls to wear themselves out", as she put the lens caps back on her telescope and placed the scope back in its pouch.

Kethera remarked, "That's an interesting telescope. I haven't seen one quite like that before."

"Oh, this old thing. It's the scope off of my sniper rifle", Angelique replied matter-of-factly, "I find it very useful for scanning things in the distance. Like the fence line out on the perimeter. It is also military-grade, so anything it sees or picks up is fed straight into my neural augments."

Those last two words caught Kayala's attention, more so than the mention of her sniper rifle. Mimasian Thols and Martians all knew about Human neural augmentation and their access to data systems, Indigenous Thols and Carlins, however, did not.

"Neural Augments?", Kayala repeated, squinting at Angelique as if the words themselves were hurting her head

"Neural Implant Technology, Kayala. It allows me to communicate with networked A.I. systems, a bit like Sarlia's telepathy, only with machines", Angelique explained.

Kayala simply nodded, not really understanding, but also not wanting to dive any deeper into the subject. Perhaps later when her hangover-addled brain was feeling a little better.

Sarlia noted just a little dryly, *"Neural augmentation is nothing like telepathy or psychic abilities."*

"You are probably right, Sarlia", Angelique agreed, "I was just using that as an analogy. Not being a member of the psi-corp, I have no idea what being psychic would even be like. No idea at all."

Sarlia sent a private thought to Angelique, *"Telepathy and psychic abilities, about that."*

Sarlia never got to complete the thought and Angelique never got to query it, as the twins came rushing over, followed by Saffiera and Kethera. Yeannah came over by wing, nailing a perfect landing.

"We're all starving", they all announced in perfect unison.

Yealah and Kayala burst out laughing, Sarlia joined in telegraphically and then commented, *"I think you just predicted this moment, Angelique."*

Angelique smirked, "And my neural augments were not even required for it."

The Mothers all got up from their lounge chairs, grabbed their mocktails and followed the girls back inside the house. Kethera took her Mum's arm and walked inside with her.

Aria commented in her usual unfiltered way, "We were supposed to have pancakes and maple syrup for breakfast, but all of the Mums were hungover, so we just had cereal instead."

Angelique rolled her eyes and glared at Aria, "What have I told you about filtering your comments!"

"Sorry, Mum, you know me. No Filter", Aria replied.

"That is precisely my point, Aria. If you are aware that you don't have a filter, you are capable of correcting for it", Angelique replied in exasperation.

Kayala chimed in softly, "We did promise them pancakes, maple syrup and ice cream for breakfast. We should at least let them have that for lunch."

Kethera chimed in, "Yes! Pancakes and ice cream for lunch!"

Angelique replied, "Really! Ice cream for lunch. What happened to real food?"

Kayala replied, smiling, "It will be a treat. In our village. Ice cream is so rare!"

Angelique addressed the three Mothers, "Okay. Pancakes and ice cream for the kids, but you three. You all look like you could do with proper food."

"Agreed", Sarlia replied, *"We were so sick this morning, we actually skipped breakfast."*

Saffiera folded her arms across her chest, *"Sick Mum! Sick! Is that the new word for hungover?"*

Angelique looked at Sarlia and Sarlia picked up Angelique's private thought, *"Saffiera's stance, her posture, her attitude. That is so unmistakably her Earth heritage standing out."*

Sarlia sighed telepathically and agreed privately, *"Yes and on Mars, it would be obvious to every Martian around her, but here, no one even notices."*

Aria and Ariel had recently had their latent talents awoken and private thoughts were no longer private around them. They heard the short exchange but lacked the full story and so did not put two and two together. Instead, their focus was on pancakes, ice cream and maple syrup. Kids be kids, after all.

Angelique took over in the kitchen, requesting Saffiera's help to show her where everything was.

"Okay. Since the decision has been made. Pancakes for lunch. Maple syrup and berries for the Mums and maple syrup and ice cream for the kids", Angelique announced.

Angelique then spoke to the three Mothers, "While Saffiera and I do the cooking, you three can have nice relaxing showers", to Sarlia she then noted with a private thought, *"Martians are Human, Sarlia and all Humans have sweat glands."*

The twins caught that one and understood, they both started snickering together.

"Oh", Sarlia replied, privately in return, *"You're absolutely right! I reek of wine and sweat. I really do need a shower!"*

The three Mothers walked down the long hallway to the bedrooms, each of which had a full en-suite and even two-person spa baths, while Angelique, aided by Saffiera cooked up the pancakes.

Yealah and Sarlia came back after quick showers. Kayala had decided to have a soak in the spa bath. Upon hearing that, Kethera ran down the hallway to her Mother. Spa baths were unheard of in Carlin villages. To Carlin folk, they were a luxury.

By the time everyone was back at the kitchen table, there were two large stacks of pancakes on the table, a couple of bottles of homemade maple syrup, a couple of bowls of mixed berries and of course, a tub of vanilla ice cream. The girls eagerly dove into the pancakes and ice cream, they were like ravenous wolves. Their Mothers, were of course, much more civilised.

"I must say, I feel so much better after a nice soak in that bath", Kayala noted, her whiskers were raised and twitching, showing that she had enjoyed the spa bath, she added, "I had no idea that they were made for two, until Kethera jumped in."

Kethera's ears lowered and she bit her lip lightly, "I splashed water onto the floor. I'll clean it up later. I promise", she admitted.

"Don't be silly, Kethera. The cleaning bots will take care of that", Saffiera informed her.

"Cleaning bots?", Kayala queried.

Sarlia replied, informing Kayala, *"Spa baths and cleaning bots are fairly standard human house features these days."*

"They can probably be adapted over to Carlin houses or even Mimasian Thol tree houses", Angelique noted, then added, "Traditional Indigenous Thol nests would probably not be suitable."

"From what I've read, the Indigenous Thols wash in natural water sources and hang their butts over the sides of their nests", Aria commented.

Astonished looks came over Yealah's and Kayala's faces, Sarlia just chuckled internally and the girls all giggled at each other.

Angelique face palmed herself and then pinched the bridge of her nose, "Aria, my little cherub, not while we're eating. Okay!"

Yealah took note of Aria's comment and thought back to a comment that Angelique had made previously, clicking and trilling, "Angelique, when you said that Thols look like Angels, you specifically said, *'Mimasian Thols'*. Don't your people find the Indigenous Thols to be Angelic?"

"There's far more to it than just looks, Yealah", Angelique replied, then explained, "Mimasian Thols not only look the part, but you're never violent, always peaceful, beautiful, poised and elegant. Your people not only look like Angels, but your behaviour is also Angelic."

"And the Indigenous Thols aren't?", Yealah's Daughter, Yeannah enquired.

Angelique was quiet in thought for a moment, then she answered, "The Indigenous Thols do look like Angels. They can be beautiful like Angels as well. Some of them can even be peaceful, poised and elegant but to be entirely honest, overall, they behave much more like Humans than Mimasian Thols."

Ariel summed up what her Mother was trying to say, "The Indigenous Thols come across as being about as Angelic as us Humans."

Yealah chimed back in, clicking and trilling, "I hadn't noticed that before, but now that you've mentioned it, it's glaringly obvious. They do behave very much like your own people."

"Yes, we Humans have our religious dogmas, some anyway and the Indigenous Thols have their ancient rules and taboos", Angelique added, remarking, "They do like to think that they are so different and yet, they are, in so many ways, so similar to us Humans."

Aria chimed in, enquiring, "And the outliers?", something that had come up in previous discussions.

Ariel pointed out, "There are outliers in all societies, Aria."

Yealah noted with some barks, clicks and trills, "The Indigenous Thols push their rules and taboos onto us Mimasian Thols. Even though we are different species of Thol and have our own rules. Unlike we Mimasian Thols, there are some Indigenous Thols that are militant. No Thol may kill another Thol, regardless of species, that rule is the same. They have no equivalent rule for non-Thols."

Yeannah elaborated, "That generally means, that if any Carlin or Human breaks one of their major rules or taboos, with regard to Thols and cross-species relations, there are outliers in their community that will take that as an extreme insult."

Yealah confirmed her Daughter's statement, clicking and barking, "They will take umbridge. Extreme umbridge!"

Angelique frowned, as the local Space Port's Head of Security, she'd had experience with Indigenous Tholish outliers, "It is worse than you may think", she commented, informing them all, "Indigenous Thol outliers also take umbridge with Carlin-Human relationships. Not all of them mind you, but enough to be of concern. We have had Indigenous Thols overflying the colony, even overflying the Space Port, which is itself a major safety concern."

Sarlia asked curiously, *"Why would they be doing that?"*

Angelique frowned once more, "The ones we've captured refused to speak in English, so we had to request Carlin translators."

Yealah trilled and clicked, "My people can provide much better translators. Why not ask us? We Mimasian Thols can speak native Tholish fluently after all."

Angelique replied, "Yealah, we don't want to put your people into that kind of position."

"But my people, we Carlins, are okay?", Kayala questioned.

"Kayala, the Indigenous Thols treat your people as if they all look alike", Angelique explained.

Kayala's whiskers stuck out straight, "That is true. They think we all look alike. They can't even tell male from female and that is pretty obvious", she replied jokingly, gesturing to herself, Carlin women have six breasts and then she asked, "So what did you find out?"

Angelique informed them all, "These so-called outliers. They wanted to know if the rumours were true. Rumours about Carlin-Human relationships and hybrids. They were actively searching for them. In the end, all we could do was warn them about their dangerous behaviour and then take them back to their forests and set them free."

Kayala then asked, as her own Sister was married to a Human and had four hybrid kits, "Are they safe? Are the Carlin-Human families safe?"

"Yes, Kayala. They are safe for now", Angelique assured her, commenting, "These outliers don't even know if the rumours they're chasing are true and they are looking for the hybrids in the Human colony. The hybrid families all live well west of the colony in their own little village and that village looks Carlinish. From the air, it looks just like any other Carlin village, right down to the dry-stone walls, native fruit trees and those weird native goat thingies on the roofs."

Kethera enquired, "Why does the hybrid village look just like a Carlin village?"

"Familiarity, Kethera. The Carlin wives are used to their village lives, so they prefer their homes to be Carlinish. Although, now they have all of the modern technological conveniences built-in", Angelique replied.

"And their Husbands?", Kethera continued, she did have a vested interest in knowing, as she was now bonded with a Human boy, Richard.

"Kethera, Human men can pretty much live anywhere and rustic Carlinish villages are actually quite appealing. Honestly, even I find Carlin villages to be appealing", Angelique informed her.

Angelique remembered something from before when they were outside talking and the girls were all playing, "Sarlia when we were outside before the girls came running over, you were about to say something to me."

"Oh, yes", Sarlia remembered, *"About telepathy and psychic abilities."*

"Yes, that's right. What did you want to say?", Angelique asked.

"Your family, your twins and yourself", Sarlia began to explain, *"You are all scions of Folcrom Tafazah, the first Folcrom, the one that created the psi-corp."*

"How could you possibly know that?", Angelique questioned.

"I am a Martian Elder, Angelique", Sarlia told her, explaining, *"One of the things we are trained to do, is to locate the scions of Folcrom Tafazah and if necessary, to awaken any latent psychic potentials that they might have. Both Aria's and Ariel's psychic potentials are now awakening."*

Both Aria and Ariel had been eves dropping in on the conversation, "It's true Mum, Aria and I can hear private telepathic conversations, just as well as Saffiera's or her Mum's normal telepathic broadcasts", Ariel informed her Mother.

Sarlia nodded, then replied, *"It appears that no telepathic conversation can be hidden from them and that is just the beginning. They will, given time, no doubt, develop much farther."*

"If I am also a scion, how does that affect me?", Angelique asked.

"It doesn't. You are now too old for me to be able to awaken your latent gifts", Sarlia explained.

Saffiera, who had also been listening, asked, *"Then how did the Martian Elders tweak Gideon Reas and Sandra Danker? They were not even naturally born psychics."*

"The answer to your question is in the very question you asked, Saffiera", Sarlia replied.

Saffiera thought for several moments, *"You can't, Mum. You are only one*

Martian Elder, but the entire Council of Martian Elders? That's a whole different situation."

"And that is your answer, Saffiera. To tweak a non-psychic or awaken adults whose psychic potential has withered, takes the combined abilities of all of the Martian Elders", Sarlia explained, then noted, *"Assuming that they choose to do so. Remember, that they did send me here to be rid of me."*

"Well, then. Sucks to be me, I guess", Angelique laughed, commenting, "I haven't needed my psychic gifts in the past, so I figure I'll continue to be fine without them."

Angelique told her Daughters, "Girls. Go out and have fun. The Suns are both shining."

Ariel asked, "Later, on the way home can we get in some flight time?"

Aria chimed in, "Yeah, Mum, flight time!"

"Okay, okay. Now go out and play", Angelique caved in, knowing they needed to get their hours up.

"Flight time?", Yealah queried with a trill

"Oh yeah, Yealah. I'm teaching the twins to fly my ship", Angelique replied, as if it was just a natural thing to teach children to fly Starfighters, "They both need to get their flight hours up before taking their pilot's exams."

Sarlia enquired, *"When's their pilot's exam? I understand pilot licenses have age restrictions."*

"True. They can sit their pilot's exam anytime after they turn sixteen in July, on the standard calendar, of course", Angelique replied, her smile tinged with pride in her Daughter's accomplishments.

"So that would make you a qualified flight trainer?", Sarlia enquired.

"Yes, fully qualified, amongst a great many other things", Angelique replied, noting, "Being that Bobby and I both have our own ships, we can teach your girls to fly as well if you wish. It just takes a bit of time and practice is all."

Sarlia commented, *"Martians do not learn to fly warships."*

"Sarlia, if I teach Saffiera to fly with my Sharona, she can get her pilot's license. Once she has her pilot's license, she can pretty much fly any ship she desires. Any ship at all!", Angelique explained.

"Sharona?", Kayala queried.

"That is the name of my ship", Angelique replied, then commented,

"Well, girls. If you want to learn to fly, you need permission from your parents first and then we can work out a training schedule."

Yeannah and Kethera looked excited, Saffiera not so much, but still seemed interested.

Ariel said to her friends, knowing that their Mothers were going to have a long discussion, "Let's go out and have some fun", and then they all rushed outside to play.

"I'm not so sure that I want my Kethera to learn to fly a warship", Kayala commented.

Yealah trilled in agreement, "Nor I. Really, Angelique, a warship!"

"Think of my Sharona as just a training ship. A complex training ship", Angelique suggested, explaining, "The aim is to pass the pilot's exam and become a qualified pilot. Taking the pilot's exam in my ship, a Starfighter, will qualify the twins as pilots with a class five pilot's license. They will be licensed to fly almost any ship and one day, could even become Starship Captains."

Sarlia caught on, she was the Martian Ambassador to this world as well as a Martian Elder, *"I think I see where this is going. With a class five pilot's license, they'll be qualified to fly almost any ship and with the high demand for pilots, they will command high salaries and always have a job."*

"And they will be pioneers, Ladies", Angelique added, commenting, "Currently, there are no Carlin or Thol pilots in this solar system. It will open doors and opportunities for both of your peoples."

Kayala's ears picked and her whiskers twitched, she snickered, "Carlins in space, flying spaceships. That sounds like pure science fiction", she mused, "Captain Kethera of the outer frontier!"

"It could become science fact, Kayala", Angelique replied with a wry smile.

"It might solve another issue", Yealah noted with a trill, a click and some soft barks, "Yeannah's, Thomas, problem! As a pilot in high demand, Yeannah could be based off-world in Cis-Luns L-Five, well away from the prying eyes of the Indigenous Thols."

"Yeannah's, Thomas problem?", Angelique enquired.

Sarlia smiled and noted, *"The Human boy with a crush on Yeannah. It is a forbidden love, but there you have it. The heart wants what the heart wants."*

"Oh, so this crush is reciprocated!", Angelique understood, noting "That would really make the Indigenous Thols wig out."

Yealah trilled, "Yes, it is and yes it would!"

Kayala asked, curiously, "The name of your ship, Sharona. It's so pretty. How did you choose it?"

Angelique replied sadly but with almost brutal honesty, "It was to be the name of my firstborn Daughter, Sharona. She was stillborn. I named my ship in honour of her. The twins do not know."

Several moments of quiet followed.

Towards the end of the day, the girls all rushed back into the house. Their mothers prepared the girls a light snack and some drinks.

Ariel asked her Mother, "On the way home can we loop around Luns?"

Angelique replied, "Ariel, my darling. Luns is almost four hundred thousand kilometres away. That will be a high-speed flight, an hour there and an hour back, at least."

Aria chimed in, "Ariel can launch and fly us there, we can loop around Luns and I can fly us back and land. It will be good practice and increase our flight time."

Ariel stepped back in, "Come on, Mum. You know we can do the math. It's just simple orbital transfer calculations."

That last statement caught the other girls by complete surprise, Mixed Martial Arts experts, Starfighter pilots, what else could the twins do? What other capabilities did they have?

Angelique caved in, "Okay, okay, I give in but I will be checking your math and only because tomorrow is Sunday", she turned to the other Mothers, gave a slight eye roll and said, "Kids!"

Ariel then told Aria, "I'll lift off and insert us into high orbit, then I'll calculate the transfer course to Luns and the orbital loop."

Aria nodded in agreement and noted, "I'll take over once we round Luns and calculate the transfer orbit back to Secundus, then it's just a matter of high orbital insertion and finally, landing approach. I'm landing Sharona!", she stressed.

Ariel agreed with Aria, "As long as I get to taxi Sharona into the hangar though", and Aria nodded.

The twins were so excited, it was a rare treat to be looping around Luns, Secundus's large Moon. The other Mothers were also quite surprised, the twins were casually talking about orbital mechanics!

"You know, Sarlia", Angelique began, "Our house isn't that much different to yours. It is a very similar design and is partially soil-covered. Our plot is much smaller though, only about three hundred metres across and we also have a high perimeter fence. The big difference is our plot is in the rolling bluegrass meadows west of the colony. That and the big hangar we have for our Starfighters and our other vehicles."

"If your plot is in the bluegrass meadows, why do you need a perimeter fence?", Sarlia asked.

Angelique smiled, "Those predators in the lowland forests, they don't just stay there. They come out when the light is low and hunt those wild native goat thingies. Both predator and prey have those bluish stripes. It makes them very hard to pick out in the long bluegrass. A good high fence is necessary."

"Mum, they're called Gudongs", Aria interrupted and Angelique nodded.

Kethera added, "Those predators, the big ones, we call them Fearlessfangs, Kyrrax in Carlinish."

"Yes, they're very dangerous. So we have the need for high electrified fences just like here", Angelique replied, then she instructed her neural implants to check the glade's perimeter fence line.

Angelique's neural implants checked the house's data logs while checking the fence line in real-time.

Kayala noted, "The land around the Carlin villages is well trodden and those predators keep well clear. If one does come close, we do not tolerate it. The problem is usually when a Kyrrax is old or sick, then it will try to take a Gudong or worse, a Kit. Our men will then go out and hunt it down."

Angelique replied, "And so they should. Animals quickly learn to stay clear of places that are dangerous for them."

"Most of the families with plots at the outer edge of villages keep Vorts", Kethera commented.

"What's a Vort?", enquired Saffiera.

"They're a Carlinish pet. A bit taller than your knees in height and they're quite solid and stocky", Kethera began explaining, "They have four hind legs and two front legs that double as arms with paw-like hands. Their heads are broad, slightly muzzled with jaws full of interlocking teeth. Oh, and they have three eyes, two in front and a third on the back of their heads between their ears", she smiled, "They have blue striped skin as well."

Kayala added, "When a family wants a Vort, the Mother will go to the breeder's house and select one. The Vort kits have to be just weened. You pick them up by the skin of their neck and if they resist, then that Vort is for someone else. If it just hangs there and yawns, it will imprint on the Carlin Mother very quickly. From then on, the Vort will treat the Carlin Mother as its own Mother and the Carlin Kits as its own siblings. They are very protective."

"And they're pets?", questioned Saffiera.

"Important pets. Vorts hate Kyrrax and Kyrrax hate Vorts", Kethera replied, noting, "Vorts will keep a Kyrrax at bay! They're funny though. They don't know what to make of Harricks. They just chase them away or even try to play with them. Wild Vorts are much more vicious though. True predators!"

"When a Vort imprints on a Carlin Mother, they seem to take on Carlinish traits. They become playful like Carlin Kits", Kayala explained.

Aria noted, "They're just like dogs, very loyal and quite intelligent. Mum has four patrolling our fence line back home. They're fully imprinted on Mum. They kind of look like a Blue Heeler Staffordshire Bull Terrier cross only bigger and a lot weirder. Don't they Mum?"

"Yes, Darling. There has even been talk about using them as guard dogs on other Human plots as well. One of the Divisions of the Dumas Corporation is looking into it", Angelique replied, then she turned to Sarlia, "I just performed a perimeter sweep and a check of your household data logs. Your fences remain hot and nothing has been approaching it. That is except for those damned Harricks. They've tunnelled underneath them. I suppose we can't blame them though, they see this glade as a safe place. At my plot, we have other measures to discourage that behaviour, including our Vorts."

"You performed a perimeter sweep? I had not even noticed. Surely I should have detected the triggering thoughts", Sarlia replied, astonished.

"You wouldn't, Sarlia. My augments are an extension of myself. It's just like opening my hand, you would have to dive pretty deep to pick up the internal dialogue", Angelique explained, as she opened her hand and splayed her fingers.

Angelique commented, "Funny creatures Harricks. They're Humanoid, only a foot or so tall, but there's a huge amount of dimorphism between their genders."

"Dimorphism?", Yealah enquired.

Angelique explained, "We've been studying them for years now with stealth drones and hidden trail cameras. Harricks males walk upright and have no tails. They hunt and gather at night. Harricks females are rarely ever seen at all. When we have captured them on camera, they are so different. They walk on all fours and have a short bushy tail, kind of like a short ferret with a humanoid head. The females are the ones that dig their burrows and tunnels. As I said, it is very rare to catch them on camera. Very rare!"

"Wait! So female Harricks walk on all fours and have tails?", Kayala asked for clarification.

Yealah trilled, "How have we not noticed this before?"

"Yes, Kayala", Angelique confirmed, then to Yealah, "The female Harricks rarely leave their burrows and when they do, it's only when the night is darkest. When Cathol, Cythol and Luns are all well below the horizon. On

Secundus, that is also very rare."

Yealah trilled and clicked, "So we've lived side by side with the Harricks forever and only ever caught glimpses of their males?"

"Apparently", Angelique confirmed, "Even stranger. We believe that the male Harricks are sapient, but the female Harricks appear to be non-sapient. This is something, that we have never encountered before, anywhere, only here on Secundus. Our people are close to cracking their language as well."

The girls and their Mothers all looked at Angelique with astonishment at this new revelation.

Kethera sighed and her whiskers drooped, "Then we'll learn what the Harricks call our world and there will be yet another name for it. Vale, Homwol and whatever the Harricks call it!"

At the end of the day after saying goodbye to their friends, the twins climbed the ladder into their Mother's Starfighter, Sharona. Angelique said goodbye to the other Mothers as well and quickly climbed aboard her ship. The small orange Sun, Cythol was already setting and the primary yellow Sun, Cathol was close behind. The sky took on mild orange hues along the horizon, while still having blue skies above.

The Starfighter, Sharona, lifted vertically into the air above the glade with Ariel at its controls. When the ship was about a hundred metres in altitude, it hovered for a few moments. Then the short shaft at the rear of the dark, arrowhead-shaped craft pulsed with blue light and the Sharona shot forward and gradually curved upwards towards space. A mere child piloting a Starfighter.

Kethera turned to her Mother and squeezed her hand tightly, "Mum, I want to learn to fly!"

Kayala looked at her Daughter, then turned to Yealah and Sarlia, while giggling, "Captain Kethera of the outer frontier!", she mused once more.

Kethera, looked at her Mother, "Captain Kethera?", she questioned.

"Just a funny thought, my little one, just a funny thought", Kayala replied, hugging her Daughter.

Yeannah commented to her Mother, "I know there a Thol pilots back in the Sol System. I could become a pilot here in this solar system."

A tear formed in Yealah's eye as she remarked, trilling and clicking, "Being a pilot offers you a path forward for many things, Yeannah, not just good employment but other things as well."

Sarlia took Yealah's hand and transmitted privately, *"This could solve Yeannah's Thomas problem."*

Yealah commented, "Well, if our girls want to become pilots, Angelique has offered them a path forward", with a few trills and clicks.

Kethera jumped up, her Carlinish legs like coiled springs, launching her four feet in the air, "Yes, Captain Kethera of the outer frontier!", she exclaimed loudly.

Kayala smiled and gently scratched the skin at the back of Kethera's ears, eliciting a gentle purr from her Daughter, "We'll discuss this with your Father and if he agrees, we can arrange lessons with the twin's Mum, Angelique", then she added, "As long as it does not interfere with your other studies."

Yealah trilled and clicked to her Daughter, "Yeannah, the same deal, okay."

Both girls high-fived each other and Saffiera joined in.

"What about you, Saffiera?". Sarlia asked her Daughter.

"I'm undecided on the issue", Saffiera replied, then she noted, *"I might be interested, we'll see."*

Kethera smiled, "I wonder if the twin's Mum will land her Starfighter in our plot when she picks me up for training."

Kayala replied, "Oh my. Little one, that will cause quite a stir."

Yealah agreed, trilling, "I cannot imagine what the Indigenous Thols would make of it either."

"All the more reason to proceed with their training", Sarlia transmitted with a wry, cheeky smile, that came across telepathically as well as visibly, she was actually going to enjoy those reactions.

At the end of the day, Sarlia drove Kayala, Yealah and their Daughters back home in her hovercar. All three Mothers agreed that pilot training since it was freely offered, would be a good path forward as a possible career choice for their Daughters. Sarlia had even convinced Saffiera to go along with the training, even though Sarlia had concerns that Angelique's Starfighter had at least six weapon pods mounted to it. Weapons with massive firepower and devastating destructive potential.

There was an ulterior motive, however, a Starfighter landing in a Carlin village home plot or beneath the mighty Jula Jula forests where the Indigenous Thols lived, would be highly visible. A subtle reminder to any potential outliers, that Humans were not to be trifled with, whilst also reminding them that Humans create opportunities that they would otherwise not have.

Sarlia as a Martian Elder and the Martian Ambassador to Homwol/Vale, had a vested interest in ensuring that peace was maintained, whilst presenting opportunities to the indigenous species. Martians, especially Martian Elders, were always pragmatic in their approach.

25. The Fall and Rise of the Horridians.

The Earth's Government and the Government of Cis-Lunar L-Five, Colonial Central Command, needed to get ahead of Stuart Dumas and his colleague, Victor Himmelstaff. In response to Stuart Dumas's and Victor Himmelstaff's monopoly on providing services to groups wanting to colonise the outer solar system, the Earth Government and Colonial Central Command came up with, what they thought was the answer.

Into the public domain, they released colony designs for O'Neil-style colonies of varying sizes, including the designs for the mega colony, Colonial Central Command itself. It was an immense colony, its main cylinder was twenty kilometres long and four kilometres wide. At each end were hemispherical caps, two kilometres in radius. The surface area of the mega colony and its outer shell had the capacity to house well over twenty five million people.

The next step was to create designs for Interplanetary *"push ships"* that were big enough to carry both colonists and all of the equipment, including mining, ore processing and manufacturing stations into the outer solar system. The idea was, that if the colonists had the designs and equipment, they could build their colonies in-situ at their target destinations, completely bypassing Dumas Incorporated and Himmelstaff Consolidated entirely. The Earth Government and Colonial Central Command would even arrange the finance for all viable colonisation plans. That, they assumed, would put pressure on Dumas Incorporated's and Himmelstaff Consolidated's colony construction yards at Cis-Lunar L-Four, manufacturing, financing and haulage companies.

Victor Himmelstaff had concerns and when he'd discussed these concerns with Stuart Dumas, Stuart had ensured him that there was nothing at all to worry about.

Stuart had stated, "Their plans are actually my plans, Victor. We just had to kick them in the guts hard enough to push them into making a move. It does appear to have worked. I've been pressuring them to do that, Victor. How else are we to fully colonise our solar system and beyond? This was the plan all along. Get our governments off of their fat bureaucratic arses. Now that they've pulled the digit out, our species can really achieve greatness. We are the catalyst, Victor and our governments have been forced to respond. Trust me, this is a good thing!"

That was a revelation to Victor!

Another corporation within Cis-Lunar L-Five was the Horridian Incorporated Industries. They were a mid-level player with three corporate colonies. All standard O'Neil-style twin cylinder colonies with the capacity to comfortably house twenty thousand people in their four end caps. Albertus

Horridian, the owner of the corporation had found a clever way to cut his labour costs.

It was technically illegal, however, colonies in Cis-Lunar L-Five had total colonial sovereignty within their colonies, so long as they obeyed the overarching governance from Colonial Central Command. Overarching things like foreign policy, defence and even things like the gravity laws were under Colonial Centrals purvey, but labour laws and internal matters were under each colony's sovereignty.

Workers, both skilled and unskilled were attracted to the Horridian Incorporated Industries corporate colonies for the high salaries and wages. The main corporate colony was set up like most. Two main cylinders produced food for the colony with colonists living and working in the end caps. Lifestyles appeared to be perfect, except the Horridians were different. Funnily enough, the hired workers all tended to be single.

Workers would arrive and be assigned apartments, jobs and pay, commensurate with their skills and positions and everything seemed normal. However, the rules in the colony were ridiculously strict and the problems would start to show around the sixth month of employment. Fines were levied for almost anything, often trivial infractions that made little or no sense. If not taken seriously and paid promptly, more fines were levied on top. It quickly became apparent, that these fines grew larger, more quickly than they could be paid and that was their underlying purpose.

Once the fines began, a worker's travel rights were removed, although at first, they had no knowledge of that. Once the fines became overwhelming and the workers tried to leave, they found they could not, until the fines were paid. Even though the constant increase in fines made that impossible, which was the very point of the fines in the first place. The workers became indebted and could not leave the Horridian colonies until the fines were paid in full. They were not even allowed to contact their friends and families elsewhere in Cis-Lunar space.

When these fines were overwhelmingly large and clearly could not be paid, the worker would be given a questionnaire, that only contained two questions.

Question one: Are you a Christian?

Question two: If not, are you willing to convert to Christianity?

Now in Cis-Lunar L-Five, there were as many religions as there were on the Earth, except for those whereby the adherents did not travel off-world. Answering the first question with a yes, had the effect of sending the worker to a second Horridian colony where all of the workers were Christian. They were assigned shared, crowded housing with other workers and could not leave until their debtors were paid.

It was literally indentured servitude and as the fines continued to grow, they could never actually leave. Answering the first question with a no and the second question with a yes, had the same precise effect, they were sent to the Christian colony. However, answering both questions with a no, was very different. It was a terrible choice.

Those who were non-Christian and had no desire to convert to Christianity were sent to the third Horridian colony, where there were no Christians at all. Their housing consisted of little more than bunks stacked in rooms with poor ventilation and their food could only be described as sub-standard and disgusting. In this third Horridian colony, the workers were literally treated as Slaves. There was no way they were ever going to leave!

Albertus Horridian never thought he'd be caught, after all, his system was cleverly crafted. If anyone from the outside, tried to contact a worker, his A.I. systems crafted a clever response based on the individual worker's first six months in the colony. This he believed, would counter any possibility of outsiders raising the alarm and it appeared to work very well indeed. Of course, most of his workers were specifically chosen because they had few if any outside contacts to worry about them.

Of course, Albertus Horridian had not considered statistics and statisticians! At a simple distant glance, the Horridian Corporate Colonies looked just like any others, except they weren't. Only the first colony actually produced food, the other two colonies had their main cylinders utilised for production, with their end caps crammed full of either indentured workers or Slaves. The first colony imported extremely large quantities of food and distributed that food to the other two colonies. This was noticeable, very noticeable.

Then, of course, inter-colony immigration records and worker movements were meticulously recorded, something that was not common knowledge among the general populous. The three Horridian Corporate colonies had a combined population capacity of sixty thousand people, yet somehow, they contained closer to two hundred thousand based on worker immigration movements.

Albertus Horridian's system was not as clever as he'd thought. It did not take into account, that some workers lied on their employment applications. Some of those *"single"* workers, had family, friends and even a few had wives and husbands to who they sent home money. The Corporate A.I. systems could not cope with the erroneous data, *"lies"*, in the system and as a result their clever responses were not so clever. For a decade and a half Albertus Horridian had gotten away with it, but slowly, gradually the alarm bells began to ring.

First, the statisticians brought word of the *"overpopulation"* and the *"massive food imports"* to their superiors. Then families, a few at first, but later many more, were filing reports for their *"missing"* relatives and friends, who'd gone to the Horridian Colonies for work and seemingly vanished. It all began to add up and finally, someone did the unthinkable.

One family member flew his personal runabout past the Horridian Colonies and skin danced his ship along the strip windows. He found that the main colony looked normal, but the other two most certainly did not. The entire central cylinder's land areas were factories and manufacturing. Through the strip windows, the air itself looked heavily polluted, obviously showing that the air filtration systems were just barely coping! He recorded everything and handed what could only be described as damning evidence to the Colonial Central Authorities.

The raids came swiftly soon after the video recordings of the Horridian Colonies were received and analysed. The evidence was just so overwhelming! The Colonial Troops move quickly, docking their Dreadnoughts at each of the twelve colony end caps across the three twin-cylinder colonies. The bottles were sealed and no one was escaping. The Colonial Troops at the main corporate colony did not find much at all wrong, however, the other two colonies were horrendous. Even the very air stank of sweat and faeces.

The workers they found were gaunt and overworked, both the men and the women. The non-Christian colony was far worse, their treatment had been harsh, very harsh indeed and the women complained of being raped repeatedly.

Albertus Horridian was cool, calm and collected, he did not panic and he and his people had Colonial Sovereign Immunity. They could not be touched! He simply instructed his people, his enforcers and those he'd put in charge not to resist, not to fight back, just let the Colonial Troops do their thing. There was nothing that Colonial Central Command could do, just as long as they stayed within their colonies and did not resist the Colonial Troops.

When the Colonial Troop Commander arrived at Albertus Horridian's office, he told him, "I should shoot you where you're standing you disgusting piece of filth!"

Albertus Horridian simply replied, "Sovereign Immunity!" and pointed to the camera mounted at the corner of the ceiling, "Shoot me and my A.I. systems will broadcast it everywhere!"

The Colonial Commander looked at the camera and stared at it for a moment, wondering if it would be worth his career and imprisonment, in the end, he just replied, "Bastard!", and then he stormed out.

Colonial Sovereign Immunity meant the Colonial Troops could do nothing and Albertus Horridian knew it. Emergency transports arrived and quickly over one hundred and eighty five thousand malnourished *"workers"* were rescued and taken to rehabilitation facilities across Cis-Lunar L-Five.

There were not enough, many had to be taken to the Earth itself.

The debate raged for weeks. Albertus Horridian's *"labour"* practices had caused an outrage and it was on the news feeds for weeks. To make matters worse, there were still nearly ten thousand workers missing, presumed dead. Yet, Colonial Central Command's laws were perfectly clear, all colonies in Cis-Lunar L-Five had Sovereign Immunity and so long as Albertus Horridian and his cronies stayed within their corporate colonies they could not be touched. To make matters worse, that same Sovereign Immunity meant that Albertus Horridian could not be touched even if he did leave his colonies, as he and his Board Members all had additional Diplomatic Immunity!

This was the first time in the history of Cis-Lunar space and its colonies that a Corporate Colonial Enterprise had abused its Sovereign Immunity and behaved in such a horrendous manner. The hands of Colonial Central Command were tied. There was little that they could do. Even the Earth Government itself was powerless, the treaties in place did not allow it to interfere.

In a meeting of the Colonial Central Presidential Cabinet, changes were proposed. The first was that no longer would Sovereign Immunity and Diplomatic Immunity within Cis-Lunar colonies apply to what amounted to crimes against humanity. It rankled the cabinet members, that such a change was even necessary, however, in the face of the *"Horridian"* situation, clearly it was. Unfortunately, they were advised that the legal changes could not be applied retrospectively.

However, some other things could be done. The Horridian's corporate licenses were revoked and all businesses with Cis-Lunar space declared that they would not do business with the Horridians. By their very own actions, Albertus Horridian and his cronies had sent themselves to *"Coventry"*. For Albertus Horridian there was only one option, they had to flee to the Outer Solar System.

There was not a single financial entity in Cis-Lunar space that would finance Horridian's plans to leave for the Outer Systems. Stuart Dumas and

Victor Himmelstaff had both taken Albertus Horridian's calls, but only to let him know what they thought of the man. Stuart and Victor had not held back. In the aftermath of those conversations, Albertus put another plan into action.

Albertus was incensed by Stuart's audacity, how dare he talk to him, Albertus Horridian like that. Albertus hired two *"espionage"* operatives, he had used them before and they were extremely resourceful. It was well known that the Dumas Corporation's research and development division was working on radiation shielding for the Jovian Dream colonies out at Jupiter.

Two methods of radiation mitigation were being researched. One involved Stackable Layered Radiation Shield Plating, (SLaReS), pronounced, *"Slayers"*. This involved radiation plating comprised of specially formulated Moncrete or Astcrete that was resistant to radiation, layered with other proprietary, including various ceramics, materials that enhanced the radiation mitigation effects. More importantly, the plates could be stacked, one atop another, which doubled, tripled, quadrupled, etc. the radiation shielding as necessary. They were still assessing the limitations of stacking.

The second was the Electromagnetic Radiation Mitigation System, (E-RaMiS), pronounced *"Eramis"*. This system worked in conjunction with the radiation plating, deflecting Jovian Radiation Particulates, such as electrons, protons, ionised molecules and cosmic rays away from the radiation plating. Which left the radiation plating to block anything that got through, including X-rays and gamma rays. Both methods showed great promise and functional prototypes had been created.

Albertus Horridian called in his two operatives, who although highly effective, of late had been collecting credits just to keep them on the payroll and handy. Aurange Sheergibbon was a tall, thin, wiry redhead, with hair the colour of a carrot. One of his past nicknames had been *"The Carrot Top"*, although few called him that these days, as those that had were all dead. Aurange did not like that nickname, people who used it, had a tendency to die, usually by violence. Aurange had once snapped the neck of an adversary with his left hand, while at the same time, beating another to death with the man's own severed arm. Violence was in his nature. Albertus had a habit of calling him the *"Orange Shitgibbon"* in private, but never, never called him that to his face.

Aurange's better half or partner, whatever she may have been, Roberta Nummus, was at least three inches shorter. Roberta was well built for a woman, quite curvaceous and also quite top heavy, very top heavy to be entirely honest. In private, Albertus had a habit of calling her *"Booby Num Nums"*, although, as with Aurange, he would never say it to her face. Roberta had been known to kill a person for staring at her breasts for too long. No one knew exactly what too long was, so nobody dared to look. The pair of them were *"talented"* pieces of work! Many of the missing indentured *"workers"* had fallen afoul of this pair. They were Albertus's perfect although extremely violent enforcers.

Aurange and Roberta had once been in the Military. They had been Special Operatives and of course, were highly skilled through years of hard training. However, there was far more to their story. During their time in the Military, they had both volunteered for *"experimental"* enhancements. These enhancements had changed Aurange and Roberta physically, genetically and psychologically.

They had become physically stronger, faster and had a sharper focus of mind. They had, of course, become psychotic as well. Their genetic changes meant that they aged much slower than most people, ageing at a rate so slow, that people could not notice them age at all. The Military authorities wanted them locked away for good, as they were far too dangerous to have *"wandering"* around. Of course, that did not agree with Aurange and Roberta. They had slaughtered their way out of confinement and later killed most of the people associated with the *"experimental"* enhancement project. The Horridian Corporate Colonies were their new home and their new boss, was to their liking, ruthless!

Aurange and Roberta entered Albertus Horridian's office. Albertus's Son, Albert was sitting to one side watching his Father issue orders to his two main enforcers.

Albertus Horridian spoke only a few sentences, not many, "Dumas Incorporated. Research and Development Division. Their Stackable Layered Radiation Shield Plating, *"Slayers"* and their Electromagnetic Radiation Mitigation System, *"Eramis"*. They belong to me now. I want them. Both prototypes and data. Fetch!"

Aurange smirked, almost a smile, but not quite, he then turned to Roberta who took on the same precise look. They were a team and they'd been given instructions. They both looked at Albertus, smiled at him and nodded, then left the office without saying a word.

After they'd both left the office, Albert closed the still-open door and asked his Father, "Why do you still keep those psychopaths around, Father?"

"They are useful, Albert, very useful", Albertus replied, adding, "And do NOT let them hear you call them that! I cannot help you if they do."

Albert nodded in understanding, but commented, "Rabid dogs will always turn on their master, Father!", thinking to himself, *"My Father the rabid dog handler!"*

Albertus Horridian never enquired about their methods, he was always happy with their results. Before the week was out, the prototypes for both *"Slayers"* and *"Eramis"*, along with their data were delivered. He wanted them and now they were his. There was something in the news feeds about twelve dead workers found in the Dumas Corporations Research and Development Division, but that of course, did not concern him. That was not his problem.

Stuart Dumas was furious that his prototypes and data had been stolen. Whoever did it, had not left any trace, no clues, just corpses in their wake. That was what infuriated him the most, whoever did it, had no need to kill anyone. They could have simply stunned them in any manner of ways, but to slaughter them in that the way they did. That made him furious. Stuart instructed Tegan to write up letters of condolences to their families and to put together compensation packages, not that would change anything, they were still just as dead!

Baron, Stuart's Son, had suggested that the Horridians were behind it, but without any evidence, there was nothing that they could do. Baron noted that the data they'd taken was all backed up, so they had not lost anything in that regard. He also noted that the prototypes that had been taken were only the first and that the next generation was already ready for production and testing. Security had been stepped up and it was unlikely whoever had done it, would find it so easy if they tried again.

While a very happy Albertus Horridian gloated at his ill-gotten gains and Stuart Dumas and his Son, Baron, were furious with the thefts and the murders of innocent people, two highly paid operatives drank, danced and enjoyed each other's company in their own private little party. Murder excited them and they enjoyed each other's company in multiple debauched ways that had no limitations. The Orange Shitgibbon and Booby Num Nums enjoyed violence in ways that ordinary folk could never truly understand.

In a lot of ways, Albertus Horridian, was quite similar to Stuart Dumas, apart from his complete lack of moral fibre and willingness to allow people to die to meet his demands, he thought fast, made quick decisions and had absolutely no regrets. Albertus and his Son, Albert, made their plans, they were simple, very simple.

Horridian colonies two and three, his indentured servitude and Slave colonies were to be sold off to raise funds. He didn't care what happened to those colonies, all he needed was enough funding to build four Interplanetary

Push Ships and as many mobile mining, ore processing and manufacturing stations as he could. That was their aim, push out to the outer system and as they now had Dumas's radiation mitigation systems, *" SLaReS and E-RaMiS"*, their destination was going to be Jupiter.

They would use their enforcers, the Orange Shitgibbon and Booby Num Nums, to pressure their *"chosen"* construction company to build everything they required and keep everything under wraps, all on the down low. It was simply too bad if a couple of executives had to die as part of the process. Albertus Horridian needed four push ships, as he had close to twenty thousand people to take with him.

People who were completely complicit in everything that had been done. They could not leave the Horridian Corporate Colonies without being arrested and charged with crimes against humanity. They had to go with him into exile and those people were entirely loyal to him. His army if needs be.

Once the four Interplanetary push ships and all of their other orbital stations were ready and docked to their respective ships, they would then be flown to his remaining Corporate Colony and docked, one per end cap docking ring. His people would then board and that final colony would be sold off to raise credits for use when they arrive at Jupiter's Moon, Himalia. The home of the consortium, the Jovian Dream and their colony, Himalia Central. Shortly thereafter, their exodus began.

Albertus had one final problem, his surname, Horridian! Any quick search would show his misdeeds, however, people could be so stupid. If you searched on *"Horridian"*, there it all was, but if searched on *"von Horridian"*, nothing came up at all. The entire Horridian family changed their surname to *"von Horridian!"*

Around the year twenty one fifteen, the four Horridian Interplanetary Push Ships arrived at Himalia Central. The Jovian Dream Consortium, by this time, had evolved into the Jovian Republic, with colonies in Himalia's trailing Trojan point and Jupiter's own L-One and L-Two Trojan points. The Jovians had already developed profitable trading relationships with the Trojan Colonists at Jupiter's leading and trailing Trojan points.

The Horridians quickly made promises, insinuating themselves into nearly every aspect of the Jovian economy, making themselves as indispensable as possible. The local authorities, led by Adam Cain and Evelyn Abel lapped up their lies, not realising at the time that they were dealing with the devil himself, Albertus von Horridian. They were naive and both eventually had mysterious accidents. Quite a few leaders of the Jovian Republic also had mysterious accidents, always those who opposed the Horridian's plans.

In the year twenty one twenty two, Victor Himmelstaff passed away, he was eighty four. His passing was sudden and unexpected, up till then, he had been in good health. With Victor's passing, his Daughter, Hypolita, inherited Himmelstaff Consolidated Industries and all of the Himmelstaff Corporations under that umbrella company. Hypolita's Husband, Baron Dumas, promised to help his wife transition into her leadership role as owner and CEO of the Himmelstaff Corporate Empire.

Susan Carter, Victor's personal assistant, adviser and confidant, had been slated to retire, however, with Victor's passing, she promised to stay on until a new suitable personal assistant could be hired. Tegan Smith, Stuart Dumas's own personal assistant, adviser and confidant, had already been training a new personal assistant to take over from herself, as she was due to retire soon as well.

Tegan's chosen replacement was someone that Tegan and Susan both trusted, a woman who was not only highly capable but also highly skilled and that person was Harmony Moon, the youngest granddaughter of Harrison Moon. Harmony Moon was not only capable of thinking outside of the box, but for her, the box barely even existed. If you needed a rabbit pulled out of a hat, Harmony would find you that rabbit and not just any rabbit either, but the precise rabbit you required. Harmony was quickly brought up to speed and became Hypolita's and Baron's new personal assistant and adviser.

As Baron and Hypolita were Husband and Wife, they were a team and would work together, with Harmony coordinating their every need. Eventually, both the Dumas and Himmelstaff Corporate Empires would merge under Baron's and Hypolita's eldest Son, Connor, and the Dumas Incorporated Industries banner, but that was still some ways off in the future.

Only one person was actually pleased with Victor's passing.

When Albertus von Horridian had received the news, he thought to himself, *"Good Riddance!"*

At the thirteenth session of the Colonisation Committee of Sol's, State of the System Report, at Eros in the year twenty one twenty five, the sixth meeting since the founding of Eros. The State of the System Report meetings were held every five years. At this meeting, the bomb dropped. The Jovian representative made note of four huge Interplanetary Push Ships owned by the Horridian Corporation having arrived in recent years. They were apparently helping the Jovians to mine the moons of Jupiter itself. At the mere mention of the disgraced Horridian Corporation, an uproar ensued in the conference room. The Jovian representative glossed over the Horridian Corporation's previous despicable history.

Mining colonies had been set up on Ganymede and Callisto, with automatic mining operations taking place on Europa, Io and even Amalthea. Something that could not have been done without the stolen Dumas Corporation's radiation mitigation technology. The Jovian representative herself, Ms Janet Keal, had of course arrived on one of those Horridian Interplanetary Push Ships. She was a true Horridian loyalist, a true believer. She even claimed the credit on behalf of the Horridians, for the achievements of the Trojan Colonists and their work in hollowing out the Trojan Asteroids, Hector, Patroclus and Menoetius. Achievements that had begun long before the Jovian Dream had found its way to Jupiter, let alone the Horridians. Such was her loyalty to the Horridians and their agenda.

By the time of the Mimasian War in the year twenty one forty, the Horridians had insinuated themselves into every aspect of Jovian life. Dissenting politicians mysteriously fell ill and mysteriously died. Operatives of the Horridians were even working as far as Jupiter's leading and trailing Trojan points. Even in those distant colonies, politicians were either bought or mysteriously died. Their influence extended to the Belter colonies as their poison and lies spread. The Belters, however, were shrewd and not so easily misled. Especially those whose family name was Moon.

The Mimasian War itself forced the Horridians into a rare moment of unity with the rest of the solar system colonies. The warlike aliens, the gargoyle-like Tarlaks on Mars and within the Saturnian Moon, Mimas, which itself turned out to be a mobile generation ship, millions of years old, could not be ignored. If humanity fell, so would the Horridians, so they cooperated for the *"greater good"*, only to revert to the usual modus operandi as soon as the War was over. With the many millions of Tarlaks now extinct and their evil Emperor, Ahriman, rent asunder, it was business as usual for the Horridians. They did not win the war, it was won for them by the sacrifice of millions of Colonial Troops.

After the devastating Mimasian War was concluded, it was covered up and concealed by the secretive and occult, Council of Shadows using their powerful psychic abilities. The War was forgotten under *"The Great Conceal"* for centuries to come. The damage the War caused became known as the *"The Great Catastrophe"* and was put down to massive interstellar micrometeor swarms. It would be many centuries before the Council of Shadows deemed Humanity ready to openly know of Aliens and the devastating Mimasian War.

President Carter of Cis-Lunar L-Five at Colonial Central Command offered twenty six heavily damaged O'Neil-style twin-cylinder colonies to the Belters as gifts, free and clear, to do with as they wished. This annoyed the

Horridians, as this goodwill gesture had unravelled years of propaganda they had so carefully put into place in one move. The Belters of course were nobody's fools and knew better.

In the year twenty one forty seven, Albertus von Horridian ran for the office of President of the Jovian Republic. He wins a majority vote of fifty two percent. For his first term, he does little, except to make sure that his own people are in places and positions of control. During that period in office, in the year twenty one fifty, word of the passing of Stuart Dumas at the age of one hundred and two reached the Jovian System.

Albertus smirked and thought to himself, *"About time that smug bastard kicked the bucket!"*

After five years Albertus's term was up and he sat for re-election. His platform for re-election involved a single issue. The creation of Ganymede Prime in Ganymede's trailing Trojan point. It was a five-year plan and a popular one at that.

Ganymede Prime was to be a huge, mega O'Neil-style single-cylinder colony, with its main cylinder being twenty kilometres long and four kilometres wide. Its two end caps would have a radius of two kilometres and the construction, once completed, could house up to twenty five million colonists.

The Horridians had the open-source blueprints for Colonial Central Command back at Cis-Lunar L-Five. They had the stolen *"Slayers"* and *"Eramis"* radiation mitigation technologies and they had the mining, ore processing and manufacturing capacity. Improvements were made to the original designs. The biggest change was the flipping of the northern and southern end caps.

Colonial Central Command had the politics, business, command and control in the southern end cap and as such was different to all of the other O'Neil-style colonies. Ganymede Prime would have the politics, business, command and control in the northern end cap, to be like every other colony of its style. Then the plans were put in place, contingent on Albertus von Horridian being elected to a second term in office.

The opposing party could not compete, as they did not have the finances, nor technical expertise to run such a project. Albertus von Horridian won the election with seventy three percent of the vote and work began on Ganymede Prime in the year twenty one fifty two.

Ganymede Prime came online three months prior to the next election in twenty one fifty seven. It was ahead of schedule and a huge success. Jupiter's radiation belts were successfully mitigated and a great many colonists were allocated housing in Ganymede Prime, reducing the severe overcrowding in the older colonies. Funnily though, it was mainly the loyalists that got to live in the luxurious new mega colony. Preferential treatment was rife and an incentive to others to be *"nice"* to the Horridians.

Towards the end of Albertus's second term in office, there was a stumbling block. The Jovian Republic's constitution only allowed for two five-year terms in office and no more. Albertus had a plan for that too. Albertus had a Son, named Albert. During the election campaign of twenty one fifty seven, Albertus's Son, Albert von Horridian ran for President on the same style of platform as his Father. Albert von Horridian promised the Jovian people, that if elected, he would build them Callisto Prime in Callisto's trailing Trojan point. Another huge, mega O'Neil-style single-cylinder colony that was equally as big as Ganymede Prime.

It was his Father's idea, after all, it worked before and surely it would work again. Grand schemes and grand gestures captured the people's imagination. The five-year plan was put in place with more adjustments and improvements upon Ganymede Prime's design, all contingent on Albert von Horridian winning the election, of course.

Without the finances and manufacturing expertise, the opposition again could not compete and Albert von Horridian, the Son of Albertus von Horridian won the election with seventy eight percent of the vote. It was a landslide victory and now President Albert von Horridian began the work on Callisto Prime in the year twenty one fifty seven.

As with Ganymede Prime five years before, Callisto Prime came online three months before the elections of twenty one sixty two. Just as with Ganymede Prime before it, Callisto Prime became an instant success. Ahead of schedule and with design improvements over the original Ganymede Prime design, it was an outstanding accomplishment. With so much room available with both Primes, even more people were allocated housing to Callisto Prime and this time, they were not necessarily loyalists.

"Good things come to those who wait patiently", President Albert von Horridian had told his people.

President Albert von Horridian was riding a massive wave of popularity and when he announced the building of a third Prime, Europa Prime, the public went mad with enthusiasm. The opposition at that point just gave up, what was the point of pretending to be an opposition party when the population barely knew they even existed.

Europa Prime was to be constructed at Europa's trailing Trojan point and it was a challenge. The radiation belts in Europa's vicinity were devastatingly potent. However, it turned out that the stolen *"Slayers"* and *"Eramis"* radiation mitigation technology was scalable above and beyond Europa's radiation challenges. The *"Slayers"* panels would be layered thicker and overlapping, their effectiveness was a testament to the Dumas Corporation's Research and Development Department, from which the designs and prototypes had been stolen.

The new five-year plan was put in place with more adjustments and improvements upon Callisto Prime's design, all contingent on Albert von Horridian winning the election. The opposition party only made a token show of contesting the election and President Albert von Horridian won the election with eighty two percent of the popular vote.

Three months prior to the next election in twenty one sixty seven, Europa Prime came online. On schedule, with thick radiation shielding, it too was a success. People applied for new apartments and housing in Europa Prime and found themselves quickly migrating across. The three Primes provided plenty of housing and the smaller colonies became the purview of those who preferred smaller colonies and more distant views of Jupiter.

President Albert von Horridian now had a problem. His second term was coming to an end and a President could have only two terms in office. Even then there was a solution. Albert von Horridian had super-control of both houses and so, he had the Jovian Republic's Constitution amended to allow himself a third term in office. Albert von Horridian then ran for his third term as President.

Jupiter had four big Galilean moons and the only one that did not have a Prime was Io, so naturally, Albert announced a new mega colony, Io Prime, to be built in Io's trailing Trojan point. The new Prime would benefit from all those that had been built before it, with improvements to its design based on past constructions.

Again the *"Slayers"* and *"Eramis"* radiation mitigation technology would come into play. Io was embedded deeply in Jupiter's radiation belts and lethal radiation doses could occur in mere seconds. As a result, Io Prime would have the thickest, overlapping, *"Slayers"* plating ever utilised and even at Io's orbital location, it was more than capable of complete radiation mitigation.

The new five-year plan was put in place for Io Prime, all contingent on Albert von Horridian winning the election. Not that it mattered, the opposition was in complete disarray and total collapse. The election was almost uncontested and President Albert von Horridian won the election with eighty seven percent of the popular vote. It was, however, a bittersweet moment for Albert, three days after his resounding election victory, his Father, Albertus passed away, he had been eighty nine years old.

At Albertus's funeral, his two most accomplished *"enforcers",* Aurange Sheergibbon and Roberta Nummus, had closed their eyes and bowed their heads to Albert. Then after raising their heads, they raid their right fists to the left breast as a salute. Albert was now their new master.

With the elections of twenty one seventy two looming and the new mega colony, Io Prime, coming online three months prior, President Albert von Horridian had his two houses amend the Jovian Republic's constitution once again to allow himself a fourth term in office.

Io Prime was the same overall size as the other three mega colonies, the main difference was the sheer thickness of its radiation plating. Europa Prime had clearly visible radiation plating, but Io Prime was something else, its thick radiation plating was clear and unmistakable.

With the other three Primes providing plenty of housing and any overcrowding issues completely dealt with, few people needed to or wanted to live in Io Prime. Those that did, however, found themselves living in opulent luxury in a highly underpopulated mega colony.

There were no more Galilean moons left, not that it mattered, there was no real opposition left at all. Still, Albert von Horridian kept the grand gestures going. He announced the building of Amalthea Prime to be built in Amalthea's trailing Trojan point. This colony would be a smaller mega colony, half the size of the Galilean Primes, shorter, but just as broad, with a population capacity of fifteen million.

As Amalthea was exceedingly close to Jupiter, far closer than even Io, its radiation shielding would consist of extremely thick layering and overlapping of *"Slayers"* plating. Far thicker than even for Io. In addition to this grand gesture, President Albert von Horridian signed an executive order for all ships in the Jovian Republic to be upgraded, with sufficient radiation shielding to be able to survive at even Amalthean distances from Jupiter.

The election came and went and there was so little opposition. Ninety three percent of the vote went to Albert von Horridian and he entered his fourth term as President of the Jovian Republic. Having lost his beloved Father, three days after his previous election victory for his third term in office, Albert had become somewhat bitter and cynical.

During President Albert von Horridian's fourth term in office, he made a lot of changes. First, he positioned his most loyal supporters into positions of power, including religious institutions. He ensured that he had absolute control and there was no opposition. Many members of the opposition or what was left of it mysteriously vanished without a trace. Something about faulty airlocks was the rumour that went around. Nobody liked faulty airlocks! People now actively avoided them.

Albert organised all of the Christian Churches, merging them into four main churches. One each for Io, Europa, Ganymede and Callisto. They were called the High Churches and the High Church of Ganymede held primacy over the rest. The Churches were given the right to levy ten percent tithes on their members and tithing was compulsory, as was membership for all Christians. As the High Church of Ganymede held primacy over the others, it also received ten percent of the tithes from the High Churches of Io, Europa and Callisto.

After this, President Albert von Horridian reformed the taxation system, setting a flat rate tax rate of twenty percent of all income across all of the Jovian colonies. As Ganymede was the Jovian Republic's main administration hub, all of the other colonies paid twenty percent of their taxes raised to the Jovian Taxation Office (JTO) at Ganymede Prime. President Albert von Horridian had all of these changes written into the Jovian Republic's Constitution.

Next, without even bothering with a pretext. President Albert von Horridian ordered the Jovian Republic's Military to send three Dreadnoughts apiece, to Jupiter's leading and trailing Trojan points. Once they arrived, they threatened the two Trojan Republics with utter destruction if they did not surrender. Neither Trojan Republic had any real armed forces, just police patrols and a space guard. They both surrendered without a fight and the Dreadnoughts were followed up with Jovian Troop Transports full of Jovian Shock Troopers. Both Trojan Republics were now occupied by Jovian Troops.

The Christian Churches in the Trojan Republics were consolidated into High Churches of the Leading and Trailing Trojans and the same tithe system was put in place. Both compulsory Christian membership and tithing. The same taxation reforms were applied to both Trojan points as well.

President Albert von Horridian now controlled all four Galilean Moons of Jupiter and Jupiter's leading and trailing Trojan points. He had them all renamed as the six Jovian Realms. The Jovian Realms of Ganymede, Callisto, Europa, Io, The Fore Trojans and The Aft Trojans.

Six months prior to the elections of twenty one seventy seven, Amalthea Prime had come online. All ships in the Jovian Republic had been upgraded to the new *"standard"* in radiation protection. Building all five of the Primes had consumed no fewer than six of the smaller Jovian Moons and utilised imports from both the Belter and Trojan colonies. Now the Primes were all completed.

Amalthea Prime itself was quickly organised to manage all mining operations on the Jovian Moon, Amalthea. Io Prime was then organised to manage all mining operations on the Jovian Moon, Io. Likewise with Europa, Ganymede and Callisto, each managing all mining operations on their respective Galilean moons.

With his fifth election looming, President Albert von Horridian told his closest supporters, "Power is means unto itself and I choose to exercise that power!", and so he did.

On the day of the election, all polling stations were closed and an announcement came over the news feeds across the entire six Jovian Realms. The announcement explained that the Jovian Republic was no more and that it was being replaced by six Principalities. The Principalities of Io, Europa, Ganymede, Callisto, The Fore Trojans and The Aft Trojans, with Ganymede holding primacy over all of the others.

Then the news feed showed a large chamber on Ganymede Prime, President Albert von Horridian sat upon a gold gilded throne. A Priest from the High Church of Ganymede, the High Priest, now the Pope of the Jovian High Church of Ganymede, held a crown high above the President's head.

The High Priest, now Pope, announced with a shaky voice, "By the powers vested in me by God himself, I hereby declare, Albert von Horridian, Prince of Io, Prince of Europa, Prince of Ganymede, Prince of Callisto, Prince of The Fore Trojans, Prince of the Aft Trojans and High Prince of the six Jovian Realms!", he then lowered the crown carefully and gently upon High Prince Albert's head.

Albert's two most capable enforcers, Aurange Sheergibbon and Roberta Nummus, stood to either side of High Prince Albert's throne, both dressed in ceremonial, yet functional armour and fully armed.

The two enforcers actually spoke, "All hail the High Prince of the Jovian Realms", and they held the weapons aloft in salute.

True to their genetic modifications, the Orange Shitgibbon and Booby Num Nums did not appear to have aged much at all.

High Prince Albert von Horridian now held six Principalities, the Jovian Realms, by his right hand and he had his Prince's fifth and his churches tenth of all revenues flowing into his *"royal"* coffers.

An elderly woman stood in the room completely unseen, her psychic obscuration field hiding her completely from the minds around her, her name was Freyja and she was a member of the psi-corps hidden, occult, Council of Shadows.

"Fuck!", she silently exclaimed, *"This was never meant to happen! The Council needs to be warned!"*, then quietly, unseen, she blinked out of the chamber and reappeared back on the Earth.

For once the Council of Shadows was caught unawares.

The Jovian Republic had fallen, it was now the Principalities of the Jovian Realms, with High Prince Albert von Horridian on its throne.

The Horridians once held in disgrace in Cis-Lunar L-Five, in the newly rebranded Jovian Realms, the Horridian Dynasty had risen, like a Phoenix from its very own ashes!

The new High Prince continued with his reign by edict. Every citizen was brought in for questioning and there were precisely two questions asked. Two very familiar questions.

Question one: Are you a Christian?

Question two: If not, are you willing to convert to Christianity?

Those citizens who answered Yes to question one or no to question one and yes to question two exited through the door on the right. They remained citizens, however, those who were not Christian were expected to convert to Christianity. That was not optional.

Those citizens who answered no to both questions, existed through the door on the left, after which they were stripped of their citizenship, all of their possessions and their rights and were re-classified as Slaves! They were then taken away for processing.

High Prince Albert von Horridian had even managed to outdo his Father, Albertus!

All non-Christian religious institutions were stripped of their property and converted into Christian Churches wherever possible. Where not possible, the buildings were torn down and their *"lands"* repurposed.

New colonists who arrived on future Interplanetary Push Ships were asked those same two questions and the same results applied. It became the Jovian Realm's dirty little secret. The once Jovian Republic, was now the Jovian Realms and it had become a staunch, right-wing Christian Society in which all non-Christians were held and controlled by the right hand!

The Jovian Realm was now a feudal society with a fundamentalist mindset and they kept Slaves!

This was not really about religion at all. For High Prince Albert von Horridian, it was purely a method of control. Something that worked and had been used previously by others, since time immemorial.

For power was means unto itself and High Prince Albert von Horridian chose to exercise that power!

26. The Saturnian Demarchy.

The girls all sat in their usual row of seats, with their data tablets in front of them. On the far left was Saffiera, to her right was Kethera and then further across were Ariel, Yeannah and Aria. The twins were sitting protectively on either side of their friend, Yeannah, whose previous week had been emotionally harrowing. The twins were fiercely protective of their friends.

Across the aisle from Yeannah, sat Yookey, who still quietly held *"forbidden"* feelings for Yeannah, his fellow Indigenous Thol friends sat to his right. In the row of seats behind them sat Richard, Thomas and their friends, not in their usual seats. They'd all moved forward two rows of seats so that Richard could sit closer to Kethera.

Richard was bonded to Kethera, as she was to him and that bond subconsciously forced him to sit closer to her, something that Kethera also needed. Thomas, who also had unrequited love for Yeannah, also *"forbidden"*, sat behind her, much to the chagrin of the twins. Thomas was the very reason for Yeannah's previous harrowing emotional week. The other students all sat around the class wherever they felt comfortable.

The emotional tension in the classroom was palpable and the changed seating arrangements told Miss Bream that something was afoot that she was not privy to. Nonetheless, Miss Bream continued with her class as usual. The emotional undercurrents around her students would need to be handled later, perhaps when more information was available. Miss Bream already had some information. Yookey's parents had already discussed their concerns about their Son's crush on a non-Indigenous Thol, Yeannah, with the year-level ten coordinator. Miss Bream, however, got the distinct feeling that something more was afoot.

It was past mid-morning when Miss Bream's presentation on the fall and subsequent rise of the Horridians had finished. Her students all looked stunned, during their own studies during the preceding week, they had all come across lots of historical information. Information that was largely about, politics, economics, technological innovation, colonial expansion, mining operations, things of a very mundane nature. For the most part, the personages involved were either very normal or even altruistic. This historical snippet about the Horridian family, however, was brutal, violent and at all times self-serving.

After watching the presentation about the Horridian's fall and subsequent rise, the class was unusually quiet. That was to be expected, the Horridians had been directly responsible for two devastating wars in the Sol System, neither of which were the subject of this term's joint assignment. The Outer Satellite Insurrection was the joint assignment for the next term, term three and the Horridian War of twenty three sixty was for next year's term two joint history assignment. For this term, however, it was the Great Explosion, the Outward Interplanetary Expansion, between the year twenty sixty and twenty one eighty two, during which the Horridians played their nefarious roles.

Kethera looked particularly distressed, her ears were flattened, her whiskers drooped and her tail was dead still. Carlins, especially young Carlins, held their emotions on their sleeves for all to see. Saffiera had picked up on her friend's emotional state and automatically took hold of her hand, transmitting soothing telepathic sensations. It helped Kethera but not by much.

Kethera's voice was shaky, she didn't even raise her hand when she asked, blurting out, "What happened to Adam and Evelyn?"

Miss Bream answered without giving any detail, "They both met with an unfortunate accident."

"No!", Kethera snapped back uncharacteristically, "What really happened to them?", she asked.

Miss Bream gave Kethera a stern look but replied softly, "I left that part out, Kethera. It's not necessary for the assignment and the Carlin students in this class may find it overly distressing."

Another Carlin girl at the back of the class chimed in, "We need to know, Miss Bream!", her feline features also showed clear signs of emotional stress.

"Okay. Are you all sure about this?", Miss Bream asked, then requested, "Raise your hands if you really want to know!"

The whole class raised their hands, they all wanted to know.

Miss Bream sighed and began to divulge Adam Cain's and Evelyn Abel's fate, "Once the colony of Himalia Central had been brought online in Himalia's trailing Trojan point. The colonists of the Jovian Dream Consortium arrived and made it their new home. Adam and Evelyn married and in the years that followed had three children, a boy and two girls", then she paused to gauge her student's reactions.

So far, so good, Miss Bream continued, "When the Horridians arrived, they lied and connived their way into Adam's and Evelyn's good graces. They did the same with all of the Jovian Republic's early leaders. Of course, lies and conniving can only last so long before the cracks start to appear. When Adam and Evelyn realised that they'd been conned, they decided to go to one of the other colonies, Jovian L-One Central, for their own safety. So they booked passage for their whole family on an inter-colony shuttle bound for Jovian L-One Central."

"So they got away?", one of the Indigenous Thol's asked.

"No. No, they did not get away", Miss Bream answered, continuing, "The inter-colony shuttle was docked at the Himalia Central's northern end cap docking ring and they followed their boarding instructions, making their way to the designated airlock. Unfortunately, when the airlock's outer doors opened, there was no shuttle and they found themselves exposed to the vacuum of space."

"What happened to the shuttle?", Yookey asked, even though he was looking a little distressed.

Miss Bream replied, "The inter-colony shuttle was docked at the airlock next door. Someone had altered the shuttle's docking instructions after the boarding instructions were issued and disabled the airlock's safety systems to make it appear accidental."

Kethera's whiskers were twitching wildly, indicating extreme emotional stress, "How old were the children?", she asked, as Saffiera squeezed her hand tightly.

Miss Bream sighed, "Kethera, they were around the same age as you and the other students here. Their Daughters were twins."

"Same-faced Kits!", Kethera sobbed loudly, same-face Kits were seen as special in Carlin culture.

The revelation that the entire family, including their teenage children, had been murdered under the guise of an accident was devastating. Several Carlins broke into quiet sobs, their whiskers trembling, while even Yookey and his friends struggled to hold back their tears.

Ariel and Aria had recently had their dormant psychic abilities awakened and Aria sent an angry thought to Miss Bream, who was extremely surprised to receive it, *"That was a very bad idea!"*

Saffiera was quick to reach out to Ariel and Aria, *"Time for some practice"*, she transmitted.

"What! How? We don't know what to do?", Ariel thought back in true telepathic fashion.

Saffiera quickly replied, *"Focus on my thoughts and feel how I shape the energies around us!"*

Ariel and Aria both gave Saffiera a telepathic nod.

Saffiera linked her mind with the twin's minds and then spread her mind outward encompassing the entire classroom. A wave of warmth and calm washed over the room, easing tension and quieting restless minds. Miss Bream, who was incredibly surprised by the sensation, somehow felt it was not just Saffiera creating the warmth and calm, somehow the twins were involved.

The twins watched closely as Saffiera worked, they were being taught, in much the same way as Saffiera's Mother, Sarlia, had taught her. They were learning as they sat and watched, lending their energies to Saffiera's skills. Within minutes most of the students in the class were asleep at their desks, as was Saffiera's intent, with the exception of most of the Human students who were far more emotionally resilient.

Saffiera confirmed what Miss Bream had suspected with a private message, *"The twins are scions of Folcrom Tafazah and they are awakening"*, she informed her, of course, the twins being scions, the message was easily picked up by them.

"Thank you, Saffiera. How long will they sleep for?", Miss Bream asked verbally.

"Perhaps five or ten minutes. It depends on how deeply they were affected emotionally by your revelations", Saffiera transmitted, noting, *"They will feel a lot better when they awaken, perhaps even a little more refreshed, with clearer minds."*

Miss Bream asked, "How, Saffiera? How did you do this? I know you're a telepath, but how?"

"We Martians are more than just telepaths, Miss Bream. We can take on the emotional burdens of others when the occasion requires it", Saffiera explained, noting, *"There was a time when we Martians were far more limited in our abilities, but that was before our liberation from Tarlak bondage."*

Miss Bream, not having any real understanding of Martian abilities, murmured, "The Mimasian War", and then cautioned, "Well, Saffiera, just so long as you don't overexert yourself in the process."

Aria transmitted almost automatically, *"Don't worry, Miss Bream. Ariel and I have Saffiera's back!"*

Miss Bream was well versed with Aria's antics and that was not reassuring at all.

As predicted by Saffiera, the sleeping students all began to awaken and within ten minutes the class was back to normal, except for a few yawns here and there. Kethera and the other Carlins were feeling a lot better, as were some of the more sensitive Humans and Thols.

"Did you have a nice nap, Kethera", Saffiera enquired.

"Yes, thank you, Saffiera", Kethera replied, still feeling a bit sleepy.

Richard was sitting on his desk and massaging Kethera's shoulders, which Kethera was thoroughly enjoying, "Sit down, Richard. This is a history class, not a massage parlour", Miss Bream told him.

Yookey yawned and noted, "Miss Bream. I think the Horridians were the absolute antithesis of Stuart Dumas and his Son."

"Yes, Yookey. That is correct", Miss Bream agreed, "Both were driven in their own ways but the methods were completely different. Miles apart in fact."

Aria thought to her friends, *"That deserves a big reward"*, then she got up stepped over to Yookey, sat down on his lap, wrapped her arms around him and gave him a huge big kiss on the cheek.

"Aria! Miss Swanson! Return to your seat immediately", Miss Bream called out.

"Miss Bream, I was just rewarding Yookey for his perfect answer", Aria explained cheekily.

Yookey's face was bright red with embarrassment.

"Yes, well, Miss Swanson. We'll have no more of that behaviour in this class", Miss Bream replied, while looking at Yookey's bright red face with concern.

"What the actual fuck, Aria", Ariel transmitted to Aria and her friends, *"Are you trying to get us in trouble?"*

Aria sighed and explained telepathically, *"Yookey has had, Yeannah on his mind all morning. Now, he has me on his mind instead."*

Saffiera checked on Yookey, *"It seems to have worked. Yookey is definitely thinking about you now."*

"You see. Job done!", Aria smiled and transmitted back.

Ariel just shook her head.

For the rest of the morning, the class discussed the behaviour and tactics of Albertus Horridian and his Son, Albert. Yookey, having recovered from his earlier embarrassment, engaged in a discussion about the change in Albert Horridian, from describing Aurange Sheergibbon and his partner, Roberta Nummus as psychopaths, to becoming their master and *"rabid dog"* handler.

Aria gave Yookey her biggest possible smile and explained, that the change came after Albertus's death and that was probably the trigger for his change. Going so far as to say, that Albert took on more of his Father's persona after his death. Miss Bream agreed and was delighted with the discussion.

Yeannah was no longer in Yookey's thoughts, now Aria was on his mind almost constantly and his crush had shifted completely. Yeannah was not sure that Aria was doing the right thing, she was too impulsive and Yookey would likely get hurt. Aria assured Yeannah telepathically, that she would not lead Yookey on and let him down gently. Although, if Aria was entirely honest with herself, she actually did like Yookey. Fickle be the hearts of young teenagers.

There was also some discussion about Stuart Dumas and his using the colonisation of the Asteroid Belt and Jupiter's Trojans to embarrass the controlling governments of the day into taking the colonisation of the solar system more seriously.

"Was it really his plan all along?", Yookey asked, he was going out of his way to impress Aria.

Miss Bream had replied, "It certainly seemed to be because it worked. After that, Saturn, Uranus, Neptune, even Pluto and the larger Dwarf Planets were, in fact, colonised."

Yookey pressed on, saying, "Yet it kind of backfired, didn't it? If those Interplanetary Push Ships had not been available, the Horridians would have been stuck in Cis-Lunar space in disgrace!", he was really trying to impress Aria.

"Yes!", Miss Bream exclaimed in absolute delight, "No Push Ships! No

Horridian Dynasty! Well done Yookey!", it was so rare for Yookey to be so engaged.

Yookey turned to Aria, to gauge her reaction, she was already looking at him and transmitted him a private telepathic message, *"I should give you an even bigger reward"*, she smiled genuinely.

That caught Yookey by surprise once more and his normal alabaster white face went bright with embarrassment, something highly noticeable on a Thol, nonetheless he still managed to smile at Aria.

Kethera had asked Miss Bream, why Aurange Sheergibbon and Roberta Nummus had murdered the twelve workers when they stole the *"Slayers"* and *"Eramis"* technology from the Dumas Corporation's Research and Development Division. Miss Bream had cautioned Kethera and the rest of the class, remembering the previous incident, that perhaps that would be best left alone.

Thomas replied, "Kethera, psychopaths enjoy killing, they don't need a reason. Just the name of that technology alone, Stackable Layered Radiation Shield Plating, (SLaReS), *"Slayers"*, was probably enough to trigger them."

Kethera was perplexed, "So just the name of that technology, *"Slayers"* and they just go and slay?"

Miss Bream gave a none committal answer, "Potentially, Kethera. We'll never really know, it's best not to dwell on it."

Yeannah chimed in, "Kethera, it's better to change the subject. This one will just make you sad."

Kethera nodded in agreement.

Yookey agreed with both Thomas and Yeannah, "Psychopaths don't need a reason, Kethera. They just kill. They just do what they like. Even I don't like to think about it. We should move on."

Aria transmitted a telepathic smile, complete with the batting of her eyelids, *"My wise Thol."*

Yookey's face went bright red once again and he looked around to smile back at Aria.

Miss Bream moved on to the next section of the term's joint assignment, the colonisation of the Saturnian system and orbital zone. Saturn, itself as a planet, had over two hundred and seventy four moons, seven rings and its

Trojan points, of which, L-One, L-Two, L-Four and L-Five were more than useful. The latter two Lagrangian zones had thousands of small asteroids, however, they were small, mostly less than twenty kilometres across.

Miss Bream began to explain to the class, using her laser point to highlight the relevant sections of hyper-text on the network pages, "You can see here that the colonisation of the entire Saturnian orbital zone, used both a combination of Dumas Corporation and Colonial Central's methods", she began.

"The Saturnian colonists called themselves the Saturnian Demarchy and they wanted to set up a direct democracy, where all decisions went to a referendum or plebiscite, whereby every person above the age of suffrage could and would vote. A democracy without any political parties and every member of their parliament was an independent", Miss Bream informed the class.

"Did they succeed?", asked a curious Yookey, without putting up his hand.

"Yes, Yookey. The Saturnian Demarchy exists to this very day", Miss Bream replied, adding, "And, Yookey, could please raise your hand if you have any future questions?"

Yookey went slightly red and replied, "Yes, Miss Bream."

Aria turned around and Yookey noticed, turning around to meet her gaze, she blew him a kiss. Yookey went bright red once more. Miss Bream just shook her head.

Aria's twin Sister, Ariel, reached over and gave her a slight elbow to her ribs, *"What do you think you're doing?"*, she transmitted, *"Yookey, is an Indigenous Thol. You are poking a hornet's nest."*

Aria sighed and turned to look at Ariel, *"I know that, but I like him. Yookey is nice!"*

Ariel slapped her palm to her face and Yeannah, who was sitting between them asked in a whisper, "What's wrong Ariel? Are you and Aria having a telepathic disagreement?"

Ariel whispered back, "My Sister, Aria, I think she has a crush on Yookey."

Yeannah blinked several times as that snippet of information sank in, "Oh, that can't be good. If they forbade Yookey from being with me because I'm a Mimasian Thol. They'll really freak out if he gets involved with Aria, she's a Human. It would be an absolute scandal. The Indigenous Elders would get involved and call a council meeting. Yookey's whole family would get called in", she whispered back.

"Excrement and turbines come to mind, Yeannah", Ariel whispered in agreement.

Aria sent them both a telepathic message, *"It will be my problem. I'll deal with it!"*

Ariel and Yeannah just rolled their eyes, knowing that Aria could not possibly handle ancient Indigenous Tholish taboos against inter-species relationships.

Ariel transmitted to her Sister, Aria, the telepathic images of shit hitting the fan and just spraying everywhere, especially on Aria.

Aria replied to her friends telepathically, *"You both worry way too much. I've got this"*, to which they both sighed and rolled their eyes once more.

Completely oblivious to the telepathic communication and whispering going on, Miss Bream continued on with her lesson. Saffiera, having picked up on the twin's telepathic conversion and the larger whispered conversion, kept their friend, Kethera in the loop, telepathically, of course. Kethera faced palmed, thinking of the looming disaster.

Miss Bream continued, "Okay class, the Saturnian Demarchy, had plans to colonise, Saturn's leading and trailing Trojan points, along with the leading and trailing Trojan points of Saturn's Moon Titan as well. Furthermore, they had plans to colonise Titan itself. Their plans were, to say the least, ambitious."

Yookey raised his hand to ask a pertinent question, "Miss Bream, that's huge! How did they manage to pull that one off?", he asked, trying his best to impress Aria.

"Yookey, if you'd just waited a little bit longer, you'd know", Miss Bream replied, then continued, "The Saturnian Demarchy contracted the Dumas Corporation for financing, construction and transport of four large twin-cylinder O'Neil-style colonies. Each one was capable of housing well over fifty thousand colonists. Dumas Colonial Financial provided all of the funding", then she paused, "Why aren't you all taking notes? Come on students, start taking notes", she implored.

Then Miss Bream continued, after watching the students pick up their styluses and put them to their data tablets, "At that distance from the Sun, those colonies required greater curvature for their strip windows to capture sunlight and more power fission reactors. Dumas Colonial Constructions and Himmelstaff Interplanetary Constructions picked up the construction of the O'Neil-style colonies and their accompaniment of mining, ore processing and manufacturing stations, equally between themselves. Of course, Dumas Corporation's, Cis-Lunar Haulage picked up the transport contract and used their latest and greatest space tugs for that purpose.

Yookey raised his hand once more, he was really trying to impress Aria, "Miss Bream. There weren't a lot of big asteroids in Saturn's Trojan points. Just lots of little ones. How'd they deal with that?"

"Honestly, Yookey. I am about to get to that part. You just need a little more patience", Miss Bream explained to him.

Aria turned to Yookey once more and blew him another kiss, which Yookey did see and then thought to himself, *"Aria, like, likes me!"*, even though, as an Indigenous Thol, he should not encourage her.

Aria sent Yookey a telepathic confirmation, *"Yes, of course, silly"*, and then Yookey went red with embarrassment, Miss Bream had noticed the exchange.

"Aria! Miss Swanson! Are you going to continue blowing Yookey kisses or can I continue with this lesson?", Miss Bream enquired, she was hoping to embarrass Aria into submission.

Aria replied, smiling, "That all depends, Miss Bream. Is Yookey going to continue looking so handsome and continue to impress me?", she asked.

The entire classroom burst into laughter. Yookey went even redder and placed his head on the table in front of him.

"Silence!", Miss Bream yelled, then she turned to Aria, "Miss Swanson, you will behave yourself in my class or your Mother will be called into the Principal's office for a meeting."

Aria begrudgingly answered, "Understood, Miss Bream. I apologise", however, inside she was laughing.

Once the class was quiet, Miss Bream continued, "Yes, Yookey", she acknowledged, "There are a lot of asteroids in Saturn's Trojan points and yes, they are all small, under twenty kilometres across. However, you may recall that the Dumas Corporation has answers for that sort of issue. Remember students, that those space tugs also contained teams of specialists to unfurl the colony's strip window mirrors, offload the orbital mining, process and manufacturing stations and set up the colonies for future occupation by the colonists."

Miss Bream looked around the class, they were all diligently taking notes, she continued, "Those same space tugs used some of the small local asteroids to create conglomerated asteroidal masses in Saturn's L-Four and L-Five sweet spots. They also travelled farther afield, hauling back smaller Centaur Bodies and other more distant asteroids to add to those conglomerated asteroidal masses. Once finished, the new colonies were placed into halo orbits around those now fair-sized conglomerated asteroidal masses in Saturn's L-Four and L-Five regions. The colonists would then be able to mine and process the materials from those masses."

Yookey put up his hand, "Yookey, you want to know about Titan's Trojan points, yes?", Miss Bream enquired.

"Yes, Miss Bream", Yookey replied.

"It was the same deal as with Saturn's Trojans, Yookey", Miss Bream replied, explaining, "The specialists in the space tugs, set up the colonies as usual and then tracked down which nearby small asteroids and even some of Saturn's smaller outer moons, that could use to build up conglomerated asteroidal masses. Then the colonies would be placed into halo orbits around those masses. The Dumas Corporation by this stage of the solar systems colonisation, were very well versed in the process."

Richard who had been quiet through the class, mainly due to his bond to Kethera, who was always in his thoughts, remarked, "Miss Bream. You did mention that the Saturnian Demarchy used *'both'* methods to colonise Saturn."

"Yes, Richard. Thank you for reminding me, but just like Yookey, you've jumped the gun. I was just getting to that section", Miss Bream replied, as she scrolled further down the page.

"Okay then. Along with the twin-cylinder O'Neil-style colonies, the Saturnian Demarchy decided to make use of the Interplanetary Push Ships. More importantly, as the designs were in the open domain, they chose the Dumas Colonial Constructions and Himmelstaff Interplanetary Constructions to construct them. Tailoring them to their own requirements", Miss Bream informed the class, then asked, "Now, can anyone tell me why this might have caused some consternation with the Earth's Government and Cis-Lunar L-Five's Government?"

Yookey was so quick to raise his hand, he had the answer and really needed to impress Aria, "Yes, Yookey", Miss Bream announced.

"The Earth Government and Cis-Lunar L-Five's Government had both conspired to break the Dumas Corporation's monopoly on end-to-end services for space colonisation", Yookey answered, noting, "Their plans had backfired when the Dumas Corporation was once again selected to help colonise the outer solar system. They were hoping that other companies would take the initiative."

"Yes, Yookey", Miss Bream applauded, clapping her hands together, "Perhaps I should allow Miss Swanson to blow kisses to you more often."

Yookey went bright red once more and before Aria could take the initiative and blow Yookey another kiss, Miss Bream pointed to her and said, "No, Miss Swanson. I was joking."

Miss Bream continued with the lesson, "The Dumas Corporation's Research and Development Division took the open source plans for the Interplanetary Push Ships and modified them for the Saturnian Demarchy requirements. They needed five push ships. Those ships needed to take the colonists to both Saturn's Trojan points and Titan's Trojan points, as well as Titan itself."

Miss Bream looked around the class, they were all diligently taking notes, she continued, "The Push Ships would all have the usual accompaniment of mining, ore processing and manufacturing stations. However, they also required survey craft to scout out locations on Saturn's Moons for resource extraction. They also needed ore transports to take the extracted ore to the processing stations and transport shuttles to travel as far as Saturn's Trojan points. The Dumas Corporation's engineers also designed the entire Titanian colony itself."

Thomas put up his hand and Miss Bream pointed to him, he asked, "So the Titan Trojan colonies didn't really need those conglomerated asteroidal masses at all?", he was hoping to impress Yeannah.

"Incorrect, Mr Mitchel", Miss Bream replied, explaining, "Having those conglomerated asteroidal masses at the Titanian Trojan sweet spots, not only gave the new colonies something to orbit but also convenient nearby masses to mine! It is so much easier to extract mineral ores when they are close by. Being able to survey and mine the Saturnian Moons and haul the extracted ore back to the Titanian Trojans for processing was just an added bonus."

Thomas nodded in understanding, "Yes, Miss."

Yeannah smiled and gave off a little smirk and giggle, even a couple of soft trills.

Miss Bream then asked the class, "Okay then, who can tell me what happens to a Push Ship when its task is completed?"

Yeannah put up her hand and Miss Bream pointed to her, "Well, Miss Bream. Once the Push Ship arrives, it is either starting a new colony, carrying new colonists or both. Once the new colony is built and online, the colonist disembark and take up their new homes. Then the Push Ship at that point becomes raw materials to be reused in further colonial constructions. They get recycled."

Miss Bream clapped her hands together, "Yes, Yeannah", then she pointed to Saffiera and asked, "Are there any exceptions, Saffiera?"

Saffiera thought for a few seconds, then answered, transmitting, *'Not usually, Miss Bream. Push Ships usually have a one-way journey. Once they've completed their task, they simply get recycled into other constructions",* then she stopped for a moment and noted, *"There is only one exception that I can think of. The four Horridian push ships, they were kept in a ship's graveyard at Ganymede Lagrangian point One"*, this was in her passed-down shared telepathic memories

"Well done, Saffiera", Miss Bream replied, noting, "The Horridians not only placed their four Push Ships in a ship's graveyard, but they also upgraded them with the latest radiation shielding."

Yeannah put up her hand and Miss Bream pointed to her, "It's as if the Horridians somehow knew that they'd be needing them in the future."

"Yes, Yeannah", Miss Bream agreed, commenting, "Having been exiled once, from Cis-Lunar L-Five, they remembered and they took precautions. After the end of the second Horridian War, in twenty three sixty two, they used those very same four Push Ships to go into exile at Eris. It's as if they knew that some day they'd need them. Anyway, that was just a side note and not required for the assignment."

Miss Bream continued with the lesson, "The five push ships that the Saturnian Demarchy had contracted were also slightly different. They were not designed to be scrapped or recycled like most Push Ships were. Instead, those five Push Ships were designed to be the backbone of the Titanian colony itself. Once a suitable location on Titan had been scouted out and the Push Ships were no longer required, they were carefully piloted into landing positions on the surface of Titan, in a pentagonal formation."

Miss Bream paused once more to let the students catch up with their notes, "Now Students, I have oversimplified this, the ground at the selected colony site did have to be prepared first. The five Push Ships were not arranged bow to stern at the landing site either."

Yookey put up his hand and Miss Bream pointed to him, "How were they arranged, Miss Bream?"

"Yookey, just a little patience and I'll get to that point", Miss Bream replied, "The Push Ships were arranged in a pentagonal arrangement, but the gap between the bow of one ship and the stern of the next was equal to the length of each Push Ship", she explained.

Thomas put up his hand and Miss Bream pointed to him, "That would mean that the overall shape of the colony site was decahedral, a decagon, Miss Bream."

"Good pick up, Mr Mitchel", Miss Bream replied, explaining, "Five of those ten sides were the Push Ships. The other five sides were connecting transportation tubes from one Push Ship to the next. Within that decahedral structure, the new Titanian colonists built several large domes and all of their required infrastructure. Once that was completed, the entire complex was backfilled and covered with Titanian regolith, except for the domes, of course. All of the structural and outer materials used were of a specially formulated *"exotic"* plasteel that could withstand Titan's extremely low temperatures."

Miss Bream looked around her class once more, before continuing, "That was the original colony structure on Titan. Of course, the colony did expand well beyond the original decahedral structure, extending well beyond the original Push Ships. By the time of the Mimasian War, the Titanian colony complex was immense, the size of a small city. Please note, our network resources do contain some quite detailed layouts, for those of you who may be interested."

Miss Bream had just finished speaking when the lunch bell chimed, "Okay class before you leave, make sure you study the next section of the notes. What became of Titan. This is pertinent as it involves the aftermath of the Mimasian War, which you all studied last term. You will find it very interesting. Class dismissed!"

27. What Became of Titan.

The girls left their history class to eat their lunch at the school's eastern quadrangle as usual. The majestic maple tree in the centre provided the girls with its usual mottled shade. Vale's primary, yellow Sun, Cathol, was high and Vale's secondary, orange Sun, Cythol, was as usual obscured by the shadow of a nearby building. That was quite normal for this time of year.

There was no breeze to rustle the leaves of the shrubbery surrounding the edges of the quadrangle. The English Box shrubs showed an ever so slight yellowing and even browning of their leaves. The Blueberry bushes intermixed with them, were taking on striking autumnal colours, with some bushes showing vibrant hues of bright reds, oranges and yellows. There were even some with purple tints.

Aria was still leaving her *"offerings"* of food at the end of each day, for the Harricks that lived somewhere nearby. The titbits of bread, berries and pieces of apple were always gone by the next morning and still not a single Harrick had been seen. Aria was disappointed, she had wanted to befriend the Harricks, but it appeared that the wee creatures were overly shy. Perhaps, it would take a week or two longer she had mused to herself.

After eating their lunches, having occasionally shared their food to try anything new that appeared in their lunch boxes, they all headed off to the senior school study hall. As they left the quadrangle, Aria sensed something unusual and she quickly turned, just in time to glimpse something disappearing behind the shrubbery. Was it a Harricks? It was about the right size.

"I think I just saw a Harricks", Aria told her friends.

"Don't be silly, Aria", Kethera replied, remarking, "Harricks never, ever come out during the day."

"No. Aria is right", Ariel noted, agreeing with her Sister, "I sensed it too. There was something there watching us eat. It's gone now though."

Ariel teased her twin Sister, Aria, "So you're going to flirt with a Harricks now are you, Aria?"

Aria did not reply, but her face showed a slight degree of annoyance at the statement.

"How unusual", Kethera replied, as they all continued onto the study hall.

When the girls arrived at the senior school study hall, it was unusually crowded. Their usual table was occupied by a group of Indigenous Thols and they had to sit at another table, one that was adjacent to a table that Richard was sitting at, along with Thomas and his friends. Kethera sat down in a chair right next to Richard, her bond mate.

Kethera asked Richard in a hushed whisper, "Did you take your pheromone blockers?"

"Yes", Richard replied and he asked, "And you, Kethera. You took your contraceptives last night?"

Kethera nodded and replied, "Yes!", as she jumped up and sat on Richard's lap giving him a big hug.

One of Richard's friends, Samuel, commented, "Really guys. Can we get you a room?"

Kethera replied back smiling, "No thank you, Sam. We don't need one."

Yeannah sat herself down close to Thomas, she liked him and he liked her, however, as Yeannah was a Thol, the inter-species relationship was forbidden. Not by her species, the Mimasian Thols, but by the vocal majority, the Indigenous Thols, the ten thousand to one and their ancient taboos and laws.

Aria was looking very disappointed, *"Where's Yookey"*, she thought to herself.

Yeannah nodded to Thomas and Thomas acknowledged her presence with an ever so slight nod in return, although they dared not speak to each other. The girls all quietly activated their data tablets, took out their styluses and connected to the school's network and its voluminous datasets.

They all quickly found the section that they were looking for, *"The Great Explosion, disambiguation four, The Outward Interplanetary Expansion, What Became of Titan."*

Morris Carpenter sat in Administrator Mark Spencer's office, he had concerns, serious concerns.

"Mark, this is not good. We've always had issues with hypo-gravitational syndromes and other gravity-related health concerns, but lately, there has been a marked uptick in these issues", Morris informed the Administrator.

"What kind of uptick do you mean, Morris", Mark Spencer enquired.

"We used to see just a few each year. You know, people forgetting to take their supplements and stimulants, not performing required exercises to combat Titan's low gravity situation", Morris explained, noting, "The gravity here is only fourteen percent of Earth's as you know, it's even lower than the Moon's, so our people have to be diligent."

"Yes, Morris, I understand all of that, but what about this uptick?", Mark asked again.

"I was just getting to that, Mark", Morris replied, explaining, "At the beginning of last year, there was an increase in hypo-gravitational disorders. It went from two or three per year to two or three per month and it's been increasing. We are now looking at two to three per week."

Mark leaned back in his chair and steepled his hands and fingers, "What about the stimulants and supplements?", he queried.

"Our people, the patients, they are taking them", Morris confirmed, noting, "I don't think they're working anymore. I have our medical researchers looking into it."

Mark Spencer, as the Administrator of the Saturnian colonies, was one of the few people, whose memories had not been altered by the Council of Shadows or by Gideon Reas and Sandra Danker. Mark remembered the Mimasian War two years earlier, a devastating War craftily hidden behind altered memories, altered historical records and currently called "The Great Disaster". Supposedly caused by the solar system passing through multiple swarms of devastating interstellar micrometeors. Mark knew that the alien species, the Tarlaks, the antagonists during the War, were extinct and that Martians lived on Mars and also inside of Mimas. Although, he didn't know about the Thols living inside Mimas. Some things, he was not privy to. Mark was the gatekeeper to Mimas and even had a hotline to their communications network.

Morris informed the Administrator, "We need to evacuate our most affected patients to somewhere with an Earth-like gravity. That is the only way that they'll have any hope of recovery."

"Well, Morris, that is going to put us in a difficult position", the Administrator noted, "We lost all of our O'Neil-style colonies to the great disaster and its micrometeor showers. So we don't actually have anywhere to evacuate our patients to. We would have to send them to the Jovian colonies."

"That's a long way, Mark", Morris frowned, remarking, "Some of them won't survive the journey and we have already lost more than a few lives. Some of these hypo-gravitational syndromes are quite deadly. Can we create something temporary?", he asked.

"I can run it past our engineers but I'm not sure what they can do", Marked replied, he added, "Perhaps some form of centrifuge? Even that wouldn't be ideal though. Any centrifuge would need to rotate fast enough to generate one g, be large enough to house the most affected patients and large enough to significantly reduce the Coriolis effects. I don't know if that can be done down here on the surface."

"What about off-world? Can we build something temporary in orbit, while we rebuild our colonies?", Morris asked.

"That is a question for our engineers. Building colonies, we talking about time scales in the years and a hypothetical *'big'* centrifuge, in the order of months, at least", Mark replied frowning.

Neither of them had easy answers, so Administrator Spenser passed the request to his engineers.

A few days later there was a meeting in Administrator Mark Spencer's office. The Head of Titan's Health Department, Morris Carpenter was present, as was the Head of Titan's Engineering Department, Pablo Ortega and The Honorable Lillian Seato, Titan's Prime Minister. The three sat around the front of Mark Spencer's desk, with the Prime Minister in the centre, Morris on the right and Pablo on the left. Mark's desk was covered in folders full of documents.

"We have good news Ladies and Gentlemen, very good news", Mark informed them, then he began, "First, these hypo-gravitational health syndromes. Pablo has a way forward on that front."

Pablo took out some preliminary designs and passed them around, "This space station will be one hundred and thirty metres across and rotate at three point seven revolutions per minute. That will provide almost one standard gravity."

Everyone looked at the preliminary blueprints, they showed a structure with a central circular docking hub that was ten metres across. Extending out from that hub, was a cross structure of hollow transport and connecting tubes, each of which was fifty metres long. At the ends of each structural connecting tube was a cylinder connected at right angles. The cylinders were connected at their central point and each was ten metres wide and fifty metres in length. Overall the whole structure would be one hundred and thirty metres in diameter.

"How long will it take to build?", Morris asked as the issue was time-critical.

"We can have the first one up and ready in orbit in thirty days", Pablo replied.

"Thirty days!", Morris was concerned, he noted, "We could lose a couple of our more critical patients. The ones with Hypo-gravitational Muscular Atrophy or Hypo-gravitational Pulmonary Insufficiency. Some of our patients have both!"

Pablo frowned, "Morris, we can only do what we can do. There is no magical solution."

Lillian enquired, "Pablo, you said the first one, yes?"

Pablo replied, explaining, "Yes. I've checked the number of patients with critical hypo-gravitational issues. There are just too many. So we build the first one in thirty days, to take care of the most serious cases. After that, we start on the second, which will take another thirty days to build, for the next most serious cases. It will be an ongoing project. I expect we can produce these gravitational health stations at the rate of one per month until we have all of the most serious cases covered."

Prime Minister Lillian Seato chimed in, "Obviously this is a public health and safety issue. There will be no need for a parliamentary vote. I'm just going to approve it and get the ball rolling."

Administrator Mark Spencer chimed in, "Sorry to steal your thunder, Lillian but I've already approved the work and the ball is already rolling. It is, as you say, a public health and safety issue."

"Yes, thank you, Mark, however, I would have liked a heads up on this approval", Lillian replied.

Mark replied, "Lillian, you are always busy and run off your feet. When was the last time you checked your email?", he asked.

Lillian checked her communicator and her emails and there it was, an email from Mark, with all of the details and files, "It appears you're right, Mark. I've been too busy lately, even to check my emails."

Morris quickly stepped in, "We have had some good luck. Mark received some communiques from Colonial Central Command in Cis-Lunar L-Five. I spent most of last night reviewing the files."

"Yes", Mark agreed, commenting, "The Lunar Mining Consortium back on the Earth's Moon has been having the same issues with hypo-gravitational syndromes as we have. They have nearly five hundred affected workers from their consortium, with fifty still in their hospitals and they've even had six deaths."

"So, it's not just us then?", Lillian asked.

"No. Definitely not", Mark replied, adding, "They even created a new Gravity Law. *'For all colonies, that derive their gravity via artificial methods, i.e., centrifugal force, that artificial gravity shall not deviate from one Earth g, by more than plus or minus ten percent as applied to the colony's main living surface. With the exception of Military Training facilities.'* We have just received official notification of this new law."

"Well then, when have some new orbital colonies, we can implement the new law", Lillian replied.

Morris chimed in, "They know what's causing these hypo-gravitational syndromes as well. It seems that some of us, not all of us mind you, are developing a tolerance to the stimulants. Which severely reduces their effectiveness. That reduces the uptake of the supplements and leads to the syndromes."

Mark who had forwarded the files to Morris, had read the same documents, "The experts at Colonial Central Command believe, that there is also a variation in who it affects and who it does not and that variation is genetically related."

Morris continued, "So for some of us, there is no issue but for others with the genetic predisposition, the stimulants will become far less effective. We can, in some cases increase the stimulant dosage, however, that apparently does not work on everyone. So it's not really a viable solution."

Mark continued, "Colonial Central Command sent us all of their files, with all of their research. Morris's people are working on it as we speak."

"So, in the end. We still need these *'gravitational health stations'*?", Lillian asked.

"Sadly, yes, Lillian", Morris confirmed.

"We've relied on that stimulant and supplement regime ever since we started the colonies here and now those measures are all failing us", Lillian lamented.

"We do have some more good luck, Lillian", Mark remarked, he was almost smiling, which was hard to do given their current predicament.

"Good luck?", Lillian queried, then asked, "Let's hear it" and Mark nodded to Pablo to divulge it.

Pablo cleared his throat, "Ah hum", then began explaining, Those micrometeor swarms didn't just destroy our four twin-cylinder O'Neil-style colonies. They badly damaged Eros, which currently does not have an active space dock. Those swarms also damaged twenty seven twin-cylinder O'Neil-style colonies in Cis-Lunar L-Five."

"Okay but how is that good news for us?", Lillian enquired.

Pablo continued, "Well, Colonial Central Command has decided not to repair those colonies. Instead, they're going to replace them with twenty seven brand new colonies, bigger ones. Of those old, damaged colonies, twenty six of them have been *'gifted'* to the Belters, two per colony, *'free and clear'* to do with as they wish. As long as the Belters arrange haulage costs themselves. It was a *'goodwill'* gesture by President Carter and the Belters have accepted it."

"Pablo! How does that affect us?", Lillian questioned.

"The twenty seventh colony", Pablo replied, explaining, "It was the most recently constructed and the least damaged one. Colonial Central Command has offered it to us *'free and clear'* to do with as we wish. They have even offered to cover the haulage costs for us."

Mark chimed in, "Considering everything that's happened and our current situation, we need it. I've already accepted it as a matter of urgency and it is on its way as we speak."

Lillian checked her emails and rolled her eyes, "Yes, I see. Another email I failed to check."

Pablo chimed in, "Lillian. I've had my people go through that colony's specifications and damage report. It will take six to eight months to arrive and up to four months the set up and repair."

"So, we will have a new colony in ten to twelve months?", Lillian asked for clarification.

Mark confirmed, "Yes and its capacity maxes out at twenty five thousand colonists."

"That's fantastic!", Lillian exclaimed.

"It also has other ramifications, Lillian", Pablo noted, explaining, "By the time our ninth gravitational health station is completed, we will be just one month away from being able to move all of our patients into the new colony. We got this covered!", he exclaimed. excitedly

"This one also comes under health and safety. No need to vote. I'll just sign off on it", Lillian noted.

"It won't be enough though", Marked noted, explaining, "Before the disaster, Titan had a population of thirty thousand people, with all of the refugees from the destroyed Titanian leading and trailing Trojan colonies, we currently have over forty two thousand people crowded in down here."

Lillian nodded, "Not to mention the hundred thousand refugees from Saturn's leading and trailing Trojan colonies. They're all stuck in overcrowded refugee camps in the Jovian Republic. Tell me, Mark, do you have a plan for that as well? It seems to me that you always have a plan."

"You know me too well, Lillian", Mark replied, then he launched into his plan for the restoration of the Saturnian Demarchy and its colonies, "I've requested a rough costing from Stuart Dumas, for four replacement O'Neil-style colonies and an extra colony from Dumas Incorporated. All of the same capacity as the others that were destroyed, maxing out at above fifty thousand colonists."

"So, Saturnian Lagrangian points L-Four and L-Five, Titanian Lagrangian points L-Four and L-Five. What's the extra colony for?", Lillian enquired.

Mark actually smiled, "Saturnian Lagrangian point, L-One, complete with a new conglomerated asteroidal mass to mine."

"Mark, that is really ambitious. And massively expensive!", Lillian replied, noting, "Something like that has to go a full plebiscite! I cannot simply sign off on something like that!"

Mark frowned, this was the Saturnian Demarchy, most decisions were made by a parliament of independent and honourable members, the really *"huge"* decisions, however, always went to either a referendum or plebiscite.

Mark hated bursting bubbles but in this case, it was clear he had to, "Lillian, you cannot possibly be thinking of having a referendum on this. We lost close to forty thousand people from the Titanian Trojan colonies during the disaster and nearly another ten thousand from the Saturnian Trojan colonies. Hell, a hundred thousand of our people are stuck in Jovian refugee camps. So you tell me, Lillian, just how is this referendum going to work? Just put it to a vote in parliament and let the honourable members decide on the matter."

Morris chimed in, "Lillian, you don't seem to fully comprehend the gravity of this situation. Just having that one *'gifted'* colony is a godsend but it is nowhere near enough. This is an emergency, we literally need to evacuate nearly everyone from Titan."

"Evacuate!", Lillian exclaimed in disbelief, "No, no, no! That can't be right!"

Mark stepped back in confirming, "Morris is correct, Lillian", he then added, "Back in Cis-Lunar L-Five and the Earth's Moon, they've instituted a new policy. *'Six months on the Moon, then two years back up in the colonies, twelve months on the Moon, then five years back up in the colonies.'* We are going to need to institute something very similar here on Titan!"

Lillian's heart sank, "You mean that we have to abandon everything we've achieved here?"

Mark reached out and took Lillian's hand, consoling her, "Madam Prime Minister. We do not have a choice", then he turned to Pablo as he released Lillian's hand, "Pablo?"

Pablo looked up from his files, "Lillian, based on Mark's concept for the rebuilding of our colonies, my people are putting together plans. We should have plenty of room to house our refugees from the Jovian Republic and our refugees from here on Titan. We should also have plenty of room to house our evacuees from Titan as well."

Lillian nodded, she was extremely unhappy with the situation but what else could be done, "And what becomes of Titan? What becomes of our colony here?"

Pablo looked to Mark, who nodded, he continued, "All Titanian infrastructure outside of the core decagon will be recycled and reused. The decagon itself and everything within it will remain as a base of operations for Titanian volatiles mining operations."

Mark chimed back in, "It will just like with the Lunar Mining Consortium, *'Six months on Titan, then two years back up in the colonies, twelve months on Titan, then five years back up in the colonies.'* The only workers allowed to stay longer will be those with the right genetic markers."

Morris stepped back in, "Colonial Central Command has yet to figure out exactly what those genetic markers are. I also have my people working on it as well."

Lillian took a handkerchief out of her handbag, her eyes welling with tears, *"What a disaster"*, she thought to herself as the tears flowed freely.

The buzzer on Mark's desk communicator sounded, "Mr Spencer, Sir. We've received a reply from Dumas Incorporated. I'm just forwarding it to you now, Sir"

"Thank you, Melissa. I'll take a look at it straight away", Mark replied.

Pablo questioned, "Didn't you just send your request off last night, Mark?"

"I sure did, Pablo. I wasn't expecting a reply until they'd completed their costing", Mark replied, noting, "I thought that would take a week or two at least."

"Well, what does it say, Mark?", Lillian enquired, while dabbing away her tears.

Mark read the email, "Well, with all of the disasters and problems we've been hit with lately, this is good news at least."

"Good news?", Lillian scoffed, remarking, "After this morning, I doubt any such thing exists!"

"The email is from Baron and Hypolita Dumas, that's Stuart's Son and his Daughter-in-law", Mark replied and then read out the email's key points, "The Dumas Corporation acknowledges our state of emergency and dire circumstances. Stuart is organising a complete recovery plan and proposal, based on my stated requirements, which should be ready in two or three weeks", he stopped.

"Is that all?", Lillian enquired.

"No, there is more, Lillian, much more", Mark replied and then he continued, "If the recovery plan and proposal are accepted, both Dumas Philanthropic and Himmelstaff Philanthropic, will each cover ten percent of the proposal's costs."

"Ten percent each!", Lillian exclaimed, checking, "So they will cover twenty percent of the costs?"

"That is what it says here, Lillian. My math says twenty percent of the costs", Mark confirmed.

"That's the entire cost of that extra colony for Saturn L-One", Pablo commented.

"It sure is, Pablo", Mark replied, commenting, "There is more. They are offering finance through Dumas Colonial Financial at the Colonial Central Command's Reserve Bank base rate, plus a smidgen more to cover their costs. Our emergency requirements will be given the highest priority."

Lillian actually smiled, she almost laughed, "So, rock bottom rates. They're just covering their costs, not making any profit on the proposal at all?"

“That is what it says here, Lillian”, Mark confirmed, noting, “When the recovery plan and proposal arrives, I will go through it with you. We will cover every point in detail and have our own people do our due diligence on it.“

“If their proposal, is as good as they say it is, then I'll push it through parliament and if anyone dissents, they'll be receiving my boot where it fits”, Prime Minister Lillian Seato of the Saturnian Demarchy smiled.

When Baron and Hypolita had sent their email, they had noted to themselves that, *“Goodwill is its own reward!”*

“This one is right out of left field but it is something a lot of our honourable members in parliament have all been asking me about”, Prime Minister Seato began, then she asked, “Why is the Mimas colony not under our jurisdiction?”

“That would be because they are their own Sovereign State. A private colony unto themselves”, Administrator Mark Spencer replied as he reached into his left-hand desk draw and retrieved a file.

“A private colony? There is no such thing. We made no allowances for it in our original charter nor in our constitution”, the Prime Minister replied.

“Read this”, Mark replied as he passed her the file.

The file contained the original charter of the Mimas colony stating it had been founded thirty years before the arrival of the Saturnian Demarchy. It was, of course, produced from the altered records in the archives of Colonial Central Command and a complete fabrication by the Council of Shadows.

Lillian quickly scanned through the document, “This simply can't be right. If this document is correct, then the Mimasians were here three decades before us!”

“That document is correct, Lillian”, Mark Spencer lied, he knew that it was the work of Folcrom Orpheus, “It gets even better, Lillian. As the first and prior colony in the Saturnian system, the Mimasian colony has primacy over the Demarchy.”

“Primacy over us! That's ridiculous! They don't hold Sovereignty over us!”, Lillian pronounced.

“No, Prime Minister. Actually, under the solar system's laws, as the first colony here in the Saturnian System, they have primacy over us”, Mark confirmed, but then he noted, “They have chosen not to exercise it. They want their privacy.”

“Send me a copy of this document, Mark”, Lillian requested, commenting, “Our honourable members are going to find it very interesting.”

Mark was okay with that, he knew Folcrom Orpheus. The Demarchy's Parliament would find the document was in order. The Martians and the Thols would remain protected and safe.

Saffiera looked around at her friends and broadcast, *"I have passed down shared memories about the events leading to Titan's evacuation. It is really quite sad. My ancestors were living inside of Mimas at the time and they could have evacuated those colonists to Mimas. However, the Council of Shadows was quite adamant about hiding our presence in the Sol system. Not just us Martians, but also the Thols. Especially the Thols."*

"Why?", Thomas asked, he was puzzled as to why it was necessary for Martians and Thols to hide.

Saffiera frowned, it was difficult to answer, *"The whole cover-up, the whole Great Conceal, was done to protect we Martians and the Mimasian Thols. During the Mimasian War, every Tarlak was slaughtered and while that was largely due to Emperor Ahriman's psychic influence. The sheer brutality of the Colonial Troops was laid bare for all to see. Nearly every Martian was fearful of Earth Humans and for the Thols it was even more poignant. Mimasian Thols and Tarlaks were and still are genetic cousins. The Tarlaks were created from the original Thols, Mimasian Thols!"*

"So an entire war was covered up and concealed?", Thomas continued questioning.

Yeannah chimed in, "All Mimasian Thols are taught about this, Thomas. The Folcrom from the Council of Shadows believed that the Humans from Earth simply weren't ready for revelations about aliens in their solar system. The Martians had been enslaved by the Tarlaks for over ninety thousand years and my people, the Mimasian Thols, were and still are the closest living relatives of the Tarlaks. We were all tared by the same brush."

"And so the Council of Shadows hid everything, covered it all up for centuries", Thomas replied, it was no longer a question, it was now an understanding.

Yeannah commented, "Yes, Thomas. The Folcrom were powerful psychics and highly skilled. They could hide evidence, change computer records, rewrite people's memories and make people believe their cover-up. They were an occult, hidden society of powerful psychic protectors."

Richard commented, "All of that work wasted. It took them decades to build that colony on Titan and by the time of its evacuation, it was a small city. I mean, thirty thousand people, that's a city!"

Thomas added on, "Forty two thousand, remember those refugees from Titan L-Four and L-Five."

Kethera looked sad with her ears pressed down and her whiskers drooping, "Nearly fifty thousand dead!", she exclaimed.

Kethera was still sitting on Richard's lap, he hugged her tightly and replied,

"Hey, Kethera. Don't dwell on it. This all happened well over thirteen hundred years ago."

Yeannah replied to Richard, "You should have seen Kethera last term when we were studying about the Mimasian War itself."

Kethera looked at Richard and she spoke in a whisper, "That was really horrible! So many deaths!"

Aria in her usual fashion blurted out, "Thankfully, we're not studying about World War One with twenty million dead or World War Two with up to eighty five million dead."

Kethera moaned and buried her face in Richard's neck as her tears began to flow freely.

Ariel chided her twin Sister, "Aria! For God's sake will stop making things worse!"

Samuel, Richard's and Thomas's friend asked, "Are all Carlin girls this sensitive?"

At this point, Yookey turned up and upon hearing Samuel's question, answered, "Yep. It's a Carlinish thing. Their women are ultra-sensitive to death", then he sat down on a chair near Aria.

Samuel replied, "Carlinish girls are pretty and all, but I don't know if I could handle all of that emotional grief."

Richard glared at Samuel, "Sam, are you actually looking for a slap or something?"

Samuel put up his hands and replied, "Just saying!"

Thomas steered the subject onto another track, "What I find interesting, is that they didn't just give up! They had real health issues with low gravity syndromes, problems with destroyed colonies, refugees scattered every which way and they had to evacuate their main colony on Titan. What did they do? They doubled down. They planned for replacements for all of their destroyed colonies and even planned for expansion!"

Richard looked into Kethera's eyes, "You hear that, Kethera. The colonists were resilient, they doubled down and rebuilt everything. They even expanded!"

Yookey was looking at Richard and Kethera and he almost laughed, "I knew you two had a thing going on!"

Kethera's whiskers raised and her ears focused, "Took you long enough to notice, Yookey."

Yookey frowned, “Hey, I'm not slow. I can see there's something going on with these two as well”, he pointed to Thomas and Yeannah, both of whom went bright red.

Yeannah asked, cautiously, “Is it that obvious?”

“No. Not really. The pair of you hide it well”, Yookey replied quietly and honestly, noting, “Which explains why Aria has been flirting with me.”

“Was I that obvious?”, Aria asked.

“More obvious than the udder on a Gudong”, Yookey replied, which being a Gudong reference, had Kethera chuckling.

“My man, Yookey, clever and witty!”, Aria replied as she batted her eyes at him.

Yookey then got serious, “Yeannah, Thomas, you guys need to be careful. We Native Thols, do have some really stupid old-fashioned taboos. Technically, they shouldn't even apply to Mimasian Thols like, Yeannah, but some of my people simply can't see the difference”, then he commented with embarrassment, “Even I didn't until recently myself.”

Thomas nodded in understanding, “That inter-species relationship hang up.”

“That's the one. No Thol can enter a relationship with a non-Thol”, Yookey confirmed, noting, “That's bad enough, but as Native Thols and Mimasian Thols are a separate species, they've even extended it to both of our peoples”, he gestured to Yeannah and himself, “Stupid effing rules.”

“You don't agree with them, Yookey?”, Yeannah asked.

“Really, Yeannah! How could I possibly agree with something so stupid”, Yookey replied, adding, “I mean, who are these people anyway? The effing love police? In the privacy of your own home, it shouldn't matter.”

That excited Aria and she jumped onto Yookey's lap, straddling his legs, “You deserve a huge reward, Yookey”, and in full view of everyone in the study hall, planted a passionate kiss on his lips.

Yookey resisted at first, then he gave in and let Aria have her way, he returned her kiss passionately. Everyone at their table almost went into shock, students around the study hall stared in disbelief. It was one thing for Kethera to sit on Richard's lap and kiss him, Kethera was a Carlin. Yookey, however, was an Indigenous Thols and Aria was an Earth Human. A scandal was unfolding in full view!

The table that the girls had usually sat at, had a group of six Indigenous Thols sitting at it, both boys and girls around the same age as Yookey. They were all in shock and began trilling, clicking and barking amongst themselves in Native Tholish, there were even a few grunts. It was loud enough to carry across the whole study hall. Kethera, Saffiera and Yeannah all blushed, the three all understood Native Tholish.

Then the Indigenous Thols took out their communicators and began videoing Yookey and Aria. Within minutes the entire scandal was being uploaded to the school's network and streamed online.

When Aria and Yookey stopped kissing, Yookey commented, "We should not have done that!"

"What's wrong?", Aria asked when she saw their faces, "What are they saying? Someone tell me!"

Kethera shook her head and so did Saffiera, so Aria turned to Yeannah, "Tell me, Yeannah! Tell me!"

Yeannah sighed and then explained, "The translation might not be entirely accurate", she tried to tone it down, really tone it down, "They're calling you a *'whore slut'* or a *'slut whore'*, maybe even something worse. I don't really know, Indigenous grunts don't really translate into Ancient Tholish."

Aria held onto Yookey tightly, she doubled down, stared at the Indigenous Thols with dagger-eyed stares, poked her tongue out at them and then flipped them the bird, "Fuck you!", she shouted.

Aria's twin Sister, Ariel face palmed herself and thought to herself, *"Aria, what have you done!"*

The video clips were spreading like wildfire. They were on the school network everywhere, they were even being shared beyond the school's firewall. They had gone viral!

"This is really bad, Aria", Ariel noted, explaining, "Those little bitches have just shared their videos within the school. They've also sent them to all of their friends and families. They're going viral!"

"Yeah, but not all Indigenous Thols have network access", Aria shrugged it off.

"Aria, every Tholish student and their families have network access. So does the Thol leadership and the Tholish High Council. All of the Tholish Elders will see those videos", Yookey informed her, adding, "We are both screwed! Right royally screwed!"

"What can they do, Yookey?", Aria asked, "Seriously, what can they do?"

Yookey did not answer, he was deep in thought.

"Yookey! It's not like they can kill us or anything. No Thol can kill another Thol", Aria commented.

"Aria! You are NOT a Thol! That law does not protect you!", Yookey replied, commenting, "This is serious, Aria! The High Council could banish my family to the Western Jula Jula Forests!"

Yeannah commented, "Shit! That is not good! That's a death sentence!"

It had only been about ten minutes since the incident, but the videos had gone viral. Indigenous Thol parents had been contacting the school. Yookey's parents had contacted the school. The shit was hitting the fan and spraying everywhere.

An announcement came over the school's Broadcast System, *"Aria Swanson and Yookey. Please come to the Principal's Office. Aria Swanson and Yookey. Please come to the Principal's Office"*, and the message continued to repeat a further three times.

28. Scandal.

Yookey and Aria made their way to the Principal's office with their friends following closely behind them. When they arrived at the Principal's Office, they found Principal Linh Nguyen and Vice Principal Seamus O'Callaghan standing in the Principal's Foyer discussing the issue.

Principal Nguyen was a smallish woman of Vietnamese heritage. Her facial features were delicate and well-balanced, her face being an almost perfect oval shape. Her cheekbones were high and softly defined, her nose was small and her full lips had a distinctive *"cupid's bow"* shape to them. She wore long dark, straight hair. She was also quite short and thin. Linh Nguyen looked far too young to be the Principal of such a large colonial educational institution.

Vice Principal O'Callaghan on the other hand had features typical of his birthplace, Ireland. His Irish accent clearly stood out. This was something that intrigued Yookey and Kethera, neither of whom had heard accented English. Seamus O'Callaghan was an older, taller, portly man with short greying hair. If it wasn't for their name badges showing their job titles, you would have thought their titles were the other way around.

Principal Nguyen looked at the group that had intruded into the foyer, "I was expecting just Aria Swanson and Yookey. Not a full entourage", she quipped, then asked, "Why are you lot all here?"

Aria and Yookey were in front of the group of students and Ariel, Aria's twin Sister, stepped forward protectively, "Wherever my Sister goes, I go."

Yeannah stepped forward as well, "Aria and Yookey are my friends. I go where they go."

Kethera was somewhat more shy, but stepped forward as well, "I go where they go as well."

Saffiera stepped forward, *"Solidarity amongst friends, Ms Nguyen"*, she broadcast telepathically.

Richard took up a position beside Kethera and held her hand, that did not go unnoticed. Thomas took up a position beside Yeannah, but kept a slight distance, not wanting to make matters worse.

Vice Principal O'Callaghan commented, "This concerns Aria and Yookey. The rest of you are not required. Go about your daily tasks."

Saffiera broadcast forcefully, *"We are not going anywhere!"*

Vice Principal O'Callaghan was about to respond, but Principal Nguyen cut him off, "Perhaps, Seamus, this is a good thing. Every one of these students was in that video clip."

The Vice Principal nodded in deference and then Principal Nguyen invited, “Students, please follow me to my conference room” and then she led the way to it.

As each person entered the Principal's conference room, the door scanner scanned their dna and registered their *“attendance”* in the room. A common, *“standard”* practice that was used across the entire school, so that in an emergency, all personnel and student locations were known and recorded. This was done for safety and security purposes.

The conference room was large and contained a long desk with a great many seats. This was usually where the Principal held her senior staff meetings. In front of each seat, embedded into the table were data tablet touch screens and attached styluses. A large screen was hung on the wall at the far end. Principal Nguyen and Vice Principal O'Callaghan sat at the two chairs at one end of the table, the end opposite the large screen.

“Students, please take a seat”, the Principal commanded, then she directed Aria and Yookey to take a seat at the far end of the table.

As the students did so, the Principal noticed Kethera and Richard sitting next to each other and then they both moved their chairs even closer together. She noticed Yeannah and Thomas sat next to each other as well, although, they were being more discrete. As she watched the student's social dynamics, she quickly became aware that far more was happening here than meets the eye. Principal Nguyen had a clever perceptiveness to her and her mind worked quickly to put two and two together.

“Okay, then. Now we're all seated, let's see who we have present”, the Vice Principal announced, as he touched his stylus to his data tablet's touch screen and the student profiles all appeared on the big screen.

“Saffiera, the Martian Ambassador's Daughter. Our whole faculty recognises you on sight, young Saffiera. Martians are so very rare this far from the Earth. Our well-known Swanson twins, Aria and Ariel. Kethera, Yeannah, Yookey, Richard O'Connell and Thomas Mitchel”, Vice Principal O'Callaghan read out the names of all of the students.

Martians, Carlins and Thols, Mimasian or Indigenous, did not use surnames.

“You all appear to be a very close-knit group”, Principal Nguyen commented, before asking, “Before we get down to the issue at hand, would you like to hear my current observations?”

The students all looked around the table from one another and back to the

Principal, Saffiera picked up on their responses and replied for the group, broadcasting a simple, *"Yes, Principal Nguyen."*

Principal Nguyen began, "Last Thursday, we had an incident, an unusual pheromonal cascade issue that required the use of our school's sickbay. Our school nurses provided me with a full report and some important recommendations. No students were named in that report, however, having seen that video clip taken in the school's senior study hall and all of you seated here today, I suspect that our *'bonded'* couple are Kethera and Richard. Am I correct?"

Both Richard and Kethera looked at each other, they were both embarrassed, Richard finally spoke for both Kethera and himself, "Yes, Ms Nguyen. That is correct."

Ms Nguyen nodded, "There are no prohibitions whatsoever with regard to Carlin-Human relationships, however, they do seem to upset the Indigenous Thol population somewhat. So can I ask you two, to be more discrete in future. Just tone it down a couple of notches. Okay?"

Both Richard and Kethera agreed in unison, "We can do that, Ms Nguyen."

"Good then", the Principal replied.

"Now then, Yeannah and Thomas", the Principal noted their names, then continued, "I can clearly see that you two have something going on. You appear to be trying to *'hide'* it, but the harder you try, the more people will talk. You're *'relationship'*, should it become common knowledge will cause significant issues. You both do understand that the Indigenous Thols have very strict laws against non-Thol Thol relationships?"

"Yes, Ms Nguyen. They've even extended that taboo to include Indigenous Thol and Mimasian Thol relationships", Yeannah replied, expanding the scope of the problem.

Thomas quickly added, "It's not right at all, Ms Nguyen. Mimasian Thols and Indigenous Thols are completely different species and each has their own specific laws and governance. The Indigenous Thols have no right to be pushing their stupid ancient taboos onto Yeannah's people, just because they look the same!"

Principal Nguyen momentarily closed her eyes and took in a deep breath, "You are right, Thomas. Absolutely right, but you have to remember, Yeannah's people are outnumbered ten thousand to one."

"That still doesn't make it right, Ms Nguyen", Thomas replied, almost, but not quite angrily, "They are a different species and have no right to dictate to Yeannah's people what they can and cannot do!"

"I am not disagreeing with you, Thomas", the Principal replied, explaining, "I'm just asking you to take into account", she paused to think of the best term, "their sensitivities. Just be even more discrete and don't give them anything else to *'complain'* about."

Yeannah readily agreed, "Yes, Ms Nguyen. We will take that into consideration. We both do understand that there are *'outliers'* amongst the Indigenous Thols as well."

Richard nodded in agreement with Yeannah.

"Good then and it's good to hear that you understand about their *'outliers'* as well. They can be problematic, to say the least", Ms Nguyen replied.

Principal Nguyen moved on to a less dramatic issue, "Saffiera, while I do understand your non-verbal telepathic communications. I would appreciate it if you would use less force when transmitting telepathically to my staff or myself. I have spent time inside of Mimas with your people. The use of too much telepathic force can cause some of us non-telepaths nose bleeds."

Saffiera was shocked, "I was unaware of that, Ms Nguyen", she admitted.

"Yes, Saffiera. I expect you wouldn't be. You are still quite young", Principal Nguyen replied, then she noted, "It's your Human heritage showing through. Hybrids can tend to be, far more forceful."

That caught everyone in the conference room by surprise, except for Principal Nguyen and Vice Principal O'Callaghan.

Saffiera thought to herself, *"Hybrids can tend to be more forceful"*, she didn't understand and then she protested, *"I am not a hybrid, Ms Nguyen!"*

Principal Nguyen now looked perplexed, "Saffiera, I have lived amongst Martians inside of Mimas. I can tell the difference at a glance. You are at least two inches shorter than a full blood Martian."

Vice Principal O'Callaghan agreed, "All Martians have a universal height of five foot ten and a level of vibrancy in their skin tones, hair and eye colour that is readily distinguishable."

Tears welled in Saffiera's eyes and Yeannah intuitively understood, "Saffiera didn't know, Ms Nguyen. She had no idea. Saffiera grew up here on Homwol. There so few Martians here."

As Ariel moved around the table to comfort Saffiera, while the Principal remarked in surprise, "I thought that Saffiera knew!"

After a few minutes of quiet, Principal Nguyen asked Saffiera, "Are you okay, Saffiera?"

Saffiera nodded in the affirmative and Principal Nguyen continued, she touched her stylus to her data tablet's touch screen and a video clip appeared on the big screen, it paused on the first frame.

"Okay. This is why we are all here", the Principal began, then after a brief pause, "This video was taken by an Indigenous Thol sitting at a table across the study hall from you guys. You can see this in this single frame. Kethera is sitting on Richard's lap, which is not against any rules but could be a little more discrete. We have Yeannah and Thomas sitting together, doing their best to not be noticed. All very good. We do have Saffiera and Ariel sitting at the table, no problem. Then we have Aria sitting on Yookey's lap!"

The students all stared at the video, taken by Indigenous Thol from their perspective.

Principal Nguyen then played the video clip.

Much to the surprise and consternation of the Thols, Aria wrapped her arms around Yookey's neck and began kissing him passionately. Yookey eventually began returning the kiss just as passionately. The kiss lasted several long minutes, during which the Thols muttered and almost shouted in their native tongue.

Then when Aria and Yookey finished kissing, there was an exchange between her and her friends. After which Aria hugged Yookey tightly once more and stared at the Thols taking the video. Aria glared at them, poked out her tongue at them and then gave them the middle finger. The cherry on top of this behaviour was Aria clearly shouting, *"Fuck You",* at the indigenous Thols!

Principal Nguyen commented, "Thank you, Aria. For that wonderful display of what NOT to do in public, when there are severe cultural taboos regarding Thols and relationships with other species."

Aria replied completely unfiltered, smirking, "You're welcome, Ms Nguyen."

Aria's Sister, Ariel, face palmed herself as Principal Nguyen rolled her eyes and shook her head.

"Aria!", Principal Nguyen chided, "This is extremely serious. That video clip has gone viral. It is everywhere. By now it's even being played in the Cis-Luns colonies. Nearly every Indigenous Thol parent has contacted the school demanding you be severely punished! They are threatening to pull their children out of our school and boycotting our colony completely. They are calling your actions an egregious insult to all Thols. Yookey's parents have contacted the school and they are furious! And you don't want to know what they're calling you. Not just Yookey's parents either, every Thol that has contacted our school over that video has given you that very same label!"

Aria's face took on a more sheepish look, "I already know, they're calling me a slut whore", she replied, her face red with a combination of embarrassment and anger.

Vice Principal O'Callaghan shook his head, "That is not quite what it means. Your translation is incomplete. Yookey, please tell your girlfriend what your people are calling Aria."

Yookey shook his head, "No. It doesn't really translate into English."

"That is not what I've been told", the Vice Principal replied.

Aria stroked Yookey's cheek, "You can tell me, Yookey. I won't be upset."

Yookey shook his head, "No, I won't say such words."

"Yeannah. You speak Native Tholish, please tell Aria the full translation", Mr O'Callaghan asked.

Yeannah put her right hand to her cheek, "Well, it's like, Yookey says, it doesn't easily translate. Tholish grunts when combined with barks, don't really translate one to one."

"But they do translate", Ms Nguyen replied, adding her weight, "Please translate, Yeannah."

"Okay. Sorry, Aria", Yeannah replied and then began the translation, "Well, the basic translation is *'slut whore'* or *'whore slut'*, there is no direction to it. The other particles, the clicks, the barks and the grunts, they translate as, *'bloodsucker'* or *'vampire'*, perhaps both. Then there are some barks and grunts that translate as *'leech'* and others that translate as *'succubus'*. The last part translates as *'excrement-covered wingless Tarlak'*. It's one big mash of insults all strung together and more of a curse, really."

Aria was really upset, "So they're calling me a *'Bloodsucking vampire leech, slut whore succubus and excrement-covered wingless Tarlak?'*. Well then, that just sucks!"

"Aria, Indigenous Tholish insults are complex and just a little colourful", Yookey tried to explain.

Ms Nguyen commented, "Aria, you've managed to insult and piss off an entire species!"

"All I did was kiss, Yookey, Ms Nguyen!", Aria protested.

"Well, Yookey's parents are on their way here. I'm hoping not to hear that insult in person", Principal Nguyen noted, "They're already on their way, by wing, that's how serious this is, Aria."

Yookey looked at Aria, "I'm screwed!"

"I think we both are, Yookey", Aria realised.

A short while later there was the distinct sound of data tablet notifications sounding. Yeannah reached into her bag and took out her data tablet, she then checked her emails and messages.

"Oh crap!", Yeannah exclaimed, then explained, "My Mum has seen that video", she looked to Principal Nguyen, "My Mum will be here soon", she then turned to Kethera and Saffiera, "Your Mums are coming too. Saffiera's Mum is picking them up."

Right on queue, more data tablet notifications chimed, Kethera and Saffiera reached into their bags.

Kethera checked her messages and emails, "My Mum will be on her way as soon as Saffiera's Mum picks her up", she confirmed.

Saffiera checked her emails and messages, confirming telepathically, "My Mum's already on her way to pick your Mums up."

"Girls, do we have an estimated time of arrival?", Vice Principal O'Callaghan requested.

"No, not really, but the way my Mum drives, they'll be here soon enough", Saffiera informed him.

Richard took his data tablet out of his bag and checked his emails and messages, he too had a message, "My Mum has seen that video as well. She's really pissed! She doesn't care about any of that Native Tholish taboo nonsense. She's upset at seeing Kethera sitting on my lap."

Kethera's whiskers drooped and she bit down on her lower lip gently before asking, "Why is your Mother upset, Richard?"

Richard sighed, "Kethera, my Mother is about as racist and specist as they come. I'm sorry, Kethera, but it's just the way she is. My Mother hates anyone that doesn't have skin tones like hers or mine!"

Kethera took Richard's head between her hands and kissed him on the lips, then commented, "You are not responsible for your Mother's shortcomings, Richard."

"Is your Mother coming here as well, Richard", Principal Nguyen enquired.

"No, Ms Nguyen. I'll be copping it when I get home", Richard replied.

Thomas was the only one whose data tablet had not chimed.

At that point, just to make matters take a surreal turn, an unusual visage appeared out of the conference room's long window behind Saffiera, Kethera and Richard. It was the sight of an Interplanetary Starfighter, a military ship silently landing on its whisper thrusters on the grassy grounds beyond the window.

Principal Nguyen stood up and walked over to the window, watching the warship land, "What in the blue blazes is going on?", she asked.

"That's Mum's ride, Sharona. It's a Broad-Head, Arrow Class, Interplanetary Starfighter", Aria replied in a matter-of-fact tone, adding, "It looks like I'm in real trouble now."

The dark, midnight black coloured warship, shaped like a broad-headed arrow point with a small blunt shaft at the rear and at least six visible weapons blister pods, slowly descended to a perfect landing on the lawns below.

Principal Nguyen turned to look at the twins, "Your Mother flies a warship?", she questioned.

"Not just Mum, Dad flies one too, although he's up a Cis-Luns L-Five at the moment", Ariel replied.

Then came the knock at the conference room door. Things were happening fast.

The conference room door opened and the Principal's Assistant, Charlotta De La Cruz, showed Yookey's parents into the conference room, "Ms Nguyen, this is Yookey's parents, Yarling and Yorvick", she introduced.

Before Ms Nguyen could even say hello, Yookey's Mother, Yarling, started verbally tearing into him, she spoke quickly in native Tholish, trilling, clicking and softly barking.

Saffiera did her best to translate telepathically for the others, *"Yarling is saying, 'What the hell have you done, Yookey! You have brought great shame upon our family. The High Chancellor of the Tholish High Council wants us all banished to the Western Mountains. We will all die there!'"*

Aria stepped in front of Yookey protectively, "You cannot speak to Yookey like that!", in English, she knew Yookey's parents could both speak English.

Yarling replied to Aria in a string of Native Tholish trills, clicks, barks and grunts!

Saffiera translated, *"Yarling is saying, 'Don't speak to me you disgusting bloodsucking vampire leech, slut whore succubus and excrement-covered wingless Tarlak.*

You should be banished to the lands of those disgusting Tarlaks, south of the Southern Mountains beyond the Southern Wastelands! You Tarlakand bitch!'", the words being translated had Saffiera in tears.

Yookey was incensed that someone should talk to Aria, someone he cared about deeply, that way, he gently motioned Aria behind him and threw back at his Mother, "You bloodsucking vampire leech, slut whore succubus and excrement-covered wingless Tarlak!", the very same insult in English.

Yarling shrieked out loudly and backhanded Yookey across the right cheek with the back of her right hand. There was a cracking sound as one of Yarling's metacarpals snapped. Yarling held her hand and shrieked out loudly in pain.

Yookey turned his face to his Mother so that she could see the red welt that she had inflicted on his right cheek, he turned to face her and glared at her, "The pain you inflict comes back to you, Mother!"

Through all of this Yorvick had remained silent, not being able to get a word in sideways, "Both of you! Enough!", he trilled and clicked, then he held his Wife's wrist and inspected her hand, "You are so quick to anger, Yarling! Now look, your hand is broken!"

The Vice Principal was on his communicator, "Nurse Yoolah, we have a female Thol with a broken hand. Please attend the Principal's conference room with your medical kit!"

"On my way, Mr O'Callaghan", Nurse Yoolah replied.

Yorvick helped his Wife, Yarling, to a seat, he was unhappy with how his Wife had lashed out emotionally and believed the situation could have been better handled.

Aria looked at Yookey's Mother, and then she told Yookey point blank, "Yookey, you have to apologise to your Mother."

"Me? Apologise? Why me? My Mother struck me. Why should I apologise, Aria?", Yookey asked.

"Your Mother was just upset, Yookey", Aria told him, "She would not have hit you if you hadn't insulted her. Yookey, what you said to your Mother was horrible."

"My Mother insulted you first, Aria. She used that same insult on you", Yookey countered.

"Yookey! Your mother was upset. The High Chancellor of the Tholish High Council has threatened your family with banishment", Aria told him, commenting, "Your Mother was just angry and scared."

"I'm not going to apologise to her, Aria", Yookey replied as he folded his arms across his chest.

Aria did not accept that, her latent psychic gifts were awake and she broadcast telepathically, quite forcefully, *"Yookey! Your Mother gave birth to you and brought you into this world. She suckled you at her breast and raised you! Your Mother deserves your respect!"*

Yookey was taken aback, everyone in the conference room apart from Saffiera and Ariel was equally taken aback. Yookey looked at Aria, then he turned to his Mother and approached her.

Yookey took a knee, bowed his head and spoke to his Mother, "I am so sorry Mother. I didn't mean what I said. I was just angry and spoke without thinking", his Native Tholish trilling and clicking.

Yarling wrapped her left arm around Yookey and pulled him closer to her and then she wrapped her wings around him and replied, trilling, "I am sorry too, Yookey. I was just angry and scared", all the while she stared at Aria, with a quizzical look on her face, *"What was this Human"*, she thought.

Yorvick stared at Aria, he too was puzzled. Martians were telepaths, Earth Humans were not, he turned to look at his Wife and said one word in Native Tholish, trilling, "Mardhin!"

Yarling looked up at her Husband and repeated back, trilling, "Mardhin! No. Cannot be!"

Yorvick replied, trilling back, "Must be Mardhin! This Human can't be anything else but Mardhin!"

Saffiera had been using her Martian telepathic abilities to translate as best she could, *"What is a Mardhin?"*, she asked everyone.

Yeannah, being a Mimasian Thol, well fluent in the Native Thol language, ought to have known, she, however, replied, "I have no idea. I don't have a translation for it."

Yookey replied instead, "A Mardhin is a mystical Wizard, a Star Strider. Mum and Dad think that Aria is a Star Strider!"

No one had noticed the open conference room door and the woman standing in the doorway. A strongly built woman was wearing blue flight pants, a sleeveless blue jacket open at the front, with a tight blue singlet underneath. She wore a utility belt with pouches containing gadgets and instruments, strapped to her left forearm she wore a *'grip'*, a portable A.I. system. She also had neural implants and augments, however, they could not be seen.

"I'm Angelique Swanson, the twin's Mum", she introduced herself, "And I see my little cherub, Aria is starting to take some responsibility for her actions. Aria, you have somehow managed to create an inter-species incident and the people above me are furious! Absolutely furious!"

"All I did was kiss a boy, Yookey, Mum", Aria replied, gesturing to Yookey.

"Aria, I have seen that viral video. You kissed a boy, an Indigenous Tholish boy. The Indigenous Thols consider that alone to be an insult. Then you just had to poke your tongue out at them and flip them the bird, not to mention your use of vile language", Angelique noted, then asked, "What the hell were you thinking, my child?"

Aria replied sheepishly, "I don't think I was thinking, Mum."

Angelique rolled her eyes, "Aria, that lack of filter excuse will only get you so far. You have created quite a mess and I have been told to fix it."

Ariel chimed him, "Mum, Yookey's parents think Aria is a Mardhin."

Angelique accessed her neural augments and they searched for references, the information was arriving and collating in real-time, "The Mardhin are ancient mythical Wizards, Ariel. Saffiera's Mother did say your latent psychic abilities had been awakened and that we three are scions of the ancient Folcrom. That alone could invoke such a reference."

"No, no", Yarling trilled, telling them in English laced with trills, clicks and soft barks, "The Mardhin were very real and they were just like your people, Earth Humans", she pointed at Angelique, "Only with gifts far greater than any Martian. They were so powerful and could stride across worlds. They last came here over a thousand years ago."

"Yes", Yorvick agreed, trilling, "We, ourselves, have seen the depictions in the Tunnels of Dread."

Angelique queried, "The Tunnels of Dread?", her neural augments quickly kicked in and began searching for information.

"Below the Southern Mountain Range", Yorvick replied, explaining, "All Thols go there on a pilgrimage at least once in their lifetime", with a series of trills and clicks.

Yookey confirmed, "We went there years ago. There are paintings on the tunnel walls. They show Humans in dark robes carrying staves and wands of great power."

The information streaming into Angelique's neural augments depicted a tunnel system under the southern mountains. It had already been surveyed, mapped and catalogued. Pictures as described by Yookey were painted along the tunnel walls. There was a section of tunnel in the very centre, several kilometres long, it was full of skeletal remains, especially at the southern end. There were Native Thol and Carlins remains in the northern end and a huge number of Tarlak remains in the southern end.

Yookey filled in any missing data with his own narrative, "The tunnels are blocked in the middle for many leagues. There are two pillars, one against each wall, beyond which is certain death. When you strain your eyes beyond the pillars into the farther depths of the tunnels, you can see the remains of those who thought they could traverse them. There are many skeletons in that dead zone. The Mardhin, set up powerful wards to keep the raiding Tarlaks at bay!"

The other Mothers, Sarlia, Yealah and Kayala arrived at that point and entered the conference room.

Kayala went straight over to her Daughter, Kethera and Yealah went straight over to her Daughter, Yeannah.

Sarlia went straight to her own Daughter, Saffiera and having heard Yookey's narration, informed the room telepathically, *"The ancient Mardhin were Psi-Corp's Folcrom from the Earth, the most powerful of Earth's psychics. The ones that had rediscovered the ability to jaunt and blink, to teleport, even as far as the exoplanets of distant stars. They were Folcrom Forkbraid and Folcrom Selene, powerful scions both. Angelique's Daughters are scions of the first Folcrom, Folcrom Tafazah himself. He was the first of the star striders."*

"You see, Yarling. It is true, this Aria and her Sister are Mardhin!", Yorvick exclaimed.

Both Yarling and Yorvick took a knee and bowed their heads to Aria and her Sister, Ariel.

"No! No, you don't!", Aria exclaimed, shouting, "I am not having anyone bow to me!"

"And that goes for me as well", Ariel agreed with her Sister.

Saffiera sent Yarling and Yorvick a telepathic message, *"Please get up, this is not what the twins want. In this room, everyone is equal."*

Both Yarling and Yorvick stood up and Aria asked them to sit down and relax.

Nurse Yoolah then entered the conference room, which was getting a little crowded with sixteen people sitting and milling about.

"Which person is my patient?", Nurse Yoolah, a Mimasian Thol like Yeannah and Yealah enquired.

Vice Principal O'Callaghan replied, "Your patient is, Yarling", pointing to Yookey's Mother.

Nurse Yoolah approached Yarling and placed a rectangular patch of material on the table in front of her. Then she gently picked up Yarling's right hand by the forearm and scanned it for broken bones.

"Well, Yarling. You have one snapped metacarpal and mild fracturing on the metacarpals on either side", Nurse Yoolah announced, explaining, "A cast will be required to immobilise the damaged bones while they heal", then she placed Yarling's right hand and wrist onto the rectangular material with the palm facing down.

"What is that?", Yarling enquired with some quick trills.

"It's a bone knitter, Yarling", Nurse Yoolah informed her, adding, "It has been configured for Tholish physiology and Indigenous Thol dna."

As Yarling watched, the bone knitter changed shape to perfectly match her right hand, wrist and forearm. Then it wrapped itself around Yarling's hand, wrist and forearm, becoming quite stiff and immobilising her wrist and hand completely.

Nurse Yoolah gently touched Yarling's chin and turned her head towards her, "Yarling, look at me, just focus on me. Look at me!", then there was a clicking sound and Yarling screeched out in pain.

The pain was quickly gone and Yarling asked fearfully, "What was that?"

"That was the bone knitter bringing together the two sections of your broken metacarpal", Nurse Yoolah informed her, "Now watch the bone knitter cast."

A red glow appeared above Yarling's right hand where the damaged bones were, "That red light indicates that the healing process has begun. Over the next three days, it will turn orange, then yellow and eventually shades of green. When the process is completed, the cast will open up and the bone knitter will come off by itself. The whole process will take three days to complete."

"And then my hand will be healed?", Yarling enquired.

"Yes, Yarling and the bones will actually be stronger than before. The bone knitter triggers and augments your body's natural healing abilities, producing a stronger bone", Nurse Yoolah explained.

"When the bone knitter comes off, my Son, Yookey, he will bring it back to you", Yarling replied.

Nurse Yoolah looked around at the others in the conference room and noticed the rather red welt on Yookey's right cheek, "Come here, Young man and sit down", she instructed.

Yookey did as instructed and he sat himself down, Nurse Yoolah scanned his right cheek, there were no broken bones. However, both Yarling's broken hand and Yookey's red welt on his cheek were completely unnecessary injuries. Of course, these were Indigenous Thols and there was nowhere to report such abuse. Nurse Yoolah reached into her bag and took out a tube of healing salve, which she gave to Yookey. Yookey automatically began reading the instructions.

Nurse Yoolah sighed and turned to Yarling, "These injuries were completely unnecessary. Please do not strike your Son in future! It is unacceptable!", she placed a trilling stress on the last sentence.

Yarling looked embarrassed and turned red, her Husband, Yorvick replied, "It will not happen again, I assure you."

"Thank you, Nurse", the Vice Principal remarked as Nurse Yoolah left the conference room.

Nurse Yoolah nodded and as her presence was no longer required, she left the conference room and walked back to the school's sickbay.

Angelique whispered to the other Mothers, "It is as I said the other day in the glade, the Indigenous Thols are more like us Humans than Mimasian Thols."

"Okay. My Daughters are both scions and Yookey's parents call them Mardhin", Angelique announced, smiling whilst adding, "I can probably use that."

Angelique's neural augments searched for two things, the contact details for the High Chancellor of the Tholish High Council and further information on the historical Mardhin and how they fit into Native Tholish laws or perhaps it was lore, due to the supernatural aspects of Tholish history.

"How can you use that?", Principal Nguyen enquired.

Angelique smiled as the information streamed in and collated, "Watch and learn, Ms Nguyen", she replied as she opened her *'grip'* and started manipulating its virtual keyboard, telling everyone, "Please be quiet and let me handle this. It is important that no one else says anything."

A large window popped up on the screen mounted to the far wall. At first, it was blank but soon an image came through of an old and wizened Indigenous Thol. The High Chancellor himself.

Angelique stood squarely in front of the screen, "Who are you? What do you want?", the High Chancellor questioned.

"My name is Angelique Swanson, Special Operative, Angelique Swanson", Angelique introduced herself, then explained, "I've contacted you to discuss the recent viral video that has been circulating."

"That insulting filth. There isn't much to discuss", the High Chancellor replied, remarking, "The Human must be punished and punished severely. The Thol family involved will be Banished to the Western Mountain Forests."

Angelique took on a stern and severe visage, it was frightful to look upon and she replied, "A young girl kisses a boy and that is your response! A little over the top, don't you think!"

"Not at all. What they did was an affront to all Tholdom", the High Chancellor replied.

"I thought you'd say that", Angelique replied, then she told the High Chancellor exactly how things were going to play out, "That *'Human'* girl, the *'insulting filth'*, you want to *'severely punish'* is one of my Daughters and I am hereby authorising both of my Daughters to use lethal force to defend themselves as necessary. They are NOT going to be punished and should any of your people ever attempt to harm them, I promise you, their heads will be mounted on spikes at the boundaries of my lot as a warning to others!"

"You would murder our punishers?", the High Chancellor replied disbelievingly.

"Self-defence is not murder, High Chancellor", Angelique replied, noting, "It is well established under Human law as a proportionate response to an attack on one's person."

That shocked the High Chancellor, "You would not dare!"

"Try me, High Chancellor and see what happens!", Angelique replied, adding with a stone-cold glare, "Fuck around and find out!", a well-known Human saying.

The High Chancellor's demeanour shifted, "Perhaps we can be lenient with your Daughter."

"And Yookey, his family, Yarling and Yorvick?", Angelique questioned.

"They must still be banished to the Western Mountain Forests!", the High Chancellor replied.

"Is that so? So, my Daughter, Aria, makes a mistake and kisses a young Tholish boy and your response is to banish the entire family, to what can only be described as certain death", Angelique replied, commenting with a daggered stare, "Your own laws state that Thols must never kill Thols, so that makes you a fucking hypocrite!", she used their own laws against him.

“Not at all if the death comes at the hands of the forest denizens!”, the High Chancellor responded.

“Okay, so you set up the death trap and let nature take its course”, Angelique responded, adding, “That would still make you one hundred percent responsible!”

“Irrelevant! The ruling stands”, the High Chancellor replied angrily.

“Sucks to be you then, High Chancellor”, Angelique replied, explaining, “It will be very embarrassing explaining to your High Council how banishing Yookey's family failed.”

“And how exactly will their banishment fail?”, the High Chancellor enquired curiously.

“As I am offering Yookey and his parents political asylum and protection, your banishing of them is superfluous”, Angelique responded with a broad smile, “The colony will provide them with housing and protection. Hell, I might even provide them with housing and protection on my lot.”

Sarlia sent an urgent message telepathically to Angelique, *“They can stay with me in the glade if they wish. I have plenty of room and even tall maple trees for them to build their new tree house.”*

“The Martian Ambassador, Sarlia, is offering them political asylum and protection as well”, Angelique passed the information on.

The High Chancellor let loose a stream of clicks, barks and grunts, it was a Tholish insult in Native Tholish, Angelique's neural augments automatically sought the translation, “Oh Mr High Chancellor, those were some really colourful insults”, then she glared at him, “Insults don't work on me and just so you know, neither will threats!”

Angelique softened her tone, her neural augments were providing her with a vast wealth of knowledge with regard to the Mardhin and how they fit into Native Tholish Lore, “High Chancellor, there is a way out for you. A way to save face”, she offered.

“In what way?” the High Chancellor questioned.

“My Daughters are both scions of the Folcrom of Earth, they are both, Mardhin!”, Angelique informed him.

The High Chancellor's eyes widened in shock, “Is this true?”

Angelique nodded to Yookey's parents, Yorvick replied with clicks, trills and barks, "Exalted one, my Wife and I have both heard the young Human girl, Aria, speak into our minds. She is a Mardhin!"

"She is a Mardhin!", the High Chancellor mused, he didn't believe it, of course, but it was something he could present to the High Council, "This changes everything. The Mardhin are above reproach. The Mardhin cannot be touched."

"And that means that Yookey and his family cannot be touched either", Angelique concluded.

Yarling trilled and clicked loudly, "The Mardhin are back!"

"Mrs Swanson, you are correct. Yookey's dealings with a Mardhin absolve him of any wrongdoing", the High Chancellor confirmed, "His family cannot be touched. I will take this up with the High Council. Yookey's family will not be banished!"

"A wise move, High Chancellor", Angelique replied, but warned, "Let it become common knowledge, that Yookey and his parents are under my protection and the protection of the Mardhin!"

"And so it shall be done", the High Chancellor agreed and the window on the screen dropped out.

Aria was smiling, her Mother had pulled a rabbit out of a hat once more, "Aria! Don't you even think this gets you out of trouble with your Father and me", Aria's smile dropped once more.

Yarling smiled and trilled in English, querying, "So we are safe?"

"As safe as I can make you", Angelique admitted, commenting, "I don't leave things to chance. I will continue to monitor your situation. How are you getting home later?", she asked.

"We will fly on the wing as we always do", Yarling replied.

"No. No, you won't", Angelique smiled back, announcing, "I'll take you all home at the end of the school day in my ship, Sharona. She's a Broad-Head Arrow Class, Interplanetary Starfighter."

"A Starfighter?", Yorvick questioned.

"Yes, Yorvick. When I drop you off with my ship, it will send two messages. First, you are under my protection and second, I mean business. It will be as clear as they can see", Angelique explained.

Yarling smiled, "And our neighbours will be jealous!"

Ariel chimed in, "My Sister, Aria, and I will come with you and see you to your nests."

"Yes, very good, Ariel", Angelique agreed, "By the time we get you home, the news will have spread across all of Tholdom. You will be escorted to your nest by a pair of Mardhin! That is so going to work in your favour!"

Yorvick gave off a Tholish chortle, "Our neighbours will see us as blessed!"

"Yorvick, that could become really annoying", Yarling replied, commenting with trills and clicks, "Our neighbours, even strangers from afar, will want us to touch their heads and give them blessings."

"That doesn't sound too bad, you could always charge them admission", Aria remarked.

"Aria! Where's your filter!", Angelique chided.

"Sorry Mum, I'll do my best to develop one, I promise", Aria replied.

Ariel noted, "When we drop them off, Mum. Give them all emergency micro-communicators. Just in case things don't pan out so well."

"I will definitely be doing that, Ariel", Angelique agreed.

Aria smiled a wry smile, "I've gone from being called a bloodsucking vampire leech, slut whore succubus and excrement-covered wingless Tarlak to a pseudo-religious figure", then she laughed.

Angelique rolled her eyes and shook her head before messing up Aria's hair.

Principal Nguyen remarked, "Well that turned out much better than I thought it would. That was most certainly not the style of negotiating that I would have used."

"Well, Ms Nguyen, perhaps if you'd been trained in the Military, your negotiation style might have been different", Angelique explained, adding, "I'm kind of used to negotiating with terrorists and using hardball tactics. That seemed to have worked perfectly well here."

"So, you treated the High Chancellor as if he was a terrorist?", the Principal questioned.

"The High Chancellor was threatening my Daughter, Aria, and her boyfriend and his family", Angelique shrugged, "I treated him as an enemy to be coerced and if necessary, chastised."

Sarlia, Saffiera's Mum, chimed in, *"Now we have both political and religious leverage over the Indigenous Thols. That in itself adds a layer of subconscious protection for we off-worlders."*

With the situation under control, Saffiera asked her Mother, *"Mum, when exactly were going to tell me that I was a 'hybrid' and that my Father was an Earthman?"*
Sarlia looked at Angelique, who simply shrugged, "Don't look at me, Sarlia."

Principal Nguyen calmly said, "Oops! I seem to have let the cat out of the bag. Saffiera's school profile didn't mention her not knowing about her heritage."

"Saffiera, I'll explain everything tonight after we get home", Sarlia promised.

"About that, Sarlia", Angelique interjected, "The girls have all had a sleepover at Yealah's place, Kethera's place and your place, I figure it's time for a sleepover at my place."

"Don't you work the afternoon shifts at the spaceport?", Sarlia asked.

"Well that's the thing, Sarlia. The powers above me tasked me with fixing an *'inter-species incident'*, so they've already covered my shift for this afternoon. As the problem is resolved, I effectively have some free time", Angelique explained, noting, "The girls can sleep over and you three could come over as well. I don't know, maybe another lady's night."

Yealah noted, "I'm on shift tomorrow at the clinic, so I can't stay overnight."

"Easily fixed, we'll have a *'smaller'* lady's night", Angelique replied, adding, "We only drink one bottle of wine and you head off home to get sleep for tomorrow. No problem."

Kayala asked, "How many glasses of wine does one bottle hold?"

Sarlia smiled a wry smile, *"That depends on how you fill the glasses. Six standard glasses or four if you fill them right up."*

"Okay then, so only one glass each", Kayala understood, agreeing, "Sounds like a plan!"

"And only one glass, Kayala", Angelique confirmed, noting, "When I saw you on Saturday morning, you did not look well at all", then she passed Sarlia a card with the GPS coordinates of her plot.

29. The Uranian Federation.

Sarlia flew Kayala, Yealah and their Daughters, first to Yealah's tree house amongst the Northern Mountain Jula Jula forests to pick up Yeannah's overnight bag and then she flew back south to Kayala's house and lot in their Carlinish village, to pick up Kethera's overnight bag. After that, Sarlia flew back to her house in the glade to pick up Saffiera's overnight bag and a couple of bottles of Martian Sweet Cherry Red wine. Sarlia then keyed the coordinates to Angelique's plot amongst the bluegrass meadows into her hovercar and placed it on autopilot. Then the hovercar took off and flew toward its destination.

On the approach to Angelique's plot, Sarlia took over control of her hovercar and began to circle it. The plot was somewhat over three hundred metres across with a double perimeter fence. Unlike the glade which was circular in shape, Angelique's plot was octagonal, the perimeter fence had eight-sides. Four Vorts could be seen patrolling in the gap between the inner and outer fences.

Angelique's homestead looked eerily similar to Sarlia's, with almost the same design and orientation and mostly soil-covered. In between the homestead and the perimeter fence, there were a number of very large, Chillic and Bell Nut Fruit trees, along with some others that Sarlia did not recognise. Perhaps another type of native fruit tree. These trees were very large and exceedingly tall. Yealah noted to herself, that each could easily support several tree houses the size of her own. Had Yookey's family been forced into exile here on Angelique's plot, they may very well have been quite happy.

The plot gave the overall appearance of having once been a smallish lowland forest stand that had undergone significant clearing and reshaping, being turned into the plot that they all saw below them. The open ground between the trees was covered in bluegrass meadows. As the hovercar circled, a herd of goat-like animals could be seen roaming the lot, feeding on the meadows of bluegrass. No, not goat-like animals, it was actually a flock of Earth Goats, not native Gudongs!

To the north of the homestead were a handful of greenhouses and fenced-off gardens. To the south was a large section of tarmac, next to which was a large hangar. It was open on the western side. Angelique's Broad-Head Arrow Class Starfighter was positioned within it.

Sarlia decided to touch down on the tarmac and manoeuvre her hovercar off to one side. As she landed her hovercar a clear view of the interior of the hangar and the Starfighter came into view. At the far end of the hangar appeared to be accommodation units.

The girls and their Mothers climbed out of Sarlia's hovercar and made their way over to the homestead. Angelique and her twins were waiting for them by the homestead's front entrance.

Saffiera sent a telepathic message, *"You have actual Goats!"*

Aria replied matter-of-factly, "Yeah, of course. Gudongs weird our Mother out. You know, having four eyes and flesh tendrils!"

"The Goats provide us with milk, cheese, meat and even skins", Ariel informed them, noting, "The bluegrass gives the milk a bluish tinge just like Gudong milk. It tastes similar, but lacks the masuli grain's infusion flavour."

Kethera commented, "Those fruit trees are way too tall for even Gudongs to climb, so your Goats won't be able to climb them either."

"So you would think", Aria replied, adding, "Look carefully, very carefully."

Kethera looked more carefully at the overly large fruit trees, there were Goats in the lower branches.

Ariel remarked, "Earth Goats are excellent climbers. If they think that those leaves or fruit taste nice, they will find a way to reach them."

Yeannah quickly asked, "How did things go with Yookey and his parents?"

Aria replied, "Yookey and his parents almost freaked out when Ariel sat down in the pilot's cockpit and started flying Sharona", she paused for a moment, "They were really impressed with her skills."

"You didn't pilot Sharona?", Yeannah enquired.

"Hmm, no", Aria sounded disappointed, "My Mum revoked my flight privileges for the rest of the week for creating an inter-species incident. I guess I deserve that, I really did screw up."

"You're sounding almost mature, Aria", Angelique remarked.

Ariel excitedly chimed in, "You should have seen the other Indigenous Thols! They had never seen a Starfighter before and when Yookey told them that I was the pilot, they freaked right out."

"It was really surreal", Aria noted, explaining, "They'd already heard on the Tholish grapevine that we were Mardhin. Everyone wanted to touch us, they wanted us to bless them. We both used our gifts to transmit messages directly into their minds. That really spun them out!"

Ariel commented, "That was Mum's idea. She said it would solidify the Mardhin image."

Angelique smiled and commented, "If we encourage the Mardhin belief, it plays to our advantage."

Yealah asked with some concern, "Were Yookey and his parents okay when you left?"

Aria replied, smiling, "Are you kidding? They have a pair of Mardhin as friends and they have been absolved of any and all of their sins and they were flown home in a Starfighter. Seriously, every Indigenous Thol in their neighbourhood converged on their tree to hear about it. Even Mimasian Thols were interested. Yookey and his parents are famous!"

Yealah checked again for confirmation, "So, they are safe then?"

Angelique replied honestly, "As safe as we can make them for the moment. We have given them three emergency micro-communicators just in case. I even gave one to your Husband, Yannick, as well and asked him to keep a watch over them. So for now at least they should be okay."

Sarlia stepped forward and handed two bottles of Martian Sweet Cherry Red wine to Angelique, "I thought we were only drinking one bottle tonight, Sarlia", Angelique queried.

Sarlia smiled and broadcast telepathically, *"One for tonight and one for the house."*

Angelique looked over at the hangar where her Starfighter was housed, her flight mechanic, her groundskeeper and his wife, could all do with a little something nice. They all worked so very hard.

Sarlia caught the thought and smiled again, *"Your people could maybe enjoy a bottle."*

"Are you sure, Sarlia?", Angelique enquired, "You don't actually know them."

"True, Angelique but you do. Let them have that second bottle", Sarlia replied.

Angelique caught her gardener's attention and called her over to introduce her, "Sarlia, this is my Gardener, Michelle Bronson. Her Husband, Sylvester, is my Grounds Keeper and Security Officer. My Flight Mechanic and Engineer over there by my Starfighter is Mike Johnson. Michelle, this is the Martian Ambassador to Secundus, Sarlia."

"It's a pleasure to meet you, Ma'am", Michelle replied.

"The pleasure is all mine", Sarlia replied telepathically and gestured to the bottle of wine.

"Yes, of course", Angelique replied to the gesture, "Here's a bottle of Martian Sweet Cherry Red wine. Kick back and enjoy the evening."

"Thank you, Mrs Swanson. We shall", Michelle replied before taking the wine back to the hangar.

Angelique smiled, "My people do work hard. They deserve some fun. Let's go inside, shall we?"

As the Mothers and their Daughters entered Angelique's home, she noted, "Our homestead has the same basic design as yours, Sarlia, just the interior colour scheme and decor are different."

"Yes, I can see that", Sarlia replied as she looked around.

"Remember, I mentioned that I was the supervisor when your glade was carved out of that forest", Angelique reminded Sarlia, "I liked the design of your homestead so much, that I copied it."

Sarlia nodded as Aria commented, "The wall between Ariel's room and mine was taken down, so we have one huge bedroom. You guys will love it, so much space."

Angelique smiled, "Well, they are twins. If I didn't knock it down, I'm pretty sure they would have."

They all slowly made their way to the homestead's kitchen.

Mike Johnson, Angelique's Flight Mechanic and Engineer stepped into the kitchen, "Excuse me, ladies. I took the liberty of running a full diagnostic on the Ambassador's hover vehicle", he stated.

Sarlia looked up a Mike, he was tall, easily five-ten, strongly built with ropy muscle and broad shoulders. His dark hair was shortly cropped in a crew cut. Sarlia took notice of the three-day growth of facial stubble and she gently bit her lower lip.

"That was not necessary", Sarlia transmitted telepathically in reply.

"Madam Ambassador, I felt obligated. That bottle of Martian Cherry Red wine is from the CCF orchids on Hebes Island above New Tortuga. Out here, this far from Mars, that one bottle is worth around two month's wages", Mike explained.

"Please don't feel obligated, it was unnecessary", Sarlia replied, noting, *"You have no obligation."*

"I still believe it was my obligation, after all, we have to ensure your safety", Mike smiled as he replied and then passed Sarlia a printed diagnostic report on paper, "Your hover vehicle is in flying order, however, there are a few minor issues that should be dealt with and it is nearly eight months overdue for its service, at least according to its maintenance logs."

Sarlia looked over the printout before folding it and placing it in her handbag, *"Thank you, Mike."*

"Any vehicle maintenance workshop in the colony should be able to perform the work", Mike informed her, noting, "They should be able to complete it in just a few hours."

Sarlia looked carefully at Mike Johnson, he was quite a good-looking Earthman, he also had that alluring three-day growth of stubble, she smiled and asked, *"Mike, could you come by my glade and perform the work?"*

Mike replied, slightly surprised, "I could, Madam Ambassador. I would need to get Mrs Swanson's approval and of course, schedule the work."

Angelique quickly agreed, "You have my approval, Mike", she could see where Sarlia was going.

Sarlia then replied, with a broad wry smile, *"Please schedule the service, Mike and let me know when you can drop by. I will accommodate your timing schedule. And please, call me, Sarlia"*, she then unconsciously tousled her golden blond locks.

"Yes, I'll schedule your service tomorrow and send you the date and time before the days out, Sarlia", Mike replied, he was not sure what he getting into, then he nodded to everyone present and left the kitchen, heading back to the hangar.

A telepathic, *"Ah hum"*, caught Sarlia's attention, it was her Daughter, Saffiera, her arms were folded across her chest and her face carried a *"cross"* expression.

"When you were talking about that 'service', you weren't talking about your hovercar, were you, Mother?", Saffiera chastised.

Yeannah's Mother, Yealah's face went bright red and she covered it with her hand, Kethera's Mother, Kayala chortled in surprise, Angelique just smiled, while Sarlia managed an awkward and unconvincing reply, *"Whatever do you mean, Saffiera?"*

Aria, Ariel, Kethera and Yeannah all giggled to themselves.

"You know exactly what I mean, Mother. I am not stupid. That man has a three-day growth of stubble and I know you", Saffiera replied, she was not impressed, *"Just make sure that I'm at school when you two start making your, noise!"*, then she turned to the other girls, *"Let's go to the twin's room and get some actual study done"*, and they all walked off down a long corridor to the twin's bedroom.

Kayala chortled once more and said, "Oh my!", red-faced Yealah did not know where to look.

Sarlia replied with a slight smirk, *"Mamas gotta do what Mamas gotta do."*

Angelique almost laughed, "I wonder if Mike knows what he's in for. Sarlia, when Mike gives you the date and time, I'll clear his calendar for the day!", then after a short pause, "Damn, now I can't wait for Bobby to get back home on Saturday! Two weeks off-world on shift and two weeks off, that's hard on this mama!"

Angelique poured the wine equally into four glasses, noting, "I'll talk to Mike tomorrow about building a fair-sized tree house in our tallest and broadest fruit tree. Just in case I need to extract Yookey and his parents from their village. He does organise that sort of thing as well, you know, house maintenance and all."

"Sounds like he's a handyman to have around. A very handyman", Sarlia replied.

Yealah commented, "That is actually a good idea. If things go south, you'll have somewhere safe all prepared for them."

"If things go south", Angelique chortled, "If things go south, we'll bring them south to safety", the four Mothers clicked their glasses together and began to drink their wine.

Kayala asked, "Angelique, do you have your own wine stash?"

Angelique smiled, "Yes, I do, Kayala, but no, I'm keeping you to one glass for your own good."

Kayala smiled, “That is probably wise.”

Meanwhile, the girls had already hooked their data tablets up to the homestead's router and their topic of study for the night appeared on Aria's and Ariel's big screen, mounted on one wall.

The Great Explosion, the Outward Interplanetary Expansion, the Uranian Federation.

Stuart Dumas sat behind the conference room table, his walking frame behind his chair. His secretary, Miss Ritu Dharma sat beside him. Stuart's mind momentarily wandering back to his previous personal assistant and adviser, Tegan Smith, now long retired and helping her own children look after her grandkids. It was so long ago, he missed Tegan, she had been a wonderful assistant over those many years of service. His mind returned from its reverie, time to focus, the meeting would start soon.

Looking to his right, now was the time for the next generation, his Son, Baron and Daughter-in-law, Hypolita, now took the lead. His Grandson, Connor, was now being mentored by Baron, as he had done with Baron, so many years before. Father to Son to Grandson, the chain and its links continued.

His Grandson, Connor, sat beside him on his right, a fine strapping lad, quite tall but not overly so, he looked much like his Father had at his age. On Connor's right was Baron and on Baron's right was Hypolita, a perfect Husband and Wife team. On the far end of the table, next to Hypolita, sat Harmony Moon, their personal assistant and adviser. Ritu sat at the end of the table to Stuart's left.

They all waited patiently for the representatives of four separate groups to enter the conference room. Each of the four groups had come to Dumas Incorporated, each with their own separate plans to colonise Uranus. Obviously, they could not all colonise Uranus, or could they? Stuart had come up with a plan that allowed them all to do so. Much to the surprise of Baron and Hypolita, who had thought that they might have to choose the group with the best laid out plans. Stuart, however, could see a way forward that could satisfy all four groups, he'd even come up with a name for them.

While they waited, Harmony passed on some news, “The Belter's have hit a milestone”, she announced, “There are now thirty Belter colonies.”

“Thirty?”, Hypolita queried, “I knew things were booming along out that way, but thirty?"

"Well, there are the original thirteen, of course, which include the big six, but now every Asteroid with a diameter of two hundred kilometres or larger has a colony. Most of the new ones are smaller, typical O'Neil-style twin cylinders, with capacities of up to twenty thousand", Harmony explained.

Baron commented, "Small, yes, but still important."

There was a knock at the conference room door and a secretary, Brenda Logan, showed the four representatives into the room. One representative from each of the four groups.

Brenda introduced their guests, "Ladies, Gentlemen", she began, "Here we have Ms Carmelita Alvarez, Mr Uric Trondheim, Mr Duarte Santos and Mr Nanuq Amaruq."

The Dumas team all stood up and shook their guest's hands in greeting, "Please take a seat", Baron Dumas requested.

Hypolita addressed their guests, "We have been looking into each of your plans and proposals and while they do seem to be more than adequate, each of your groups wants exclusive control of Uranus and its orbital zone. That in itself, could become problematic."

Ms Carmelita Alvarez replied quickly, "Then it is easily fixed. You choose the most viable proposals and lock the others out. The problem is then solved."

"And if that choice does not go in your favour, Ms Alvarez?", Mr Duarte Santos enquired.

"It will. Our plans are the best choice. That much is obvious", Ms Alvarez replied.

Mr Nanuq Amaruq rolled his eyes at that pronouncement, then asked, "So, which have you chosen?"

Stuart Dumas stood up and leaned forward, facing his guests, "We have chosen none of your plans. They each include aspects that are not currently achievable and although they are viable overall, they will cause issues later down the track."

"How so, Mr Dumas?", Mr Uric Trondheim questioned.

Stuart scoffed, "We choose one of you, then the other three will go off somewhere else and you'll all end up at Uranus fighting over territory. It is a recipe for disaster."

The four guests looked at each other, it was true, none of them was going to give up just because the Dumas Corporation chose only one of them.

Mr Trondheim was a pragmatist, "I assume that you have a solution, Mr Dumas?", he enquired.

"Yes, Mr Trondheim", Stuart replied as he sat back down, "We do have a solution", he nodded to his Son's Wife, Hypolita.

Hypolita took out four rectangular cards, each about the size of a *"playing"* card. The backs of the cards were golden in colour and their faces could not be seen. Hypolita shuffled the four cards several times then placed them face down on the table, sliding them across to Baron. Baron proceeded to slide the cards around on the table, mixing them up so much that no one could ever know what the faces of the cards looked like, even if they had seen them. Then Baron slid the cards across to their guests, one in front of each of them.

"In front of you are four cards all nicely shuffled. The card you get is purely random, pure chance", Baron explained, then instructed, "Pick up your card and look at them."

Ms Alvarez picked up her card and looked at it, it had a picture of the Uranus Moon, Oberon, depicted on it, along with its diameter and orbital parameters, "Oberon, fifteen hundred and twenty three kilometres in diameter", she muttered with a puzzled look.

An equally puzzled Mr Trondheim picked up his card and turned it over, it depicted the Uranus Moon, Titania, he read it out, "Titania, fifteen hundred and seventy eight kilometres in diameter."

Mr Santos quickly picked up his card and turned it over, "Ariel, eleven hundred and fifty eight kilometres in diameter", his face took on a puzzled look.

Mr Amaruq was last, he slowly picked up his card and looked at it, he scoffed, "Umbriel, eleven hundred and sixty nine kilometres in diameter", then he asked Baron, "What is this, Mr Dumas?"

Baron Dumas looked to his Father, Stuart, who answered, "Random selection has assigned each of your groups a Moon of Uranus", he explained.

"But each Moon is not equal, Mr Dumas", Ms Alvarez critiqued in reply.

"Yes, but don't complain too loudly, Ms Alvarez. Oberon is the second largest of the Uranian Moons", Stuart replied calmly, noting, "Chance has been kind to your group."

"Chance could have been kinder, Mr Dumas", Ms Alvarez replied back quickly.

Mr Santos commented, "Chance could have been less kind, Ms Alvarez. My Moon, Ariel, is the smallest of the four. Yet, I am not complaining."

"It was a blind chance selection, Ms Alvarez and you got lucky", Baron chimed in.

Mr Amaruq enquired, "So, each of us gets the Moon we drew. What about all of the other Moons?"

Hypolita answered him, "The other Moons of Uranus will be shared resources for all four groups."

Ms Alvarez nodded in understanding, then asked, "And the leading and trailing Trojans?"

Those Trojan points had been a big part of her group's proposal, which had largely been based on what had been achieved in Saturnian orbit.

Baron smiled and replied honestly, "The leading and trailing Trojan points of Uranus are not a realistic option at this point in time. Perhaps, in the future when your colonies are more developed and our technology has advanced further."

Hypolita chimed in and added, "At which time, they too, will be a shared resource."

Uric Trondheim, Duarte Santos and Nanuq Amaruq all nodded in agreement, Carmelita Alvarez, not so much, she asked a simple one-word question, "Why?", more of a demand really.

Baron sighed almost imperceptibly, "Orbital dynamics, Ms Alvarez, orbital dynamics."

Stuart chimed in and explained, "Both Saturn and Uranus suffer from the same affliction, Ms Alvarez. They both sit between Jupiter and Neptune. In both cases, Saturn's and Uranus's leading and trailing Trojans have a dearth of asteroids in those libration zones. The gravitation heft of their neighbouring planets on either side makes asteroids in those zones, unstable concerning their orbital properties. Simply put, those asteroids drift away into unstable, chaotic orbits around the Sun, becoming Centaur bodies for the most part."

"And yet, you did manage to create conglomerated asteroidal masses for the Saturnians in their leading and trailing Trojans", Ms Alvarez replied, folding her arms across her chest, she thought that she had him.

Stuart smiled wryly, "Ms Alvarez, Saturn has one advantage over Uranus in this regard. Saturn is far closer to Jupiter than Uranus is. We were able to pull some of Jupiter's asteroids out of their orbits and use those to build those conglomerate asteroidal masses. As you probably know, Jupiter has thousands of Trojan asteroids. We chose asteroids from the outer regions of Jupiter's leading and trailing Trojan points and even the opposing libration zone, which itself contains thousands of transient asteroids. That is not feasible at the present moment in time for Uranus, it is something for the future."

"If that is the case, why are those conglomerated asteroidal masses now stable?", an unconvinced Ms Alvarez continued to question.

"We placed those conglomerated asteroidal masses right in the heart of Saturn's leading and trailing points, right in the sweet spot, where they'll stay for a very long time", Baron Dumas chimed in, he added, "The Trojan points of Uranus are perturbed by Jupiter's, Saturn's and Neptune's gravitational heft and there is not a vast reservoir of asteroids floating around like there is in Jupiter's orbital zone."

Ms Alvarez looked at Baron, "Thank you, Mr Dumas. I needed to fully understand the situation to explain it to my board. They won't simply accept a no, they will need to hear the reasons why."

"Ms Alvarez, the full explanation can be found in the proposal documents, that we will be providing", Baron Dumas informed her, understanding that she had accepted his answer but had no need to explain why she had been so '*prickly*'.

"Talking about the proposals, what are we looking at?", Mr Amaruq enquired.

"We have four identical proposals. One for each of your groups", Hypolita Dumas replied, noting, "As we speak, they are being adjusted to take into account the selected Uranian Moons."

Baron Dumas then took over, "We will provide to each group, the following. An O'Neil-style twin-cylinder colony, capable of housing over fifty thousand colonists. The new colonies will have their long strip windows modified to capture every possible skerrick of Sunlight and sufficient Faster Breeder Fission Reactors to maintain optimal power."

Baron paused for a moment to let the information sink in, then continued, "We will provide all of the requisite orbital mining, ore processing and manufacturing stations necessary for resource extraction and processing. Our people will perform all of the necessary onsite set-up, installation and training as required. We will also provide interplanetary push ships to take your colonists to the respective colonies. Those push ships will be rather large and they will be designed, so that when your groups decide, they can be recycled into the skeletal structure of a new colony, for colonial expansion."

Hypolita chimed in, "The new colonies, orbital stations and push ships will be constructed at our Cis-Lunar L-Four construction zones by both Dumas Colonial Constructions and Himmelstaff Interplanetary Constructions. Dumas Colonial Financial will provide you with all of the necessary finance at excellent rates. Have I left anything out?", she paused, then noted, "Ah, yes. Dumas Cis-Lunar Haulage will handle the haulage of the colonies to their final destinations."

Harmony Moon had already adjusted the proposal documents to reflect the selected Uranian Moons and printed them out at secretary Brenda Logan's printer. Brenda knocked on the conference room door, entered and passed the freshly printed and bound documents to Harmony before retreating back to her desk in her office outside. Although Harmony trusted Brenda's work, she quickly ran her eyes through each folio to make sure that they were kosher, before passing them one by one to Hypolita.

"Ms Alvarez, Gentlemen, here are the proposals", Hypolita passed them across to their guests, ensuring that they each received the correct copy, "Everything we have noted and more is covered in those proposal documents."

Their guests thanked Hypolita and began thumbing through the folios.

After several minutes, Ms Alvarez enquired, "I suppose it's buried in here somewhere, but you didn't mention colony placement", impressed with what she had skimmed, she was using a much softer tone of voice.

"Yes, of course", Hypolita replied, explaining, "We will use a standard colony placement for each Uranian Moon. Each colony will be placed into its Moons, trailing Trojan Point, in a halo orbit. Each colony will be designated by its Moon's name followed by Central, which is, of course, the standard naming convention."

Uric Trondheim questioned, "Where do you envisage the push ships residing when they are eventually repurposed?"

Baron Dumas answered, "In the proposals, we do recommend each Moon's leading Trojan point, which gives you colonies on either side of the relevant Moon in its orbit. However, ultimately, you get to decide. If you wish you can place it in the relevant trailing Trojan point, you can make that choice. Ultimately, the choice is yours."

Nanuq Amaruq was still perusing the proposal, he asked, "What if we want to make variations?"

Stuart Dumas replied, by answering, "Any variations you submit will be run through our engineering department and if they are workable, a variation to the proposal addendum document will be provided outlying the changes."

While Nanuq Nodded, Duarte Santos noted, "These look very thorough", then asked, "Is there anything else we'll need to know?"

"Yes, of course, there is, Mr Amaruq", Stuart Dumas answered him, explaining, "Uranus has twenty eight known moons and the fifth largest, Miranda, which is four hundred and seventy kilometres in diameter, is the most important part of this entire proposal."

That caught their guests by surprise, it was likely a salesman offering them steak knives, only they were more valuable than the product.

"The most important part of this entire proposal?", Ms Alvarez enquired, her ears had picked up.

Harmony Moon took out four folios from her briefcase, they were each labelled, *"Joint Uranian Colonisation Initiative, JUCI, pronounced, Juicy"*, and she passed them to Hypolita.

Hypolita passed the folios across to their guests, "These four proposals are identical to each other. They also match and compliment your *'specific'* proposals for each of your selected Moons."

Baron explained, "We envisage that the Uranian Moon, Miranda, will have an identical colony set up as with your selected Moons. The main difference will be that this is a joint project that you each invest one-quarter of the cost."

"Why on Earth would we do that, Mr Dumas?", Ms Alvarez questioned.

"Well, Ms Alvarez, for one, it will give you a fifth colony in Miranda's orbital zone", Baron replied, then he elaborated, "A shared colony where all four groups can come together."

Stuart chimed in, "Oberon Central will be the centre of governance for Oberon's orbital zone, your group's zone, Ms Alvarez. Likewise, Titania Central, Ariel Central and Umbriel Central will be the centre of government for their respective orbital zones and their respective groups. Mr Trondheim's group, Mr Santos's group and Mr Amaruq's group."

Hypolita chimed in, "And Miranda Central will be the centre of government for the entire Uranus orbital zone. Decisions made in your individual group's orbital zones will cover your individual groups, however, decisions made at Miranda Central will cover all of your four groups."

Baron chimed back in, "The Uranian Federated Colonies! My Father came up with that idea."

Stuart looked at his guests squarely and stated, "In this, the Miranda proposal, there is an important political component. Each of your groups must come up with its own Constitution and you must also work together to develop an overall Constitution for your Uranian Federation. It is recommended in the proposal, that you work together on your individual Constitutions as well, to make them all compatible with each other."

"And what if we refuse? What if we can't work together?", Ms Alvarez asked.

Stuart chuckled softly to himself, "Ms Alvarez. When you check these proposals in detail, you will find they all hinge on you working together to develop those Constitutions, your individual ones and the one for the whole Federation."

"What does that even mean?", Ms Alvarez demanded.

Stuart signed, "Ms Alvarez, it means that this is not negotiable. No Constitutions. No Colonies."

"What's to stop us from just going somewhere else?", Ms Alvarez asked.

"You could try, but it won't work", Stuart replied, then he explained, "We are not in the habit of enabling disparate groups that cannot cooperate together to colonise an orbital zone. That would be an absolute disaster. If you cannot cooperate on this, you cannot colonise Uranus!"

Baron chimed in and noted, "If you fail in this task, we will use our economic leverage to prevent your group from colonising Uranus. You will not find finance or construction companies willing to help you. If one group drops out, we will find another group that is willing to cooperate with the others."

Uric Trondheim, Duarte Santos and Nanuq Amaruq all nodded in agreement, with Nanuq stating, "Mr Dumas is correct, Ms Alvarez. If we cannot do this, we have no business even attempting this venture. We have to come together and work on these Constitutions."

Ms Alvarez ran both of her hands through her fiery red hair, "I am not disagreeing with any of you. I'm just wondering how to push this through my board. They would not have even considered any political components to any of this."

"Ms Alvarez, make them understand, that going into deep space as four separate groups that do not cooperate with each other, is just setting them up for failure", Stuart explained, "We cannot have a single colony or colonial group member fail. Not ever!"

"Consider it done, Mr Dumas", Ms Alvarez replied to Stuart, "I'm not sure how I'll get the board on side with this yet, but I'll find a way."

Stuart replied with a scenario, "Tell your board this. Uranus is almost three billion kilometres away. If there is no cooperation and things go wrong, no one will be there to help them. People will die!"

"Yes. I understand", Ms Alvarez replied nodding.

All four groups managed to work together, each developing their own individual colonial Constitutions. They all cooperated on developing an overarching Uranian Federation Constitution that covered all four groups as a united people. Construction of the relevant colonies, associated orbital stations and push ships began and in the due course of time, the Moons of Uranus were colonised.

Once the Uranian Federated colonies were online and operational, another, lesser-known company under the Dumas Incorporated Umbrella, Dumas Astro Resources Ltd, kicked into gear. Searching for suitable small Centaur bodies in chaotic orbits that brought them close to Uranus, for possible relocation to Uranus's Trojan points.

With time quite a few Centaurs were located and telescopic observation from Cis-Lunar L-Two, where Dumas Astro Resources was based, deemed them suitable. The Miranda Central Command colony, the capital of the Uranian Federation, was notified and new plans were developed to capture and make use of those Centaurs.

This was going to be more difficult than usual, due to the nature of the Centaur bodies themselves. They weren't like the asteroids in the main Asteroid Belt, nor were they like the asteroids in Jupiter's Trojans and libration points. These Centaurs were far more volatile, more loosely packed together and resembled comets more than anything else. Hauling them into Uranus's Trojan points, into their sweet spots, would not be an easy task. Due to the gravitational perturbations caused by Jupiter, Saturn and Neptune, keeping them there would be a challenge as well.

Stuart Dumas had always believed in the KIS principle, Keep It Simple! The problem was moving the small Centaurs without them breaking apart into dozens of smaller fragments. So instead of locking onto the Centaurs and gently *"hauling"* them, as they had done with the previous asteroids, they decided to gently *"nudge"* them into their new locations.

To prevent the Centaurs from breaking apart, the Dumas Research and Development Department, came up with a net-like webbing that could be deployed around a small Centaur to hold it together. The nets had to be easily deployable, flexible and capable of stretching for full coverage. The nets also needed to be easily removed once the Centaur was in place in its new location. The nets were created using various newly developed nanomaterials, shape-memory alloys and high-tensile polymer composites.

Being more volatile than other asteroids, the Centaurs once positioned in the sweet spot of Uranus's Trojan points, had to be compressed and pushed together, to prevent them from coming apart. A process that would require at least three space tugs at each Trojan point. Baron Dumas allowed for no fewer than eight space tugs in all to ensure such processes would proceed smoothly.

Then it was just a matter of how to ensure that the Conglomerated Centaur Masses stayed put, in the sweet spot and were not perturbed out them by competing gravitational forces. This too came back down to the space tugs. There was to be one space tug always in Uranus's Trojan points to *'nudge'* the Conglomerated Centaur Masses back into the sweet spot should they start to drift out of them. This of course meant that space tugs needed to be on station permanently.

The Dumas Corporation was not in the business of selling space tugs, however, as the long-term stability of the project required it, six of the eight space tugs were sold to the Uranian Federation. Their crews would teach the Federation personnel how to pilot them as part of the process, bringing them up to speed. Then when the task was completed, the Dumas employees were to return to Cis-Lunar space in the remaining two space tugs, or if they wished, stay behind as new Uranian Federation colonists.

Parallel to the development and management of Conglomerated Centaur Masses, the Dumas Corporation constructed two more O'Neil-style twin cylinder colonies for the Federation, along with a full complement of orbital mining, ore processing and manufacturing stations. Each of Uranus's Trojan points was to receive one set.

They were to be placed in halo orbits about the Conglomerated Centaur Masses. These colonies were identical to the five colonies already online in the trailing Trojan points of Uranus's major Moons. They were both *"shared"* Uranian Federation colonies under the governance of Miranda Central Command itself.

Stuart, Baron, Hypolita and Connor had read through the Constitutions that the four groups had developed, along with the Uranian Federation's overarching Constitution. Each of the group's constitutions was consistent with each other, with only minor differences. The Uranian Federations Constitution was impressive, it contained multiple pathways for dispute resolution concerning *"shared"* Uranian resources and other issues that might crop up.

They all thought that it was great to see Ms Alvarez and her group come around to their way of thinking. Carmelita Alvarez had even suggested, flirtatiously, that Connor should come to live at her colony, Oberon Central Command, in the Uranian Federation. Her logic was impeccable, after all, Connor Dumas had helped to create the Uranian Federation and its colonies, surely, he should be a part of the result, surely, he should live there. Connor was flattered but politely declined. Carmelita was way too fiery for him, although he had to admit to himself, that he found Carmelita with her fiery red hair and personality quite intriguing. Connor Dumas was smitten!

30. The Neptunian Commonwealth.

A thoughtful look came over Aria's face, "So these four separate groups each wanted to colonise and control Uranus, yet they all ended up working together and forming a federation?", she questioned.

"Apparently, Aria", Yeannah replied, noting, "And it seemed to have worked as well. Very successfully in fact."

"It's kind of like wanting to eat the whole pie, Gudong pie of course. Then somehow they decided to settle for one-fifth each and then share the final fifth", Aria explained with an analogy.

Ariel just shook her head and rolled her eyes at her twin Sister, "Very good, Aria. Now why the hell couldn't you have been this thoughtful at lunch, instead of creating that inter-species incident!", she chided her.

Kethera chortled, before bursting out laughing, then she stated softly, "Oh, I love it when you two get angry with each other", she smiled, then commented, "I know that same-face kits never mean it."

"Same-face kits?", Saffiera asked telepathically.

"Ah huh, same-face kits", Kethera confirmed, explaining, "After a Carlin Mother's first litter, the kits come in twos and then in threes. They can be same-face or different-face, sometimes both, if there's three or more in the litter."

Yeannah replied, commenting, "Kethera, they're called twins, triplets, quads etc."

"I know that, Yeannah. The twins are Sisters with the same face, so same-face kits", Kethera confirmed she understood the concept quite well, then she noted, "When I'm older. I want Richard and me to have some kits with the same face, just like the twins. I'll call them Aria and Ariel."

Both of the twins smiled at Kethera's compliment.

Yeannah sighed, "We Thols never have twins, never more than one youngling at a time."

Aria remarked, "I fully comprehend why Carlins have six breasts. Before we Humans turned up, I expect five and six kits to a litter would have been normal."

"Hmm, sometimes, but not often", Kethera confirmed.

"Kethera, you have as many kits as you like, just as long as their Aunty Yeannah gets to cuddle them", Yeannah replied with a smile and Kethera reached over and hugged her.

Yeannah then brought the conversation back to the topic of the term assignment, "So, we're all good with how the Uranian Federation was set up?"

"Yep", Saffiera replied, noting, *"They were assigned the four biggest Uranian Moons using a random process, then shared everything else"*, she smiled, *"They actually drew cards!"*

Yeannah nodded in agreement, but added, "Keep in mind, that each group developed their own individual Constitutions and ensured that they were compatible with each other, before drawing up an overall Constitution to cover the Federation. I have a feeling that the political side of this will be important for the assignment."

"Quite likely", Ariel agreed, noting, "It's too important to leave out. I don't want to lose marks just because we neglected the political angle, so yeah, let's keep it in mind."

All of the girls nodded in agreement, Ariel's previous chiding of Aria was completely forgotten.

Aria commented, "I loved the way they solved their Trojan problem. The Centaur bodies were too unstable structurally, I mean they were pretty much, just fluffy snowballs with a bit of aggregate. Wrap them up in a net, just like putting on a stocking and just gently nudge them into place. So simple!"

"Except for the need to keep at least one space tug on location to ensure that their Conglomerated Centaur Masses stayed on station and didn't drift", Ariel replied, noting, "That was probably something they'd need to do constantly. Nudge their major resources back into their sweet spots over and over."

Kethera giggled, "I'm thinking you'd like Yookey to wrap you in a stocking and gently nudge you into place, Aria."

Aria smiled and laughed, "Maybe! Hmm, yeah, maybe."

Ariel rolled her eyes, "Kethera, please don't encourage my Sister. Remember that incident."

"Oh, Ariel. I'm not going to fuck Yookey, at least not until we get to know each other", Aria replied.

Saffiera just shook her head and replied, *"The Uranian Trojan points are probably the least stable of all of Sol's Gas Giant's Trojans. So you would expect more effort to be involved. Continuous effort."*

"And that's another point to keep in mind. The colonisation of Uranus was not only difficult politically but other aspects of it required true grit", Yeannah remarked.

"It couldn't have been easy. They were pioneers. True pioneers", Kethera agreed, then remarked quite whimsically, "Maybe, just maybe, after the Twin's Mum trains us as pilots, Richard and I will be pioneers. Captain Kethera of the outer frontier!"

"And your loyal mate, Richard", Aria added.

Yeannah chortled, "You want a house full of kits and be a pioneer. We'll put you and Richard in a Conestoga with all of your kits and off you all go to colonise the unknown worlds of the outer frontier", and then the girls all laughed.

"Will there be room for all of our future kits?", Kethera jokingly asked, adding to the laughter.

Aria laughed and remarked, "Captain Kethera and her faithful side-kick Richard, conquer the Planet of Doom!"

Kethera's whiskers drooped, "I want to conquer a nice Planet, Aria. Like this one, Vale!"

Aria's twin, Ariel reminded her, "Kethera, your world has Fern Dragons, Sleimorps, Chitten, Kyrrax and Tarlaks. All sorts of nasty predators. You do remember?"

Kethera's whiskers twitched and her ears flicked forward, "Well, Aria. No world is perfect."

After the laughter died down, Saffiera noted, *"I've got all the key points noted down, we should move on to Neptune."*

"Agreed", replied Yeannah, adding, "I've been looking at the orbital dynamics of Neptune's Moons. If you thought the Uranian Trojans were an issue, well, Neptune tops that one" and then she brought the relevant documents up on the screen.

Stuart Dumas's office was just a little crowded, his Secretary, Ritu Dharma was present, always ready to assist the now aged and frail business mogul. Stuart's Son, Baron and his Son's Wife, Hypolita were also present, along with their personal assistant and adviser, Harmony Moon. Stuart sat in his favourite chair, with the others sitting in chairs around a central coffee table.

Each of them had a glass of Martian Sweet Cherry Red wine in front of them.

They were discussing a new group that recently formed, on the back of the colonisation of Uranus. They had seen all of the planning and construction going into the Uranian Federation and the ongoing Uranian colonisation efforts and the reports that had been presented in the inner system news feeds. They felt that their new group could colonise Neptune. This group was very new, it had grown very quickly and had a burgeoning membership. They called their diverse community, the Neptunian Commonwealth! They were also very naive!

"So how is the Uranian Federation going?", Stuart enquired.

Baron replied, "Our boys, Connor and Daniel, are working closely with them to ensure everything goes smoothly. So far everything is going to plan."

"That is good to know. Uranus is over nineteen astronomical units away and we need everything to go perfectly. At that distance, we can't have a single thing go wrong", Stuart commented in reply.

"Well, Neptune is over thirty astronomical units away. That is so much further", Baron noted, adding, "This new group, the Neptunian Commonwealth, are also underestimating the sheer distances involved. Most people don't understand the sheer scale of the solar system."

"Anything out beyond Saturn is dangerous territory, Baron", Hypolita noted, adding, "They're thinking that Uranus and Neptune are just little steps further out and it's nothing like that at all. Uranus is double Saturn's distance from the Sun and Neptune is more than triple! These guys have no idea!"

"Even the trade logistics are a nightmare. The Neptunian Commonwealth will want to trade with both the Uranian Federation and the Saturnian Demarchy, perhaps even as far afield as the Jovian Republic and the Jovian Trojans", Baron noted, adding, "Those are very long-distance trade routes."

Harmony Moon chimed in, "Mr Dumas, Sir. Unless they can find a source of Uranium and they can refine and enrich it, they'll be reliant on Uranium fuel rods from Earth. Their trade routes will reach as far as the Earth at least."

"Yes, Harmony. That's a good point. The Neptunium Commonwealth will need Faster Breeder Reactors, to extract every skerrick of energy out of the uranium", Baron Dumas replied, noting, "We provided no less for the Uranian Federation, so we'll do the same for them as well."

Stuart felt the stubble on his chin, he hadn't shaved of late and his hands weren't as steady as they used to be, he decided to ask his nurse to shave him later, "When we put together our colonisation proposals to the Neptunian Commonwealth, we'll have to include information about the distances involved, the inherent dangers and the issues of long trade routes. They need to fully comprehend every issue involved."

"I have concerns about our Son, Connor", Hypolita remarked, explaining, "That Alvarez woman is very persistent."

Baron tried to reassure her, "Hypolita darling, Baron has already told us that he has no intention of following Carmelita out to their Oberon Central colony."

"Oh, Baron, don't be so naive. Connor is sleeping with that woman. Connor is not thinking with his head!", Hypolita replied, she was seriously concerned that their eldest Son was going to end up in the Uranian Federation, over nineteen astronomical units away.

"Hypolita my love, I have observed their relationship. They argue, they break up and then they reconcile and have make-up sex. Then their cycle repeats and it does so every week. Their relationship is rocky, to say the least", Baron tried to assure her, concluding, "I doubt very much that he'll follow her out to the edge of the solar system."

Stuart Dumas stepped in, "Baron, Hypolita, I'll talk to Baron", he assured them both, that he did not want to see his eldest Grandson at the far edges of the solar system either.

"Dad, the problem with the Neptunian Commonwealth, is that they think all planets are equal", Baron was trying to explain to his Father, Stuart, remarking, "They think that what worked at Saturn and Uranus is just repeatable at Neptune and that is simply not the case."

"I can understand that, Baron. A lot of our earlier methods translated almost directly across the inner solar system, as far out as the Asteroid Belt and Jupiter's Trojans", Stuart replied, he understood the problem, but this new client was unable to see intricate details that allowed that to happen.

"Triton is the problem, Dad", Baron declared, explaining, "If Neptune had never captured Triton, the system would probably mirror Uranus with its Moon. The problem is that Triton was captured and any earlier native Moons similar to those of Uranus, would have been scattered into Neptune itself or kicked out into the Kuiper Belt."

"Baron, honey", Hypolita interjected, "We have to work with what we've got. There is no choice."

Baron squeezed his Wife's hand, "Darling, Triton is a spoiler. Its retrograde elliptical orbit will destabilise anything we put in its Trojan points. The Tritonian Trojans are a no-go!"

Harmony Moon looked at Baron and chimed in, "Mr Dumas, Sir.

Neptune is kind of like Uranus turned inside out. Uranus had four big stable Moons and another one that was not quite as large but nonetheless useful, while its Trojan points were problematic, to say the least. With Neptune, it's the Moons that are the problem and the Neptunian Trojans are a very viable option."

Stuart Dumas agreed, "Harmony is correct. We need to work the Neptunian Trojan angle and do what we can with Neptune's Moons."

Harmony was already on top of it, "Sir, there are at least five leading Trojans above seventy kilometres in diameter and over in the trailing Trojans at least another five. When we actually get out there, I'm confident that we'll find hundreds, perhaps thousands more."

Stuart commented, "There, that's our starting point, Baron. We won't create conglomerated masses. We'll use what we find in situ and live off of the zone. So all we need is a pair of O'Neil-style twin cylinder colonies and their retinue of mobile mining, ore processing and manufacturing stations."

Harmony chimed in, "Sir, we should quadruple the number of mining stations and include a few survey ships, four per colony should do it."

Baron considered that for a moment, "Neptunian orbit is a long way out. The curvature of those long strip window mirrors will need some careful modelling and engineering, not to mention the fission reactor requirements."

"And there you have it, Son. Our plan is coming already together", Stuart Smiled.

Baron smiled, he could see the plan coming together and then he sighed, "The jewel in the crown is Neptune. So we have to figure out what to do with Neptune's Moons."

Harmony was quickly gathering information, "Mr Dumas, Triton's Trojan zones are unstable. We can't use either of them, however, inside of Triton's orbit, that is another matter."

Baron Dumas enquired, "Well then, Harmony, what have you got for us?"

"Well, Mr Dumas. Galatea at one hundred and eighty kilometres in diameter and Despina at one hundred and forty eight kilometres in diameter look fairly good. Both have stable orbits, so both trailing Trojans look usable", Harmony informed them all, noting, "There's also Thalassa at eighty two in diameter and Naiad at fifty eight kilometres in diameter. Useful as nearby resources, but probably too small to make use of their Trojans."

Hypolita smiled, "Harmony, you never disappoint. Now, what about the Moons outside of Triton's orbit", she enquired.

Harmony rattled off a list, "Proteus at four hundred and twenty kilometres in diameter is probably the most likely prospect. Then there's Larissa at one hundred and ninety four kilometres in diameter, which is smaller and further out, so that's another. We can use both of those."

"So, Harmony, that's four, yes?", Baron requested confirmation.

"Yes, Mrs Dumas, four", Harmony confirmed, noting, "There's also Nereid. It's big, three hundred and forty kilometres in diameter, however, it has a less stable, eccentric orbit. Another resource world."

Stuart Dumas chimed in, "Every other Moon orbiting Neptune is a resource, along with the biggest, Triton itself. So that's four more colonies, Galatea and Despina on the inside and Proteus and Larissa on the outside. It won't be pretty, but it does sound workable. Baron, have Dumas Astro Resources perform the necessary modelling. If that works out then hand it over to our engineering team and we'll prepare the proposals."

Baron chimed in, "That's just the trailing Trojan zones, the Neptunian Commonwealth will be utilising push ships to get their colonists out to Neptune. So they will be recycled and become the backbones of new colonies, probably in those Moon's leading Trojan zones. Just like with Uranus."

Hypolita picked up her glass of wine and Baron did the same, they clinked them together and she announced, "Cheers to the new Neptunian Commonwealth", and all of the others joined in.

Over the next few weeks, the Dumas Astro Resources Corporation, from their Cis-Lunar L-Two location, scanned the entirety of Neptune's Trojan regions and Neptune's Moons themselves. A combination of telescopic, radiometric, spectroscopic analysis, gravitational measurements and thermal imaging were used in the process amongst other techniques.

Quite a few more asteroids, many dozens, were discovered within Neptune's Trojan regions, adding to the resource availability of the entire Neptunian orbital regions. These would become extremely important for the new Neptunian Commonwealth upon their arrival. Astro Resources then studied and modelled every aspect of both Neptune's leading and trailing Trojan regions, along with the orbital dynamics of Neptune's Moons.

The orbital dynamics of Neptune's Moons, most notably the four Moons chosen for the installation of O'Neil twin cylinder orbital colonies, were found to be within acceptable parameters. The chosen Moons did indeed all have usable Trojan zones. All of the other Neptunian Moons were either too small or had orbits that were too unstable, including the massive Neptunian Moon, Triton, so they were all relegated to be used as *"resources"*. Triton's gravity was far too low for permanent surface colonies due to the effects of low gravity on Human physiology.

Dumas Astro Resource then passed the information back to Baron and Hypolita. The Husband and Wife team studied it intently, then promptly organised the Dumas Corporation's Engineering Department to prepare detailed colonisation plans for the Neptunian orbital zone. Plans based on their earlier discussions with Baron's Father, Stuart, his secretary, Ritu Dharma and their personal assistant, Harmony Moon. All up, it took around twelve weeks for the colonisation proposals to be prepared and then the Neptunian Commonwealth's representatives were called in for a meeting. If the Dumas Corporations colonisation's proposals were accepted, the colonisation of Neptune could begin.

The Neptunian Commonwealth sent three representatives to the meeting with at the Dumas Corporation. Stuart Dumas and his secretary were present, as were Baron and Hypolita, their second Son, Daniel and their personal assistant and adviser, Harmony Moon. Before handing them the Neptunian Colonisation Proposal documents, they first discussed with them the particular difficulties in colonising Neptune's orbital region.

It was a slow and arduous meeting, their guests were fixed in their beliefs and how they wanted to proceed at first, not understanding the enormous challenges that Neptune presented. First, they had to explain the tyranny of distance and how it would affect both the setting up of the colonies and their trade with their neighbouring colonies once they were established. Just that alone took nearly an hour to explain. Most people look at a book and say, *"Look there right next to each other"*, explaining the sheer scale of the distances involved took time but eventually, they understood the problem.

They were more than happy to hear about the plans to utilise the Neptunian Trojan points, which to them had been something insignificant. Daniel had explained to their guests that Jupiter and its Trojans had been colonised separately and were essentially three separate colonies. However, with Saturn and Uranus, both their Trojans and their system of Moons had been colonised at the same time, hence, both colonies had complete autonomy over their respective orbital zones. It helped that Daniel had just finished work with the development and construction of the Uranian Federation's Trojan colonies.

They liked that idea, it made a lot of sense. There were asteroids with raw materials to be mined and covering an arch of one hundred and twenty degrees of Neptune's orbit, mitigated some of the *"trade route"* issues. Having a pair of O'Neil-style twin cylinder colonies at those locations now made perfect sense. One of them had noted, that setting these Trojan colonies up from the get-go, would prevent squatters from attempting to move in later. Taking possession now avoids problems later.

The biggest sticking points were the Neptunian Moons. Stuart Dumas and his Son, Baron, along with the others, had all known this would be the case. Their guests were comparing Triton to Saturn's Moon Titan and the four large

Moons of Uranus. They did not understand that Moons with regular circular orbits were a completely different kettle of fish to Triton and its elliptical, retrograde *"spoiler"* orbit. Baron Dumas actually used that very term. Titan and Triton may sound similar, but they were completely different Moons!

Stuart had noted, that before Neptune had captured Triton, it likely would have had a whole retinue of fair-sized Moons like Uranus. However, Triton was captured and when that happened, it sent those hypothetical moons either careering into Neptune itself or off into the Kuiper Belt. Triton had created a chaotic lunar system which was very difficult to work with.

Harmony went through the four Moons that they had selected and meticulously explained why they had been chosen. The guests learnt that Triton's Trojan points were not stable and that its gravity was far too weak for permanent habitation. Harmony also explained that they would have two colonies inside of Triton's orbit and two colonies outside of it, positioning Triton in the perfect position for resource extraction. Triton, although a *"spoiler"* Moon, was still a useful resource.

After well over four hours of argy-bargy, they finally had reached the stage of being able to pass the Neptunian Commonwealth the proposal documents. Stuart's secretary, Ritu, passed them each their own copies, her face was beaming with a smile. It had taken so long to get to that point. During the meeting, jugs of water and glasses were available, but now they wanted to go over the proposals in greater detail. So Ritu organised drinks and sandwiches.

Their guests scanned through the proposal documents, asking many questions. Most of which had been answered during the previous four hours. None of Stuart's team rolled their eyes or sighed, they all stayed attentive and even Stuart himself, who was of advanced age well into his nineties, refused to nod off to sleep. Eventually, after more than six gruelling hours, their guests were happy and the meeting came to a close.

Their guests agreed to present the proposals to their board of directors and lobby for their adoption and signing. After the meeting had finally ended and their guests had left, all five of Stuart's team sighed in relief. The colonisation of Neptune and its Trojan points was finally going to happen!

"Stuart looked around the conference room, "Now, could someone please tell me where my Grandson, Connor is? He was meant to be here today?"

Daniel sighed and looked at his Grandfather, "Granddad, Connor is with that redhead. You know the one from the Oberon group that's going to head out to Uranus with the Uranian Federation."

Hypolita sighed and commented, "That Carmelita Alvarez has her hooks into my Son!"

Daniel laughed, "Don't worry too much, Mum. The last time I saw them they were both arguing. Connor had told Carmelita, that in no uncertain terms, would he be going out to Uranus with her."

Baron shook his head, held his Wife's hand and squeezed it, "Let's hope he sticks to his guns this time and doesn't make up with her again."

Daniel laughed out loud, "What Dad? You think Connor is going miss out on angry makeup sex!"

Baron squeezed his Wife's hand once more, then replied, "Daniel! That is not helping one bit!"

Saffiera picked up a telepathic message from her Mother, Sarlia, *"Hey guys, my Mum is taking your Mums home. She's going to come back and pick us up in the morning to take us home"*, she passed the message on to her friends, telepathically of course.

Kethera enquired, being overly concerned having seen her Mother, Kayala, waking up at Saffiera's house the previous Saturday morning massively hungover, "They did stick to only one glass of wine, yeah?"

Saffiera smiled and replied, *"Yes, Kethera. Only the one glass, although just one appears to be enough to get your Mum pretty tipsy."*

Kethera's whiskers drooped slightly, "Carlins and strong wine do not mix, Saffiera."

Aria quickly blurted out, no filter as usual, "Maybe your Dad's going to get lucky tonight, Kethera", and then she burst out laughing.

Ariel and Yeannah both burst out laughing as well and Kethera replied, "I do not even want to think about that, Aria!"

Saffiera frowned and transmitted, *"Guys, Focus. The Neptunian Commonwealth remember!"*

Aria noted thoughtfully, "I'm learning just as much about the orbital dynamics of the sol system as I am about history. I mean, I would never have known the differences between the orbital zones of the outer planets otherwise."

Ariel shook her head, "One minute you're creating inter-species incidents, the next you're indirectly learning about orbital dynamics while studying history. Aria! I swear, you may be my twin, but I'll never understand you. You make absolutely no sense."

Aria shrugged, "I'm just complicated!", then after a short pause, "And hey, at least I'm leaning."

Kethera giggled, "Same-faced kits. Always poking fun at each other, never really meaning it", then she reached out and wrapped an arm around each of them and pulled them both into a hug.

The twins both hugged Kethera back, "Love you to bits too, Kethera!", they stated in unison.

Yeannah decided to get back on topic, "I like the way Neptune is described as like Uranus, but inside out. When you wade through the complexities of both systems, one, Uranus has a sweet set of Moons and a dearth of Trojan asteroids. The other, Neptune, has a sweet set of Trojan asteroids and really crappy lunar dynamics caused by a *'spoiler'* Moon, Triton."

Saffiera agreed, commenting telepathically, *"Yeah, that's really noticeable but look at how the Gas Giants were colonised. Jupiter's Trojans were colonised on the back of the Belter Colonies as two separate entities. Then Jupiter itself was colonised separately by those Jovian Dream people."*

Aria chimed in uncharacteristically, "And Saturn, Uranus and Neptune were all colonised as whole orbital zones at once. The Saturnian Demarchy, the Uranian Federation, the Neptunian Commonwealth, one group for each of those three gas Giants."

Ariel sighed in exasperation, "How do you do that, Aria? Go from crazy to brilliant in a heartbeat?"

"I don't know, Ariel", Aria admitted, then smiled wryly and replied, "How do you even walk with that stick up your butt, Ariel?"

"Really, Aria, really", Ariel replied, disappointed at how short Aria's period of brilliance lasted.

"Do I have to hug my favourite same-faced kits again?", Kethera enquired.

"Yes!", both twins said in unison as they reached out to Kethera and hugged her while they all tumbled backwards to the floor giggling.

Yeannah and Saffiera looked at each other and just rolled their eyes, *"Twins"*, they both thought.

Kethera frowned, her whiskers ever so slightly lowered, "What happened to Connor Dumas and Carmelita Alvarez? I don't remember seeing that anywhere?"

Saffiera was also curious, *"Yeah, I'd like to know that one as well. Did Connor follow Carmelita all the way to Oberon Central in the Uranian Federation?"*, she transmitted.

"We do have a hyperlink attached to them. It would be a shame not to follow it", Yeannah agreed.

"Yep. Follow that link", Aria and Ariel both answered in unison and they cracked up laughing.

Carmelita Alvarez and Connor Dumas were arguing, it was loud, fiery and their worst blow-up yet! Carmelita was having a major meltdown. Everyone in the Dumas mansion kept well clear of the toxic couple, lest it spread to them all like an angry toxic plague. Stuart and the rest of their family were at the Dumas Corporate Tower, working on various projects, they were the lucky ones. The Dumas mansion's household staff not so much!

Carmelita was shouting profanities at Connor in Portuguese. She called him everything she could think of under the Sun. Connor had no idea what she was saying, but her face was exceedingly red and angry. All Connor had done was reiterate once again, that he had no intentions of going to Oberon Central, that he had no intention of joining the Uranian Federation. That he was more than content being a colonist in Cis-Lunar L-Five in his Grandfather's Corporate colony. He had of course reiterated his position rather strongly. Angrily telling Carmelita to fuck off and go to Oberon Central on her own, was probably what triggered her. Carmelita was as fierce and fiery as her long red hair.

Carmelita was a woman in love! She was torn between the two most important things in her life, her group, the Oberon group and its ambitions to colonise Oberon's orbital zone with Oberon Central, as a part of the Uranian Federation and the man that she loved, Connor Dumas.

Connor was so frustrating, he was infuriating, why would he not go with her to the colony?

Carmelita could not understand it, Connor had expressed his love for her in so many ways and yet, he was unwilling to follow her to Oberon Central. Time was running out, the interplanetary push ship, the Oberon, was ready, it was leaving in mere days!

Why would he not follow her to the new colony?

What was his problem?

Carmelita had tried everything to convince Connor to follow her. She had professed her undying love for him. She had tried to ply him with her feminine wiles. She had even performed extreme acts of sex in their bedroom to convince him, that she was the only woman for him. Sexual acts that she would never have performed with anyone else. It all seemed to work, then every time Carmelita asked Connor to follow her to Oberon Central, in the new Uranian colonies, he declined and said, in no uncertain terms, no. He was completely adamant, his position fixed in stone!

Finally, Carmelita gave up. She was broken. She could not fight anymore. She had called him every vile name in Portuguese that she could think of. Her tears flowed freely and she threw herself to her knees. Their fight had lasted for hours and Carmelita was exhausted. Connor looked at Carmelita and his tears welled. Slowly he walked over to her and knelt down in front of her. Connor took Carmelita into his arms and held her tightly. Then he leant back and looked directly into her eyes.

Connor spoke softly, asking Carmelita, "Why do you have to go to the ends of the solar system, Carmelita? Why don't you stay here with me in Cis-Lunar L-five? Just stay here with me and be my Wife? Marry me, Carmelita?"

Carmella's tears still flowed, but now they were turning to tears of joy, this frustrating and infuriating man, her Connor, had just proposed to her.

Carmelita wiped the tears from her eyes with her sleeve and replied, "Yes. Yes, Connor", then she gave off a little chuckle, "That is all I really wanted, to marry you, Connor. I thought we would be in the colonies, at Oberon Central, but I was wrong. I will stay here with you in Cis-Lunar L-five."

And that was that, three days later, the interplanetary push ship, the Oberon, left without Ms Carmelita Alvarez. Just like that, the once firebrand woman of the Oberon colonisation group had become a Wife and eventually a Mother. To the amazement of everyone who knew them. After their marriage they never argued again for the rest of their lives and between them, they raised nine children. All Great Grandchildren of Stuart Dumas.

The girls read through the historical pages about Carmelita Alvarez and Baron Dumas.

"Wow! They had nine children! That's a lot", Saffiera noted.

"Not for a Carlin family", Kethera smiled.

"They weren't Carlins, Kethera", Yeannah reminded her.

"Humans are like Carlins in a lot of ways, Yeannah", Kethera replied, with her own observations.

Ariel noted, "Mum says that the Indigenous Thols are a lot like us Humans."

Aria gently punched her Sister in the arm, "Ariel, silly. Carlins and Indigenous Thols are a lot like us Humans."

Yeannah then remarked, "It says here, that they had three sets of twins and a set of triplets!"

Kethera squealed with delight, "They had lots of same-faced kits!", she exclaimed, she so loved same-face kits, perhaps that was the reason that she loved the twins so much.

"Guys, if you could just focus for a few more minutes", Saffiera implored them, *"I've taken some pretty detailed notes and tied in a lot of links back to the other Gas Giants. I'll send you all copies"*, then she tapped on the document twice with her stylus and her data tablet automatically copied the document to all of the other data tablets in the room.

Ariel jokingly remarked, "Saffiera, note taker extraordinaire", laughing.

Aria looked to Kethera, "Captain Kethera of the outer frontier and her loyal mate, Richard", and began laughing.

Kethera began laughing as well and Yeannah and Saffiera joined in as well.

The rest of the night was spent talking, laughing and joking around.

31. The Darklings.

The Tholish High Council upholds the laws of all Thol kind. Their laws against inter-species relationships, yes, but most importantly, their ultimate law. No Thol may kill another Thol. By and large, their laws had been upheld across countless millennia. Yet, even as this was so, there was a dark secret within the Indigenous Thol clans.

Far to the west of the westernmost Thol villages, was another, separate clan of Indigenous Thols, a clan that did not adhere to the rules of the Tholish High Council. This clan, the Darklings, lived in the canopy of the tallest Jula Jula trees, just barely east of the territory of the Chitten. A harsh insectoid species that looked like giant Ants.

The Chitten had segmented bodies, with an abdomen, thorax and head. Six agile legs extended from their thorax and a sizeable deadly stinger extended from their abdomen. Their head contained two antennae, two compound eyes and a pair of giant vicious mandibles. The Chitten had no wings and could not fly and although they could climb, they preferred not to.

Their workers were roughly four feet in size and largely harmless, not so much their soldiers, who were two feet larger and whose mandibles were like massive, sharpened pincers. They were capable of bringing down their prey by spitting formic acid with deadly accuracy. The Chitten Queen lived safely in the deepest chamber of their tunnels with her Princesses, controlling their hive with her pheromones. The Chitten were quite possibly sapient and the Darkling clan kept well clear of them. They taught their foundlings, never to cross a Chitten barrier, that would be certain death, something the Chittens did not tolerate.

Other denizens of the dark Western Mountain Forests could also be dangerous. Almost as common as the Chitten and just as deadly, were the Sleimorps. These were bipedal creatures with a muzzled head, with two forward-looking eyes and a mouth full of sharp, pointed teeth. They had short, strong arms, with three-fingered, clawed hands. Their legs were long, ending in three-toed, clawed feet and a fourth toe held a sharp, sickle-shaped, retractable talon.

They had a long tail, the end of which contained a retractable, sharp bone sword hidden beneath a sheath of skin. The Sleimorp instinctively wielded their sickle-shaped talons and bone swords with absolute precision. Running, their tail aided their balance and when fighting, it sliced and diced like a natural sword master. The Sleimorps were highly skilled and deadly. Their dull, grey colouration matched perfectly with the shadows of the forest in which they lived.

The Sleimorp were natural pack hunters, they were extremely territorial and intelligent, yet nonetheless, sub-sapient. They were the most efficient killers in the deep Jula Jula forests of the Western Mountains. Even so, the Sleimorp would not cross a Chitten boundary unless they had no other choice. The Darkling clan kept well away from the Sleimorps as well, except at the time of their passing of age, when a male foundling became a man.

At the passing of age, the hunters amongst the Darklings, separate a single Sleimorp from its pack, a difficult task, that can take up to thirty men of their clan. Once separated out, the male foundling must ritually fight the Sleimorp and slay it in combat, such was the rite of passage. Most survived this one-on-one combat, but some, more than a few did not.

Once the rite of passage was completed, the foundling became a man. His chest was adorned with a tattoo of a Tarlak skull, black ink against his alabaster white skin. The Tarlaks being a malevolent sapient species, more troglodyte than Thol, resembling a cross between a Gorilla and a Winged Gargoyle and at seven feet tall, were far more powerful than the other species on the planet. Both Thols and Tarlaks were genetic cousins, yet only the Darklings worshipped them.

The new Darkling man then received the two sickle-shaped talons and the long, bone-sword as his prize. Each of which was soaked in resin, which filtered into every pore and crevice and then was allowed to harden. Once treated in this way, all three could be shaped and sharpened to hold s sharp, keen edge. A hilt was added to each and scabbards of Sleimorp hide were made for their keeping. The pair of sickle-shaped talon knives could be joined at the hilt, to create a double-bladed weapon. These were the weapons of the Darkling clan and they were all Murderers and Assassins!

It was long believed that those few Thols who broke the ancient taboos and laws and were subsequently banished to the Western Forests, would either survive, highly unlikely or more likely be killed by the denizens of the forest. The reality was, that they were more likely to be killed by the Darkling clan, who held to no authority but their own. A handful of the Tholish High Council members knew of their existence, a few made use of their skills. None talked about them. None dared, to openly mention their existence was asking for the visitation of death incarnate!

Yvainyurei was a Darkling, he was a master assassin and he also had been contracted! Yvainyurei sat in a large Bell Nut Fruit tree, carefully surveilling the compound in which the tree grew. The compound was over three hundred metres across. It was surrounded by eight doubled, chain-link fences all joined and linked together. He smiled to himself, as he had just flown straight over those perimeter fences, flying low and coming in behind the cover of the huge Bell Nut Fruit tree. He had approached unseen!

His great wings were now comfortably furled and he was recovering from his long flight. There had been strange creatures in the tree, eating leaves, fruit and nuts. They looked similar to Gudongs, but had hair and only two eyes? They must have been something that the Humans had brought with them from their world somewhere up in the sky, amongst the highest clouds.

Sky people? What were they? Where did they come from? Did they truly live in the highest clouds?

These hairy creatures did not seem to be bothered by sharing the tree with him.

Yvainyurei touched the Cress tooth that he wore on a leather cord around his neck. It had been his Father's and his Grandfather's before him, back to the dawn of time itself. It was a symbol of his high status amongst the Darkling clan. To Yvainyurei, it was his lucky talisman.

The Cress kind of looked like a Sleimorp, only they were much bigger, a little of twenty feet tall. They had a huge muzzled head and their mouths were lined with sharp nine-inch fangs. They had strong hind legs, the feet of which had three clawed toes. They had no sickle-shaped talons on their feet, but their tails were long and powerful and they were tipped with three, two-foot-long spikes. The Cress used those to strike with great and deadly effect. Their forelegs were short, but nonetheless dangerous, with clawed hands that were capable of crushing a man or ripping a man in two. It was good that they were solitary hunters and only came together to breed. They were also a denizen of the Western Forests.

Yvainyurei made himself comfortable for the night. He wore only a pair of short-legged trousers made of softened Sleimorp hide. His belt contained his scabbarded, Sickle-Knives and Bone Sword. Yvainyurei took out the picture of his target from one of his pockets and looked carefully at it. On the back were written instructions on where to find his target. This was definitely the place. The large hangar in the distance and the soil-covered abode matched perfectly. The target's house was just a little way further to the south.

It was curious though, his target was a simple Human child, a she-child. Hardly worth his time to slay her, except of course he was being paid, *"most high"*! The price to kill this one child was ten times higher than the going price for anyone else. She was a *"paid high"* target! He smiled to himself as he considered his luck, to be paid such a high amount for such easy pickings.

The orange glow of Homwol's secondary Sun, Cythol, was giving way to the bright rising primary Sun, Cathol, whose mottled yellow light filtered through the leaves from the east. The time of the kill was fast approaching.

Yvainyurei considered, would the target come to him? Or would he have to go to the target?

Yvainyurei most certainly did not want to risk going into the target's abode, which was largely covered in soil and meadow. And that hangar? What was it for? It all looked so out of place!

Yvainyurei watched as a Human hovercar landed and what looked like three younglings climbed into it, a she-Carlin kit, a she-Thol, one of the strange new ones and a weird she-Human with golden-hued skin. Then the Human hovercar lifted off from the ground and sped away into the distance to the south. Yvainyurei watched it disappear and then he refocused on the task at hand, ending his target.

Then Yvainyurei heard laughter. From out of the abode came two she-children, Human she-children. They were cheerfully playing on the bluegrass meadow, some sort of Human game perhaps. At least one of them looks exactly like his target. They were coming closer, they were soon between him and their abode.

Yvainyurei's wings unfurled with a snap and he leapt from the tree into flight towards the two young girls. Yvainyurei covered the distance quickly, gliding to a landing on the bluegrass meadow in front of the two girls, his doubled sickle-shaped talon knife in his left hand, his bone sword in his right hand! Yvainyurei faced his target, this kill would be so quick!

Yvainyurei stood in bewilderment, both girls looked identical? He actually raised his left hand to his head and scratched his scalp below his long white-blond locks.

Two targets? Is that why it was *"paid high"*?

Were these Humans like the Carlin folk, pushing out children, sometimes with the same faces?

Was there some sort of magical cloning going on here?

Was this a trap?

One of the she-children shouted something at him, though he understood it not. Then before Yvainyurei could act, the two she-children moved.

Aria and Ariel saw the Thol landing before them, he was tall, five foot nine, way too tall for a Mimasian Thol, so obviously he was Indigenous. They both saw the Tarlak skull tattoo on his chest, which was not a good sign and the weapons he carried in his hands weren't either. Aria nodded to her twin Sister, Ariel, who took the lead.

Ariel shouted at Yvainyurei, "Stand down!", the Thol did not move, "Stand down now!", she demanded again.

When Yvainyurei failed to heed her warnings, Ariel made her move without the slightest hesitation.

Astonished, Yvainyurei watched as the Human she-child moved with impossible speed, were all Humans this fast? She was NOT running away in fear!

Ariel was the fastest of the Swanson twins, she closed the gap quickly, stepping inside of Yvainyurei's defences for close-quarters combat. Yvainyurei barely had time to move, when he was pummelled in the chest with five solid rapid-fire punches. Yvainyurei felt at least two ribs crack! Then a sudden, solid uppercut caught him squarely under the chin. He literally felt it break! Yvainyurei was involuntarily pushed backwards by the onslaught.

Ariel stopped her pursuit and let her sister, Aria take over. Aria spun around at high speed and her right foot caught Yvainyurei squarely on the right cheek! Yvainyurei flew to the ground in a crumpled mess, stunned and in shock.

What the fuck had just happened? Do all Humans hit that hard? Where's my fucking bone sword?

Yvainyurei's mind was full of questions, none of which he could answer and of course, he was now awash with pain! There was absolutely no way he could fly out of here, not with cracked ribs!

Yvainyurei was no longer holding his bone sword, although he still held his sickle-shaped talon knives in his left hand.

This was NOT over, Yvainyurei's anger boiled within him. I am a master assassin! How dare they! These Human she-children bitches are going down!

Yvainyurei forced himself through his pain and began to stand up. He could see his bone sword lying on the ground, not too far away, but given the speed of his targets, still too far. Yvainyurei separated his doubled sickle-shaped talon knives and held one in each hand. Yvainyurei felt a wave of pain from his broken jaw and shattered right cheek as he shook his head to clear it.

Yvainyurei looked to his right, the target who had kicked him in the face, now squared off with a rock-solid side-on fighting stance. Her legs were held slightly apart and her knees were slightly bent. The she-child's hands were held out in front of her and moving in small circular motions, with her fists not yet closed.

Yvainyurei turned to look at the other she-child, the one who had cracked his ribs and broken his jaw. Her stance was completely different. This she-child faced him square on, perfectly balanced on her left leg, which was ever so slightly bent at the knee. Her right leg was drawn in, cocked like a coiled spring. Her arms were held apart at either side of her chest and they were raised, with her hands held out as if holding the very air to stay balanced. What the fuck was this? These are fucking children!

Yvainyurei had a decision to make, the rock-sold stance on his right or the weird air-hanging stance on his left. He didn't know it of course, but neither stance was good for him. Yvainyurei forced himself through his pain and lunged towards Ariel, with his sickle-shaped talon knives carving the air in broad arcs. He would overwhelm with power and main force!

Ariel let Yvainyurei close the gaps, his knives carving dangerously and then at precisely the right moment and without any hesitation, she struck! Both of her arms and hands drew into her chest as her left leg quickly pressed upwards. Her right leg unfurled like a whip, the flat of her right shoe striking Yvainyurei squarely in the face. Yvainyurei's nose shattered with the sheer force of the impact, he heard and felt the resounding crack of cartilage and bone.

Yvainyurei reeled backwards, but it was not over yet. Ariel's twin Sister, Aria, spun around once more and struck Yvainyurei squarely on the back of the head with another resounding crack of bone. Now Yvainyurei was reeling forward from the force of that blow and landed flat on his face amongst the bluegrass of the meadow. What the fuck was that? Was he that outclassed?

It took Yvainyurei several long moments to recover. One hand was under his face and covered with his own blood. Yvainyurei winced in pain, noting his broken nose, cheek and jaw. The blow that had broken his right cheek had caused swelling and that was now engulfing his entire right eye. Yvainyurei was now blind in his right eye. Somehow, he still held both sickle-shaped talon knives and as he turned his head, he spied his bone sword just in front of him and within easy reach.

Both of the Human she-children had now begun circling him as if they were closing in for the kill, yet they didn't. Their fluid martial arts fighting stances were in readiness, but they were not pressing the attack. They had honour, something that Yvainyurei did not have, they would not strike him while he was down! Slowly, Yvainyurei pushed through his pain and rose to his knees. He looked around and the she-children continued to circle him warily. They were still not attacking.

Yvainyurei locked his sickle-shaped talon knives back together and held them firmly in his left hand, he then reached out and picked up his bone sword. If he was going to die, he would die fighting. Slowly, pushing through the pain, he rose to his feet. The Human she-children still did not attack him, they circled him but maintained their distance. These bitches were going to make it hard for him!

Yvainyurei caught sight of someone else approaching. It was an adult male Human and he was tall, strong and rapidly approaching from the hangar. In his right hand, he held something that Yvainyurei did not recognise. The man's left hand also held it at the side. What the fuck is this?

As the man approached he shouted out something that Yvainyurei did not understand.

Sylvester Bronson approached the incident scene, he shouted at Yvainyurei, "Stand down!", while pointing his pulse laser pistol at Yvainyurei's chest, his centre mass.

Yvainyurei noticed a small red light coming out of the device, he followed it and found a small red dot in the middle of his own chest. What kind of magic is this?

Sylvester Bronson shouted at Yvainyurei again, "Stand down now!", while still pointing his pulse laser pistol squarely at Yvainyurei's chest, however, Yvainyurei had no English language skills and Sylvester did not speak Indigenous Tholish either.

Sylvester Bronson shouted at Yvainyurei one final time, "This is your final warning! Stand down now!", he saw no movement of compliance at all.

Yvainyurei stood there still brandishing his traditional weapons, "Fuck!", Sylvester Bronson exclaimed, then he squeezed the trigger of his pulse laser pistol.

Veeeee-wack! The pulse laser pistol shot out an intense super heated blue beam of coherent light. It was so quick and Yvainyurei flinched when it struck. He felt a distinct pain in his chest, but also out of his back. The pulse laser's beam had cored right through him. Yvainyurei looked down at his chest. The red dot was now gone and in its place was a small, centimetre-wide hole bored into his chest! It did not bleed, as if it had been cauterised by the Human's weapon. What the fuck!

Yvainyurei's knees buckled and he started to crumple to the ground, then fell to his right, landing on the bluegrass, his lifeless purple eyes staring back at Sylvester Bronson. Sylvester approached Yvainyurei and prodded his body with his boot. No movement, the assailant was down.

Sylvester then scanned the plot, his head on a swivel, "Girls. Get back to the house. Full lockdown! Get into the panic room and lock yourselves in!", he ordered, adding, "This may not be over!"

The girls broke their stance and bolted for the homestead as instructed.

Sylvester spoke into his micro-communicator pinned to his collar, "Police dispatch. Do you have your ears on?"

"The line is still open, Sir", the Police Dispatch Officer replied.

"Sylvester Bronson, Security Officer at the Swanson plot back again", he replied, adding, "The assailant is down! I repeat the assistant is down!"

"And the assailant's condition?", the Police Dispatch Officer enquired.

"The assailant is deceased. A morgue unit will be required", Sylvester informed the Police Dispatch Officer.

"Mr Bronson, a police cruiser is on its way at high speed. It should arrive in less than ten minutes", the Police Dispatch Officer informed him, then added, "A morgue unit is being dispatched now."

"Police dispatch, the entire incident has been captured by stealth surveillance drone", Sylvester informed them, "I'll give you full access to the video shortly."

"That will be appreciated", the Police Dispatch Officer replied.

Sylvester replied, "I'll stay on station until the police cruiser arrives. Over and out", then he signed off and patiently awaited the arrival of the police.

While waiting, Sylvester checked in with the twin's Mother, "Mrs Swanson. The assailant is down and the twins are safe. A police cruiser and a morgue unit are on their way."

"Thank you, Sylvester", Mrs Swanson replied, adding, "I'm just jumping into my ship now and should be there shortly. Over and out."

The police cruiser arrived first and landed about thirty feet from the scene of the attempted assassination. Two Police Officers stepped out, one male the other female, both Human. As yet, no Carlins, Thols (Mimasian or Indigenous) had joined the colony's police force, they had no interest in it. The two Police Officers walked straight over to the crime scene and Sylvester

Bronson holstered his pulse laser pistol.

"Geez, he's a right bloody mess", the female Police Officer noted, while taking pictures of the scene.

"That is what happens when an assassin attempts to assassinate a pair of twins, ones that have been trained in mixed martial arts since the age of two", Sylvester matter-of-factly replied.

"They took down the assailant?", the male Police Officer enquired.

"No, you'll find the kill shot was mine", Sylvester informed them and tapped his holster.

"That thing licensed", the male Police Officer asked.

"Yes, as am I", Sylvester replied, noting, "Military Security", as he flipped out his credentials.

The male Police Officer nodded and asked, "Couldn't you have shot to disable him?"

"You have been trained right? I mean, what's the first rule when facing off with an armed assailant?", Sylvester asked.

The male Police Officer was slow to answer and his female partner quickly stated, "Aim at the assailant's centre mass. Don't try to be fancy, it will get you killed."

The female Police Officer looked closely at Yvainyurei's weapons. The Policewoman was about to pick them up when a message came through on Sylvester's neural implants.

"I wouldn't touch those if I was you, Miss", Sylvester advised, explaining, "Our surveillance drone is detecting neurotoxins. Those knives and the sword are coated in them."

The Policewoman stepped back, "That is good to know, however, we will be needing those weapons as evidence."

"Incorrect. Those two knives and the sword are now the property of the Military", Sylvester told them firmly, "We will need to investigate that neurotoxin. It's not in our database. It's something new and we need to understand it."

"That is highly irregular", the Policeman commented.

"Perhaps, but not my call. I'm in contact with my bosses. The higher-ups in Military command as we speak by neural augment", Sylvester explained.

The Policeman replied, "We will need to interview the assassin's targets."

Sylvester replied protectively, "Sorry, but that is not going to happen either. Both girls are traumatised by this event. So you can forget that."

The Policeman looked at her partner, who then replied, "Well, we can't very well leave here without any evidence", she was quite adamant.

Sylvester opened up his A.I. *'grip',* which was strapped to his left arm and activated its holographic keyboard. A few keystrokes later and the surveillance drone was hovering close by, fully uncloaked and in full view, only five feet from the ground.

"There's your evidence right there. The full incident was captured on video and uploaded to our networked servers", Sylvester informed them, "I'm sending a complete copy to your people as we speak. You'll have access to it before you leave here."

Both Police Officers nodded, at least they'd be getting some evidence.

They all looked up as a warship began circling the plot, it was a broad-head arrow class interplanetary starfighter and it was fully armed. It flew around the plot three times before hovering to a soft landing on the nearby tarmac. The twin's Mother climbed down the ladder and began running over to the crime scene. Angelique Swanson was not very happy, someone had targeted her Daughters.

"And who is that?", the Policewoman enquired.

"That. That is my boss", Sylvester informed her, "She is the twin's Mother."

The Policeman recognised her, "That's Mrs Swanson. She organises the martial arts and hand-to-hand combat training for the Police recruits."

"That's Special Operative Mrs Swanson", Sylvester corrected.

Angelique was quickly on the scene and straight away flipped out her credentials, "This entire crime scene is effectively under Military jurisdiction."

The Police Officers looked at each other in confusion.

"Don't look so upset", Angelique told them, commenting, "You've got the assassin's body, your photographs and a complete copy of our surveillance. That's pretty much all you guys need."

Another of Mrs Swanson's workers came running over, it was Mike Johnson, her flight mechanic and engineer. He was carrying an ten-foot star picket, a two-pound mall hammer and a small step ladder with four steps.

"Are you sure you want to do this, Mrs Swanson", Mike asked.

"Absolutely, Mike. I made a promise to the Tholish High Chancellor and I intend to keep it. I need to show him what it means to cross us", Angelique Swanson replied, then she enquired, "Sylvester, which way did he come from?"

"Surveillance shows he came from the north, Mrs Swanson", Sylvester replied.

"Mike, set up that picket ten feet inside the inner northern perimeter fence. Make sure it's fixed solidly into the ground. Right in the centre point of the northern fence line", Angelique instructed.

"Yes, Ma'am", Mike replied and then he jogged off towards the northern perimeter fence.

A few minutes later, banging could be heard as the star pick was driven into the ground.

Angelique reached around her back and pulled out a short kukri sword, "Sylvester, hold up the assassin's head", she instructed.

Sylvester held up Yvainyurei's head by his white-blond hair and as the two Police Officers looked on in abject horror, Angelique swung her kukri sword across Yvainyurei's neck and in that one move the deceased assassin was beheaded.

The female Police Officer shouted out, "Mrs Swanson. The desecration of a corpse is a crime."

Angelique ignored her, she passed her kukri sword to Sylvester and he passed Yvainyurei's severed head to Angelique, who then stalked off towards the northern perimeter fence.

The Policewoman started to protest, but Sylvester just held up his hand to silence her.

Angelique reached the picket that Mike had installed, she climbed up the step ladder and then with grim determination, firmly planted Yvainyurei's head on top of the picket facing north.

Angelique walked in front of the picket and using her neural augments, captured an image of Yvainyurei's head mounted on the spike. This was a warning to all other would-be assassins. Angelique then walked back to the crime scene as Mike carried his equipment back to the hangar and his workshop.

As Angelique walked back to the crime scene, the two Police Officers began reviewing the video surveillance footage that they now had access to. Sylvester had already cleaned Yvainyurei's blood from her kukri sword and was ready to present it back to her when she arrived.

As soon as Angelique returned, the Policewoman began protesting, "The desecration of a corpse is a crime! The improper disposal of a corpse is also a crime! We should be arresting you!"

"Those are crimes under Human law and they cover Humans, both Earth and Martian, as well as Mimasian Thols", Angelique replied, adding, "Those laws do not cover this world's native species, Carlins or Indigenous Thols. You might want to check that", she tapped her temple, "I did!", her neural augments had been working overtime.

The Policewoman continued protesting, "We have just reviewed that footage. Your Daughters were brutal, methodical and efficient!"

Angelique had had enough and she snapped back at the Policewoman, she pointed to Yvainyurei's headless corpse, "That bastard came here with poisoned blades to murder my Daughters. To right my girls were brutal, methodical and efficient! When some prick comes after you, perhaps you'll want to be brutal, methodical and efficient as well!"

The Policewoman fell silent, she had no answer for that.

"Sylvester, stay with these two until everything is cleaned up. I don't want my girls to find a single drop of blood if they come by this way tomorrow. Remember to take charge of those weapons. I want them analysed, we need to know where this prick came from", Angelique instructed, then she added, "From now on I want two of our Vorts patrolling the inner grounds. Keep just two on border patrol."

"Yes, Mrs Swanson. I might recommend picking up two more Vorts. I'm thinking up-scaling is a good idea at this time", Sylvester replied.

"Yes, great idea. I'll pick out a couple of Vorts for imprinting tomorrow", Angelique agreed and then she began to walk towards her home but stopped and turned around.

"What's your name, Officer?", Angelique asked the Policewoman.

The Policewoman was surprised and answered, "Officer Harrington. Officer Anne Harrington."

"Sylvester, I like this one. Speak to her superiors and have her seconded over to our team", Angelique instructed.

"Seconded to your team?", Officer Harrington enquired.

"Yes, Officer Harrington, for all of your lip, you have potential. I've been using my neural augments to review your profile", Angelique informed her, commenting, "Your first duties here are going to include mixed martial arts, hand-to-hand combat and pilot training."

"Martial arts, hand-to-hand combat and pilot training?", Officer Harrington repeated questioningly, then she asked, "Are you going to be my instructor?"

"Hell, no woman. I'm far too busy for that. My girls and Mr Bronson will instruct you", Angelique replied.

"Sylvester, make sure Officer Harrington's training fits in with my girl's schedules. If she's as good as I think she is, she'll also need a ship, maybe even neural implants", Angelique further instructed before turning and heading back to her house, "I have a few calls to make", she replied in parting, as she walked off.

"Neural implants?", Officer Harrington queried.

Sylvester looked at Officer Harrington, "Military grade neural augmentation. The full suit. Mrs Swanson likes you, so you are in for a career boost."

The other Police Officer had taken offence, "What am I, chopped liver?"

Sylvester smiled, "Don't feel too bad lad. The boss lady is picky is all."

As Mrs Swanson walked back to her homestead, she adjusted her micro-communicator and sent out a simple message, "Sheppard to Sheep Dogs! Sheppard to Sheep Dogs! Bring home the Flock! Repeat. Bring home the Flock!", then she adjusted her micro-communicator once more.

"Yookey! Yarling! Yorvick! Have your bug-out bags ready. Your ride is on the way and should be there in fifteen minutes", Angelique informed her flock, "Please acknowledge."

Yookey, Yarling and Yorvick all acknowledged that they'd received the message.

After which they quickly got ready, each of them taking out their two bug-out bags. This was something that Aria and Ariel had explained to them after the previous inter-species incident. How to prepare bug-out bags in readiness for possible emergency extraction. Aria and Ariel had provided their Mother with precise GPS coordinates and a complete scan of the area in which Yookey's family lived. Yookey and his Parents waited patiently for their extraction.

Angelique looked toward the large hangar and in particular its roof, she adjusted her micro-communicator once more, “Mike, you got your ears on?”

“Yes, Mrs Swanson”, Mike replied.

“Mike, we need a *'Sweep'* mounted on the hangar roof. If more assassins try flying in here, I want to see them coming”, Angelique noted.

“I'll order one in right away, Mrs Swanson”, Mike replied, commenting, “The *'Sweep'* I'm thinking of will pick up anything larger than a crow approaching at two clicks.”

“That's just the ticket, Mike. Mount it on top of the hangar roof as soon as it arrives. We need eyes on the skies and we need them yesterday”, Angelique replied.

“Is there anything else I can arrange while I'm at it, Mrs Swanson?”, Mike queried.

“Yes, Mike, we have guests arriving soon. That tree house I mentioned earlier, we'll be needing it”, Angelique replied as she scanned around her lot, she then added, “Have it built in our tall, Bell Nut Fruit tree to the south of our homestead. Our guests will be inside of the perimeter fence, nice and secure. They'll feel right at home.”

“I'll arrange it straight away, Mrs Swanson. I even have a nice Mimasian-style tree house design ready. It will have all of the mod cons as well”, Mike informed her.

“Excellent, and Mike, I want this to happen fast, so use an Android work crew”, Angelique instructed, she then enquired, “What's the estimated build time?”

“A Humaniform Android crew, an Alpha and five Betas can have it completed in three days”, he replied with certainty.

“Make it so, Mike”, Angelique confirmed and then signed off.

Next Angelique adjusted her micro-communicator to contact her Daughters inside their panic room, “Girls! It's safe to come out. We have guests arriving. Yookey and his family, and girls, I want you both carrying side arms”, she informed them.

Both twins replied in unison, “Yes, Mum”, then they thought to themselves, “*Side arms?*”

The morgue unit had already arrived and taken away the body. Sylvester and the two Police Officers approached Angelique. Sylvester was carrying the two sickle-shaped talon knives and the bone sword in his now, carefully gloved hands. He was also carrying what looked like a nine-inch long dagger-toothed pendant on a leather string. Sylvester passed the pendant to Angelique who studied it thoughtfully.

“This came from a rather large beast”, Angelique commented, then enquired, “Do we know of any such creatures on Secundus?”

"None that I'm aware of, Mrs Swanson", Sylvester replied.

Officer Anne Harrington, offered, "We have only been on this world for a quarter of a century, it could be from something we haven't come across yet or perhaps it's an extinct species."

Angelique smiled wryly, "Already making yourself useful I see, Officer Harrington. You will make a great addition to my staff."

Aria and Ariel appeared from out of the homestead.

Straight away the Policeman noticed their side arms, "Are they licensed to carry those?"

Sylvester almost laughed, "Yes and they also have a higher clearance than you do. Trust me, the twin's proficiency is of the highest standard."

Ariel commented, as she and her Sister, Aria, flipped out their credentials, "Although, we don't usually carry side-arms. Today is just, well, you know, you saw the assassin."

And of course, both Police Officers had, nonetheless, they also wondered, how the two teenage girls had security credentials.

Officer Harrington's communicator buzzed and upon checking her messages, she found out that her secondment to Mrs Swanson's team had been approved by her superiors and had been activated immediately. Officer Harrington was now firmly under Mrs Swanson's command.

The update came through Mrs Swanson's augments even before reaching the officer's communicator, "Yes, Ms Harrington. You are now officially an Operative in training. We have rooms and accommodation available at the back of the hangar. You may grab your things from the colony and move in tomorrow morning", it was a done deal.

These were whirlwind changes, *"Operative in training"*, the thought ran through her mind.

A ship approached from the northeast, it was a military drop ship, the kind of ship used for deploying troops or used for extractions. It approached the lot's tarmac and hovered to a soft landing right beside the starfighter, after which Yookey, his Mother, Yarling and his Father, Yorvick alighted along with their bug-out bags.

As they all walked over to Angelique, the drop ship lifted off and Aria bolted towards Yookey.

Aria wrapped her arms around, Yookey, "You're safe", then she planted a strong kiss on his lips.

Yookey dropped his bug-out bags, he then wrapped both of his arms and his wings around Aria and returned the kiss just as fiercely.

"Isn't this what started this mess in the first place?", Yarling quietly trilled to Yorvick, "They broke a sacred taboo! A sacred law! It was the cause of all of this!"

Yorvick was more pragmatic, "What you or I think no longer matters, Yarling. The heart wants what the heart wants", he trilled back.

The Police Officers began walking back to their Police cruiser to return to Police headquarters.

Angelique reminded Officer Harrington, "Remember, be back here tomorrow before noon."

Officer Harrington turned around momentarily and nodded in agreement, she was now an Operative in training and this new opportunity both frightened and intrigued her.

Angelique smiled at Yookey and his Parents, "Aria and Ariel will show you to your rooms. We will have your new tree house ready for you all in three, maybe four days", she informed them.

Yorvick asked with a few trills and clicking words in English, "We thought we were safe. The twins are Mardhin. The High Chancellor agreed. What has gone wrong?", he queried.

Angelique frowned, "I'll let Aria and Ariel explain the details to you. However, suffice to say, my hand was forced and I found it necessary to place you all under my protection here, where I can see the enemy coming."

"Enemy?", Yarling trilled questioningly.

"Come", Aria requested, "My Sister and I will explain everything once you're settled in."

Yookey and his Parents noticed that the twins were wearing side arms and quickly realised that the situation was far more serious than they understood. They said nothing and followed the girls.

Angelique informed them as they left, "Guys. I will be speaking with the High Chancellor on this matter, to clear a few things up. He needs to answer quite a few questions."

Mike Johnson informed Angelique, "Ma'am. After the tree house accommodation is completed, High Command has decided to *'gift'* the Humaniform Androids to us, to *'serve and protect'*. They believe they will be of assistance."

"Serve and protect, they're metal men, Mike. They adhere to the three laws of robotics", Angelique almost laughed at the suggestion, despite their current situation.

"Ma'am, those laws of robotics have never been updated to extend beyond humanity. The laws of robotics only cover Humans, Earth or Martian. They don't even cover Mimasian Thols, let alone Indigenous ones", Mike explained, noting, "If an Indigenous Thol assassin gets cornered by them, they'll tear him apart."

"Seriously, Mike! That's news to me", Angelique replied in surprise, "I thought those three laws of robotics covered all sapient life."

"Ma'am, check with your neural augments", Mike tapped his temple, then he explained, "Mimasians Thols have always been few in number outside of Mimas, so no one has bothered to update the three laws. Think about it, Mrs Swanson. Every single Android would need to have been recalled and of course, we've only been on Secundus for two and a half decades. So the native inhabitants of this world aren't even on anybody's radar."

Angelique did check her neural augments and found that Mike was one hundred percent correct. The three laws of robotics were purely Human-centric.

"Mike, after the metal men have finished the tree house, introduce them to our guests. Have them sniff our guest's dna and instruct them to treat our guests as Humans. Make sure that the metal men fully comprehend that. If they don't, I'll shut them down myself."

Angelique walked off towards her home, thinking, *"God damned difference engines!"*, concerning Androids, if it came to a choice between saving a Human as opposed to a Thol or a Carlin, the metal men would choose the Human every damned time, no matter the circumstances.

Angelique entered her home and went straight to her office. Once inside she shut the door and locked it, this was to be a private conversation and quite likely an unpleasant one at that. Angelique printed out two photos from the images obtained by her neural augments. One was a photograph of the deceased assassin's body and the other was the assassin's head mounted on the spike. Angelique placed them on the desk and then sat down on the edge of her desk beside the photos. Using her neural augments, she called the Tholish High Council's, High Chancellor.

The Tholish High Chancellor appeared on the large wall screen. He did not look very happy to see Mrs Swanson at all, probably due to his last encounter.

"Yes, Mrs Swanson, what can I do for you today?", he enquired with trills and clicks.

Angelique frowned, "We had an encounter with an assassin this morning, High Chancellor."

"An Assassin!", the High Chancellor exclaimed, he sounded genuinely surprised and Angelique's neural augments indicated his surprise was, in fact real.

"Is everyone alright?", the High Chancellor asked, his concern also appeared to be genuine.

"Yes, High Chancellor. All except for the assassin", Angelique held up the photograph of the assassin's head mounted on a spike, "As I did promise you", Angelique explained.

The High Chancellor was genuinely aghast. The assassin's face was severely bruised, most especially around his right eye socket and it looked as though he'd been beaten to a pulp. Now all Thols, have alabaster white skin, like pristine white marble, except for their creamy-coloured wings.

Angelique watched as all of the colour drained from the High Chancellor's wings, they were now as white as his face ought to have been, except his face was now ashen grey in colouration.

"What is the meaning of this?", the High Chancellor demanded with trills, clicks and barks.

"Your assassin attacked my Daughters with poisoned knives and a poisoned sword. Apparently, he did not know that my Daughters were able to defend themselves. His persistence led to this result. It is called self-defence, remember that High Chancellor", Angelique explained.

The High Chancellor caught two words out of Angelique's explanation that stood out the most, *"Your Assassin"*, he quickly responded, "He was NOT my assassin! I did NOT send him!", Angelique's neural augments indicated that he was not lying.

Angelique frowned, "Then who did, High Chancellor? Who sent the assassin?", she questioned.

Angelique held up the other photograph of the assassin's battered and bruised corpse, "Who sent this assassin after my Daughters? I need to know, High Chancellor!"

The High Chancellor stared in both shock and disbelief at the photograph, he still had not recovered from the shock of seeing the assassin's head mounted on the spike, "That, that, that tattoo!", he mumbled, "By all the Gods, that man, that assassin, he's a Darkling!"

"A Darkling! You will need to explain that one!", Angelique responded, requesting information.

The High Chancellor approached his screen's embedded camera, he looked around as if checking that he truly was alone and began his explanation in a loud whisper, "All societies have their dirty little secrets, Mrs Swanson. The Darklings are ours. A dirty little secret that we barely even acknowledge to ourselves. They are a clan of Thols that does not recognise the High Council's authority. They follow their own ways, their own rules and murder is just a part of their lives."

Angelique was actually shocked by this revelation, *"Thols must never kill Thols"*, the thought crossed her mind as she did her best not to appear shocked, these Darklings did NOT adhere to the laws or the rules, only their own whims.

"Now we are getting somewhere, High Chancellor", she replied smiling, "Now, tell me all about these Darklings and leave nothing out. I will know if you do."

The High Chancellor stepped even closer to the screen, he whispered loudly, "If a Darkling came for your Daughters, then there must have been a contract. The assassin is dead and that contract is now unfulfilled. Another assassin will pick it up and come for your Daughters. If he is also killed, another will take his place and then another and another and so on, until the contract is fulfilled."

Angelique smirked and replied, "High Chancellor. What you are telling me is, that I'm going to have a whole lot of assassin's heads mounted on spikes around my plot of land!"

The High Chancellor nodded in agreement, "Yes, that is the most likely outcome, Mrs Swanson. They will keep coming until the contract is fulfilled or until they are all dead!"

"Why? Why do they do this?", Angelique enquired.

"That tattoo is of a Tarlak skull. The Darklings, they worship the Tarlaks like Gods", the High Chancellor explained as he checked over his shoulders again to make sure he was alone.

Angelique nodded, understanding there was no rationality behind them, just dogma and profit, that was their motivation, "This assassin appeared this morning, straight after yesterday's inter-species relationship incident. That implies quick communications, High Chancellor."

The High Chancellor replied again in his hushed tones, "There are some in our Tholish society, even amongst the council itself, who know how to contact the Darklings and hire them for their nefarious purposes. Not every Thol obeys the laws and when they break them, they always do so side-ways, obliquely!"

"Okay. So you have a problem you cannot solve", Angelique replied, then suggested, "We can solve this problem for you."

"How? How can you solve this problem for us, Mrs Swanson?", the High

Chancellor questioned.

"Simple really, High Chancellor. You tell us where to find the Darkling's nest and my people will go in and eliminate them", Angelique's face took on a serious visage, like the anticipation on the face of a serpent about to strike!

"We, we, we, don't really know. These Darklings are the boogeyman that no one speaks about", the High Chancellor replied using a Human metaphor.

"You must have some idea, some notion of where they come from?", Angelique pressed.

"I'll tell you what I do know", the High Chancellor looked around himself once more and then whispered, "Here in the Northern Mountain Range, if you travel beyond the furthest Western Villages of Tholish society, you will find a place beyond which no sane Thol will ever travel. Towards the Western Mountains, the place where the banished Thols are sent. That is the region where the Darklings live. It is a vast region."

"The place where you were going to send Yookey's family, you mean?", Angelique questioned.

"Yes", the High Chancellor admitted, "But we reached an agreement on that, didn't we?"

"Yes, we did, High Chancellor, but you neglected to mention these Darklings", she replied.

"I admit that. I should have considered the Darklings", he replied, he was truly remorseful, remarking, "We barely acknowledge their existence ourselves."

Angelique considered his, *"my bad"* excuse entirely inadequate, "High Chancellor, I don't give a flying fuck about your fears or your foibles! I need to know where these damned bastards live!"

"You do not understand, Mrs Swanson! The mere mention of the Darkling clan can end up in death!", the High Chancellor exclaimed, firing back, "The banished Thols that go beyond the farthest villages, some fall prey to the denizens of the western forests, some are killed and eaten by the Darklings. They are cannibals, Mrs Swanson, just like the Tarlaks they worship!"

That caught Angelique by surprise, not only were the Darklings dogmatic, transactional killers, but they were also cannibals!

Angelique enquired, "High Chancellor, would I be correct in assuming, that if a Thol travels far beyond the westernmost Thol villages, that they will eventually run afoul of the Darklings?"

The answer from the High Chancellor was a resounding, "Yes!"

"Exactly how far?", Angelique questioned.

"That, I do not know. Seriously, we just don't know", the High Chancellor admitted, noting, "Which is why we cannot solve this problem. The Darklings live far beyond our borders. I can tell you this much, look for their nests in the canopies of the tallest Jula Jula trees."

"Thank you, High Chancellor. You've given me a starting point", Angelique thanked him, assuring him, "We will work this problem to its ultimate resolution."

Before signing off, Angelique held up the nine-inch long dagger-toothed pendant, that the assassin had been wearing around his neck, "High Chancellor, do you know what this is?", she curiously asked, noting, "The assassin was wearing it around his neck."

Without any hesitation, he replied, "It's a Cress tooth."

"What's a Cress?", Angelique enquired.

"Think of a Sleimorp, only five times their height", the High Chancellor replied, then he walked across his office and took a painting from off of the wall, when he returned, he held it up, "This, Mrs Swanson, is a Cress."

Angelique studied the creature, her implants recording the painting in great detail, so it was taller than twenty feet in height and had three long spikes on the end of its tail, "That, High Chancellor, looks like an extinct species we once had on the Earth, only with a spiked tail. It was called an Allosaurus and it died out well over a hundred and forty million years ago."

"Well, Mrs Swanson, our beast is called a Cress. They live in the far western forests. The same place as the Sleimorps, the Chittens and the Darklings", the High Chancellor explained, adding, "They are solitary ambush predators and they are said to be able to sense, *'life force'*. It makes them extremely deadly predators."

"Thank you, High Chancellor. I'll give you a heads up when we have the Darkling issue resolved", Angelique replied and then the connection dropped out.

Angelique adjusted her micro-communicator and contacted her head of Security, "Sylvester, we need to organise some stealth drones. A couple of dozen."

"Two dozen stealth drones?", Sylvester queried, asking, "What are we hunting, Mrs Swanson?"

"Two things, Sylvester. It's better if I transmit you a transcript of my discussions with the Tholish High Chancellor", Angelique explained and her neural augments went to work.

Sylvester's neural augments received the information and streamed it directly into his brain, complete with the image of the cress, "Yikes! So that tooth belongs to one of these, Cress?"

"Apparently, Sylvester", Angelique confirmed, commenting, "We are trying to confirm the existence of another top-tier predator here on Secundus. More importantly, the Darkling clan from whence the assassin came. I want discovery and eyes on the targets, with the priority on the assassin's nesting sites."

"Yes, Mrs Swanson, although, I may have to beg, borrow and steal, to get two dozen stealth drones", Sylvester replied, wondering where he would acquire so many drones.

"Use my authority and the drones will come to you, Sylvester", Angelique replied with assurance, noting, "We'll be searching the Western Jula Jula forests beyond the farthest known Thol villages in full stealth mode. We will find their nesting sites and then we'll deal with them."

"Understood, I'll make it so", Sylvester agreed and confirmed.

Angelique adjusted her micro-communicator once more, and sent a message to her husband in Cis-Luns L5, "Bobby, I'm sending you a shit tonne of information. Some bastard has put a contract out on our Daughters. We've taken down one assassin so far and we are expecting many more. I want to nip this in the bud and wipe out their whole damned nest. These are legitimate targets and maximum prejudice is authorised. Have someone take over for you and return home as soon as you get this message. We should have eyes on our targets within a few days."

Angelique sat down quietly and let her neural implants transfer the voluminous amounts of data to her Husband, Bobby. The Darklings have declared war, now they are going to pay the price.

Angelique then went to the rooms that she had prepared for Yookey and his Parents. Aria and Ariel were with them, which was good, as she could explain the situation to them all together.

"Guys, I have some good news and some bad news", Angelique explained, "You're getting the bad news first. Someone in the Indigenous Thol community, perhaps even a member of the Tholish High Council itself, has placed a contract on Aria and Ariel."

"Is this true?", Yarling trilled.

"Yes, Yarling and it probably gets worse", Angelique replied, explaining, "This same unknown individual has in all likelihood placed a contract on Yookey as well. Perhaps, even on you and Yorvick as well. We were lucky we acted quickly."

Aria quickly answered, “Then extracting Yookey and his Parents was absolutely necessary!”

“Yes, Aria. That does appear to be the case”, Angelique agreed.

Yarling trilled and clicked, questioning, “The assassin is now dead, so we can go home, yes?”

Angelique was brutally honest, “Yarling, one assassin is dead. The contract was unfulfilled. Other assassins will come for my Daughters and your family. They will keep on coming until they are paid for their contractual obligations. They won't stop until the contract is fulfilled. I have been told as much by the High Chancellor himself. The danger is not over yet.”

Yorvick enquired with a few quick trills and clicks, ”Then what is the good news?”

“Yorvick, while we don't know who has contracted the assassins, we do have a fair idea of where the assassin's nests are”, Angelique explained, noting, “Sylvester is sending stealth drones into their territory to locate them and gather intel. Once we have eyes on them, we will wipe them all out in one fell swoop. Without the assassins to worry about, we can track down their contractor!”

“Where do these assassins live?”, Yorvick enquired.

“The High Chancellor says that they live in the far Western Jula Jula forests, far to the west of the farthest Thol villages”, Angelique informed them, “He called their clan, the Darklings!”

“No, no, no! The Darklings are just scary stories we tell our younglings to make them behave themselves”, Yarling replied, then she gave examples, “If you go out late at night, the Darklings will catch you and eat you. If you don't behave, the Darklings will snatch you up and sell you to the Tarlaks. That sort of thing.”

Yookey agreed, confirming, “Mum told me those stories as a youngling.”

“Excellent, Yookey. Describe a Darkling for me”, Angelique requested.

Yookey looked down to his left, straining to remember the stories told to him as a youngling by his Mother, he closed his eyes and focused, “They're like Thols, yet they're not like Thols. They wear Sleimorp hides instead of clothes. They use the sickle-shaped talons and the bone swords of the Sleimorp as their weapons. They eat other Thols, that are not of their own clan. They worship the Tarlaks and paint or tattoo Tarlak skulls on their chests. Is that right, Mother?”, he asked his Mother for confirmation.

“Yes, Yookey. You remember very well. Darklings are mythical monsters, not real people”, she replied with trills, clicks and soft barks.

Aria and Ariel looked at each other and then Ariel spoke, "Yarling, that assassin that was killed this morning, looked exactly like Yookey's description of a Darkling."

Yarling waved her hand in dismissal, trilling, "That cannot be. Darklings are a myth!"

Angelique did not want to do this, but she had no choice, she took the photograph of the dead assassin from out of her jacket pocket and passed it to Yorvick and his eyes widened in shock.

"Yarling!", he clicked in exclamation, then he trilled as he showed her the photograph, "It was a Darkling. Look! See! There is no doubt about it!"

Yarling stared at the photograph in disbelief, "It is true. Our worst nightmares are real", then she quickly passed the photograph back to Angelique, so as not to become cursed by it.

"Everything you know about the Darklings is true. All of it! They are murders, they are assassins and they are even cannibals", Angelique reiterated, then remarked, "We must find them and end them, for the good of all!"

When Robert Swanson landed his starfighter on the tarmac at his plot in the bluegrass meadows, his Daughters, Aria and Ariel, were quick to rush out and greet him. He checked his Daughters to make sure that they were okay and then hugged them tightly. He left his starfighter in the hands of Mike Johnson, who taxied it into the hangar with the use of his A.I. *'grip"*, that was wrapped around his left forearm. Angelique waited patiently for Robert to come to her. He was a tall man, with broad shoulders and a pleasant face. Once he was in front of Angelique, he held his powerful arms out wide. Angelique stepped into his arms and they wrapped around her.

"Bobby, it's been so horrible!", Angelique exclaimed and then they kissed and hugged for several long moments before Angelique remarked, "Bobby, we have to find these bastards!"

"Then let's get to work, shall we", Robert replied.

"I watched that surveillance video by the way", Robert informed Angelique as they walked towards the homestead, noting, "Aria's stance was strong and solid, a warning to the assassin to stay away. Ariel's stance, though", he looked at Angelique with concern, "Her stance was wide open, she was actually inviting him in."

"What are you saying, Bobby?", Angelique asked.

"I'm saying, Ariel's stance, drew the assassin in and away from Aria. A deliberate move to protect her younger Sister", Robert explained.

Angelique smiled and almost laughed, "Younger by two minutes", she replied.

"True. Still, Ariel is very protective of Aria", Robert replied, noting, "It was a huge gamble. One nick from either of those blades and the neurotoxins would have killed her in mere seconds!"

"So, we could have lost our Ariel", Angelique understood, adding, "I'll talk to her about it tomorrow. Ariel didn't know about the neurotoxins on those blades at the time, so she didn't know about their danger. I'll ask her not to take so much risk next time."

Robert smiled and replied, "Angelique, we both know Ariel. She would have done the exact same thing, even if she had known the risks. So, let's just make sure that the is no next time."

Robert entered Angelique's office and sat down at her desk to begin reviewing the data they had on the Darklings. His neural implants were of the same military grade as his Wife's and he was quick and thorough, his augments sharing his conclusions with Angelique.

The resin used to treat and harden the assassin's bone weapons was a clue, however, analysis had shown that the resin was from a native vine that grew on the Jula Jula trees. It was a vine that grew everywhere in the northern, the western and even the southern Jula Jula forests. A useless clue!

The neurotoxin was another matter, another clue, it was something new and unseen before. Except, of course, the Mimasian Thols had knowledge in this regard, although, they had never seen the toxin used as a weapon before. They had found that both perplexing and frightening, as the toxin was so easily found.

The toxin came from the seeds of the Jula Jula trees themselves. When the huge seeds dropped to the ground, their outer casing fractured and to protect the seed inside, it exuded a deadly neurotoxin. No animal of any kind could eat the seeds as a result. The Jula Jula seeds were everywhere in the mountain forests and anyone with skill could safely collect the neurotoxin. The neurotoxin was also necessary for the life cycle of the Jula Jula trees for another reason. Another useless clue!

The soil in the mountain forests was a thick mix of rotted humus up to six feet deep, below which was a bedrock of granite. The seeds would gradually sink into the humus and on contact with the granite, the neurotoxin would begin to dissolve it. Then the seed would sink deeply into the granite and sprout, its roots *"melting"* into the rock every which way, while the new sapling reached up for the light of the twin Suns of Homwol.

The deeper the granite, the taller the Jula Jula trees and the granite ran deeper, the closer one got to the Western Mountains. This was why the Jula Jula trees only grew in the mountainous regions, their seeds could not germinate in the Masula Valley with its sandy soils and layers of clay. The cut-off between the mountain Jula Jula forests and the lowland forests was a stark line that was clearly visible from the air, clearly visible even from space.

The third clue of course was the nine-inch long Cress tooth. Sylvester's surveillance drones had already proven the existence of the Cress. They were real, they were deadly and they had something extraordinary. The Indigenous Thols believed that the Cress hunted by sensing their prey's *"life force"*.

However, a quick study of their anatomy provided by Sylvester's stealth drones, showed their muzzled snouts contained large olfactory glands, with their nostrils covered by large prehensile directional flaps. Speculation was, that the Cress could *"sniff"* out their prey from up to twenty kilometres away, perhaps even further. Being the Cress was a stalking and ambush predator and also highly mobile, this was unfortunately not a helpful clue to find the Darklings.

"You know, Angelique, our most promising leads and unfortunately the worst, are those damned contracts", Robert announced, explaining, "The inter-species relationship incident happened around lunchtime yesterday. The assassin was on our property with Cathol rise, perhaps even earlier. Whoever issued the contracts, not only had the means to contact the Darklings but were able to do so almost straight away!"

"Yes, Bobby, but we have no idea who the contractor is. We don't even know where to look", Angelique replied, it was a frustrating situation.

"That inter-species relationship incident by the way. Remind me to talk to Aria about that", Robert requested, commenting, "Aria needs to stop stoking fires and poking bears!"

Angelique nodded in agreement, "Aria doesn't seem to consider where her actions will lead. Seriously, Bobby, she broke one of the Thol's most important taboos!"

Robert brought up a holographic map of the Northern Mountain forests and a great many dots appeared on the map, "Those dots represent the known, mapped Thol villages in the Northern Mountains. You see over here in the far west, there's a sharp line of villages, beyond which there is nothing. That is where those Darklings live, somewhere in that vast expanse of forest beyond those Thol villages."

"Bobby, that is a vast area. They could be in the far western reaches of the Northern Mountains or even further west, in the Western Mountains themselves. How are we going to search all of that?", Angelique questioned, noting, "It will take forever, even if we had two hundred drones!"

"I know. I even considered using satellites to scan for clustered heat signatures and biosignatures", Robert replied

"That actually sounds like a good idea. We should give that a go", Angelique smiled.

"Except for the Fern Dragons", Robert replied with an exasperated look.

"Fern Dragons? They are on par with the Harricks in size. We'd hardly mistake a Fern Dragon heat or biosignatures with that of a Thol", Angelique replied in protest.

"Well, Angelique, there are the Fern Dragons you know and the Fern Dragons you don't", Robert replied cryptically.

"I don't get it, Bobby? What does that mean?", Angelique enquired.

"The Fern Dragons come in multiple species. The ones around here are about the size of a Harricks, bright green in colour and you can even catch them and use them as pets. In the Northern Forests, they're larger, duller in colour and vicious", Robert explained, adding, "In the forests further west, they are larger still, grey in colour and as big as a man. Those ones are called Wyverns and they hunt in packs on the wing. They hunt in the forest's understory and they are dangerous."

"I get it, Bobby. We scan the forests using satellites and we won't know the difference between a Darkling village and a Wyvern nest", she sat down and sighed.

"And there are a lot of Wyvern nests. They are everywhere", Robert added.

"Angelique, my love. We are left with one option", Robert informed her.

"I think I know what it is and I do not like it, Bobby darling", Angelique replied, noting, "I do not want to use our Daughters as bait."

"Angelique, darling. I was not suggesting that", Robert replied, then he asked, "Your base defences are breached, your VIP is exposed, but you manage to take the assassin down. What is the usual procedure, Angelique?"

"Move the VIP to a more secure, unknown location", Angelique replied as she began to get it.

"And what did you actually do, Angelique?", Robert asked her.

"I doubled down and beefed up our defences. I did not move our VIPs. I even brought three more into the existing base", Angelique replied smiling, then she added, "That is not what they'll expect."

"You acted as a Mother would, not as an Operative, Angelique", Robert smiled back.

"So, the Darkling will be looking for intel on where we moved their targets!", Angelique replied.

Robert Swanson nodded, "We need to do three things. One, keep our heads on a swivel here in our plot, just in case. Two, station our people undercover at the colony's school which is an obvious place they'll try and three. Yookey's family's nest, we need it under constant surveillance. Not from Yookey's tree though, from the one next door."

Angelique smiled, "I have just the place. My friend Yealah. Her tree house is in the tree next door and according to the twins, there's a clear line of sight to Yookey's nest cluster."

"And of course, mature Jula Jula trees are hollow. Indigenous Thols don't use those hollows, only Mimasian Thols do. So we can secrete our troops inside the tree and lay in wait", Robert explained.

"Bobby", Angelique smiled, "It looks like we have a plan. Let's capture one of those bastards!"

"We won't even need to interrogate our captives. The Martian Ambassador and her Daughter are both telepaths", Robert smiled and almost laughed.

"About that Bobby. Aria and Ariel are both telepaths as well", Angelique informed him and Robert's jaw literally dropped, then she commented, "I'll explain it to you later. For now, I have other things in mind", then she walked over to him and sat on his lap, stating, "You have duties to perform, Bobby."

Robert then gently picked up his Wife and carried her across to a large plush, faux fur rug, that covered a large section of Angelique's office floor.

32. Pluto and the Dwarves.

Yvainyorin and his cousin Yvainyasha had flown in low on their approach to the compound where their primary target lived. They landed in the long bluegrass of the meadows and crawled cautiously towards the perimeter fences. Their cousin Yvainyurei was missing, he had taken a *"most high"* contract and not returned. Now they could see why. Just beyond the inner perimeter fence, mounted on a spike, was the bloodied, bruised and broken head of Yvainyurei.

Yvainyorin and Yvainyasha looked at the photograph of their mark, their *"paid high"* target.

Did this Human she-child do this?

The amount of damage was extreme!

It was perplexing for them, yet Yvainyurei was dead, clearly he was dead!

Yvainyurei was their best assassin!

Where was Yvainyurei's body?

Did they spit roast it and eat it like the Darkling clan does?

Obviously, now there had to be revenge! There had to be a vendetta!

Yvainyorin and Yvainyasha stared into the compound before them. Beyond Yvainyurei's head, was a tall, massive Bell Nut Fruit tree. There were strange hairy Gudong-like creatures that only had two eyes gathered around its base. They could not see anyone in the actual tree, but there could be people concealed within its foliage.

The compound was secured by two perimeter fences and between the two fences, there were two patrolling Vorts. Inside the compound itself, there were two more Vorts! All four of the Vorts were in line with the spike mounted with Yvainyurei's head. The Vorts knew that they were there and were staring into the long bluegrass warily. The Vorts were snarling, growling and scraping the ground with their front paws. Yvainyorin and Yvainyasha looked at the Vorts and then at each other.

"They will have moved the *'paid high'* somewhere safer", Yvainyorin trilled to his cousin.

Yvainyasha trilled back, "Yes. The Human she-child will definitely be at an unknown location."

Yvainyorin trilled and clicked, "I will go to the nest of our secondary target. The boy Thol and his parents will be mine! I will collect their bounty."

Yvainyasha nodded, trilling and clicking back, "The parents are *'paid same'*, the boy is *'paid little high'*, three times normal. Three Thols will give you five!"

Yvainyorin agreed, "The target family is worthy of my time and effort."

Yvainyasha trilled and clicked, "I will go to the Human school and watch for our targets. If they turn up, they will die. Maybe I get lucky, maybe I kill the *'paid high'* worth ten Thols!"

As the pair slunk away from the compound back into the depths of the long bluegrass, Yvainyasha trilled to his cousin, "Remember, one small cut is all you need. Be quick and be out!"

Before midday, Mrs Swanson's new recruit, Special Operative in Training, Anne Harrington, arrived at the compound in her personal hovercar. Michelle Bronson, Mrs Swanson's Gardener and Goat herder, greeted Anne and showed her to her quarters. Mike Jonson, Mrs Swanson's Flight Mechanic and Engineer, used the A.I. *"grip"* wrapped around his left forearm, to taxi Anne's hovercar into the hangar.

By mid-afternoon, Mike Jonson had received the *"sweep"* that he'd ordered and he busied himself, installing it on the hangar roof. By the end of the day, anything approaching the Swanson's plot from the skies, that was bigger than a crow, would be detected at at least two kilometres out. The detection would result in notifications to every operative on Mrs Swanson's team.

Mrs Swanson's Ground Keeper and Security Operative, Sylvester Bronson, was patrolling the grounds, keeping an eye out for anything unusual. Anne had noted on her arrival that everyone was now carrying sidearms of pulse laser pistols. Mike, Sylvester and even his Wife, Michelle had kukri swords sheathed along the utility belts at their backs, easily accessed and ready for use. Everyone at Mrs Swanson's plot was prepared for anything. The atmosphere was tense and they all had their heads on a swivel. The attempted assassination of Mrs Swanson's Daughters, Aria and Ariel, had created quite a reaction.

Between the homestead and the southern perimeter fence, there was another tall, broad Bell Nut Fruit tree. Three forty-foot high cube shipping containers of lumber and tools had been delivered and were nearby, along with six Humaniform Androids. An Alpha and five Betas. They were currently surveying the tree to ascertain the best way to construct a Mimasian-style Tholish tree house.

Upon the arrival of the Androids, Mrs Swanson introduced the *"metal men"* to Yookey and his parents, Yarling and Yorvick. Angelique's instructions were clear and simple. She ordered the Androids to scan Yookey's and his parent's dna and to recognise them on sight. Then she instructed the Androids that the three Indigenous Thols were Humans and to be treated the same as Humans. After this, Mike Johnson gave the Androids the task of building the tree house.

While Yookey's family, Aria and Ariel, relaxed inside the soil-covered homestead, Angelique and her Husband, Robert, organised two teams of Colonial Marines. One to stake out Yookey's nest complex in the Northern Mountain forest village and the other to stake out the Colony's School. Their given task was simple, watch and wait. If any assassins turn up, disable and capture them. Consider them armed, dangerous and carrying neurotoxin-coated weapons. They needed them alive.

Neither Yookey, Aria, nor Ariel went to school that day. It was simply far too dangerous for them with Darkling assassins flying around. Mrs Swanson notified Yealah, who was Yookey's neighbour and her friend. Yealah of course informed her Husband, Yannick and her Daughter, Yeannah, the twin's friend. Yeannah took it upon herself to inform, Kethera and her boyfriend Richard, Saffiera and even her own paramour, Thomas. Saffiera then notified her own Mother, Sarlia. Kethera decided not to tell her parents, she did not want to worry them.

They were all quite shocked that just a simple kiss between Aria and Yookey could have led to not just an inter-species incident but also assassination attempts! They found the situation to be quite surreal, even bizarre. For that entire Tuesday, the whole group was eerily quiet during every one of their classes.

Yeannah's Mother, Yealah, went to her work at the colony's medical clinic as usual. While Yeannah was at school and Yealah was at work, seven Colonial Marines arrived at the giant Jula Jula tree where Yeannah lived. Aria and Ariel had both been to Yeannah's tree house previously and so, had explained how to access the tree, which, like all mature Jula Jula trees, had a hollow trunk.

The seven Colonial Marines entered the hollow tree at its main access door built into its base. They used the elevator inside the hollow to access the level at which Yeannah's tree house was located. There, inside the hollow tree, the Colonial Marines in full tactical armour and wearing jet packs waited patiently.

As the hollow within Jula Jula trees was only ever used by Mimasian Thols and not Indigenous Thols, they were unlikely to be detected. Especially as the elevator within the tree's hollow was largely for receiving guests who could not fly. Thols, both Mimasian and Indigenous, of course, had wings.

Lieutenant Salaam Baker left his squad and made his way to Yeannah's tree house. It was easy to locate as Yeannah's Father, Yannick, had been given a micro-communicator previously and he simply did a location trace. The Lieutenant then made his way to the tree house with a heavy rucksack of specialised equipment.

Yannick, who was ready and waiting for him, greeted him when he arrived. Yannick showed the Lieutenant to a room that had a clear view of Yookey's nest complex from its window. The Lieutenant smiled, it was perfect. He set up his surveillance equipment, which had rollout screens, optical, active night vision, thermal detection and other surveillance methods.

Yookey's whole family had been extracted that very morning and the extraction team had left audiovisual micro-cameras with motion detectors built in, in every one of the five nests in the nesting cluster. Lieutenant Baker had his equipment all ready and linked up with the micro-cameras.

Indigenous Thol nests were like large bowls constructed of tightly woven branches, with a second larger upturned bowl over the top as a roof and canopy that was covered in strong, durable leaves. Thols would fly up between the walls of their nest and the canopy and slip over the side for access.

Most Indigenous Thol nests had only one nest. Yookey's Father, Yorvick, however, was considered *"progressive"*. He could not build a Mimasian-style tree house, but he could build Indigenous nests, so he built five of them in a cluster and linked them all together. These were built on a solid, broad branch in the next Jula Jula tree over from Yannick's.

There was one nest affixed to the branch at its precise split point, where it split into two branches. Two more nests were affixed along those two branches and connected to the first in such a way that once inside, you simply strolled between nests. These three nests together formed a triangular shape base. The other two nests were affixed to other branches above the first three. Once inside the nest cluster, one could leap up into them or drop down out of them. They were used as bedrooms.

And so the Colonial Marines waited and they waited patiently.

While this was all happening, another team of seven Colonial Marines, along with the twin's Father, Robert Swanson, all in plain clothes, secreted themselves into positions within the colony's school. They were in plain clothes, yes, but heavily armed nonetheless.

One of the Darkling assassins, Yvainyasha, had already reached the school before the arrival of the Colonial Marines. He had landed on a rooftop where he had a good view of the school and its students. There was a dormer window behind him, that he had checked. It led to an attic storage room. Yvainyasha could secret himself within the attic room if necessary.

Two things Yvainyasha did not know or understand. Some of the adult

Humans wandering around on the school grounds below him were Colonial Marines in plain clothes. The other, Colonial Marines used stealth drones. Nonetheless, Yvainyasha was still highly cautious. This was well within the Human colony, after all, and everything around him was alien in its very nature. When the primary Sun, Cathol, was low on the horizon, Yvainyasha crawled through the attic's dormer window to make himself comfortable for the night. So too did the Colonial Marines.

It was a long, slow day and slowly, Secundus's primary Sun, Cathol, began to set. Secundus's distant secondary Sun, Cythol, was still above the horizon. Between Cythol's eerie orange glow and the silvery light of Secundus's large Moon, Luns, one could see quite well, if not all that clearly. Indigenous Thols, of course, had evolved in this world that they called Homwol, so their eyes were used to the eerie nights. Yeannah had already returned home from school, as had her Mother, Yealah returned home from her job in the colony. They were not surprised to find Lieutenant Baker in their tree house when they'd flown up to their landing and walked across their small suspension bridge to their front porch. Yannick had already requested they be notified ahead of their leaving the colony.

Yvainyorin flew swiftly into a neighbouring tree to Yookey's nest tree and secreted himself amongst the branches and foliage. It was already dark and Yvainyorin's eyes had already adjusted to the lower light. He waited patiently. The Thols in this neighbourhood would soon be asleep and then he could get down to business completely unseen.

Yvainyorin checked the photographs of Yookey and his parents, Yarling and Yorvick. One was *"paid little high"* and the other two were *"paid same"*. Yvainyorin smiled to himself, three gives him five. Patiently, he waited until all of the surrounding lights had gone out. Not yet, not yet, one must wait until everyone is sound asleep. Waiting, waiting, waiting, patience brings its own rewards. Then all he needed to do was fly in and give them each a little nick! They would be dead even before they realised he was there. It was nice of them to live in such an atypical nest cluster. Easy for him to target!

It was now the middle of the night and Yvainyorin was ready, he took a deep breath to steady his nerves, then dove out of his hiding spot. Yvainyorin glided across to Yookey's nesting tree, down and then up between the walls of the nest and its canopy. Yvainyorin was inside.

Lieutenant Baker had just reached for his thermos of coffee at that precise moment and missed it entirely but then the micro-motion-cameras in the first nest came online. Two windows popped up on the screen and there in active night vision and infrared was the Darkling assassin.

"Pappa Eagle to Eaglets. Pappa Eagle to Eaglets. The target is in the nest. Repeat. The target is in the nest", he spoke softly into his comms, adding, "Give the Target time to get comfortable. We'll make our move on my mark."

The soft reply of, "Roger that", came back from his squad's team leader.

Yvainyorin found the first nest was empty, he sighed and then checked the second nest. Disappointment, it was empty as well and then to make matters worse, upon checking the third nest, it was also empty. Yvainyorin frowned.

Yvainyorin looked up, perhaps in the bedrooms.

Yvainyorin leapt up into the first bedroom, it too was empty. What the fuck! So he checked the final bedroom nest only to find it was empty as well. Yvainyorin scratched his white-blond locks, Yookey and his parents must have gone to ground. Shit! Those bastards! Yvainyorin's blood boiled with anger!

Yvainyorin looked around. They must have left some clue as to where they'd gone. He started to ransack the nest complex, rummaging around and tossing things about. This was not normal assassin's work. Yvainyorin was an assassin, not an investigator!

Where were my kills?

"Pappa Eagle to Eaglets. Pappa Eagle to Eaglets. The target is in the top right nest. Repeat. The target is in the top right nest", he spoke softly into his comms, adding, "Use your thermals. Surround and capture. We need him alive, Eaglets. On my mark!"

The soft reply of, "Roger that", came back from his squad's team leader.

Lieutenant Baker softly spoke one word, "Mark!", then followed with, "Eaglets are go!"

In quick succession, the Colonial Marines left the concealment and leapt towards Yookey's nest complex, their whisper-quiet jet packs taking them straight to their target. The Darkling assassin was still ransacking the same bedroom and they had him on their thermal night vision goggles.

One by one the Colonial Marines quickly swooped between the nest's wall and its canopy. Five into the same nest the assassin was ransacking and one into to nest below to block any egress in that particular direction.

"Fuck!", Yvainyorin screeched in his native Tholish.

Five Humans were all around him and they held these strange things in one hand and supported their wrists with the other. He did not recognise what they were holding.

Five little red dots appeared on Yvainyorin's body, "*What magic is this?*", he thought to himself.

One of the Humans was shouting at him, "Drop your weapons and stand down!"

Weapons, that he had not realised he'd pulled out of their scabbards, *"instinct"*, Yvainyorin held a Sickle-Shaped Talon Knife in each hand.

Again, the Human shouted at him, "Drop your weapons and stand down!"

Yvainyorin had no idea what the Human was saying, so he dove for the exit to the lower nest.

"Target heading down, target heading down", the squad's team leader spoke into his comms.

Much to Yvainyorin's surprise, the was another Human in the lower nest and he collided with him. There was a strange sound, Veeeee-wack, and he felt a sharp stinging pain in his right shoulder.

Whatever it was had bored straight through him. Yvainyorin looked down. Both of his poisoned sickle-shaped talon blades were deeply embedded in the Human's neck. Instinct or luck, it did not matter! The Human was dead! Yvainyorin laughed a deep guttural, almost a Tarlak laugh!

Then "Fuck!", Yvainyorin screeched once more in native Tholish.

The five Humans from the upper nest had surrounded him once more and those strange red dots were on his body again. They moved so fast for such big people, these Humans did.

One of the Humans was shouting, "Pappa Eagle! Man down! Pappa Eagle! Repeat! Man down!"

Lieutenant Baker sighed, he had one man down and there'd likely be more to come, he made his decision and then replied, "Eaglets! Take down the target! Eaglets! Repeat! Take down the target!"

Veeeee-wack! Veeeee-wack! Veeeee-wack! Veeeee-wack! Veeeee-wack!

Yvainyorin felt sudden intense pain raking through his body, he looked down at his chest, *"Why are there holes in my body?"*, he thought to himself, he'd never seen a pulse laser pistol before

Yvainyorin collapsed to his knees and then his body toppled backwards, his lifeless purple eyes staring upwards at the main nest's canopy.

Lieutenant Baker shone a spotlight on Yookey's family's nest complex providing the Colonial Marines with plenty of light. The Colonial Marines then removed the two bodies from the main nest and lined them up along the nest's broad supporting branch, ready for retrieval. All of the violent commotion had awakened every Thols within earshot, Indigenous and Mimasian.

The Indigenous Thols climbed out of their nests and watched from their tree's branches or their nest's canopies. Mimasian Thols watched from out of their tree house's windows. They all had one thing in common, they watched in abject disbelief. Below them was not only a dead Colonial Marine but something out of their nightmares. The Tholish boogieman that Indigenous Thol parents warned their younglings about to make them behave themselves.

The Darkling assassin was easily identified by the Tarlak Skull Tattoo on his chest. By rights, he should not be there! He was a thing of myth and legend, not something real to be seen with Tholish eyes. Yealah, Yeannah and her little Brother, Yarris, all tried to get a look but Yannick was having none of it and wouldn't let them near the window.

Yannick told the Lieutenant, "That Darkling looks just like our nightmares", he then paused before adding, "According to our myths. If you turn him over, his name will be found tattooed down his spine in between his wings. That should tell what family he comes from within their clan."

Lieutenant Baker took note and then looked farther afield at all of the frightened onlooking Thols, "Sargent! Cover those bodies up. The locals are getting freaked out!"

Within two minutes the Sargent and another marine had retrieved some blankets from the bedroom nests and covered the two bodies. Then, twenty minutes later, a military morgue hover bus arrived to take away the bodies. It was a sad night, the Lieutenant's team had lost one of their own.

The incident was quickly reported to Angelique and her Husband, Robert. They were not happy with the loss of the Darkling as an intelligence asset but understood it was the right call. Robert was shocked when Angelique requested the Darkling's head and noted that she was going to mount it on a spike ten meters east of the other one. Angelique had neglected to mention the first one to him.

"So, Angelique, we're mounting Darkling heads on spikes now, are we?", Robert asked.

Angelique was unrepentant, "As a deterrent and a warning, Bobby", she paused and then added, "I will do anything it takes to protect my Daughters!"

"Angelique, that is just so medieval. What's next, fucking crows cages?", Robert responded.

"Oh, get over it, Bobby. It's happening", Angelique replied, before sending instructions to Mike Johnson to prepare another spike in advance of the head's arrival.

Angelique told Robert straight up, "Every assassin that comes after my Daughters. Their head is going on a spike", and she was extremely adamant about it.

Robert just frowned and walked away in disgust. This was a side of his Wife that he simply did not want to see!

As Robert walked away, Angelique remarked loudly, "Bobby, these Darklings. They're cannibals. They eat their victims!"

Robert paused, he considered that, *"Cannibals"*, he thought to himself, before continuing.

Miss Bream looked around her classroom, there were empty seats, a lot of empty seats. She knew why, it had been all over the colony's news feeds from the crack of dawn onwards. The Indigenous Thol's nightmares were real. The Darkling murderers, assassins and cannibals were real and one had been killed inside of Yookey's family nest complex.

Yookey was one of the missing Thol students, "Yeannah, you live in the same village as Yookey. Is Yookey okay? Is his family okay?"

Yeannah smiled more unsettledly, "Yookey and his family live in the next tree over from mine, Miss Bream. Nearly every Thol in this class is Yookey's neighbour", she replied.

"Yes, Yeannah. I am aware of that, but are Yookey and his family okay?", Miss Bream asked.

"Yes, Miss Bream. Yookey and his parents were extracted from their nest complex early yesterday morning and taken somewhere safe", Yeannah informed her, not mentioning anything about where Yookey and his parents currently were, "Last night, when the assassin came, he was flying into a trap. The Colonial Marines were waiting for him."

"Well then, that explains Yookey's absence. Now, where are the twins?", Miss Bream enquired.

Yeannah shifted uncomfortably in her chair, "Yesterday morning, before the Colonial Marines extracted Yookey and his parents from their nest complex, an assassin came to the twin's plot. He was killed on site. That's what led to the extraction of Yookey's family, Miss Bream."

Miss Bream pinched the bridge of her nose, "My understanding was that the incident on Monday had all been sorted out with the Tholish High Council."

"It had, Miss, but apparently, not all Thols agreed with their High Council", Yeannah informed her, noting, "There are still contracts out on the twins, Yookey and his parents. If my understanding is correct, the Darklings won't stop until those contracts are fulfilled and the bounties collected."

"So, Yookey and the twins won't be attending class for a while, I take it", Miss Bream pinched the bridge of her nose once more, "I simply cannot fathom in this day and age how a simple kiss between a boy and girl can lead to such violence."

One of the few remaining Thols in the class, a boy who lived farther afield from Yookey, commented, "Yookey and Aria broke one of our most sacred taboos, Miss Bream. The High Council may have been okay with it, but it looks like some of my people took umbridge."

"Yorlock, I seem to remember another of your people's taboos. A Thol may not kill another Thol", Miss Bream replied.

Yorlock shrugged and replied, "The Darklings don't obey our laws or our taboos, Miss Bream."

Miss Bream looked back to Yeannah, "You said the assassin that went after the twins was killed. So the twins are both okay, yes?", she was seriously concerned.

Yeannah was slow to answer, she was having a should-she and how-much moment, finally, she settled on, "The twins are not what you think, Miss Bream. They are far from simply helpless school girls. Their parents have trained them in martial arts since the day they could walk."

That caught Miss Bream completely by surprise.

Yeannah continued, "Aria and Ariel defended themselves and dealt with the assassin until their security was able to take him down", she was hoping word would get around that the twins could and would defend themselves with main force.

"The twins fought off an assassin?", Miss Bream asked incredulously.

"Yes, Miss Bream and they caused him quite a lot of damage in the process. They beat the assassin into pulp", Yeannah replied.

This revelation told Miss Bream three things, the twins were okay and that they were formidable. The third thing was that the twins belonged to a military family, which explained the swift and deadly responses. The military would be harsh when protecting their own!

Yorlock trilled a laugh or two, "Thols don't have same-face younglings. The assassin would have been looking for a single Human girl, not twins. That would have confused the Darkling", he trilled another laugh.

Miss Bream looked around what was left of her history class, "Students, please take notes for your absent classmates. Recent events aside, we still have a history class this morning."

In the year twenty one fifty, Stuart Dumas passed away at the age of one hundred and two. It was now three years later and another series of groups had formed, wanting to colonise distant solar system objects. Most of the solar system had colonies in place as far out as Neptune. These new groups did not want to join a colony, they wanted to create new colonies themselves. There were only the Kuiper Belt objects left, Pluto and the other Dwarves.

There were fifteen different groups and each of them wanted the biggest slice of the pie, that slice was Pluto with its five Moons, including the large Moon, Charon. That system provided a beautiful analogue of the Earth-Moon system, with the Charon L-Four and L-Five points being exceedingly stable. There were, however, only thirteen Dwarf Worlds, including Pluto to be had and not all of them were equal, let alone viable options. The Dumas Team was preparing a random selection, a binding random selection.

The Dumas team sat in their conference room. It was one of their larger conference rooms with a large circular table capable of seating up to twenty five people. Stuart Dumas's Son, Baron Dumas and his Wife, Hypolita, sat in the centre on their side. Their Sons Connor and Daniel sat to their left and their personal assistant and adviser, Harmony Moon, sat to their right. To Harmony's right sat her assistant, Ritu Dharma, who had been Stuart Dumas's secretary. They were patiently waiting for their fifteen guests to arrive.

Ritu Dharma had sent their organisations binding contract agreements, that all had to be signed, scanned and uploaded to Cis-Lunar L-Five's Colonial Central contract registry before their representatives could be present at the table. The contract was a binding agreement, that the organisations would agree to and abide by, the allocation of the Dwarf Planets in the Kuiper Belt, irrespective of the Dwarf Planet they were allocated, if any. Failure to comply and the relevant organisation forfeits their seat at the table. The document was a legally binding contract once it was registered at the contract registry.

Ritu checked the registry for compliance. One of the organisations was delinquent.

The fifteen representatives filed into the conference room and began to take their seats, which had been prepared and labelled.

Jason Marrakesh of the *"Outer Realm Consortium"* found that he did not have a seat, labelled or otherwise, he looked around and then asked, "What gives? I have no seat?"

Ritu replied in a very matter-of-fact manner, "That is correct, Mr Marrakesh. Your Consortium has not signed the contract and registered it."

The Outer Realm Consortium saw no need to sign that contract", Jason Marrakesh simply replied.

Baron chimed in, "Then the Outer Realm Consortium does not get a seat at this table."

"Wait a minute! That's not fair!", Jason Marrakesh protested.

Hypolita replied calmly, "It is perfectly fair, Mr Marrakesh. Your organisation did not comply with a legally registered business process. Non-compliance means no seat at the table.

Connor commented with equal calm, "Your organisation screwed up, Mr Marrakesh. Now you can leave of your own accord, or we can call security."

Mr Jason Marrakesh swore something under his breath as he left the conference room.

After the door closed behind Mr Marrakesh, Baron Dumas smiled and noted, "And then there were fourteen."

One of their other guests asked, "What if his group causes problems for the rest of us?"

"The Outer Realm Consortium has been excluded from a legally registered process", Danial replied, noting, "If they interfere, they will be breaking the law."

Baron Dumas chimed in, "In which case they will find themselves running up against Dumas Legal and an economic black listing."

Hypolita held up a stack of cards with golden backs, there were fourteen cards in all.

"On the front of these cards is the name of a Dwarf Planet, its most recent photograph and its Astrometric details", Hypolita informed them all as she shuffled the cards and then spread them out, face down on the desk in front of her Husband, Baron.

Baron swirled the cards around on the table in front of him while he noted, "Only ten cards have actual Dwarf Planets on them. Four are blank. You will get what you choose and there will be no complaints", he explained and then he informed them, "This meeting is being videoed and your selections will be recorded."

Harmony chimed in, "And documented with the Colonial Central contract registry. Your selection will be legally binding. Any non-compliance will be illegal."

"Okay then, starting on the right, one by one come and select your card. Then we'll move on to the left. Do not look at your chosen card. Just pick it up, return to your seat and place it face down on the table in front of your seat", Baron instructed.

The circular conference room table was open at the side closest to the door. One by one, their guests walked into the centre of the table and approached the cards in front of Baron. Some hesitated before choosing, some were quick to snatch up a card and a few took their time before picking up a card. Once they'd chosen their card, they returned to their seats and placed their chosen card face down in front of them. It did not take long before they were all seated once more.

"Okay, Ladies and Gentlemen, turn your cards over", Hypolita instructed and they all did so.

The delegate that had chosen Pluto mouthed the word "Yes" and then he pumped his fist. Four delegates were extremely disappointed, they chose blanks. The other nine were in various states of disappointment, none of them picked Pluto.

The other Dwarf Planets were a varied bunch. Some were quite large and some weren't much more than big rocks. The smallest, Chaos, was a mere four hundred and fifty kilometres across, while the largest was Haumea, at nineteen hundred and sixty kilometres across. Five of them had Moons and one of those, Haumea, had two Moons. However, none was as impressive as Pluto.

"All selections are final", Hypolita announced.

As all fourteen cards had turned over, the video camera above the table captured all cards and all nameplates, registering which delegate had chosen which Dwarf Planet, if any. The conference room's A.I. system translated the information and added it into fourteen documents.

Binding contracts acknowledging the chosen cards and thus, the allocated Dwarf Planets, if any, were updated accordingly. Those documents were printed out on a printer conveniently located behind Ritu on a small table. Ritu picked up the fourteen documents and carefully distributed them to their matching delegates.

Harmony instructed the delegates, "Please check that your selection matches your document. Then sign the said document and then return it to Miss Dharma."

All of the delegates did as instructed. Those you drew blanks or perceived, less desirable Dwarf Planets, grumbled nonetheless.

One of the delegates, who'd drawn a blank card, had been looking around the table and he noted, "I've noticed that Gonggong, Sedna and Eris weren't included in the draw."

"They are not suitable", Connor replied, explaining, "Gonggong is sixty seven astronomical units away and Eris is ninety six. They are too far away for our current level of technology to reach in any reasonable amount of time. And at that distance, there would be no possibility of trade whatsoever."

Daniel added in, "Even Makemake, which at close to forty six astronomical units out is pushing the limits of what's currently possible. Its inclusion was debatable."

The delegate that chose Makemake smiled, "I'm glad you did. Makemake is one of the bigger Dwarf Worlds."

"What about us poor mugs that chose blanks?", one of the delegates enquired.

"It's not over yet, not by a long shot", Baron replied, commenting, "You could choose to walk out now or perhaps, you might just want to take one of your fellow delegate's business cards. Merging with another group is an option."

The delegate who'd chosen Pluto slid his business card around the table, "Give me a call. We are always looking for more colonists and to be honest, Pluto is a cherry of a world."

Baron gestured to the delegate that had drawn Pluto, "You see there. That's what I'm talking about."

"Now, how many of you have done your homework?", Baron asked.

"You mean all of the information you provided about how Saturn, Uranus and Neptune were colonised?", the delegate that had drawn Pluto responded.

"Yes, exactly. I need to know how many of you actually comprehend what we actually do. This is very important", Baron explained.

Every delegate at the table nodded and a few replied with a "Yes."

"Okay. Then you understand that we construct O'Neil-style twin cylinder colonies and that we haul those out to their destinations and set them up before the colonists arrive, yes?", Baron asked them for confirmation.

All of the delegates at the table nodded, with a few replying with a "Yes."

"Okay, so far so good. Each colony is engineered to suit its destination. We even provide the orbital mobile mining, ore processing and manufacturing stations", Baron commented, noting, "And of course the interplanetary push ships to take your colonists out to the new colonies."

The delegate that had drawn Pluto asked, "We are probably all well versed on what the Dumas Corporation can do for us, Mr Dumas. So why am I getting the feeling there is a major issue?"

"That would be because there is, Mr Silvertail", Baron admitted, explaining, "The Dumas Corporation is a business and all of the finance for these ventures will be financed through Dumas Colonial Financial."

Mr Joshua Silvertail nodded in understanding, "We are the clients. We borrow the credits. We then have to service those loans."

"Precisely", Baron confirmed, explaining further, "When a colony is close to forty astronomical units out, any trade routes are going to be very long and quite stretched. Dumas Colonial Financial will need to see your business modelling. Your trade routes, your trade partners. How you're going to earn the credits to service your loans. With Saturn, Uranus and Neptune, this was a relatively simple exercise. With the Dwarf Worlds, not so much!"

Hypolita chimed in, "The outer gas giants all trade with each other and via Jupiter's Trojans and the Jovian Republic. They then trade with the Belters and the inner solar system worlds. Your trade routes will need to leverage the Neptunian Commonwealth and their Trojans for trade and access to Uranus and Saturn. Your trade routes will be long and extended, like fragile, stretched tendrils."

Mr Silvertail understood, "I see. Even with Pluto and its Moons, my group is in the same boat. You want us all to go back to our groups and work out how we're actually going to make a living at the far edges of the solar system", he laughed, "Now I can definitely see why you left out Gonggong, Sedna and Eris. They're simply too far out! They are not financially viable at all."

Hypolita smiled and chimed in, "The long-term viability of the colonies is of paramount importance. So we do recommend working together on this. Look at where your selected Dwarf Planets are concerning each other and Neptune's Moons and its Trojans. Use the Neptunium Commonwealth as your gateway. Work out the most efficient trade routes from your orbital zones and work together on everything where Humanly possible. Cooperation is the key!"

Hypolita's wise words had all of the delegates nodding.

One of the other delegates, Ms Belinda Snoddgrass, who had drawn Haumea, the second largest Dwarf Planet up for grabs, with its two Moons, Hi□aka and Namaka, had another idea.

"Look, guys. I went through all of the documentation you handed out. I was especially impressed with the Neptunian costing examples", Ms Snoddgrass told everyone, then remarked, "Better than ninety percent of the cost is the O'Neil-style twin cylinder colony and its haulage to site."

Mr Silvertail caught on, "If we use a single cylinder format instead, we reduce capacity but at the same time, we lower the costs down to fifty five percent!"

Baron Dumas stepped in, "It's not just about population holding capacity. Counter-rotating twin cylinders are more stable and require less fuel expenditure to keep them on station."

"Yes, but as we already know, the volatile fuels are plentiful in the Kuiper Belt objects. So that is no longer an issue", Mr Silvertail noted.

Baron looked at his Sons, Connor and Daniel, then back to Hypolita, Harmony and Ritu. Their curated discussion about trade, trade routes and financial economics was quickly descending into a crazy cost-cutting exercise.

Ms Belinda Snoddgrass then said something that made their heads spin, "Why do we need to O'Neil-style colonies at. Cut them out and build our colonies from scratch. It will take us longer but we'll save ninety percent and maybe, just maybe, be able to finance everything internally ourselves."

Was this woman serious?

Harmony was the first to speak out, "Ms Snoddgrass, if you don't have a colony, a stable home to go to when you push out to the Kuiper Belt, you will be running a massive risk. Push ships are not designed for long-term habitability. The push ship takes you out to your new colony, you offload the colonists into their new colony home and then later, you recycle your push ship into the foundation of a new colony at your leisure. Having an O'Neil-style twin cylinder colony as your target gives you a base to go to, already in place and prepared to your specifications."

Ms Snoddgrass, however, was an even faster thinker, "I see what you mean, Ms Moon", she paused momentarily in thought before continuing, "We will need the Dumas Corporation's Engineering Department to redesign the push in a few ways. One will be increased supply storage and life support systems. The second, we'll need long-term habitability and the third, we will need two of them per Dwarf Planet colony."

Harmony was flabbergasted at how quickly Belinda Snoddgrass thought, "Two push ships?", she questioned curiously.

"Yes, Ms Moon. When we push out to our destination, we'll only take one-third of the capacity in terms of colonists but a full complement of supplies in each push ship. When we get to our destination, we'll offload all of the colonists from the second push ship into the first. The first push ship will be at two-thirds capacity, so we'll all have plenty of room", Ms Snoddgrass replied.

After a short pause she then added, "We can then recycle the second push ship as the foundation to construct our first colony. Once completed, we can do the same and recycle the other push ship and we'll end up with two colonies. After all, push ships are designed to be recycled into colonies. That is their final end purpose."

Harmony Moon had no idea what to think. Was this Snoddgrass woman brilliant, or was she insane?

Harmony let it out, "Ms Snoddgrass, are you serious? I don't know if this idea of yours is brilliant or completely bonkers", she said.

That was such an unusual response from Harmony that the rest of her team just looked at her.

"Guys!", Harmony frowned and broke with protocol, "Baron, Hypolita. Ms Snoddgrass's concept is not the way we do things. It's reckless, bloody reckless! And remember, I'm a Belter and we do reckless! If anything goes wrong way out there, people will die and there is no one, no one at all out there to help them."

Ms Snoddgrass smiled and calmly replied, "Thank you for candour, Ms Moon. I really do appreciate it. And I do understand your concerns, but at the end of the day, isn't it our choice? After all, the customer is always right."

"Ms Snoddgrass. I think what Harmony was trying to say is that our methods work, they are tried and tested. They work. What you are suggesting would require very careful consideration, careful modelling and will no doubt, have a significant number of engineering challenges", Baron explained.

Mr Silvertail chimed in, "So, you will at least entertain Ms Snoddgrass's ideas, Mr Dumas?"

"Yes, Mr Dumas, have your engineers perform their modelling. If they can solve their engineering challenges and make it all work, then I'm all for it", Ms Snoddgrass piled on.

Connor noted, "Dad, if they do this, they'll need blueprints to build Fast Breeder Fission Reactors. Uranium mining stations, processing plants, enrichment plants and manufacturing plants dedicated to making Uranium fuel rods. They can't take this stuff with them on a push ship! No way!"

"Thank you, Connor", his Father replied, thinking to himself, *"Fuck! What a mess!"*

Hypolita picked up on Baron's and Harmony's concerns, "Ms Snoddgrass. Mr Silvertail. Even if our engineers work this problem to ground and figure out a way to make it work, the Dumas Corporation will require waivers to absolve us of any liability should things go horribly wrong!"

Harmony Moon entered Baron's and Hypolita's shared office with a huge folio of blueprints and specifications, "Mr Dumas, Mrs Dumas. You'll both be very happy to see these", she announced.

Harmony placed the oversized folio on top of the office's coffee table and opened it up, then beckoned Baron and Hypolita over to see what she had discovered.

Harmony looked at Baron, "When I was twelve. My Grandfather, Harrison and your Father, Stuart, were both enabling the Belter Colonies to avoid the jurisdiction of the Colonisation Committee of Sol and the Security Committee of Sol, based at Eros. They managed to create a historical precedent, which in turn created a loophole."

Baron smiled and replied, "Yes, Harmony. I do remember. Keeping the final loan payment from ever happening and the colony never officially coming online. I also remember that was your creation."

Harmony smiled back, "It's not the legal loophole that's important here, Mr Dumas. It was the reaction of the Earth Government and the Colonial Central Command Government. Both Governments thought they could break your Father's colonisation business model by releasing blueprints and specifications to the public domain. Blueprints for Bernal Spheres, Stamford Torus, O'Neil Cylinders and orbital stations, like mobile mining, ore processing and manufacturing stations. A lot of infrastructure blueprints, all released into the public domain!"

"I remember that one as well, Harmony. It blew up in their faces in the end if I remember correctly", Baron noted in reply.

"Yes, but here's the rub, Mr Dumas", Harmony replied, pointing at the blueprint, "That is an interplanetary push ship and its blueprints and specifications are all in the public domain!"

Baron and Hypolita looked at the designs, while Harmony brought the blueprints up on the office's main screen alongside the current equivalent Dumas push ship. The differences were stark!

The Dumas push ship design was smaller, longer, thinner, elegant and sleek. The public domain design was twice the size, long and thin but blocky, almost brutalist in appearance.

Harmony explained, "Our basic business model is to build the infrastructure here in Cis-Lunar L-Four. Then haul everything out to the target location and set it all up, ready and waiting. Our push ships are used to get the colonists, the '*passengers*', from here to there", then she paused a moment.

Harmony continued, "The Government release of those blueprints was meant to create a new business model all hinging around that push ship design. The push ship, the orbital stations, the supplies and then the colonists push out to their final destination with no infrastructure in place. Then, using the colony blueprints, they construct their new colony themselves, in-situ! That is the complete reverse of what we do here", she paused once more.

"Both of these designs are meant to be recycled into new colonies once their primary purpose is met. Our design is meant to become the foundation of a smaller colony. This public domain design, though, gives the colonists the option of building a larger colony from scratch, or if they have more than one push ship. The surplus push ship becomes the foundation of a much larger colony."

"Harmony, this is exactly what Ms Snoddgrass is wanting", Hypolita realised.

"Yes, Mrs Dumas and it has already been tried and tested successfully", Harmony replied, noting, "All of the engineering challenges we're facing, they've already been solved in this old design", she pointed to the screen and the push ship blueprints.

Baron chimed in, "And that is also why the government's plan backfired."

Harmony nodded in understanding, revealing, "The one and only time these designs were ever used was when the disgraced Horridian Corporation built four of these push ships and fled into exile in the Jovian Republic. That took the wind out the Government's sails and poisoned the waters for any further attempts to trash the Dumas Corporation's business model."

"The Horridians quite literally poisoned the well in that regard", Baron added.

"I think we should pass that design onto our engineering department", Hypolita suggested.

Harmony smiled, "Way ahead of you, Mrs Dumas. Our engineers are already studying them. They will need upgrading, of course, for the latest technology and safety standards, but this all looks very viable. Ms Snoddgrass should be very pleased!"

The older, larger push ship designs were overhauled and brought up to modern standards. Then the resultant designs were incorporated into the colonisation proposals for the ten teams with the ambitions to colonise the Kuiper Belt. Two of the new push ships would be sent to each Dwarf Planet along with all of the colonists, their supplies and all of the orbital stations that would be required. The proposals were all accepted.

The four groups that had drawn blanks merged with the other groups. Two merged with the Plutonians, one merged with the Haumeans and the last merged with the Makemakians. Mr Jason Marrakesh and his Outer Realm Consortium begged for inclusion in the process and the Quaoarians relented and took them in. So in the end, all fifteen original groups had been included.

The construction and launching schedule was determined by two things. Which groups had the finances ready first and then signed their indemnity waiver, absolving the Dumas Corporation and its subsidiaries of any fault or blame should things go horribly wrong. Total autonomy meant each group was solely responsible for its own fate. Baron and Hypolita didn't like it but in the end, they had no choice and had to protect Dumas Incorporated's interests.

Starting in the year twenty one fifty seven, the Kuiper Belt colonisation began. First to launch were the two Pluto-bound push ships, the Plutonians. The following year two push ships launched toward Haumea, with the Haumeans. The next year, it was the Makemakian's turn to launch their two push ships out to Makemake. Then, in twenty one sixty, the Quaoarians launched their two push ships out to distant Quaoar.

Then, over the next six years the remaining groups each launched their two push ships toward their respective destinations. The Orcusians to Orcus, the Salacians to Salacia, the Varunans to Varuna, the Ixions to Ixion, the Huyans to Huya and then finally, the Chaosians to Chaos. All ten colonial groups were on their way and they had the better part of a ten year journey ahead of them.

From the Dumas Corporation's perspective, the task was completed. From the perspectives of Baron and Hypolita Dumas, their Sons, Connor and Daniel, and even Harmony and Ritu, they foresaw a series of long, highly dangerous journeys, the outcomes of which were far from certain. Their fears were not allayed when nearly ten years later, all communications with the Kuiper Belt Colonists went dark. No one knew what had happened. Were they dead? Were they alive? Nobody actually knew!

At the back of the class, Yorlock asked in an agitated fashion, "Miss Bream! Miss Bream! What happened to all of those colonists? Did they all die?"

Miss Bream waved her hand dismissively, "They were fine, Yorlock. The folks back home just didn't know it was all."

"That makes no sense, Miss Bream. Surely if they were all okay, they would have kept in contact with Cis-Lunar L-Five?", Yorlock insisted, he was truly puzzled.

"You don't know much about us Humans, Yorlock", Miss Bream noted, then explained, "Yorlock. Those Kuiper Belt colonist took their whole families with them. There was no one back home to talk to, not related to them at least. So when they finally arrived at their chosen Dwarf World, they all got down to the business of building their colonies. They simply didn't bother to call back home. They had no family back home to actually call."

"Miss Bream, you have no idea how ridiculous that sounds", Yorlock replied, he thought it was an absurd explanation.

"Yorlock. You have no idea how ridiculous we Humans can be when in tight-knit groups", Miss Bream replied.

Saffiera laughed telepathically, *"Earth Humans, Miss Bream, Earth Humans. Not we Martians!"*

Finally, Yorlock asked, "So, when did the people back in Cis-Lunar L-Five find out that the Kuiper Belt colonists were okay?"

"Well, Yorlock, it wasn't until around twenty three sixty two, some two centuries later during the second Horridian War", Miss Bream began, explaining, "During the first Horridian War, the Outer Satellite Insurrection as it was called, the Saturnian Demarchy, the Uranian Federation and the Neptunian Commonwealth all supported the Jovian Realms. However, during the second Horridian War, the Jovian Realms stood alone and the other Gas Giant colonies were all neutral."

Miss Bream paused for a moment before continuing, "The Earth Defence Forces and Colonial Fleet contracted with the Dumas Astro Resources company in Cis-Lunar L-Two to surveil the Jovian Realms. Even though the colonies farther out were neutral, they were surveilled as well to ensure that they were, in fact, neutral, which they were", she paused again to check that she had their undivided attention.

"Now imagine you're in charge of all of that surveillance infrastructure and it is all largely automated and controlled by A.I. processors", Miss Bream remarked, then she smiled, "The guy in charge simply got bored and started surveilling Pluto and its five Moons. He discovered that the Pluto-Charon system had a colony set up analogous to Earth's Cis-Lunar colonies. There were ore processing and manufacturing stations in the Charon L-Four zone and colonies in the Charon L-Five zone. The biggest colony was fifteen kilometres long. After that, there was a concerted effort to scan all of the other Dwarf Planets for their missing colonies. They were eventually all found and communications were reestablished after the conclusion of the second Horridian War."

Yorlock simply shook his head, "No offence, Miss Bream but your people be crazy. Seriously Harricks crap crazy."

"No offence taken, Yorlock", Miss Bream replied, she was almost laughing.

Yeannah took note of something interesting, "Miss Bream. The Kuiper Belt colonies went silent between twenty one sixty seven and twenty one seventy six. So that was right before the start of the Outer Satellite Insurrection in twenty one eighty two. That War largely destroyed trade routes, immigration, communications and trust across the entire solar system. It wasn't until two centuries later, after the second Horridian War ended and the Horridians went into exile that things actually normalised."

"You are quite correct, Yeannah", Miss Bream agreed, "Both Horridian Wars created turning points in Human civilisation. Ironically, the exile of High Prince Heinrich von Horridian and his Brothers led to the colonisation of the distant Dwarf Planet, Eris. The descendants of his Horridian Dynasty are still there to this very day."

Yeannah nodded and then commented, "I'm certainly glad they lost that War. I'd hate to be living in the Horridian Imperium. They had a Slave based society, it would be beyond comprehension!"

"As are we all, Yeannah. As are we all", Miss Bream agreed.

Yvainyasha had chosen a good position to surveil the school's main courtyard. The school's hover bus station was over to his left. Students alighted their buses and walked directly from the station into the courtyard below him and then into the various buildings within his field of view. It was a very good position indeed.

Yvainyasha held a photograph in his hand, it was a still shot taken from Monday's video of the *"paid high"* kissing the *"paid little high"*. He found it disgusting but this was his only clue. The others in the photograph, all *"paid nothings",* were not worth the killing nor the effort that involved. Although they might just contain information that he could use to locate the *"paid high"*.

By now, his cousin, Yvainyorin, should have killed the *"paid little high"* and the two *"paid sames"* and headed back to their clan with his reward. Yvainyorin was a highly skilled assassin, perhaps even better than himself or his cousin, Yvainyurei. The other *"paid nothings"* in the photograph had all passed by, through the courtyard below him. They were now somewhere in those buildings before him, hidden from Yvainyasha's sight.

Behind Yvainyasha was a long gabled roof, covered in slate tiles. Every ten metres, there were dormer windows, one of which was behind him, slightly off to one side. Yvainyasha had already managed to unlock the window and left it slightly ajar. In between the dormer windows were maintenance ladders lined against the roof. They were used for easy access to and the repair of the slate roofing tiles.

The roof itself sloped down to a ledge, it was three feet wide and Yvainyasha had plenty of room to sit comfortably. At the outer edge of the ledge ran a low brick wall, which Yvainyasha cautiously peered over. The roof was symmetrical, with an identical setup on the other side of the gable. Between the dormer windows, penetrating the low wall, were small tunnels. Yvainyasha had inspected more than a few of those narrow tunnels. They extended through the low wall and into ornate stone carvings that were shaped like the head of a Tarlak.

Yvainyasha had no idea that they were Gargoyles and that their purpose was to channel water from off of the roof and away from the walls of the building. Nearly all of the school's buildings were largely of the Gothic style, with square towers mounted with tall spires. The lower walls were supported by ornate flying buttresses.

"Do these Humans worship the Tarlaks like his clan? If so, could there be allies of his clan within the Human society like his?", Yvainyasha thought to himself, it was a mystery to him and he considered investigating the subject.

There were a lot of things Yvainyasha did not know.

Yvainyasha did not know that Yvainyorin was dead, that his body was riddled with holes and that his head was now mounted on a spike ten metres to the east of Yvainyurei's own head.

Yvainyasha did not know that he had been detected by cloaked stealth drones. He had no idea that such things even existed.

Yvainyasha did not know that two Colonial Marines in plain clothes had taken up position in concealed locations and that they were armed with high-powered laser sniper rifles. Should Yvainyasha attempt to flee by flight, the Colonial Marines would use those lasers to slice through his wings and force him to the ground. The Colonial Marines wanted him alive.

Yvainyasha had no idea that two Colonial Marines and their Lieutenant had quietly snuck into the attic room behind him and that they all carried pulse laser pistols and taser pistols.

Yvainyasha had no idea that on the other side of the gable, there were two Colonial Marines and his target's Father, Special Operative Robert Swanson. They were climbing the maintenance ladders lying against the slate tiles. They were all armed with the very same weapons as the Colonial Marines inside the attic room.

Yvainyasha had no idea how right royally fucked he really was!

Yvainyasha simply did not know!

Yvainyasha did not know the well-known Humans saying, *"Fuck around and find out!"*

Yvainyasha was about to find out exactly what that meant!

When Robert Swanson reached the peak of the gable, he trained his taser pistol on the centre mass of Yvainyasha's back and shot him in the dead centre of his spine!

It was done!

Yvainyasha collapsed with violent convulsions and spasms from a weapon he could never hope to understand. Yvainyasha, now unconscious, pissed himself reflexively.

With swift motions, the two Colonial Marines accompanying Robert Swanson were on either side of Yvainyasha. They grabbed his arms and wrapped them around his back, cuffing his wrists. Yvainyasha could not unfurl his mighty Tholish wings. His own arms held them tightly furled. His own long tail with its rounded prehensile tip would prevent him from slipping his arms under his feet. When Yvainyasha came to, he was trussed up and helpless. Once a master assassin, now a prisoner!

One of the Colonial Marines disarmed Yvainyasha with carefully gloved hands. Yvainyasha's sickle-shaped talon knives and bone sword, coated in a deadly neurotoxin as they were, were then sealed in a locked box specifically manufactured for that task.

Once Yvainyasha's weapons were secured, the other Colonial Marine grabbed Yvainyasha by the neck and lifted him to his feet. Yvainyasha was surprisingly light, then again, all Thols had hollow bones like birds. Robert Swanson stood before Yvainyasha, he was probably the tallest, most broad-shouldered Human that Yvainyasha had ever seen.

"You bastard! So you wanted to murder my Daughters, did you!", Robert Swanson spat at Yvainyasha and then he punched him solidly across the jaw.

Yvainyasha collapsed unconscious, while the Colonial Marine still held him up.

The two Colonial Marines dragged Yvainyasha through the dormer window, the Lieutenant asked Special Operative Swanson, concerning the punch, "Was that really necessary, Sir?"

Robert Swanson replied coldly, "I tell you what, Lieutenant. You take this bastard to my Wife. She'll rip off his head, shit down his neck and have his head mounted on a spike before you can even blink!"

The Lieutenant stared at Special Operative Swanson in abject disbelief, Robert told him, "Trust me, Lieutenant, when it comes to cubs, the Lioness is always far more savage than the Lion."

The Lieutenant simply replied, "If you say so, Sir."

"Now, we need the location of the Martian Ambassador, Sarlia and her Daughter, Saffiera. Whichever is closer", Robert Swanson asked.

The Lieutenant touched his right temple as his neural augments searched for their locations, "The Martian Ambassador, Sarlia is off-world, Sir. Cis-Luns Colonial Central Command, Sir. Her Daughter, Saffiera, is here in the school. I have her location."

"Well, ain't that fucking brilliant. Lieutenant, lead the way! It seems our telepathic interrogator is a fucking sixteen year old girl! Shit!", Robert Swanson replied as they all headed off the Saffiera's history class with Yvainyasha in tow.

When Special Operative Swanson entered Miss Bream's classroom, he did not knock, he just walked straight in. Two Colonial Marines took up station by the classroom door in the passageway outside. Two more Colonial Marines took up station by the classroom door inside of the classroom. The Lieutenant and Special Operative Robert Swanson stood in front of Miss Bream's desk.

Two Colonial Marines appeared to be holding a Darkling Assassin between them. He was easily identified by the Tarlak skull tattoo on his chest. The two Colonial Marines and the Darkling were standing midway between the desk and the door.

Special Operative Swanson's augments quickly gave him the names of everyone in the classroom, "I apologise, Miss Bream, but we do have an ongoing military operation and time is critical", he informed her, while she stood there in shock.

Special Operative Swanson looked around the class, "Not many Indigenous Thols in class today, Miss Bream?", he asked.

Miss Bream replied, her voice shaky, "After last night's military operation at Yookey's family nest complex, their parents have decided to keep them home."

Special Operative Swanson nodded, "Understandable, Miss Bream. This is nasty business", he replied, then he asked the class, "Which of you Students knows the most about", he paused and gestured to Yvainyasha, "Darkling assassins?"

Yorlock stood up and commented, "I know some stuff, Mr Human Sir"

"Good lad, Yorlock", Special Operative Swanson, gestured to his men to turn Yvainyasha around, "The tattoo down his spine, what can you tell me?"

"That is his name, Sir", Yorlock replied, noting, "His name is Yvainyasha. It literally translates as Yasha of the Yvain family."

Special Operative Swanson nodded, then he called up a photograph of another assassin's back on the classroom's main screen, which was behind Miss Bream's desk, "And this one?"

Yorlock looked at the photograph.

The Darkling assassin was obviously dead and he had a single hole bored through his chest, without hesitation, he responded, "His name is Yvainyurei. Yurei of the Yvain family."

"We are getting somewhere, only one more photograph. I promise, Yorlock", and then Special Operative Swanson called up another photograph on the screen, "And this one. He's the reason so many of your classmates are absent."

It was another dead Darkling assassin, his body had six holes bored through it, "His name is Yvainyorin, Yorin of the Yvain family. These names are in an archaic format, that hasn't been used since the days of the Tarlak raids well over a thousand years ago."

"Are they Brothers, Yorlock?", Special Operative Swanson asked with true curiosity.

"No, Sir. We Thols usually have only one youngling, when we have two, they are always different genders", Yorlock replied, noting, "Those three are likely cousins, although I cannot tell how close."

"Thank you, Yorlock. I really do appreciate your help in this matter",

Special Operative Swanson replied, he even managed a smile, not much of a smile under the circumstance, but a smile nonetheless.

Special Operative Swanson turned to Yeannah and noted, "Yeannah, you are a neighbour and friend of Yookey, also a friend of my Daughters, Aria and Ariel, yes?"

"Yes, Mr Swanson, that is correct", Yeannah replied, she had seen him in the family photograph on the wall in Aria's and Aria's house.

Special Operative Swanson pointed to the Darkling assassin, "This particular man was one of three assassins sent to murder Yookey and my Daughters, Aria and Ariel. They are your friends, Yeannah. I need this Darkling assassin to fully comprehend the precarious position he is in. Now, how is your contemporary Tholish?"

"I am fluent in multiple languages, Mr Swanson, including contemporary Tholish", Yeannah replied, wondering what Mr Swanson was going to ask her to translate.

Special Operative Swanson instructed, "Now, I know this will sound strange, even barbaric and medieval, but I need someone to explain to this assassin what might happen if he doesn't cooperate. Can you do that, Yeannah?"

"Potentially", Yeannah replied, being a little noncommittal.

"Okay. Tell this assassin that if he doesn't cooperate, my wife will mount his head on a spike just like his cousins. She will have her retribution", Special Operative Swanson further instructed her.

Yeannah looked at Mr Swanson in shock. *"Was he serious"*, the thought ran through her mind, this was her friend's Father, *"Would Mrs Swanson really mount the assassin's head on a spike?"*

"I know. I know. It is a really crazy request, but I need this assassin to understand his precise current predicament. He either talks to me, or I hand him over to my Wife", Mr Swanson explained.

Yeannah trilled, clicked and barked in fluent native Tholish and the Darkling assassin immediately reacted, his eye widened and he began struggling to get free.

Special Operative Swanson looked at Yvainyasha, "And now he understands!"

Yvainyasha struggled but he was going nowhere, pound for pound, Humans, especially those with military training, were far stronger than Thols, no matter what species of Thol they may be. Yvainyasha was also handcuffed with his hands behind his back. Even if he managed somehow to get free, his wings were immobilised and running would be difficult with hands handcuffed.

Yvainyasha resigned himself to the fates, he trilled, barked and clicked in native Tholish.

Without thinking, Yeannah began translating, "I don't care! Do what you will with me! I will tell you nothing, you filthy wingless Chitten food!"

"Thank you, Yeannah. You need not translate any further. This assassin, Yvainyasha, has stated his clearly fixed position. I suspected he would", Special Operative Swanson commented, before remarking, "Which unfortunately means I need to take another approach."

Robert Swanson frowned, he had no wish to do this, he looked to Saffiera, sighed and then noted, "Saffiera. I would much prefer to ask your Mother, Sarlia, to do this but she is off-world at Cis-Luns Colonial Central Command."

Saffiera nodded, she understood, her Mother had left just two hours earlier on a diplomatic mission.

"What do you need?", Saffiera asked telepathically.

"We've dealt with three assassins so far, however, we have been told that they will keep sending more assassins until the contract is fulfilled and they get paid. So, Aria, Ariel, Yookey and his parents are still targets and in serious danger. Worse, Yeannah, Kethera, Richard, Thomas and yourself are all in that viral video. Assassins won't hesitate to extract information from any of you. If they perceive that you have pertinent information, then they will come for you. Any of you. Do you understand the situation?", Robert asked.

Saffiera nodded, she understood, the stakes had risen and she asked again, *"How can I help you?"*

"We need to know where the Darkling villages are. That information is in his, Yvainyasha's head", Robert informed her, "You are a telepath, Saffiera and you can access that information directly. It's the quickest way. Military interrogation methods take much longer and the results are never guaranteed."

Saffiera informed Mr Swanson, *"These Darklings, they aren't just assassins and murderers you know? They are cannibals as well! Even now, this, this, Yvainyasha, is looking at us as little more than food!"*

Mr Swanson nodded, "I understand that and yet, we still need that information."

Saffiera nodded in return, *"Then I shall have to retrieve it for you."*

Special Operative Swanson grabbed Yvainyasha by the throat, picked him up and slammed him down on his back on Miss Bream's desk. He then placed his left hand firmly on Yvainyasha's chest and pressed him down. Yvainyasha could not get up, he was firmly held in place.

"How can these Humans possibly be this strong?", Yvainyasha thought to himself.

Saffiera stood up and walked over to Miss Bream's desk, she placed her hands on either side of Yvainyasha's head, gently touching his temples and then she entered his mind.

Saffiera normally perceived minds as a golden ball of tightly woven and threaded thoughts. Yvainyasha's mind was not, it had threads of greys, reds, purples and blacks. The mind of a Darkling was indeed dark. It was a dark, foreboding place and it was a terrifying place for a telepath, most especially one as young as Saffiera.

Yvainyasha's mind was full of memories of assassinations, murders, hunts and cannibalism. Yvainyasha's memories of his family spit-roasting a murdered Thol over an open fire and tearing strips of flesh off to eat were particularly disturbing.

What was that poor Thol's Crime?

The Tholish High Council had banished him and his family to the far western forests. The Thol had lost his Wife and only Son to the Sleimorps and then he had run afoul of Yvainyasha's family. These memories were truly horrifying.

Nonetheless, Saffiera had to dive deeper, into the memories of Yvainyasha's journeys from his family's nest within his village to the east across the forestscape to where he found his victims. Saffiera carefully studied all of these memories until she found the most important one of all. The memory of Yvainyasha's journey from his family's nest with his two murderous cousins that led them close to the Human colony.

Then from the Human colony were Yvainyasha's memories of his journey to the Swanson's plot with his cousin, Yvainyorin. It was here that Saffiera saw Yvainyasha's memories of his cousin, Yvainyurei's battered and beaten head mounted on a spike. Saffiera quickly pulled he mind out of Yvainyasha's mind in shock. Saffiera stood there, not fully comprehending what she had seen.

Saffiera collapsed to the floor. Special Operative Swanson picked up Yvainyasha by the throat and passed him roughly to the two Colonial Marines, who took him back into custody. Robert went to Saffiera's side, he took out a handkerchief and began wiping away the trickle of blood oozing out of Saffiera's nostrils.

"Are you alright, Saffiera? Are you okay?", Robert enquired.

Saffiera's eyes opened wide in shock and horror, she mumbled telepathically, *"Your Wife, Angelique. She stuck that assassin's head on a spike! It looked like he had been brutalised!"*

"Yes, Saffiera", Robert admitted, trying to explain, "She did it as a warning to the other assassins that she knew were coming for Aria and Ariel", he paused for a moment, should he tell her, then he continued, "That assassin came across Aria and Ariel in our plot on their own. It was a fight to the death and the assassin had no idea how well-trained our twins are."

"The twins, they killed the assassin?", Saffiera questioned.

"No. Our security man, Sylvester, delivered the kill shot", Robert explained.

Saffiera's eyes brimmed with tears, *"I have this assassin's memories in my mind and I do not want them. They are so horrific!"*

A few tears welled in Robert's own eyes, "Unburden yourself, Saffiera. Dump all of those horrors onto me. I should never have involved you in this."

Saffiera reached up as Robert lowered his head and then she touched Robert gently on the temples and then transferred all of Yvainyasha's memories into the Special Operative's mind, "*Taken them, Mr Swanson. These horrors are not for me to hold.*"

Special Operative Robert Swanson felt Yvainyasha's memories flowing into his mind.

Saffiera caught a glimpse of two minds in one. Robert Swanson's own mind with its golden tangle of tightly woven golden thoughts and embedded within it, was a second, much smaller tangle of tightly woven processes, silvery machine thoughts. Neural augments? Saffiera let the glimpse drift away.

Special Operative Swanson stood up and he shook his head several times. His neural augments were collating the transferred memories but their sheer horror was hard to behold. Eventually, after more than a minute, he rolled his head around on his neck. His neck gave off some cracking and popping sounds as the horrors and tension were released.

Robert helped Saffiera to her feet, he turned to Yeannah and Kethera who had been sitting on either side of Saffiera's chair at her desk, "Yeannah, Kethera. Please take Saffiera to sickbay."

Yeannah and Kethera both stood up. Thomas and Richard followed suit and all four were quickly by Saffiera's side.

Special Operative Swanson turned to his Lieutenant, "Lieutenant! Accompany these students to the sickbay. Call in a counsellor, someone well-versed in psychic trauma. Protect and serve!"

"Yes, Sir. Straight away, Sir", Then the Lieutenant quickly led Saffiera and her four friends to the school's sickbay.

Next Special Operative Swanson turned his attention to the Colonial Marines holding Yvainyasha, "Take the assassin to the lockup. Grab the two Marines by the door to assist you. He is not to be harmed! Make sure he is guarded around the clock. And for God's sake, keep him away from my Wife, S.O. Angelique Swanson!", and thought to himself, *"Two heads on a spike are more than enough"*, he did not want to see any more.

The two Colonial Marines left with Yvainyasha in tow and the two Marines at the door followed.

Special Operative Swanson then turned to Miss Bream, "Ma'am. I apologise for this intrusion. Hopefully, we will have this situation under control. Good day, Ma'am", then he left the classroom and the two remaining Colonial Marines outside the door fell in behind.

As Robert walked down the passageway, he called his Wife, Angelique, "Honey, we have the information we require."

"So you caught one of them?", Angelique queried.

"Yes, a Darkling assassin named, Yvainyasha. We have him in custody", Robert reported back.

"Excellent, Bobby! When can I interrogate him?", Angelique requested.

"That's a negatory on the interrogation, Honey", Robert informed her, "We already have the information we need."

"How, Bobby? Sarlia is off-world at Cis-Luns L-Five", Angelique asked in reply.

"Sarlia's Daughter, Saffiera, ripped it straight out of his head", Robert explained, commenting, "Then she transmitted all of the assassin's memories straight to me. They were truly horrific."

"Bobby darling, Sarlia is going to be really pissed!", Angelique informed him.

"I know, Honey. I'll take full responsibility", Robert told her.

"Is Saffiera alright?", Angelique asked.

"Saffiera is now in the school's sickbay. I've requested a psychic trauma counsellor to attend her", Robert explained, then concluded, "Saffiera is incredibly resilient. She'll be okay."

"Let's hope so, my love. Otherwise, my next conversation with Sarlia will be very awkward", Angelique replied.

"On another note, Honey. My neural augments have worked out the most efficient path to the Darkling's villages. That information is being delivered to our stealth drones as we speak", Robert informed her, he then added, "We should have eyes on our targets in around three hours."

"That is most excellent, Bobby! Good work!", Angelique exclaimed, "I might have to wrap myself up as a gift for you tonight."

Robert laughed, "Honey, you don't have to do that. That's completely necessary."

"Perhaps, my Darling. Maybe I just want to", Angelique countered.

"Anyway, something else we need to consider", Robert informed her.

"What would that be, Bobby?", Angelique asked.

"I met two students in the school today, one you already know. Yeannah, Daughter of Yannick and Yealah. A Mimasian Thol and friend of the twins. The other was an Indigenous Thol named Yorlock. He's apparently a neighbour of Yookey", Robert informed her, further explaining, "Both appear to have the potential to become excellent data analysts. At least based on their school profile and reports. Something to consider."

"Bobby, honey, I don't know this Yorlock boy but Yealah is actually a friend of mine and I'm currently teaching her Daughter, Yeannah, to fly", Angelique informed Robert.

"Are you teaching her in Sharona?", Robert asked.

"Yes, of course, Bobby", Angelique confirmed.

"So, Yeannah will have a class five pilot's license. With a bit of data analysis training, Yeannah could become an asset on our team", Robert commented.

"Bobby, darling. Thols, Mimasian or Indigenous are not usually interested in military positions", Angelique reminded him.

"Just saying, Darling, just saying. Mimasian Thols don't usually become pilots either. Yeannah is being trained in a broad-head arrow class starfighter. That in itself is highly unusual", Robert replied, then instructed, "And take those damned heads down. We'll have this all wrapped up by nightfall tomorrow", then he dropped the connection.

33. The Council of Shadows.

The stealth surveillance drones had eyes on their targets ahead of schedule. Fully cloaked and whisper-quiet, they surveilled the Darkling villages. There were six villages in all and each contained a great many nests. Each and every village and nest had precise GPS coordinates registered, and the number of Darkling occupants per nest was recorded in detail. There appeared to be two to four occupants per nest.

The region where these villages were located was dangerous enough in the far western forests. However, it was made all the more hazardous by the Darkling's habit of disposing of the uneaten remains of their victims by simply dumping the carcasses over the sides of their nests to the forest floor far below. Their nests, as expected, were high up in the canopy of exceedingly tall Jula Jula trees.

As a result, the denizens of the western forests treated the area under those trees as a buffet. Chittens, Sleimorps and Wyverns alike all knew there was food aplenty for the scavenging. And even though the Wyverns were the only denizens that might be a threat to the Darklings, as intelligent sub-sapients, they knew better than to bite the very hand that was feeding them.

As Angelique and Robert viewed the data coming through in real-time, they could see a nice pattern emerging. Every Darkling assassin was male, above sixteen years of age and easily identified by the Tarlak tattoo on their chest. That appeared to mark them as having transitioned into adulthood. The females and younglings were not tattooed in this way, although, all of the Darklings had their names tattooed down their spines between their wings.

"Easily identifying markers for cataloguing", Angelique had noted.

"These Darklings may be murderers, assassins and cannibals, but their women and children are still civilians", Robert replied, noting, "They are not to be targeted", he told Angelique firmly.

"I agree entirely, Bobby darling. However, that does complicate matters," Angelique replied, agreeing with her Husband and then commenting, "And yes, I've had those spikes taken down and had the heads buried with their bodies. Once this is over and the threat is removed, we'll have no need for any more warning spikes."

Robert nodded, thank the Gods his Wife wasn't the monster he'd been thinking she was.

"That Tholish boy I mentioned, Yorlock. He approached Yeannah's

Father, Yannick", Robert commented, explaining, "They went to the Tholish High Council Archives. They researched the Scrolls of the Banished. They're all written on a specially treated parchment. The Yvain family was banished to the western forests along with five other families over a thousand years ago. They were banished for working with the Tarlak Slavers that were raiding the Masula Valley from the south."

"So the Darklings have a back story and the Tholish High Council are responsible for creating these monsters", Angelique noted, concluding, "They banished them. They survived and being tainted by the Tarlaks, they took on Tarlak brutality and cannibalism."

"That appears to be the case, although my point is that Yorlock is a natural researcher, an analyst. He sought out information off his own bat, his own initiative. The boy has talents that we can use", Robert replied.

"A career path stands before that boy. Have our recruitment people talk to his Father. Perhaps, Yorlock might become our first Indigenous Thol recruit", Angelique suggested.

"We need to talk to Yealah and Yannick about their Daughter, Yeannah, as well", Robert remarked, "Yeannah is being trained as a class five pilot and I suspect her analytical skills are a level above Yorlock's. Being a Mimasian Thol, she might be more easily convinced."

"Two career paths for Yeannah, a pilot and an analyst. Hell, why not both?", Angelique agreed.

"Time to game this out, Bobby", Angelique announced, then she explained her plan, "Squads of six marines and a Lieutenant. A squad for each village. Each marine controls one stealth attack drone. Armaments. Two needle guns per drone, one with the needles dowsed in a knockout agent, the other with needles dowsed in the Darkling's very own neurotoxin. What do you think?"

"Poetic justice. Take down the assassins with their own neurotoxin and knock out the civilians", Robert replied, "It is acceptable. They won't know what hit them. It will all be over in less than an hour. Although, I can't imagine what the civilians will think when they wake up and find that their menfolk are all dead."

"That is unavoidable, Bobby. We cannot let a single assassin escape", Angelique noted, then continued, "Step two, Bobby. We round up what's left of the Darkling clan and ship them out to that large island in the Eastern Sea. The surrounding waters get infused with nutrients from the outflow of the Masula River. So there's lots of fish and the island itself is a paradise with abundant food."

"And no one lives there because of all the reefs and shoals. We'll be trading one form of exile with another, Angelique", Robert replied, "I am not okay with that."

"Isolation in the western forests of terror and hardship or isolation on an island paradise", Angelique commented, then asked, "I know which I would prefer."

"We can't leave them isolated. We'll need to help them to readjust to a pescatarian diet and send in teachers so we don't repeat past mistakes", Robert explained.

"In the future, they could even reintegrate", Angelique replied.

Robert replied, "Agreed then, let's make it so."

Early the next morning the Colonial Marines were all in place, one squad per Darkling village. They were located several miles away and so there was no danger of being seen. When the attack drones arrived, the surveillance drones fell back to perform their surveillance from a distance. Then the marines went to work and the attack drones were in play.

The cloaked attack drones watched with their thermal imaging systems, waiting for the Darklings to awaken. Once they were awake and standing, it would be far easier for them to distinguish targets from civilians. Then, when the right moment arrived for each nest, the attack drone's A.I. processor kicked into the attack.

One by one the attack drones popped up between the walls of the nests and their canopies. They were cloaked, completely invisible and could not be seen. Homwol's primary Sun, Cathol had risen and the eerie light filtered through the Jula Jula tree's canopy. The Darkling Thols were caught unawares.

The A.I. processor had its targets in sight. Zing, zing and the two civilians, a Mother and Daughter, were knocked out instantly. Zing, zing and the two Darkling assassins, a Father and Son, dropped to the nest's floor dead. The drone's operator sent the attack drone to its next designated target nest. There were many nests in the village, all lined up in a tight sequence.

The dawn attack was carried out swiftly, efficiently and without any remorse. If an assassin was found outside of his nest, he was taken out and left to fall to the forest floor five hundred feet below. Most of the assassins, however, died within their nests, their minds barely awake and their eyes still filled with sleep. Any women or children found outside of their nests were left alone, although most were knocked out within their nests. From start to finish, the entire process took around fifty minutes and all six villages were subdued. Then the Colonial Marines moved in and the attack drones went into automatic *"protect and serve"* mode with the Darkling survivors designated as *"possible hostiles"*.

The Colonial Marines moved in with their whisper-quiet jet packs, taking no chances, they used *"electro prods"* to coerce any *"un-nested"* Mothers or younglings back into the nearest nests. They took no chances because they did not know the level of training that these civilians had received. They could still be a threat, especially with their known use of neurotoxins. Once in the Darkling nests, the unconscious civilians were handcuffed with their hands behind their backs, as were the *"un-nested"* civilians who had been rounded up.

Then, as the unconscious Darklings began awaking, the transports arrived and they stared at the flying machines in abject terror, having never seen such things before. The Colonial Marines, under instructions to be gentle, carried their prisoners onto the transports and gently locked their handcuffs to rings mounted on the interior fuselage. These Humans were tall, broad and impossibly strong and the rings to which they were secured seemed to be *"almost"* overkill.

The prisoners were not going anywhere and as they were in shock at their current predicament, they could not even think to escape. More than a few of the Mothers peed themselves in fear and a few even soiled themselves. The Colonial Marines did their best to keep Mothers and younglings together. Scans were taken of the tattoos running down the Darkling's spines, which were later translated into their names. There were the names of the six Tholish families banished over a thousand years ago. They were the Yvain, the Yootak, the Yikzark, the Yyork, the Yvilkra and the Yslorn families. All of them were exiled long ago in the past by the Tholish High Council.

The bodies of the Darkling assassins were left where they fell and to the eyes of their Wives and Mothers and their younglings, they appeared as if they were sleeping. Yet they all knew that their Husbands and Sons were dead. Then when all of the Darkling Thols were aboard the transport ships, they switched from hover mode to flight and flew swiftly to the east. The view of the landscape flashing past through the ship's portholes was itself frightening.

After the civilians were flown away, the bodies of the Darkling assassins were thrown over the walls of their nests to the forest floor five hundred feet below. This was in exactly the same way that the Darklings themselves had disposed of the uneaten remains of their victims. The Darklings had inadvertently altered the ecosystem in a way that now expected this. It was only fitting that the Chittens, the Sleimorps and the Wyverns would receive their final buffet.

How these denizens would take this final banquet, no one could tell. The Chitten were sapient ant-like insectoids and both the Sleimorps and Wyverns were intelligent sub-sapients. Those who had been the providers of food for the forest's denizens were now themselves the food!

After an hour of flight, the transport ships landed on what was literally named, *"Big Rocky Island"*, in the only clearing available on the Island. The climate here was tropical with abundant rains and the Island was covered in thick forests with many fruiting trees. Bell Nut Fruit and Chillic Fruit trees amongst many others. The surrounding waters were full of various species of fish and what animals did exist were generally small, except a native species of Gudong. There were no predators on the island.

The surviving Darklings were carefully carried out of the transports and then their handcuffs were removed. Many of them rubbed their wrists. Special Operative Robert Swanson had suggested bringing in Yeannah's Father, Yannick, as an interpreter, as he was a Mimasian Thol and was fluent in both the Mimasian and the Indigenous Thols languages. Yannick was more than happy to help.

With all of the Darkling Mothers and the younglings standing in one large group, Yannick greeted them using a megaphone.

Yannick greeted them by telling them their new situation with trills, clicks and soft barks, "You are no longer Darklings. You will no longer eat people. Here on this island, you have plenty of native fruits, vegetables, fish and wild game. You will learn to live in peace and the Humans will help you to prosper. This island is now your home!"

One of the Darkling Mothers yelled out, trilling, clicking and grunting, "Why did you do this thing? Where are our Husbands and our Sons?"

Yannick sighed and replied, "Your most recent *'contracts'* involved a pair of Human same-faced younglings. How did you expect the Humans to react? You brought this upon yourselves by your own actions", he trilled, clicked and softly barked, then he added, trilling and clicking, "The bodies of your Husbands and Sons were given back to the forest."

"Burial by beast", the same Mother responded, nodding with a few trills and clicks, understanding their fate, "It is the way of our people."

“How long will we stay here?”, another Mother who was tightly clutching her youngling Son asked with soft trills and clicks.

“Until you have learned that eating people is bad, very, very bad”, Yannick trilled and clicked in reply as if he was talking to small children who had seriously ingrained bad behaviour, additionally trilling, “Your people may be here for several generations to fully comprehend that lesson and to understand how bad your Darkling behaviour has been.”

“And just where will we live?”, another Darkling Mother asked, trilling and clicking as she held tightly to her two younglings, a boy and a girl.

Yannick pointed to a large stand of tall trees, native trees that were not Jula Jula trees, but nonetheless nearly three hundred feet tall, “The Humans have Androids, metal men, building nests for you in those tall trees. They are not the same as your old Jula Jula trees, but they will suffice. The new nests will be the same as the ones that you are used to. Here you will be safe and the Humans will teach you to fish. Any fruits, vegetables or fungi that you are not familiar with, the Humans will tell you which are safe to eat and which are not”, he trilled, clicked and softly barked.

“And you trust these, Humans?”, another Mother trilled and clicked, she even grunted.

“I am a Mimasian Thol. My people have lived alongside the Humans for far longer than your people were banished in the western forests”, he clicked and trilled back, he added with more trills and clicks, “Remember this, the Humans did not have to spare your lives. They could have killed you all. Instead, they brought you here to learn a new way to live. So, leave all of your violence behind. You no longer need it. You will learn new ways!”

Yannick paused for a moment, then asked, trilling, “Who can tell me about the contracts?”

One of the Mothers scoffed, trilling back, “That is the business of the Skull Sworn! Not the business of women and younglings.”

Yannick nodded in understanding. The Skull Sworn's chests were tattooed with a Tarlak skull.

After Yannick explained the situation to the Darkling survivors, Human civilians, mostly women, provided them with food and water. This was important, woman folk helping other woman folk. It was designed to be a psychological way to gain their trust. At first, the Darklings didn't eat or drink, but after a lot of assurances, they began to do so.

Yannick reported back to Robert, trilling and clicking, "Those contracts. Only the assassins knew of who the contractors were."

Robert looked at the group of Darkling Mothers and their children, "With mercy comes great responsibility", he told Yannick, then noted, "Our colonists will take good care of them."

Yannick replied, "As long as you remember to do so for as long as it takes for them to change."

Robert agreed, "Of course, their reformation is a long-time goal, Yannick", then he changed the subject, "Your Daughter, Yeannah. She looks like becoming a skilled pilot and perhaps even has skills in data analytics."

Yannick smirked, "Robert, we Thols have no interest in the Military. You know that."

"There are other non-military pilot positions and data analytic positions, Yannick", Robert assured him.

"Then those we can discuss, Robert", Yannick agreed, noting, "Although, it does all depend on Yeannah. It will be her decision, after all", he finished with a trilled flourish.

As Yeannah's Mother, Yealah, had become a close friend of the twin's Mother, Angelique, it looked as though her Father, Yannick, would become a close friend of Robert, Angelique's Husband.

While Robert was over at Big Rocky Island with Yannick, helping the surviving Darklings settle into their new home, Angelique informed Yookey and his parents of the good news.

"Yookey, Yarling, Yorvick. I have some great news. Bobby has just informed me that the operation was a success and that the Darkling assassins have been eliminated. So you guys should be somewhat safer", Angelique announced.

Angelique's twin Daughters, Aria and Ariel, who had been standing in the doorway of the room, both replied, "Yes!", in unison.

"So we're all safe now?", Yarling replied in English, laced with trills and clicks.

Angelique frowned, "Somewhat safer, Yarling, somewhat safer", she replied, carefully noting, "The operation couldn't take into account any assassins that were away from their villages at the time and those contracts are still out there."

"So we can't go home yet, I take it?", Yorvick asked, trilling, he understood the situation.

"That is correct, Yorvick", Angelique confirmed, then added cheerfully, "Tomorrow, my metal men will be finished building the tree house. Your family is more than welcome to stay there for as long as you wish."

Yarling smiled, it was a small bitter-sweet smile, but a smile nonetheless, "We can all treat it like a holiday, Yorvick. It's a Mimasian-style tree house. I've never seen inside of one. It will be nice to see how the Mimasian Thols live. Our own nests appear to be so much simpler."

Aria interrupted, "Wait! You mean, you've never seen inside a Mimasian tree house?"

Yarling's Son, Yookey, replied in perfect English, "No, Aria. We Indigenous Thols would never presume to poke our noses into another Thol's nests or tree houses."

Aria smiled, "Then you guys are in for a treat. Ariel and I stayed in Yeannah's tree house with Kethera and Saffiera. It was really cool!"

"And you'll be really safe, too", Ariel chimed in, "Mum will assign the Androids to protection duty. Day or night, no one, no one at all will be able to harm you."

Aria commented with a fierce look in her eyes, "If any more assassins turn up, Ariel and I will beat the tar out of them. No one is hurting my Yookey!", which made Angelique roll her eyes.

Ariel quickly added, "I've got your back, Aria!"

"Which reminds me", Angelique stepped in, "The assassin that we took down at your nest complex. He ransacked your nest looking for information. After the tree house is finished, I'll assign the alpha Android to go there and clean things up a bit. Maybe even grab some more of your belongings for you as well. Having your own things around you might help you feel more at home."

"How will it know what to bring back?", Yorvick queried.

"Easy, Yorvick. You and Yarling tell me what you need", then Angelique touched her right temple, "Then I transmit that information directly to the Android using my neural implants in such a way that it understands."

Yarling smiled at Angelique, feeling somewhat more secure yet still uneasy.

Later, Yookey, with Aria's guidance allowed, Yarling and Yorvick to view the surveillance drone's footage of the assassin, Yvainyurei's, attempt on the twin's lives. What they saw was both shocking and reassuring, yet equally perplexing. Two teenage girls had managed to disable the highly skilled and trained assassin with both skill and ease, they were methodical. The assassin had been clearly outmatched!

"You see. Ariel and I will not allow anyone to harm any of you", Aria explained.

Yarling and Yorvick both wondered how two sixteen-year-old younglings, Aria and Ariel, could be so fierce. Aria's mention of their training didn't seem to explain it. Were all Humans like this?

By mid-afternoon, Robert Swanson had dropped Yannick off back home at his tree house in his northern forest village. Shortly after Robert was back at his plot amongst the bluegrass meadows. Angelique was there to greet him with a stern look on her face.

"What are you doing back here?", Angelique enquired.

Robert looked surprised, "Nice to see you too, Angelique. Now, what's with the attitude?"

Angelique frowned, "Bobby, our girls have invited their friends over. Their Mothers are coming over as well. Everyone wants to know what's going on, Bobby. Sarlia will be bringing them. So naturally, you had better make yourself scarce!"

"Okay, so we're holding gatherings in a crisis now, are we?", Robert asked, then he questioned, "Wait! Why do I need to make myself scarce? Sarlia is a Martian. I'll apologise and she'll move on."

Angelique rolled her eyes and tapped her right temple, "Bobby! Sarlia drinks! She has a penchant for drinking Martian Sweet Cherry Red wine."

"Don't be ridiculous, Darling. Martians don't drink!", Robert replied and then it dawned on him, "Wait! Sarlia is a hybrid!"

"Bingo, Bobby! If you used your neural augments for more than just military matters, you would have checked the genealogical archives. You'd know that Sarlia's Grandmother was a Folcrom. A very powerful psi-corp operative!"

"Okay then. I'd better do more than an apology, I'd better grovel", Robert replied, he understood!

"Here's her backstory, Bobby", Angelique started, then divulged, "Sarlia was the youngest Martian Elder selected for their Council of Elders. After her Husband was murdered, she turned to drink as a crutch. The Council was responsible for her Husband's death, it was a diplomatic mission that went tits up. That's why the Martian Council of Elders shipped her all the war out here. A Martian Elder with her potential and a penchant for drinking. They made her our Martian Ambassador and shipped her off! Sarlia isn't an alcoholic, but she does have an Earth Human side to her nature. So don't forget that!"

Robert nodded, "I'll try not to anger her. I have no wish to be psychically lobotomised."

"Good then, Bobby. I prefer to keep you just the way you are", Angelique replied.

Sarlia's hovercar landed in the plot shortly after. Saffiera, Kethera and Yeannah quickly alighted and rushed over to the homestead. Yeannah even took the opportunity to spread her wings and fly. Their Mothers, Yealah, Kayala and Sarlia, took their time to step out of the hovercar and walked over to the homestead at their own Motherly pace. Once inside the homestead, Aria and Ariel greeted them and then led them straight down the long hallway to their bedroom to tell their friends everything that had happened. Yookey followed along after them, he and Aria were emotionally attached to each other.

Yealah and Kayala entered the homestead and greeted Angelique and Robert. Sarlia, however, walked straight up to Robert and, before anyone could act, slapped him right hard across his left cheek. It was such an odd sight. Sarlia was tall, five ten and very slender. Robert was easily six foot six and built like a muscular, solid brick shit house. Years of military training at three gs in military training cylinders, yet he took the slap without responding. Yealah and Kayala both stared in shock!

Angelique was about to instinctively respond, but Robert raised his right hand up and remarked loudly, "I completely deserved that. My actions were unconscionable!"

"What the hell were you fucking thinking asking my Daughter to rake through a cannibal's mind for fucking information?", Sarlia snarled telepathically, she was livid!

"I sincerely apologise, Sarlia. We had a time-critical operation ongoing and the telepath I needed was off-world at Cis-Luns Colonial Central Command",

Robert both apologised and explained.

"You should have waited until I got back!", Sarlia snapped back, asking, *"Couldn't you have waited until nightfall, when I was back planet-side?"*

"In hindsight, Sarlia. I probably should have and again, I do apologise", a contrite Robert replied as his left cheek turned red where Sarlia had slapped him.

"Apology accepted! You get to keep your frontal lobes. This time!", Sarlia replied, then she asked, *"Did you get what you needed?"*, a very telling remark about Sarlia's abilities.

"Yes, we did. The operation at first light, took down the assassins and the Darkling civilians are now in a rehab settlement", Robert replied, hoping this new information would settle Sarlia down.

"Good. At least there's that. I spent half the night fixing the fucking mess those cannibal memories did to Saffiera's psyche", Sarlia replied and then she warned, *"Never again, Robert! Never again!"*

Robert nodded in agreement, then commented, "While you're here. I'll have Mike service your hovercar for you."

Angelique smiled, "Belay that, Bobby. I believe that Sarlia would prefer Mike to service her hovercar back at her glade. Sarlia has other things in mind for Mike, I do believe."

Robert nodded to his Wife and then left in the direction of their spacecraft hangar. He was more than happy to remove himself from an angry Sarlia's presence.

Angelique looked at Sarlia, "I have never seen Bobby look so contrite! You really rattled him."

Sarlia smiled back, *"I could really use a drink, but I didn't bring any wine!"*

Angelique smiled back at Sarlia, "No wine today, Sarlia. We have active operations in progress."

Then, Angelique began explaining everything that had happened since the inter-species relationship incident on the preceding Monday. When Yealah, Kayala and Sarlia heard all of the details of the events, they were quite shocked!

Saffiera and the twins, Aria and Ariel, were sitting in stunned silence. Saffiera had picked up on her Mother's angry broadcasts. So had Aria and Ariel, they were scions of Folcrom Tafazah and they had recently had their latent psychic potentials awakened by Sarlia, Saffiera's Mother.

"Did your Mum just beat up our Dad?", Aria asked with incredulity.

Ariel rolled her eyes, "You exaggerate everything, Aria. Dad just copped a slap. A hard Slap."

Saffiera replied in her usual telepathic way, *"Yep, my Mum just gave your Dad a huge slap!"*

Kethera's eyes lit up and her whiskers twitched, "That is so weird. The twin's Dad is huge."

Yeannah's face took on a thoughtful look, "Saffiera, I know your Mum's a bit different. I mean, she does drink wine and Martians normally don't, but physically hitting someone. That's so un-Martian-like. I was born inside of Mimas and the Martians, they are so different to your Mum. Are there any differences between Martians from Mimas and Martians from Mars?"

"No, there's no difference and my Mum was actually born inside of Mimas", Saffiera responded.

"I'm sorry, Saffiera, but that doesn't make sense", Yeannah remarked.

"Hmm, my Mum does hold a lot of secrets. I just found out on Monday afternoon that I was a hybrid and my Mother has neglected to explain that to me, even though she said she would", Saffiera replied with a somewhat disappointed look on her face.

Yeannah smiled, it was a wry smile, "I think it's time we worked around your Mother, Saffiera. Something just doesn't add up."

Saffiera nodded and replied, *"Let's do that, shall we?"*

"I'm surprised you haven't thought of doing this yourself, Saffiera", Yeannah told her as she connected her data tablet to the Earth's Interstellar Alliance genealogical database, "You actually once told us about this data site", and the site came up on the screen in the twin's bedroom.

"I know, Yeannah. I've just been too scared to look", Saffiera replied and then Kethera reached out and held her hand in support while Yeannah performed a few searches.

The data came up on the screen, there was Saffiera, her Mother, Sarlia and her Father!

Yeannah smiled as she read out the data, "Saffiera, your Father was Anthony (Tony) Beaufort. He was the Earth's Ambassador to Mars, not the planet Mars, specifically to the Martian people on Mars. So it looks like your Mother emigrated from Mimas to Mars, met your Dad and actually married him. It was an official marriage! Not just the usual living together. You know what that means, don't you?"

"Not really, Yeannah", Saffiera replied.

"Saffiera! You and your Mother have the right to use the Beaufort surname", Yeannah explained.

Yeannah frowned, "Saffiera, it says here your Father was killed during negotiations to free thirty Martian hostages. They were scientists held for ransom by Neptunian pirates. They blew him up along with the hostages! You would have been only two, not yet three at the time."

"Which explains why I don't remember him", Saffiera understood, she squeezed Kethera's hand for comfort and Kethera quickly wrapped her arms around her.

"That might explain your Mother's drinking. Grief does that", Kethera noted.

"Okay, we now know about your Dad, let's look more closely at your Mum", Yeannah commented.

The data came up the screen, "Your Grandparents on your Father's side were both Martian. Ziltack was your Grandfather and Vilny was your Grandmother. On your Mother's side, again both Martians, Tivling was your Grandfather and Carol was your Grandmother", Yeannah reported.

"Wait! Carol is an Earth Human name! Not Martian at all", Saffiera exclaimed in confusion.

Yeannah drilled deeper and the data came on the screen, "Holy crap!", Yeannah exclaimed and then she turned to Saffiera, "Your Great-grandmother was Lady Folcrom Silvana! Her occupation is listed as psi-corp operative!"

"My Great-grandmother was a Folcrom from Earth!", Saffiera telepathically exclaimed.

"It says it right here, Saffiera and there's a hyper-link", Yeannah replied as she clicked on the hyper-link, another window popped with Silvana's psi-corp profile, "Holy fuck! She was a scion of Folcrom Tafazah as well!"

"If your Great-grandmother was a scion, then so was your Grandmother, your Mother and you, as well, Saffiera", Ariel explained.

Ariel noted dryly as she looked at her Sister, Aria and Saffiera, "That means that we three are all distant cousins!"

All the pieces clicked into place, *"It all makes perfect sense! My Mother can detect scions because she is, in fact, a scion herself!"*, it was quite a revelation.

Kethera noted, she had just done the math in her head, "It also means your Mother is one quarter Earthling and with you having an Earthling Father, that makes you five eights Earthling!"

"Thank you, Kethera. Sadly, I can do the math as well", Saffiera remarked.

Saffiera's friends watched as Saffiera got up, marched out of the bedroom and headed straight to her Mother. Her friends followed close behind.

Saffiera walked up to her Mother, crouched down and before Sarlia could react, she touched her forehead to her Mother's, transmitting, *"This is what I know, Mother. You can explain it all to me later, along with your apology!"*, then she pushed everything she'd leaned directly into her Mother's mind, before stalking off outside the homestead with her friends in tow.

"Oh shit! The cats are all out of the bag now!", Sarlia exclaimed telepathically, *"Excuse me, Ladies, I have something rather urgent to deal with"*, then she got up and followed her Daughter.

Sarlia approached her Daughter cautiously and Saffiera's friends moved aside to give them plenty of space.

Sarlia started off with an apology, *"Saffiera, I am so sorry. I was hoping to keep all of this from you because it is so painful for me and I didn't want you to suffer as I have"*, then she leant in and gently touched her forehead to Saffiera's.

Sarlia very gently transferred all of the relevant information. How the Earth's psi-corp has affected their family with their endless missions and responsibilities. How the Martian Elders were responsible for her Father's death by their dreadful decisions. That was why she drank and the reason for her pent-up emotional pain and frustration. Why they were on Secundus. Sarlia was an Ambassador in exile, never to return home. There was so much more on top of that as well. Sarlia transferred all of it and at the end of it all, Saffiera collapsed onto the bluegrass of the meadow in tears. Sarlia sat down beside Saffiera, wrapped her arms about her and rocked her in her gentle embrace.

Now Saffiera knew everything, except now she wished that she didn't!

It was around a half an hour before Saffiera could compose herself enough to get up. Saffiera stood up and wiped away her tears on her sleeve.

"Well, Mother. Since we're fucking exiles and we're stuck out here, then we'd better make everyone safe", Saffiera's face took on a look, fierce with determination, she marched back into the Swanson's homestead, she was on a mission.

"Mrs Swanson. Is it okay if my Mother and I stay overnight?", Saffiera requested.

"Yes, of course, Saffiera, but why?", Angelique asked curiously.

"I was raking around inside a cannibal assassin's mind, remember. So we need to visit the Tholish High Council in full session. Tomorrow morning, before they've had time to really wake up", Saffiera announced the beginning of her plan.

"The Tholish High Council?", Angelique enquired.

"Yes, Mrs Swanson. We'll need yourself, your Husband, Aria, Ariel and a squad of Colonial Marines", Saffiera listed off her requirements, *"Oh, we also need to let them know that we are coming. We want every last one of them to be there. The Council session is compulsory, not a single Councillor can be absent."*

"Okay, Saffiera. I'll make the request", Angelique agreed.

"Request? Hell no, Mrs Swanson. Demand that they all be there. Absolutely no exceptions", Saffiera corrected, explaining with a wry smile, *"Someone put out those contracts on the twins and Yookey's family and my bet is, it was one or more of the Councillors themselves!"*

Saffiera then turned on her heels and went out to play with her friends, leaving Sarlia, Angelique, Yealah and Kayala all wondering what in the blue blazes had just happened.

Saffiera smiled to herself as she played with her friends. If she was a scion, then hell or high water, she was bloody well going to behave like one!

The next morning, Saffiera, Sarlia, Aria, Ariel, Angelique and Robert climbed aboard Angelique's starfighter, Sharona. Kethera, Kayala, Yeannah and Yealah had also stayed overnight and they, along with Yookey and his parents, watched as Angelique's starfighter prepared to leave.

Saffiera requested to fly Sharona to the meeting with the Tholish High Council. Angelique had looked to her husband, Robert, who messaged his Wife via his neural augments in the affirmative. Saffiera took the pilot's seat while everyone else strapped themselves in. Angelique used her neural implants to check Saffiera's navigation settings before she launched.

"Saffiera, I'll be logging this flight against your training flight time", Angelique commented.

Saffiera then launched Sharona, hovered for a few moments at thirty metres altitude, before punching the throttle and flying off to the Tholish High Council's chambers. The trip took around twenty minutes.

What did take longer was flying low under the Jula Jula forest, flying under the towering trees and dangerously low branches to their final landing place. When they arrived and touched down, they found the squad of Colonial Marines had already arrived in their colonial troop transport. Lieutenant Salaam Baker and his six-man squad were waiting for them.

When they'd all alighted from the starfighter, Sharona, Lieutenant Baker saluted Special Operatives Angelique and Robert Swanson. Robert shifted his eyes to look at Saffiera, however, the Lieutenant was slow to understand.

"Lieutenant. Brevet Special Operative Saffiera is in charge of this mission", Robert announced.

"Miss Saffiera Beaufort", Saffiera corrected telepathically.

"Miss Saffiera Beaufort", her Mother, Sarlia, thought to herself, she'd used her Father's surname.

The Lieutenant snapped to attention and saluted Saffiera, who then returned the salute before they all made their way to Tholish High Council Chambers.

When they entered the Council Chambers, Saffiera walked boldly to the centre of the stage where normally the High Chancellor himself would be standing at his podium. Aria and Ariel took up flanking positions in front of Saffiera, while Angelique and Robert took up flanking positions behind her. Her Mother, Sarlia, stood proudly by her side and the fully armed Colonial Marines blocked all of the exits. Lieutenant Baker stood to one side, making sure his marines were well placed. No one was leaving the Council Chambers!

Saffiera's telepathic broadcast boomed in the Councillor's minds, *"You have traitors in your midst! Traitors who thought to assassinate the Mardhin!"*, she gestured to Aria and Ariel, *"Traitors who thought to assassinate a Tholish family! Today, those traitors will be brought to book!"*

The entire council chamber erupted in chaos and shouts of condemnation at the accusations.

Saffiera's telepathic mind boomed in the councillor's minds, *"Silence! Do NOT try to leave this chamber. If the Colonial Marines don't get you, either I or the Mardhin will lobotomise you!"*

Fear took over the councillors and they all quickly retook their seats.

Saffiera looked to her friend, Aria, who was forward on her left, *"Seek out the contractors"*, then she looked to Aria's twin Sister, Ariel, who was forward on her right, *"Seek out the contractors."*

The twins moved forward towards the frightened councillors, their recently awakened latent gifts reaching out. They were the Mardhin, they were scions of Folcrom Tafazah, they could do this! One by one, they scanned the councillor's minds.

Aria pointed out one of the councillors, *"That one there. He wrote the contract!"*, her thoughts resonated across the chamber and the increase in fear was palpable.

Saffiera's mind boomed out once more as she pointed to the councillor, *"You! Come to the front and prostrate yourself on the chamber floor!"*, the councillor did not move, *"Aria, if he does not move, burn him where he stands!"*

The councillor quickly found his legs, ran to the front and threw himself face first to the ground.

Aria continued scanning for any other traitors.

Ariel pointed out another councillor, "*That one, up there near the back. He extracted the frames from the video and printed them out. The photographs of Aria, Yookey and our whole group!"*, her mind also resonated across the chamber.

Saffiera's mind boomed out again as she pointed to the councillor, *"You! Come to the front and prostrate yourself on the chamber floor with your fellow traitor!"*

He first stepped back but then noticed the Colonial Marine raise his pulse laser rifle.

Ariel's thoughts bellowed out, *"Colonial Marines do not miss!"*

The councillor changed his mind and made his way to the front of the chamber and laid himself down on the floor next to his fellow traitor. Ariel then went back to scanning the councillors.

Saffiera's mind boomed across the Tholish High Council chamber once more, *"Are there any more traitors amongst you? Do I have to scan your minds as well? You will find me to be most unpleasant!"*

Aria smirked and then pointed, *"You there, trying to hide under the seats. You know that doesn't work! Get down here with your fellow traitors"*, her telepathic voice commanded.

Ariel smiled, *"Saffiera, that one was the leg man. The go-between who contacted the assassins and handed them the contracts"*, she telepathically informed.

Saffiera held up her hand and beckoned him forward with her index finger and then as he approached the front, she pointed to the floor where he laid himself down beside his fellow traitors.

Saffiera instructed the twins, *"Aria, Ariel, keep on scanning. I want to make sure we've got them all"*, then she turned to her Mother, *"Mum, you scan too. Just in case we've missed any."*

All four of them scanned the councillors once more to make sure they'd gotten them all.

They had the three corrupt and treacherous councillors and Saffiera asked the High Chancellor telepathically, *"Are you certain that every councillor is present?"*

The High Chancellor bowed before Saffiera, Aria and Ariel, "Yes, Mardhin. All of the councillors are all present", he, once a sceptic, was now a true believer.

Special Operative Robert Swanson sent a message to Lieutenant Baker via his neural augments. His marines converged on the stage and handcuffed the Tholish councillor's hands behind their backs. Their wings were furled and unable to move. Then the Colonial Marines led them out to their transport and locked the councillors to the internal fuselage prisoner rings.

Saffiera's mission was now complete.

The contracts put out on Aria, Ariel and Yookey and his family were as good as dead!

The Colonial Marines had left, but something was still amiss. Saffiera could not put her finger on it and asked her Mother and the twins if they could feel it as well.

Sarlia replied with softer telepathic tones, *"I feel it too, Sweety. Someone else is here!"*

Aria and Ariel both nodded in agreement, with Ariel replying, *"There's something behind us!"*

Saffiera, the twins, Sarlia, Angelique and Robert all turned around.

Saffiera reached out telepathically, "*You there, show yourselves!*"

The two interlopers didn't move. They'd been there since the councillors had arrived, watching as they always did. They'd watch the previous day at the Swanson's plot, unseen as always. They'd both been to Sarlia's glade many times as well. Yet today was different.

There were two Earth psychics and two Martian hybrid psychics standing before them and the young girls were now almost fully awakened. Their sheer power was palpable, much as was their own.

The Lady Folcrom Carol spoke to her colleague silently, *"Well then. They see us, don't they? We should make an appearance. How about we make it flashy!"*

"Flashy is always good", Lord Folcrom Scintaro replied.

There was a sudden flash of light that stretched between the chamber ceiling and the floor, then all of a sudden two people appeared. They both wore long, hooded robes of shimmering black, like the shimmering of raven feathers.

Robert's and Angelique's first reaction was to draw their pulsed laser pistols and take aim, but they quickly re-holstered them again when Sarlia's mind shouted out, *"Mother!"*

Every councillor in the chamber, including the High Chancellor himself, prostrated themselves on the floor, muttering, "Mardhin! Mardhin!", over and over.

Sarlia raised her hands and asked telepathically, *"Where the hell did you come from? I thought you were back on the Earth with psi-corp?"*

"I was, Sweety, but when those horrible Martian Elders sent you here, I blinked across space to follow you. Myself and my colleague, Folcrom Scintaro", she answered and gestured to Scintaro.

"Seriously, Mother! I've been here eleven years and you never once thought to, I don't know, stop by and say hello?", Sarlia chided.

"You know we Council of Shadows members are supposed to stay hidden, Sweety", Sarlia's Mother, Carol, replied.

Sarlia was about to say something more, but Saffiera held her arm and said, *"Grandmother?"*

Tears welled in Carol's eyes, and she stepped forward, wrapping her arms around Saffiera, *"Oh, Baby girl. I've missed you so much!"*

Folcrom Scintaro looked around the chamber at the Tholish High Councillors, still prostrating themselves on the floor, *"Carol. We probably should hold this reunion back at the glade."*

"You are probably right, Scintaro", Carol agreed.

The Lady Folcrom Carol's mind boomed with authority across the council chamber, *"Esteemed members of the Tholish High Council. I hereby task you with rooting out corruption and treachery from amongst your fellows. Do these things as I instruct, lest we have to come back and do them for you!"*

Carol gestured to her Daughter and Granddaughter, then to the twins and their parents, Angelique and Robert, to form a circle, which they did.

"Okay, everyone, all hold hands", Carol instructed telepathically.

They all joined hands and as they did so, Carol jaunted the whole group back to the Sharona, Angelique's starfighter. They found themselves inside with perplexed looks on their faces.

Carol looked around, *"Good, we didn't lose anyone. Okay, my Darling Granddaughter, fly us all back to the Swanson's plot and we can talk in a more cordial location."*

Saffiera flew the Sharona back to the Swanson's plot and they spent the rest of the day talking about what the Lady Folcrom Carol and her colleague, Lord Folcrom Scintaro, had been doing on Secundus. As legend had it, there was a tower called Kiltain, far to the west of the farthest western forests, beyond the Western Mountains, in a place called the Mardhin Plateau. A place that only the Mardhin or the foolhardy might go!

That was where the Folcrom lived on Secundus, hidden under psychic obscuration fields and cloaked technologically in splendid isolation. The Tower Kiltain had originally been built by the Lord Folcrom Forkbraid and the Lady Folcrom Selene, well after the second Horridian War ended in the late twenty three hundreds, over eleven hundred years earlier.

It was they who had rediscovered how to blink and jaunt. A talent that had been lost nearly two centuries earlier due the genetic psychic dilution of the Council of Shadows around the year twenty one eighty. Apparently, they had set up towers like the Tower Kiltain on many habitable worlds within fifty light years of the Earth, each with its own psychic teleportation portal.

Folcrom above level ten were capable of jaunting across the star fields, while those at level nine and the non-Folcrom, who were even lower, needed a psychic portal and often years of training. In every world where Earth had colonies, the Folcrom from the Council of Shadows were present as well.

Occasionally, Carol and Scintaro would jaunt around the planet to keep tabs on things. Making sure everything was okay and making adjustments as necessary. Over the past couple of weeks, they'd been watching three budding young psychics develop their potentials. One of course being Carol's own Granddaughter, of whom she was very proud.

Aria and Ariel were both surprised when Scintaro told them that one day they too would become Folcrom and likely be inducted into the Council Shadows alongside Saffiera. Most of the scions of Folcrom Tafazah join the Council of Shadows, if they're gifts are realised, but not all of them. It is a choice. This was something that Saffiera's Mother, Sarlia, had declined many years ago, when Saffiera had been born.

Robert headed over to the hangar to check things with Sylvester, Michelle, Mike and Anne, to let them know how the operation had gone. Meanwhile, the Mothers. Angelique, Kayala, Yealah and Yarling listened with wrapped attention as Carol and Scintaro gave them quick history lessons of Secundus, since the first Folcrom arrived over eleven hundred years ago up to the present day.

Aria, Ariel, Kethera, Yeannah and Saffiera, along with Aria's boyfriend Yookey, listened in as well. After all, the Folcrom were real, the Mardhin were real, the Star Striders were real and so was the Council of Shadows. They were all largely one and the same to a huge degree, except, of course, there were psi-corp Folcrom who were not so gifted as those who were inducted into the Council of Shadows.

Only level ten psychics and higher were eligible. The Council of Shadows remains hidden to this day, even from the other three branches of psi-corp. The watchers who watch the watchers and guide the greater mass of humanity across the star fields.

Yookey, of course, wanted to hear about the Tunnels of Dread and the tales of the Tarlak Slave raids and the Tarlak Wars that followed. Sadly for Yookey, they declined to tell of those horrific and bloody days. Their stories and tales lasted most of the day and eventually late into the night. Finally, for the first time since the murder of her Husband, Tony, Sarlia felt content.

Saffiera ended up falling asleep in Sarlia's arms. The world seemed changed somehow, different, but in a good way. Eventually, a content Sarlia fell asleep with her Daughter still asleep in her arms. Sarlia had pleasant dreams for once. She dreamt of a man her height, five ten, with ropy muscles and a three-day growth. Three years later, Sarlia married that man, Mike Johnson, who was the Swanson's flight mechanic and engineer.

Saffiera had decided to use her deceased Father's surname as her own. So naturally, Special Operative Angelique Swanson sent a record of that information into the Earth's Interstellar Alliance archives using her neural augments. That then transferred automatically into the Alliance's genealogical database, amongst many other interconnected databases. This triggered an immediate alert!

Saffiera's deceased Father was Ambassador Anthony Beaufort of the Dumas Beauforts and as such, he was a direct descendant of the Dumas family, of Stuart Dumas himself. A legal notification was automatically sent to Dumas Legal Incorporated and it was immediately actioned upon. Before the day was out, a legal representative was sent from the Earth to Xi Bootis A Secundus, otherwise known as Homwol, Vale and Tarlakand.

Saffiera Beaufort had been confirmed as the sole legal beneficiary of the Beaufort Family Fortune. Saffiera was also a Dumas Family Legacy, with all of the ramifications thereof. Saffiera was soon to find out that she was extraordinarily wealthy! Wealthy beyond belief! Planet purchasing wealthy! And the Dumas Legal Representative would arrive in just three days!

Saffiera had no idea what was coming and it was coming quickly. Life-altering changes were heading her way. As a Martian telepath and a scion of Folcrom Tafazah, a powerful psychic, Saffiera was well-positioned to deal with them all. So she did, with her proud Mother, Sarlia, standing by her side!

Special Operatives Angelique and Robert Swanson received an urgent message via their Neural Augments, *"Saffiera Beaufort! V.I.P. Status. Immediate Protect and Serve!"*, which kind of caught them both by surprise.

Sixteen-year-old Saffiera was far more than she appeared to be and now, the Interstellar Alliance was ordering an immediate around-the-clock protection detail!

Special Operatives Angelique and Robert looked at each and shook their heads, *"What next?"*, they both silently questioned, didn't Angelique just update an archive?

Yvainyasha was removed from his cell and taken by Colonial Marines to a waiting colonial troop transport. A Mimasian Thol interpreter informed Yvainyasha that he was the last of his people and that all of his Darkling assassin relatives and friends had been killed by the Colonial Marines. The translator did not mention that the Darkling women and younglings had been relocated to Big Rocky Island to be reformed. Where Yvainyasha was going, he did not need to know.

Yvainyasha was shoved inside the door and immediately noticed three other Thols. They all wore the robes of High Councillors and one of them he knew. They were also prisoners! The go-between who brought his people the contracts! So the contractors had been caught and any contract was now null and void! Yvainyasha's handcuffs were locked to a ring against the troop ship's inner hull and within minutes, the ship took off.

Yvainyasha's people had believed that the Humans and the strange new Thols, the Mimasians, lived somewhere on top of the highest clouds, but now he was in for a shock. Yvainyasha could see out of the troop ship's porthole opposite him. The porthole was large enough to afford him a good view. The former Tholish High Councillors could see out of the portholes opposite them as well. The troop ship flew up through the various cloud layers. Then, when it got to what Yvainyasha thought must surely be the highest clouds and their destination, instead the troop ship continued onwards.

A very few confused Yvainyasha watched as the troop ship flew higher and higher, as the sky outside the porthole began to turned dark. Soon, it was so dark that the sky outside was inky black. If Yvainyasha strained his eyes, he could see the stars amidst the inky blackness. Yvainyasha's heart beat hard with fear. Where the fuck was he going? His eyes shot wide open in sheer terror.

The former High Councillor, who had been the go-between, spoke to Yvainyasha with a few trills and soft clicks, "The Humans and the Mimasian Thols. They travel the void between the stars."

Yvainyasha did not understand what that even meant, but something told him he would not be returning to Homwol anytime soon.

After many hours of travel, the colonial transport began to circle something that made no sense to him at all. It was a large Stamford Torus space station. A penal colony simply called, the Stamford Penal Colony in the Cis-Luns L-Four orbital zone. The troop transport circled the space station three times before it had permission to dock.

Yvainyasha and the three councillors found themselves being led down a long corridor and then led down several other corridors before reaching a bulkhead with a door built into it.

The sign above the door read, *"Sector twelve, cell block thirteen. Dangerous Prisoners. Caution at all times"*, not that any of the Thols could read it.

Yvainyasha and the three councillors were led to a large cell and shoved through the door, which was locked behind them. The cell could easily hold twelve people, yet there were only four beds set up. Beyond that, there were seats, a table, a bench with a sink, a toilet and a wash cubicle. Everything was fixed to the floor. Along one wall, there was a section that was open and tightly lined with bars.

Yvainyasha and the three councillors walked over to the opening and looked through the bars, beyond which was a corridor and another cell opposite it.

Two guards looked at the Thols and one of them said, "These ones are not a problem. They're just Indigenous Thols, no problem, really. Although, that one with the tattoo is an assassin and a cannibal. He's the last assassin of the Darkling clan."

As the lead guard, he knew exactly who the prisoners were, it was his job to know.

The other younger, newer guard nodded in understanding, then a commotion occurred in the opposite cell and to the shock of Yvainyasha and the three councillors, six Tarlaks appeared. They grabbed the bars, reached through them, snarling and barking at them in Tarlak.

To the new guard who had never seen a Tarlak before, they looked like a cross between an angry gorilla and an angry gargoyle. They were grotesque, which is precisely how they were genetically designed to be six million years ago. To think that the closest living genetic relatives were the Thols was hard to believe. Tarlaks had been genetically altered from Thols!

The lead Guard pushed the other guard slightly back and commented, "These Tarlak fuckers. They look big. They are seven feet tall and the sheer length of their arms gives them power and leverage, but you've received a year of three G training in an O'Neil military colony. If one of them grabs you, just break its fucking arm. Their bones are hollow, which makes them weak. Thols have six-fingered hands grouped in three pairs and the outer pairs are opposable. So, for a Thol, that gives them great dexterity. Tarlaks have the same kind of hand and that gives them great grappling abilities, but they can't make a fist! Tarlaks are designed for flight, not hand-to-hand or melee combat."

The younger guard asked, "What if one of them gets out?"

"Fuck lad, use your training. You are faster and stronger. You know how to kill with a single strike! Just step inside and punch the fucker in the ribs. Once one or two of their ribs are broken, they back down right quickly. It's all about their bio-mechanics. Broken ribs for a Tarlak means no flight and difficulty breathing. Just one solid punch to their sternum can kill them!", the lead guard replied with brutal honesty.

"I'm not sure I'm comfortable with hurting them, Sir", the newer guard replied.

"Look, if one them get their teeth into your neck, you're dead. I know it's brutal, but brutality is the only thing that they respect", the lead guard explained, noting, "Look, if you injure one, we tranq the lot of them and then extract the injured one and fix it while it's still unconscious."

The new guard nodded, then asked, "Why are they even here?"

The lead guard shook his head and sighed, "There was a group of researchers in the south lands, well east of Tarlak territory. A place called Korland. They thought that they were safe. These fuckers caught them, tortured them, killed them and then ate them. To a Tarlak, we are all just food. I've seen the drone footage from the Korland incident, it was a totally unprovoked attack. It was straight out of the blue! No survivors!"

Then the guards moved off further down the corridor, the lead guard continued talking, "The Tarlaks aren't intelligent sub-sapients. They are fully sapient and nearly as smart as you or I. Never, ever underestimate them. You do that and you're a dead man. No one wants to become a Tarlak turd!"

The three councillors all understood English and that Humans were capable of killing Tarlaks!

The six Tarlaks looked across the corridor at the Thols.

One of the Tarlaks pointed at them and in Tarlak, he said one single word with a grunt, "Food!"

Yvainyasha and the three councillors walked away from the bars into a section of the cell from which they could not be seen by the Tarlaks. This was their life from then on.

Towards the end of term two, Miss Bream had been grading her history class's group assignment, "*The Great Explosion – The Outward Interplanetary Expansion"*, it was good to see that every group had chosen the correct, *"Great Explosion"*, there were four they could have chosen from across history.

Part of the task, the most important task, was choosing the right one, not they she expected anyone to get that wrong. The last on the list of reports to grade had been the girl's report.

Miss Bream had left theirs till last, as they were the only mixed species study group in her class. Miss Bream noted as she read through their report, Aria's brutal honesty and conclusions, Ariel's carefully crafted arguments, Saffiera's extraordinary detailed notes, Yeannah's analytical insights and even Kethera's deep emotional understanding. Their report was extraordinary and she gave them an A++ at ninety-nine point five percent!

Miss Bream had noted that Saffiera, a Martian, was now using her deceased Father's surname, something that was highly unusual for a Martian.

Kethera achieved her class five pilot's license shortly after her sixteenth birthday. She was the first Carlin ever to achieve a pilot's license, let alone a class five license. A few years later, Kethera and her bond mate, Richard, married. With the help of Ambassador Sarlia, Kethera was able to purchase an interplanetary space freighter. Kethera was now the Captain of a space freighter and she made Richard her first mate, whom she then trained as a pilot as well. Kethera's freight business was booming and they were doing extremely well.

When Kethera and Richard finally had hybrid kits, they were born in space. Kethera raised them on her freighter. Kethera and Richard homeschooled them as best they could. When they were back at Colonial Central in Cis-Luns L-Five and between freight runs, they would fly down to Vale to visit Kethera's parent's plot and visit the twins at the Swanson's plot. Richard rarely visited his racist and specist Mother, leaving her to his long-suffering Father.

Kethera's Mother, Kayala and her Father, Krylor, doted on the hybrid kits, they spoiled them rotten. Kayala was amazed by their features. They largely took after Kethera, being most recognisably Carlin, with cat-like ears and whiskers, even a Carlinish tail. They even walked on the pads of their feet, giving them a digitigrade walking gate. Where they differed was the lack of blue stripes, the luxurious sandy blond hair and the girls having only two breasts instead of six, their eyes also had Human circular pupils instead of cat-like pupils slits. Their eyes were a delightful hazel colour like their Father's. The first pair of same-faced girl kits that were born, Kethera and Richard, named them after their friends, the Swanson twins Aria and Ariel.

Kethera's Mum and dad were delighted to have them around and more than happy to look after them. Even if Kethera and Richard were to go off on an interplanetary freight haulage assignment. Every time that Kethera and Richard landed their ship's shuttle in Krylor's and Kayala's plot, all of the neighbouring kits would line up along the plot's dry stone wall, wanting to get a look at *"Captain Kethera of the Outer Frontier and her loyal First mate, Richard"*. The name once used by Kayala as a joke had stuck and become a reality. Carlins from all over the Masula Valley suddenly took far greater interest in the Human colony and visited in their droves, looking for opportunities.

Yeannah also achieved her class five pilot's license shortly after her sixteenth birthday, although as a Mimasian Thol, this was not so uncommon as with the Carlin folk. Yeannah and her boyfriend, Thomas, moved off-world to Colonial Central in Cis-Luns L-Five and married, far away from the prying eyes of Homwol's Indigenous Thols. Yeannah worked as a class five pilot and fully trained data analyst for the Earth's Interstellar Alliance Military, although in civilian capacities. This was among Mimasian Thols, highly unusual, almost unheard of.

Much to their surprise, Yeannah became pregnant. Something that they had both believed impossible. In all the time that Mimasian Thols had lived amongst Humans, Earthling or Martian, there had never been a Mimasian Thol-Human relationship. Whether it be within Mimas during the Great Conceal or amongst the Earth's solar system after the Great Reveal, such a thing had not been recorded, not even once. It had been expected to be impossible.

Mimasian Thols had originally evolved on Homwol, long before arriving in the Sol System, hidden aboard the generation ship Mimas in frozen cryosleep. Genetic testing had found that the very same or a very similar pathway existed for genetic compatibility with Humans, as with the Carlin-Human hybridisation, only ever so slightly different. This had never been expected.

When Yeannah's youngling was born, he looked very Tholish, with a beautiful set of wings and tail with its round prehensile tip. Testing even showed that his bones were hollow, as they would be expected of Thols. However, he was also different. His skin was not alabaster white like his Mother's, he was instead fair-skinned with a slightly rosy or ruddy complexion. His hair was not the expected white blond either, he had his Father's ginger hair and instead of Tholish purple eyes, his were green. They named their Son, Ysmar, meaning the Emerald Eyed One.

Thomas worked from home in the apartment in Colonial Central and so looked after their youngling when Yeannah was at work. They made frequent trips to their village in the Northern Mountain forests in the tall Jula Jula trees so that Yeannah's Mother and Father, Yealah and Yannick, could see their Grandchild. They doted on him, as they would also, with Yeannah's later younglings.

With every visit, they found themselves surrounded by curious neighbours, amazed by their Son. When the local Indigenous Thols learned of Yeannah's work off-world, many flocked to the Human colony seeking further information. Were there opportunities for the Indigenous Thols as well as the

Mimasian? This did unnerve the Tholish High Council, who had long maintained the ancient taboos of Thols against having relationships with non-Thols. This was a problem, as Yeannah was a personal friend of the Human Swanson twins, as they were Mardhin and so also sacred!

Yookey's Family had been so impressed with the Mimasian-style tree house they'd been staying in, high in a Bell Nut Fruit tree within the Swanson's lot, that they cautiously asked if they could stay there. Their old nesting cluster, high in the Jula Jula trees in the Northern Mountain forests, was so much less and this new tree house was so much more. That was the only way that Yarling and Yorvick could describe it.

Mrs Swanson had, of course, said yes straight away. Yookey's family being present was good for two reasons. One, just having another family around was a good thing, normalising the plot and making much less *"military"*. Two, Yookey was her Daughter, Aria's paramour and so Aria was both delighted and excited that they were staying. Mrs Swanson instructed her Android *"metal men"* to bring across the remainder of their belongings. Yookey's family then sold their old nesting cluster to another family of Indigenous Thols.

Eventually, Aria and Yookey married, which was against the Indigenous Tholish taboos and customs. The marriage ceremony was a Human one. Aria and Yookey moved into their own bedroom within the homestead itself. This did cause some disturbances. Aria's and Yookey's nocturnal predilections, Aria with her moaning and groaning, both auditory and telepathic, along with Yookey's grunting and the flapping of his Tholish wings, were quite *"noisy"*.

Robert had played it down, noting that he and Angelique had been just as noisy when they were newlyweds. Aria's twin Sister, Ariel, put it into perspective when she told her parents that Aria and Yookey were, *"extremely loud and embarrassing!"* Angelique frowned and instructed her Android *"metal men"* to expand their homestead and build Aria and Yookey their own *"wing"*, so that they could have their own *"privacy"*. A code word for, let's put them a lot further away from everyone else to dull the sound! Soundproofing was, of course, included as a part of the build.

It wasn't long after Yeannah found herself pregnant up at Cis-Luns L-Five that Aria found herself pregnant on Homwol in her home in the Swanson's lot. Yookey was completely confused, as he had thought it was an impossibility. Aria had recently heard from Yeannah only a few days earlier about her pregnancy, so she had a heads up that it was possible but nonetheless unexpected.

The colony's local medical clinic studied Aria extensively and their genetic studies ended up confirming that the same genetic compatibility pathway that had allowed Yeannah to become pregnant was also responsible for Aria's pregnancy.

Aria's pregnancy was monitored to full term and when the baby was eventually born, it was quite a shock. Aria's pregnancy had not only followed Human norms, lasting nine months as opposed to Yeannah's, which had lasted eleven and a half months, following the Tholish norm.

Aria's and Yookey's baby was a girl and she appeared to be quite Human in basic appearance, although there were some differences. The baby girl had no wings or tail, yet her skin was a beautiful Tholish alabaster white. The baby's hair was pure white blond and her eyes were a pure creamy purple, both Tholish traits. Tests showed her skeletal structure was Human with solid bones, unlike the hollow bones of a Thol, which were so necessary for flight.

Doctors had wondered if that was the pattern. A female Thol and a male Human led to offspring that took after the Mother, more Thol than Human. A male Thol and a female Human led to offspring that also took after the Mother, more Human than Thol. They had no idea, it could even have been something to do with the differences between Mimasian Thols and Indigenous Thols. The two were different species of Thol after all and not themselves genetically compatible. Only time would tell and so far, they only had two examples to study.

Yookey's Father, Yorvick, was accepting of the baby straight away, while his Mother, Yarling, was more coy. Yarling stared at the baby in disbelief. She was so Human and yet the wingless youngling also looked so Tholish. In the end, Yarling rushed over and picked up her Granddaughter, kissing her over and over and cradling her gently.

Tears flowed down Yarling's cheeks as she exclaimed how beautiful her granddaughter was. In typical Indigenous Thol fashion, Yarling named the baby then and there, Yin! She wasn't sure where she'd heard the name, it was a Human word after all. Aria and Yookey both agreed with her choice.

The following year, Aria gave birth to her second baby, a boy and just like the first, he was Human-like with alabaster white skin, pure white blond hair and creamy purple eyes. Yarling was so ecstatic and named her new Grandson, Yang! Both Aria and Yookey agreed to the name and Aria noted, laughing, our children are *"Yin and Yang!"* Yookey had to look up the meaning to understand the reference. Yin and yang are opposite but complementary forces.

Not long after that, Yeannah gave birth to her own Daughter, who appeared to be a Thol, except for being fair-skinned with a slightly rosy or ruddy complexion, red hair and this time, blue eyes. Yeannah and Thomas named their new Daughter Yasna, meaning Blue like Sky! So far, the pattern continued. The offspring of Human-Thol relationships, thus far with only four examples, were taking after the Mothers for their base biological and genetic traits, with genetic variations coming from the Fathers.

All of the attention Aria's children were attracting was also becoming a security issue. The mere fact that Aria and Ariel were now *"Mardhin"*, meant that Indigenous Thol pilgrims were collecting at their lot's perimeter fence line just to get a glimpse of the twins.

When the news feed began divulging news about Aria's and Yeannah's children, even more Indigenous Thols began making their pilgrimage to the Swanson's lot. They could not go off-world to see Yeannah's children, but the hybrid children of Aria the Mardhin were quite a draw. Hundreds were arriving outside the perimeter fence daily!

In the end, they had to place signs in native Tholish along their perimeter fence line, requesting that pilgrims turn back and instead go to the Human colony and to respect their privacy. The twins, Aria and Ariel, made themselves available, along with Yookey and the hybrid children, Yin and Yang, to meet with Tholish pilgrims at the Colony's town hall on Sunday afternoons. There were so many of them that they literally had to allocate bookings.

While in the Human colony, the Indigenous Thols tried Human foods, drinks and entertainment. Some even looked for other opportunities. The Human-Thol hybrids were creating quite a stir with the Tholish High Council. Yeannah's hybrid younglings were one thing, she was a Mimasian Thol living off-world, but now one of the Mardhin, Aria, a Human, also had hybrid younglings. That was most disturbing!

Aria and Ariel were both Mardhin and Indigenous Thols considered the Mardhin to be sacred. The ancient taboo against non-Thol relationships was also sacred. The two were incompatible with each other. At a meeting of the Tholish High Council, the High Chancellor himself declared, that if a Mardhin, who was Human, saw fit to have younglings by a Thol, then the ancient taboo against non-Thol relationships must be false! The entire chamber voted on the matter and the ancient taboo against non-Thol relationships was rescinded. There was no dissent!

More Human-Thol relationships began developing almost straight away.

Times were a changing!

Two and a half decades into the thirty five hundreds, a new entry was added to the Interstellar Alliance's databases and its historical list of *"Great Explosions"*.

"Disambiguation 5. The Great Explosion – The Great Hybridisation Event."

"The rapid expansion of Human-Carlin and Human-Thol Hybrids across the Star fields."

The Girls had created their own Great Explosion and Captain Kethera of the Outer Frontier with her loyal First mate and Husband, Richard, along with their kits, had led the way!

It was the year twenty one seventy seven and a major disaster had unfolded, one that, due to deteriorating circumstances, could not be prevented by the Council of Shadows and their powerful Earth psychics, the Folcrom.

Folcrom Freyja dragged her reluctant Husband, Folcrom Gideon Reas and her Sister-Wife, Folcrom Sandra Danker, along with her other Sister-Wife, the Martian, Winchilly, to the Council of Shadow's main meeting place on the Earth.

The meeting place itself was deep under the sandstone of the South Australia outback, about fifty kilometres from the township of Coober Pedy. A town that was largely built around underground dugouts. Even the pubs and hotels of Coober Pedy were underground. The meeting place was a huge underground complex, where the Council of Shadows lived, ate and slept. Their meeting hall was a huge underground cavern, which, like the rest of the complex, was literally carved out of the sandstone.

Reluctant because quite frankly, Gideon, Sandra and Winchilly were simply getting too old for this *"bullshit!"*

Gideon and Sandra had not only been instrumental in the ever-ongoing process of terraforming Mars but had also defeated the evil Tarlak Emperor, Ahriman, which concluded the now *"buried under the rug"*, Mimasian War. Hell, Sandra and Gideon had together prevented the evil Emperor from taking over the Earth and turning it into his own private version of Hell!

Then they had even terraformed the interior of the Saturnian Ice Moon, the generation ship, Mimas, to give the Martians a new home. They had helped to resurrect the Mimasian Thols from six million years of cryosleep. Of course, after Folcrom Orpheus had inducted them into the Council of Shadows, they had helped out with every cockamamie Council of Shadow's request concerning the Mimasian War's Great Conceal.

Sure, the Great Conceal kept the Martians and the Thols safe and it even prevented a solar-system-wide panic, but they were tired and they had had enough!

It was simply time for them to finally retire and let the new blood deal with all of this bullshit!

“Okay, Freyja, what do you want us to fix this time?”, Gideon asked, he was quite blunt and then he softened, “I mean, we three love you and all, but we're simply tired, Freyja. Why is it always us that has to fix this shite? It's time for the younger generation to step up to the plate?”

“You think you're tired, Gideon?”, Folcrom Orpheus chimed in.

Gideon looked over to Orpheus, “No offence, Orpheus, but you look old. Old and tired!”

“Ya think. I'm at least twenty years older than you lot and yet, here I still am”, Orpheus noted.

Freyja answered Gideon's question, “We don't have a younger generation to take over, Gideon!”

It was Sandra's turn, “For God's sake, Freyja, what haven't you told us?”, she asked.

Winchilly placed a calming hand on Sandra's arm and telepathically commented, *“Please let Freyja explain it. I'm sure she will. Our anger is not going to help.”*

Orpheus rolled his eyes and chimed in with, “You haven't told them, have you, Freyja?”

“How could I, Orpheus? No one really believed the prophecy and well, you know, now the Council of Shadows is kind of fucked and all!”, Freyja replied with the use of her expletives.

“Prophecy?”, Gideon enquired.

Folcrom Orpheus chimed in as the expounder of knowledge, “As you know, when Folcrom Tafazah created psi-corp, he created four internal organisations, three overt and one covert.”

“Yes, Orpheus, we know all of that”, Sandra confirmed.

Orpheus continued, repeating things that they already knew, "The overt organisations, of course, were the psychic teaching academies, the psychic old scholar outreach program, the remote viewing teams, you know, the wyvern covens that keep the Earth safe. Our Council of Shadows was to be covert, unknown to everyone but us. We were always the silent watchers, watching over the overt watchers", he paused, waiting for their memories to catch up.

Orpheus continued, "Every Council of Shadows member was meant to be a descendant, a scion of Folcrom Tafazah himself. The pair of you are the only exception. Freyja, you can continue with the prophecy side of things."

Freyja began explaining, "The children of Folcrom Tafazah were all powerful psychics. Not just his six Earth children but also his six children on Mars. When Mars was evacuated before you terraformed the planet, we lost track of those scions during the chaos of those evacuations."

"Freyja, just get down to the gist of the matter", Orpheus chimed in.

"For fuck sake, Orpheus, I am getting there", Freyja replied angrily, she did not like to be interrupted nor pressured, so she continued, "Folcrom Tafazah prophesied, that as the generations of scions continued into the future."

Sandra caught on and quickly chimed in, "Their psychic potentials would become diluted. We've reached that point, haven't we, Freyja?"

"I don't appreciate being interrupted, Sandra, but yes, you've nailed it in one", Freyja confirmed.

Sandra, Winchilly and Gideon all sat down, defeat in their eyes.

"Why would Tafazah create a system that would so quickly collapse?", Sandra enquired.

Orpheus answered matter-of-factly, "Tafazah had six children with each of his two Wives. One Wife here on Earth and his other Wife over on Mars. If not for the terraforming process and the chaotic evacuation of the Martian colonies, we would not have lost track of those scions! Nobody has any clue as to where all of those evacuees ended up! They ended up scattered across the whole inner inner solar system."

"So, we're to blame, are we now, Gideon and I?", Sandra asked.

"No, it's not about blame", Orpheus assured her, "This is just something that Tafazah could not have foreseen. With that branch of the family, we could have continued for another two generations. Tafazah predicted failure, yes, but not the timing of that failure. Tafazah got the timing completely wrong! We weren't supposed to reach this stage until around twenty two fifty."

"Okay, Orpheus. Exactly how bad is it?", Gideon asked, stating, "Spill the bloody beans!"

"I'll explain it, Orpheus", Freyja chimed in, simply stating, "The first generation, the children, all good. The second generation, the grandchildren, also all good. The third generation, ours, the great-grandchildren, is a bit hit and miss when it comes to the levels of our psychic power. The fourth generation, the great-great-grandchildren, just forget them. Not a single one of them can blink or jaunt off-world! They have psychic abilities, yes, but they can't use their abilities off-world at all. After we're gone, the Council of Shadows is limited to the Earth. We can manage the Earth but nothing off-world."

"Wouldn't that have been the same, even with the missing branch of scions?", Sandra asked.

Orpheus chimed in, "We were supposed to fix this problem ourselves, but no one took the prophecy seriously. The scions were meant to marry other psychics out of duty, instead, they chose to marry for love, marrying mundanes. That watered down the psychic bloodlines in a major way and psychic potentials plummeted as a result."

"Well, that makes sense, Orpheus. Sandra and I weren't naturally born psychics and of the four children I have with Freyja, only two are psychic and they're both level nines. Too low to be inducted into the Council of Shadows", Gideon commented.

Freyja noted, "If we had managed to keep track of the scions from Mars, we could have cross-married with them to maintain a higher degree of psychic potential. Both bloodlines descend from different Wives of Tafazah, so having them around would have been very useful. Again, unforeseen circumstances. Tafazah did give us fair warning though, he always said, that the Council of Shadows was never meant to be forever."

"The ironic thing is, we were never meant to operate off-world in the first place. Our mandate was to watch over psi-corp to keep it honest. That was our job", Orpheus remarked, explaining, "If it wasn't for that damned Mimasian War, we probably wouldn't have left the Earth at all."

Freyja nodded her head, "Yet another unforeseen circumstance. That one was way out of left field. Seriously, way out. The whole concealment was about hiding that. Protecting the Martians and the Thols and not letting the

Earth know that it was nearly taken over by an evil disembodied spirit, Emperor Ahriman, that could possess anyone at will, even in their millions."

"We all went out on a limb with that one. It had to be done", Orpheus admitted.

"Still, imagine all of the chaos if the word actually got out", Freyja reminded everyone.

"So you were never meant to be doing any of this up here?", Sandra asked incredulously.

"No. Our mandate was purely the Earth. If there was no Mimasian War, we would have happily stayed on Earth", Freyja admitted, then commented, "No one could have predicted evil Tarlaks in a generation ship orbiting Saturn as one of its moons. Unforeseen circumstances!", she reiterated.

"Yeah, but the Tarlaks are all dead, their Emperor Ahriman has been rent asunder. So why is it a problem that you're now all stuck on Earth?", Gideon questioned, noting, "You are just back to your original mandate."

Freyja smiled a wry smile, "Oh Dear Husband, because our duty never ends and shit happens!"

"Shit happens?", Sandra repeated, then she asked her Sister-Wife, "Why am I thinking that the shit is already in motion?"

Freyja frowned and replied, "Because it is, Dear Sister-Wife, because it is."

Orpheus's face took on a hardened look, "You notice that our cousin Tina isn't around?"

"No, I hadn't, but now you mention it. Tina doesn't seem to be here", Sandra replied, looking around the cavern.

Freyja frowned, tears welled in her eyes, "Tina's dead, along with another one of our Cousins."

"What the fuck!", Gideon exclaimed, then asked, "When did this happen?"

Orpheus answered, "The Jovian Republic fell just three days ago. They are now calling themselves the Jovian Realms. They've annexed both of the Jovian Trojan points and enslaved all non-Christians within their realms. They're now controlled by High Prince Albert von Horridian", he divulged it all in a stream that sounded like pure nonsense.

"How the hell did that happen?", Sandra demanded.

Freyja wiped her eyes, "We were so busy with everything else that we didn't find out until way too late."

Winchilly asked telepathically, *"What happened to your cousins?"*

"I was there when the High Prince Albert von Horridian was crowned. I jaunted straight back here to report the issue. I kind of considered it an important matter", Freyja replied while wiping the tears from her eyes, then she noted, "Tina and another Cousin jaunted straight out to gather more information, as we usually do", her eyes shed tears once more and she couldn't continue.

Orpheus took over, "As usual, they would have used their psychic obscuration fields to hide themselves. Except the Horridians keep dogs amongst other things. In this case, it is Dobermans. Dogs can see straight through a psychic obscuration field, apparently. Tina and our other Cousin found out that the hard way. We believe that they were attacked on the High Prince's Palace grounds inside Ganymede Prime's Northern End Cap by the Dobermans. They were still being mauled by the Dobermans when the Jovian Shock Troops arrived and beat them both half to death."

A teary-eyed Freyja chimed in, "They declared them to be sorcerers and even before they'd recovered consciousness, they hung them from a gallows! They murdered them in cold blood! They didn't have a chance!"

"It gets worse! They've declared the event to be an assassination attempt against High Prince Albert von Horridian himself, by the Earth's Demon Government", Orpheus pronounced.

"How do you know?", Winchilly enquired telepathically.

"When we hadn't heard from them, I jaunted to Ganymede Prime. It was broadcast all over their internal news feeds. The execution was public and it was all recorded. They replayed the execution over and over every thirty minutes. I only saw the news feeds, but it was horrible!", Freyja replied while still crying.

"And that's why you need Gideon and me", Sandra nodded.

Orpheus stepped in, "I am far too old to deal with these things anymore. My jaunting days are far behind me. You, Gideon, both you and Sandra are the most powerful of us!"

"We are also old Orpheus, maybe not as old as you, but honestly, what are you asking? Do you want us to assassinate High Prince Albert von Horridian?", Gideon replied, questioning.

"No, not at all, Gideon. That's not what we need", Orpheus replied.

Freyja chimed in, "Maybe that's what I need, Orpheus!"

Winchilly walked over to Freyja and hugged her with her usual calming effect, *"No, Freyja, My Love. That is not what you want. That is not who you are!"*

Freyja responded more positively, "You're always right, Winchilly. You're always right! We need to steer the Jovian Realms back to their old Jovian Republic using powerful psychic intervention. That is what is required."

Sandra remarked, "There are only two of us and honestly, at our age, you are asking for failure, Freyja. Seriously, you are."

Freyja actually did have a plan, but it could not be implemented without help and she looked at Gideon and Sandra, "You guys weren't natural-born psychics. The Martian Council of Elders psychically genetically tweaked you. They created the very conditions for you to evolve and develop your gifts."

Gideon pinched his nose, "Freyja, we've had this conversation in the past. Many times, in fact."

Winchilly frowned at Freyja and noted, *"Freyja, the Council of Elders is not going to tweak any more Earth Humans as they did with Sandra and Gideon. They have even made it illegal under Martian law."*

"So I have been told, but hear me out. If we had ten Gideon's and ten Sandra's, we could have the Jovian people back on track with their old Jovian Republic in no time", Freyja suggested.

"Only you won't get ten of me or ten of Gideon, Freyja. For good or for ill, you'll whatever you'll get", Sandra warned her.

Winchilly held onto Freyja's hand, *"Freyja, My Love, Sandra is right. Gideon and Sandra could very easily have turned out differently. Things could have gone horribly wrong!"*

"Freyja, you have no idea. The Tarlak Emperor, Ahriman, his influence was intoxicating. We came within a hair's breadth of joining him or, much, much worse, replacing him. We could very well have ended up as psychic monsters! Powerful psychic monsters!", Gideon explained to Freyja as he had many times before.

Sandra piled on, "The Martian Council of Elders got lucky. We could easily have taken a turn for the worse, an evil turn and that would have been disastrous for the whole solar system."

"Then what are we supposed to do? How are we to fix this?", Freyja asked.

Gideon replied bluntly, "You said it yourself, Freyja. The Council of Shadows is fucked!", and then when Freyja burst out into tears, he reached out and held her in his arms to comfort her.

Orpheus had the final word when he stated sadly, "Perhaps, Freyja, not all things can be fixed. Perhaps, they just have to run their course."

And, of course, things did run their course.

High Prince Albert von Horridian used the execution of the psychic cousins and his lying narrative about his attempted assassination, along with the Earth's banning of fission reactors and their replacement with the newer, more reliable and far safer fusion reactors, to launch the Outer Satellite Insurrection. The first Horridian War, a mere five years later.

Pretexts make perfect!

www.ingramcontent.com/pod-product-compliance
Lightning Source LLC
Chambersburg PA
CBHW050838030726
47503CB00007BA/2231

* 9 7 8 1 7 6 3 7 2 7 7 3 1 *